TALKING WHITE OWL

TALKING WHITE OWL

—‹A NOVEL›—

VALERIE HAGENBUSH

This is a work of fiction. Names, characters, places, and incidents are either the product of the author's imagination or are used fictitiously. Any resemblance to actual persons, living or dead, events, or locales is entirely coincidental.

Copyright © 2024 by Valerie Hagenbush

The author reserves all rights to be recognized as the owner of this work. You may not sell or reproduce any part of this book without the written consent from the copyright owner.

Cover design and title page by David Provolo

Book formatted for print and ebook by Phillip Gessert (gessertbooks.com)

CHAPTER 1

"Leg hold traps...on people?" gasps Mrs. Bentgrass through locked fingers held prayer-like over her lips in a show of horror. Our frantic neighbor dropped by Grandmother's house early this morning, upset by news of the latest attack on our Lakota reservation. When the part about the hunting knife comes up in their conversation, and how it was used to carve into the victims' chests...I'm outta here, eager to race my horse Jim at breakneck speed across the wide-open plains. This summer's visit is turning into such a downer!

"Off to Billie's for the day," I say as I grab a piece of toast off the plate.

"Viktor, please leave Billie alone," my grandmother begs, flipping her long braid over her shoulder and out of the way as she clears the breakfast table. "With Billie, trouble can only follow you home." I shouldn't have mentioned where I was going as I flew past them. She has good reason to fear.

Billie Spotted Horse, the center for our flag football games, is said to have joined a gang on the reservation. It can only be to retaliate against the power-hungry Mérodders from up north in Canada. They've slowly been working their way down through the Dakotas, annihilating the homegrown squads that stand up to them. They've finally reached us here near the Nebraska border. I need to hear it from Billie himself. Why else would he do it? He's the oldest in our group, a guy as big and square as a tractor, the one we kids always looked up to. He made us swear we'd have each other's back if any rez boys "gone gangsta" tempted us to join them. We had known the brothers when they weren't bad, before they left with their families for the big cities. There aren't jobs here in Indian country. They went north to Rapid City, east to Sioux Falls, with some going as far away as Chicago and Denver. After a time, each came back, claiming there was the same nothing there as could be found here. They had found something, though—drugs, all kinds, and they were easy to unload. Their connections just kept the supplies rolling in.

Normally, riding Jim fast always clears my head, but not today. Our people's future, in question way longer than my short fifteen years on the planet, seems doomed more than ever. I can't shake the gory image of mangled hands and feet that Grandmother's been dealing with as a nurse for a mobile clinic on wheels. She and my Uncle William, the only doctor within miles, have had to amputate some. Hunting traps, believed too cruel for animals, are what the gangs have resorted to using. "Ho," I order, pulling gently on the reins as we near Whiteclay Creek. I stop to pay my respects to our wide receiver, Ron Léglise, who died last August. There it is, poking out of the dry earth: a makeshift cross of two-by-fours that marks the spot where the old truck he was driving hit a boulder and rolled over, pinning him and his three friends inside. The navy jersey with Léglise in yellow letters still hangs where it was nailed to the wood, even after the winter's heavy snows and strong winds. Broken strands of beads and ragged feathers honor the others.

"What an ending, eh, White Owl—drowning in a few inches of water?"

I look up and see Ron casually perched on the wide branch of a maple around thirty feet away. I don't think my mind is playing tricks on me, that I'm hallucinating, although he's in one piece, and not bloodied. There's no seeing through him like one expects with a ghost. His presence doesn't scare me. Growing up among my Indian relatives, I'd heard many stories about people visited by the dead. I don't understand how the wind blows through his long hair.

"My sister just left. It's a monthly ritual. She still needs to finish making her peace with me before I can move on."

"Is this your only hang out?" I wonder aloud.

"For now. I watched the wake held at the school gym right after the accident. Matt had Neil and Mark in stitches when he said dumb ole Ron couldn't miss a rock the size of a bull."

"They were high."

"Yeah…aren't we all."

The memory of our team makes me sad. No one cares about football anymore.

"Always high, except for our sensible Viktor." He pulls his leg up and rests his hands on his knee. "I predict jerseys with their names, Gray

Cloud and Moreau and High Flying Arrow, will soon hang from patched-together crosses like mine, and in as lonely and forgotten of a spot."

Can't argue with that. Wish I were leaving on a happier note. "It's beyond me," I mutter to Jim, my one true friend for all time.

"I heard that," yells Ron after me. "Stay strong, brother."

We pass over the last hill that borders Billie's neighborhood, a run-down HUD project that once had actual sidewalks and doors and windows that weren't kicked in or shot out. The gaping holes are boarded up and decorated with gang tags. They look condemned and empty, but people live inside. I see Billie with his new homies. Jim is sure-footed along the steep, winding path. I wave back to Billie, when suddenly I realize he's motioning wildly for me to back off. There's some fierce yelling going down. Baseball bats are being swung around ... and metal pipes.

Scared, I get Jim turned around, but he stubbornly twists right back figuring this was the way we were headed—the fool riding him must be confused. "Un-hee! Holy shit, Jim!" He bolts upright, angry at the jab to his ribs. The seriousness of the moment registers and he charges up the hill we'd just come down. Those idiots seem hell-bent on destruction and are probably jacked up on meth to boot.

As we near the top, a couple of vehicles crammed with bodies are beating up the dirt road. They're coming from the direction of Billie's house. Riders hanging halfway out the windows are pounding the doors like maniacs. Their war cries scare the birds. I don't recognize the taped up old heap. The driver of the white pickup floors the engine and tears around the clunker. I reckon the truck must be stolen—looks new. The guys in back go flying. The air's so thick with dust it's hard to make out faces, but I can see some are streaked with yellow and red war paint.

After riding a distance, far enough to feel safe, Jim and I take a breather on Nolan's Butte. The prairie grasses have turned light brown and go on as far as the eye can see, just like the huge sky. Hawks circle overhead. So many critters below to feast on. It's a spectacular view. Even so, for the first time ever I'm longing to leave the reservation: my first home, and true home. The yearly ritual of going back and forth between Texas for the school year and the rez here in South Dakota for holidays and summer break is no longer fun. We've all changed too much, my Indian brothers and me.

"Bullies...that's what they are." Jim's stuck listening to my grumbling.

"Who on earth terrorizes their own? It isn't natural." He snorts in agreement. My lungs appreciate the clean air. I'm struck with profound respect for the generations of ancestors whose spirits are alive everywhere and whose DNA is carried on through me. I call upon our Creator.

"Great Spirit Wakan Tanka, please keep Billie in mind. He's so talented and funny...and good. If only the lost brothers of our Nation could find a way to reconnect with our Great Spirit and become men of honor..." Ah hell, it's a frickin' pointless prayer.

These warrior wannabees know nothing about the virtues of our history's Lakota braves other than they had awesome names and used symbols that make for wicked tattoos these days. Jim trots along at an easy pace while I continue to stew. Banking on a slim chance that I might also catch sight of my dead grandfather today, I glance around with the hope of spotting Pahpie on a boulder, or up a tree like Ron. I think about what it means to have unfinished business with a person who dies. Did Grandmother? Off to my right, not that far, a thin trail of smoke curls upward in the sky. There's a loud boom, then lots more smoke.

"Al's!" I yell, fearing the worst. An eerie mushroom-shaped cloud hangs above the spot of our favorite hangout. It's crazy! There's no follow-up explosion, only a rumble deep in the earth that Jim finds unsettling. His instincts don't stop him when I steer us toward the smoke. My heart's racing. Was that where Billie and the psychos were headed? *Please, no,* I pray.

I'm certain no one saw me creep under the old Wells Fargo Pony Express stagecoach that sits off to the side of Lazy Al's Trading Post. A row of monster Harleys stand parked in front of the wagon like a unit of linebackers waiting for the signal to attack. The bikes are covered with the Mérodders trademark decals: a sideways 8 infinity symbol copied from the flag of the Métis, proud Canadian mixed bloods who must hate these jerks for using an image that belongs to them. From the looks of things, they're hammering the shit out of the idiots who had passed me in the truck. Some *war.* Beyond them, at the corner where rural Goose Neck Road intersects the two-lane County Highway, orange flames shoot above the white-hot insides of what had been the truck and car. The fumes from the burning tires are nasty. I keep my nose close to the ground and try not to puke. Jim better stay safe behind the trees on the other side of the highway. There's no let up to the insanity. From my keyhole view between the spokes of a big wheel, and squinting from the dust, I wonder who the lifeless body belongs to that keeps getting kicked over and over. His attackers fall over themselves laughing. More crazed bikers head toward the fire that's grown huge. They cheer it on like that could make it bigger. The heat doesn't faze them.

I nearly jump out of my skin as a chopper thunders through the smoke. Police cars surround the store. Everybody scatters. The cops outnumber the bad guys so there's no chance for escape. I half expect a movie director to yell *Cut!* But when I see Miss Audra and Takodah being led from the porch on the arm of an officer, it's definitely not make-believe. They're hobbling toward the stagecoach as quickly as their aging bones can move.

The wind is fanning the fire north. Al's might be saved. Miss Audra's feet are within touching distance, but I'd freak her out, and Takodah, too, if they saw a hand on the ground grabbing at their ankles.

"Miss Audra! Takodah!" I shout at the top of my lungs.

There's no answer at first; next I hear: "Who's down there?"

"It's Viktor."

I no sooner begin to crawl into the open when waiting arms scoop me up and hug me tight. Holding them by the waist, we head across the highway to the picnic table and trees where Jim is. They collapse on the bench, clutching each other as well as their chests, which makes me uneasy. While they collect themselves, I check on Jim.

"Viktor, come." Miss Audra raises her thin arm and motions for me to sit beside her. She holds my hand loosely in hers. They're both shaking like a hound spooked by thunder. We watch a firetruck come screaming down the road.

The fingers slide off mine, and Miss Audrey starts crying softly into her hands. They've got dark bulging veins. I look at Takodah and say, somewhat surprised, "Can you believe help arrived this fast?"

He acts as if he didn't hear. His left eye is clouded by cataracts. He once had bright brown eyes. Seems like they've both been old forever.

"After the turquoise got stolen last year," he says with his thick Lakota accent, "the police have been good about sending a patrol here every few days. We also got an alarm that goes to the station in Mundersen." His arm moves from his wife's small back to me. He places his hand on my shoulder. "Sam was shot."

I stare in disbelief. "Sam would never get mixed up in a brawl," I insist. "He's the most peaceful brother there is." I then realize he means shot dead. This can't be happening. I'm numb.

Takodah tells me that Sam had been checking out magazines when a biker came in and got upset...told Sam to stop looking at him weird. "All Sam did was glance up at him," says Takodah, his voice breaking up. "The guy just wanted a reason to pick a fight. He demanded an apology. Poor Sam didn't know what he was talking about and next thing he was getting slammed into the wall. Right then, Billie showed up and pulled the troublemaker off him. He thought he was helping Sam when he came up with a quick excuse, telling the biker the kid wasn't right in the head, and that he shouldn't take anything he did personally. The man shot Sam between the eyes so fast, none of us saw it coming; and then he said the kid was all right in the head now. When he heard the sirens, Billie tripped him as he ran for the door. Audra and I hurried outside. An officer grabbed us and helped us down the steps."

We sit in silence, overcome with sadness. Even Jim stares across the highway as firefighters work to put out the flames and save our magical childhood stomping ground from becoming a pile of ashes. For me, it's all good memories. This was *the* place —the crossroad of America—where tourists and truck drivers went from one side of the state to the other... and where we kids had planned on getting discovered by some important person traveling through. We played flag football in the field beyond the picnic table, within view of the highway so college scouts could see Ron and Billie and sign them up on the spot. Dad coached our teams. My dream had been to headline my own Wild West Show. In a big riding ring behind Al's, I impressed everyone with my knife throwing skills and trick riding acrobatics. Jim loved galloping at full-throttle in circles. I had planned to hire native entertainers, though not necessarily Sioux, and take the show on tour like Buffalo Bill did. Visitors used to tip me good, but instead of saving for this future "extravaganza," I bought comics, not just for me, but for all my friends. Al's was the only place on the rez that sold them. *"We could use you now, Wingfoot."*

"What?" asks Takodah.

"Nothing, Takodah. I was wishing for a real superhero. Remember how as kids we used to go on about Wyatt Wingfoot, the college-educated Indian from the Keewazi tribe who helped the Fantastic Four on their missions? He was in your son's Marvel collection you gave us." As soon as I say it, the words sound stupid considering what's happening in front of us.

He squeezes my shoulder. "You are right, Viktor; no Superman on the reservation."

"We hoped to be heroes one day," I tell him. "When we were old enough to understand how drinking hurt our people, me and Billie and Sam and the others made a solemn promise to always represent the Lakota in a good way. We even held a ceremony where we cut our hands and mixed our blood, making a pact that was intended to unite us for all time."

"Those comic book stories meant that much to you?" asks Miss Audra.

"You bet! Using their words for inspiration, we swore to travel the path leading to moral victory while lesser souls caved to temptations."

"And did you smoke?" asks Takodah matter of fact.

How'd he know! I tell him about the chants we held during secret meetings in Neil's broken down barn where we naïvely puffed on Chanunpa, the sacred pipe filled with tobacco that we snuck from our elders' containers. We wanted to connect to the spirit world so we could talk to our great chiefs, Sitting Bull and Rain in the Face and Running Antelope, about their legendary deeds. The old man offers a knowing smile, like this rite of passage is something he did in his day. Then I think of Sam. So does Miss Audra.

"Sam and his guitar," she whispers. "He lived for the day when he'd find himself traveling the world with a famous band." She pats my cheek. "He had a wild way of playing."

That pretty much sums up his existence—*summed up*. I listen in my head to Sam strumming his heart out in the backroom at Al's. He loved Hendrix and put his own unique twist on songs. Since his own home had no electricity for his amps, he was allowed to practice in the store. That's just the way Miss Audra and Takodah were…still are. This better not mean they're calling it quits. The place is an institution in these parts. Takodah's father, Al Chankoowashtay, which means Good Road, built it back when my own grandparents were teens. Later in his life, diabetes caused him to get his lower leg and other foot amputated, which landed him in a wheelchair. Before then he had been a Lakota cowboy on his family's cattle ranch. No one made it through the front door without first seeing the big photo of him bronc riding.

News about the fire has spread. Folks in the area are riding up on horseback. A few in cars are pulling off the road to watch. When some of the neighbors notice us on the bench, they head over. I ask to use a guy's cell phone to call Dad to pick me up. Jim will stay the night in Takodah's barn, which lies a good distance behind the store. Before I leave with Jim to get him squared away, Miss Audra asks me what it's like where I live in Texas.

"We're in an older neighborhood outside the city near the Air base where Mom works, around a three-day drive from here, with tall trees and brick homes...mostly Jewish. I think they're the only ones in all of Wichita Falls. The families are well-off, but they don't play it up." Hmm. That was dumb to add. I've heard Dad say it.

"How about gangs?" she asks. "Are you far enough away from them?"

"No gangs; we're safe."

She stands and steadies herself against me. "Viktor, our smart Viktor. Don't come back again—not to this. If I weren't so old..." She shakes her head. I hug her tight before letting her friends step in for me. As Jim and I are about to cross the highway, I turn around and see that she still has me in her sight. Wishing and praying won't change things; Al's is history.

Miss Audra's words stick with me as I walk Jim past the riding ring. The fires seem under control, but the air is bad. Yeah, gang life and getting wasted, it just can't be stopped. It's tragic to see the way the babies are affected by their parents' poor choices. Starting with day one, the cards are stacked against them. I think of my older sister, Iris, who is studying ways to help the kids' mental development in a specially designed program at the University of Wisconsin.

Jim isn't bothered by the strong smell of smoke and seems glad to be in the stall. I find a big bag of carrots, his idea of heaven. "You're getting a bath tomorrow." His beautiful white and chestnut coat is covered in soot. "Promise you won't ever allow the negative vibes on the rez to change you, Jim, you hear?" He whinnies on cue, like that could ever happen. An old-time boombox was left on top of a bale of hay. I turn it on and wait for Dad. A Lakota DJ reports that Germany is wild about a local rapper. Somewhere it's cool to be Indian. That's why the brothers and sisters look to music as their ticket out of here, posting their songs on YouTube. Before growing disillusioned, they can be just as starry-eyed as the rest of America's kids.

While the talk back at my school in Texas usually includes what colleges we students plan to attend, which is a given, few on the rez consider finding success through education. Miss Audra is right; it's time to break ties. The Indian culture I hold dear has survived only in a remote section of the reservation where Grandmother lives. In reality, her people's origins are not Lakota. My elders' ancestors called themselves Rawakota, and they believed like the Lakota that the mountains they had come across in this region of South Dakota were sacred. Their tribal members were taken in by the larger Lakota community when the Europeans drove the Plains Indians onto reservations. Somehow, though, my grandmother's clan managed to preserve a bit of their identity on their corner of the rez. It really hits me that my classmates don't have to deal with making a clean break from home when deciding their futures. The situation on the reservation, known for its crushing poverty, makes it near impossible for anyone to get ahead. And without obtaining a solid educational foundation, there isn't much hope for a decent life on the outside.

I better leave; Dad should be here by now. I spot him through the haze. He's standing by the stagecoach, coughing loudly. The area in front of the store has been taped off. What's to become of all those bikes, I wonder.

"Jim all set?" He can't clear his throat enough.

My upper chest and throat are beginning to burn. As we walk to the truck holding our shirts over our nose and mouth, we notice Billie alone in the back of a cruiser, his head hanging down. It's impossible to approach the car. We're close enough to see that he's focused on the back of the driver's seat. From the way he's sitting, his hands must be cuffed behind him. He's gotta be feeling guilty as hell over Sam's death. Dad holds my arm to stop me from throwing a small stone at the window.

"But Dad...Billie's got to see how thankful I am for him giving me the heads up this morning." No deal. He practically drags me alongside him while I try telepathically to get Billie to glance up, at least long enough to make eye contact.

Once in the truck, we immediately gulp down a couple bottles of water he brought in the ice chest. The windows stay closed. Dad reaches for my long, dust-coated braid and sniffs it, then smells his own shirt and declares that Grandmother is going to throw us in a tub of vinegar and baking soda, we reek so bad of smoke. Al's finally disappears in the side view mirror. If the loss hurts me to this degree, what must it be like for the elders? Dad concentrates on the long, empty road. Normally it's fun the way my insides hang suspended as we sail over the hill tops. Right now, my stomach feels queasy.

"It's so pointless joining a gang," I say after a while, more or less thinking out loud. "Either you end up dead or in jail. Why can't everybody find joy in just being?"

Dad is quiet. Maybe I struck a nerve. At fifteen he was in juvie and a few years later in prison. And he didn't even grow up on a reservation, but in Kansas City, Missouri, where he was raised by Christian parents in a loving home on what is still a pretty street with nice sidewalks that aren't busted up. I drop it and rest my head against the window. It's nice and cool from the air conditioner. The road's a blur. Dad's voice floats in space:

"You're one of the lucky ones, son. Most of us are hard-wired to get bored easily, especially when we can't figure out what we want. People, especially kids, will turn to anything that makes them feel something. Makes no difference, good or bad, as long as it isn't *nothing*."

CHAPTER 2

Fall semester flew by, mostly because I threw myself into playing football, in order to forget the sad events that happened on the rez during the summer. It worked, for a while. As the quarterback, I led the team to a perfect winning season. It put the spotlight on our league which is made up of independent schools. But now it's winter break, and here I am again in South Dakota. A recent arctic blast stayed north and for once spared us from minus zero degree temperatures. With no one left on the rez to hang out with, boredom has set in, to the point of causing physical pain. I've been ripping up the park with some skateboarders, which has been a blast—damned cold but fun. It was encouraging to find kids who don't do drugs, hardcore drugs that is; they're into vaping. It's my fault for not wanting to make new friends. There's just no energy for it, especially knowing I won't be returning as often anymore. Sister is back from Wisconsin, and she's good company, but there's only so much Iris is inclined to do with me. We still love racing our horses together, but her thoughts are on completing grad school, which makes me anxious to get on with my own college life. I'm still riding high from having tested out of the last two years of high school. That, along with the unexpected surprise of having won a full-tuition scholarship to Ohio State, has got me daydreaming about starting classes in just a half year. Staring out the window with no plans for the day…guess this morning is as good a time as any to go say bye to *mithá khola*, my oldest friend, Daniel. I've put it off after hearing about his current situation. He didn't have much to say to me last summer.

Pushing open the flimsy outer screen door to Daniel's place is a shy, dirty-faced toddler wearing an over-sized sweater but no pants. He looks way high up to me, big-eyed, straining his tiny neck to the point of falling backward. I catch the little guy and lift him to the side. The room is dark. It's a gray day and the windows are small. It can only be Daniel's shadowy figure sprawled across a cot, waving me over. "Hey Kemosabe," he teases, which he knows bugs me. My shoe catches on the ripped edge of the buckling linoleum floor. I'm bowled over by the change in his personality. The empty beer cans everywhere are the last straw.

"Couldn't you have held-out a little longer, Daniel, at least until you got your diploma? What options do you have now?" On the table beside him a candle burns low, making me nervous. The stub has almost sunk inside the empty plastic bottle. Wax is pooling around it.

"Don't knock it, brother. I'm happy." He says it with a drugged tongue rolling inside the smirk stuck on his face. He acts like he possesses a secret and I am the unenlightened outsider—like wasichu, a *white* man. His half-closed, deep-set eyes catch the light and shine black, but they never completely settle on mine. Daniel's girlfriend, a cousin who came to live with his family almost a year ago, is four months pregnant with their baby. He's my age; she's already sixteen. Both have quit school. Their three-bedroom graffiti-scribbled trailer, nothing more than a dilapidated box with an outhouse, is shared with over a dozen relatives who are dropped off and picked up when it suits somebody. Most are second and third generation grandchildren of the tired and mentally slow woman who cares for them. She is humming a tune in the corner, trying to get a whimpering child to forget about the cold and go to sleep. The older kids tend to the needs of the younger ones as best they know how. The parents either left for good, having deserted their children, or they're in jail.

When his girlfriend leaves for the outhouse, I rail against his irresponsible behavior: "Is this the legacy you want to leave for your unborn child? You learned like I did that babies are sacred, and that while they're still spirits in the beyond, they choose a particular woman and man to be born to, being a blessing to their union."

With difficulty, he props himself up on an arm and pats my cheek. "If I have been chosen, Viktor—and Eileen—then plainly there's a reason you just don't see, *right?*" The smug attitude continues. "Look around, brother, at the hungry and cold little ones here. Check out Kimimela, my niece, who my kind grandmother is singing to over there. She was born addicted. Her name means Butterfly, but she'll be staying a prisoner in her cocoon forever. You really think she wanted the parents she got? C'mon, Viktor. Wake up." His head wobbles and he slips back down on the stained and tattered mattress.

I really don't understand—the poverty and problems were as widespread when we were growing up as they are today, so how were we able to have fun and laugh so much and picture exciting lives for ourselves? I guess it was mostly on account of our hormones not having kicked in yet. I just want to escape quickly before my disgust gets the better of me. I'm ready to grab Daniel by the throat and shake him till he comes to his senses, but it's only his limp hand I end up shaking. The foul smell of weed is going to stick to my hair and clothes. The littlest kids must be wasted from inhaling the built-up smoke in the room. I'm struck by the realization that our long-standing friendship is definitely over. I do wish him well, even though he's as good as dead. I grieve the loss of the tribal brother I shared such a special understanding with since as far back as I can remember. We were told we took our first steps together on the same day.

I mount Jim outside and take off flying down the road. His hooves as they pound the hard cold earth feel like life hurling its best punches. Anger, sadness, disappointment, and, unbelievably, love of the deepest kind, merge into one confusing emotion that must have its own name.

A light goes on. I can tell through my closed eyelids. It's too early; my alarm didn't even go off yet. Dad tosses something on my chest. It's his car keys. I look up at him in sleepy disbelief when he says, "What? You don't wanna drive to Rapid City?" There's no chance of me turning him down, and I leap out of bed to shower. My learner's permit has been burning a hole in my wallet for a month. There haven't been many opportunities to practice behind the wheel. Dad was busy fixing up cars in his shop before Christmas, after which business slows and we immediately leave Texas and head for the rez. Mom would gladly have offered to supervise me, if she were home. Her being a fighter pilot doesn't allow for long visits with us. She is currently flying missions somewhere over the Middle East or Afghanistan. And Iris, who was here last week on break from UW, would have taken me out, but we had fun on our horses instead.

After the painful meeting with Daniel two days ago, I spent yesterday reading about Ohio State to improve my mood. It didn't prevent images of Daniel's lost life from surfacing now and then. He had agreed months ago to come along with Dad and me to Rapid City for a clothes-buying spree at the mall. I can't wait to be done with khakis and navy shirts, my school's uniform, all of which I've outgrown after gaining a half foot in height since last spring. The latest measurement taken by Coach at the end of football season in November had me at six foot, five inches. It happened so quickly. I can't get used to being taller than Dad, even though it's only by a forehead.

No one on the rez pays attention to following laws about the driving age. It's normal to see a young kid swerving around in an old model car or truck which is shared by different families. I've done it myself, but it's completely different than driving with the concentration required on busy city streets, especially like those in Texas. And I've never done it while drunk, which is more often the case here.

This trip to the big city today is special, a guys' outing, the last Dad and I will be able to share for a while. Daniel doesn't know what he's missing. He stood to benefit, too. How can he not miss Dad? All my friends who Dad coached over the summers loved him. During winter breaks, when it was too snowy outside for football, he showed us how to spar and wrestle. Dad hasn't spoken to me about the situation, but I've overheard him tell Grandmother he's devastated by the fact that he couldn't help turn the boys' lives around and keep them out of trouble.

By the time we reach the highway, the sun should be up. Iris got the newer Toyota 4Runner to drive back to Wisconsin. My parents wanted her to have more reliable transportation because she needs to travel a distance for an internship this semester at a remote camp for troubled adolescents. That means we're stuck with her eight year-old Ford F-150 pickup truck. Based on how we're bouncing around in the cab, it's way overdue for new shocks. It's good for a laugh, though—until Dad all at once orders me to exit the upcoming turnoff and I take it too fast. The unpaved road leaves our bones rattling like loose marbles under our skin. *"Jesus criminy, Viktor!"*

"I'm sorry...I'm sorry." As soon as I hit the brakes, the truck skids toward a tall tree stump fixed in the ground like rebar.

Miraculously, we miss it. My hands are welded to the steering wheel at the eight and four position. It's quiet for a second, when I hear, "Shit, Viktor." But it isn't said mean-like. Dad even laughs a little. The humor escapes me. He leans over and wipes my chin. I taste blood and realize I've bitten my tongue. I check it out in the rearview mirror along with the inside of my cheek, which also stings. I'm instructed to take a deep breath and relax my shoulders. Dad then motions to continue down the narrow road, having always been curious about the amount of traffic going in and out of here on his previous trips to Rapid City. I'm angry and tell him he could've given me fair warning. My confidence is shot, and I'm overly cautious now when it comes to maneuvering around one deep hole after another. Lord knows where I'll launch us next time. Two ATVs come from behind a curve and swerve around us. Next a motorcyclist careens past, gunning his engine. Dad insists we keep driving to see what lies ahead. It's obviously a hot spot for off-roading.

The trees are thinning out, which is good, but this old truck is no match for the rutted terrain. I swear I see smoke rising from under the hood on my side, but Dad says it's nothing. He finally agrees to head back to the 44. I aim us in the right direction...but that's as far as we get when the truck sputters a minute before dying altogether. Something is seriously wrong.

I look over Dad's shoulder as he inspects under the hood. He's mad at himself for not replacing a sensor of some kind before the trip. We're relieved when a passing biker calls for a tow truck. Shortly after a driver comes and hooks us up. He takes us deeper into the woods to a place called the Horse Rustler. It's a gas station with a snack bar that is well-known to regulars, but it doesn't appear on any map. Dad tells me to go check out the food while he heads around back to the garage. This is a run-down joint, a hangout for bikers. Depending on what's wrong with our Ford, there might not be the right car parts to fix it here.

In big red letters, now faded, "The Horse Rustler" stretches across the entire side of the building facing the road. Bleeding through the name is a ghostlike image of two horses reared up on their hind legs and fighting each other. The bright white gas pump out front, with no brand name posted anywhere, looks surprisingly new. I walk around it and hop up the wobbly, open wooden steps when suddenly I hear a hissing sound coming from under them. A cat's paw shoots out and strikes my shoe. Inside, the sight of hot dogs turning on a spit makes me really hungry. My sore tongue will hurt when I eat. It's not yet nine o'clock, and I would prefer breakfast with eggs. The only guy working here, maybe he's the owner, is talking to a customer seated at the short counter to my right. He eventually moseys over to me. As I ask about other stuff they serve, like pancakes or omelets, since there's no chalkboard or menu, I'm struck by the serious way this old dude is staring at me. He was laughing loudly with the customer, likely a buddy of his, now he's as deadpan as an undertaker. He tells me my choices, and then he eyes me a good second longer while I wait for him to turn in the order. He's got wiry tangled eyebrows and a shaggy walrus moustache that droops over his mouth, making it hard to read the expression on his face.

My first thought is he doesn't like Indians, but this is where we all live. That can't be it. Next, I figure it's the yellow color of my eyes, which everyone I know ignores by now. When strangers mention how unusual they are, I tell them they're contacts to avoid more questions. This is different. I'm really given the once-over. He's checking out my neck—probably the pulse pounding away in it. Then he looks at my hands that are in plain sight beside the cash register. I feel self-conscious and hate that my cheeks are scalding hot. I can't think of a thing to say. I'm grateful when he goes back to the kitchen, except now his pal eating at the counter is staring at me the same way.

That guy looks every bit the stereotypic outlaw biker. Being older, his tattooed bare head is probably bald instead of shaved. He's solid, with big shoulders, and he's got a fuzzy beard that reaches the middle of his chest. His leather jacket has all kinds of patches on it. He's wearing a thick chain necklace and a wide leather tooled wristband with yellow and red flames, which the man who took my order had, too. I might be taller, but mean makes stronger. Then again...he isn't looking at me in a mean way. *God, Dad, what's taking so long?*

"Did you get something good?" comes the welcoming voice as the door creaks closed behind Dad.

"Bacon and egg sandwich okay?"

We head to one of three small tables crammed in the corner where there's a window. Lots of picnic tables are stacked in rows a distance beyond the wrap-around deck. "Must get pretty busy during the summer months," says Dad when I quickly ask about the truck. I need to know if we can leave anytime soon!

"I spotted a leak," he says, "which isn't the main thing wrong, but the temporary fix will get us to Rapid City. I can use a friend's shop there to work on her. I'm glad Iris didn't drive it back."

Dad looks at me and shakes his head, chuckling over the events. "How's the tongue? Christ, what a morning, huh!"

"Coffee?" The man at the register who left for the kitchen is standing right beside Dad with a coffee pot in hand, presuming the customer with me wants a cup…which he does. I don't dare look up.

"What's wrong, Viktor?" Dad asks. "You brooding over getting us nearly killed?"

My brain is elsewhere.

"Hey…no harm done," he says. I shoot a quick glance over my shoulder as the two men lock eyes. A different person, the cook, limps toward us with our food. As he places the plate in front of me, he looks me square in the eyes—right square into them. Dad is too busy fumbling with the stuck napkins in the metal holder to notice.

At this point I'm nervous. *Three of them against us.* Dad is by no means a lightweight. But then I remember there's also the driver in the garage who had towed us.

"C'mon, eat Viktor. The faster we can get out of here."

Amen to that. I do my best to chew on the left side of my mouth. It's slow going. A couple of cars drive through to buy gas, but no one else stops to come inside. Who would find our bodies out here?

Before leaving, I follow the directions to the restroom that's outside in the back of the building. I can't believe it's clean. Being alone grounds me. As I head back, a guy who just parked his Harley close-by and is walking a few steps in front of me turns to check who's behind him…which is when he turns completely around and stops dead in his tracks, which forces me to stop. A weird expression registers on his face. Not again, I'm thinking. This time I'm looking at an Indian. It seems he wants to say something. When he reaches for my face, I lose it and hop to the side to bolt, but he jumps in front and blocks me, holding fast to my coat sleeve. Before I can escape, he says in a low voice, "You're Constance Howling Wind's boy…aren't you? And Lukas's… Lukas Sun In Eyes." Talk about being thrown for a loop!

From around the corner I hear: "Viktor! Let's hit the road! Move it!" Perfect timing. Without answering, I brush the hand aside then sprint to the front where Dad is waiting by our truck. He can tell there's something off with me. I must be looking wide-eyed and panicked. My neck is wet with sweat. "Let's just go," I say as though my life depended on it.

"Hey, son. What happened?"

The Indian rounds the corner at the same moment the man who runs the place kicks the screen door open and steps out, followed by his buddy at the counter. Dad takes one curious look at me, and then looks back at the Indian who had been behind the building with me. For whatever reason, he doesn't like what he sees, and all at once he storms over to the men on the porch, making a beeline for the Native biker who instinctively holds up his arms in a defensive move and oddly tries to calm him, telling him it's not what he thinks. Keeping my distance, I'm now pleading with Dad, too, agreeing that it's not what he thinks, which is dumb because I don't know what to think. He must have it in his head that the guy tried to hit on me.

"Whoa...whoa..." says the Indian as I call out to Dad a couple more times begging for us to leave. "*You're* the boy's father?"

"You gotta problem with that!" Dad spits out the words, he's so angry and very much still in attack mode. It's unnerving.

What probably surprised the Indian was not that I had another father after all these years, but the fact that my dad, Solomon Davis, is a Black man. Dad has no idea that my birth father's name was mentioned. The subject of Lukas Sun in Eyes has never come up in my family, not in front of us kids, that is. And to think he is known here ... and Mom, too.

In no time, I suddenly find myself on the porch. "Please, Dad. Let's just go...please." I reach out and tug on his jacket. "Please."

"I'm Rex," says the man who was at the cash register, taking advantage of the break in the yelling. "This is AJ and Scratch." He cocks his head toward the Indian. "We were his father's best friends—I mean—I understand you're the kid's dad now, but...you know..." The biker called AJ nods in agreement, and then asks for Dad's name.

Awkward silence follows. Shaking his head in disbelief, Scratch says to me, "You're the spitting image of Lukas. Sorry to have scared you back there, but...it's like you're wearing his face. You're as tall as he was, and your eyes...I wouldn't believe anyone else could have eyes like his."

Again there's silence. No one has ever said that to me...that my eyes are like my father's. I stare blankly at the man.

"There's a picture inside; you can come in and see for yourself," says Rex. "So sorry, man," he tells Dad, and then continues, "Him—the kid—walking in here out of the blue...it was like seeing Lukas. That two people can look exactly the same—I mean exactly. You gotta understand it's mind-blowing."

I'm beyond curious. On our own, Iris and I had read old newspaper stories online about our biological father's capture. I must've been around nine, an age when one starts wondering about things heard in passing while growing up. Lukas Sun In Eyes had confessed to kidnapping our mother and holding her in a cabin in the Black Hills, so there was no trial. That charge alone sent him to prison. The rumor of her having also been raped remained just that, a rumor. I was still too young to fully comprehend the circumstances, even with Iris's explanation. According to Sister, Lukas had raped Mom once before when she was fourteen, but being a confused and embarrassed young girl, she refused to press charges against him. As soon as she learned she was pregnant, she moved off the rez to go live with a missionary couple up in Canada. Mom returned long enough for Iris to be born on the reservation, after which she went back up to Canada with her baby. Lukas had no way of finding her. A few years later, Mom came back to the reservation to get her papers in order to apply to the Air Force Academy. She planned to leave Iris in our great-grandparents' care. Lukas learned she was back in the area and stalked her, nabbing her during a trip she made to Rapid City. Because the crime happened outside the jurisdiction of the tribal authority, U.S. law enforcement became involved. Lukas had held her for a month until the location of the cabin was discovered. He died in jail shortly after I was born on the rez. In photos of him on the courthouse steps, Lukas had worn sunglasses and a wide-brimmed hat that shadowed his face. The press had not been allowed inside the building. Mom's resulting pregnancy stayed out of the news since she remained on the reservation until I was born. I can't help wondering if the picture these guys have is in color. I really want to see it. I don't know how to tell Dad without hurting his feelings.

"Go on, Viktor; it's okay to be curious."

I'm relieved, but I want him to come along. The men no longer scare me, but I want to share this with him, mostly because I can't guess how I'm going to react. He straightens his shirt under his jacket then turns to me. "Go," he orders, "I'll wait in the truck. Take your time."

Rex holds the door open for me. I'm led to a back room with a stocked bar, a pool table, and a couple of ancient pinball machines. The air smells stale. A large bristly-haired dog is sprawled across a threadbare plaid couch that must be decades old. He raises his head, having caught a whiff of something other than cigarettes. The old nose twitches, but then he goes back to sleeping. I take it all in, trying to conjure the image of the man.

Biker brotherhoods are a foreign world to me, one which holds no interest. Rex raises the blinds, letting in the morning light. It's cloudy today, but still bright. Framed photos hang on every wall. Then he points to the one, a large 8x10 print, and yes it is in color.

"*Wow!*" I blurt out, hardly believing what I see.

"That was a great ride," says AJ, "a 93 Sportster. Lukas put his heart and soul into that machine. The girl behind him is Constance. It seems a lifetime ago since I said her name: Constance Howling Wind." He turns to me. "Your mom. You're probably around the same age she was when that picture was taken."

My father. He's magnificent looking. Powerful. His legs are outstretched along the sides of his red Harley and he's holding on to the handlebars. He's wearing jeans and an open black leather fringed vest, no shirt. His arms are thick and muscular. He's got really broad shoulders and ripped abs. Mom has an arm around his waist. Her knees are hugging his thighs. Her other hand is keeping her blowing long hair out of her face. My father's black hair falls clear to his waist. Behind his ears he has a few long, thin braided strands bound together with beaded ropes that have three white-tipped brown feathers dangling from them. They're laughing and looking so happy, crazy happy. This is too much, especially when I wonder how soon after Mom became pregnant with Iris.

"You can have it." Rex reaches to lift the frame off the wall, but I quickly say no to the offer. For some reason I don't want Dad to see me with it. I could hide it under my coat...no, I don't want it, but I do snap a picture with my phone. I thank them and head out. AJ calls after me when I'm in the doorway:

"No matter what people have told you, boy, you have to understand that Lukas worshipped your mom. It was never his intention to hurt her. She was so young...just a girl."

"No other woman could ever take her place," adds Rex. "His love for her was his downfall."

I don't understand...probably never will. I hurry outside to where I find Dad already sitting behind the wheel of our truck, which is idling. Once I'm in the passenger side, and before he takes his foot off the brake, he wants to make sure I'm okay. I don't know what he was expecting... an emotional breakdown of some kind? I just nod, and he starts driving slowly down the pitted road that will get us back to the highway. We talk a little about my final months at school. He will stay behind the wheel until we arrive in Rapid City, which is fine with me. My mind is cluttered with questions I can't put into words yet.

Because the truck needs to be fixed, he has to get to his friend's garage. He drops me off at the mall and hands me a credit card to buy clothes with. We've been invited to stay at the guy's home, so he'll pick me up later. This wasn't the plan. When he pulls out, I stand forlorn at the curb like a stranded five year old. Gone is the enthusiasm I woke up with. The last thing in the world I feel like doing is shopping for clothes...by myself.

The world suddenly turns noisy. Strangers' eyes follow after me. No, this isn't how today was supposed to turn out at all.

It's chilly, but I sit outside on a bench under a tree and debate whether I should see a movie. My mind won't be able to focus on that either. It's impossible to shake this sinking feeling. My thoughts turn to a comfy bedroom in Texas and the few good friends there I'll miss when I go away, especially Bernie who himself is off to MIT next fall. Hillel doesn't separate students into grades like traditional schools, and he got stuck with me as his partner for projects in our engineering class. Bernie Lieberman, who's a year older and a math genius, is the sole child of Jewish parents that had him late in their lives and dote on him as if every day could be their last with him. Mr. and Mrs. Lieberman actually started Hillel Academy, just for Bernie. The regular public school didn't meet their high standards. With the help of a Rabbi who was stationed at Sheppard Air Base, they opened the school over a decade ago with only eleven students. Bernie's father is a banker, and he got lots of donations to turn Hillel into a first rate school with outstanding instructors. Their family's ancestors immigrated to the U.S. from Russia in the late 1800s. Somehow they ended up in northern Texas along with other Russian Jews. Because of Bernie, I picked up a bunch of Yiddish expressions, my favorite being "fercockt." Our teacher, Mr. Schwartz, is forever on Bernie's case about him using the word so much. I'm to blame for things getting fercockt, or fucked up, as often as they are in class, mainly because I'm not big on building structures or robots. Overall, Bernie is patient with me. Microscopes are my thing, which gets me sidetracked thinking about Cornell University's awesome new scanning detector that lets you see at the atomic level. *Did someone just touch my arm?*

"Hey! I've said your name twice!"

I know the girl's face but can't place her. It must show because she reminds me that her brother is Levi Tall Elk, a kid who joined our team a while back. He didn't stay for very long. I remember that Levi had yellow eyes like mine.

"I can't believe who I run into way up here!" Her cheerful attitude is a godsend. She has no idea how great it feels for me to finally smile today.

Marnie must be at least nineteen. I recall now that she had gotten stuck with the job of driving Levi to football practice. Sometimes she'd invite a few of us to get ice cream afterwards. She'd sit with her friends at another table. Marnie says she is enrolled at Black Hills State University. She plans on working in the fashion industry and is taking business and marketing classes. Her shift just ended at her job in the mall and she was heading to her car when she spotted me on the bench. I explain the mission I'm on, to buy new shirts and jeans, and that my friend Daniel was supposed to have come with me on the trip. She remembers him and isn't surprised to learn that he along with some of our other players have dropped out of school.

"It's a wonder I survived going to North Valley," she says, "but then my nose was always in books. Our parents decided Levi needed a different environment and sent him to Bright Cloud. You and your dad never stuck around after the summers. You have a sister, right? Have you ever considered going to Bright Cloud? It has lots of opportunities for kids who can't handle the BS that goes on in the other schools. Jesuits run it, but they don't cram religious nonsense down the students' throats."

I'd sound like I was showing off if I tell her that the opportunities at Levi's school don't compare to the ones at mine. Mom made certain to find the best ranked school in town for Iris and me, unfazed by the fact it was Jewish. I explain that my mother works out of Sheppard Air Force Base and that Dad owns a couple of auto repair shops near Wichita Falls, Texas, which makes staying down there more practical. Marnie has obviously seen Dad on the football field, but I'm surprised when she says that Mom gave a speech at her high school once. I mention that my family discussed the pros and cons of Iris and me remaining on the reservation with my grandmother's parents. "Because our grandmother worked full time as a nurse, they took care of us until I was five and Sister was ten, which is when Mom got sent to Texas and we moved." It's also when Mom and Dad got married, but that's nobody's business. As we talk, I'm aware that

I have her full attention. No longer am I one of her kid brother's little friends.

Marnie always tries to find the right words to convey her thoughts, which causes her to hesitate a lot when she speaks. The fact that she has a big vocabulary is kind of a turn on. I'm blown away when she volunteers to help me find clothes. While she reels off the names of different stores, and who has what, the word convoluted pops into my head. I had used it to refer to the plot of a movie Daniel and I watched last summer, to which he moaned, *not another one.* He told me to stop being so annoying and using big words he didn't know. I hated myself for apologizing, because at that point I was getting upset with him and the other guys, too. They might as well have dropped out of school in the fifth grade because that's when they quit learning. I had no idea that language of all things could divide us. Cussing became the norm with them. I wasn't above swearing for a while, repeating the words I kept hearing around me. When Daniel spelled out the nasty meaning behind some of them one day, because they were in the lyrics to my favorite rap songs, I thought he was joking. No longer could I enjoy the rhythm of the syllables. And when I went back to Texas, I really believed people on the rez had different sex than the parents of my Hillel classmates, because those weren't the same facts of life I was learning about in health class at my Jewish school.

Just as I stand to follow Marnie, she gasps bigtime and raises her hand over her mouth.

"What!" I ask, scared by the look of surprise. She measures an imaginary line from the top of her head to the middle of my chest. Reactions to my growth spurt haven't been as dramatic as hers, but then she hasn't seen me in forever, and she is on the short side, not typical of someone whose background is also Rawakota like mine. The short genes must come from lots of intermarriages with outsiders.

What the attention of a girl can do for a lousy mood! I thought the mall was loud and ugly, now it's colorful and the people seem happy. The events of the morning are history, as is the promise of Dad meeting up with me later. All that matters is a pretty girl—make that a young woman—is definitely flirting with me. I finally force my mouth muscles to relax after developing cheek pain from constantly smiling. It still smarts from when I bit it earlier. I tell Marnie about the incident and she gives me some ibuprofen.

We talk continuously and I learn Marnie is a staunch separatist, wanting the reservation to break ties with the U.S. and form its own Republic of Lakota. Once she graduates and gains more business experience, she wants to return to the rez and create a company that manufactures Native products using local resources. I admire her entrepreneurial spirit. She asks how I intend to give back to the community in the future. "Whoa, Marnie, stop right there," I tell her. "I can only think as far ahead as surviving my first year at Ohio State, as a sixteen year old no less." She laughs and changes the subject. There's no bothering to ask about the circumstances that led to my starting college early.

After several hours we head to the food court. It's the longest this growing boy has gone without eating in a while. Four bulging bags take up a chair. I didn't give a second thought as to how much I was charging to Dad's VISA card. He can't complain; he didn't set a limit. During the shopping process, I discovered what colors go best with my dark skin and black hair, the style of jeans I look good in, as well as what colognes are a hit with the girls; things I'd have otherwise missed out on if it were only Dad and me at the mall today. Whenever I stepped out of a dressing room for advice, Marnie tucked in my shirt, or checked the waist to see how snug the pants fit. She helped pull sweaters over my head. I loved the sensation of her touch. I've never dated anyone yet. There was one horrible encounter with a girl that I wish to forget happened. Outside of school, this is the closest I've been to a girl, especially one who lights up my insides the way Marnie does. My phone rings. Dad asks whether I can hold out an hour more for the truck to be finished. I tell him shopping was a success, that I met someone from home and not to hurry.

Marnie again brings up the subject of an earlier train of thought, which irritates me. "Viktor, even though you have a lot of other things to think about now, being mindful of your Native heritage should always come first, especially since you, like me, are directly descended from the same people who established our sacred city under the mountains. That is unique to us and incredibly special."

She reminds me of my sister when she's trying to drive home a point. Isn't it obvious to her that I simply want to enjoy her company? I'm tired. I find comfort in her pretty light brown eyes that have taken on such a serious look.

"It isn't fair that only boys inherit golden eyes. Aren't you proud of being identified as Rawakota simply because of your physical appearance?"

She comes off sounding like an elitist. Fighting a yawn, "Marnie...there are too many accounts about our origins. Don't give credence to the stories. They're about as real as the gods on Mt. Olympus." I'm caught off guard by a strong desire to kiss her.

It's around five o'clock, but the winter sky is already dark. I'm growing impatient with this conversation. I would ask to sit outside but the temperature is dropping. Marnie's nationalistic sentiments turn into a rant against white people. Aargh! Too many complex ideas to delve into right now. Besides, I haven't decided where I stand on a lot of the issues. *Darn!* I'm forced to speak up after this last comment. Marnie shows her biased version of history when she talks about the European traders who purposely offered the Indians blankets infected with smallpox. I tell her there aren't enough facts to support the claim, which upsets her and puts her on the defensive. Again I interrupt her long-winded argument, in order to report that virology will be my major at school, and that I've researched the topic in detail. Since the seventh grade, when we learned how diseases wiped out most of the Native American population, as well as other groups, the subject became all-consuming. "After the country was colonized, Indians were exposed to a host of new agents that can't all be attributed to smallpox. For example, Leptospirosis infections spread by rodents likely contaminated stored foods and water supplies that were commonly shared. Indians had stopped being hunter-gatherers."

"Yeah, thanks to the Europeans forcing us on reservations. I guess I've been one-upped." Her voice is flat.

I'm not about to say I'm sorry, instead I tell her, "It's understandable to believe something is fact if it helps one's cause. For the most part, our history was passed down orally. Without written reports made by eyewitnesses agreeing to what they saw or heard, the stories can't be considered credible." I rub my eyes. It's impossible to think another thought; I'm wiped out. The day was already overwhelming as it was, and now I have to deal with this? Surprisingly, she doesn't counter with another remark. We sit watching the people in silence. They all blur together at this point.

"Where are you spending the night?" she asks.

"At a friend of Dad's." I prop my head up with my hand. "I'm fading fast, Marnie."

"I can see that." She looks friendly, not like we had a major disagreement. "Call'm up and get the address. I don't mind taking you there." I'm speechless at the offer. "Go on. Call."

I do, after which I manage to find my second wind. We leave the mall to go to a nearby Best Western, not dad's friend's house. That was unexpected. He appreciates that I've got a ride and tells me to thank the person for him. In only a few minutes we arrive, but instead of pulling up to the front office, Marnie parks in the lot far from a lamp post. My breathing picks up. She scoots sideways behind the wheel so she can face me, and then brings a knee up to rest her leg between my thighs. After helping her out of her coat, I manage to get my arms out of my jacket right as she reaches for the lever to make the seat go back. I can only think about the breasts squished against my chest. Soft lips brush my eyelids, then my ears. When she kisses me full on the lips, I'm a goner.

CHAPTER 3

A blur of knives whiz past my ears, having missed their target—namely me. I can't keep this up, zigzagging this way and that to keep from getting struck. I escape the dangerous forest only to find myself standing exposed in a small clearing with nothing but sky beyond it. Out of breath and sweating, I inch back, watching for the slightest movement in the underbrush, wondering why someone has it in for me. A bad step too near the ledge sends me hurtling over the cliff toward certain death. Terror takes hold as the rush of air forces my useless arms and legs up and away from my body.

"Damn it, Viktor! Wake up!"

Who's shouting so far off in the distance? I pray to our Creator to please let me blackout before getting dashed to bits on the rocks below. *Ow!*

My eyes pop open. Dad looks upset. I don't know why. The sky appears again ... I'm still freefalling to earth!

"Christ, Viktor. Shit!" His saving hands shake me awake. "If I didn't know better," he yells, "I'd swear you were on something!"

Grateful to be conscious, I shoot forward off the pillow to throw my arms around him. "I had a dream, a nightmare! God, it was horrible!" My heart feels ready to burst and my jaw is shaking. "I fell off a cliff...and there was nothing to hold on to."

"Hey, son..." His tone changes, in order to calm me. I'm called *son* whenever Dad is worried about my well-being. I manage a weak smile and wipe his shaving cream from my ear. He was getting ready and is in his undershorts with a towel around his neck.

"They say you'll wake up before actually dying in a dream, but my heart would've stopped for good if you hadn't been here."

"From the looks of it, I'm inclined to agree." He dries his chin and goes back to the bathroom. "You were moaning when I went to clean up. I assumed you were thinking about something enjoyable. Next you're screaming and waving your arms all over and kicking your feet in the air like a maniac." He shakes his head and tells me to shower so we can grab breakfast somewhere.

As I clamber out of the jumbled bed sheets, he says he's sorry for squeezing my arms so hard to wake me. Okay, so that pain *was* real.

Standing under the hot water and breathing in the warm steam relaxes me. For some reason I start thinking about Iris, specifically when she left for college after high school. Getting called *son* a few minutes ago probably sparked the memory. I had just turned twelve. Following a stint in Greece that lasted for nearly a year, Mom came home to Texas to see Sister off. During her absence my voice had changed. We also stood eye-to-eye; I had grown to her height of five feet ten inches. There was no great show of emotion upon seeing me like there'd been other times. She barely brushed my cheek in a hello kiss. Worst of all, I didn't even get a hug. We talked together just fine, but the lack of physical contact continued, to the point where I couldn't take it anymore and asked whether I had done something wrong. She stated that I had become a young man and shouldn't expect to be treated as if I were still a boy. Dad hit the roof when I told him. He called me son for weeks, maybe even months, hoping it would help me get over feeling dejected, but it didn't.

We head across the parking lot to a coffee shop. The sun will probably lose out today. Every so often a sliver of light breaks through the low lying clouds. A soft layer of snow swirls around our feet. A couple of kids are catching fat snowflakes in their mouths. I'm not above such childish behavior and stick my tongue out as far as it'll go.

"Jesus, Viktor...*really!*"

I get a kick out of embarrassing him. "Open the hangar, Dad! They're flyin' in!" I tug on his chin to pry his mouth open.

"You're hopeless," he laughs, swatting my hand away as he opens the door. "I guess you don't mind people thinking you're a little touched in the head."

Besides smelling great, the fresh pastries under the glass counter are works of art, like in Kreuz's Deli down the street from my school. Dad orders a cappuccino for starters while I ask for hot chocolate...with extra whipped cream. The winter weather is definitely bringing out the kid in me. We settle in a corner with its own free-standing stove. The puny little fire is enough to set the mood. The place is empty except for those few customers who were in line behind us for take-out. It's still early.

"This is perfect," I tell him, looking around. The ceiling has big solid wooden beams that make the room cozy, as does the pinecone wallpaper. "So, why didn't we stay with your friend?"

"Bob is having marital problems." He then asks whether we should take advantage of this time to discuss what happened along the way yesterday. I agree, but am not sure how to begin. We watch the blue flame in the stove. A jarring loud pop in the overhead speakers prepares us for some music. Willie Nelson's soothing, weathered voice fills the space. "Nice," says Dad. The woman who took our order comes over with our drinks. Not to be mean, but she's built like one of those hardy Bavarian waitresses I've seen in pictures who can haul a dozen liter beer glasses on a tray. Her breasts are incredible. They jut out over the top of her blouse and jiggle as she walks. It's hard not to stare. Dad waits until she's gone then says, grinning, "You can stick your eyes back in their sockets."

He goes on to say that he thought the mall was just down the road from the motel. "I wanted to have a sandwich with you, but then went ahead and ate. I didn't feel like waiting up anymore."

"Sorry." I sense my face getting hot. I wonder if it's noticeable. I tell him a little about Marnie and add that we stayed in the car after driving here…to talk. He gives me a knowing smile and sips his coffee. We watch out the window as more snow starts falling, taking in Willie's rendition of *Blue Skies*.

"You're so young, Viktor," he says, as if to himself.

"What do you mean?" I laugh. "Just because of the silliness with the snowflakes?"

He looks at me with concern. "You think you'll last at OSU? It's such a big school, Son…and so far away."

This is the first time he has expressed any misgivings about my going to Ohio State. I assure him I'll be fine.

"Uncle William will be there," I remind him, if only to comfort myself. I knew his wife better, my Aunt Loretta—Auntie and her humongous cats. Ovarian cancer killed her a couple of years ago. I haven't given a second thought as to what living with him will be like, figuring classes are going to take up my entire day, and nights, too, more than likely.

Three people come in and sit along an opposite wall. They immediately set up laptops and stick their ear buds in. Dad waits quietly for me to start this conversation about my reaction to what the men at The Horse Rustler had to say about Lukas. I'm stalling, which is unusual; it's always been easy to talk to Dad about everything—at least until this past year. It's been a rough period for both of us in terms of dealing with the things that have happened to my group of friends, boys he took under his wing so many years ago. They've either died, been arrested, or, like in Daniel's case, are headed nowhere. It wasn't easy for him to leave his business in the hands of his employees for long stretches every year while he brought Iris and me up to South Dakota. He felt so fortunate for having straightened himself out in prison that he wanted to help others find a purpose. Dad went so far as to invite Daniel to come live with us in Texas, to keep him from getting caught up in the gang culture. It's hard to believe that the idea of leaving the rez scared Daniel more than dealing with criminals.

"I do have a question…but it means describing the photo, and you didn't want to see it."

"Shoot." Dad has switched to wearing what I call his Denzel smile, his all-is-right-with-the-world smile.

"Okay." This might be easier if I were older, and we could discuss this in a bar over whiskey. I'm not sure about calling Lukas by his name, but I can't go on saying my biological father. It's weird either way. It must have been upsetting for Dad to hear that I'm a dead ringer for Lukas. It was for me, but that isn't the thing that's bugging me, the main thing that is. All right, here goes! "In the picture of Lukas on his motorcycle with Mom behind him, they appear to be having the best time." I won't reveal to Dad that they looked very much in love. I lean in and cross my arms on the table, lowering my voice so no one around will hear—not that anyone can, but it is a private matter. "Mom got raped by him, which doesn't make sense. You know what I mean?"

Dad sucks in a big breath then lets it go. We must look like we're plotting something serious. He sits forward and puts his cup on the table.

"Viktor, I'm not going to guess what you're asking. Be specific."

He's got me there. How to word this without using names. "If two people really love each other, how can their having sex ever be considered rape?" He looks thoughtfully at me.

"Do you think couples are always in the mood at the same time?"

I take a moment then answer truthfully, "I would hope so…" The short laugh, rude the way I see it, seems as though he's making fun of me, which I don't appreciate, and I tell him as much. "I can't help it if I don't have any experience to draw from…that's why I'm asking."

"You're right. That was uncalled for. It's hard going back to your age and remembering what it was like coming to grips with such powerful emotions for the first time. I was high most of the time anyways, but you know that. The girls I was with all blur together. Have you had sex yet?"

I am struck dumb. It's obvious the question made me uncomfortable.

"Sorry, Viktor, that's your business."

Maybe having this talk isn't such a good idea. Normally, Daniel and I would've gone on all night about stuff like this. There's no one in Texas that I'm that tight with. Even Bernie, who's older, has never had a girlfriend. I don't want this phase of my life to be the start of Dad and me growing apart.

"Let me tell you what your mother, and to some degree her family, too, shared with me about what happened to her. It was before we got married."

He has my full attention.

"Your mom hit puberty early, so I was told, and she liked to make eyes at the boys. During the summer before her freshman year in high school, your grandparents wanted a porch built on the house and some roofing work done, so they called a neighbor who was a handyman. He brought Lukas to help with the job. Constance immediately fell for him. He was her first crush. And Lukas apparently played along, something a thirty-plus-year-old man should have known better about doing. Today he'd be arrested.

"In any case, Lukas took her for rides on his Harley behind her parents' back. She blew up when Benjamin and Victoria told him not to come around anymore. In the meantime, he decided she was the girl for him, to the point that his interest in her became obsessive, which pretty much matched her emotions. Your mom confessed she worshipped him."

That's hard for me to picture, or maybe I don't want to. I'm jealous of people who knew Mom before her career took over her life. Once upon a time this mother and son did have fun together, back when I was little. She'd come home on leave and we would dance and sing and play the piano…and teach the horses tricks. She taught me to shoot with a bow and arrow and to throw knives. It seems forever ago. I sometimes wonder if I made it up.

Dad continues. "There was no police...no authority on the rez back then. We're talking over twenty years ago. Your poor grandfather went out nights and drove around for miles trying to find her, following leads about parties they might be at. This lasted for months until he realized it was useless. By then your mom had quit showing up at school.

"After a couple of months, Constance finally returned home. She didn't speak to anyone, barely ate...just sat in her room and cried. I'm sure you've gathered it's when she realized she was pregnant. She told her parents that she hadn't really wanted to go all the way with Lukas, but he didn't listen. He in fact wanted a child, and he tried to convince her that she was meant to be the mother of his baby. The thought terrified her. One night after he had fallen asleep, she ran to the highway and hitched a ride home."

I imagine her on a dark road making her escape. "She must've been scared out of her mind. Did she wind up hating him? So then...how can someone tell the difference between a crush and true love?"

He sits back in his chair and ponders it a second. "Honestly, Son..." I'm hanging on his words. "It's mostly luck when you find that person who loves you back the same. If it were easy, it wouldn't be special, and that's what adds magic to the relationship. And for love to last, well, that *is* up to you. That's a conscious decision."

"But what if one person falls out of love?"

"There are reasons when that happens. You both have to get to the bottom of them. You can fall back in love with someone, if you choose."

Guess more living needs to be done on my part. That made no sense. I worry I'll never enjoy that magical moment, mostly because of my fault-finding tendencies that Iris has pointed out a number of times. Mom's behavior as a teen really bothers me.

"I don't think it was right for Mom to get that involved with Lukas, and then opt out when he wanted more from her. Do you? Girls who do that get a reputation for being a tease."

"An immature kid can't weigh consequences. A grown man is plain stupid for taking advantage of that kind of ignorance."

The tables are filling quickly. We decide to let others enjoy our spot. Outside the snow is beginning to stick. It also feels colder than an hour ago because it's windier. Dad decides we should stay another night, which works for me. He asks if I want to spend time with the friend from the mall. I tell him Marnie works today and is busy tonight. I don't know whether she is.

We hit the exercise room before a swim. This is a terrific motel. It's Wednesday and the parking lot is empty, but based on the hubbub going on in the convention rooms, there must be some large groups expected for the upcoming weekend. Today, however, we have the equipment and pool to ourselves.

Taking a break on a bench, Dad asks, "I've thought about what you said. Tell me, would you go ahead and force yourself on a girl if she's led you to believe she wants to have sex, but then changes her mind, even when you're right *there*, ready to go in?"

Un-hee! Do I really want to go down this road with him? My left leg starts bouncing up and down, a nervous habit that's hard to break. We've had discussions about this predicament at school...with outside speakers who've come in from the police department and women's organizations.

"I used to think a girl was just as responsible as a guy for letting things go that far, and so she shouldn't suddenly be unwilling to go all the way. But I've learned that when a gut feeling tells you no, not now, it should be respected. I mean...a guy might want to back out at the last second, too." He looks curiously at me. I've hinted at something too personal. Damn my bouncy leg! That's as far as I'm willing to go on the subject for now. The gym is *not* the place for this discussion. Dad drops it and gives my neck a friendly squeeze.

We actually swim laps and don't horse around in the water like we normally do. The nice thing about our tight knit neighborhood in Texas is that everyone knows Dad personally, and therefore knows that this Black man is my father...and of course, Iris's, too. When we travel, however, he keeps his distance in public, more so now that I've grown taller than him. He says that people might assume there's something improper about our relationship if he shows me affection. I just don't see it that way and often forget, placing an arm around him, simply because I like being physically close to him. He makes me feel good, safe. Iris understands his position on the matter, but then she's never sought love from him like I do. As we've grown older, I realize I'm the needier child.

We return to our room after stuffing ourselves at a nearby Olive Garden where their unlimited breadsticks are my downfall. Dad tipped the waitress extra on account of the basketfuls I polished off. He searches for a TV program while I roll onto the bed, hoping the digestive process hurries along faster.

I think back over what I ended up revealing to him. We had gone to the restaurant during non-peak hours so it wasn't packed and felt private enough to talk. I brought up the week in December before we left Texas to come up here. It was the start of winter break, and a girl I was friends with from the Honor Society invited me to her house for a party, or so I thought. When I showed up at Ashley's place, no one else was there. Dad looked to know where this was heading. She said her parents were out of town, her brother was at sleep-over, and would I consider having sex with her. She was older than me, a senior, and she didn't want to be a virgin when she entered college in the fall. There was no boyfriend in the picture, so she wondered if I was willing to do this favor for her. I told Dad that I wanted her more than anything, which he confessed he would've, too.

I went on to tell him that after we got undressed and had been going at it a while, it hit me that I wished I were experiencing what I was feeling with a girl who meant something to me, a girl I loved. There was no way for me to know beforehand it would bother me to such a degree.

Dad sat quietly listening during this tell-all, swirling his beer in the bottle. Up until then I had managed to describe the details as though I were talking about somebody else. But when I reached the part of the story when I slid inside her, I relived the panic I had felt at the time. I just wanted to escape out the door. It had been a humiliating experience, one I wish I could take back. I told Dad that I pulled out in time, not because I hadn't worn a condom, I had, but because I didn't want to give her that emotional part of me. He asked if it upset her. I told him I doubted she noticed. She just seemed glad it did the trick. At that, he held back a smile, and I found myself laughing a little. I needed to know from him if there was something wrong with me, figuring that's the last thing any normal guy would do. Before he could answer, I thought I might as well give him an account of what happened with Marnie in the car last night.

There again, like with Ashley, I couldn't believe my luck when the fantasy I'd had at the mall about kissing Marnie was really going to play out in the motel's parking lot. Everything was great, until she unzipped my jeans, which is when I grabbed her wrist to keep her from going any further. I didn't want to stop kissing her, though. When I thought about my reaction later last night in bed, it really bugged me, and I wondered if I have a psychological problem that counselling might help me overcome. Dad didn't think so and suggested that I merely set high standards for myself. He admired me for not going through with something I wasn't one hundred percent sure about doing—which sounds like a good thing, but isn't that the same as Iris stating I'm too picky? I could wind up alone for the rest of my life.

A sudden bold knock at the door has Dad and me looking at each other. He goes to open it. "Hello, Mr. Davis." Marnie! Fuck! If her ears aren't burning because she was just in my thoughts, mine certainly are from embarrassment. That Dad has a mental picture of the two of us all over each other is more than I can take. It didn't matter when I assumed that she and I were never going to see each other again. What could she possibly want? To go out...in a snowstorm? I hop off the bed, wishing it were possible to make her disappear at the snap of a finger.

While Dad shows Marnie into the room, they discuss her brother, Levi. He recalls him, despite the fact that he played on our team for such a short time. So Levi is going to study agriculture after high school *blah-blah-blah*; get on with it already! I compose myself, if only slightly, managing not to shake when she comes over and transfers a kiss carried on her fingertips from her mouth to my lips.

"Hey, Marnie. How'd you know we'd still be here?" I sound calm, or so I think.

"I didn't, but the place is so close to the mall, I thought I'd stop and check on my way home. Bet you're wondering why," she teases. Her eyes catch the light from the TV and shine real pretty. I wish I shared her easy-breezy manner. She's got some nerve pulling out the chair from the desk after dropping by uninvited. While Dad hangs up her coat, she holds out a bag I forgot to take with me last night, which I hadn't noticed yet.

I'm relieved to hear that she can't stay more than fifteen minutes. Let the countdown begin! Her cheery disposition turns more serious. Apparently, something I said yesterday stayed with her, to the point that she felt compelled to swing by and get it off her chest. This ought to be good. Dad turns off the TV and takes the corner chair after tossing the clothes clumped together on it into his duffle bag on the floor. That leaves the bed for me to sit on.

She gets right to the point. "Remember what you said at the mall about the Rawakota's oral history not being as reliable as written history?"

Is she serious?

"Anything that is written," she continues, "is as inherently biased as an oral narrative that's passed down. The people who put pen to paper to record events for posterity were influenced by the times they lived in, the same as they are today…how do you not get that?"

The memory of my exact words is lost. It was the end of a long day, and I was exhausted. I can only restate what I likely said. "How can a story told over the course of centuries retain details from the original version?" The frown on her face better not be a sign of a longer visit, in order to what—change my mind?

"You must agree," she says, "that the written Bible is no truthful account of history, but it is reliable to the extent that followers believe the events that took place in it were based on actual occurrences. It's the same with Indians. There were always special members in the tribe who were responsible for maintaining the accuracy of our oral histories. At the core of these stories were important ideas that have held true through the ages."

Dad hasn't chimed in. I push my hair behind my ears and straighten my back. "Why should it matter at all what I think?"

She quickly checks the time on her phone, then looks back at me. "You strike me as a guy who accomplishes what he sets out to do. One day, Viktor, you might become a meaningful role model for Native boys. I just think it's wrong of you not to acknowledge your Rawakota roots more. They go back further than any other indigenous tribe's on the continent. You told me that your great-grandparents on the reservation cared for you during the first years of your life. That is such a formative period. There must have been customs they clung to that influenced you. How can it not feed your spirit today?"

My jaw tightens. How can she presume to know squat about my upbringing. I glance at Dad, just to see if her comments are registering with him. He raises his eyebrows, as if to say the ball's in my court. I can't tell whether he views this situation with humor or genuine interest. I seldom think back that far to when Sunkwah and Winnie looked after Iris and me, the years before Solomon Davis entered our lives. I was five when we got a dad, which was all I'd ever been wishing for, and it's the most vivid memory I have from my childhood.

"Of course they influenced me," I tell her. "When I was around nine, my Mom's father and grandfather taught me how to hunt pheasants and bison and deer. I learned to skin and prepare a hide, as well as butcher the animal in the old way and preserve the meat. It was the Lakota who taught my Rawakota relatives' ancestors the techniques when they chose to make this territory their home, too." Why am I bothering to defend my position? I find I can't stop.

"You see, Marnie, our traditions aren't lost on me. In fact, for my college essay I described what growing up in a white Texas community was like compared to being raised on a Lakota reservation. I have a unique perspective on both worlds. Certain aspects of my Indian culture will always be important to me, and I include them in my daily routines."

"I'm impressed," she says, sounding sincere.

I add that once I'm going to Ohio State, I'll try to find people who might consider financing Native youth programs here in South Dakota. With that, her eyes narrow. The wheels are once again turning in that head of hers. *Not good* I'm thinking.

"Taking money from non-Natives only encourages tribal members to continue being dependent on outsiders. It should be outlawed! Look at how the government has ruined reservation life with their federal subsidies. How will you know where the money is really going from your rich, probably white, new *friends*?"

God, she's exasperating! "The Lakota and other tribes belonging to the Great Sioux Nation aren't that admirable, historically speaking. They booted the Cheyenne out of the Black Hills. They're guilty of their own infighting. Every group has blood on its hands. Maybe outside money isn't the solution to our problems, but it will give us the means to build medical clinics and more schools. There's no moving forward if you aren't healthy and educated."

As Marnie stands to leave, she makes this annoying clucking sound with her tongue to show what she thinks of my ideas. "You're talking about changes that are decades in the making, Viktor. We can't wait any longer to stop this downward spiral." She shakes her head and looks at Dad. "We need the kind of activism there was in the sixties, with leaders like Bobby Seale and Stokely Carmichael." *Who?* She says it like he should know them. I stand now, too, thinking I might have to resort to pushing her out the door, especially when she opens her mouth to speak some more. "Understand this, Viktor, wasichu—white people—always have an agenda. Never underestimate them."

"Well I have my own agenda, too, Marnie!"

"And don't believe for a second that the good folks at Ohio State won't recognize it and figure out how yours can best serve theirs!"

I'm done. Dad, too. He goes to grab her coat out of the closet. After slipping into it, she faces me again. "Something else just crossed my mind. How can you play football for a big name university when you're not part of a top division high school?" Boy do I regret telling her that OSU was going to allow me to try out as walk-on when I felt ready. "I know you've got a good arm. Levi used to go on and on about your throwing abilities...but this is a huge country with lots of outstanding players, proven players. I don't mean to downplay your talent, but doesn't that make you suspicious of their motives? Why would they make you such an offer?"

On that note, Dad opens the door. He's definitely biting his tongue. She offers me a hug then says, in a kinder voice, "Dear Talking White Owl, Hinhán ska, have fun at college. Wear your feathers and beads once in a while, and please don't ever fall for a white man's promise. Don't be a dimwitted Indian. Watch who you trust, that's all I'm saying." Next she shakes Dad's hand and tells him how fortunate his son is to have a man like him for a father, and that Levi and the rest of her family appreciated his support following the untimely death of their own father in a tractor accident, news that jogs my memory.

Dad and I remain in the doorway, watching Marnie as she heads down the hallway. I can't explain it, but something overcomes me, and I grab my jacket and race to catch up to her. We don't say a word on the elevator ride down. Once outside, the beauty of the night stops us in our tracks. The snow is falling so lightly the flakes seem suspended in the air. The white ground glitters as if covered by a sheet of sequins. A busy snowplow is nearby. We hold on to each other, stepping cautiously to her car which is parked directly in front of the lobby. Before climbing behind the wheel, she turns and faces me. I think she's waiting to be kissed. I don't want to misread the moment. Taking hold of her with a tight grip, I hoist her up until our lips meet. Despite her headstrong personality, she still excites me. The sensation is short-lived when next she says goodbye. There's no invitation to join her inside the front seat for a repeat of last night's passionate make-out session.

Dad can't hide his surprise over my swift return. As quickly as the shoes come off, I'm on the bed. "Does her brain operate in overdrive 24-7?" he asks, not trying to be funny.

He sized her up right. "She is beautiful, though, don't you think?"

"Very. Is she someone you could be serious about?"

"Daaad!"

"I know… just curious if that type interests you." Can there be a type at my age I wonder. He falls onto his bed and rests against the headboard, pleased to have found some old black and white WWII movie. As for me, I close my eyes and pick up where I'd left off on that kiss.

Dad tosses me the keys. "Time to blow this pop stand."

"All right!" I feel up for driving. We managed to fit in a last minute workout this morning. Ate a huge breakfast. Now it's goodbye Rapid City. The snow has begun to melt on the streets and freeway, helped along by scads of sunbeams stretching from the clouds to the ground. It looks downright godly. Iris left a CD of traditional Lakota music in the truck, which runs great now. I join in the chants and drum the steering wheel. Dad is already asleep and quietly snoring. Guess he isn't used to exercising so early. He doesn't even budge during the loud wailing choruses. I'm a coyote howling in the wind. I picture myself riding Jim at full speed. Life is good. "This song's for you, Jim." I keep at it, pounding the wheel, glad that Grandmother will be taking care of him from now on. He won't have to face getting hauled between Texas and Dakota anymore, even though he likes traveling, and he did enjoy the ranch where we boarded him. My thoughts turn to college. I am so psyched about going to a big campus. And to think, one day, a face will stand out from the crowd, one that makes my heart stop. I'll be bouncing off the walls until it happens. Forget what Iris says about me being picky, there's bound to be somebody for me among the tens of thousands of girls at OSU. Seems the odds are in my favor.

CHAPTER 4

"We call upon the Spirits of our ancestors," begins Chairman Black Horse, a Mohawk, speaking in his native tongue as he officially opens the Council of First Nations' meeting. *"Help guide us in our efforts to maintain our traditional customs. Too many children right now feel hopeless because they are losing their cultural connections. We pray that those who become agents of change for the future recognize you in the wind, in the trees, and in the rivers... grace them with your wisdom."*

When he finishes, the impassioned voices of the mostly male attendees, four are women, fill the great room of this fishing lodge that's located in the Canadian Province of Manitoba. Together in English they pledge to win back full independence from the U.S. and Canada, the culprits of a devastating colonial legacy that left their people powerless on their own land. The impressive wooden log structure and its furnishings, which includes the long rustic pine table they're seated around, were recently willed to the Council by a generous, unmarried and childless member, who, remarkably, became a successful Indigenous entrepreneur in the construction industry. The remote backwoods setting is a pleasant change from the impersonal conference centers inside loud casinos where the group normally holds its meetings.

Twenty-eight out of the fifty-two members who comprise the Council braved the elements and traveled to the secluded site this blustery and frigid final week in January. The leaders, roughly half of whom are actual chiefs, are voted to the position by their people. They represent the most populous Indigenous Nations on the continent—Métis, Choctaw, Sioux, Apache, and Iroquois, to name a few. No matter their individual differences, all commonly refer to home as Mother Earth, which serves as the basis for most policy-making. Being good stewards of the environment has been, and always will be, central to decisions that affect the quality of life on reservations, or reserves as they're called up here. In recent years, though, tribal leaders have been getting criticized by the young people who feel they're being ignored when it comes to helping solve the problems that impact them. As a result, teenagers have resorted to creating their own inter-tribal youth movement, using the Internet. The Council now wishes to rectify that oversight.

Back when the organization was known as the Circle of Elders, and only tribal chiefs possessed authority to run things, leaders actually got together with one another to work out trade deals and hunting ground disputes, until the Europeans arrived. The Indians' age-old systems of governance ended when the pale-skinned newcomers drew up their own self-serving boundary lines in the 1800s. With predatory zeal, the colonists laid claim to the entire continent, and did it aggressively with guns and written laws. Evidently, a god in their holy book gave them dominion over these lands inhabited by "heathens." The whites called themselves Christians, and after they successfully moved most Indians onto reservations, the group of tribal chiefs never saw each other again. The entire Indigenous population in the northern hemisphere had to face the fact they were going to be stuck on these lands forever, lands that held no significance to them. Fast forward to today, when plenty of Native people have mobilized to contest that gross injustice. Holding title to property is key to building wealth the white man's way. Without it, one has no collateral for securing loans, and you stay poor. To the Council's credit, tribal representatives have been working diligently for decades with the government to change the demoralizing paternalistic features of past treaties and doctrines. The very idea that the U.S. believed it had to "protect" Indians by holding their lands in trust for them fuels the current separatist movement. Although the Council of First Nations has made considerable headway to date when it comes to bringing tribal issues to the forefront, their detractors argue that progress has been too slow in coming. And they'd be right, which is why the organization is crafting new strategies.

The first item on the Council's agenda during this particular session is to consider the names of a few bright young hopefuls they'd be willing to support in whatever way they can. Topping the list is a Lakota boy named Viktor Talking White Owl, who at age fifteen was awarded a full-tuition academic scholarship. His college essay gets read aloud, which expresses why his Native background is so important to him. And although Talking White Owl is admittedly quite young, there is no question that he is a standout student.

Three other individuals are mentioned as well. One is an 18 year-old Iroquois tennis player of the Turtle Clan, who is an advocate for Native children in foster care. There is the 20 year-old Kiowa champion swimmer at the University of Florida. Because an older brother got locked up following a run-in with police, she seeks to start a program to help reintegrate jailed kids back into their communities. And then there's Jason Red Moon. Everyone seems most excited about the 22 year-old Apache actor who's on the verge of becoming an international star after the release of a big Hollywood special effects movie. For years, Red Moon has been vocal about protecting a sacred Arizona site from a copper mining company.

The leaders agree that if even one of these young persons could successfully pitch the value of higher education to the upcoming generation, it would change the landscape entirely. Viktor obviously sets a good example. These ongoing problems that strip the dignity from their people must be solved or the Nations can never hope to attain total sovereignty. The task appears daunting, mostly because the Indian DNA has grown muddied over recent times, a matter that takes precedence during the biannual meetings. The leaders are constantly asked: How much *Indian* does a person have to be, in order to qualify for Native status within the tribes? In the late 1980s a committee was formed to deal with the question. Some resolution is finally forthcoming. It was decided that biological markers alone do not classify one as true Indian, that tribal identity should also be based on how an individual incorporates traditional customs and culture into his or her life. Because tribesmen routinely adopted children from conquered enemies, both Native and European, and warriors took their women for wives, ethnic purity based on bloodlines cannot be the sole determinant used for Native American documentation.

The caterer hired for the occasion interrupts the group to announce that lunch is ready. The buffet-style meal is served in a huge kitchen that includes an impressive commercial-size range with double ovens. The place was obviously built for entertaining. As the leaders wander the rooms with plate-in-hand, they discuss the scope of their influence in different cities. It was inevitable that at some point Roger Bertrand's name would come up, along with the bus accident that killed him last year. He inspired people on so many levels. The likable, articulate, 26-year-old Canadian pro hockey player was passionate about his sport as well as his Haudenosaunee background, the name he preferred over Iroquois. During the off-season, he continued to live among the families he grew up with on a reserve in Ontario. That is really the main question on everyone's mind: Who can match the hockey player's influence and generosity?

Upon reconvening in the great room around the long table, William Horse That Walks Backwards raises his hand to speak. He thanks the members for wanting to support his nephew, Viktor Talking White Owl. "My sister-in-law and I have already finalized plans for him to live with me while he goes to college." Horse That Walks Backwards holds no illustrious title, but his words carry weight. He is here in place of the boy's mother, U.S. Air Force pilot Captain Constance Howling Wind, an honorary member. Her ability to bolster the confidence of disillusioned boys and girls raised in squalor on reservations has long been lauded, as is her knack for getting corporate bigwigs to bankroll needed projects on the reservations, like replacing a flooded school gym floor, or purchasing squad cars and modern equipment for tribal police departments.

One thing the Council is completely in the dark about concerning the distinguished Captain Howling Wind is that her main loyalty does not lie with the U.S.A.—as her uniform would suggest. Years ago, at the outset of her military career, Howling Wind aligned herself with an altogether different Nation, an enterprising one with a bold vision of what Native communities should look like in the 21ST century. It's no secret that both she and her brother-in-law trace their ancestry back to them, but learning that the Rawakota Nation exists intact to this day would astound the Council members, especially those from the nearby states of South Dakota, Montana, and Wyoming, where the Black Hills mountain range is located, the region once home to the people. It's common knowledge that the yellow-eyed tribe broke up around a hundred and fifty years ago, joining nearby bands of Indians that comprise the Lakota—which is exactly what the shrewd Rawakota wanted everyone to think, colonists and Indians alike. It wasn't a deception intended to undermine their fellow tribesmen; rather, a means by which they could continue their close watch over the area, having withdrawn to their sacred city beneath the granite mountains. They found ways to communicate with their scouts on the outside who had allowed themselves to be captured by European armies, and who were then assigned to live on reservations like every other Indian.

The Rawakota's reach these days extends beyond the oceans. They keep tabs on a top-secret world, having infiltrated the security agencies and companies that work on protecting countries from all kinds of military threats, a strategy that informs them of ways they can shield their own territory from outsiders in the future when they reclaim the Black Hills for themselves and the Lakota. It's a cause so close to Howling Wind's heart that she's willing to use her position in the Air Force to obtain intelligence for the tribe. The mountains, known as He Sapa to the Indians, are believed to hold remarkable spiritual power. They are part of a bigger parcel of land that was granted to them by the U.S. Government in the Fort Laramie Treaty of 1868, land that was later unlawfully confiscated by a Congressional Act when whites discovered gold on it. The tribes were subsequently insulted by the monetary settlement offered to their people in 1979. As if money could possibly make up for such a reprehensible criminal act. They refused the sum even though the amount exceeded one hundred million dollars. Their sacred hills were never for sale. And the dispute continues. A day of reckoning is inescapable, but it won't be Indians who are caught off-guard; the Rawakota will see to that.

The first Rawakota to inhabit the region were an uncommon people. Enveloped in myth, they occupied a subterranean place filled with multilevel chambers and countless corridors that took them centuries to completely explore. One particular two-mile long passageway that had an extremely tall ceiling led them to believe they had reached Chohkahn, the life center of Mother Earth. This all happened long before today's scientists think the Americas were first populated. The Rawakota, who back then went by a different name, routinely journeyed to the forests above to hunt and collect nuts and berries, which is how they sometimes encountered later arrivals to the area—nomadic tribes who came and went with the seasons. Over time, a few of them stayed. They lived in peace, except when a community believed another to be encroaching on its hunting grounds. Occasionally the Rawakota sided with tribesmen they felt a kinship with, the final time being at the Battle of Little Big Horn in 1876. Their warriors aligned themselves with the Sioux and fought side by side with the Lakota, Northern Cheyenne, and Arapaho for the survival of their buffalo culture. The victory was short-lived. When whites broke promises made with the Indians, and reservation life became a reality in the late 1870s, the demoralized Rawakota retreated to the safety of their underground city.

Remarkably, defeat fired them up. Soon after, more of Chohkahn's men and women volunteered to go live on reservations, in order to offer additional accounts about the goings-on within the confines of the borders. Their presence did not go unnoticed since the golden eyes of Rawakota males were a dead give-away. Physically, too, they were taller and more robust than other Native peoples. Their story of bluecoats apprehending them in the forests was the same as that of the scouts who had been captured earlier. Aided by sympathetic trappers who saw the desperate conditions on reservations when they came with furs for the soldiers and missionaries, the Rawakota spies got them to deliver messages back to their own people about the white man's plans for the Indian.

And what was it they witnessed over the decades? That assimilation was destructive to the soul. Anything having to do with Indian culture was outlawed. Children were stolen from their parents and taken to the outside where they were schooled in the missionaries' language and religion. Time-honored stories and songs passed on orally were losing importance. The golden-eyed Rawakota came to be viewed no differently than any other tribe: they were all trapped in this hell together—no *wanikiya*, no savior among them. Elders had to resign themselves to a future that would be shaped by their Christian, English-speaking offspring. Rawakota spies had no means of fighting this policy. They did manage to work out a deal with the government whereby they could move their own families to a corner of the reservation, if they promised to limit their interaction with the other tribes. Such a privilege wasn't granted on a whim; it came with a price. Besides knowing English, Rawakota tribesmen revealed they spoke several Indian languages and offered to work as translators for the military, making them privy to all kinds of schemes the white man had up his sleeve. The Rawakota never mentioned they could read and write, and no one suspected they could.

Missionaries liked the idea of keeping the Rawakota separate from other Indians, believing them to be demons, what with their extraordinary unflinching stares and eyes a color unlike any known humans. They encouraged other Sioux to view them the same, but too many remembered the valuable role the Rawakota had played in their history. And then of course there was the fact that Rawakota families willingly hid other tribes' children in their homes, sparing the lucky few from going to the distant mission boarding schools. Government agents made periodic sweeps of the reservation, hoping to catch kids that had been previously overlooked.

One thing the colonists didn't anticipate was that the Black Hills would continue to matter to the Sioux, even after they got them to convert to a new faith and forget their uncivilized ways. Despite the brainwashing, He Sapa, the Black Hills, would always maintain its sacred status to the Indians. The mountains, believed to hold the womb of time past and time to come, spoke to their oneness with creation. That visceral connection to the place of their origin could never be stripped from them.

Each of the Council of First Nations' members has his and her own sad account of that period in history. And at some point during every gathering, the stories invariably get relived and discussed, as they presently are. The remainder of the afternoon is devoted to examining services provided by The Bureau of Indian Affairs, the long-beleaguered government agency that they must deal with on a regular basis. Its website is projected. There's a blurb about the Council's meeting here in Canada, in which the allocation of this year's budget will be decided. It also mentions the hundred year celebration of its name change from Circle of Elders to the better suited Council of First Nations, affirming the truth that non-whites came to these lands before Europeans. The leaders up here in this cold Canadian backwoods recall the time their forbearers were finally permitted to assemble again. Under the pretense of having accepted Christ as their savior, the powerless chiefs were allowed to gather in the churches erected on the reservations. It was assumed they were learning scripture when all the while they'd been plotting ways of ridding the white man from the land. Such a ruse. Too bad they never managed to outfox their adversaries.

Taking a page from those previous chiefs' playbook, the Rawakota are using the white man's view of the red man's shortcomings to its advantage. The idea that today's Indians are capable of organizing to a degree necessary for retaliating en masse against the government is too farfetched for almost anyone to consider. Time and again the Indian is proven deficient. The sacred symbol of the circle meant to reflect the natural order of the universe has lamentably been replaced by the circle of poverty, a trap seemingly impossible to break out of. There is no control over the lawlessness in many of their communities. That perception of them is exactly what the Rawakota are banking on, in order to achieve their lofty goal of establishing absolute control over the land surrounding and including the Black Hills. They must continue to lay low during the planning stages and not draw any undue attention to themselves and their growing power. When they sense the time is right, the Indians' decades-long campaign for reclaiming stolen lands, that up until now has been ill-defined and ineffective, will at last come to pass. And it won't allow for compromise. Should their action provoke an attack by the U.S., it will be met with a stunning counterstrike. An operation of such magnitude requires getting local tribes up to speed on the technologies needed for this feat, which will take at least a decade, if not more.

William Horse That Walks Backwards leaves Canada for Ohio, his mind filled with thoughts about his nephew. He agrees with the Council's assessment of him: Viktor truly is exceptional, but he is still a teen, which means he's just learning to manage the ups and downs of his emotions. It seems a bit premature to believe that he could become the unifying voice for the country's Indigenous populations. Regardless of his personal opinion, the boy is set to become an unwitting participant in a grand plan. With luck, after Viktor is older, the expectations placed upon him by the Council's leaders will be the same as those he holds for himself.

Although Viktor still has five months left in Texas, William plans to drive around Columbus and the university campus, explore the neighborhoods, and find an apartment for the two of them. Joining him will be a Council member's friend, a policeman. William was hoping to provide the fledgling student with a network of Indians to assist him during his studies at OSU; however, the number of Native Americans is insignificant not only in this city, but throughout Ohio. He learned there are likely Wyandot and Lenape in the region, but they aren't organized, and he isn't about to waste his time searching for them. It's not that important. As the plane begins its descent, William looks at the scrap of paper with the name and number of his contact. Who knows, he thinks, it might prove beneficial having a liaison within the police force. There is so much at stake if Viktor should slip up. It wouldn't hurt to have him watched now and then. He has yet to face enormous challenges that no one—not even enlightened elders—can anticipate. This is a period in a young man's life that requires inordinate discipline. Viktor wasn't above being influenced by the bad behavior of his troubled Indian friends a few years back.

William heard all about it from the boy's grandmother, who was his nurse in the clinic on the rez. Victoria Birdsong is also William's mother-in-law. Thankfully, the sudden streak of defiance was short-lived, amounting to nothing more than backtalk and swearing. No alcohol or drugs or stealing was involved. The uncle, who was born and raised in the sacred city of Chohkahn, is glad that the boy has had more interactions with the outside world than he personally ever did when he left the Black Hills for the University of South Dakota to become a doctor.

Because Viktor did not grow up in a typical Rawakota family structure with his birth father, he won't be celebrating Otiwota, the tribe's time-honored male-bonding ceremony, a milestone in a boy's life when he learns ways to channel this powerful emerging energy. Girls have their own comparable ceremony. It takes place between the fifteenth and seventeenth year, depending on one's level of maturity. A son will learn in detail what to expect during his momentous first sexual encounter, an experience only to be shared with his life partner. The conditioning is begun at birth when babies are ceremoniously taken outside every evening to behold the great mysterious space above, the source of all existence. Later, adolescents are taught that this special bond between a man and woman will last throughout innumerable lifetimes, as many as the creator Wakan Tanka intends for them. Sex is described as a mesmeric experience. If one spouse passes on before the other, he or she trusts they'll be reunited, and their adventure together continued. In this respect, Otiwota is unlike other rites of passage that may involve hunting a ferocious beast, fighting a stronger opponent, or enduring some form of physical pain. Rawakota people prize the courage of one's convictions, and that can't be determined in the course of a day or a week. The youth learn that life advances in stages and every level involves facing unique moral dilemmas that the more experienced elders will have encountered and learned from. The ritual creates special, positive relationships within a family. That said, Viktor's mother has openly criticized Otiwota because of its emphasis on finding the right partner at too early of an age. What she can't deny is that her own father, Benjamin One Horn, along with her grandfather, Sunkwah, have been strong, admirable role models for her boy. They imbued her son with the very same Rawakota principles that inspired their own lives. Constance Howling Wind is less worried than William as to how Viktor will fare when left to his own devices at college. She made it clear to her brother-in-law that he take a wait-and-see attitude when it comes to Viktor's conduct and not overwhelm him with rules.

CHAPTER 5

To braid or not to braid? I study myself in the mirror before heading down to breakfast. It's the first day of what will be the final semester of my sophomore year, and also the end of my time at high school. Thanks to Marnie, I'm much more conscious of my looks. I spent the entire trip from Dakota back to Texas thinking about the initial impression I make on strangers. My height probably intimidates a lot of people. It happened so fast. Being tall is one thing, but I don't want to be labeled a giant, which to me, for some reason, starts at six-eight. I'm thin, but I've got strong arms and legs. The photo of Lukas is reassuring. My chest is bound to fill out, I hope. My eyes are the exact copies of his. Did the girls tell him they were awesome? Did Mom? What did Lukas see when he looked back at himself? I expect people will continue to wonder about my race, because of the dark skin. I have to laugh...a sales guy at the mall in Rapid City asked if my background was Samoan! It made sense when he said I reminded him of his favorite NFL player, a wide receiver who happens to be an islander. There are several more who play football. Hmm, *Samoan*. Maybe I should try on a new identity at OSU. I've never completely fit in with the close knit Jewish community here at the Hillel Academy. And these days, reservation life holds little interest for me. I'll lie about my age, too, since everybody will assume I'm at least eighteen. Complicating things is the fact that I'll be entering as a junior in the fall after I earn credits for two English courses this summer. No way will a twenty-year old girl want to go out with a guy who's only sixteen. Marnie is older, but she was just having a fun day with me...we'd never date.

There's no point dwelling on something I have no control over. I shake out the braids I had started making and think about Sam and Daniel and Billie, and the dreams we shared of getting discovered. No football recruiters or music agents were ever going to stop by the road or at Lazy Al's to sign up an Indian kid for anything, a sad truth I'm only too aware of now. Even if an academic scholarship wasn't in the cards for me, if you're talented in a sport like I am, the likelihood of meeting a college athletic recruiter is greater in Texas than on our little-known Buckthorn Reservation in South Dakota. Here, students at small private or parochial schools, even home-schooled ones, can choose to play for another school with a sports programs if it's in their district. Four other guys at Hillel besides me play on the football team for a magnet high school. We're the Burnett Lions. Burnett doesn't have a top Division ranking, so there's a fat chance of getting on the radar of a big name university. Coaches, though, particularly Texas coaches, can make it happen, and our team has a great one. Coach Wheatley's enthusiasm for the game is contagious. I'm sure I'll think of him often when I'm at OSU, especially if I hit a roadblock. My biggest takeaway from playing for him is, you have to be proactive, no matter what setbacks you encounter, and that includes off the field. When last year's season ended, Coach Wheatley, with Dad's help, put together a spectacular highlights reel of me and sent it off to a number of the best college football teams. I heard back from six schools in the Southeastern Conference, impressed that a freshman was a varsity team's starting quarterback—add to that the Lions 10-0 record, which we duplicated this year. But then I received the Herrington Scholarship from Ohio State, an honor that my teachers and parents said couldn't be passed up. Dad and I about lost it when I was told that I'd be allowed to try out as a walk-on for the Buckeyes football team at some point down the line. What a perk! It's hard wrapping my head around everything that's happening in my life. I'm going to a place where people aren't aware of my athletic abilities. There won't be kids my age in class. I'll be living with my uncle, a man I respect but don't know very well.

    I'm still staring at myself in the mirror. No one at Hillel has ever seen me with my waist-length hair braided with beads and feathers, or pinned with strips of fur, the way I wear it on the rez. And they won't today. As usual, I gather it in a pony-tail, loop it around, and then tie it together with a leather rope at the neck and go bounding down the stairs.

    Reports of bad weather from coast to coast are the lead stories on TV. The pan is already hot. I crack open six eggs and drop them in. Dad is enjoying his coffee and Danish. I kiss his cheek before sitting across from him at the table. That smile of his always starts my day off on a good note. Mom isn't here. She's serving a short stint at an air base in North Dakota.

    "That was some trip we had us!"

"You said it! Wish I could wear my new clothes. I can't wait to shed these ho-hum khakis and navy shirts. All I can think about is getting my license this spring. I bet the next four months are gonna drag!"

"Let them drag. Soon after your birthday, you'll be leaving for college …and I'll be all alone in this house." It's true, we've never been apart, but he won't be sitting around twiddling his thumbs as he waits for my return; he's got a business to run. No more handing things over to someone else while he takes me to the rez for the summer. I reassure him that I'll be checking in constantly. "I'm glad your mother can see you before she heads overseas," he says. "Better not be for as long this time."

Up pops the toast. We eat and listen to a report about a Taliban suicide bomber in Kabul, Afghanistan, a place Mom knows and might be sent to again after I'm squared away in Columbus. I try not to think about her job. On the phone, she sounded like she was really looking forward to touring the campus and seeing our apartment. I had no clue before this last trip to the rez, when Dad and I met my birth father's old friends at that seedy joint on the way to Rapid City, that I resembled Lukas so much, a man Mom ended up hating. I need to believe that her son's happiness is important to her, and that my looks as I've gotten older have nothing to do with the lack of hugs I receive from her.

Throughout the day, fear of passing Ashley in the hall makes me nervous. It isn't until last period that I learn she's still on vacation with her family in Hawaii and won't return until next week. Had I only known that in the morning! I've decided to drop out of Honor Society, in order to avoid further contact with her. If only I could wish away the memory of that night with her at her home in her bed. It was all so awkward.

Just about everyone I know at Hillel takes first-rate vacations over school breaks. I suppose our family could. My parents don't discuss their incomes, but they earn decent salaries. Growing up, it never occurred to Iris or me to go anywhere but the reservation. Along the way we always took a detour through Missouri to visit Dad's many relatives. They're an entertaining and outgoing bunch. Considering how welcome Mom and Iris and I were made to feel when we first met them, it was hard to believe Dad had ever been as estranged from his family as he led us to believe. His parents were done with him when he joined a gang in Junior High, which landed him in big trouble after its members got caught dealing drugs. Luckily for him, and for our family later, he reformed himself and got back in their good graces.

Dad grew up in a respectable suburb of Kansas City where his father and uncles work for the railroad industry, just like their father before them, except they earned business degrees and never get their hands dirty. I forgot that his Uncle Roy didn't go to college; nevertheless, he's in management, too. There should be a BNSF Railway on the reservation to offer jobs with good pensions instead of a few grocery stores and fast-food places that don't pay squat. Dad's parents, Grandpa Cyrus and Grandma Junie, once joined us for a short visit to the rez to meet our side of the family. They swore never again! Not because they didn't like my grandparents or great-grandparents, they did, but the isolation, poverty, and alcoholism they observed in the rest of the Native community broke their hearts. Of course, they didn't ride horses for miles on end or climb trees or shoot arrows and dance in powwows. Being kids, we thought it was the best place ever.

Living the life of an Indian was a welcome escape from Hillel's controlled environment, especially for Iris, who had been older when we moved south. Dad, in order to win her over when he and Mom announced their marriage, let her pick out an old line of Nakota breed horse she had been wanting. Iris rode Ola from sunup till sundown, often letting me sit behind her. Mom suggested the name for her mare. Ola Mildred Rexroat was a WWII Lakota female aviator. Jim didn't become part of the family until much later. Riding around the plains was positively liberating because our lives in Texas were all about academics, even when Iris played volleyball and I started football. We used to attach a horse trailer to the truck and bring Jim down so I could ride him in the fall. He stayed at a big cattle ranch located west of the city near Lake Kemp. Then we'd haul him back over winter break. Grandpa Cyrus and Grandma Junie thought it was neat having a horse in the backyard during the stopover. Ola freaks out in trailers and had to always stay behind. There was too much going on this past year for Jim to come along.

The bell rings; school's out. Isaac, who lives a few doors down and drives, drops me off at my house where I make a beeline to the kitchen to wolf down a couple of sandwiches and a quart of chocolate milk. I check my email. Ohio State sends lots of stuff. It keeps me daydreaming about walking around the Oval at the center of campus. I picture studying at the library and eating at all the hang-outs. I can't wait to watch a football game inside "the Shoe." My leg's bouncing like it's spring-loaded.

"Viktor!" Dad yells as the door bangs open. "Didn't you see the packages on the front porch?"

"No," I yell back, "I was in a hurry to eat."

"They're the ones you've been waiting for...for your teachers."

"Un-hee!" I meet him at the hall table where he begins to cut through the tape of one of the boxes with his key. I pull out the insides before he's done.

"Oh, wow! It's awesome! Feel how soft." I hold the brown leather jacket for Mr. Reuter up to my shoulders and stare in the mirror. The short fringe along the sleeves isn't overdone like on many Native outfits. It's trimmed with colorful beaded geometric shapes. Dad starts in on the second box, which holds an embroidered saddle blanket for Miss Omara's horse. "It's gorgeous!" I exclaim, running my fingers across it. The teeniest, sparkly glass beads were strung onto bright blue, pink, yellow, and white threads to create the flowers and dragonflies. I can't wait to see my teachers' faces light up when they're given these tomorrow. Without Mr. Reuter's and Miss Omara's deep-rooted faith in my abilities, the Herrington scholarship would not be mine. They nominated me for it.

After school I get the presents from the office where I was allowed to stash them for the day. First stop, Mr. Reuter's room. His back is to me as he fusses with cramming more things into an already overstuffed briefcase, which is clearly testing his patience.

"Mr. Reuter, mind if I interrupt you a moment?"

"Sure, Viktor," he says, recognizing my voice, "just give me a sec."

I take a seat at a desk and look the perfect student: with feet planted on the floor and posture straight, the package set square in front of me. Finally he turns, brushing aside the hair on his forehead from the workout.

"What's this?" he asks with eyebrows raised, peering over the top of his half frame reading glasses knocked crooked.

"It's for you, Mr. Reuter...so you have something to remember me."

"You're a teacher's dream, young man. How foolish to think I'd ever forget you."

"I had fun trying to figure out what you might like." I lift the box for him to take. He shakes his head in a *you shouldn't have* way, and then carries it to his desk, pushing stacks of papers out of the way before he plops on his chair. His wiry white moustache doesn't hide the smile. I think to myself how old he's become. He arrived at Hillel a decade ago, having left the Centers for Disease Control in Atlanta, where he had worked for twenty years as a research scientist. When his elderly mother got sick, he came to care for her. He wouldn't hear of having his students call him Doctor even though he had a PhD in immunology. His enthusiasm for teaching science hasn't lessened over the years, but caring for his looks sure has. Kids started taking bets on days he'd show up wearing a change of clothes. He has everyone's respect, though. The school was lucky that circumstances brought a scientist of his renown to its door. I'll be forever grateful.

"All right then…hmm, where to start?"

His stiff and clumsy stogie-shaped fingers pull at the ribbon. I made sure to tie the bow loosely. He lifts the lid off and parts the tissue paper, revealing the contents. Next he explores the beaded collar with his fingertips. It's like watching a blind man use braille. I wait for him to speak. And continue to wait.

He takes hold of it by the shoulders, and then swivels his chair to the side for some room to shake it out.

"You've always complimented me on my coats," I tell him. He was someone who took the time to examine the craftsmanship, and he was always curious about the historical significance of the symbols that decorated them. "The skin is from a buffalo I hunted. A Lakota artisan in Sioux Falls created the patterns and finished it."

"This is a treasure—an honest-to-god treasure. Thank you from the bottom of my heart." He stands to try it on. I go over to help him. He's a big man, a tall man, with a broad round back and barrel-shaped chest.

"How on earth did you get it to be such a perfect fit!"

"That's top secret. Look at you! You could be mistaken for Buffalo Bill, with your long white hair. You should grow a beard."

He pinches away the tears from the corners of his eyes and lets go a sniffle. We exchange hugs. I really do love him. I want us to part on a lighter note and search my memory for anything to put a smile back on his face. "Mr. Reuter, besides opening my eyes to the world, I also have you to thank for saving me from the most humiliating experience here at school."

He looks at me questioningly. I remind him of when I learned that all the boys at Hillel were circumcised, except me, and that this fact came out in front of sixth grade girls. I about died on the spot. Even after four years, I find my cheeks turning hot from embarrassment. Instead of the expected chuckle, though, he responds with a *tsk-tsk*, and then asks, "Are you serious?"

"It was horrible! Besides believing I was going to get AIDS, I imagined everyone picturing my dick, along with its foreskin." Now he does laugh and pats my cheek.

"Oh, the trials of youth. When you reach my age, Viktor, I guarantee that the things you once thought so consequential will be long forgotten." Cradling my hand in both of his, he gives a firm handshake. "Thank you, again," he whispers. "Wait until I walk into the office wearing this!" I smile big, grab my backpack, and tuck the other box under my arm. He guesses that it's for Miss Omara.

Just as I'm heading out, he wants me to explain why the devil I thought I was going to get AIDS. He vaguely remembers the incident.

"Before we left your room that day to go to health, you told the girls to go to a separate room from the boys because puberty was going to be discussed. Rudy then asked you, because you'd been with the CDC, if it was true that Jewish men couldn't get HIV since they were circumcised. First you set the record straight, stating that anyone could contract STDs, but then you mentioned the studies that Rudy was likely referring to… that showed an increase in HIV among guys who weren't circumcised. I freaked out, and with that my arm shot up and out spilled: *I'm going to get AIDS because I'm not circumcised!* The room went dead quiet, and then the giggling started."

"Oh, my…that must have been rough," he admits.

"You went on to explain why different cultures don't circumcise, which turned out to be enlightening."

As I rush over to the other building, I think about what I kept to myself. Even though no one made fun of me after that, the reservation took on a deeper meaning—it was about going home to families whose men had foreskins. *My people.*

I run through the hall to catch up to Miss Omara, who's locking her door to leave.

"Heavens, Viktor, where's the fire!"

I hold out the box covered in bright wrapping paper with a white owl's feather strung through the bow.

"For you," I say, catching my breath.

Her hand automatically goes to her chest where she clutches the key against it, and a look of total surprise crosses her face. It's a beautiful face. She has the warmest brown eyes and the biggest smile, with teeth that radiate whiteness against her coal black skin. Unlike Mr. Reuter's humility, thinking a gift wasn't warranted for anything he'd done, Miss Omara has the door unlocked and gets to opening the present on her desk in nothing flat.

"This is so thoughtful of you." She tickles her chin with the feather.

"But you don't know what it is yet." I pretend to sound worried that she won't like it.

And in seconds, "Ooh, Viktor, how exquisite!" Based on its shape, she knew right away it was a saddle blanket for her horse Kipro. Our horses always come up in our conversations. Kipro is the nickname of Stephen Kiprotich, the Olympic marathon runner from Miss Omara's homeland of Uganda. I had told her that my horse, too, was named after one of my heroes. Although Jim Thorpe wasn't Lakota, I learned at an early age that this Indian had been called one of the greatest athletes of the 20TH century, and by some accounts, *the* greatest. Miss Omara was the person who recommended the ranch where Jim could stay when Dad and I were looking for a place close by. Around twenty years ago, her family was able to immigrate to America because the local synagogue, in partnership with other Texas synagogues, helped bring African refugees here to resettle in their neighborhood communities. Both of her parents got jobs on the ranch. They still work there, along with some of Miss Omara's brothers and sisters. She's got lots of them.

I go on to describe the details of the blanket. "The yarn is a combination of bison down and merino wool, and the needlework along the edges is typical of Lakota." I sound like I'm reading from a catalogue. Because Miss Omara often wears traditional African dresses with these crazy, abstract prints, I knew she would value something that represented my background, although, gathering from her initial reaction, I could have given her a second-hand potholder and she'd have been thrilled.

"Kipro will look so handsome."

Long arms embrace me in a natural, unselfconscious manner. She smells good, like orange blossoms. Her high heels make her nearly as tall as me. It wasn't so long ago that I was looking up at her, back when we worked together one-on-one to "elevate" my writing.

Miss Omara motions for me to sit. Wagging a finger, she orders, "Just because your plans are set for going to the university does not mean you can relax now and forget your studies! It is a matter of character." I miss her already, especially her way of enunciating every syllable. She never uses contractions.

"Oh I know," I tease, "at my age, demonstrating impeccable character is all I think about."

"Smart Aleck White Owl should be your name," she laughs. "Did you have a good time in South Dakota over the break? If only my country were not so far. Why the sad eyes?"

I don't want to ruin the moment by complaining, but at the same time, she did ask. Miss Omara has these soul searching eyes that make it easy to open up to her. We met during my angry period, when I'd had it with school. The way I saw it, my Native history goes back thousands of years before the Europeans came, and yet our school's history books glossed over all those centuries. In them was stuff that mattered only to the whites who wrote them. Miss Omara understood and was sympathetic to my feelings, as I'm sure she'll be when I tell her how disconnected I've become from my Indian friends.

"Bet you never thought you'd hear me say that."

She plays with the feather as she contemplates my problem. "You had good reason for your rebelliousness back when you began to understand how incredibly unfair life often is. I suspect this is different."

"It is different. Guys I've known since I was little are wanting nothing to do with me. Trust me, I feel for them. They see that I don't have to try and study when I'm hungry. I'm able to go to movies and different kinds of restaurants. Most families on the rez don't even have access to the Internet. When you're a kid, you simply don't understand what being poor means. Thank goodness, when I was at my worst, you and Mr. Reuter came to my rescue."

"Yes," she says. "It was my first year teaching here, and Mr. Reuter approached me because he believed your genuine curiosity about the world would be your salvation. We put our heads together to find a way to interest you in school again. You appeared to have an affinity for science."

"No kidding. So that's why he introduced me to his friend at the college." Miss Omara and I share what a life-changing event that turned out to be. The researcher, a former colleague of Mr. Reuter's, had invited me down to Midwestern State University to take a look at an electron microscope. The small field of view fired up my imagination bigtime. Above all else I wanted to understand how the tiniest cells, invisible to the naked eye, were capable of destroying any form of life.

"You have come a long way, Viktor. Besides excelling in mathematics, your vocabulary is exceptional…English and French."

I stare down at my feet. "If only I weren't so lonely."

"I know, dear boy. You must get over this hump. New, exciting relationships await you."

She's right, but I'm feeling sadder than ever. "Daniel, who's like a true brother, told me outright that I've come to think I'm better than he is and my other Indian friends, and maybe he's right. I figured if they saw how excited I was about biology, they might start taking their own schooling more seriously. It's been so frustrating. They don't care about speaking Lakota anymore … or having fun at the powwows."

"You made a noble effort."

"It's been a useless effort. And look at the backgrounds of the faculty at Hillel. We're exposed to such a wide range of unusual subjects that can lead to careers we'd otherwise never know about." And then the real game-changer occurs to me. "The biggest difference is that the students here have parents who are concerned about them and track their progress."

Miss Omara places her hand on my arm. "My poor Viktor, you have outgrown these friends and that is truly difficult. Nothing can be done except to explore the loss within yourself and to keep moving forward. One person's journey is not the same as another person's, nor is the rate at which lessons are learned."

"It sucks."

"Your friends have made their choices. Their moment of enlightenment may come yet. Life is full of surprises. You have seen that already."

"Still, I should have been more understanding. I could kick myself. If I faced such bleak conditions year round, and someone tried to make a case for me to stay in school like I did with Daniel, I'd have said *screw you,* too."

"You could have…and you would have been none the wiser as the saying goes. No amount of encouragement will produce the desired result, if first the light bulb does not go on." She points comically to the top of her head. "You became interested in diseases because understanding them was suddenly relevant due to their impact on your people. And thankfully you were not on drugs at the time, or nothing would have happened."

I see what she's saying. It makes me think of the phrase about leading a horse to water.

She goes on to say, "It is a tragedy that so many children are born into poverty and cheated out of happy lives, and here in America of all places. There are some success stories on your reservation. You are one after all, and from what I know about you, the rest of your family."

"True." I mention the students at a private school on a bordering reservation who have received Bill Gates's scholarship, which is huge. "Lately, more people who went away to college are returning, with the hope of turning things around. A Navajo tribesman from New Mexico is partnering with the Sioux to build solar installations on our land. He's training locals to do the work. Maybe I can play a role in a project like that someday. You know, Miss Omara, I would have had a different circle of friends on the rez if my dad hadn't chosen to coach kids from such poor backgrounds. Because of that, they're the ones I'm tight with … was tight with." Next I break out with a big grin, and add, "I'd never trade my childhood, though. When we imagined ourselves fearsome warriors and rode our horses together at lightning speed across the wide open fields, or hunted small game in the Black Hills, life was magical."

She sees it. Even a crowded and dirty refugee camp like the one she lived in for a while is probably an amazing playground to a kid. Children can always create something out of nothing. She reminds me of the good friends I have at Hillel, the guys I play sports with, and of course there's Bernie. They're supportive and kind and respectful. It's not the same, though. Miss Omara understands the need to be around one's own people. It's beyond me how she manages to stay upbeat. How would I fare if

I had to move to the other side of the planet and learn a new language? Before they arrived in Texas, her family was displaced several times because of political conflicts in her country. We learned from her that Uganda was one of the poorest countries in the world. I don't want to know poorer than what I've seen. It hurts too much.

I glance at the wall clock and tell her I need to get going.

"Thank you, again, Viktor. If anyone understands how much Kipro means to me, that he is family, it is you."

The short days add to my depression. I love the daylight. It's only seven at night and I'm in bed listening to a new Dakota Sioux rap artist. Dad stayed late at work. When Mom is here, she practically lives at the base. Dad goes to have lunch with her, but I can't because of school, which is okay. The couple of times I joined them everyone ends up asking whether I'm going to be a pilot—in front of Dad. As if his being the owner of an auto body shop is nothing. The Air Force has never been a career option. I hate flying, preferring the solid earth under my feet.

This song is awful. The lyrics are all about what this guy wants his bitches to do to him. Sex is too much on my mind. I picture Daniel screwing his pregnant cousin. The longer I listen, the more turned off I get, so I choose to sit in silence. A conversation comes to mind that I had with Mr. Reuter when I was awarded the scholarship. At the time I was trying to build my French scientific vocabulary and was reading a lot of French biology journals. I didn't understand the big deal behind me discovering a paper in an American journal that clearly plagiarized one I had read on a French scientist's work, a Dr. Bonnaire. The woman, who was a PhD candidate at Ohio State, got expelled. Mr. Reuter warned me that research is a cutthroat business, not unlike football. Just be aware, he said, that one's reputation within the science community means *everything*.

In between thoughts of basketball practice resuming tomorrow, and wondering what it'll be like to face Ashley next week, and rerunning conversations with Marnie, and what I want for dinner, I find that I'm also grieving the loss of my fictitious love interest, Liliana Broken Wing. For whatever reason, I'm unable to conjure up the picture of us making love, which was always gentle and wonderful. The sex part happened only recently, following a lengthy platonic relationship, because at nine and ten, or even at twelve, I would never have touched her private parts. We used to climb trees, swim naked in a lake, and cuddle close to each other beside a fire at night, all of which eventually led up to me inside her.

My favorite spot included a waterfall that dropped from an incredible height. The scene had to have sprung from the rich Lakota legends I grew up hearing, as well as Edgar Rice Burroughs' descriptions of the jungle in his Tarzan books, because that's what I read at the age I dreamt up this Otherworld. Then *Avatar* came out, and the lush trees and plants of Pandora blew my mind! The movie showed my innermost fantasy come to life …only Liliana's skin was violet, not blue like the film's character, a minor detail; and her long, shiny hair was the purple-black of a raven's feather. She seduced me with gorgeous lavender eyes that peered out from the shadows of a similar mist-filled forest.

During these past weeks, the emotion connected to my made-up world has evaporated. I crave the real thing. There's a desperate need to substitute Liliana with an actual physical version of her, but what girl can remotely resemble my weird idea of beauty!

CHAPTER 6

Minot Air Force Base, North Dakota. Remembering the historic security breach on August 29, 2007, is cause for suppressed mirth among the three U.S. Air Force personnel responsible for the brazen heist that played out like the perfect whodunit, minus the discovery of their involvement. It's a quirk of fate that nearly a decade later the guilty parties, a pilot and two technicians, are back together at Minot. This time the leader of the Rawakota Nation, Chief Rolling Thunder, has assigned each of them individual missions and, as usual, the United States Air Force remains in the dark. The pilot, Constance Howling Wind, routinely sees her Rawakota co-conspirators throughout the day on the base, without a word exchanged between them. When their eyes connect, however, they light up like pranksters on a college campus who, after disassembling a car, just put it back together inside the Dean's office. To this day, no concrete evidence has turned up that could pin the theft of six cruise missiles loaded with live nuclear warheads on any suspects. Their disappearance from a bunker was a blunder that went undetected for thirty-six hours. The military term used to describe such an incident when it involves the transport of nuclear material is "Bent Spear." Certainly the initial response made by top brass when they learned of the situation was more along the line of "Holy Bentspear-mother fucking-shit!"

Years have passed since the Rawakota first began quietly observing Constance Howling Wind. She was watched for the duration of her student life at Colorado's Air Force Academy, and then later at flight school in Laughlin, Texas, where she was becoming quite an extraordinary pilot. Their plan back then was to carry out covert operations at Ellsworth Air Force Base in South Dakota, near the Black Hills, where they had ties to an influential Native American officer who could arrange to have her sent there. To their dismay, he got transferred before seeing it through. When Howling Wind landed a position at Minot Air Force Base instead, they felt relieved. After some research, it turned out the location suited their needs even better.

It was considered a daring move on the part of such a secretive people to approach Howling Wind, but the timing was perfect for the Rawakota to enlist her help in their grand plan to recover stolen tribal lands. The concern over how much to disclose to this woman was hotly debated among the tribe's governing members. It was after all one of their own men from Chohkahn who had kidnapped her when she was nineteen. Who's to say she wouldn't turn on them one day? Chief Rolling Thunder chose to rely on Howling Wind's brother-in-law to make the call whether she could be trusted with the knowledge of their existence. William Horse That Walks Backwards had been her doctor on the reservation. He was also the one who found her chained to the bed in a remote cabin where Lukas Sun in Eyes had been keeping her. There was no one better to assess her emotional and mental state.

For this current mission, the newly promoted Major Howling Wind is faced with a task not nearly as daunting as stealing missiles. She's been ordered to fly a B52 Stratofortress bomber to Wright-Patterson Base in Ohio. Fixed to the aircraft will be a stolen sample of the latest highly-confidential Russian radar absorbing paint. It will be imbedded in a foam-filled hard rubber shell comprised of unique properties that is also of interest to the Rawakota. The product was developed by Germans and is sealed together with the Air Force's own complex epoxy. The Major will never see the thing. The Rawakota just need her flight path. Tribesmen on the ground will activate a sensor causing the unit to disengage from the aircraft, dropping it into their waiting arms. Easy.

A deck of playing cards left behind on the cafeteria table is inconspicuously pocketed by Constance as she sits to eat.

"Major, you're going to be impressed with Wright Patterson's flight simulators," says Colonel Bedford, taking a seat across from her. "You normally don't transport planes. How'd someone convince you to leave F22 Raptor training for *this*?"

True to form, Constance replies in her typical no-nonsense way, "I asked to do it. My son is moving from Texas to Columbus to attend Ohio State. I wanted a chance to see him before heading overseas."

"I see. I figured there had to be a good reason." He knew of her children. "He can't be college age already?"

"He'll be sixteen when he starts this summer."

"You must be a proud mom. Not to downplay his father's contribution, but the brains and ambition could certainly have come entirely from you."

Constance ignores the compliment and switches to the topic of Wright Patterson's Research Center. She isn't interested in getting personal with co-workers, though many have tried to get closer to her, and tried hard. Her husband and children aren't alone when it comes to recognizing the increasingly serious behavior the Major has exhibited over the past year. One might surmise that her reputation for getting the job done is a trait she holds dear, when in fact she merely appreciates the challenges that flying offers her. She derives focus and clarity of thought from it. Her instructors are constantly impressed by her inherent "oneness" with an aircraft. In her charge, the machine seems organic. The trade-off on the other hand is that the pilot is growing more machine-like.

At this phase of the Major's life, family takes a back seat to the political events affecting the greater global arena. Constance is every bit the quintessential U.S. Air Force officer, one who is definitely headed for overseeing units someday soon. Because of the recent clandestine nature of the Special Operations Squadron she was ordered to be a part of, she knows the Combatant Commander believes she can be trusted. It's crucial that she be held in high esteem. Her goal is to eventually work within DCA, Defensive Counterair, perhaps joining NATOs Allied Air Command. There she'll learn how enemy forces penetrate friendly air space. With the advent of drones, gaining the advantage over the enemy using stealth technology is a priority, especially among powerless nations faced with ongoing border threats. Critical information that will help the Rawakota protect the perimeter around the Black Hills.

Following a late afternoon meeting, Constance retires early to her quarters. She pulls the cards out of her jacket and removes the deck from the box. Next she counts to the ninth, tenth, eleventh and twelfth cards, and again from the twentieth through twenty-third ones, which translates to: 4369 and 9Ace56. She checks a physical map mounted on the wall and matches the numbers with the coordinates 43.69° N and 90.56° W. It's the location of Wildcat Mountain State Park in southeastern Wisconsin, the designated area for the secret air-drop and ground recovery. She has only to fly the plane; no active participation is needed. She won't know if co-pilot Major Cabrera, whom she's never met, is involved. The Air Force has them testing the structural fatigue on the low altitude flight of the refurbished B-52. It shouldn't be difficult for her to spot the five bursts of smoke sent twice, indicating the expelled device successfully cleared the aircraft and was retrieved. Considering the advanced technology used in this era of high-speed communications, the simplicity of employing archaic smoke signals, a Native wireless resource, demonstrates the wry nature of the Rawakota character. And they needn't encrypt their messages. That's rich. The irony entitles them to a degree of smugness generally observed in those who've gained the upper hand.

The following day, the mission goes off without a hitch. The pilots land in Ohio. Constance turns in early, mainly to stretch out on a bed after sitting in a cockpit. She should have rented a car and driven the mere hour it takes to go from Dayton to Columbus. She opted to stay in a room on the base tonight because a friend who runs an air taxi service offered to fly her up in his Beechcraft Baron in the morning. Only now is she aware of what that sounds like…it's as if she wanted to see the plane more than Viktor. The mother reflects on her son's upcoming entry into academia. Viktor is an inherently good boy. Solomon can be credited for enhancing their son's life, but not for shaping his morals, evidenced by his concerns as soon as he could talk. Viktor always questioned the fairness of a situation. *How dare a hawk dive down and steal a mouse from the owl's talons!* A scene she had recounted to him about the day he was born, and one which he loved to hear repeated. She hears herself saying: "The Great White Snow Owl had wings that spanned the length of a man's arms…and with its keen, golden eyes, big and round like the full moon, it watched across the fields and listened for the slightest movement…"

Constance knew before Viktor took his first breath that the Great Spirit had a design in mind for the baby. During the final days of her pregnancy, the majestic owl sat dutifully on the fence post in the back yard and remained there for the additional weeks needed for her recovery. In her darkest hours, when she believed her personal dream of flying would never be realized, for which she had been studying so long and hard, the owl, with its hypnotic calming gaze, offered a sense of peace. They peered at each other endlessly through the bedroom window, that's how closely he perched. Sometimes when she was reduced to tears, the creature took flight and swooped in circles and called to her in barking like fashion, as if admonishing her for feeling sorry for herself.

    She turns to the side and draws the blanket up to her chin, wondering if Viktor can sleep as he begins this exciting new period in his life. It's a pity she knows only what others tell her about him these days, and downright shameful that she needed to convince herself it was important to go to Columbus and share the milestone with him. This is normally a bittersweet chapter in parents' lives—when the last child leaves home. And for Solomon it is. For her, it's been mostly an inconvenience. Things at work had to get rescheduled. She better nip these waning maternal feelings in the bud, or she stands to lose the respect of her family. Her mother and brother-in-law have voiced how distant she's become. Their opinions still matter. She doesn't wish to lose her humanity. Regardless, putting up a front is wearing thin. Her speaking engagements, that she used to look forward to with enthusiasm, have gone by the wayside. She is currently shouldering a ridiculous amount of responsibility at work, because that's how you advance in your career. This is the age to make one's mark, she tells everyone (including herself). *Whatever*, she mutters, as she closes her eyes and waits for the welcome refuge of black mindless sleep, just as she had when Lukas held her captive.

CHAPTER 7

"...wet male sheep..." reads Rajeev from his report about renewable energy systems.

I look around the classroom for signs that others are as baffled as I am. He seems confused himself. That's odd. This is only my second week of a French 5000 level course at OSU, in which we translate scientific and technical reports. Each of us has to stand before the class and read the original French article, and then what we wrote in English paraphrasing it. Besides taking the mandatory English Composition class that's needed before I can enroll full time, I chose this elective, thinking it'd be fun.

Rajeev, an engineering student, had been talking about bélier hydrauliques, which are hydraulic rams. It can't be...he wouldn't miss that! A snort of laughter escapes my lips. The teacher, Madame Dubois, a petite and dignified lady, shoots me an annoyed look. "Monsieur White Owl." She definitely sounds pissed off. "Do you have a problem with M. Kapoor's presentation?"

I shake my head no, but she won't drop it.

"Do you believe your pronunciation is so perfect! We are here to learn!"

"No, sorry," I say, my leg bouncing like crazy under the desk. "It isn't that." Raajeev mutters something in his mother tongue. I feel terrible.

"Rajeev, I mean no disrespect..."

He cuts me off. "I know," and then he proceeds to tell Mme. Dubois that I happened to catch an inaccurate translation of a technical term.

In the hallway after class, Rajeev stops me by the steps. He's smiling, thank god. "You, Viktor, are an astute listener. I am embarrassed by the oversight on my part." His green eyes appear bloodshot and glazed over. With an arm against my back, he leads me down the stairs. "I was not about to tell Mme. Dubois that someone else translated the text so I could go to a wedding this past week. Since the girl *is* French, I trusted her and never bothered to review the paper. Isn't it funny how words can be interpreted so differently? To me, bélier, a ram, is a pump or cylinder. An animal wouldn't cross my mind. And "wet" for hydraulic...really? Why not just say water, or choose a different fluid like oil?"

I tell him that I personally associate RAM with computers. "And let's not forget RAM pickup trucks."

We have a good laugh over the multiple meaning of words, when out of the blue he asks, "Have you ever been to an Indian wedding, Viktor?"

"No," I reply, amused by the question. It certainly makes more sense for the citizens of India to call themselves *Indians*.

"The dancing and drinking goes on for days." He describes the extravagant atmosphere in typical Indian sing-song fashion. His accent is unusually thick, making the story hard to follow. We reach the front sidewalk when he asks if I want to meet with several of our classmates for lunch on Tuesdays. Only French is permitted.

"Yes! Definitely!"

Although the others are getting their master's like Rajeev, I welcome feeling part of university life. His invitation made my day, and I greet each passer-by with an enthusiastic hello, including the bus driver who'll be taking me clear across this sprawling campus to talk to a professor about a pathology course that's available this fall. *More* older students. I need to find an interesting organization to join with people closer to my age. We pass magnificent old trees—ever-present spirits to commune with. They remind me I should never feel alone here.

The third-floor apartment Uncle found for us is across the river in a university building repurposed to house mostly grad students and married couples—aargh! I can't catch a break. It overlooks our ugly parking lot. At least when you're on the couch you can see the tops of the giant oak trees and the sky. The place comes with a shuttle to campus.

Growing up, I called the husband of mom's older sister Leksi, short for *lekshila,* which means "uncle." Uncle William called me *tonska,* the word for nephew. During our first meal together, Leksi asked if I might be okay with addressing him as "uncle" since we're no longer on the reservation. He liked the sound of it, which was fine with me. It's what I call Dad's brothers. We agreed that I could leave off his name, seeing as how he is the only uncle around. I did give it a Lakota spin by exhaling on the second accented syllable, pronouncing it un-khal´. He nodded his approval and smiled slightly.

My history with Uncle is tied strictly to the reservation, so it's been interesting to watch how people respond to him when we travel around the city. Kids my age probably aren't familiar with the Buffalo nickel and its iconic Indian head, but many from the older generation have come up to Uncle and remarked how much his profile matches the face they remember. The resemblance is uncanny. The artist used three different models for his design, but Chief Iron Tail, an Oglala Lakota Sioux, looks most like the sketch that was chosen for the coin. Uncle William stands as tall as Dad, so that makes him a little over six feet. He hasn't turned fifty yet. The few gray hairs by his ears are hardly noticeable. They're wound into braids that reach the middle of his chest. He wears true distressed Levi's that come from years of his own washings. White shirts fill his closet, each trimmed with colorful designs and beadwork. His hard-soled, cuffed buckskin moccasins are handmade by a family of leather crafters who live somewhere in the Black Hills, a part I've never explored. Women are really attracted to Uncle, even girls who work in the stores and restaurants on campus. They talk up a storm together. I watch, figuring to learn a thing or two. Uncle claims he was simply born with "roguish charm." A trait he obviously thinks I lack.

Uncle is a different man around me compared to the joking and tender husband and father I witnessed growing up. Maybe because he had three daughters and no son, showing affection toward me is difficult. I remember once standing fixed in place by the kitchen window of their home while getting a drink, in order to study him and *tunwicu*, my aunt, lip locked out back in the hammock. They kissed a lot.

My cousins openly showed love for their father. And he didn't hold back his feelings for them. Uncle must miss Aunt Loretta so much. I don't know how close Mom was to her sister. They are…were…ten years apart. They clicked on some level to have laughed together like they did. Aunt Loretta got honest-to-goodness belly-laughs out of Mom.

The knock on my open bedroom door means food's ready. We no longer eat at the small flimsy table in the kitchen, where we comically sat sideways to avoid hitting each other's long legs. A bigger new dining table stands against the wall in the living room. Traditional Lakota music plays.

Uncle claims the flute and gentle rhythm of the drumbeats have a peristaltic effect and aid digestion. There's no TV until later.

The grilled chicken and roasted corn and potatoes is a typical dinner. "This smells great! I'm lucky you like to cook."

"You should check out the dining halls and cafeterias. The experience would be worth it...to be around students you can make friends with."

"Maybe later."

"If you change your mind next spring, you know you can move to a dormitory."

"I seriously doubt I'll reconsider...too much partying goes on, or so I've been told." Changing the subject, I ask, "Do you like your program?"

"Very much. I'm surprised there are a few students as old as I am who also have a medical background. There's a veterinarian learning acupuncture."

"And he's switching to physical therapy?"

"No, he wants to apply what he learns on animals."

Uncle is to be admired for taking on a new challenge. "Isn't it hard for you," I ask, "already being a doctor...to go back to the classroom?"

He leans back in his chair and thinks about it. "Much has been discovered these last decades. There are new medicines, new procedures...and the research that goes on today would have been unimaginable when I began med school. This is an extraordinary opportunity for both of us." He sounds satisfied, then adds, grinning, "I better know how to treat you when you're a football player, right?" And for the first time ever, he taps my chin in a playful way.

"I hope it isn't often," I joke.

When the dishes are cleaned, I excuse myself to study, glad that Uncle William is so positive. Before moving to Columbus, I had felt somewhat sorry for him, like he had pulled the short end of the stick and got stuck with the job of watching over me. But after twenty plus years of serving the people on two reservations out of a mobile van, with the help of his two nurses, my Aunt Loretta and Grandmother, he said he was ready for a change. They did everything from pulling teeth and delivering babies to filling out forms for addicts and victims of abuse, so they could get help in rehab centers and shelters, even going so far as to treat farm animals. It was noble work for little pay. Medical assistants were hard to come by. Government subsidies didn't cover the services. Administrators in the department were repeatedly caught stealing supplies and drugs. I'm reminded of how Uncle got his name. He was born William Half Moon. One of his first patients couldn't pay him and offered what he could, a useless mare. Every time anyone mounted her, she turned twice in a circle, and then stepped backwards, which is how the man got his foot broken. He had been in the way when his son suddenly jumped on her back, launching the horse into her routine. The horse eventually did go forward, after about twenty steps. Despite her compulsive behavior, Uncle agreed to take her. The animal was well-proportioned with good bones, and had a remarkably nice disposition, even around children. He named her Horse That Walks Backwards. Soon people on the rez started calling him that, which he liked. It endeared him to folks who weren't accustomed to seeking medical help, especially those who lived in isolated areas. Getting to them on horseback was a more practical solution than driving.

Following my aunt's death, the old horse died. By then Uncle William's daughters had married and moved away. They were busy raising their own families. When Grandmother decided to work in a new medical center, Uncle volunteered to stay with me at college because I was too young and had to have a guardian.

I call Dad to let him know that things are falling into place. A knot forms in my gut I miss him so much—not home, just him. I sit up in bed for a while, wondering what Mom is doing right now on the other side of the world. The sheets get pulled up when the air kicks on. My Target sheets. Mom surprised me with a shopping trip during her short two-day visit earlier in the week. There was no guessing what to expect before she came. I was filled with nervous anticipation, which I revealed to Iris. Being the sympathetic older sister that she is, she found a last-minute flight from Wisconsin that would arrive close to when Mom's plane was expected to touch down—a small private plane that took all of twenty minutes to get here from Dayton. Boy, that irked Uncle, who saw absolutely no reason for it. After he and I picked them up at the airport and were driving to the apartment, Mom said that she needed to stop at a research company along the way. With that, Uncle suddenly pulled over on the shoulder of the highway and proceeded to glare at her in silence for a good long minute. Iris and I sat perfectly still in the backseat, afraid of what might happen next. We ended up stopping at the place, and Mom did keep it short. Later, Iris insisted that Mom take only me to the store, which I had my doubts about. I'm grateful now to have gotten that "alone time" with her. As I searched through shelves of towels and pillows, stuff I had never thought about buying before, I'd catch her staring at me out of the corner of my eye. I wondered what she was thinking. It could've been that she wished she were anywhere else, doing something else, but I needed to believe she was here solely for me, and honestly, she had me convinced for a few hours that she was.

When my head sinks in the pillow, I thank our Creator for my sister. It was thoughtful of Iris to come. After Mom left, Sister stayed a few more days, leaving late yesterday. We explored the shops and galleries and pubs along High Street in a district called the Short North, walking as far as downtown. It's a straight shot, and maybe two miles. The things we saw triggered deep discussions that lasted into the night. Iris treated me as an equal, which made me feel grown up. There was no talk of boyfriends, though. Iris is way too pretty and smart to have gone this long without someone showing an interest in her. When I pressed her about it, she simply ignored me. It occurred to us that we never would have enjoyed talks of this nature if we had lived during our great-grandparents' time. Brothers and sisters weren't allowed any close physical contact with each other once they reached puberty, or for that matter anyone of the opposite sex. The relationships resumed only after they found their partners and got married. It didn't amount to a whole lot of years since they married really young. Iris said that several of her childhood friends on the rez still honor the Rawakota tradition. We had some thoughtful conversations about the family, both our Native and Dad's. A great aunt apparently had a big impact on Iris's life. I have no memory of Pahpie's sister having lived with us at Sunkwah and Winnie's home until I was almost four.

Gazing out the window, the full moon captures my imagination. I beg the stars to quickly turn to dreams. This Buckeye can't wait to get into the swing of things here.

Un-hee! Campus is loud and confusing and overcrowded, but at the same time electric. It's like after a torrential downpour when all sorts of desperate creatures are forced from their flooded holes. Nothing could have prepared me for the official start of the school year this third week of August. It took all of June and most of July for me to find my bearings, which also, thankfully, coincided with the peaceful summer term. I squeeze my ass on the end of a crammed park bench that faces High Street, eager to watch the craziness.

It's godawful hot. Big clouds of steam escape from the roof vents of restaurants, adding to the stifling humidity. Then there's the car exhaust that makes the street look wavy. Peoples' deodorants aren't holding up in the brutal heat. When I fan the air with my hand, whiffs of liquor sicken me. The smell is coming from the guys beside me. They're all wearing Greek letter fraternity shirts. My attention turns to the amount of exposed skin in sight, girls' skin. The continuous stream of bouncing breasts and fleshy thighs ignite my primal brain. I home in on a face at the intersection. The girl finishes crossing the street and is heading this way. Her big brown eyes meet mine. She continues to watch me. My breathing picks up. When she's only feet away, she gives me the once-over, and then offers a beautiful smile that shows off her perfect teeth. In a bold move, I prepare to introduce myself when large colorful butterflies jump out at me. They flit along her shoulder; small ones climb up her calves from the ankles. I stay put as she makes her way down the street. What a bummer! The tattoos were pretty—still, to me they're disfiguring and a turn off.

I'd be curious to know her thoughts. Today I decided to wear my hair loose. It falls to my waist. Sections are braided with falcon feathers and ropes of beads just like Lukas's hair in the photo of him on his bike with Mom. Did the girl see me as a throwback to the '60s hippies? Thinking about the thousands of people here, I wonder how many have actually met a true American Indian ... one off a reservation.

Knowing my dislike for tattoos, Dad once told me if I really meet the right girl, things that once bothered me, won't. I'll take his word for it and accept this wasn't the one for me. It seems nearly everybody expresses themselves through body art.

The sharp corner of the bench is killing my tailbone. Time to head for class anyway. A part of me is jealous of the incoming freshmen. Regardless of my second-year status, I feel like one of them when it comes to being new on campus. I'd love to go out and act a little wild to mark the occasion, dance like I do at powwows. I miss it.

Within a week, the population thins out and there's a semblance of order, except at night. Binge drinking on a regular basis is a way of life for a lot of kids. The garbage they create overwhelms the city's ability to stay on top of the clean-up. When walking off-campus, a person is always having to sidestep the empty beer cans and broken glass along the sidewalks and curbs, not to mention the spots you have to hold your breath, the stench of urine is so bad. It's totally opposite OSU's main campus, which is beautiful and clean. Students caught trashing the surrounding community should be expelled from school for causing unlivable conditions.

Not only am I starting to feel disconnected from reservation life, but I'm beginning to feel estranged from here as well. I wake brooding. Fortunately, Uncle isn't around much to notice, or else I'd have some explaining to do. I like moping, lying sprawled on the couch, taking in the tops of the trees, and listening to sad songs. It isn't like I'm having trouble adjusting to college; I'm simply lonely at the moment, until I make friends—one true friend will do. The lunch group from French class has turned out to be fun, but there's no clicking with anybody in particular. I look forward to seeing Iris over Labor Day weekend. So much so that it's worth facing my fear of flying. Dad is also going. We're meeting my Indian relatives in Rapid City for a reception that's being held in Sister's honor. Iris is going to be recognized by the governor for her work with children with intellectual disabilities. She had told me that the strategies she developed for her thesis have produced remarkable results. I try and picture being that far along in my schooling.

Man! I gotta laugh...pondering my future when I can't get a handle on the here and now. Maybe it's exhaustion kicking in. I've had to work my butt off this last year to start college early. *Yeah...that's it.* I roll over and hug the pillow, and next picture those wonderful brown eyes coming at me from down the street. Only now I approach the girl as she goes past, and we continue walking together. We laugh. I place an arm around her, having mentally erased the butterflies...and drift off to sleep.

CHAPTER 8

I quietly take the aisle seat next to Dad's that he saved for me inside the city's Council Chambers. There's a look of relief on his face as I peck him hello on the cheek. Heavy fog delayed departures in Columbus, but I still managed to catch my connecting flight in Chicago to Rapid City. I won't miss any of the speech praising Ms. Iris Racing Water's educational program, which is set to begin in a minute. Iris looks every bit the grown-up. I lean forward to acknowledge Grandmother and her parents who are farther down the row. Winnie blows me a kiss. A few great aunts and uncles are seated in back, all beaming with pride over Iris's accomplishment. The sight of them lifts my spirits. We haven't seen one another since last year's powwow.

After the Board President of Education explains what the study entailed, everyone, including me, is awed by the strides Iris's students have made in such a short amount of time. Because of the five-year age difference, I paid little attention to what Iris finally ended up studying in college. According to the handout, she is an Interventionist for Exceptional Children. Iris looks beautiful, regal in fact, with her thick hair pulled back in a French braid. She's wearing a dark blue dress and heels. Standing next to her is the governor who presents her with a plaque. His wife, a former teacher herself, applauds enthusiastically then shakes Iris's hand. Iris moves to the lectern and thanks the Office of Indian Education for partnering with local agencies to improve the lives of children on reservations. She's acting pretty subdued, even for a serious event like this. Iris typically loves the spotlight and lights up anytime there's a chance of going onstage. It's surprising she didn't go into theater. Where's that dynamic person today? Maybe she's not feeling well.

After the ceremony, Iris immediately spots me as the small crowd heads toward the reception area. Her long embrace is nice, although one might think we hadn't seen each other in years rather than a few months.

"Viktor, you're going back to the rez, aren't you?" She asks as though it isn't up for discussion.

"Uh, no...I've got classes."

"You can miss a couple days. No one takes attendance. Something important has come up that I need to discuss with you...and it can't be over the phone."

I don't care for her flip attitude. It matters to me if I miss school. I want to call her out on it, but other people interrupt to offer congratulations and discuss her work. My great-grandfather Sunkwah directs me to the food. The rest of the hour is spent describing campus life to my relatives. They plead with me to visit home for a couple of days, enticing me with the prospect of riding Jim. They know my weak spot.

"Okay, okay," I answer in defeat, getting swept up in a circle of hugs, which is just what this lonely boy needed to beat the doldrums I recently found myself in. However, I don't like giving Iris the satisfaction of me staying, although she has piqued my curiosity.

The region of the southern Black Hills where my elders live is beautiful. The rolling hills are altogether different than the open plains that make up most of the one million acre Buckthorn Reservation. Home is a small enclave of land that was allocated to the Rawakota tribe by the government in the 1800s, in return for the people's service as interpreters after they'd been captured in the woods by federal soldiers. Sunkwah told me that before then, his Rawakota ancestors used to divide their time between an honest-to-god underground city and the earth above, where they hunted. There are presently a hundred or so families descended from those Rawakota living in an area that covers around twenty square miles, half of which is bordered by pine forests. The nearest town, which takes all of two minutes to drive through, is just northeast of here. I have vivid memories of my first years at Sunkwah and Winnie's house, when Daniel's parents used to drop him off early every morning on their way to work, and we played our hearts out until we dropped. I don't remember him ever getting picked up in the evening. In those days, Pahpie was still alive and farmed the land behind his and Grandmother's house, when he wasn't away protesting. Grandmother had her job as a nurse. After Mom married Solomon Davis and we moved to Wichita Falls, Texas, which was his home, and where he had met Mom during her training at Sheppard Air Base, Iris and my visits back here to South Dakota were spent in totally different neighborhoods, at least for me. Iris continued to stay with Sunkwah and Winnie, because that's where her friends were that she had grown up with. Their community didn't experience the troubles that had already destroyed other parts of the reservation. The Rawakota had always placed a high value on education, and no members ever deserted their families. By then, Daniel's father was out of the picture, for reasons I didn't question as a child, which is when Dad took it upon himself to make sure these best little buddies stayed together. And that meant living in a small paper-thin, box-like house on the other side of the rez, which I learned much later was the poor side, the druggie side. It's where Dad rounded up several more Lakota boys and began coaching us in flag football. Dad and I still made it back for family dinners two nights a week. Winnie cooked terrific meals.

Though their numbers are dwindling, great-grandparents like my own, nearing ninety, still recount the stories told to them by their parents, people who had lived during the turn of the twentieth century and who had survived the Wounded Knee Massacre. Their stories also included the heartbreak of having their children stolen in plain sight and sent away, often by missionaries, to become civilized like whites.

It still amazes me that the Rawakota were able to make a deal with the government that spared their kids when everyone else's were forced to stay at boarding schools. Too bad they couldn't fight the legislation that put an end to our people's nomadic ways. It totally changed how we viewed our territories. When I was growing up, I seldom heard anyone on the rez refer to me as Rawakota, the lineage being so important to Marnie for some reason. My relatives and neighbors insisted on calling themselves Oglala Lakota, because the Lakota were the people they lived among, and whom they liked. Oglala simply means that we are one of seven tribal bands that make up the bigger Lakota tribe, which is part of what outsiders called the Great Sioux Nation; those outsiders being the French, who botched the pronunciation of *Natowessiwak*, calling us the "Nadouessioux." Then the English adopted the name Sioux.

I wake in Grandmother's house to a rare cool summer breeze that chills my toes. Back under the sheets they go. It's a cozy log home. Dad's in another spare room. Iris is staying with a friend. I told her I'd meet with her early, but I don't know about leaving this cushy bed.

Grandmother enters flanked by Hank and Zunta, two loveable very old Newfoundlands. They make several wholehearted attempts at jumping on the bed to greet me, only to slide back to the floor. Arthritis be damned! They don't let it thwart their efforts. I roll over and bury my head in their necks.

"See how they've missed you…my precious sleeping owl."

"Aye-yi-yi!" I laugh, wiping drool off my face. "God, they're funny. Please don't close the window. The air feels too good." She comes over and sits on the edge of the bed. Her faded scrub uniforms eventually become work clothes for around the house. Today's top has orange and green splotches that were once bright flowers…they always have flowers.

"Look how strong you've become, like your grandfather."

Even though I still carry memories of my grandfather Pahpie, who died when I was around twelve, the muscular image of Lukas pops into my head. Grandmother continues to be in top form, but then everyone on Mom's side is tall and sturdy. She could retire, but insists on staying as active as she's always been, working part time in the clinic while still maintaining her home and animals. Besides the dogs, she keeps Jim and Ola, Iris's horse, plus one for herself to ride. Can't forget the chickens and goats.

"The girls must be all over you."

"I wish."

She looks at me adoringly as only grandmas can, and then assures me, "They will." A framed photo on the nightstand of her and Pahpie has her sighing. "If you should fall in love with an outsider—be sure she's not simply infatuated with the idea of you."

The idea of me? "I don't understand, Unci."

"Not to worry." She waves off the comment. "The biscuits should be done any minute. Get up so you're ready when Iris comes over. I'll see if Sol's awake." Giving a slap to the thigh, the dogs jump to her side. On her way out, she mutters *unci* under her breath and chuckles. I haven't used the Lakota word for grandma in ages. Even when I'm thirty I'll feel like a kid here, in a good way.

Iris could plainly see I was just sitting down for breakfast when she entered all keyed up and ready to go, demanding that I hurry so we could make the most of the day riding in the hills.

"For God's sake, Iris! Stop rushing me and telling me what to do!"

It's no wonder that Dad and Grandmother are put off by my rudeness, being ignorant of Iris's behavior at the reception. Ours is not a relationship prone to drama. Does Iris even get why I'm annoyed? I apologize. It sounds as insincere as I'd hoped. Just great! Grandmother invites her to stay. I chew real slow without looking up.

"Thanks, Mémé," she says, her name for Grandmother, "but Ola is waiting."

"*To **her** she sounds nice?*" I grumble under my breath in a Yiddish dialect learned at school.

"Viktor!" says Dad, getting irked. "What gives with you this morning?"

"It's okay, Dad," says Iris. She hugs him and kisses Grandmother, then asks me in a pleasant voice if I'll meet her up at Eagle Point, a huge granite peak with a challenging trail, *whenever I'm ready*, she adds. She intends to stay the day and maybe swim in the lake.

After she leaves, I continue eating at a leisurely pace, catching up on the local news as Grandmother fills us in. The big story is the new Engineering and Physics program at both high schools on the rez, funded by a state university. The goal is to prepare Native youth for careers in building the kind of infrastructure most Americans take for granted. They're following a model from India that has kids learning math as early as age three. Grandmother says she heard that students could one day land jobs at the Sanford Underground Research Project, a ginormous cavern in the nearby town of Lead that's used for finding dark matter in the universe.

Boy, if that doesn't sound like a pipe dream! Before committing to such an undertaking, don't they first have to deal with the poverty and gangs? And when it comes to building infrastructure, indoor plumbing would be a good start. Too many Indians still have no running water. Considering the scope of the plan, I'm sure the university must have done its homework. I wish the idea didn't seem so far-fetched.

Grandmother packs a lunch while I shower and get Jim harnessed.

After twenty minutes at a decent gallop, Jim decides he's had enough and abruptly starts walking, bypassing the trot mode. I know to hang on tight to keep from toppling over. Until I was able to read him better and learned to brace myself, this quirk of his caused me to get thrown hard, resulting in lots of sprained wrists and bruises. I never suffered any broken bones, though.

Instinctively, Jim steps with caution among the boulders leading to the clearing that opens up to the lake below Eagle Point. I see Iris drying out in a patch of sunlight. Her soaked shorts and top cling to her body. Jim nudges Ola when I dismount. I wipe the sweat from his neck then throw the blanket on the ground beside Iris.

"How can you stand freezing like that?" I ask. She's covered in goose bumps.

"It's worth it...to then feel the heat of the sun. I guess you won't be taking a dip."

"It's torture. Bet the water isn't 70 degrees. You're not human."

High above, feathery clouds float along. Nature is loud here, especially the piercing calls of some of the birds. One for certain is the Killdeer. It's almost ten o'clock and the temperature at this elevation is probably in the mid-sixties. We remain silent. It goes on too long. I'm antsy and want to know what's up with her.

She starts reciting the opening verse of *Mitakuye Oyasin*, a Sioux prayer every child learns that praises the interconnectedness of all things. The theme fits the moment. I join in and we say all its verses. Next, she sits so she can face me, and then draws up her knees.

"I realize I've been short with you," she admits. "When you spoke up at breakfast, it occurred to me that one more day or week or month won't make any difference when it comes to what I've discovered."

Could she be more mysterious?

"The accolades and attention I've gotten are without merit. None of it is deserved." She is quite emphatic.

The long pause might be my cue to respond, but without more info, nothing pops into my head.

"Viktor, I believe there's a conspiracy taking place, one that is using our Indian children to experiment on, but I can't figure out who's behind it."

Whoa! I did not see that coming!

Before it can sink in, she takes me by the neck and draws me toward her, and next whispers in my ear, "Dear brother, the woods could have eyes and ears. I don't know who to trust."

She's gotta be pulling my leg, and I snicker, "Oh that's good, Iris. You got me good."

"You think I'm playing a game!"

I push her hand away because she's actually hurting me. This is getting old, me being annoyed with her.

She stands and walks to the edge of the lake. Meantime, I'm growing impatient. She continues to stare at the water.

Finally I roll to my feet and go to her side. "Okay, Iris. Talk."

She repeats what I already know about the backgrounds of the twenty-three kids she had used for her study. I guess it's so I'll truly appreciate the severity of the challenges confronting them—which I did the first go-round during her talk in Rapid City. They range in age from five to twelve and suffer serious neurological problems caused by things like fetal alcohol syndrome, having been born to addicted mothers. Some were harmed by inadequate nutrition. Others have inherited defects. And yes, it's sad they were orphaned because the parents, battling their own demons, are out of the picture. The kids live in government subsidized group homes where Iris says she has been following their development over the past three years, having taken over a colleague's research when he became too frustrated by the poor results he was obtaining.

Iris should be glad that they are now literate and able to communicate. "Why do you claim the children made such gains without your help? Sounds like you've worked around the clock with them."

Her eyes narrow and she takes a deep breath, and then reveals that, unbeknown to her, some kind of device has been imbedded under the scalp of sixteen of the Indian children. Alarmed by the discovery, she inspected the other subjects she works with at the University of Wisconsin, non-Native ones. Several kids there had them, too. Unlike on the reservation, where the children were orphaned, at the university parents *are* involved. They signed their children up for this particular experimental program, and it didn't include any gizmo being placed in their children's heads. Iris's eyes fill with tears. She hadn't said much about the students in the UW study in her speech, since the focus was on Indians.

It feels a little strange to be comforting my big sister, but I take her in my arms, finding the circumstances to be as bewildering as she does. After a few minutes, she collects herself and takes the bottom of her shirt to dab her eyes. I feel sorry for her.

"You can't be the only one questioning what's been going on. Has anyone else felt their heads? Wouldn't the parents in the university program have noticed?" And before she can answer, I add, "How on earth did you detect them?"

Choking back tears, Iris goes to sit in the tall grass where the horses are grazing contentedly, unfazed by worldly concerns. My stomach growls super loud, making me aware of my own hunger. "Go eat," she says smiling, knowing darned well that Grandmother made sandwiches for us. "You're still a growing boy. Nothing for me, thanks." The break in the conversation allows her to compose herself. Once I'm situated, she goes on to answer my question.

"On the reservation, it's mandatory to do monthly checks for lice. Usually a house parent does it; they're easy to spot." I'm thinking, what a gross job. "We've recently been asked to do more thorough checks, in order to see if there are signs of physical abuse. Since house parents are often accused, it's strictly nurses who handle the inspection. I was also given authority because of the nature of my work. That's when I discovered these bumps along the hairline, one at the top of the forehead and one on either side behind the ears. They're barely noticeable."

Iris looks exhausted. I believe she's lost weight, too. Her unloading on me like this will no doubt be helpful, and I'm glad I stayed, as much as I had wanted to talk more about me and my issues, which are nothing compared to this.

"Why weren't all the kids subjected to getting these...implants?" I ask.

She shrugs. "From what I gather, those with aggressive tendencies weren't included. The kids diagnosed with autism don't have them either."

"How might it have been done?"

Again she shrugs and shakes her head. "Maybe they're injected with a syringe...the way animals are micro chipped."

"Anyone would feel a poke," I say, "besides actually *seeing* the device! Who'd want that? The kids were probably sedated, if only long enough to do it."

"Then it has to be by someone who has access to them. It could be any number of people at the university. But way out here? I don't know."

I allow for the free flow of ideas while I munch on my food, then casually ask: "Do they get their teeth checked?" Sister's posture straightens and she shoots me a look—obviously a eureka moment.

"Viktor! The mobile dental van travels to the homes four times a year! And it goes to the rehab centers as well! What if this is more widespread than I thought?"

"Don't get carried away, Iris."

"It's perfect. They have the stuff to knock them out for a brief period, and no one would suspect a thing."

"I still don't get why you can't take credit for the children's success. They couldn't have learned anything if you weren't teaching them."

"Viktor, Viktor..." she says in a hushed voice, rubbing her temples. "It's not that simple. Yes, I taught them, and will continue to." She looks searchingly into the sky. "Let me use Sarah, a ten year old, as an example. Before the program, a milestone for her would have been to go to the bathroom without help, to be able to pull her diaper down and back up. She had never spoken, but she could match words with corresponding pictures. In less than a year, this girl is working at her 4th grade level academically. She speaks. Her arms don't flail all day long. This kind of progress is unheard of, no matter how great a teacher I am. The other kids' stories are just as remarkable. Granted, I designed the procedures, and I monitored and adapted their lessons using the approach that Dr. Abrams developed and then gave up on; but honestly, his theories weren't so unique or ground-breaking. Minor improvements in their behavior would be noteworthy, but this? No, Viktor. What these children accomplished isn't possible without some kind of outside intervention. Do you see there's something sinister going on?"

"So tell me, Iris, how do the children at the university fit in? They aren't Indians, right?"

She answers quickly. "I believe similar results had to be obtained at UW, in order for me to appear credible. How would it look if only one group exposed to the same set of conditions advanced, and the other didn't? Whoever holds a stake in these children's futures has me playing a key role because I get the funding."

"Any ideas?" I ask, unwrapping the brownies that Grandmother also packed.

"The Bureau of Indian Affairs came to mind first. Maybe those heading the agency are trying to figure out a way whereby future generations can be made employable. As things stand, liquor and drugs have ruined the physical and mental health of our people to such a degree they're not fixable."

To me, if true, this seems an altruistic undertaking; everyone benefits.

"That got me wondering," Iris continues, holding her hand out for a brownie, "if the scheme was more diabolical. Remember learning in history that the CIA was behind the experiments in the 1950s that used LSD on prisoners, without their knowledge? What if mind control is the goal? These are throw-away kids, Viktor, with parents who are either dead or close to it, or in jail. No one is going to step up and rescue them. It's a perfect scenario: a population in the middle of nowhere that will bend to their oppressors' will...nothing more than obedient slaves."

There's a bone-chilling prospect. "What are you going to do? Why don't you confide in Mom or Dad?"

Her eyes stay fixed on mine. They're so penetrating. Just what the heck does she expect out of me? I'm no expert in this. I'm waiting to hear why she hasn't involved our parents. Instead, she drops the subject for now and asks what it's been like to live with our uncle.

We discuss movies while sitting in a tree, the kind of afternoon I was hoping for during my visit. Iris describes the personalities of the friends she's made at college, and says she looks forward to hearing about the people I'll be getting to know in the coming years. Her enthusiasm is uplifting. We decide to head back, taking the long way around the eastern side of the lake. The ground is flatter, and a pretty creek veers off towards Grandmother's house. We ride quietly for a stretch when Iris reminds me of the place near campus where Mom wanted to stop off after we left the Columbus airport...when Uncle William got upset with her. "It was on King Avenue, but the name escapes me. She was just stopping in to say hi to a friend who worked there."

"It was Battelle," she says. "Battelle Memorial Institute."

"Right. What do they make?"

"It isn't a company that manufactures stuff. I googled it. Once in a while Battelle comes up in conversations at school when students or professors search for grants. I was blown away when I read it's the biggest nonprofit research organization in the world. Think of the implications. "

"No shit. It didn't look that big from the street."

"Battelle has a global network made up of all different sized companies. Some have contracts with the Department of Energy. They have a center that's not only in cahoots with the country's biodefense and cybersecurity industry, but it also deals with agencies that handle DNA and RNA research involving human and plant genomes. What if it uses hospitals and universities to serve as front organizations...like the CIA did for one of its projects that secretly carried out human medical trials? They're no doubt masters at keeping things under the radar. What do you think about Mom knowing a person who works there?"

Dare I believe where she's going with this? "Are you insinuating *Mom* is behind this plot with the kids, simply because a friend of hers works there!" I steer Jim in front of Ola, who rears and needs steadied. "That's one helluva serious allegation, Iris!"

"Not directly, mind you. But in some capacity."

"Based on what? Where's your evidence...your facts? You can't honestly think Mom would do that to you!"

"Maybe," says Iris, "if there were something bigger at stake. Isn't that why people sign up for war?"

"Un-hee, Sister!"

A firm yank to Jim's reins sends him flying down the path, which was mean of me to do to him. It was a reflex response; Iris got me so doggone upset. Suddenly Ola's beside us, bumping into Jim for the fun of it. He turns his head and playfully nips her neck. Next thing the horses start stepping sideways down the stream, whinnying and splashing as they go. Because they're facing each other, Iris and I are, too. We can't help but laugh over their clowning. I don't want to be angry with Sister, and I realize it wasn't her intention to get me riled up. Using a kinder tone, I ask if anything happened to give rise to this crazy theory of hers. There's no other word for it.

We can't talk while the horses are carrying on like this. Ola and Jim stubbornly resist our efforts to end their game. A firm hand is needed to direct them back to the path. By now, fortunately, they're ready to take it slow, which makes for a relaxing end-of-day ride.

Iris looks at me and asks, "Do you know the name Rolling Thunder?"

I shake my head no. "Should I?"

"No," she says, "just curious if you did. I used to overhear some of my friends' parents going on about this man, Rolling Thunder, and with such excitement in their voices. I was around nine or ten when I picked up on it, which is when I became consumed with learning Rawakota. Winnie had lots of books in Rawakota, and I started speaking it with her and Sunkwah. And I liked that I could understand what was being talked about in homes where it was still spoken."

"Yet you didn't learn who this guy was?" I'm guessing there's a reason that she's bringing him up.

"I mentioned the name Rolling Thunder once to Pahpie. He wondered *where* I had heard it, and next he asked *what* was said about him, to which I answered, nothing. I told him that people just seemed real happy that they were going to get a chance to see this man on their vacation. Pahpie said that many of our neighbors continued to visit their Rawakota relatives in an area of the Black Hills that is off limits to anyone but family. He said that Rolling Thunder was the community's leader."

"That's pretty unbelievable," I say, wondering how a place could be kept secret.

"I had been questioning my results for months, and didn't give Rolling Thunder a second thought," says Iris, "until we visited you and Uncle William in Columbus. I caught Mom on the phone telling somebody that she was going to find out more about the experiment after meeting with Rolling Thunder. When I asked her who Rolling Thunder was, she said, 'Just forget what you heard.' Imagine! She didn't say it mean-like, but I knew not to pursue it."

"So, Iris...when you began to question your data, you immediately jumped to the conclusion that Mom and this mysterious Rolling Thunder were somehow responsible? That doesn't jibe."

"Mom deals with things that none of us has an inkling about; I bet not even Dad. I don't want my suspicions to be true. I'm at a complete loss over how to proceed with my studies in the future."

I don't think I have ever used the word conundrum in my life, but it seems appropriate in this case. After thinking about Iris's predicament, I tell her she should confront the dentist. We both agree that it's highly unlikely he would admit to something so preposterous. He might even laugh in her face.

Clippety-clop, back and forth, my lids grow heavy. Iris yawns. Luckily for us, the horses can find their way home. The scent of Grandmother's blueberry pie in the air means we're close. Ola and Jim know from experience that there are always little freshly baked tarts with their names on them.

CHAPTER 9

"...and for the first time, the Buckeyes take the lead!" The announcer's voice is muffled by the roar of the crowd that includes me, yelling my brains out, high-fiving strangers. It's no less thrilling sitting in the nosebleed section of the football stadium watching what looks to be tiny LEGO action figures scrambling across the field. Surprisingly, you get a better total picture of the plays as they develop from this far up. And what a view of the city's skyline! As I look around in awe, it's ironic that the thing that holds people's attention is their tiny cell phone screens, even when there's a huge jumbotron flashing in front of them.

I came with two guys I barely know. We met last month while shooting hoops at the rec center on south campus. Jackson Cole, who goes by Jake, belongs to a fraternity and will be in the starting lineup of the OSU basketball team this year. Theo Doggard, "The Dawg," a jittery kid from the inner city who has lightning bolts shaved on his scalp, is on athletic probation with hopes of playing alongside Jake as a second-year freshman. Dawg's mumbled speech is incomprehensible, which he realizes, and is smug about. I was glad when he sat to the other side of Jake, who laughs it off.

Failing to attend the first home football game would not have been the worst thing to happen, but I needed to come to let loose in a big way. Iris was right in that I wouldn't miss much in class by being absent for a couple of days. That same evening after our ride back from Eagle Point, we enjoyed a relaxing, drawn out dinner that included our great-grandparents. Dad woke early to get us up to Rapid City in time for his return flight to Texas, and mine back here to Columbus. That was three days ago.

Iris and I parted on good terms. Throughout that meal, I thought about the things she had brought to light. Her fears weren't baseless. But jumping to the conclusion that Mom would deceive her? There had to be another angle.

What Iris really wanted from me was the name of a top neuroscientist at Ohio State, someone trustworthy. In the future she intends to bring a couple of kids to be evaluated. The trip would take place under the pretense of a normal visit between sister and brother. The children would be invited along as a reward: like a field trip for having earned good grades. Iris put thought into her plan. At least she doesn't expect this right away. I have my own pressing problem to deal with, like finding a girl to kiss. With any luck, it'll happen tonight.

Uncle sits glued to a cooking show. At no time while getting ready for the party does he say anything. It's exciting because there will be younger students in the mix. Trusting Marnie's judgement, I wear the deep purple V neck tee shirt she had picked out. My hair's in a single braid with colorful beads running through it. And although I prefer sandals with shorts, I opt for sneakers…they're better for breaking. After a final quick once-over of myself in the mirror, I'm good to go. God, I can't wait! Jake messages that he's in the lot. On my way out, Uncle yells something about drinking, but the door slams shut too fast to hear it.

As we drive over to the southeast side of campus, I admire Jake's shiny black Nissan Murano, a high school graduation present. He says his parents, both lawyers, bribed him with it so he'd study law. He's fine with that and decided his specialty will be negotiating athletes' contracts. He is already networking with coaches since they have an in with professional team owners. Now that's planning! Jake operates in high gear nonstop. I like his gung-ho attitude. It's just the thing I need to keep me psyched about trying out for the football team one day.

Come to think of it, my future is mapped out as well. Get my PhD in Biochemistry, and be a quarterback. I don't have the chutzpah to share my football aspirations with anyone here, especially after Marnie made a case regarding why a Big Ten Conference School would want me. I clearly have to find a way to maintain my athletic skills during the interim.

"Hey, Jake, do you ever wonder whether things will turn out like you expect?"

"Oh they will," he states with supreme confidence, the same confidence that wins him the last parking spot, which he barely squeaks into, and without a scratch. He whips his head to the side to flick his long blonde bangs off his forehead and taps my arm. "C'mon, Viktor, let's go find us some action."

Getting to the place takes some walking. Doors are propped wide open along every block, with homes crammed to the max. The hard-driving bass of hip-hop is everywhere, and so amplified it seems the sound could shake the old and crumbling three-story brick structures to the ground. They look dangerous to live in. It's a beautiful evening despite the humidity. The sun's rays extend outward from below the horizon. When we arrive at the address, Jake throws an arm around my shoulders and high-fives his way through the crowd, showing I'm his friend. Maybe that entitles me to some respect. Size-wise I'm in my element. A lot of guys are at eye-level for a change. Jake is even a couple of inches taller than me. I'm assuming they're his teammates. I'm swept up in a swirl of bodies dancing to James Brown of all people.

It isn't long before the call goes out for participants in a break dancing contest. We used to have a blast holding matches on the rez...before teams started to identify with gangs, and the friendly competitions turned ugly. I was shorter and much thinner, and could spin on my head endlessly. Daniel's and my performances almost always clinched it for our Bboy crew, the Wingfoots. Daniel defied gravity. He'd get to bouncing and twisting so high in the air, and then land with perfect splits. I check out the wood floor, debating if it's worth it. Everyone has moved to make space and is shouting for a contender. Old school stuff sets the mood. A guy across from me takes his stance inside the circle. Nelo is his name, and his friends bait the crowd, asking who'll take him on. He's gotta be damned good. I in turn take a slow, deliberate step toward him, accepting the one-on-one challenge. The playlist switches to a great funk track. A groundswell of enthusiasm fires me up, and I launch into a set of acrobatic planches that I haven't practiced in a while. The recent growth spurt has affected my speed, but I'm stronger than ever.

"*Viktor, Viktor, Viktor...*" chants Jake, prompting others to join in.

My opponent takes to the floor. Nelo's a wiry, medium-sized Latino kid, who wears trendy baggy pants and a skintight cap. He's definitely got his following, and I can see why. I don't go for his dance style of popping, but it's fun to watch, especially his chest and neck pops. We go at it for a while, back and forth, me sticking with lots of knee drops, until it's time for the fast and furious suicide moves. Judging is based on applause. The result: a tie. Nelo and I, dripping in sweat, nod respectfully then walk to the center for a quick handgrab-fistbump. Normally, ties aren't acceptable. It's understood that you keep going until there's a clear winner. But that isn't what it's about tonight.

"Get *out*!" exclaims Jake, bumping his head into mine too hard. "Indians know that shit!" Man, he's plastered! He shakes me by the neck in a good natured way then heads to the porch with a girl. Suddenly lots of girls close in on me from all directions.

"Hi, I'm Cheryl," says the fastest one to me, cutting in front of the others. The alpha female slides an arm around my waist; her other hand cradles a beer. "That was awesome," she says in my ear, stretching on tiptoe. Her lips glide across my jaw until we're looking directly into each other's eyes. She's tall and thin and has long, sparkly, green-streaked blonde hair. Her strapless top barely covers her nipples. The song is a slow one. Cheryl sets the beer on a table then holds my hips tight to her. We rock side-to-side. I stroke her soft hair. Her breasts fit snug against my chest. I'm somewhat aware of guys downing jello shots in another room. There's a group huddled in a corner lost in video games. Some giggling girls dancing with linked arms tumble into us.

A hallway that leads out back provides an escape. Others had the same idea and are making out in the dark. Cheryl and I start kissing. She doesn't taste good, but not bad enough for me to stop exploring.

"Ow! Shit!" A lip bite coupled with a go-for-broke grab of my crotch snaps me back to reality. While my body yields to fierce instincts, my brain is firing signals to brake.

"God Cheryl!"

"What?" she laughs as I unlock her fingers and push her hand aside. Unfazed, she says, "You Indians *must* have a wild side."

Did I hear right? Disappointment doesn't stop my hormones from catching me off guard. Turning to the side, and with my hands spread flat on the hood of a car, there's no stopping the release of my longstanding pent up cravings. Behind me I hear Cheryl's footfalls as she walks away. Then loudly she yells back, "Screw you." Do I care? I can't move. I can't think.

It takes a few minutes to regain my senses. I shuffle down the alley, still spaced out, relieved to be out of the clutches of such a bimbo. Everywhere people are wasted. They're stumbling around and laughing out of control.

I just want to be home, but I'm not about to bother Jake for a ride. Calling a cab might be smart, but the walk is beginning to clear my head. I check the time on my phone: it's only a little past midnight.

The air is heavy. I bet it's still in the nineties. At a fast pace it might take me forty minutes to get to the apartment. But I don't speed up, enjoying instead the freewheeling sensation of a late night stroll. I grab a bottle of water and manage a quick clean up in the men's room of a gas station. My hair and shirt are still damp from the dance-off. The sidewalks are fairly empty once I reach High Street. There's enough traffic though to be worried about a drunk or texting driver running a red light. I race across the intersection where I decide to take a shortcut behind the student Union to get to Mirror Lake. From there I'll follow Neil Avenue to Lane. Mapping it out in my head, I realize, realistically, this could turn into a trek lasting well over an hour. Uncle never said he was going to wait up for me, so I continue.

The overhead clouds reflect the light making it easy to see. I rest on a bench and pick up small rocks to skim across the water. A few ducks bob on the surface, unconcerned by my presence. More ducks are sleeping on the grassy bank, with necks tucked in and beaks resting on their chests. The ripples travel to the stone wall, only to bounce back creating new smaller ripples. It makes me think of Mr. Reuter. He introduced us to the Law of Precession using Buckminster Fuller's stone in the water example.

Such a nice memory. I smile at how we kids used to compete for the daily job of getting our teacher sidetracked. Mr. Reuter knew what we were up to, but indulged us anyway. We loved where he took us. Whether ripples of water or gravitational waves rippling through space and time, he taught us that we're all wave catchers and wave emitters. "God I miss you, Mr. Reuter." He's the most knowledgeable person I've ever met.

"Are you alone?"

Lost in thought, I'm startled by the form that seems to materialize from out of nowhere. Forget that he heard me talk out loud to—nobody. At the moment, it's the uniform that leaves me speechless. My heart goes wild.

"Sorry," says the cop, "didn't mean to spook you. Figured you saw me coming down the path."

I look up toward the street. There's the silhouette of his partner leaning against the trunk of their patrol car. From this distance, his arms and ankles appear crossed, a relaxed pose as I see it.

"Has something happened?" I ask, not sure whether they consider me a suspicious character.

"No. Just making the rounds. You didn't notice us trailing behind you over by the Union?"

I shake my head, not so much to answer him, but in disbelief over my own lack of awareness. Letting my guard down like this in the Black Hills would make me easy pickings for a bear or mountain lion. Never again, I promise myself.

"Mind showing me your ID." It isn't a question.

Countless news images flood my thoughts with things gone wrong when minorities are stopped by police. Instantly, memories of the night get replayed, and for the life of me I can't think of a reason to be worried. As I stand to remove my wallet from a back pocket, the officer by the car takes some steps toward the path. He can see that I'm much taller than his partner. His hand is for sure resting on his holster, although the one questioning me hasn't shown any concern. He merely takes my school ID and driver's license.

"Texas, huh?" He examines them carefully with a flashlight. "Don't you have a car?"

"No...my parents didn't see a need." I look back up the hill for movement. I answer more questions about the party...where it was. There's a long pause.

"It's past curfew."

"What! I'm a student here."

"You're also only sixteen." He returns the IDs. "How much did you have to drink?"

"Nothing." I replied too quickly, which sounded guilty to my own ears.

"Here," he says, "know how to use this?"

I'm staring at a breathalyzer. "No, I don't; and no, I'm not going to." I know for a fact they aren't reliable, and I don't want to incriminate myself; although, refusing this request might have serious consequences.

"It's meant for *my* safety, that's all," says the officer. "I need to get you home and, let's face it, you're a big guy. But...since I don't smell alcohol. C'mon, we're gonna drive you to your address."

He points his light at the path, leaving me no choice. I'm dreading how Uncle will react.

"Do you have to file a report whenever anyone gets in your car?" I ask, growing sicker from worry by the second.

"Don't be paranoid...Talking White Owl is it? You're not in trouble. But you shouldn't be out here unaccompanied by an adult. What tribe do you belong to in Texas?"

The question throws me. The disappointment on Uncle's face when police show up at the apartment is all I can think about. "Uh...I'm originally from South Dakota. I'm Lakota."

Cops must have a secret code for nonthreatening situations. Without hesitating, the partner goes to the driver's side and gets behind the wheel. Opening the back car door for me, the officer says he's got some Indian blood in him: "Delaware, from up along Lake Superior. My great-grandfather was French. He brought his Indian wife down here to Ohio. Then, in the early 1820s, they got booted off their land and told to go west of the Mississippi, even though he was white."

I crouch to climb in the back seat. When we're all buckled in he says, without turning around, and more to himself it seems, "It's the same old story for all our elders. Downright criminal." The use of *our* strikes me as odd. He must still hold a strong connection to his Native American side.

In less than ten minutes we pull into the parking lot where I beg the cops to let me go upstairs alone, but they won't hear of it. I'm insistent, "...but you can watch the lights go on in the apartment..."

I trudge alongside them up to the third floor. The door opens before I even get the key in the lock.

"What's this?" asks Uncle. My head lowers, a reflex reaction, and I find myself staring at his moccasins.

The Indian cop tells him there's a curfew in Ohio, and that I was picked up for walking alone on campus.

"Thank you for driving him home," says Uncle.

That's it? I walk inside. The door closes. Uncle tells me to take a shower, which I balk at because I'm exhausted, and my nerves are spent over this ordeal. But I have to because he says I stink; and I'm still the obedient child. I'm also ordered to place my clothes, which admittedly reek, on the balcony, a three-foot-wide slab of concrete outside the sliding doors that I thought fairly useless until now. As I go about the business of undressing, Uncle returns to bed.

My relationship with Uncle is getting better, the more I learn what to expect from him. This past Sunday, after I woke up around noon following the cops scare, the two of us sat eating at our table as usual. "Now we know," were his only words regarding the reason for my escort home earlier in the middle of the night. Yep, we do. Bummer for me, having a curfew at college.

Uncle William had informed me a few days ago that he was going to the Black Hills today, Thursday, to celebrate the birth of another granddaughter. Before the sun rose, I drove him to the airport in his new VW Golf Sport Wagon that he said I could use for the next couple of weeks. And just like the night of the party, the offer came with no cautionary advice. As a parent of three girls, did he instill in them such morals that he could always trust them? Because that's my take on his behavior. I admire him tremendously, as I do Dad, to the degree that I would be crushed if I did something so stupid it would reflect poorly on them. Now that I'm older I understand the pain Dad put his family through with his self-destructive choices. By my age, he was already addicted to heroin and living with anyone who'd let him stay with them.

I love having the apartment to myself. A smorgasbord of meats and veggies line the kitchen counter for a two foot sub. I'm all smiles as I hum and chop to a lively Boston Pops concert playing in the background on PBS. A culinary maestro I am, waving my knife through the air like a baton. I'm happy that my classes make sense to me, that the weekly French get-togethers for lunch are interesting and full of laughs. The six of us are getting to know each other really well. I have Jake and his buddies to shoot hoops with. Life is good I must say, and so is this sandwich. *Ta-da!* It's a work of art.

And now dinner on the couch in front of the TV, just like with Dad. Switch to the news, local comes on in five minutes. This is great. My jaw pops, I have to open so wide for a bite. Mmm—out of this world. This is going to take a while to polish off. Radar shows Columbus is minutes away from a downpour with the likelihood of severe flooding. Not my worry. I'm hunkered down in a cozy spot, safe on the third floor. I love storms. There are none more dramatic than on the Plains.

Next the news anchor at the desk speaks about a follow-up to last night's tragic story, the drowning death of Ohio State freshman Jackson Cole. A chill travels my spine. Surely, I hadn't heard right; but there's Jake with his winning smile looking back at me from the screen.

"...a 911 call made after midnight by a friend..."

"Jake..."

"...the accident occurred at Marble Cliff, a quarry known to be dangerous..."

"Jake..."

"... his head struck a sharp rock under the water. The student was found to have a high blood-alcohol level, which likely contributed to him ignoring the no diving and no trespassing signs posted on the property. He was pronounced dead at the scene."

I sit frozen on the spot, half-listening to the promising future that lay ahead of him; how he had served as a youth leader in his Church, organizing a group to build homes over the past couple of summers for poor families in Appalachia. I didn't know that. His parents are OSU alumni...

The chills continue in waves, so strong they set my shoulders to shaking. The remaining food in my mouth ends up in the napkin, which I put on the plate with the giant sub I barely started, and then I curl into a ball, reaching for pillows to make a fort around me. The roll of thunder continues and grows louder. I close my eyes and hear Jake's voice, his friendly voice. In plain sentences, I hear him talking on the basketball court. The scene changes to his dorm room, to him in his car, his snazzy new Murano. I can hear his voice over the phone. Just late yesterday afternoon he was asking me to join him and some guys for an evening swim in the Scioto River. It's been so hot and humid. He almost convinced me, but I had a late lab to go to. Besides, I wasn't keen on the idea of exposing my body to muddy river water. The springs in the Black Hills are clear and sparkling.

The crack of a lightning bolt with its loud boom rattles the windowpanes and shuts down my brain. The couch vibrates. I bury my face in a pillow.

My eyes open to a horizontal view of the room. A different news team warns of flooded streets to avoid during today's early Friday commute. I grab the remote to turn off the TV. I don't question whether Jake's death was dreamed; it's true. The lettuce hangs wilted off the sides of the bun, which is soaked through from the Italian dressing. Leg cramps cripple me when I try to straighten out. My right side hurts from having slept in the same position all night. My stomach rumbles from hunger.

I ease myself to my feet, which is when I really feel I've been twisted in a knot. I shower. I dodge huge puddles on the way to the bus stop to take the shuttle to campus, with a stomach still empty. The professor's lecture in my first class is gobbledygook. Dazed, I march on to the next class where I take a test. Working out math problems offers somewhat of a break from the sadness, which is not my intention to escape. I want to feel sick at heart. Someone I liked a lot is no more. Fat tears keep falling on my paper, blurring the type on the page. I get lost in how they spread, how they leave the paper slightly buckled. I go turn in the exam.

"Are you all right?" asks the professor with genuine concern.

"Jackson Cole was a friend," I answer.

It takes a second for the name to register. Anyone would know it from the news. "I'm so sorry, Viktor. Such a terrible loss."

For some reason, saying Jake's name out loud and referring to him in the past tense was necessary. I nod, accepting his condolence, and then go home to sleep, thankful it's the weekend. I only wake to pee. By Sunday, I've had enough. It's cool outside and smells like fall. I drive for hours northwest of the city, past the zoo, winding among beautiful farms with magnificent clusters of trees. Some leaves are already turning colors. The brilliant Robin egg blue sky is filled with fluffy cotton ball clouds. My soul aches to share the scene with someone—even if it's Jim, especially when I see horses grazing in open pastures. I think of Jake, of all that lost potential. Fuck the need for getting high! What's with people? And not just here, but the world over. It's one thing to grow up in a war zone where daily you're faced with losing all your possessions, or your life, but when you're surrounded by this...

Fall semester is a blur, but winter break was memorable. To think that this time last year in January I was looking forward to starting college in the summer. And now, coming to the apartment feels perfectly natural. I met Dad at his folks' place in Missouri for Christmas. A blizzard made it impossible to travel to South Dakota. Iris left college early enough to stay with the family on the reservation before getting snowed in. Mom was a no-show, apologizing in a message we received on New Year's Day. Again a mission took precedence; but we're used to it. Dad and I missed Iris's company. The three of us have never been separated over the holiday. Thanks to Grandmother having Internet on her corner of the rez, we settled for an online celebration that included Sunkwah and Winnie.

Uncle has been more approachable since becoming a grandfather for the third time, another girl. Each of his three daughters now has a girl. He himself has four sisters and no brother. When he married Mom's sister, my Aunt Loretta, he was surrounded by even more women. *Man!* That's worth a conversation some time. When he returned from his visit he was fired-up about us watching football together. To my surprise, he's incredibly knowledgeable about the rules.

I had stopped shooting hoops at the rec center after Jake's death because it reminded me too much of him. I feel ready to go again, but now it's to lift weights and increase my strength for football.

It's Friday night and I have no plans. I'm enjoying the movie *Greystoke: The Legend of Tarzan* on TV when Uncle places dinner on the back table. I get up the nerve to ask: "Would it be okay if, just tonight, I eat in front of the TV?"

He grunts a few syllables, which is like swearing in Lakota since we don't have any real curse words. I roll my eyes in defeat and start to stand when he puts the plate down on the coffee table.

"It's your home, too," he says, "more yours than mine. Sit."

"Uncle, don't say that...just once in a while, you know?"

His tone softens. "I'm not angry with you, Viktor, but mad at myself. My children have been on their own for years, and with Loretta gone...I am used to my own schedule and routine. I try to give you space..."

"You do! You absolutely do." This is the first insight I've had into his thoughts. And it's greatly appreciated. He prefers to stay and eat at the dining table but watches the story, sometimes adding a comment. It's not awkward.

When the movie ends, and before turning in, I worry that the advanced calculus class this term is going to test my patience. I need to buckle down and throw myself into my studies. I got approved for a degree that combines the master's with the bachelor's. At this rate, having tested out of freshman and sophomore courses, I should be able to complete the four-year program by summer and move right into post graduate work. Around then, thinking optimistically, I'll be ready to join the football team. I haven't figured out how to integrate a doctoral thesis with the rigors of training...cross that bridge later. John Urschel, the former Baltimore Ravens guard, is for sure an inspiration. If he was able to pursue a master's degree in math while playing for Penn State, it *can* be done. From what I've read, he sounds like a grounded individual, even though he is reported to be super competitive in everything he undertakes, not only sports. I have to believe that when I'm actually on the field and facing goliaths who are hell-bent on eating me alive, survival instincts will kick in.

A day doesn't go by without Jake's name entering my thoughts. The worst is at bedtime. He's standing in the darkness on a stony ledge, looking down into the black water. I try to envision his state of mind that night. Did he leap high into the air with his usual inherent confidence, or did he question the recklessness of the act and hesitate for the first time in his life? Perhaps his foot slid, throwing him off balance. Was there a moment's panic? Truth is he was too shitfaced to think anything.

At least he went out knowing what it felt like to be inside a girl. I'd hate to die without having a good experience. The possibility plagues me during my waking hours. Why can't I just do it like everybody else? Why does love have to figure into it for me?

"Good grief, Iris. Please stop asking whether I have any names for you whenever we talk. You can look up researchers yourself now that you've finished your thesis. I barely have a minute to breathe; I'm carrying such a load."

"I'm sorry, Viktor. Every time I follow a lead, it ends up going nowhere."

She's afraid to say the word *children* or anything on the phone that might be construed as suspicious, believing that the "implant Nazis" could be listening in. I tell her that in December or January I'm supposed to assist in a research project at the Medical Center. "Maybe I can be more helpful then." I quickly change the subject. "Dad said you're serious about a guy. That you're thinking about marrying him."

She says she has known Hashkedasila, Hashke for short, since the eighth grade. They met at the two week summer camp for American Indian kids in Minnesota. He was a high school senior, and one of the counsellors. His mother is Apache, his father Menominee. Their family lives on his dad's reservation near the town of Keshena, Wisconsin. Hashke has a master's in engineering. The reason she chose to go to the University of Wisconsin was because Hashke was there. "He's busy putting together a business proposal to open his own construction company near their reservation," she says. "We plan on dividing our time between South Dakota and Wisconsin."

"You did a good job of keeping the lid on your relationship. Why wouldn't you at least have confided in your brother?"

"It's complicated, Viktor. I fell head over heels in love with Hashke around the same age that Mom was when she met Lukas. She initially believed that she was in love with him. The circumstances were by no means the same, but I needed to see if Hashke's and my feelings for each other would withstand the test of time. Plus, I had always assumed growing up that I would marry a man with some Rawakota in him. It might sound silly to you, but I had to come to terms with that."

Sister is more grounded in the romance department than I'll ever be. After our goodbyes, there's no time to reflect on the news; I've got to get to class.

And so it goes, this maddening schedule I willingly took on, just to keep my mind off of dying young like Jake did...without knowing what loving a girl felt like.

CHAPTER 10

Almost a mile below the town of Lead, South Dakota, 4,850 feet to be exact, in a hidden cavern tucked behind a 500 foot granite divide that separates it from a massive underground research laboratory, sit two Rawakota physicists and their guest, Constance Howling Wind. More than a century ago, it was the site of the largest gold mine in North America. Nowadays, the deep pit has been transformed and is used to hunt for theoretical subatomic particles. While the place was undergoing construction in the 1960s, Rawakota operatives secretly concealed pin-sized cameras throughout the structure to allow for ongoing surveillance of the experiments that were to be conducted inside. It proved a boon to their understanding of a new field that the outsiders called quantum physics. The Rawakota ran with it, to the point that, following decades of eavesdropping on speculations put forth by world-class scientists and engineers, their own knowledge on the subject is about to supersede that of everybody else's on the planet. Tribal members are currently gleaning news about construction of Sanford Lab's LUX-ZEPLIN: an upgrade to the Large Underground Xenon facility. It is being touted as the next generation search for dark matter in the universe. Today, however, there is an air of levity to the otherwise sobering business of spying. Howling Wind and the physicists are observing a few LUX scientists who are in the deepest part of the laboratory. Connected by phone, they're answering questions posed by school children high above at ground level. Sarah, a thoughtful girl attending junior high in Sioux City, has just asked how it's possible to measure the amount of dark matter and dark energy believed to exist in space, if it can't be seen.

It is Sanford Lab's Annual Neutrino Day, an event intended to excite the imagination of all attendees, but in particular youngsters. Visitors enter the mindboggling realm of particle physics, which will hopefully entice many of them, including local Native children, to pursue any number of possible scientific career paths.

"The participation increases every year; it's encouraging," says Spotted Tail, one of the Rawakota scientists. "Having a tech savvy workforce can't happen soon enough. To think that the Lab's partnerships with the area's schools are funded by the federal government. It's on their dime that our children on the reservation will learn what's needed to work here someday, a place built by outsiders on our land."

"It would happen faster," says Howling Wind, "if the regional high schools and colleges could find the teachers for advanced calculus and chemistry courses. There aren't enough willing to move here."

"We'll work on it," says Spotted Tail, "even if I have to leave my home below in Chohkahn for a period to teach them myself."

The three share a laugh when a grade-school boy asks with utmost sincerity whether his little brother's invisible friend is in fact real…*could he be dark matter?*

While continuing to watch the web-feed from Sanford Lab's computers, Spotted Tail casually asks about one of their own tribe's experiments. "What does the data reveal about the *altered* children? Do the chips help facilitate cognition?"

"It's promising," says Howling Wind, who is never addressed by her military rank among the Rawakota. "The device generates a unique pattern of connections that bypass damaged areas of the brain. Forty-seven of Dr. Devreau's patients are learning at the appropriate age level. Fifteen others who were recently added to the study show similar progress. It takes around six months for them to catch up."

His face lights up. "Excellent news." Showing no constraint, he next enquires about her son, Viktor. "How is he getting along at the university?"

"Good," she replies. "He caught a bug this winter that laid him up a spell…had to drop a lab, but it isn't a setback. If I have time to stop at Battelle next week, I'll see him. My brother-in-law is confident he'll be ready to play football as planned after next year."

Constance understands what Spotted Tail really wanted to know by his seemingly innocent question. *Has Viktor found his mate?* He is after all marrying age. The Rawakota believe the union should happen by the time a person reaches twenty, by twenty-one for sure. It's a gentle reminder that should he not find a partner during this period, he runs the risk of acquiring a condition called *yahzahn choh lah*, which translates to "the pain of being without" in English. The preoccupation with finding an everlasting relationship while one is relatively young is a fixed part of their people's collective temperament. The idea is introduced early in childhood, and then cultivated over the next decade. Using age appropriate stories, toddlers begin learning about this great love from the time they begin talking. When boys and girls reach puberty, they are introduced to the concept of *theeich ihilah* in their coming-of-age ceremonies. It describes the promise that a husband and wife make to each other, which is not unlike most traditional marriage vows. In Rawakota culture, marriage offers the most fulfilling life, a life that continues beyond this world. There is no till death do us part. Through a couple's eternal union comes a deeper understanding of Wakan Tanka, the mystery of all creation.

Spotted Tail knows to tread lightly when it comes to bringing up the subject with Howling Wind. She is all too familiar with how this "pain of being without" can manifest itself in unacceptable ways. Lukas Sun in Eyes, Viktor's father, chose alcohol when faced with the profound loneliness that took hold of him when he didn't find his partner early on. He was after all thirty-two when he met Constance, whom he designated as the one for him. Sadly, a decade's worth of drinking had eroded any remnant of clear-mindedness. Up until he met her, he had also engaged in sex merely for the physical pleasure it brought him, thereby denigrating the act believed sacrosanct between a man and woman. Constance came to understand the intense shame Lukas bore only when she was much older.

With evening approaching, the scientists and Howling Wind travel to Chohkahn in one of the many comfortable coaches that make up their underground high-speed transit network. Dubbed the "Loozh," it's the abbreviated name derived from a longer phrase meaning *to ride on air*. The magnetic people-mover connects territories under the Black Hills to places deep within Canada's interior where the land meets the sea. This particular tunnel, half a century old, was begun after Rawakota tribesmen began noticing human activity at the old Homestake Mine. The mine, built illegally on Indian land, had been boarded up ever since the area's gold rush ended in late 1870s. When scouts went to investigate, they confronted a pleasant, harmless-looking middle-aged white man who appeared to be in charge of the construction being carried out. He told the scouts that he was a chemist, and that the Homestake Mine was being turned into a laboratory to run experiments. His workers were in the process of building huge pumps because so much water was required. The man certainly didn't think for a moment that Indians could grasp his explanation, but he went on to say that his "neutrino detector" required an environment that's shielded from the cosmic radiation in the atmosphere. What better place than at the bottom of a deep mineshaft.

While en route to Chohkahn's central district, Howling Wind and the physicists engage in a lively discussion about one of the things they overheard today, a plan to connect the Sanford Lab here in Lead to another research center called Fermilab in Batavia, Illinois, where invisible particles are also studied. The project is called LBNE for the Long Baseline Neutrino Experiment. It will follow neutrinos as they travel an eight hundred mile tunnel through the earth. This is viewed as a complex, history-making endeavor, which it assuredly is. But the Rawakota have them beat, having successfully completed a comparable tunnel system back in the mid-1950s.

Their operation at least didn't require the drilling of massive holes into Mother Earth. The tunnels already existed. Some excavation was necessary to connect them. They wound under the forests of the Black Hills from the western border of the state into North Dakota where they continued below the Yellowstone and Missouri Rivers, eventually reaching Minot, South Dakota, right when Minot Air Force Base was getting established. The distance was an impressive four hundred and fifty miles. That's when the Rawakota began sneaking onto the protected military base and stealing highly classified intelligence. Aided in recent times by Howling Wind, their people are well on their way to becoming a powerful Nation.

After spending the night in Chohkahn, Howling Wind parts ways with her hosts by the elevator that will transport her to the outside. Once on the surface, she slips through a narrow mountainous passage that leads to a waterfall. From there it's a one mile hike down to the stall where her horse is cared for during her dealings with the Rawakota. The final ten mile ride to her mother's house on the Buckthorn Reservation is always enjoyable. It gives her time to reflect.

CHAPTER 11

"S'cuse me, brother."

"What the...!" A dark hulking figure is looming over me, right as I was drifting off to sleep, which was my sole intention when I plopped down on a lush bed of grass beside Mirror Lake. It took everything I had to drag myself to my favorite spot on campus today. I thought I was suffering from another bout of a respiratory infection that led to bronchitis over the winter; turns out it's only allergies. *Only.* The pills for treating them make me dog-tired.

The light jabs my eyes as soon as the guy squats down beside me. He had been blocking the sun that poked between the tree branches behind him. I blink hard. White-hot dots are swimming everywhere I look. He extends his hand. "I'm Ishmael, and you are?"

I prop my lazy self on an elbow and automatically shake it. "Viktor," I answer, irritated as can be for the disruption to my recovery process.

His black eyes stare into mine. Both sides of his head are shaved to the skin. A black Mohawk strip runs along the middle of his skull. It isn't spiked like some guys wear them, but looks soft...like a shoe brush. I can't make out the tattoo on the side of his neck.

"*What's with you!*" I bark, still hoarse from weeks of coughing. "You woke me *because*?"

"Sorry, bro. Really, I'm sorry. About a month ago I heard stories about this big Indian dude on campus who can dance like nobody's business. I did a double-take just now walking by. You've gotta be him."

I'm not remotely curious where this is going ... just grateful that the dull headache which has persisted for days is suddenly gone. My heart's been set on coming here, in order to relax after my only class. I decided to take it easy this summer. With patience wearing thin, I ask, "What does that have to do with anything?"

"Have you run into any Natives here?"

"No," I reply, pausing. "If I did, it doesn't follow that we'd have anything in common."

He grins; it's a wicked grin, and then he makes himself comfortable. *Shit!* Just leave, I'm thinking. "I've been involved with the dance department," he says, "but I have yet to find the right partner for this piece we've been working on. That's why I'm here, to meet with Hayden and Skyler. That's their dance troupe." He motions toward the outdoor amphitheater to our left where a handful of performers are entertaining passers-by who sit to watch them. "Seeing you up close, you're even more perfect for what I had in mind."

I ignore him and lie back down. He blabbers on—to himself. His words trail off. I concentrate on the soft swishing sound made by the leaves. Across the way, I hear the dancers' music, a familiar adagio by Albinoni. There's the vivid memory of the sheet music, and of following Iris's fingers on the piano keys as she practiced. She liked the calming effect of slow music, as do I at the moment.

I'm jiggled awake to find two new strangers seated close by, a man and a woman with towels draped around their necks. Anger builds. I had been blissfully passed out for around twenty minutes and would gladly have enjoyed sleeping through the entire afternoon—I need the rest. Grabbing the backpack from under my head, I roll to my feet in search of a more secluded place.

Immediately the Indian jumps up to block my get-away. He's roughly my size. It's an aggressive move on his part.

"Just hear me out," he orders, holding his arm straight out in front of him to within an inch of my chest. "Please!"

The guy on the ground tells his friend to leave me alone, but asks me if they could get my phone number, in order to talk later. He seems pleasant enough. I think back to the Indian's name. Did he really say Ishmael? Still ruffled from being woken, I try to make sense of what he'd been going on about. "Are you talking about dancing in front of an audience...a paying audience?"

"Just listen to the idea, okay?"

Exasperated, I let out a dramatic sigh. "Later...*bro*, I've got to go eat."

"I'll buy," he says, quickly adding, "anything you want...Viktor."

"God, you're relentless!" He at least took note when I told him what my name was before and used it for a change. *Bro* and *dude* drive me nuts, especially coming from someone decked out in a metal spiked choker collar and matching upper arm bands.

"C'mon. Say where." He turns to the couple. "We can all use a bite to eat, right Hayden? Skyler?" Only now do I notice the colored gemstone studs that outline the edge of his right ear. A pheasant's long tail feather hangs from it to his collarbone.

The man and woman, both regular-looking white people with no crazy hair, ugly face piercings, or extreme tattoos, stand to introduce themselves. Hayden informs me that I might as well give in because Ishmael isn't going anywhere. The mention of a pricey Thai restaurant is a game changer. It's too far to walk so Hayden offers to drive. I figure if he and the woman are professors in OSU's Department of Dance, they must be on the up-and-up. As we talk on our way to the car, I learn Skyler is Hayden's wife.

For the most part, I've made a point of not running anything by Uncle or Dad first, reckoning it's important to my personal growth to deal with matters on my own.

I decided that the long hours I had spent on academics this past winter was the reason for the chest cold I couldn't shake for months. A vicious cycle unfolded when the weight training schedule I pursued, with the belief that my health would be restored, probably ended up lowering my resistance. I can't say if my condition had finally run its course or if the acupuncture needles I allowed Uncle to insert all over me did the trick. He was supervised by a doctor with thirty years of experience who is integrating classes into OSU's medical school curriculum. I was ready to try anything, and Uncle needed someone to practice on.

At any rate, the twenty pounds of muscle that resulted from all the reps was worth it. I feel manlier, as manly as a seventeen year-old can possibly feel. My voice, too, has gone down another register. I think it's from the constant hacking; my vocal cords got irritated. That could be temporary.

It's only summer, but I'm looking forward to turning eighteen next spring. I may decide to live with friends after all, providing I make some. Guy friends are as hard to come by as a girlfriend. It seems nearly all incoming freshmen drink hard liquor, and not just on weekends but for any reason and no reason. It's alienating. I still go places to dance sometimes, but leave before the drunkenness gets out of control. Uncle picks me up since the darned curfew still applies. For the most part, students who are party animals get weeded out by junior year. When the material finally gets harder, many vanish. The remaining kids realize a certain degree of sobriety is required in order to graduate. Then I'm grateful for knowing a bunch of older students, many of whom are foreigners. It seems there's more at stake for them. It's a wonder how some American students even get admitted to college. Their poor knowledge of U.S. geography is unbelievable, which becomes evident the minute you meet someone and ask each other where you're from. South Dakota might as well be in Canada. I could see mixing up Iowa with Nebraska, maybe. It's also inexcusable how many are ignorant about our own country's historical timeline, and they really don't know squat about Native nations. Nothing new there. I probably would be as clueless about things had I grown up on the rez. Under the influence of my tribal brothers, I'm certain I'd have reached the same conclusion they did about school, that the system designed by white men for white men was pointless to us. Though true, it doesn't justify them turning to gangs and drugs and destroying what was so precious to the Lakota: the family. I refuse to believe I could reach such a low.

Something does puzzle me about the outlying region of Buckthorn Reservation where everyone with Rawakota blood running through them lives. Why did our particular tribe place such a high value on education? Indians scorned anything associated with whites, and yet, people from Pahpie's and Grandmother's generation went to college. Pahpie farmed, but he studied crop science at South Dakota State University. All their children who were Mom and Aunt Loretta's age earned degrees. Many went abroad to study, and still do. That our great-great-grandparents who were captured and forced onto the reservation saw fit to encourage this kind of book-learning is remarkable to me. Being that they had served the whites as translators, I assume they must have realized the benefits from knowing how to read and write. But who taught them? Sunkwah can fill me in on my next visit. It's also odd that nowadays many with Rawakota backgrounds return to the rez after graduating from college, to a place with few opportunities. They end up commuting to jobs that are outside of our Indian territory, but they won't move there. What is it about the rez that draws them back?

The fact that those of us with Rawakota roots also completely abstain from alcohol sets us apart from other Indians, not just the Lakota. I have no desire to try it, and fortunately at Hillel Academy, the college party scene was not criterion for anyone's choice of university. If anything, such a reputation would be grounds for a university getting crossed off their lists. In that respect it was the perfect environment for me, even if most were Jewish. That isn't to say no one got drunk at parties; I just don't remember anyone ever passing out or puking from too much. And the frequency with which the kids did it was nothing like at the bigger high schools.

Hayden and Skyler and Ishmael don't drink. That alone makes them worthwhile company. And they're all passionate about music and performing. I love watching them. They're incredibly focused. Each is a highly creative force. They try to communicate ideas that are hard to translate. Hayden, who is thirty-two, along with Skyler, a year older, are excellent teachers.

I think of myself as focused. Even when I was a kid, it took discipline to ride Jim and do tricks on his back. I went all out. The idea though of finessing my act would have struck me as laughable. But that's what these guys do. They rehearse and rehearse and rehearse some more, analyzing their movements as they go. Even when I break dance or take part in our powwows, it's simply a physical response to the music. I never think about conveying subtle moods or emotions that will touch the soul of the person watching, which is the effect they're going for. Being welcomed in their circle is going to pay off down the road. Ishmael should be thanked for ambushing me at Mirror Lake weeks ago, but I can't bring myself to telling him. His rudeness is but one of his many ugly traits that I've observed in his behavior since that afternoon. He is so full of himself.

I don't like admitting it—walking with the man, the way people respond to us is a rush. Alone, each of us commands attention simply because of our height. Together we're a show of might. It's a heady sensation. The fact that Ishmael likes to wear buckskin vests on a bare chest to display his muscles only adds to the picture. Keeping up with his fast power strides is a workout. My hair, slung over a shoulder at his suggestion, hangs past my waist and bounces against my thigh as I keep pace. I'll return a passing stranger's smile, but that's it.

Guys…girls…doesn't matter to Ishmael; he loves being gawked at, encourages it actually. Those black eyes of his are penetrating. I've been on the receiving end and felt how jarring his look can be. And if a girl really impresses him, he'll tap her arm as she goes by, sparking a response between her thighs for sure. He worships a tight ass and will stand in place, brazenly following a girl's backside until she's out of sight.

So anyway, Ishmael's got this grand idea about a battle between a celestial deity, that being me, and the Lord of the Underworld, him naturally. We're vying for the affections of the goddess that rules Earth, Camila Queipal, who is supposedly drop-dead gorgeous, and whom he can't wait for me to see. The premise sounds trite, but I'll try to be open-minded… for now.

The overcast skies offer relief from an August that started out with a couple of clear sunny weeks and blistering heat. I'm sitting in front of Sullivant Hall and sketching, anxious to meet Camila as soon as her dance class lets out. I'm brainstorming ideas that are based on Lakota legends as well as traditional Seneca tales that Ishmael heard growing up as a member of the Deer Clan, part of the Iroquois Nation. I love attending powwows and want to integrate the ceremonial dances into the performance. Ishmael has been vague when I've asked about the kinds of dances done at his tribe's celebrations.

In high school, after reading *Moby Dick,* Ishmael decided his tribal name Ojimaahl sounded close to the narrator's name, so he changed it. At twenty-seven, he seems older, Ishmael vows one day to be as iconic as his adopted namesake. In my opinion, the tattooed cannibal Queequeg in the tale would fit him more, but then, as I recall, Queequeg was a friendly, good-hearted guy, someone with noble character.

The sound of tolling bells from Orton Hall at the top of the hour has me eagerly waiting for our Earth goddess to appear…and she's right on cue with Skyler beside her.

Before I can even stand, Skyler says, "Something's come up, Viktor! Brian hurt his back in a lift, and I need to get back." Looking to each of us and out of breath, "Camila, Viktor. Viktor, Camila. So sorry guys. I'll call later." And away she runs, leaving the two of us to shake off the awkward moment with a short laugh. I pull out a chair for Camila. She smells freshly showered and her shiny espresso-brown hair is still wet.

I sit. Camila extends her hand to make the introduction official. We get right down to business, but not without me first noticing the widow's peak in her hairline, her perfectly shaped face, and the points of her upper lip I've heard called a "cupid's bow." As she looks over my sketches and notes, I confess: "It never occurred to me that a South American might answer Ishmael's ad. How narrow-minded on my part. When he asked for Native Americans to try out for the dance company's project, I was curious who from around here might respond."

"Well...it is understandable." Her accent adds to her sexiness.

I admire her lovely hands. She has no lines whatsoever on her face, not even at the corners of her amazing eyes when she smiles. They're big, dark brown, almond-shaped eyes, really unusual. Camila *is* beautiful, but her slender body doesn't resemble what I envision an Earth goddess to look like. To me, the character should be more full-figured, like the typical female fertility figures in art.

Sticking with her background, I add, "There must be as many indigenous peoples in South America as here in the U.S."

"Yes," she says, "and as equally disenfranchised."

It's easy to see the fascination she holds for Ishmael. There's definitely something seductive about her, besides those incredible eyes. She is light-skinned, which might be typical of her people.

"What tribe is your family?" I ask.

"Mapuche, from southern Chile."

We discuss the similarities between our Creation myths, which we laugh is the same for just about everybody in the world. There are the great floods, along with miraculous births and comparable tricksters and supernatural creatures.

Pulling an iPad out of her duffle bag, Camila finds the list of suggestions Ishmael wants us to toss around. We could be doing this online with a video meeting, but our conflicting schedules make it hard to agree on a time...plus I wanted to see her in person for myself. I glance over his ideas with interest.

"What's that mean?" she asks, regarding my little grunt.

"It's just that his view of the relationship among the three deities isn't at all what I pictured. He sees Earth as a judge, a balancing force between the struggle of good and evil. To him, good and evil inhabit characteristics of the other, so you can't tell them apart. I think the symbolism should be cut and dry. We're dealing with basic carnal desires. Bottom line, it's a story about two guys competing for a girl's attention. She ultimately chooses who her partner will be. Humanity then faces the consequences of her decision. His approach is too intellectual. I can hardly believe he came up with this."

"Interesting." She smiles slyly. "Your take on Ishmael is that he's one-dimensional."

I hadn't thought about it, but I guess I do. Words that come to mind to describe him are crude, vulgar, raunchy...horny. She must realize it. Everything out of his mouth has some kind of a disgusting sexual connotation. And the way he has of staring people down.

"I gather you believe the Earth Spirit will undoubtedly fall for the more exciting outlaw type, the Lord of the Underworld. And that the union will produce events of cataclysmic proportion, like earthquakes and hailstorms..."

"Exactly! Isn't that more fun!" It makes me want to switch roles with Ishmael.

"Not to worry. There is an erotic subtext, but it's expressed through music rather than story."

"I'm not buying it," I tease. "Look at this wrestling scene," I continue. "Every step is mapped out. There's a gazillion of them; it's so technical."

"But that's what dance is: choreography. I take it you've never studied technique."

"No, I do what I feel. It's spontaneous. It doesn't mean I don't believe in practicing. A lot of time goes into learning and perfecting a particular move."

As she listens, her eyes cast a dreamy spell. My breathing picks up. I'm done with talking; I just want to keep staring at her. Camila holds my gaze. The situation creates the kind of physical response in me that any guy in my shoes would experience. It feels incredible. I'm tempted to ask her out...except the way Ishmael raved about her, he must be interested in her for himself.

Camila hands back my papers, then says, "It's going to inconvenience us, but we need to start meeting together to finalize the concept so we can move forward. Then we have to think about rehearsals. Hayden and Skyler said that Tuesday and Sunday afternoons are best for them. I'd say we commit to those days."

It hits me that I'm dealing with professional dancers. "Camila, do you think I'm getting in over my head?"

She considers my question. "Ishmael and Hayden have seen you dance, right?"

I nod.

"Do you question their judgment? They must have liked what they saw."

"True." Once more I find myself hooked by her gaze. If we meet this Sunday, it's four days until I get to lay eyes on her again. That's too long.

We part and I catch the shuttle back to the apartment. Uncle will be home late. He enjoys the company of Dr. Nate, the veterinarian classmate of his whose wife is currently in hospice care. I immediately head for my room and throw myself on the bed so I can start kissing Camila. Her hair is silky and soft. The clean soapy smell of her skin is still fresh in my mind. I picture those long, pretty fingers gliding across my chest and stomach. She is someone I could love.

CHAPTER 12

Using a secure channel linked to one of the Rawakota Nation's own communication satellites, William and his sister-in-law carry on a conversation about a matter that is troubling him. "Constance, this new acquaintance of Viktor's poses a serious threat. I can't explain why, but I believe there's more to the man's motives than meets the eye. The situation must be dealt with, and soon," he cautions. "If Viktor gets blindsided and things don't go as planned, he won't be the only one affected. There are thousands of young Natives across the land who stand to benefit from Viktor's successes."

"Sure you're not overreacting, William? There is after all no evidence to go on. Maybe you're fixating too much on Viktor's future...it's causing you unnecessary worry." Their connection isn't the best; her voice sounds faint, but then she is on the other side of the world from Ohio.

"Don't act like you don't know the score. Your son stands on the threshold of becoming a prominent, inspirational leader. My senses went on high alert the moment I looked into that Indian's eyes, if in fact he really is an Indian. Viktor is no match for the brute. Plain evil, that's what he is."

With seemingly not a whit of maternal concern, Constance tells William, "If Viktor can't handle himself under duress, he doesn't deserve to be the role model we envisioned."

"You've hardened, Constance. If it's because of your military training, you really need to rethink things. Viktor isn't you. Just because you were able to overcome an unspeakable act. The boy could at least be warned."

"No. A heads up won't test his mettle. Just let it play out."

William isn't about to ignore his gut feeling.

The idea of a football player studying ballet strikes me as funny, especially after watching YouTube videos of muscle-bound linebackers taking a stab at it. That's the hook Hayden came up with when he invited me to his house for dinner, in order for us to get to know each other better. I wasn't expecting such a traditional neighborhood when we turned onto his street. The 1950s two-story brick home is about twenty minutes north of campus. He sits beside me on a corner couch and opens his high school yearbook. We're in what was once the living room. Now it's a dance studio with a large mirror that runs the length of the wall. The ceiling has been fitted with recessed lights. Skyler declined our offer to help with the meal and is busy in the kitchen. Whatever she's cooking, it smells great.

"You saying you don't believe me? There...proof!" Hayden plops the book on my lap and asks me to find him among three long rows of forty players wearing dark green jerseys and holding their helmets above their heads. Studying the faces, I make one wrong guess after another. "Try left side, top row." Seems easy now, except the camera's too far away, and the quality of the photo isn't the best to spot his pale blue-gray eyes. Hayden says the photographer insisted they copy the Hulk's angry scowl. He laughs, "Seeing us after all this time, we look more constipated than intimidating." Two blonde players are ruled out, leaving just the one with medium brown hair; but whose neck is wider than his jaw.

"Eighty-three?"

"Bingo! Best defensive end ever to have played for the Cave Creek Comets, although we averaged only two wins a season during the four I played."

There's no resemblance. "So you kept your dancing on the down-low?"

Hayden loses it. "God, no...my thighs were so huge I'd have crushed my nuts attempting a mid-air cabriole at that age. My mother taught ballet and used my brother and me when we were in grade school to partner with the girls."

"How'd that go over in your little rural Wyoming town?"

"The ribbing was all in good fun. The boys would get in trouble with their parents if they dared pick on Matt and me since their sisters took classes at mom's studio. People loved her. She was also our school's third-grade teacher. And everyone knew Dad. He used to run the John Deere dealership in town."

I mull over the picture of him and his teammates. "You had to have taken anabolic steroids."

Hayden looks thoughtfully at me. "Yeah, some of us did."

"*Why!*" The guy is so admirable; I don't want to believe it. I don't care how I come off sounding.

He leans back and sighs. "Because it gave us an edge. It was our moment in the sun. We were farm kids livin' the dream. Our parents couldn't have been any prouder of us."

This insight into him is disappointing, despite the fact he obviously knows better now.

"A few bronco riders on the rodeo circuit used. Drugs were easy enough to come by and not expensive. I won't lie; we were scared at first. Then we started seeing results, and fast! It was amazing. We bench-pressed around the clock. The side effects that we were so afraid of never happened. I mean, testicles *do* shrink, but we could live with that. No one went on "roid rages" or got super depressed." He pauses a second. "I don't think."

I close the book and set it on the table. Out of curiosity I ask what he ended up weighing.

"Two-fifty…from one-eighty. And I'm six foot-one."

"Holy shit. When did you get back into dance?"

"I came home after a year at the University of Wyoming. My mother got sick and I wanted to help out my dad. School had been a waste of time and money. I didn't know what to major in. I thought it would be smart to combine a business degree with agriculture, but I couldn't get excited about it."

"Was it serious…what your mom had?"

Hayden nods: "Ovarian cancer. But she pulled through. It was rough-going, though." There's a loud clanking noise, and suddenly we see Skyler scurrying past the kitchen door. Then immediately again the other direction. Hayden's eyebrows go up. He assures me it's best to leave her alone. "My Mom's illness turned out to be a blessing in disguise," he says. "She obviously couldn't teach then. After putting in hours at Dad's store, I'd go into the studio, which was in a converted barn behind our house, and I started to remember what I had learned years ago. Dancing became a great outlet for everything I was going through at the time. Mom saw me from her window and came in one evening. Without any discussion, she started to give me pointers, and it took off from there. There was nothing I could've done to make her happier. Eventually I enrolled in Central Wyoming College, sticking with business. I was sitting in my favorite coffee house when I noticed a girl who I was convinced had to be a dancer, just by the way she moved. I struck up a conversation with her…turned out I was right."

"Skyler? You met her in Wyoming…at a community college?"

"She was taking theater classes. There was no dance program, so she was earning credits to move on to a four year university. She grew up in Cleveland, but went to live with her dad in Wyoming after her parents split when she was in high school. She didn't get along with her mother. Anyway, I brought her home and we ended up dancing together in the studio, and, well…there you have it. She and my mom talked endlessly about ideas for dance routines, which in turn fired up my imagination. Being from Ohio, Skyler dreamed of going back and enrolling at OSU. I tagged along. "

Un-hee! The circumstances that lead to the love of one's life! I want to ask more about Skyler. I have only observed her in a class setting, and I thought that she was overly critical of the dance students she was teaching, to the point of being mean. So far Hayden has been in charge of the rehearsals with Ishmael, Camila, and me, but that is due to change. I'm curious how Skyler will act with only me here tonight.

"For a while there," says Hayden, "I thought for sure you must be on steroids."

"What! *Me*?" The allegation is beyond upsetting.

He looks me long and hard in the eyes, as though waiting to see if I'm going to come clean, then, leaning in, he wraps his hands around the circumference of my elbow and asks: "You're really like this…without HGH?"

My self-consciousness returns. I had finally started to feel comfortable in my skin, especially when marching alongside Ishmael across campus. I dismiss Hayden with a shake of the head and a seldom used *Jesus*. His suspicion threw me for a loop, and now I wonder if people truly think that. *They probably do.* I only made the comment about him after comparing the before and after picture in his yearbook because he's lean now. Still muscular, but not in a stocky way.

"Viktor, please…forget what I said. Lucky for you to have been blessed with an extraordinary physique."

But I can't let it go.

He pats my knee. "Hey, c'mon, don't make a big deal out of it. You should feel flattered."

I guess I should. I forget how it came up, but one day I confided in him about wanting to play football after next year. That's when he invited me to his house. We were going to discuss how studying ballet would give me an advantage on the football field. I *had* to hear this.

Skyler calls us to the table. It's covered in a pretty blue paisley tablecloth and there are linen napkins. The bouquet of flowers I brought her is set beside a big cast iron pot filled with Hungarian goulash. Mozart is playing in the background. We make small talk about Columbus neighborhoods and restaurants and films we like. They ask about my scholarship and how I became interested in science. The meal is terrific, and Skyler is pleasant. I never saw her smile before. When she does, it's quick, easy to miss.

Over coffee, Skyler explains the renovations done to the downstairs, how three walls were removed leaving only support structures. The single piece of furniture by the front door, the cushy burgundy velvet couch where Hayden and I had sat looking at his yearbook, is the waiting area for students who pay for individual instruction.

The tour continues when Hayden asks me to follow him upstairs to watch a video. The carpet is the color of moss.

"Whoa! This is beautiful!" I do a full 360 at the top. The wallpaper in the hallway looks 3-D. Lavender wisterias surround us. I poke my head in a room and admire the oversized carved wooden furniture. Being familiar with Lakota quillwork and embroidery, I can appreciate the artistry of the elaborately woven fabrics on the chairs.

"Can you tell we like the Italian Renaissance period?"

"It's really cool, Hayden. I've never seen such a colossal four poster bed. How'd you ever move it in?"

"In pieces. Same with the chandelier." Before I can ask where he bought them, they had to have been pricey, he says that a gay couple, both physicians and big OSU arts supporters, sold him the pieces for a song when they decided to retire and move to Taos, New Mexico.

I follow him into the last room, the TV room. It's super bright. Transparent curtains catch a breeze from a cracked window and twirl in the air. A snow white L-shaped couch is set off by the palest blue walls. Snoozing on the armrest, camouflaged, is a white cottony cat curled up tightly in a ball. I think it's alive. A wall-to-wall painting depicts a row of various shaped clear glass jars that reflect a rainbow of colors. Each holds the single stem of a different kind of flower. The beige hardwood floor reminds me of sand.

Hayden turns on the TV. The cat complains. While he searches for the segment of the video, I think about him and his wife, and what a difficult person Skyler appears to be; and yet he *loves* her. First off, it's hard to get past her seriously skinny body when you're talking to her. When we went to the Thai restaurant the first day we met, I was surprised by the amount of food she put away, even just now at dinner. It made me wonder if she's bulimic, and I didn't want to go there; it's too disgusting. I'm angry at myself for thinking that considering Hayden assumed I take steroids. Skyler, after all, has the metabolism of a hummingbird. She's in constant motion, and Hayden says she makes do with a mere four hours of sleep. They're so opposite. Both are perfectionists, but he's diplomatic when it comes to his students. Skyler is an impatient taskmaster and will put dancers through the wringer until their efforts are up to her standards, which can mean additional hours of grueling repetition. Her favorite line is: "Suck it up!"

I'd characterize Skyler as an overbearing drill sergeant, with a repertoire of the most humiliating insults to boot. Her drawn out *shheeeeit!* has to be the stuff of jokes; although, any of her students would be wise to imitate her out of earshot. To watch her though, in classical pieces like *Sleeping Beauty* or *Swan Lake,* is a treat. Her limbs move like ribbons floating through air. And her expression miraculously transforms into one of such softness that I forget I know her. The poetry of the moment pulls at one's heartstrings, which is why I guess students willingly tolerate her badgering. They wish to emulate her on stage.

I respond better and am willing to work harder for Hayden. He looks so unconcerned and relaxed, always sitting with knees apart, one arm bent at the elbow with his hand resting on his hip. The other arm lays draped over a thigh. Unflappable, that's Hayden summed up. He watches the world and sizes things up in deliberate fashion. "I know *you know* you can do better," he offers kindly, whether directing a pro or a novice like me.

Hayden found the section he was looking for. "Pay close attention to the fast footwork and how the dancers rotate their bodies in the air. Think about executing these moves yourself... while throwing a football."

I'm intrigued.

What Hayden neglected to mention, and what fascinates me, is this ball that's constantly getting flung across a full stage. Not once does it touch the ground. The dancers maneuver around each other at dizzying speeds, all the while keeping the ball in motion. It's a short piece, not even five minutes. Cirque du Soleil comes to mind.

"So? Whaddya think?"

"Uhh, sorry... I couldn't help following the ball..." Hayden rolls his eyes while grinning and cues it up again. Skyler would've served up a tongue lashing for wasting her time.

I realize now that the Tuesday and Sunday rehearsal schedule was a ploy to get me to commit to the dance project. The two days turned into three the following week, and soon five days will be required. I loved that Camila worried I would quit when it became apparent how much of my time was getting taken up by these sessions. I'm actually having too much fun hammering out ideas with the group to consider it. The work is demanding. I race to the dance department in between my academic classes, and wake up at five in the morning to stay caught up on my assignments. The workouts have also produced measurable results with regard to my quarterbacking abilities. I'm jumping higher and throwing with greater accuracy. I'd have remained clueless if Hayden hadn't suggested that the two of us toss a ball around once in a while, just for the hell of it. He found us a flat open space in a remote area along the Scioto, a different river from the one that flows through OSU's campus. He's thrilled to grip a football after more than a decade, while I'm amazed over my "tours en l'air" and "jetés," although I won't oblige him by using dance lingo. A spin is a spin and a jump, a jump. The time spent with Uncle analyzing films of impalas and zebras twisting and turning when they're under attack has also paid off. As the quarterback, my goal is to achieve predictable, repeatable trajectories when throwing the ball. A clock face serves as my frame of reference. If I run to the right and push off for a spin with my left big toe at 2:00, and then whip my right leg around for momentum, my arm is in position to release the ball when my body rotates left to 7:00. There's a short window of opportunity when I can control the direction and distance of the ball, assuming there's a receiver in the right spot to catch it.

Uncle William encourages this friendship with Hayden. For whatever reason, though, something about Ishmael rubbed him the wrong way the only time they met. Uncle wasn't even aware that I didn't particularly like him. Ishmael had stopped over to talk about ways of advertising the show, which still has no title. Instead of shaking Ishmael's hand when I introduced them, Uncle turned on his heel unexpectedly and said he was off somewhere. His action had been abrupt and out of character for him. I stood there speechless.

Ishmael laughed. Though I have grown no fonder of the Indian, I am thankful that he pressured me into doing this show. So far, it has been an incredibly gratifying experience. I've met people in completely different fields. Besides dancers, there are graphic artists, musicians, and set designers, plus carpenters and technical engineers who handle the lighting and audio. Best of all, many students are closer to my age. And now I'm learning about the business end of marketing the event. It's proving a valuable association.

It was during that visit when I asked Ishmael if he was going out with Camila. Amused by my interest, and with his black eyes flashing, he answered, sometimes, when it suited them both. Neither was interested in being tied to any one person. That gave me something to think about. Maybe she'd reconsider if I were to become involved with her. But could I handle being with a woman who obviously has a sexual history that includes many partners? And with Ishmael, too, a guy whose bravado when he finishes probably matches that of a chest-thumping gorilla. He's so damn cocksure of himself—always.

Camila is truly beautiful. She's smart and dedicated to the cause of her people's independence, much like Marnie back in South Dakota. Maybe girl activists are my type. Her brother in Chile still manages to organize demonstrations from his jail cell. He and a band of protestors were arrested for occupying the home of a wealthy landowner who was descended from Spanish invaders. They had thrown the man off his ranch, which was never rightfully his. The thousands of acres had been in Camila's family for generations before the Spanish seized the property for themselves a century ago. These takeovers were permitted by officials who were never elected by the indigenous Mapuche. Their story is my people's story, and how many other native peoples' worldwide who were exploited by the European colonials of the time.

Because she feared for her own safety, having taken part in violent protests, Camila ended up in Columbus after meeting a traveling Ohio State geology student who had offered to help her.

I wish I hadn't learned that she's promiscuous. During rehearsals, I wonder who besides Ishmael has seen her naked, touched her, been inside her. I stare at the men on stage and the male musicians in the orchestra pit, homing in on the slightest eye contact one of them might make with her that would give him away. I ask myself why I do this; why torture myself? How can there be no jealousy? Are people being honest with themselves? I hate admitting that the prospect of a future with Camila is unrealistic. I have to resign myself to the fact that any physical contact between us will only be happening on stage.

CHAPTER 13

I can't play down the hurt. After Uncle witnessed the countless hours of practice as well as my mounting excitement as the date drew nearer, he told me this morning that he wasn't going to attend the show tonight. I'm proud over what I've accomplished in the past months, and I want him to see the end result. Ishmael remains the source of the problem, yet Uncle still won't explain. He has only suggested, *strongly suggested*, that I keep my guard up around him. Why the shadowy warning?

Dad should have arrived in town yesterday, but storms in Texas delayed his flight. He's coming directly to Mershon Auditorium when he lands. I doubt we'll even have a chance to say "Hi" before the curtain goes up.

There's been little time to spend with Iris, too, who flew in three days ago. She somehow finagled her way into Battelle Institute's headquarters in search of a contact who can explain the latest technology behind brain implants. There'll be no mention of her students. Using the cover of wanting info to apply for a grant, she's keeping her eyes and ears open to follow leads. The same weather pattern that pushed back Dad's departure time has also grounded flights as far away as Wisconsin, where Iris's husband is waiting for word to see if and when he can take off. Iris's *husband*...if that isn't weird to say! I'm anxious to meet him. Normally that wouldn't happen until the families got together at the next powwow, which isn't until spring. We have no customary wedding ceremony. There is only the husband and wife's private exchange of vows, and the request to have their union blessed by our Creator.

The media blitz begun around six weeks ago has turned Ishmael, Camila, and me into campus celebrities. The publicity isn't new to Hayden and Skyler, well-known for their troupe called the *ABCs of Dance*. Using their last names, the company's official title is *Adler and Banks' Consortium of Dancers*.

My brief experience in the limelight as quarterback for our high school doesn't begin to compare to the amount of attention I've been receiving, thanks largely to Efrem Zukor, a professor of art who designed our show's poster. He idolizes the fantasy artist Frank Frazetta and was overjoyed when asked to come up with a *Conan the Barbarian*-esque type of world for the three of us to inhabit. In true classic Frazetta style, Efrem painted us, bulging muscles and all, intertwined in a dynamic pose where the anti-hero is shown below ground holding on to the legs of the Earth goddess as he tries to drag her down among the gnarled roots and molten rocks of his lair. At the same time, the voluptuous goddess, whose curves in the painting challenged the costume designers to find ways to make Camila look more shapely, is held firmly in the clutches of the Sky god hero, who struggles to hold her above ground with him. Dramatic gold and crimson clouds frame them. The result is spectacular—lustful. Indigenous faces depicting the unquiet spirits of long-departed ancestors are cleverly worked into the scene. The images take me back to the *Tarzan* books I reread countless times growing up, with illustrations by Frazetta.

The two thousand seats sold out in four days, faster than Hayden or Skyler could believe.

Ishmael deserves a lot of the credit. He is masterful at selling himself. Self-promotion embarrasses me. Those skilled at it seem arrogant. But, as Skyler posed, why expect anyone to come see you if you aren't psyched enough to flaunt what you can do? Perhaps if I'd been at this longer—acting that is—I could step inside another skin and believe. Skyler managed to mold this innocent into a character brimming with repressed sexuality that the Earth goddess alone can invoke. If only that scenario would play out in real life. At first I felt a fraud. Early into this venture I figured I looked the part therefore I could pull it off. But Skyler wasn't buying it. She said I was a eunuch in a bullring. *Ow!* Then she stated flat out, in a corner where thankfully no one could hear, if I didn't become more assertive, I might as well kiss my football career goodbye. 'You're a god in the show,' she stated bluntly. 'You *will* walk the walk, *understand*? Revel in the fact you're stronger and wiser than everyone. Now buck up and own it! And without Ishmael's handholding!' The wake-up call was necessary, though it smarted.

I thought long and hard about her criticism. She was right to an extent, the way she described me here among outsiders, but that's hardly how I am on the reservation—where my identity is never in question. There I'm one hundred percent Indian one hundred percent of the time. And bragging is okay among the Lakota, as long as you don't exaggerate about what you can do. One must prove himself. My friends and I were always trying to outdo each other, whether target shooting with bows and arrows on horseback, or running foot races across the plains. We would climb cliffs to see who could reach an eagle's nest the fastest and claim a feather. I didn't think about it too much once I found my calling in science, in Texas. It was right at the age when coaches were noticing my athletic abilities. Although I was encouraged by them to go after a football scholarship, I was quietly relieved when I received an academic one, so my future wouldn't depend on me playing football exclusively. It turned out that I'm naturally coordinated, but it was my insatiable curiosity about microbes and disease and general interconnectedness of life itself that lured me from my cozy bed every morning.

Unlike me, the dancers and everyone else involved in the production are pursuing *their* passion, and they give it their all. As one of the principal characters, I do them a disservice by approaching it like a hobby. Skyler is right; unless I change my attitude and totally commit to whatever it is I'm doing at the moment, whether it be dance or football, I'm always going to get called out on it. Following that revelation, I was struck by a deeper one. There are often times, if truth be told, I feel out of place in the white man's world. It's his education system serving me, his rules that govern my life, and although the college audience for our show is diverse, it will ultimately be white people's perception of what qualifies as good that determines whether it's a success. Hayden once said something about most theater critics being white. If we get rave reviews, I'm not sure how well that will sit with me.

It's a balmy fall evening, the second day of November, 6:45 p.m.. A single strip of cloud has cut the full moon in perfect halves. Wonder if that means anything. It's my final view outside before entering the stage door. Showtime is at 8:00. A stack of programs was forgotten on a cabinet. I grab one as I continue on my way. *WAKAN* — it's a catchy name, all right.

Pronounced wah–kahn, the title didn't get my vote because it doesn't do justice to what the concept means to the Lakota people. It is not an individual supreme ruler's name. Other indigenous gods' names we researched were either too long or they contained odd letter combinations, or we simply didn't like the sound of them. It finally came down to Ishmael, who said the five letters would stand out on the poster, making it memorable. Hayden was afraid people would say it using a short "a" vowel and wanted to include an "h" after the first a, which is how it is sometimes spelled. Ishmael assured him that once the show got advertised, no one would mispronounce it. Wakan Tanka, our Creator, embraces many entities. There's Taku Skanskan, a life force, and the powerful Nagi Tanka, or Blue, which refers to the sky. Wakans can be good or evil. They can have form or be invisible. In the end I conceded, rationalizing that maybe theater-goers would be inclined to learn more about them on their own. The story draws on heroes and demons from Greek myths and African legends as well. Camila's character, *Piedra Volada,* comes from an ancient Mexican culture. It means Balancing Rock, which is fitting since she serves as the humans' moral compass. Her loyalties are forever getting tested by the ruler of the underworld and his adversary, Wakan, the ruler of the heavens. At one point in the story, when Piedra Volada is confronted with a world in turmoil, she must choose between joining forces with Wakan to save mankind, or being with Ishmael, er...the god of the underworld, the lord of lost souls, so she can explore her own deepest and darkest desires. He naturally uses all of his deceitful wiles to seduce her. Will she abandon her responsibilities? Without her presence, all earthly life stands to wither away. I personally think that the plot is kind of a jumbled mess. Skyler isn't concerned...says we can tweak it later.

    The opening line of the summary reads: *WAKAN* embodies a universal theme as old as time, the conflict between good and evil. I've seen the program before this evening, but holding it in my hand right now, knowing this is it, makes the moment real.

    Backstage, there's subdued excitement. I hurry to my small dressing room to escape the busyness. Sitting quietly, except for a bouncing leg, I try to review some steps. It's hard to focus. I think of how beautiful, more like spellbinding, Camila looked yesterday when she practiced her solo dance to a haunting melody played on the oboe. Wearing a see-through copper-colored dress, she appeared to float across the stage as she moved. Suddenly the floor rumbles, which means everybody's seated. Thanks to the wizardry of our audio engineers, the audience is presently experiencing what I am, but to a much greater degree. The noise and vibrations are meant to imitate a nearby stampede. Using technology that once would have cost too much money, the theater seats were embedded with these little pulsating devices that get triggered by sounds coming through the speakers. A deafening surge of cicadas is up next, after which fast and chaotic violins will open Act I. A Navajo musician created the musical score.

What follows is going to blow people's minds. The visual elements of the production *were* expensive, well beyond what the university could afford. Along with the sound, they're what make *WAKAN* the "immersive experience" it's been billed as. Hayden convinced a private company to design holograms of us for the show at a greatly reduced rate, in exchange for marketing its newfangled laser projection system to other businesses. No headgear or goggles required. Our bodies briefly appear in digital form and don't look transparent or ghostly. There's a scene at the end when we've got arrows and spears that look real as can be flying across the heads of the audience.

Not so much as a glimpse has been allowed between Ishmael, Camila, and me since our final dress rehearsal yesterday afternoon. There's a knock. It's time. Taking a deep, slow breath, I mentally go to my domain in the heavens. The image is indisputably clear. *I am Wakan.*

Here it is the closing scene, and all appears lost. Following a tumultuous war, in which no one makes it out alive, not even Piedra Volada, I watch from the wings as our audience sits quietly murmuring. What's left, they must be wondering. The stage is strewn with corpses. In the aftermath of the tragedy, in the eerie silence, bizarre novel creatures rise slowly from the ground. A few take flight into the theater's auditorium and soar toward the ceiling.

The takeaway is that the Greatest Wakan, the Creator, cannot alter the cycle of life once it is put into play, and that death is but a part of the universe's continuum, holding the promise of future possibilities. Regardless whether people get it, the applause is thunderous.

Unlike the despair that accompanies an actual disaster, our exhausted cast and crew behold the debris-riddled auditorium and smile. Some stroll around the empty theater while I sit with a couple of dancers in a corner. There were countless things in the final scene that went all wrong during the trial runs, but, in the end, crossed fingers worked the magic. Emotions are running deep. It's done. We pulled it off. I have such respect for my talented colleagues. They'd been planning this long before I came on board.

Iris latches on to me first. I barely get a foot in the door when she throws her arms around my neck. "Viktor, Viktor...baby brother. That was extraordinary, absolutely amazing!" Dad embraces us both and plants a kiss on my cheek.

"That was somethin' else, Son." As he steps away, he pulls Iris with him. "Let him get some air."

I look in the room and am shocked to see Grandmother seated on the couch. Before she can stand I'm beside her, just about sitting in her lap, kissing her hands and hugging her to pieces.

"You came to see me! Why didn't anyone tell me you were coming?" I'm suddenly aware of the air boot on her right foot.

"Got in the way of Jim." With a hand lovingly cupping my face, she adds, "Clumsy me...not his fault."

I feel all warm and fuzzy and hug her again. That she would come all this way to watch me...wow. I notice a stranger over in the corner.

"Viktor," says Iris, I want you to meet Hashkedasila, my husband. He got a seat on the first flight after the airport reopened and arrived in time to the theater."

He steps forward as I stand to shake his hand. "So pleased you arrived safely. I'm happy to meet you. Congratulations on your marriage." I take note that he's Dad's height, just over six feet.

"Thank you. And congratulations to you for a job well done! I had no idea what I was coming to see."

Uncle invites us to eat. It's only appetizers, but there's enough to feed at least fifty. Stories and laughter fill the room. Dad and Hashke describe the irony of surviving the line of storms that ran from Texas to Wisconsin, only to be hit by a violent one in the theater that they were convinced would *really* do them in. "How on earth was it done?" they ask in unison, referring most likely to the erupting volcanoes. Besides believing there was red-hot lava oozing off the stage, they would also have felt the tremors and the heat and the strong winds that accompanied the action. Iris chimes in, "That was fun the way you rode a star to Earth." I watch Uncle's response out of the corner of my eye. So far he has not looked at me directly. It's beyond strange. I want to shake him by the shoulders and demand an explanation. He sits between Dad and Hashke and seems to be having a good time.

"Tomorrow," says Grandmother, "Iris and I will prepare a feast. There's so much to celebrate."

During the next hour I observe my family. And now Hashke is a member. Iris called him handsome, and I see it, with his strong jaw and straight white teeth. He looks friendlier than I imagined, probably because of the dimples in his cheeks. His shiny black straight hair is cut blunt at the shoulders and worn behind the ears. He is comfortable in our group, easily taking part in the conversations. Every so often he and Sister give each other a lingering kiss on the lips, which I've never witnessed her do. There's nothing Native about his clothes. He's in jeans, boots, and a plain deep green sweater. The design of his gold and silver wedding band does however incorporate the Apache cross. Iris chose a Lakota symbol for hers: a simple silver version of braided sweetgrass, which is a traditional purifying herb used in ceremonies. My eyes meet his. He smiles while chewing his food. They're warm brown eyes. Definitely kind eyes. He's on the thin side, which I wouldn't expect Iris would like. What a dumb thought. He seems all things good. Iris catches me, perfectly aware of my scrutiny. She knows when I blush.

Grandmother, who is beside me at the table, is constantly squeezing my arm; she's so happy to see me. She hasn't spoken much. This is late for her to be up, and me. It must be way past midnight. Dad says it's 2 a.m.! I'm trying to remember how old she was on her last birthday... must be nearing seventy. She looks great. A few deep creases run along the outer edges of her eyes and the sides of her mouth, otherwise her face is smooth. She still ties her long gray braid into a knot at the base of her neck. It supposedly keeps her hair out of the way when she works, but we all know she loves to show off her necklaces.

Mom comes up in conversation. I mention that she called to wish me well. I'm curious what Hashke thinks of his mother-in-law. Considering how long Iris has been with him, he's had time to form an insightful opinion. I look forward to talking alone with Sister tomorrow, which, come to think of it, is already here. The late hour catches up to us. Uncle is driving them to a nearby motel. Before we part ways, I announce I'm sleeping in. They're all for that idea.

CHAPTER 14

"What the hell are you watchin', Major?"

Earbuds block the voice. The man wearing the rank of colonel leans in, his eyes glued to the computer screen. He rests his left arm on the back of the Major's chair.

Surprised, Constance yanks the buds out, allowing him to hear the rollicking music the figure is dancing to.

"Is that Viktor?" he asks, his voice hoarse from ongoing problems with throat polyps. "Why...he's a man!"

His incredulous tone is understandable. She watches along with him for another minute then admits: "I can't believe it myself. He was in a show at OSU this week...parts of the rehearsal got posted on YouTube."

"He's damn good. What a transformation from the gangly kid I met at Sheppard. He was like a young giraffe. A couple of years sure make a difference at that age."

Constance reminds him, "Try five."

Colonel Tom Nally's eyes open wide in disbelief. "Along with all my other health problems, I'm getting senile, too?"

Constance pats his hand and assures him he is not. The two go way back to when she was a first-class cadet during her final year at the Academy in Colorado, and he was just a major, there to assess the newly graduated officers who qualified as pilots. She stops the video. It's around her tenth time viewing it. He heard that she had arrived at the base and figured on finding her somewhere inside the rec center. Tom knew that her dislike for the outdoor boardwalk at Kandahar Airfield matched his own aversion to the theme-park atmosphere, what with its chain restaurants and over-priced souvenir and food shops run by the local Afghan merchants. More than once he had voiced his disdain, saying their slogan here should be "Come Play War." He believes in boosting the morale of soldiers, but basketball and volleyball courts in addition to fully outfitted gyms, not to mention a hockey rink for the Canadians! How many ways are required to get away from the daily grind? In light of the current administration's decision to limit America's military role in the region, Tom is grateful that he needn't have to contend with the nonsense much longer. By year's end the drawdown of U.S. troops will transform the once bustling NATO base into a ghost town. The British forces have already vacated. Americans, too, have begun tearing down the prefabricated buildings and hangars.

Tom asks his friend back to his office for a drink of soda or coffee since alcohol is forbidden in the region, not that Constance would want it, but he'd appreciate a good Scotch whiskey. He relaxes beside Constance on a vinyl couch that has stood the test of time much better than he has. On their way over, they had noticed a poster that advertised an upcoming dance and trivia contest, to which Tom had growled, "More nonsense. Look at 'em trying to recreate a lifestyle like the one they left. It isn't conducive to the job at hand." Constance wonders why he gets so worked up. Although she never went in for the "camaraderie BS," she has understood how it helps people work through the utter absurdity of war.

Sipping a Coke, she asks, "Are you still working on the dams?"

He rubs his face and then folds his hands on his lap. "It's a frickin' nightmare, Constance. The two projects that were begun have already cost American taxpayers around 750 million dollars, and god knows if they'll ever be completed. I sat in on a meeting yesterday where a solar power plant was discussed. Our engineers and Kandahar officials realize it could never generate enough electricity for this city's needs. I mean...why bother bringing it up. Finish first what's been started." A few officers darting past the open door wave a quick hello when they notice them inside. The familiar faces provide a cohesive element in a place that has otherwise seen thousands of deployed troops from over fifty countries.

Tom wonders why Constance is stationed here. She tells him straight-faced, "For some R&R"— like he's going to believe that. She nods it's true.

"Seriously," he says.

"Seriously. After tomorrow I'm flying to Kashmir where I'm going to stay in a comfy bed in a swank hotel, have normal conversations with civilian tourists...and finally, if there's time, stop by an army base to help them figure out ways of securing the grounds better against militant attacks."

"Shit, Major! I knew it!" he laughs. "It's no doubt the other way around: first work, and then if you're lucky there'll be an hour for yourself."

When Tom goes to sit sideways to face her better, he immediately straightens his back and freezes, having been struck with an awful spasm that he attributes to a pulled muscle. Alarmed by his expression, Constance grabs him by the arms and encourages him to exhale. The severity of the attack left him holding his breath. When she yells for help, Sergeant Kurtz appears promptly followed by Private Herrero. A wheelchair is ordered. Tom almost passes out as they lower him down on the seat. Constance zeroes in on his desperate eyes as he is wheeled to a hospital tent. He works hard to hold her gaze.

She waits until her friend is made comfortable before leaving. It's no heart attack, thank god. There's an obvious disconnect between the capable, burly figure of a man she has known her entire career to the one lying so helpless on the bed. He reaches for her hand, and then peacefully drifts to sleep. The lines of distress on his forehead soften. He's at least fifteen years her senior, but Constance still considers him handsome. The full head of graying hair blends into a straw colored stripe that borders his tanned neck. It looks interesting, especially since his eyebrows and moustache are brown. She glances at the clock. Lacking a private space of her own here, she returns to Tom's office to meet with a pilot arriving from Australia who has information that she personally requested from him. He should have landed by now.

Lieutenant Colonel Blacksnake arrives hungry and asks if Constance, or CW as he calls her, wouldn't mind going to the canteen. The habit of using two initials became customary under their commander at Sheppard Air Force Base, Brigadier General Robert Jordan, who claimed it helped him connect names to faces. As they walk, Blacksnake tells her that he thought he'd be addressing a fellow Lieutenant Colonel. "Two months," says Constance, regarding her promotion. Other than having trained together for six months in Texas, their paths have not crossed in years. And although the two airmen belong to different Indian Nations, Jim Blacksnake being a Seneca from the New York area, there exists a unique bond that can never be fully realized with non-Native brothers and sisters in arms. Blacksnake is officially enroute to Israel to observe the latest technology used for their UAVs, unmanned aerial vehicles. He could have emailed the info that Constance had asked for, but he wanted to stop off at Kandahar, in order to see how surveillance here is accomplished in populated towns. He reverts to calling the UAVs drones, which all the military branches avoid doing. Drones to them are no more than radio-controlled flying objects pursued by hobbyists, nothing like the highly sophisticated computerized systems that require actual pilots to operate them, grounded pilots that is, who sit in rows of desks and stare at 3-D screens, often half the world away from the action. Blacksnake and Constance thank their lucky stars for not having been relegated to the *chair force*—not yet anyway. It's a pilot's nightmare.

"We're relics, CW, an outdated work force model." Blacksnake holds the door open for her, typical of his gentlemanly manners. "To think that the skills of an F-35 pilot might amount to nothing more than overseeing a fleet of drones from his cockpit. It's ludicrous."

"We must continue to prove ourselves indispensable, that's all," says Constance. "We belong to an elite group who can fly like nobody's business. Unmanned aircraft don't have anywhere near the rapid response dynamics in a combat situation that manned ones have demonstrated." The major's resolute stance on the subject reassures him. They quickly buy some burgers and return to Tom's office to eat.

It's enjoyable chatting about their respective professional lives. Constance was recently at Nevatim Israeli Air Force Base before flying to Afghanistan and tells Blacksnake about the most recently planned underground "doomsday bunkers" that are reportedly being financed by American dollars. "They are not a conjecture," says Constance, having recognized faces from U.S. corporations visiting there to obtain contracts for building them, men whose names she learned via diligent Rawakota espionage units, which she would never disclose to Blacksnake. He is clueless when it comes to the Rawakota. Suddenly Constance finds herself grinning when she remembers another pilot in their group, Peter Uber, PU.

Laughing a little, Blacksnake says, "Poor kid. I think the General had it in for him. He could easily have called him Pete; don't you think?"

After a short conversation about the whereabouts of some others from that flight training stint, Blacksnake brings up the business that Constance eagerly awaits hearing about, namely the background of a guy called Ishmael, whose last residence before ending up at The Ohio State University was in Sydney, Australia, close to Base Williamtown where Blacksnake had been stationed.

Pushing aside his food tray, Blacksnake holds out a flash drive for Constance. "This guy's a piece of work, CW—a cold-hearted SOB. First off, let me say...*he ain't no Indian*."

Hearing those words, that Ishmael is an imposter, gives rise to a protective maternal instinct—for once. Throughout her student life and professional career, Constance found comfort in knowing that her children were in the good hands of her relatives while she followed her dream. They took care of any problems that arose, as did Solomon after they married. When William expressed his distrust for this Ishmael whom Viktor had met, she realized later that she had better heed his misgivings and not shirk her responsibility. William is reliable, she reasoned; if he senses danger, it's justified. This didn't sound like anything the family could deal with. They don't have the many resources at their disposal like she does. Jim Blacksnake sees the day of reckoning in her eyes. He doesn't know why CW had to find out about the man, but he's certain that the calculating bastard will pay for whatever offense he has committed.

Maintaining her composure, she thanks Blacksnake for his assistance. "I thought it was going to be a fairly straightforward investigation," she tells him. "When I learned that Ishmael claimed to be a member of Seneca's Deer Clan, I assumed you would make a few calls, not to confirm his background, which I didn't doubt, but to tell me what locals thought about him and his family. I'm sorry you took so much of your personal time to do more digging, though I appreciate it."

"I got sucked into the story while trying to unravel the mysteries in his life," says Blacksnake, sounding like he had a vested interest in pursuing the man's trail. "He was born Hammad Bishara in the United Arab Emirates," quickly adding: "He could be viewed as a spy of sorts, just not like the ones we're accustomed to dealing with. I discovered some things that turned out to be beneficial to the Seneca as well. You'll see."

Now that he has sparked her curiosity, she's really impatient to learn what's behind the deception. A rush of adrenaline boosts her heart rate as she anticipates implementing a course of action. Perhaps her help will arrive too late. Blacksnake excuses himself. Constance is anxious to view the info, but not before checking in on Tom, who continues to sleep.

In all likelihood, evidence of cruel behavior would have surfaced long before Hammad Bishara turned fifteen, that is if anyone had bothered to go looking for it. The man now called Ishmael had likely been a cunning child from the time he could talk. He learned early how to play his parents and siblings against each other, in order to gain the things that he wanted. The preponderance of reports that attest to his nature is well-documented by Jim Blacksnake. The findings were corroborated by religious and academic teachers, close relatives, neighbors, and household staff.

The Bishara name in Abu Dhabi represents one of a few families in whose hands the mindboggling wealth of the country's oil industry is concentrated. And like many in Arab High Society, they flaunt the fact they can buy the costliest items on the planet a thousand times over. Their displays of outrageous ostentation when shopping at the priciest stores in the world, whether for a custom sports car or exotic perfume or a diamond studded baby rattle, is fodder for international tabloids.

Constance views Hammad's birth certificate. She studies images of the palatial estate he grew up on that was also home to an extended family of a few uncles, aunts, and their children. His father belonged to a corps that advised international companies about, what else...oil. Hammad joined his dad on one of his visits to New York City, where the teen stayed and attended a private high school for foreign diplomats' children. His mother, three older brothers, and a younger sister remained in the Emirates.

Blacksnake included a note about the sister's death, a tragic episode that occurred several weeks after her father and brother's departure to the U.S. An obituary stated that the thirteen-year-old girl had died in an accident. No mention was made of the type of accident. Former servants believed that the depressed child committed suicide, that her jumping off a balcony was done on purpose. There were rumors about her being pregnant, and it was unthinkable who the father was believed to be. Hammad did not return for his sister's funeral.

Her curiosity piqued, Constance goes on to read that in the States, Hammad got into trouble immediately for carrying out mean pranks that got him and other unscrupulous students suspended repeatedly. To prevent criminal charges, school officials were paid off by the boys' families. Everyone eventually got nailed in a scandal that involved the death of a sixteen-year-old student who "accidentally" fell out of his upper dorm room window. Messages appeared online afterward, in which friends of the deceased reported that he had been the victim of bullying. It had become so bad that he talked about killing himself, an allegation which was never substantiated.

Constance runs out for a candy bar and drops in again on Tom, who, at almost midnight, is sitting up but still quite drowsy.

"Getting old stinks," says her bleary-eyed friend. "I need to hold on for a few more years...to receive a better pension. I don't think I'm gonna last, Constance."

"Jeez! You're not even close to sixty—if that's old!" She sits on the edge of his bed and offers him ice chips, doing her best not to think about getting back to the computer. Tom mistakes his woes for her serious face. He shakes his head, wondering how he'll be able to perform his job of evaluating projects since it requires that he walk across uneven construction sites. The four surgeries on his pelvis and hips after a parachute training mishap halfway into his career resulted in the formation of scar tissue, the cause of his worsening pain. The thought of being confined to a wheelchair depresses him.

Constance whispers, "I have something you can take, Tom. There are no side effects, but you can't be caught with the capsules. They're not approved; no pharmaceutical company has them."

He stares into her lovely light brown eyes, showing the same trust she once found in his when she asked him to help her obtain Social Security numbers for Iris and Viktor. Because prospective candidates applying to the Air Force Academy cannot have dependents, she had lied about the existence of a daughter on the school form. Then, when she was finally accepted into the elite program, and wound up a no-show, an administrator called their home for an explanation, which her father gave the man. The kidnapping had made the news in South Dakota after all, and therefore couldn't be kept secret. Even if it were assumed that Constance had been raped, there was no mention of it in any reports. The Academy was willing to give Constance all the time she needed to recover from the terrible ordeal, which turned out to be a year, long enough for the pregnant mom to give birth to her second child, a boy she named Viktor. It worked to her advantage that both of her babies were born on the reservation and not in a city hospital where their births would have been entered into a U.S. data base. Things only got complicated years later when she met Solomon, and he accepted *her* proposal of marriage, on the grounds that he adopt her kids. Iris and Viktor would have a legitimate father albeit one with a record of incarceration, not unlike Lukas, their biological father. Constance wasn't sure if that fact would affect the court's final decision. No matter, at some point the kids would need to be fully documented citizens. Although she possessed tribal birth documents signed by her brother-in-law, William Horse That Walks Backwards, the doctor on the reservation, she feared that the process might turn into a bureaucratic nightmare. Normally, doctors and midwives register births with the county as standard practice, but there's no law stating they must. And what about her having lied to the Air Force Academy? Was it possible to keep the Admissions Office from finding out? Enter Tom, who at the time felt compelled to confront her about the sudden worrisome behavior he was noticing. She seemed preoccupied, distracted, not her usual sharp self. Given her job as a fighter pilot, that could spell disaster. He asked if she could use his help. Would there be strings attached, she wondered. By saying yes to his offer, he'd come to know the circumstances surrounding events in her life that she had hoped to always keep private. Her gut feeling won out, which took a load off her shoulders. For Tom, learning about the challenges that Constance had overcome was a testament to her fortitude. It made him admire her more than he already did. Tom need not have become involved at all if her relationship with the Rawakota scientists from Chohkahn had been more established. The Rawakota would gladly have done anything for the U.S. pilot following the recent success of the Minot "Bent Spear" job, her first mission for them. Both sides were still feeling each other out. It was too early in the game for them to fill her in about the nature of their various dealings, and too soon for her to understand that these were people she could totally trust, personally as well as professionally.

Tom Nally was smitten with Constance the moment he first laid eyes on her at the Academy. She, however, was supremely focused on flying, and he was married with two small children. She had the shiniest black hair and the most wondrous smooth skin he'd ever seen. Constance never asked how he managed to show up in the places she was later assigned, but he did, until the day of the accident, which put the kibosh on his flying. That's when an engineering degree came in handy. There was no expectation of anything ever happening between the two of them; he simply enjoyed her company and looking at her.

"Can you at least tell me what they're made from?" he asks.

"Spruce evergreens."

"Christmas trees are going to be my salvation? I don't understand the big deal; why so secretive?"

"Gee, let's see… my people were guaranteed ownership of the Black Hills in an 1868 treaty, but as soon as gold was discovered in the mountains, droves of white people ignored it and mined the region, claiming the land for themselves."

"But there are enough trees, right?"

"There's always enough of everything; does that stop the greedy from depleting a resource? Besides, the medicine is proprietary. It belongs to the Indians. Several therapeutic chemicals have been isolated. A lot of research was done to develop the products."

Tom rests his head back on the pillow and looks thoughtfully at her. "They've got labs tucked away somewhere…the Indians?" There's no response from her. He looks up at the IV bag, thankful for the current drug giving him relief, fully aware that every remedy so far has serious side effects after prolonged use.

Constance stands and whispers: "You'll get the pills as soon as you're out of here."

His eyes convey such affection for her.

Although it's late, Constance hurries back to Tom's office and picks up where she left off in Jim Blacksnake's report. She fortunately has the day free before flying to the Kashmir Valley.

The next image, from a casino's security camera, shows the Bishara patriarch playing baccarat. Blacksnake writes that Hammad accompanied the father on these bi-monthly trips to western New York. Because the teen was underage, he was never allowed on the gambling floor. Instead, he helped out backstage with things like props and sound equipment for the musical acts that were hired to perform at the resort. Apparently, the Muslim father didn't want to attract attention to his gambling, which of course was prohibited by his religion, so he traveled clear across the state to enjoy his addiction. During this period, Hammad became good friends with many Seneca Indians whose Nation runs the place. This routine continued until Hammad graduated from high school, which is when a new identity emerged, that of Ojimaahl Atoga, complete with Social Security number, a driver license, and, oddly, tribal enrollment status, something not easy to obtain. Just like that, he now belonged to the Seneca Deer Clan from Coldspring, New York, with ties to the Allegany Reservation. One can only wonder why? Had he finally done something so abominable that these extreme measures were necessary?

According to his faked documents, Ojimaahl was three years older than Hammad. As a twenty-one year old, Ojimaahl could get hired as a valet and cage cashier at the casino. He never again worked in the area of theatrical production. The young man's appearance was altered enough so as not to get mistaken for Hammad, or anyone from the Middle East. His thick black wavy hair is straight on his new ID and grown out to the shoulders. The eyebrows were reshaped, giving him an altogether different expression, one less brooding. His skin looks to have been lightened, too.

Constance gets up to stretch and pulls the wrapper off a second chocolate bar. It's 1 a.m. and she's wide awake. What is likely a roadside bomb has just exploded in the distance, no doubt the handiwork of the Taliban as they continue to target security forces. Civilian casualties are the norm. The situation will become increasingly dire as more NATO troops leave. The Afghan local police and army are no match for insurgents and infiltrators, especially jihadist martyrs. Who is?

"Shit," mutters Constance as she scrolls down and reads of yet another death: a young Seneca woman. One of the casino's card dealers. It's a good thing that Blacksnake fills in the gaps in these articles to give her more background. The female employee was accused of cheating on behalf of the elder Bishara. Details are a bit sketchy, but what it comes down to is that the senior Bishara was likely going to be expelled from the U.S. if he got linked to the woman's death. He could never be found complicit due to diplomatic immunity, but he also didn't want to become embroiled in a scandal, so he quickly left the country to avoid the drama. Might it truly have been a murder, wonders Constance.

The diplomat's son who had changed his identity was not connected to the investigation, although Blacksnake says he'd been secretly seeing the card dealer. The two would meet in a cabin on a dead end road in an isolated stretch of the reservation. In order to obtain this information, Blacksnake had sent a photo of Ojimaahl and the Native woman to all the gas stations between the casino and the rez, including a few small grocery stores. He got lucky. Apparently, the Bisharas used the gullible woman in their scheme, and then walked away, the father having disappeared in time before his involvement came to light. He had plainly incurred huge gambling losses and owed somebody big time. With his dad out of the picture, Ojimaahl turned up at a university in New York City where he got himself enrolled as a theater major. His student ID shows him now sporting a closely-cropped Mohawk hairstyle. New eyebrows, too. An open shirt reveals a tattoo on the side of his neck. Most would think him handsome, devilishly so with his intense black eyes and smug smile. Constance thinks this is a good stopping point to call it a night, when she catches a blurb about him having a roommate, a young Native American student from South Dakota. She hurriedly skims over the paragraph until her suspicion is confirmed. It was believed that the young man took his own life. He left a note begging his family and his people, *the Rawakota*, for forgiveness. "What the...?" This bit of news fills her with apprehension. Does Hammad, or Ojimaahl, or whatever he goes by, possess some kind of diabolic power? A call to William is in order. Perhaps he or members of his family remember hearing rumors about the boy's death.

CHAPTER 15

Oy vey, this makes the third go-round: "...*each new piscine host studied has revealed the presence of*—try to remember—*a phylogenetically unique*—close the eyes and see the words—*chlamydial pathogen...*"

"Shh."

I look up. The guy to my right shushed me politely. "Sorry." I didn't realize I had resorted to reading out loud. It's hopeless. Learning the disease-producing groups of fish disorders is the last thing I want to be doing now. Did I really believe aqua medicine would be interesting? Or has my life taken such an exciting turn, crazier than I ever could have imagined, it's making me seriously rethink my major? But then I'd lose the scholarship.

I love my quiet little study space in Thompson Library overlooking the Oval. There's an away football game this afternoon so campus is peaceful. Uncle didn't bother to ask to watch it with me, knowing how behind I've gotten. We're on limited speaking terms. He seems relieved the show is over. I sat here yesterday and got nothing accomplished, hoping today would be different. It's too easy getting lost in the clouds. They're super low and fast-moving. Tonight is the cast party at Hayden's house. A research paper is due in a week. I can't hold a thought. The past months have caught up to me big time. I can barely move my pinky. I'm curious to see if other dancers feel as drained and out of it.

Enough with the pretense of studying. I turn off the computer. Another five minutes is needed to ease my overtired body out of the chair, and that's motivated by the bed waiting for me at home.

Eventually I make it outside where I plod along. The cold winter air slaps my cheeks and keeps me alert. While waiting at the bus stop, three girls stand huddled together giggling while staring at me. Finally one asks if she can have my autograph. "What?" Is she really serious? It's Saturday, only the third day since the performance at Mershon. I haven't really been out in public. Thursday was spent with the family.

"Did you go to *WAKAN*?" I ask.

"I wish!" says the pretty blond one all excited. "I bought the poster, though. It's awesome."

They're hanging on my next words to them. It would be more flattering if they didn't seem so flaky. A disturbing thought comes to mind. It's as though Ishmael is beside me, talking in my ear: *Take on all three.* Based on the girls' wild-eyed expressions and enthusiastic body language, I stand a good chance of pulling it off, if the idea were suggested...which I would never actually follow through with.

I'm grateful when the bus pulls up and we board without them mentioning the autograph again. Even when seated they flirt, glancing at me constantly and smiling their hearts out. It's so weird...like having groupies. A few snowflakes begin swirling around. I look forward to the party; it should be interesting. I wish Camila weren't the main reason for going.

I place the keys to Uncle's car in a safe pocket inside my coat and walk the block from the church lot to Hayden and Skyler's place. I didn't want Uncle to drive me tonight and was ready to take a cab when he handed the keys over and told me to have a good time '... *and be sure not to drink from bottles or cans that have already been opened.*' Worn advice to which my head bobs up and down when he says it like a karaoke bouncing ball following lyrics. Music from a live band fills the air. They must be in the huge tent that's behind the house. A light snow is falling. I take a deep breath and hold it in my lungs a second; it's so fresh and invigorating. Cars are lined up end-to-end on both sides of the street. There's barely room for anyone to drive down the center of the road without sideswiping one. Fat chance if a person wants to leave early. This is some turnout. I follow a couple up the stairs. Someone pats my back. I turn to greet *WAKAN's* musical conductor, Dr. Kassel, who appears to be alone.

"Good evening, Viktor. Come down out of the clouds yet?"

He's a good-natured man, close to sixty I'm guessing, whom the students love. Ishmael mostly dealt with him. I'd say hello in passing. We shake hands and enter together when immediately we're surprised by cheers of congratulations. I'm assuming it's strictly for the maestro, who is also the director of OSU's Jazz Studies Program. I'm somewhat embarrassed to be beside him, feeling as though I'm detracting from his glory. In a startling move, he grabs my hand, lifts my arm in the air, and continues to shake it while folks raise their glasses for a toast.

"Please, Dr. Kassel," I beg, forcing my arm down. Naturally, Skyler recognizes my discomfort and makes a beeline in my direction, the last person I want to have doing the rescuing. She plants herself right in front of me. *Uh-oh...here it comes.* Using her index finger to motion me closer, I'm informed that there are certain *influential* people in attendance who expect to meet Talking White Owl, the star. I straighten up. There's no mistaking her thoughts: *I damn well better not let her and Hayden down!* Smiling, she offers to take our coats. Dr. Kassel, who was in a conversation with a gentleman during my short but meaningful exchange with Skyler, starts to make his way through the crowd, with me on his heels. We're immediately encircled by some extremely well-dressed individuals, clearly highfalutin patrons of the arts, who think they're entitled to touch us as they speak. Dr. Kassel probably knows them, but I don't. I catch Skyler observing me from the entranceway, our coats still in her arms. I glare back: *I hear you loud and clear!* I watch and learn from Dr. Kassel, realizing he must attend a lot of functions like this. I dive in and proceed to schmooze with the best of them; assuming that's what Dr. Kassel's half wink meant before he left me on my own. Camila shows up at my side. Now I do feel rescued.

Damn if she isn't an expert at this. Together we work the room. In the process, countless people ask where they can donate to help the Mapuche in Chile, and at the same time ask what is needed on my reservation. Where to begin?

Hayden corners me while I take a breather in the hallway. Camila went to find her friends

"Hey, you...go dance! It's a great band. We took a chance with the neighbor's son. He's only in high school. Go check it out."

"Am I allowed?" I'm not being sarcastic. I get that mingling among the moneyed helps keep Adler and Banks Consortium of Dancers afloat. Hayden laughs when he realizes that I'm serious.

"Don't tell me Skyler commanded you to make nice to our fancy guests?"

What am I supposed to say; she's his wife.

"Oh, hell, Viktor. I'm sorry. Shit."

"It's okay, Hayden. Probably a good lesson for me." I keep it to myself that I was with Camila most of the time. He has no idea how deep my feelings run. I'm led to the buffet where I stack the prime rib on my plate. They went all out for this. The food makes up for having to hobnob with their generous benefactors, whose promised donations to the Indians on the Buckthorn Reservation I humbly accepted on behalf of my fellow tribesmen and women, which I acknowledge was hypocritical of me. As it turned out, I did end up enjoying our conversations. Besides being well-read, well-traveled, and articulate, they were nice rich folks. After chowing down, I join a few of the show's stagehands and we make our way to the tent, which has an industrial size space heater inside. A wooden dance floor has been laid over the lawn. The band is good. The faces are familiar. When the group takes a break from playing hard core Rock 'n' Roll, a recorded track of waltzes completely changes the mood. I'm game. I look around for a partner. Ballroom dancing was mandatory at my high school. Our principal convinced the parents that it was a civilizing activity. Because my idol Jim Thorpe had won a ballroom dance competition in college, I was inspired to be as good as he was. The violinist I'd had my eye on during rehearsals floats across the floor with me. Thank god I napped after the library; it's given me my second wind.

I stand to the side when the cast comes together for a number from *Rent,* the show the company performed before *WAKAN*. If only I'd known Hayden and Skyler then. If that wasn't enough to get everyone fired up, a hard-driving Salsa piece with blasting horns has the room jumping. I'm psyched, but not sure how to begin. The fox trot was part of my high school's repertoire, not steamy Latin dances. Camila and Ishmael sneak up from behind and spin me onto the floor. They're a blur, everyone's a blur, they've got me twirling so fast. Camila and I have a go at it. Ishmael grabs her and performs a new step, then tosses her back in my arms. I love this music, especially the hesitations, my favorite thing in all dances.

Finally there's a time-out before the band starts another set. I'm soaking wet and dying of thirst. Someone's on top of it and has begun to pass around bottles of water. Camila pours a handful over her face and neck.

"Viktor...some friends are going to my place. Come, too."

"Now?"

She dumps more water in her hand and pats it on my neck and forehead. God, she's beautiful. Her top clings to her breasts. I don't pretend not to notice the hard nipples.

"Who'd you come with?" she asks.

"No one." I'm torn between leaving and staying and dancing my legs off. If Camila had wanted to spend the evening alone with me, well…that's another story; I'd be outta here in a flash. "Aren't you having fun?" I ask, hoping she'll stick around longer.

"I'll text you the address. You come when you want, okay?"

The band starts tuning up. I can't drink enough water. Camila places her cool, damp hands on the sides of my head and looks directly into my eyes, turning this lovesick boy into mush. She glides her thumb slowly across my lips. I touch it with my tongue. Ishmael interrupts the momentary trance. Some other girl is on his arm, a dancer in the show.

"We've got to find a ride for Laura," he says to Camila, "since we're taking Viktor and Eric." He assumes I'm coming and knows I don't own a car.

"I've got a car tonight," I inform him, "so that leaves an extra spot in yours for her." Laura, however, quickly invites herself to go with me…to give directions, she says. I guess I'm okay with that.

"Great! Let's head out!" says Ishmael.

Camila seems ready to tell him that I had wanted to stay, but I don't give her the chance. He motions to some others across the room. We thank our hosts, and then go grab our coats.

First and foremost, Constance Howling Wind wants to hear from her brother-in-law that Viktor is in fact *not* alone with Ishmael this evening.

"*It's a big crowd,*" William assures her in Lakota, "*a party for everyone involved with the production. There haven't been any signs of trouble over the last months; however, the boy needs to start concentrating on his schoolwork. What have you discovered, Constance? Were my instincts right about Ishmael Atoga?*"

Constance is relieved to have gotten hold of William before boarding the plane that will take her to the airfield in Kashmir. It's Sunday morning for her, but not quite midnight on Saturday back in Columbus. She describes everything that she's learned about the thirty-plus-year-old Arab who was born Hammad Bishara. Apparently, Ishmael changed his birth status yet again, since William says he is currently passing himself off as a twenty-six-year-old student at Ohio State. She tells William that Ishmael once went by the name of Ojimaahl when he was enrolled at a college in New York City, wondering if that alias might elicit a response from him, but it doesn't. The name Hammad Bishara didn't resurface until years later in of all places, Sydney, Australia. Before going into the details of his life down under, Constance wants to know if William had ever heard of a young man called Jonah Plain Feather, who died years ago while away at college. She doesn't mention the word suicide, or that the student referred to his Rawakota background in a short note of apology that the police found in his pocket.

William does in fact recall the circumstances and says, *"Jonah Plain Feather wasn't truly from a Lakota reservation, even though there was proof of his being born on it. He grew up in Chohkahn."* Constance understands that William is referring to the Rawakota practice of falsifying their infants' birth records. In order for Chohkahn to remain secret from outsiders, parents create documents for their babies that show they were born on the reservation of a federally recognized tribe. They started doing this back in the 1940s to make it easier to move around the country later in life should a person wish to travel or hold a job elsewhere in the States. These days, as enrolled tribal members, their young people also have access to lots of college scholarships. *"Our families didn't know each other,"* says William, *"but word spread fast about what had happened to Jonah. It was such a terrible tragedy. The boy killed himself, Constance. He jumped off the roof of his dormitory. I'm guessing you know this…and brought him up for a reason."*

"Yes. His roommate's name was Ojimaahl."

They're both quiet a moment as they reflect on the boy's despair. Jonah Plain Feather must have been so excited about starting college in New York and exploring what the world outside the Dakotas had to offer him. His future held such promise. At his age, he would also have been struggling with the emotions associated with *wakuwa*, an especially important stage in young people's development when they're on the hunt—for a partner that is, not prey. It is a strictly Rawakota tradition that leads to theeich ihilah, the initial coming together of a couple as husband and wife.

William says that Jonah mailed his parents an in-depth letter explaining the terrible action he was prepared to carry out. *"If only he had called* them, they would have gone to his side and helped him. His parents felt compelled to share its contents with everyone in Chohkahn because Jonah believed that he had compromised the location and safety of our city."

"Oh?" Constance lets him in on the note that the police found in his shirt, but says it didn't offer any real explanation.

William clears his throat. "Their son accused his roommate of having drugged him. When he came to, Jonah discovered that he had told the guy about the hidden entrances leading to Chohkahn. He had also given him descriptions of our private culture, which included aspects of the ritual Otiwota. The roommate knew everything about the coming of age ceremony. Worse yet, Jonah disclosed to his parents that he had been spiritually ruined, and that he could never enjoy the anticipated union between him and his future wife. That's how he worded what was unmistakably a rape. And you're saying that Ishmael was this fellow Ojimaahl?"

"Whatever he goes by, Ishmael—Ojimaahl — Hammad—he finds perverse pleasure in driving people to suicide," says Constance. "He has an uncanny knack for honing in on a person's vulnerabilities. It must give him an incredible sense of power."

"Something like this happened in Australia, too?"

"Yes, and with a high-profile family named Randolf. Again, nothing could be proven. The Randolf name is synonymous with wealth there just like Rockefeller is in the States. Hammad could go back to being a Bishara because it would help him get close to Australia's elite Upper Class. He targeted a fortyish woman, Evelyn Randolf. She was the unmarried granddaughter of the man who built the mining empire. She suffered from anorexia most of her life, which did not stay private thanks to the tabloids... reports of it probably made her condition worse. Anyway, her older brother, who had taken over the running of the business from their late father, died suddenly in a boating accident. This happened over a decade ago. It was assumed that the next fellow in line would take over the operation; instead, Evelyn got her shit together and took charge. She held controlling interest in the company. The responsibilities were all-consuming. It apparently left no time for her to be self-absorbed by her body image the way she had been. Company profits grew. The public admired her."

"Then she met the man who now goes by Ishmael." It's obvious to William where the story was headed.

"Yes; she met Hammad, perhaps at a party where anyone would have *been familiar with the Bisharas' background. He was a considerably younger man, and a handsome one at that, who showed a serious interest in her. He came from money, so Ms. Randolf likely felt confident that he wasn't after hers. Following a few months of dating, he proposed marriage. They had a civil ceremony as soon as Hammad's paperwork went through for a marriage visa. Within the year they became parents."*

"*That fast!*"

"*He didn't waste time.*" Constance speaks so quickly and talks about things that don't exist in the Lakota language, like anorexia, tabloids, and civil ceremonies that much of the conversation has reverted to English.

She continues: "*For whatever reasons, Evelyn's insecurities returned... and the anorexia. I'm guessing that Hammad made her feel self-conscious about her weight gain during the pregnancy, and kept up the harassment after the birth of their son.*"

"*I don't get it, Constance. What did he have to gain?*"

"*To see if he could ruin another life, I imagine. You'd have to ask a shrink why. I just know that she no longer cared about the business. Hammad called her an unfit mother. He openly criticized her, which of course made the news. He wanted a divorce and full custody of their boy so he could raise him back home in Abu Dhabi. Evelyn ended up overdosing on pills.*"

"*Poor thing. How long ago?*"

"*Around two years.*"

William adds what he knows. "*Ishmael has been here at OSU for about a year. He's been involved with a couple and their dance company. The address on his license is St. Regis, New York, which is part of the Mohawk Reservation along the Canadian border. They belong to the Iroquois Confederacy up there, but they're not Seneca, which is what he told Viktor he was.*" Jim Blacksnake had told Constance as much.

The two take a minute to mull over the facts. They worry if Viktor is going to be the calculating Arab's next intended victim. Or maybe he has set his sights on either Hayden or Skyler. Did the man sit bored back in his palace in Abu Dhabi and choose a person at random to target next? Constance pictures him spinning a globe and traveling to wherever his finger lands. No matter, insinuating himself into others' lives is definitely fun for him. Isn't that what sociopaths do? William is no fan of puzzles and hates that he can't fathom a motive. Someone yells in the background for Major Howling Wind. The plane is ready and its pilot is waiting for her. William, who is normally in bed by now, realizes he may never sleep tonight; his mind is racing a mile a minute. And just when they are about to hang up, he has a light-bulb moment. *"They have yellow eyes, Constance ...both Jonah and Viktor. Somewhere along the line, Ishmael could have read a piece about the American Indian boy who discovered that the research work of the noted French scientist, Dr. Bonnaire, was being plagiarized by an OSU student. There were photos of Viktor ... along with details of his background, especially when he got the Herrington Scholarship. The yellow-eyed kid, born on a South Dakota reservation like Jonah, was all that Ishmael would have needed to connect the dots. It surely made the news in France, where the popular Dr. Bonnaire is known outside scientific circles for his TV show about peoples' ancestry. Being a diplomat, Ishmael's father might even have met Dr. Bonnaire on occasion. The French collaborate on all kinds of projects with the Middle East. It isn't a stretch to think that the elder Bishara at times plays a role in the negotiations between their two countries. Ishmael must believe that he can gain more information about Chohkahn from Viktor. What if Jonah alluded to the rare crystals found deep under the Black Hills that power everything in our city?"*

Constance needs to hustle. She wishes she could tell her brother-in-law that his theory sounds preposterous, but she can't. *"Hold that thought, William, and I'll get back to you as soon as I land, okay?"*

"You're not on Facebook!" shrieks Laura on our way to Camila's apartment. "How can anyone not be on Facebook! Don't you stay in touch with your high school friends?"

I'm baffled by her reaction to something I don't give much thought to. Traffic is heavy on High Street as we near campus, so I don't bother to answer. Walking as much as I do, I know people drive right through red lights and stop signs. I don't want to die, or worse, yet...get in a wreck, because then I'd have to face Uncle William.

"After the next light, get ready to turn left," she says, all bouncy and excited.

I do as told, and continue down a street that I'm not familiar with. The neighborhood is quiet until we reach Camila's place. It's right before a short overhead bridge. There's a clearing by the bushes for me to park in. As we get out, Laura won't drop the subject and insists she's going to help me set up a Facebook account. *Good grief!* We run to keep from freezing our butts off.

It's dark inside. Tiny purple lights have been strung around the windows and pushed inside empty wine bottles. They stand in rows on the sills and give the room a club-like atmosphere. Laura and I lay our coats on a heap of others that are balanced on a chest next to the door. The place is packed. We weave through the bodies to get to the light at the other side of the room. The music is slow and bluesy, and the dancing—if you can call it that—is about as raunchy as it gets.

In the kitchen I'm introduced to Camila's roommate Anne, a computer science major, born and raised in a Columbus suburb. She was living in a sorority house and needed a change. She met Camila on the Oval and the two hit it off.

"I thought you didn't drink." My comment is directed to Camila who is having fun creating all sorts of martinis with a guy I've never seen before.

"Sometimes," she says, with a giant smile, and then she flicks a fingertip in the glass and dabs my lips with her concoction. "Wanna try one? Taste the blueberry?"

"No thanks." I grab a coke in the fridge and lean against the counter to watch as I wait for someone else to start talking to me. I'm not sure about staying. Camila glances my way a lot. The smile hasn't left her beautiful face. Who's to say that I couldn't convince her to date only me? The lights suddenly go up in the living room...time to play a game. I'm curious what a crowd made up of such an assortment of individuals finds entertaining.

There's an easel with over-sized paper and a hat with clues. Really? Win, Lose, or Draw? We divide into teams. So far, no one appears too drunk; but then the night is still young. Once we start calling out our guesses, which get quite obscene, the laughter doesn't stop. A joint gets passed around. I refuse to let it bother me because I'm actually having a good time. A few other people hand it off without taking a drag just as I do. That's encouraging, until one of them produces a baggie filled with pills. I decline the offer. Could it be I've gotten stoned from the second-hand smoke in the room? It sure is hazy in here.

The game finally runs its course. The lights dim again and this incredible voice fills the space. It belongs to a female singer I don't recognize. Nina Simone, says the guy beside me, and in a such way as to make me feel like a real dumbass. I ask if he's heard of Keith Secola, knowing full well he hasn't. "How do you *not* know *NDN Kars*! What a maroon," I mutter, shaking my head as I continue toward the kitchen. It's no longer bright like before. My hand searches for the light switch when I hear sounds of people making out in a corner by the sink. Damn if Laura doesn't corner me by the fridge! I grab a bottled water and gulp it down. My eyes adjust to the dark, thanks to a bulb in the hood over the stove. I ignore the couple in the corner, although I think it's the guy who helped with the martinis when I arrived and was never introduced to. He's lip-locked to another guy.

"Let's dance, Viktor."

Laura rests her hands on my shoulders and starts swaying to the music. My hands settle on her small hips. The singer, whatever her name, has an unusually deep and erotic voice that is soft one moment, then grows powerful and dramatic the next. Laura's babbling is wearing thin. It's an instance when alcohol might come in handy, to shut her down, or for me not to care. It figures that out of the few people at this party who aren't drinking, she's one of them. I wonder if Camila is dancing with Ishmael. We rock back and forth while Laura blathers on. "Do you have any idea how many of us dancers were jealous over your duets with Camila? I don't see why you can't partner with anyone else. That could easily be written into the story, right?"

"Ah...I guess. Talk to Skyler."

"She'll just say no. Hayden needs to speak up more; don't you agree? I mean..."

"I hate to cut you off, Laura, but I've got to use the bathroom." It's a convenient excuse to call it a night. I move quickly without turning back, worried that she might be trailing me.

As I zigzag my way out of here, I pass by a couch with Ishmael's long body sprawled across it. His head is on a girl's lap with his face touching her naked breasts. He sees me and grabs my pant leg. Just then Camila appears and slides an arm around my waist. I shake her off and pull my leg free, but not before witnessing another girl mounting him. I just want outta here and instantly push past people to get to the door. Fuck! My coat's somewhere under this huge pile. Camila followed me. I can't think I'm so upset. I'd like nothing better than to hurl her cheap, slutty body all the way back to Chile. Next thing she's on my chest with her legs locked around my hips, breathing in my ear. I've got a firm hold of her ass under her skirt. The pressure of her body against my penis makes me crazy. When her lips meet mine, my fingers go searching. They slip inside her. This is what I've dreamt of and longed for…for Camila to want me as much as I want her. It's not in the kind of place I pictured, though. There's nothing romantic about any of this, and yet I am powerless to stop it from happening.

Sunday, 3:47 a.m. EST, William sends Constance a message that Viktor returned home.

CHAPTER 16

In a cold, stark room filled with war-weary soldiers who continue to eye her suspiciously, which they do with outsiders anyway, but in this instance it's because she is a female, newly promoted Lt. Colonel Howling Wind sits listening to a TV news account broadcast in English of a recent surprise attack at the Indian and Pakistani border. An Indian Army Colonel and two policemen were killed by a grenade. This is normally not business of particular concern to an Air Force pilot, but because of her unexpected involvement in a ground operation last year that prevented a disaster at an outpost in Yemen near Saudi Arabia, the U.S. asked her to offer strategies that would help the army from India better recognize threats to isolated camps like this one in the future. It's an austere place with inadequate resources. As if she didn't have enough on her plate, her superiors in the Air Force are counting on her to learn who in this distant country is continuing to supply Yemen with air power and tanks. The situation called for a higher ranking officer, but because one wasn't available in the district, and Howling Wind's promotion had already been approved by the Board, it became effective the second she boarded the plane to come here.

Constance didn't have to accept the request to go to this highly charged part of India; it wasn't an order, but the Himalayan region has been of personal interest to her ever since she visited a village last summer near Srinagar, an area north of her present position in the Pulwama district, when her jeep stopped for a boy who was crossing the road with his goats. If he hadn't raised his head, and the sunlight not struck his eyes at the exact moment, she would simply have driven on, unaware of their golden color. Spurring her curiosity, she followed him on foot. The boy returned the animals to the farm of an elderly couple. The old man had but a single leg, and the woman suffered from extreme curvature of the spine. She walked with a stick, her lowered head tracking her own steps. Constance counted eight other structures a good distance from their house. After herding the goats into a stall, and then feeding the chickens, the boy was met by a man in a rundown cargo van. The age of the driver couldn't be determined—maybe an older brother or his father? She was too far to see if the eyes were similar. Man and boy drove north.

When she returned to the village, she asked a trusted local interpreter to find out all he could about the goatherder, and she gave him money to give the couple for information. It was a lot to ask of poor farmers. The smallest hamlets throughout the entire Kashmir Valley, of which there are hundreds, harbor militant groups that represent numerous tribal and religious interests, including Taliban fighters and operatives from Al Qaeda. Trusting the right person is crucial to staying alive. In this case, money talked.

Constance smiles at the newest recruits as she sits down to a meal of lamb stew. Only one soldier offers a welcoming nod while the rest remain engaged in small talk, mostly in broken English since they come from different regions where the dialects are unfamiliar to each other. The killings at the border are the center of conversation. The men, boys really, look nervous; not a good sign thinks Constance, who senses she is the cause, and not because she is the sole American. The idea of sending a woman when their lives are on the line is anathema to their way of thinking. Her credentials are meaningless. At least they are somewhat polite to her face.

Constance must wait to reply to William's message. As soon as she read Viktor was home safe, about fifteen minutes ago, the local cell phone towers got bombed again. They will always be prime targets. Time to use her backup, the superior and dependable Rawakota technology. Unfortunately, she has only a short window in which to communicate from this remote location. The roving and intermittent signals of their spy satellites elude any country's abilities for tracking them. Later this evening, after Pulwama's coordinates are scanned, she'll tell the Rawakota to send word to her brother-in-law that Ishmael needs to be out of the picture *completely*. Ishmael—Hammad, knows more about being Rawakota than Viktor, although she doubts the Arab realizes it. Viktor is the same age Jonah Plain Feather was when his conniving roommate, using the alias Ojimaahl, took advantage of their friendship and drugged him, in order to learn things about his background. Unlike Viktor, though, Jonah was profoundly influenced by his culture in Chohkahn. There is no way at present to determine how deeply Viktor has been affected by the Rawakota teachings that her father and grandfather instilled in him. She heard about it only after the damage had been done, or she would never have given her consent. Regardless, this is an extremely vulnerable period in his life. If the Arab should get to Viktor before he has a chance to experience *thee-ich ihilah* with the woman he chooses for his wife, his future might be ruined like Jonah's. It's imperative that William intervene before this can ever occur, which he fully understands now that he's aware of Ishmael's connection to Jonah.

After dinner Constance retires to her quarters. Somebody improvised a room from a tiny closet to provide her privacy among the males. Furnished with a wobbly cot and a tin barrel for a table, she gladly accepts the inconvenience of the tight accommodations for the luxury of being left alone. For a second, she pictures the plush mattress and smooth sheets of a hotel not even five kilometers from here, which is where she had planned to stay for a week. Her agenda changed just minutes before departing from Kandahar. Even though the telecommunications systems are down, she still checks for "hidden bugs" in the room with an Israeli designed detector that can also jam signals. An all-clear registers, and she prepares to send her message. Unbuttoning the top of her military blouse and then lifting her left breast out of her bra, she wiggles the nipple until the bottom part detaches from the areola. Using tweezers, she extracts a thin bendable stamp-sized disk kept buried within the fleshy tissue, and then quickly buttons up. Next, she licks both sides of it. The protective coating reacts with substances in her saliva. Once dry, a needle and small magnifier help to accurately poke the tiny spot that in turn projects a keyboard. She could speak into the thing if she wanted, but there might be an ear glued to the other side of her door. The fact that she isn't using English would make the soldiers more leery of her than they already are.

Typing quickly, her message is immediately received by Chief Rolling Thunder himself, who assures her that he will personally contact William about Ishmael, the man the Rawakota now know was responsible for the death of one of their own, Jonah Plain Feather. Next, he tells her that the news she had passed along to them about the goatherder being from the northern Dras Valley in Kashmir has paid off. The geologists in Chohkahn concluded after further research that her catching sight of this particular boy was a fortuitous event. Howling Wind had stumbled upon what was for certain the site of their original people. It was the tribesmen and women from that ancient culture who embarked on the great journey across Asia to Khéya Wita, their name for America. The revelation astounds Howling Wind as well. The goatherder serves as proof that descendants from that tribe still reside under the Himalayas today, people genetically linked to the Rawakota in the Black Hills. According to the map, Tiger Hill, the highest peak near the town of Drass-Kargil in the Kashmir District, corresponds to Black Elk Peak in the Black Hills of South Dakota, the highest point east of the Rockies; what Constance grew up calling Harney Peak before the name change. Like every child descended from the Rawakota, she learned from her parents and grandparents that over the course of their history their people finally ended their search for a new homeland when they reached *He Sapa*, the Black Hills. The area was imbued with the same life-giving force as the far-off mountains their predecessors had journeyed from. This knowledge, this blueprint, was passed down through songs and stories that were later recorded using words when the Rawakota became literate. During the epic odyssey, tribesmen charted points on the ground and matched them to unique patterns of stars that they incorporated into their stories, thereby preserving the survival of their society. Because of the long held belief that Mother Earth mirrors the sky, and the importance of the number seven to them, the locations of all entrances to Chohkahn were based on the seven visible stars called "Winchincala Sakowin," or seven little girls, known to Constance and the western world as Pleiades. It's presumed that the main entrance in the Asian mountains must be in line with the constellation's most prominent star, Alcyone, just as it is in South Dakota. It follows that the other openings are linked to the positions of the remaining bright stars, best viewed in the northern hemisphere during winter. Howling Wind is told that a Holy Man named Sleeping Buffalo will travel to Kashmir in the spring. Because their scientists have been able to close in on the coordinates, thanks to her, Chief Rolling Thunder believes the spirits of their ancestors will guide Sleeping Buffalo to their distant relatives' exact location.

He adds that nothing can be corroborated until the heavy winter snows melt in the Drass-Kargil region. If Sleeping Buffalo should need her assistance, will she be available? Constance types back: *not sure. tricky business here. A paramilitary police force continues to antagonize the local citizens with their heavy-handed tactics. They're always raiding neighborhoods, which is creating an explosive situation.* In other words, it's damned dangerous, and there's no guessing the outcome, especially if those in power start redrawing the political maps. Rolling Thunder says he is sending two operatives from Islamabad. They can be there within a day. He won't divulge their covers. Lay low, he advises.

The time has expired, the signal gone. Constance takes a tube labeled as petroleum jelly from her bag and rubs the special high-tech oil on the disk so nothing can locate it, not even the sniffer of the best trained dog, and then she reinserts it in her breast.

CHAPTER 17

Uncle's bedroom door opens. With any luck, he's still half asleep and won't notice me on his way to the bathroom. But he does and asks the time.

Glancing at the laptop, I tell him, "8:22." I figure he's surprised to see me up already on a Sunday morning, busily working at the dining room table…and on a paper for class, of all things! Notes are laid out neatly everywhere including the floor and along the back of the couch. He grumbles something and goes to pee.

I'm just as surprised at myself, awake and alert on less than four hours sleep. Suddenly his hand pats my head, my damp head.

"Showered, too?"

"Uh huh."

He shuffles back to his room, looking like he's the one who needs to rally after a late night. It's out of character for him. Uncle William is normally an early riser, even on the weekends. I continue to organize and make sense of pages of data. It feels good having this renewed sense of purpose. I know exactly what I must do. I knew it as soon as I left Camila's.

I work through noon, not paying attention to Uncle's movements around me. He did offer a proper "good morning" after he got dressed, but that was it, until now when he announces he's going out for groceries. Iris calls. It's only been a couple of days since she was here with Hashke, Dad, and Grandmother. She's curious about the cast party. I tell her it was fun, but spare her the details, knowing full well why she really called. I then ask her what she had discovered.

"Zilch, Viktor! Can you believe it! Do you have any idea how much research is carried on around the world using implants in people's heads? And it's all documented, above board."

"So…there's nothing you learned from anyone at Battelle about the possibility of the government using Indigenous kids for any kind of testing?"

"No. I checked into names of scientists who work with improving the cognition of brain damaged children…but nothing struck me as Orwellian."

"God, Iris, will you just go to the Bureau of Indian Affairs on the rez and talk to somebody! Better yet, meet with Dr. Devreau, the dentist you suspect is involved. If he isn't, he could at least examine a few of the kids' bumps…maybe even give one a local anesthetic, in order to remove the thing…just to see what it is and take pictures."

To me, this seems the obvious thing to do. She called right when I was almost done reviewing my bibliography. I take advantage of the silence on her end and scan some final entries before forwarding the paper on to my professor. What a weight off my shoulders. Next I locate the notes of all those fish diseases I couldn't get a handle on when I was at the library. I'm anxious to bring this conversation to an end because she's refusing any advice.

"I don't know, Viktor. The BIA deals mostly with land rights. And I don't trust anyone who would go work for them. They're just another corrupt government agency."

Now she sounds like Marnie, although a lot of Indians actually think that, and with good reason—Sunkwah being one of them. I want to believe there must be some honest individuals in the organization who genuinely try to help. I need to get off the phone and study. "Iris, I understand you're upset and want to get to the bottom of this, but face it, whoever is behind the conspiracy seems to be doing more good than bad."

"I'm sorry, Viktor. This shouldn't concern you, but there are even more kids with them in their heads. It's alarming, you know?"

"Why on earth haven't you spoken to Grandmother about it? Think of all the people she's come into contact with over the years. She might have an idea who's responsible."

"I would…if everyone weren't so darn proud of me. If this comes to light, all the hours and effort spent on my thesis won't amount to a hill of beans."

"I don't recognize this person I'm talking to! Are you insinuating that you plan on keeping the criminals' identities to yourself after you learn who they are? Iris, do you care more about the children or your status? Wouldn't you think that this discovery will enhance your position in the scientific community? Minors are being used without adult consent!"

"You're right, my dear brother. I'll figure something out. This is tying me into knots."

"Iris, I don't mind being a sounding board…but you have a husband. Have you discussed it with him? It isn't that I don't care; I do, you must realize that. It's just that this has been going on for such a long time, ever since you got the award from the governor. You're driving yourself crazy. And worse, you don't listen to my suggestions."

She wishes me good luck on my finals and says goodbye. Her voice sounded flat.

It's early in the evening and Uncle wonders whether I'm ever going to leave my chair. He was out the one time I got up to collect my piles of papers and to go to the bathroom. I haven't eaten the entire day, afraid that a break might hamper my momentum. Besides, studying has kept me from thinking about last night. I quickly accept his invitation for dinner. My choice. Hmm.

I'm as happy as a pup with two tails, as they say, with a stack of pancakes a foot high and a plate of bacon…at our favorite IHOP. Sunday evenings are always nice and quiet here. After downing half the plate, I casually mention that Iris called; and then also casually mention that she has been worried for a long time about something she has observed about the kids used in her research. That doesn't produce any reaction out of the ordinary. He simply chews his steak and spears the eggs and potatoes on his fork, and looks at me like *so what*?

"You must know Dr. Devreau, the dentist on the rez?" He nods. I'm not sure how to explain the problem without it sounding stupid, like science fiction. "Iris discovered these raised bumps on some of her students' heads, and she can feel something under the skin. The only person to have had contact with all of them is Dr. Devreau. Could you ask him about it?"

"Why doesn't she?"

"That's what I told her."

We go on eating like the subject was never brought up. When we're finished, and after he's had his dose of fun flirting with our waitress Naomi, he stretches back in the booth, rubs his full belly then says, "There's no mind control involved; nothing sinister going on. Parts of the injured brain are stimulated to facilitate learning. That's all. Someone still has to teach the youngsters. Now they can learn and become productive adult Lakota. Your sister is doing an admirable job."

What the...! If Iris were here, she'd shit a brick, as Dad loves to say when he's beyond ticked off. In Uncle's defense, he was kept in the dark about Iris's concerns. To think that he's known all along about this.

Folding his hands on the table, he says, "You're going to catch flies."

I close my mouth.

My anger grows during the ride home. We don't speak. Once inside the door, I block Uncle's path to the living room. I realize I'm a sight, what with my hands in my hair ready to pull it out and the way I'm darting in front of him like an idiot.

"Hunta yo," he says with quiet authority. "Get out of the way. What's with you?"

"What's with me! What is with me? Really?" I'm trying hard not to cuss. "You have no idea what Iris has been going through! Christ, she's gone so far as to talk to people at Battelle to find out who might be behind this scheme. Why the hell didn't you or Dr. Devreau ever tell her about the implants? It skews all her data." For a moment, shockingly, it does occur to me how Iris feels ... exactly how I would feel if it happened to me. I just stare at him and try to get a handle on my breathing. He didn't take a swing at me for raising my voice to him. It's driving me nuts that he won't say anything. I refuse to move until he answers.

He walks around me and goes to the couch.

"Come," he says and motions for me to sit in the chair across from him.

I'm not quick to oblige him. He no doubt wants to put me in my place with one of those stern intimidating looks the older men on the rez learn to master. Sunkwah and Pahpie were no exception. It's meant to squash defiant behavior. Dad's *"this is the last straw"* face doesn't come close. I do as he says.

Sitting face to face, he asks with total sincerity, "How was I to know?"

He sounds hurt. Not what I expected. "Are you in on it?"

"No, Viktor. Not in the way you think."

"Then who?"

"Winter Crow's lab in Rapid City developed the technology. Doctors tested the thing for years before placing them in the youngsters. They aren't guinea pigs."

"It doesn't make sense that Iris wasn't informed. Wouldn't you be pissed!" I'm speaking as softly as Uncle, though clearly frustrated with him.

"In all honesty, Viktor, from what I understand about the project, the researchers never imagined finding the degree of success they encountered. The speed at which the subjects started to learn was incredible. In no time, they were able to grasp abstract concepts. It's unprecedented. And I do believe Iris's efforts contributed to that."

"What role did you play?"

"I gave them physicals—that's all...to make sure they were in good health before the team went ahead and put them in. Your grandmother wasn't involved."

That was my next question, since she was the nurse with him on the rez. I lean back and cross my arms. "Does Mom know?" He doesn't have to answer; I see it in his eyes. *Oh, Iris...*

"Go to your room, Viktor. Get a good night's sleep after your long day. You deserve it. I'll call your sister. We'll discuss it."

Bed...sleep, that's a great idea, but somehow I can't get this body to move. I want more answers, but I suppose I'll get them from Iris after Uncle talks with her.

"Now that your work is finished for your classes, will you be rehearsing for a future performance of *WAKAN*?"

God! WAKAN! It completely escaped my mind today. "No. I won't be taking part in any more shows." He doesn't ask why, thankfully. I start wondering how I'm going to break the news to Hayden and Skyler. Uncle stands and heads for the kitchen while I go to my bedroom. Before closing the door, I hear a goodnight. I hesitate a moment, then respond in kind. "G'night."

"She is understandably upset," declares William Horse That Walks Backwards in a video call to Chief Rolling Thunder. Echoing Viktor's sentiment, *"It was wrong that my niece wasn't made to feel a part of Winter Crow's study since it impacted the outcomes in the research she oversaw at the University of Wisconsin. In all fairness to her, tell the lead scientist that every detail relating to the development of the implants on their end at the lab must be disclosed."*

Chief Rolling Thunder's primary concern is whether Iris Racing Water, upon being told this news from her uncle, has confided in anyone else. Is her husband trustworthy? William insists she will keep the matter confidential, but she wants to speak to the researchers behind the experiments. The question then arises about whether Iris should be told that many of the Rawakota scientists involved are from the hidden city of Chohkahn. The several Lakota scientists from the surrounding reservations who work alongside them had to be thoroughly vetted before being allowed in on the project. When Iris and Viktor were little and in the care of their great-grandparents, they read stories and learned songs about the ancient sacred city Chohkahn that was home to their Rawakota ancestors. Although some of their family's neighbors occasionally traveled down to Chohkahn, the visits were never openly discussed, nor are they today. White men are never to suspect it's a real place, and present-day Lakota cannot be trusted with knowledge of its location. These are not the same Indigenous peoples that once ruled the Great Plains over a couple of hundred years ago. Too many have lost the spiritual connection to their past. They could easily be bought for the information, and for only a beer.

Rolling Thunder thinks the decision to enlighten Iris about Chohkahn should be made by her mother. In the meantime, the Chief tells the uncle that Howling Wind wanted his word that Viktor will never have any future contact with the man called Ishmael.

"She can put her mind at ease," says William. "*Viktor has just informed me that he has no intention of participating in future productions. He means to cut his ties with the performers, which would include Ishmael. He seems genuinely recommitted to his studies.*"

"That isn't good enough," states Rolling Thunder. "*Howling Wind said to make certain that their paths never cross. Do what you must.*"

———

"What do you mean you don't have the Lakota breastplates and the buffalo hide drums!"

"What do *you* mean you've quit *WAKAN*! We're finalizing the dates for a three night event in March at an arena at the fairgrounds!"

We're like strangers, glaring at each other in awkward silence. There's nothing funny about this scene. My heart's set to explode. Hayden's got a vein bulging from his forehead ready to burst. And it's all because each of us believes a wrong has been committed against him.

Realistically, both of us know that neither would do anything intentionally to upset the other, and we do finally come to our senses. It was simply the immediate shock of the news. For me, it was hearing that many of the personal and priceless Lakota items I had lent him for the show were picked up by Ishmael, who said he would take them back to his place for safekeeping. I've been so busy I overlooked the email about dropping by Mershon to collect them. I just assumed all the props would stay together and I'd get my pieces later.

For Hayden, it was disbelief over my abandoning *WAKAN*. He slumps onto a stool and lowers his face into his hands. We're in his cubbyhole of an office in the dance department. The only other chair is the nice ergonomic one at his desk, and I don't feel right taking it, so I continue to stand in the doorway. There's a large window with a view of the open studio. I watch a few students going through their warm-up routines while I collect my thoughts.

Without looking up, Hayden asks, "Is it because of Camila?"

I'm dumbfounded. "*Nooo*. It *isn't* because of Camila." My cheeks suddenly grow hot from embarrassment. "You do realize I have a full-ride scholarship. There's no way I can keep up the kind of schedule I've had. The rehearsals nearly killed me."

"Can't you take a six month break? You're already far ahead of the game for someone your age."

"It doesn't work that way. It's not like I'm leaving you in the lurch. My understudy, Steven Heartsong, is up to the task."

Hayden groans as he stands. "Yeah, Steven will do...any number of people will do..." he says, planting himself in front of me in a rare power pose with his hands on his hips "...but I'd be accepting mediocrity." He shakes his head. "How is football gonna be different?"

"For one thing, by the time I want to try out, I'll be close to finishing my master's. There are too many classes right now." It hurts to witness the depth of his disappointment. "I'm sorry, Hayden. It was an unbelievable experience, a once in a lifetime experience."

"But, Viktor—it can *be* for a lifetime! You're an incredible performer!"

"I love science, man...love it. It means a lot that you think so highly of my abilities, but I'm happy with the field I've chosen."

He resigns himself to my decision, and then holds out his hand for me to shake. At least we've reached a friendly parting of ways. I feel guilty, but only to a degree. I was after all pursued and roped into doing the show.

This wasn't my life's calling. Now—I just want to go get my stuff back from Ishmael and split before Skyler makes an entrance.

Boy, Hayden's got my number when it comes to Camila, which I hadn't realized. Before heading to Ishmael's place, I need to make a quick stop at the Bio Sciences building. I'm fighting the memory of Camila's legs wrapped tight around me. As exciting as it felt to kiss a sexy woman like her, I hated myself at the same time for taking part in what could only be described as an orgy. I never want to see anyone connected with that night, ever. Thank god my clothes stayed on, unlike the others going at it in the dark. The tender emotions I felt for Camila had been reduced to a vulgar display of lust. I was merely a curiosity to her, no more special than the other guys she has screwed, although, technically, no actual intercourse took place, which I'm relieved about. My breathing picks up as I recall the sensation of the erection in my pants against her pubic bone. I acted like a madman, pumping furiously until I came. The feeling of remorse was immediate.

The decision to end my association with the dance department, which occurred during the drive home, must've been the right thing to do, because I then enjoyed the deepest untroubled sleep that I'd had since before meeting Camila.

Now that I'm in the building, I'm wondering what the Director of the Microbiology Department wants to see me about. I've never met him; I think it's a "him." My stomach's growling. Glancing at the time, it's too late to grab a bite to eat.

Before there's a chance to ask how to correctly pronounce his or her name, a man sees me step off the elevator and invites me into his office. Introductions follow, which include the head of Biophysics, a tall man dressed all in black. He has a goofy, wide grin along with big, soulful puppy-like brown eyes. The Micro Professor's accent sounds Russian. He has tented eyelids with the clearest blue eyes. His nose is straight like a ruler, as are his thin lips. I take a seat, completely clueless about the nature of this meeting.

I listen to a glowing summary of my contribution to science merely for having detected a serious case of plagiarism that led to my receiving the coveted Herrington Scholarship. When the Director finally finishes, the men simply stare at me, friendly-like, not threatening. Okay, I'm thinking, now what? Rewind to his last sentence...if this is my cue to talk, I didn't hear a question.

"So, Viktor..."

The Director gets up, walks around his desk, and then sits on the edge of it so he's facing me. I'd be worried, if it weren't for the fact that these guys are smiling ear-to-ear like they'd just won tenure.

"Dr. Bonnaire is intrigued by the young man who rescued his reputation, so much so that he wants to organize a research team right here at OSU, and he insists that you be a part of it."

Wow—blindsided a second time today. That was over three years ago since I read those articles in high school and uncovered the fraud, which in reality Mr. Reuter and Miss Omara handled after I brought it to their attention. These men, these distinguished cheerful white men, continue to be elated over *my* good fortune—or is it in fact theirs? OSU stands to benefit bigtime if a doctor of Bonnaire's stature chooses to come here. Not wanting to sound ungrateful, I explain that I've already made plans to pursue my studies with Dr. Sharma in virology. Bonnaire's expertise lies in the field of chromosomal anomalies. He's more of an evolutionary biologist. As I recall, his work was fascinating to read because it included anthropological studies. It was way over my head, but I got the gist of it; enough to recognize that the French terminology and sentences completely matched an English version—word for word—a paper that had been published in an OSU departmental newsletter of sorts, in which a doctoral candidate described the exact same theory Bonnaire was working on. In high school, my conversational French was good, but it didn't include much of a science vocabulary, so I began reading things on all kinds of different topics. I politely tell them that I want to stick with cells and how they behave under attack.

"But Viktor..."

And the pitch begins. *Oy Gevalt! Get me outta here!*

The Chair of Biophysics adds his two cents. He tries to convince me how much I stand to learn about methodology from Dr. Bonnaire, that the position would provide a unique opportunity for making international professional contacts; but my brain has moved on. Marnie's warning from ages ago pops into it. What was it she said? Beware that the good folks at Ohio State...are figuring out how my agenda can best serve theirs. It's true that many a doctoral candidate would sell his or her soul to be accepted onto a prestigious research team. The field becomes extremely competitive at that level. Why would a renowned French doctor want an unproven student like me, one without even a master's? Smells fishy to me.

Besides, it's lousy of these guys to lay a guilt trip on me. They say OSU will contribute more money, much more than they already have, to expand medical services and educational programs on the rez...if I sign on. Of course I'd love to see that happen. If I refuse, though, I guess that generous offer goes out the window.

I tell them I'll think about it, but I won't. I like Dr. Sharma. I like the field I'm in. End of story.

Making my way down Neil Avenue, I pass on eating. Ishmael's street is close by. I want only to get my Lakota headdresses and shirts and drums from him. It's doubtful that Hayden called or texted him so soon after I said I was leaving the show. I won't bring it up.

William woke early and saw that Viktor had already left the apartment. Immediately a sinking feeling took hold of him, and presently, at two in the afternoon, the sense of impending doom persists. The first three calls to his nephew had gone unanswered. He resorts to texting. At last. He reads Viktor's message.

Sorry, been busy. Collecting props from show. Home soon.

The uncle stares out the living room window at the gathering gray clouds, menacing clouds that spell trouble. Loretta, his wife, his dead wife, sits weaving at her loom as she does every day in her spot to the left of the window. Viktor had put a standing piano keyboard there after they moved in. He had kept up his piano lessons throughout the years and still liked to play. Without explanation, William set it in a corner that was already taken up with a bookcase, which puzzled Viktor because the open space by the window was perfect. William seeks guidance from Loretta. She agrees with her husband; Viktor must be located—immediately!

Seriously? Not again. I've purposely been avoiding Uncle's calls. There's too much to think about today. I quickly text him back as I round the corner to Ishmael's apartment, which I've been to only once. It's on the left half side of an old brick two-story with its own sectioned-off porch. He might not be home. I almost wish he weren't. We haven't seen each other for a week, not since the party. My finger hesitates before ringing the bell. It's quiet inside, no TV, no music. At the sound of the bell, the neighbor's dog starts barking like crazy. The door swings open, and without so much as a hello, Ishmael heads back to the kitchen, leaving me to let myself in and, I guess, to follow him. He acts as if he expected me, but then…he is in possession of important things that he knows I want back. They're true treasures.

"Finished with classes?"

"Yeah."

"Wanna drink? There's Coke and apple juice. No chocolate milk." He smiles, knowing I could drink jugs of it.

"Water will do." I find a glass in his cupboard and turn on the faucet. He promptly turns it off.

"The water tastes nasty. The city has been working in the streets to fix it. I've got bottled water. Go have a seat. I'll bring it in."

On my way out, I go right past the fridge. As I reach for the handle, he pushes me on towards the living room. "Go." I apparently interrupted him as he was putting away groceries.

The living room doesn't reflect his large personality. He inherited the previous student's used furniture, nothing but odds-and-ends. The loveseat feels lumpy. The one across from it looks the same. There's a big photo book to thumb through. Interesting. *The United Arab Emirates*. Of all places…

Ishmael comes in, sets the water on the table, and then goes to the opposite lopsided couch.

"Is that your idea of a dream vacation?" I ask, removing my jacket.

"Yes. Yes it is."

I was joking, but he seems serious. No matter, I state my purpose: to pick up the Lakota items I had lent Hayden.

"I figured. They're upstairs. I'll help you carry the boxes to your car." He stands.

"I need to call an Uber first."

"You walked?"

"I was just down the street…"

"I'll drive you home."

But I don't want him to. "That's okay. I'll come another day."

I'm thirsty and go to grab a quick swig before leaving, when I hear Uncle's voice in my head ordering me *not to take anything that's been opened!* How stupid—his paranoia is now mine. That red-flag is so ingrained...this is ridiculous. I want a drink; I need one, but the bottle has no cap. Now I'm actually trying to remember if I've ever removed the cap before handing someone a bottle of water. I don't believe so. No one does, or do they? What must Ishmael be thinking, watching me stall like this? My instincts tell me to leave this second.

"Sorry I bothered you. Next time I'll call." Grabbing my jacket, I make my getaway, but not faster than Ishmael can slide between the door and me, pushing my hand from the knob. We're chest to chest, and I'm forced back a step.

Gone is the habitual sarcastic smile. He leans against the door, slouching to one side, his arms behind him. He cocks his head. I'm struck by the full force of his gaze. Without turning, I gauge how quickly I can reach the back door in the kitchen.

"Is this some kinda game?" I try to laugh it off.

"You tell me."

I never saw it before, having taken him for his word that he was twenty-six, but he has lied about his age. I've been around enough grad students at this point to realize this guy's older than they are. I see it in his skin, his neck, the folds of his eyelids, in his power...

He speaks in a measured tone: "A girl must absolutely savor winning the prized emotions of a Rawakota boy." There's a tender tone to his voice, which is creepy. "How do you manage it, Viktor...to hold in your carnal desires? Don't you find the lofty expectations of your culture unreasonable? More than anything you wanted Camila to be the one, didn't you?"

Where is this coming from? Deep down, is he jealous? And what's this about me being Rawakota? Not once during all the planning for *WAKAN* did I mention that part of my background. I always say I'm Lakota. The phone in my coat pocket goes off...Uncle William again, I'm sure.

With lightning speed, he locks an arm about my waist and tries undoing my belt. I struggle to push him off when next I'm punched hard in the middle. It leaves me doubled-over in pain, unable to catch my breath. What follows is a series of unrelenting savage blows that I deliver with the same force dealt me as my survival mode kicks into high gear.

Our wrestling takes us from the center of the room to a wall, to the kitchen...and then back to the front entrance. It's all a blur. There's pain, and more pain. My fists are destroyed. Even as I scramble up the stairs in a clumsy backwards crawl, I realize it's a stupid move, one that leaves me vulnerable. Ishmael leaps and nails me with the full weight of his body. I fight the urge to cry out when the edge of the stair digs into my spine. It's too easy for him to fold an arm behind my back in a Hammerlock. With my elbow ready to crack, I beg him to stop. But he holds firm.

I lay motionless and concentrate on the ceiling, furious with myself for getting trapped. I'm better than this. Ishmael's hot breath keeps blasting across my cheek. No way can I accept what's going down! "If you dare bite my tongue," he warns, speaking against my lips, "there goes your arm."

My right foot is free, the only part of me that is. If I could get enough leverage from pressing it against the wall, I should be able to escape the clutches of this monster. My body's at an awkward angle, kind of sideways. In order to move my arm down, I'll need to push myself toward the top of the staircase. Even though I don't struggle, Ishmael knows not to relax his grip. Anger fuels me. I explode like a bull bucking the damn rider from his back.

It works, for a second. Then we're at it again. The dizzying speed of the blows has us both reeling, to the point that our tangled bodies drop over the banister. As I'm hurled above the couch, I manage a mean kick to his balls. Next thing I'm in a corner with Ishmael on top again, straddling my chest. *Shit!* He's got a chunk of hair and lays into me, striking my head on the floor over and over. I grab something sharp, maybe broken glass, and wave it frantically as I go for an artery. I don't know if I pushed him off, or if he slid off, but I make my break for the front door, only to get tripped up by my jacket on the floor. I kick it outside as I fall and roll off the porch. Hugging it to my chest, I stumble down more steps to the sidewalk where I hobble ape-like on my knuckles. I fear passing out. *Look for a safe spot...a safe spot...* It's hard to see. I'm terrified of going blind.

A distressed William Horse That Walks Backwards charges into the OSU dance class without apology and demands that Hayden tell him when he last saw Viktor. He knew his nephew was coming by to pick up some things.

Seeing how rattled the uncle is unnerves Hayden, who has been around Viktor and William enough times in their apartment to think him an even-tempered individual with a fun sense of humor.

"He probably went to Ishmael's place. He has them."

The answer produces a look of such abject misery that Hayden grabs the man by his arms to hold him upright.

"What can I do? I'll take you over..."

But there's no time, and William flies out the door.

Crouched behind a dumpster, I try hard to find my bearings. The hospital's close...so is the rec center. Since I can remember that, maybe there's no concussion. It's so quiet. My breath fogs the view, what little there is to see with one eye. My fingers don't bend. The thought that my left eyeball might be hanging out of its socket turns my stomach, and I begin to heave, which hurts like hell. Using my elbows against the brick wall, I manage to climb to a half-standing position. I limp through the alley, clutching my jacket close. I land on a different street. No one drives by, and so I shuffle down another alley. I must look a fright. *Somebody, please help.*

Damn it's cold! I made it! The long building has to be the rec center! The sight of it boosts my spirit but my legs don't care, and I plunge flat to the ground. My phone is ringing in my jacket. I hear people around me. A siren grows louder then stops.

While medics go about their business, gently shoving me onto a stretcher and doing whatever they do, someone keeps patting me on the shoulder and telling me it's going to be okay. His voice is familiar to me. Everything's fuzzy, but there's no mistaking Dawg's wild Medusa-dreads. Theo Doggard, "the Dawg." It's been ages. He's with another guy who says he's Jasper...tells me to hang in there, that he'll stay with me until family shows up. *Family*...there's a thought. My eye closes. I'm in good hands. I can drift off.

So much commotion...lots of instructions: careful with the legs, stabilize the neck; give CCs of this and that. I realize I'm inside, and warm. The guy is still there—Jasper. He's standing out of the way next to Uncle. Reality sets in big time. My chest tightens, to the point of suffocating me. I don't take my eye off Uncle, my desperate eye...

Hearing Lakota has a calming effect. Uncle leans in close and repeats my name in our language. The hospital staff work around him. I fixate on his face and listen to his steady voice.

"*Hinhán Ska*, breathe with *lekshila*. Not too deep. In, now out. Again. Good. You have been unconscious for a few hours. X-rays have already been taken and an MRI. Your sight will be fine. You can't see because of the swelling from the hits you took to your forehead and cheek. Nothing is broken except some ribs. Do you understand?"

"*Hua*...yes".

He strokes my cheek with the back of his hand as he gazes intently into my eye. When it seems I've collected myself he adds:

"The doctors are concerned about your kidneys. There's blood in the urine, but they aren't lacerated. You have a catheter right now." He mixes the medical terms with the Lakota.

"Nothing's broken?" I whisper, the first real words I've attempted. "Not my hands?"

"Your bones must be steel. The kindly Spirits acknowledge your good heart and saw fit to protect you."

He knows Ishmael did this. He's always been suspicious of him. "Please don't tell Dad I'm in a hospital."

"He's on his way, Viktor. I'm not your legal guardian, and you are not yet eighteen."

Uncle is asked to move aside so I can be wheeled to a room on an upper floor. Before I can get too upset over Dad coming, the room starts spinning, and then it's lights out.

"Have the police learned anything?" asks Solomon of William. "Was it racial?"

The questions don't stop as the men wait for Solomon's bags to appear on the carousel. William hadn't explained much over the phone, only that Viktor had been found on the street, beaten. The fact that the boy had been pounded almost beyond recognition was deemed unnecessary at the time.

"Solomon, it's the middle of the night and the rain is changing to snow.

It would be best if you come back to our apartment. He'll be sleeping now..."

Solomon cuts him off. "Really? Really, William! If this was your child that's what you would do!"

William is embarrassed for suggesting it; he's simply exhausted. For the past two days he's been at the hospital tormented by guilt for not getting to Viktor sooner. Solomon would have arrived earlier but due to the Thanksgiving holiday weekend, flights had been booked far in advance. He had to be routed through Atlanta then Pittsburg to get to Columbus. He could have driven up from Texas in that amount of time, but it would've been dangerous. He was too upset to be behind the wheel.

Fortunately, the roads are empty and still passable. Upon pulling into the hospital parking garage, Solomon has the door open and a foot out when William quickly shifts to park and grabs him by the arm.

"Sit and listen."

Solomon resents the order and still tries to climb out, but William holds him now with both hands. "Listen to me!"

Solomon's jaw is clenched so tightly he could break teeth. He glares at the man who has been able to sit with his son when he should have been the one here comforting him.

"Viktor will be extremely emotional when he sees you, Solomon, which makes it difficult for him to breathe. It's true that no important bones are broken, but several ribs are. The x-rays show his lungs aren't punctured." He eases up on his grip. "Just don't mention the fight, or that you're going to find who did this. The police have all the information. His appearance is shocking. It wouldn't have served any purpose if I told you just how frightening he looks right before you had to sit on a plane for hours."

Solomon fights back tears. He nods to William.

On the elevator, William says he won't stay. "Call when you're ready to leave."

Hospital floors at three a.m. are the eeriest places. No different than prisons at that hour thinks Solomon. William accompanies him down the corridor, but no farther. He then walks back to the elevator. A nurse confirms that Solomon is family. When he hesitates in front of Viktor's door, she quickly steps over and, with a hand on his back, gently leads him inside.

He thought his own experiences with street fights would prepare him for this scene, not so when it's your own child. He remains standing by the side of the bed, horrified by the damage that was inflicted, yet relieved his son is able to sleep. His handsome, strong son. The nurse scoots a chair behind him, offers a kind smile, and then quietly exits. Solomon has to believe the swelling will go down. The hands are double, no triple, their normal size. And his face is unrecognizable.

He sits and looks at all the monitors. In the background, he can hear the conversations at the nurses' station. Someone is scolded for laughing too loudly. The slow, hypnotic drip of the IV has a therapeutic effect on him, and at last his body relaxes after hours spent in suspense while stuck on planes. This time to himself is good because he can't be looking this sad, this scared, when Viktor wakes up. Constance should be here. The Air Force promises to notify her of her son's hospitalization as soon as communications are up and running again at the base where she's presently stationed in northern India. Solomon tries to put the conversation he had with a commander at Sheppard Air Force Base in Texas out of his mind because it gets his blood boiling. How can the U.S. with all its advanced technologies not have the means to contact one of its own airmen anywhere in the world?

On that tragic day, when William raced out of the Dance Department in a panic, he had continued to try and reach Viktor while enroute to Ishmael's apartment. He had learned where the Indian lived right after meeting him, having had initial misgivings about his character. He intended to keep track of him as best he could, with the help of Officer Latham, his contact from the Council of First Nations, the same OSU policeman who once brought the teen home for breaking curfew, and who had been entrusted to keep tabs on the student's whereabouts. Unfortunately, his duties precluded him from tailing Viktor around the clock, or he, too, could have intervened in time to prevent the grisly confrontation. When a call at last went through, William's relief was short-lived. The individual on the other end told him that the person he was trying to reach, namely Viktor, was being transported to the hospital. The fellow introduced himself as Jasper, and said he was using the phone that he found in Viktor's jacket. At that point, William got hold of Officer Latham and asked if he would go over to Ishmael's place.

While William met the ambulance at the ER and was being apprised of Viktor's condition, Officer Latham went alone to Ishmael's home, intent on apprehending him. Latham had been told the student's real name, and that he was an Arab, not an American Indian. William hadn't offered more details; the story was so complicated. And he would never divulge information about Ishmael's connection to the Rawakota, which wouldn't mean a thing to this local Native policeman anyway. When Officer Latham walked into the apartment and saw the blood-spattered mess, and then encountered Ishmael's imposing frame seated upright in the corner of a couch, he reached for his gun. For a moment, he thought Ishmael was dead. The guy sat motionless with a fixed stare. He stepped with caution, using the other upturned couch as a barrier between them. It was then that those keen vulture eyes locked on his. Latham remained wary of the man's strange calm. A bone poked through his shin, and one would have thought him defeated. And yet Latham believed the sonnuvabitch might have a secret move left in him. Dead snakes can still bite. Ishmael read the officer's thought, and he privately smiled. Latham wasn't rattled. Throughout his long history on the force, he'd witnessed his share of maniacal expressions.

Next, Officer Latham unscrewed a spring loaded pen, removed the slim ink cartridge from its barrel, and then placed a hair-thin wire inside. He took aim for the center of Ishmael's chest and pressed a button on the end that released the wire. It shot out and pierced the skin of its target, going straight to the heart. There was no reaction on Ishmael's part, other than he turned his attention to a book lying on the floor. Its cover showed a swath of smooth golden sand with men riding camels. In the distance, a glistening modern city crowned the horizon. Latham kicked it to the wall. After the misery this character Hammad Bishara caused Viktor, he shouldn't be allowed such a pleasing final picture to ease him into the next world. Latham resisted bashing in the Arab's skull with the end of his gun. But it was already too late; the poison was fast-acting. He called William for further instructions.

Within the hour, two men and two women that Latham didn't know entered the back door. The hoodies and big scarves they wore covered their faces. Hardly a word was spoken. Together they lifted the dead man the few feet to a rug and rolled him up in it. One of two cargo vans stood open in the backyard, ready to receive the bundle. Buckets were filled with water and strong smelling chemicals, which is when Officer Latham was thanked and told he could leave; they had this. Stepping outside, in order to give the surroundings the once-over, he determined that the activity inside the apartment hadn't garnered any suspicion from the neighbors. Most students had already gone home for the long holiday weekend. Besides, people are always moving at the end of the month. A van wouldn't draw any undue attention. Latham had parked his own patrol car blocks away on Neil Avenue. One may wonder how many other dead bodies have routinely been removed and escaped notice.

CHAPTER 18

Great...I'm expendable, thinks Constance to herself. In a manner of speaking, everyone in the service is. The reality, unfortunately, is that certain personnel are at greater risk of getting killed than others, airmen not being among them. Training pilots is expensive. Lieutenant Colonel Howling Wind reached that conclusion shortly after arriving at the military post in the Muslim-majority district of Pulwama in the Kashmir Valley. The U.S. clearly isn't viewed favorably in this part of the world at the moment. Besides the sudden unexpected withdrawal of its troops from the region, American leaders have decided to negotiate with a despised militant group in Pakistan, which the locals believe has its own self-serving agenda that will adversely affect them. Their people's cultural differences involve issues that faraway nations can't relate to. They need to mind their own business. For decades, both Pakistan and India have sought control over this big geographical region that lies to the north on the Indian subcontinent, with China later entering the picture, subjecting the defenseless Kashmiris to untold suffering. Howling Wind presently finds herself in a precarious situation, which she hadn't counted on when she agreed to come here. Following elections back in the States, a new administration has had to make good on its promises to voters by deescalating the war in Asia. Given that the nuclear-armed countries of India and Pakistan are constantly at odds with each other, with meddling China as a neighbor, the U.S. Armed Forces believes it is in the best interest of America and the world that they maintain a strong military presence in the area. Bottom line is they need a reason to reengage its troops, one the public will support. Typically an air strike is ordered in response to a specific heinous atrocity that's been committed by terrorists. Howling Wind's gut tells her that this base is a perfect target, and that the U.S. Army has gotten wind of an attack, and they're going to use it to their advantage rather than prevent it from happening. There will be civilian casualties, including children, a fact that garners tremendous sympathy from folks back home.

Mention the name "Taliban" in the report, and the troops will start pouring in again. Her best chance for survival depends on whether help from Chief Rolling Thunder arrives as promised, if it hasn't already. The trust she places in the Rawakota has never been violated, which is something American service men and women can't necessarily say about their own government that on occasion has invented a crisis or two as a means to further its own ends.

"*Bullshit!*" shouts Howling Wind as she walks the room, looking each man in the eye. "Do you understand? This is bullshit!"

Standing almost six feet tall, the formidable American female officer holds their attention. They're definitely familiar with "bullshit," but why she said it was lost on them. There's no snickering in response to her rant. Perhaps the soldiers recognize the exasperation in her tone. Howling Wind has had it with the level of incompetence she's observed in her short time here. It isn't the soldiers' fault they lack adequate training. Now she realizes why the French and British diplomatic peacekeeping teams that were to have arrived yesterday won't be showing up. They were obviously forewarned of major trouble and decided to play it safe.

With cell towers temporarily down, creating a communication blackout—the perfect ploy for keeping the "operation" under wraps—Howling Wind sets her mind on figuring a way out of this deathtrap. She leans against a window and stares at a fixed point somewhere in the middle of the vast landscape that surrounds the main guard house. No citizen gets beyond the massive iron gate without undergoing a complete search. Grenades and guns are easily hidden under phirans, the loose fitting garments worn by men and women alike that fall to the feet like a gown. Phirans have been outlawed, but that doesn't prevent Kashmiris from wearing their traditional clothing. Double rows of barbed wire fencing go on forever. About a dozen soldiers man the station around the clock. Howling Wind doesn't bother to explain to the interpreter that even without the cell towers, satellites continue to transmit intelligence that the U.S. military collects, in order to plan their next move. She surveys the scene with binoculars. The twenty or so men surrounding her in the room watch in silence. After a couple of days with the Lt. Colonel, they have witnessed a level of professionalism that impresses them. Howling Wind is confident they will do her bidding, once she determines what to do.

Sitting on the edge of the bed, she rubs her eyes and closes them for a moment, afraid of going directly to sleep if she were to lie down for even a minute. Outside Howling Wind's tiny room, the soldiers wait for instructions. They're eager to fight. That's good. The leader who commands this regiment and enjoys the men's deepest respect, Major General Balhami, was to have returned from a meeting in Pakistan's capital city of Islamabad on the day she arrived. This morning, she and the soldiers learned of his fate. Families from a small nearby farming community came here seeking help after members of a radical group forced them at gunpoint into the countryside at night. The people reported seeing dead soldiers and overturned jeeps and trucks along a path that led them to the base. It's presumed the General was a casualty. He played a vital role in maintaining order among the disparate groups that occupy the valley. His death complicates the situation. The rumble of approaching military vehicles alerted the villagers, and they ordered their sons to run to the hills and lay low until a trusted voice came calling for them. Boys are known for getting kidnapped and exploited by extremist groups. The younger the better. They're impressionable and easier to make martyrs to the cause. The parents ask if some soldiers here at the Pulwama post would accompany them to help find their sons.

Constance permits herself a moment to picture her own son. William better have been sure when he told her that Viktor had ended his association with Ishmael. She sighs as she gets up from the bed, wishing she could linger alone with her thoughts, if only for an hour.

The parents will get but two days to locate the boys. Everyone understands the urgency of the situation. Besides having to worry about their children getting kidnapped, Kashmiri families can't trust their teenagers not to run away from home to join ISIS fighters. The youth are angered by the three decade-old conflict in Kashmir, and are readily swayed by the terrorists' politics and fervor. "That could be it," thinks Howling Wind out loud, regarding the reason behind an air strike. The problem is serious enough to warrant outsider interference. With youth membership on the rise, things appear to be getting out of control—high time to eradicate the anti-India rebels. Protesters of the bombings will be pacified when they hear ISIS members were killed. A general will apologize for the casualties, and life will go on.

Not on my watch, thinks Howling Wind. There has to be a way to spot a suicidal terrorist, some behavior that will betray him or her. And what about ensuring the soldiers' survival, if indeed the base gets hit? She jumps when the door suddenly flies wide open. In strolls a tall, battered-looking gentleman, generating all the enthusiasm of a cricket match.

"Smitty! Smitty! Smitty..." shout the men, laughing as they skip over to the fellow who is obviously a dear friend. There's a lot of back-slapping and hand-shaking. The visitor calls out their names and speaks to them in what is assumed to be Kashmiri. In the meantime, there's a crisis looming and Howling Wind's brain is going a mile-a-minute as it works through ways to avert it ... when all at once she finds herself standing almost nose-to-nose with the stranger who's holding out his hand to her.

"Major Howling Wind. Honored to meet you. I'm Nigel Smith, or Smitty, as you've likely gathered."

He has a pleasant voice. Having removed his hood, she inspects the newcomer. His hair and skin and clothes are filthy, but shining through the dirt is a radiant smile, an infectious one that prompts one from her, which is quite reserved by comparison. She shakes his hand, thankfully clean because of the gloves he'd worn. She guesses he's blond, and that his striking blue eyes belong to a face with a fair complexion. He's a pilot; how else would he know of her?

"Are you with the British?" she asks, after correcting him on her rank.

"Yes, and the Norwegians. We're part of the UN's peacekeeping mission."

"You're alone?"

"Sadly, yes."

He takes a seat at the table and pulls a chair out for her. A soldier brings him tea. A cup has thoughtfully been brought for her. Smitty removes his ragged parka then tells her he's going to explain to the men what happened to him. He asks Mahtab to translate for her. Of course he knows Mahtab, too, the civilian schoolteacher who resides on the base. First Howling Wind wants his rank, so she can address him properly.

"I've been "Smitty" in these parts for over a decade. Please, it's just Smitty." He gets comfortable. "Don't worry, I won't call you Connie." The smile never completely disappears; it's like part of his uniform.

This can't be who the Rawakota sent me. She doesn't want to appear rude, but story hour is wasting precious time.

"The truth of the matter is," says Mahtab after Smitty begins, "the

Lockheed C-130J Hercules crashed because of pilot error." His English is flawless. He goes on to tell Howling Wind that Smitty was a crew member on another aircraft that was one of three planes conducting a training exercise for low level penetration. "They were flying at around three hundred feet when the C-130 ran into wake turbulence from the plane Smitty was on, forcing it into a hillside. The debris from its crash flew into them, causing their pilot to lose control and crash, too. Smitty says that Lady Luck smiled on him. His seat was right where the plane broke apart, and he simply rolled out onto the ground, barely clearing the fireball that engulfed the wreckage."

Out of respect for the lives lost, the soldiers are permitted a moment of silence for their comrades, a very brief moment.

"On your way here, Smitty," asks Howling Wind, "did you notice anything that could help us? I'm certain we're going to be rained on with missiles shortly. A group of diplomats never showed up."

"That *is* a bad sign."

Smitty holds a quick conversation with the soldiers, one in which they do most the talking while he nods in response.

"There's been talk in town about an increase in the number of *fedayeen* squads sneaking into other camps and then opening fire. The attacks seem to run in cycles."

She has heard of fedayeen-style suicide attacks...they involve a large quantity of explosives. "Bottom line," says Howling Wind, "we have to be more aggressive during searches, and do them farther away, before people reach the guard house. If anyone seeks asylum within our walls, they must consent to such searches, as will the families when they return from looking for their sons. It's that or they remain on the outside, exposed and vulnerable."

The interpreter shakes his head. Mahtab claims that the modesty of the women is so great they would risk death over the shame of being frisked by a male. Other than Howling Wind, there are no female soldiers for the job. She asks for nurses and is told they're too afraid to do searches.

Howling Wind makes a derogatory sounding tsk noise with her tongue, which Mahtab sees as an insult to the various religions and cultures that exist here. He himself wears the peaked turban of the Sikh minority, which most males have given up. Based on his severe expression, he obviously supports the women's way of thinking. The two stand glaring at each other unflinchingly when Smitty intervenes.

"Colonel...can I just call you that? Lieutenant Colonel is a mouthful. How about we set up a tent for the arrivals where they can open their coats and raise their phirans, in order for us to see if they're carrying weapons? These suicide attacks aren't usually the kind where bombs are strapped to the body. The militant outfits move in numbers that overwhelm the soldiers at the guardhouse. Grenades are thrown from a distance that reach inside the camp. Next, the boys that have been radicalized enter swiftly and start firing the guns they've been given. They accept it's a battle to the death."

Howling Wind is so done with all of them. Gazing out the window again toward the gate, there's an air of militancy she doesn't recognize in herself. Why not simply start shooting at everything, including the birds? She turns to Mahtab. "Tell the soldiers we have as much to fear from America's drones as from the Taliban."

He looks at her questioningly then relays the message.

Smitty makes the connection. "Wireless drones don't need towers. The U.S. can see anyone approaching this camp on foot...and know the precise second an attack occurs. Enter their fighter jets to demolish us all. They get their terrorists, with the added bonus of silencing any witnesses to their attack." He grins, "Killing two birds with one drone."

"That's grounds for arrest," says Howling Wind, dryly. Scanning the faces around her, she asks who the best sharpshooter is. Mahtab and Smitty exchange looks and answer in unison:

"Bandhu."

A buzz of excitement fills the room. The name invokes a call to action, and though Howling Wind worries about the soldiers' combat readiness, their zeal is commendable. She reacts to Smitty's wink with a stone-face, which causes him to flash those bright teeth in an ear-to-ear smile as he chuckles. He hopes she doesn't view it as him mocking her; he really likes her. Perhaps a symbolic gesture might be in order, to show his respect for her, especially in front of these men who for the most part regard themselves superior to women. Smitty stands straight to salute her, and then formally announces himself as Squadron Leader Smith. Next he asks if he may be excused to go eat and get cleaned up. A bewildered Howling Wind manages a quick salute, realizing only after he has left that he did her a big favor.

Mahtab dismisses the soldiers upon her order. They will reconvene in two hours. Howling Wind goes to her room to make plans for a military action that she never dreamed herself doing. She knows her purpose and remains calm, drawing strength from her ancestors' war experiences. Oddly, while strategizing, an image comes to mind of her confronting Hammad Bishara—Ishmael—of her shooting him dead.

CHAPTER 19

It's only a flight of stairs, but I might as well be staring at Mt. Everest.

"You insisted on coming home from the hospital earlier than what the doctor recommended," says Uncle, fully aware of how daunting going up three floors was going to be. I'm the dumb-ass that overlooked this part, wanting so badly to be in my own bed and on my own schedule. "Picture your room." He gingerly places his arm around my waist and holds my elbow with his other hand. I drag one foot up a step, and then the other. If Uncle hadn't borrowed Dr. Nate's high-riding SUV, I'd have stayed stuck in the seat of his car.

"And to think you wanted to be off the pain meds before leaving."

"Yeah, yeah, I know, Uncle...I'm an idiot. You know best. *Leksi always knows best.*"

He grunts back at me. God, how I hate feeling so feeble, and my size makes it worse. Dad was expecting to accompany us today, but there was a fire in his shop, and he had to return to Texas. I hope I can talk him out of coming back. I just want to be left alone.

This is a ridiculously slow process. We haven't even made it to the frickin second floor and the sweat's rolling down my face. My armpits are soaked. Becky and John stick their heads out of their apartment, having heard my pitiful moans. Uncle asks for a stool and a glass of water for me.

While I take a break, sitting there on the landing, which looks really stupid, the three of them discuss the storm due later this afternoon, which makes me glad to have left the hospital when we did. Couldn't travel in a blizzard.

Onward and upward we go. My legs are shaky. Our door is in view. In the excitement my left eye pops open. Uncle sees it and gently hugs me. The sense of relief gives me a second wind.

Once in bed, I don't want to shut my eyes, in case it was a fluke the one opened.

"Thank you, Leksi. Thank you so much." I got used to calling him that in the hospital. Uncle William said I spoke Lakota for a week, even to Dad, which I have no memory of.

"Rest. Let me put another pillow under you."

I hate having to sleep almost upright until my ribs heal. My fingers finally bend enough to make loose fists. That's encouraging. I still won't touch my face or look at myself. The sleet sounds like lead pellets being shot at the window. I can't hold a thought, which is probably a good thing.

"It's eight thirty," says Uncle.

I slept the entire day. He helps me to the bathroom then stands waiting by the door until I'm done peeing. It's hard ignoring the mirror on the way out. *"Holy shit!"* I resist Uncle's effort to pull me along and go on staring at the freak looking back at me. I step closer to inspect the damage and suffer a flashback of the slugfest with a deranged Ishmael. The police said he's nowhere to be found, that he apparently just up and left...leaving his belongings behind. After the way I laid into him, that's hard to believe—unless he really is a supernatural monster.

"How 'bout a bath?"

"Huh?"

"Look...I bought a hand shower with a hose attachment for the faucet."

Uncle pulls back the shower curtain. He sounds proud of himself for thinking of it. He even included a plastic step stool that's in the middle of the tub. I do feel gross. Sponge baths just don't cut it. There's still dried blood under my fingernails, and my hair is so stringy.

"Take a pain pill and get some food in your stomach. You'll be good to go in a half hour."

"Leksi...I appreciate the thought, but you can't do it alone. If you twist your back or fall, I'll feel worse than I already do. I'm nothing but trouble..."

"Stop! We'll take our time."

I'd love to feel clean. I begged Dad to hire a nurse to help me out at home, if only for a week. A big guy named Tim was assigned to me in the hospital. Uncle wouldn't hear of it.

I ate an egg and took a pill, and now we both stand facing the bathtub. We're a sight! Two tall men—me naked, Uncle's in undershorts. It's a job getting me seated. We can't help but start laughing, which hurts my ribs but does the spirit good. I'm covered in bruises. They look black on my dark skin. Uncle holds the sprayer above my head as he tries, without success, to get comfortable on the edge of the tub. There's no room for both of our long legs. As soon as the warm water hits my head and runs down my shoulders and back, I relax. It's beyond wonderful. I worried it might sting at first. Uncle lathers me up but good. If I don't look like Digger! He was a loveable, shaggy haired mutt that wandered into Dad's auto shop one day and never left. Cars that were beyond repair and headed for the junkyard usually leaked oil, and Digger loved rolling in the puddles. To get him clean, Iris and I would dunk him in this huge sink filled with enough suds to cover him completely, like in a cartoon.

After a bit, Uncle says, "We've come full circle; here I am cleaning you up again."

"What do you mean?"

"I was the first person to hold you and wipe you off after you were born."

"Didn't Grandmother deliver me in her house?"

"It's true your mother had you at home, but there was a problem and Loretta called me to help. You were sideways and couldn't come out. Constance refused to go to the hospital for a C-section, which I advised. We had her lie in different positions and even crawl on the floor, which helped, and out you slid into my hands."

"No kidding! That must've been incredibly painful for Mom."

Uncle gently massages my scalp. To think he held me as a newborn. Seems somebody would have informed me of that sooner in life. Now I'm really curious.

"What did you do then? Did Mom hold me right away? Did she want me?"

"Did she *want* you?" He shakes his head like…what a thing to ask, and goes about his work of untangling my matted hair. He'd never suggest cutting it. He then wants to know if I recite the names of my elders when I braid it, a young person's way of showing respect. "Not always," I admit, hoping he appreciates my honesty. "I mean, there are at least a hundred of them. We're no longer hunters and gatherers with loads of free time." That gets no response.

"Does it ever bother you, Uncle," I wonder, "living among outsiders?"

"Don't forget that I lived with them when I went to the University of South Dakota. But yes, I find that too many of them never seem to get enough of what they want, when they already have more than they realize. People's focus on money is worse now than when I was in med school. I can't say, though, that I encountered the best of the Indians' world while I lived on the reservation."

"True." We're finished, but I hesitate standing. Uncle gets behind me, holds his arms out straight under my arm pits to hoist me up, and *voila!* He tosses the stool onto the bathroom floor with his foot, and then guides my legs over the side of the tub.

By now it's almost midnight, and I'm exhausted. I sip tea on the couch while the sheets get changed. There's a big box of get-well cards on the coffee table. They were mailed to the hospital. The first few I open are from fans of *WAKAN*. It's weird to imagine people hearing my name on TV just like I had heard Jake's when he died after diving in the quarry.

The rest of the cards will have to wait. My eyes are sore. Although they remained mostly closed in the hospital, everything I heard is still vivid, especially Skyler's voice. Over and over she sobbed, '*I can't believe it.*' Hayden couldn't console her. It was too emotional for me, so I asked Dad not to allow anyone but family to visit. I didn't want Camila to see my mangled body. Iris must've been given fair warning about my appearance. She was stoic and mostly talked about what life was like on Hashke's tribal land in Wisconsin. I appreciated that.

Once I'm squared away under the covers, I bring up Mom for the umpteenth time this week. How is it possible for her not have learned by now that I was in the hospital? I don't buy the story that she can't be reached. It's never been the case before. What happened to me was damned serious...surely *somebody* has the means to contact her. Uncle swears it's the truth.

Before turning off the light, I have to ask: "Uncle William, did you suspect Ishmael was attracted to me when you first met him?"

He pauses by the door.

"No...regardless, it isn't the kind of attraction you're probably thinking of. Do you remember if your grandfather Pahpie or Sunkwah ever mentioned theeich ihilah when you were growing up?"

"*Theeich ihilah?*" Hmm. This isn't an especially good time for me to be thinking hard about anything. If it relates to the fight...maybe it has to do with proving oneself. "Is it associated with manhood, like when boys are strung up on poles using needles in their chest, and they have to endure the pain until their skin tears and they fall to the ground."

With that, he clearly uses an expletive to convey my stupidity. No translation needed!

"It's difficult to explain," he grumbles. "Sunkwah and Benjamin, your Pahpie, were of an age when it would have been discussed during Otiwota, their traditional celebration for young males, which is nothing like the Indigenous coming-of-age rituals you're referring to that test a boy's stamina. Theeich ihilah is about gaining insight into the very nature of creation. It's about synchronous interactions that spark new life, earthly and heavenly. Sexual intercourse is a component of a couple's ongoing relationship with the universe."

"What..." I almost laugh, "... like the Big Bang?"

He takes a moment. "Think superstring cosmology. It's about perceiving all dimensions."

Aye-yi-yi...is he serious? I have always believed Uncle to be of sound mind, until now.

"The Lakota didn't know squat about physics," I argue, sounding like a wise-ass. "Whatever you are describing, how does Ishmael fit in with this ...this...?" I can't even dream up a word for what theeich ihilah is.

"I'm referring to your Rawakota background, which Winnie and Sunkwah were closely connected to, not your Lakota identity. Your great-grandparents took care of you and influenced you during your formative years. Because of them, you and Iris were taken outside every night to recite a poem to the wakan spirits who reside in the skies. It's a child's introduction to the idea of what theeich ihilah represents. Understanding it is a process that occurs in stages over time. Ishmael knew things about the Rawakota, and in particular this important concept. He assumed you grew up in its culture, based on the color of your eyes."

"You make it sound like the Rawakota tribe exists as a community to this day. The Lakota accepted our ancestors into their circles when they were all forced onto reservations. Did Ishmael belong to a clan that historically hated us?"

"No, Viktor. I don't think it was his plan to actually fight you. He wanted to harm you spiritually. He was a wicked Unktehi, a Trickster. And he was not Iroquois like he said he was."

Before I can ask why he used "was" with Ishmael, who left town according to police reports, and I assume is still alive, I'm ordered to sleep. Man, he's intense.

"When you're back on your feet," he says, as he turns to go, "you will return to the reservation to spend time with your Elders. It's criminal what you don't know at your age."

I'm wondering what good it will do. Uncle lingers by the door. *Now what?*

"Consider this, Viktor. What would you have done if Ishmael had won?"

"Nothing, I'd be dead."

"Not dead," he says. "Think! What was he set on doing to you?"

This is totally awkward and embarrassing. He apologizes for upsetting me and heads out, leaving the door cracked open. Thank you for that! Now I'll never sleep. Staring into the darkness, I've not allowed myself to picture the other outcome. The very idea leaves me nauseous, like when I was trapped on the stairs with that foul breath on my face. If Ishmael *had* succeeded, if he had penetrated me, *I would have wanted to die afterward.* Sounds drastic. Mom didn't kill herself after she was raped, or when she ended up pregnant. It would be humiliating. A girl isn't strong enough to fight back, but a guy? And what if I'd been drugged? Reason tells me it isn't worth dying over, and yet ... shit! Why on earth would my being Rawakota make any difference to Ishmael? And how did Uncle know that, unless I said things while I was out of it those first few days in the hospital. "Yeah, okay, Uncle," I mutter out loud to any spirit listening in, "I'll go see my ninety-year-old great-grandparents like you want. This oughta be good. Ow! Fuck!" Without thinking I took too deep a breath. It feels like a knife in my chest.

My eyes open to a new day, with no memory of dreams. I manage to stand, go pee, and walk to the table for breakfast by myself. I'm wobbly, and I missed the toilet, but still...

We eat in silence. Homemade oatmeal with peaches. Can't complain.

As Uncle reaches for my empty bowl he says, "You put up a good fight, Talking White Owl."

I did. When he returns from the kitchen he asks if I'm ready to cut back on the meds.

"The pain hasn't been bad, until this very second. My forehead just began throbbing."

"Want to try acupuncture?"

"How about tomorrow?"

He hands over a pill and gently rubs my neck muscles before sitting again. He then leans forward and crosses his arms on the table.

"It's absolutely true when I said your mother would be here if she could. I won't allow you to go on thinking that she doesn't care."

He speaks slowly and deliberately and looks grave.

"She has recently gotten involved with more highly classified assignments, which troubles Solomon; but he isn't going to share his concerns with you at a time when you need to concentrate on regaining your health. The last we heard she was on her way to a hotel in northern India. Her orders were changed at the last minute. There's been no word from her for a couple of weeks…and the Air Force isn't helping."

I listen with interest and feel sorry for Dad.

"Going back to what you asked about last night…you took to nursing as soon as you were placed at your mother's breast. Constance kept repeating how beautiful you were. I can see it like yesterday. She cradled you like the most precious thing in all creation and whispered in your ear nonstop. She said it was between her and the snow owl that watched her from outside the window. One might have thought her a bit touched in the head. You brought her great happiness then, as you do now."

I admit I'm warmed by the image of maternal love. As a child I had witnessed this side of Mom. It wasn't often that she got back to the rez, or in later years to our home in Texas, but she had always acted lovingly toward Iris and me, until that day she saw me at the airport after a long absence, and I had undergone that dramatic growth spurt.

Uncle adds, "During those first three months, before your mother left for the Air Force Academy, no one could hold you except for when she slept."

"Our relationship changed when I started looking like Lukas. I saw a picture of him for the first time just a few months before coming here. I can't help it that we're identical. Don't tell me you wouldn't feel hurt if your mom kept you at a distance."

He's quiet, not even a cursory grunt. Finally, he says, "Don't believe for a moment that Lukas is the reason. It's much more complicated." I'm surprised when he takes my hands. He examines them with doctorly interest. When he looks up, it seems he's on the verge of maybe saying something about Lukas, instead he simply advises me to get strong so I can travel to South Dakota. What a letdown. This theeich ihilah business and how it relates to Ishmael does make me curious. Problem is, do I want to be reminded of the incident? It's history and best left forgotten.

CHAPTER 20

"Shoot, now!" orders Lt. Colonel Howling Wind. Without hesitating, Bandhu and fellow sharpshooter Raahil fire at the heads of three girls and two veiled women. From a trench dug a safe distance from the guard house, these females had been under their scrutiny for the past fifteen minutes. The targeted peasant women blended in with the returning group of parents who had left to find their sons and were among the throng of new arrivals seeking aid, hill dwellers whose homes were just destroyed by mudslides following the recent rapid snowmelt. Several guards run to the victims. Howling Wind expects to see a sign indicating that the shootings were warranted.

The deadly decision was not based on any superior technology, only hunches. It required simple old-fashioned observation. Howling Wind enlisted the help of a few local soldiers' moms and grandmas from the city of Pulwama, who gladly volunteered their services. The Kashmiri soldiers agreed to the plan, as long as their dear *ma* and *nani* weren't expected to do battle. Smitty's influence couldn't be underplayed when it came to coaxing the soldiers to do this. Using long range military binoculars, the women were asked to report any suspicious behavior among the steady stream of survivors winding their way toward the base.

The ladies in the trench had remained dutifully focused when suddenly they became excited. Mahtab, the translator, explained that they thought two women in the far-off crowd walked too straight and took steps that were too big. Other families trudged along in tight knit groups, but not those individuals. And though the three girls who accompanied the adults looked like girls, Howling Wind was told to study their headscarves, the way they were tied, and to watch how they ran beside the women, not taking their hands. They didn't act like the other grieving people who'd lost everything, or the happy ones holding their dear sons close to them. While Bandhu and Raahil maintained vigilant surveillance and kept the five in their gun sights, Smitty, Howling Wind, and one of the regiment's leaders used two way radios to communicate with the border guards as they checked each person who came through the gate—a tedious and extremely dangerous process. Particular attention was paid to eyes, to their quickest glances. When Bandhu noticed one of the young girls touching something inside her cloak above the waist, something wide …like perhaps an automatic rifle, Howling Wind didn't wait, nor did she have doubts. A similar experience in Yemen endowed her with confidence.

A wave of a guard's arms signals the all-clear. However, it isn't time to relax just yet. Right now, the displaced families who were marching toward what they believed was safety are still lying on the ground, parents atop children, having dropped at the sound of gunfire. No one had taken off running. At this point, hunger and exhaustion influence their actions. Mahtab listens to the radio and announces that the victims were indeed terrorists. Though they had not worn suicide vests, guns and grenades were found under their clothes. Like previous attacks in the region, the five had planned to open fire as soon as they reached the guardhouse. Lt. Colonel Howling Wind breathes a sigh of relief. The use of deadly force was justified.

"Now the money will really flow into the hands of the terrorist cells," complains Colonel Yadev, the replacement sent here this evening following the confirmed death of the previous commander, the much admired Major General Balhami. He is referring to the impacts from the devastating floods that were caused by the fast melting snow and ice. Smitty and Howling Wind sympathize with him, knowing how easy it is for munitions to get smuggled in during relief efforts—money, too, and food and medical equipment sent from good Samaritans around the world who naively believe it will go toward humanitarian aid when, in reality, most gets siphoned off by military leaders and are given to their own fighters. The U.S. President as well as other European leaders actually addressed the abominable act after recent floods in Turkey, which displaced thousands of citizens. The relief agencies are damned if they do help and damned if they don't.

The new colonel's brusque, loud manner doesn't go over well with the men in this unit. During dinner, Yadev speaks his mind on topics of grave importance that divide the soldiers, men who come from different districts with different cultural ideologies, but who call the Kashmir Valley home. Without any consideration shown to them, Col. Yadev states that the current border disputes which have troubled Kashmir for centuries are to be decided solely by Pakistan and India. "Kashmiri separatists should never be included in the talks."

Smitty fights the urge to roll his eyes after the unconscionable comments and proceeds to tap Howling Wind's boot under the table to grab her attention. They take note of the soldiers exchanging looks with one another that could well be construed as mutinous. A messenger enters the room none too soon to report that the cell towers are operational. Normally there'd be a swell of emotion from the young men who miss having the connection to the outside world; instead, they finish their meals and walk out in tense silence. Yadev follows after them to begin work in his office. He's a wiry man with intriguing green eyes who speaks with passion. Unfortunately, the subject of his rhetoric will only incite violence in this splintered region of northern India.

Mahtab offers a moment's levity when he quips, "Time to get the hell outta Dodge. Isn't that what you say?"

Smitty grins. "You know it, sheriff! No cavalry here to the rescue, that's for sure." As soon as the sentence leaves his mouth, the irony hits him, but it provokes no reaction from Howling Wind. "Speaking of which," he continues, directing his words to her: "Why *would* an American Indian fight for the U.S.?"

Howling Wind takes stock of this Brit with his rather self-effacing charm. Mahtab, oblivious to their conversation, soaks up his bread with the last of his soup and bids them good night. It's time for his evening prayers. The dimly-lit mess hall is empty except for the cooks scurrying to get the kitchen cleaned. The lone aviators sit sizing each other up from across the table. They appear rather amused by the exercise. After several minutes of deliberation, there's no question they are comrades in arms. She is fine with Smitty addressing her by her first name. Constance believes he is one of the operatives the Rawakota sent to get her out of this hell-hole. The blonde hair and blue eyes admittedly threw her off.

Constance pinches the corners of her strained eyes. She's ready to call it a night. As she scoots her chair back, it accidentally bumps into the jawan with KP duty who was coming to collect their trays. The soldier bows to her and displays a bashful smile as though he had been at fault. He then rubs his chin back and forth and mutters something to Smitty in Hindi before walking away.

"Now that was a truly impressive sleight of hand," says Constance about the pack of playing cards left behind on the table. "Did you catch that?"

"I did, although I was expecting it at some point."

Of course, she thinks, he and the jawan are in cahoots with each other. "Where to now?" she asks, seeing that the staff is ready to lock up the building and neither of them has an office. It would be improper for her to have a man in her room or for her to be seen going to his, even if the door remained open.

"The community center?"

They run the short distance, trying to stay warm in the freezing temperature. The place is crowded. They squeeze into a corner where others are drinking and playing cards and board games. Unlike Pakistan, the liquor flows freely in the Kashmir Valley, which baffles Constance.

"The military has easier access to liquor than regular civilians," explains Smitty. "The government promotes the sale of it. Alcoholism is a growing problem among all the Kashmiri peoples. Some believe it's a conspiracy designed to weaken the society. After their long-standing conflicts with China, Pakistan, and the rest of India, the people in this region feel hopeless. Drinking has always served as an escape from one's daily misery. An inebriated population will make it easier for India to finally gain control."

"There's a familiar story," she sighs.

Smitty gets them tea then sits and slides the cards from the pack. It makes sense that he's in charge of the coded deck. He acts like he's dealing them, but stops here and there to show her the numbers, which she scribbles on a notepad as though keeping score. Occasionally she scans the room to see whether they're being observed by anyone in particular. To be sure, Smitty is doing the same. They examine a map he unfolds from his jacket. Depending upon how one looks at it, the coordinates of 34.257° N and 75.412° E, just northeast to their current location in Pulwama, might seem close or far, depending on the season. The site is a campground for pilgrims who make the annual summer trek to worship at the Hindu shrine in the Amarnath Cave, which lies in a glacial valley. Traveling in the Himalayas in winter is a different animal altogether.

Before discussing the mission, Constance asks Smitty to look at the bottom card, always a seven, and one that sometimes carries an additional message. It's news to him, never having been given such instructions. Penciled along its edge is *beeta theek hai*. "Son is fine," he tells her, which means nothing to him. Constance slumps in her chair and closes her eyes. He's grateful to see the hint of a smile, otherwise he'd be worried. She leans into him and hugs his arm, which he has gathered by now is uncharacteristic of her.

"Good news, I take it." He gently squeezes her hand and glides his thumb across the knuckles. "All this time I've ignored the bottom card," he says, still holding the seven of clubs as he watches her with interest. "I wonder what vital intelligence I've missed. Are there any other cryptic messages we need to find...like what we're supposed to do there?"

"I was hoping you'd know," she says, still wearing a look of relief.

Constance lets go of him and sits straight. "My orders were to stay here and coordinate the flight training. I can't just pick up and leave."

"Like hell you can't! Your orders nearly got you blown up along with everyone else in this camp!" He looks around at a roomful of high-spirited, unsuspecting soldiers. "We disrupted a strategic military action. The Americans have cooked up something with the Indian army."

"Are you certain your crash wasn't part of the scheme?"

"More like an accident waiting to happen. Trying to teach these blokes how to fly sophisticated planes is pointless, and that leads to accidents. This isn't the first time a plane has followed too closely behind another. These lads don't get it."

"*They* don't get it?" she chuckles. "Their ineptitude is a boon to defense contractors like Lockheed Martin, Boeing, and Northrop Grumman, the top arms-producers and manufacturers of military aircraft. This is what I now "get", Smitty. The worth of my years of experience as a pilot is the same as that of a two hundred million dollar fighter jet, basically zip. We're both subject to being nothing more than collateral damage. These days, ground troops and airmen merely serve as a front for the cyber warfare being carried out secretly around the globe. When will the military truly be confronted about its outrageous budgets and misguided programs?"

"Indeed, that's the million dollar question. It definitely is a new age."

"The so-called mistakes are occurring with more frequency, and yet the investigations by news media are more superficial. Nothing came of the recent downing of the U.S. Apache helicopter by North Korea. A whole bunch of investors made an obscene amount of money off of the mishap because the chopper had to get replaced." That causes Howling Wind to rethink the reason she was given about coming to this base, which was to learn who is arming Yemen from this part of the world. She believed it was a legitimate concern. No more. She hates that she was used as part of a ruse. She does a double take when Smitty abruptly starts speaking Rawakota:

"We're expected to go to this location…together. ASAP."

"You mean tonight? After the day we've had?"

"No…early tomorrow morning. I overheard that Australian troops are expected to arrive by noon. They shouldn't see us. One of the guards at the gate recorded the shooting on his phone and has likely already sent the video to a major Indian news agency, seeing that we're back online. Of course the soldiers will claim credit for spotting the terrorists, but that's cool. It makes it harder for the U.S. to say that the Kashmiri Army can't tell the difference between militants and your run-of-the-mill peasants, especially if Americans intend to secretly fire upon innocent civilians in the future, simply to spark an uprising. We avoided a tragedy here today, however, some other unit is going to have to pay the price. Sadly, it might be the Aussies. I enlisted in the Royal Air Force in order to fly, not to kill. It's a terrible thing to admit that the adrenaline rush I feel during combat is exhilarating. You and I may hate how profitable war is, but we contribute to the endless nature of it."

"I need to still act the good soldier, Smitty, and complete my assignment in Pulwama. Plus, my job is far from over when it comes to collecting intelligence for the Rawakota."

He mulls over her words while dealing the cards for a game of rummy. "We'll travel to the mountains and find whatever it is we're supposed to find. I don't believe the Rawakota themselves know exactly what's there, or they would've told us. We'll block our cell phone signals so our governments can't trace us. We've got lots of time to come up with a story for you. People disappear from the Kashmir Valley routinely. You'll simply be another casualty… that is, until you surface again."

Their conversation is interrupted by a drunk jawan who calls out from a nearby table, "Smitty…do you not realize you are dead? Dead soldiers are not permitted to drink and have fun anymore here on earth, only in Paradise."

"What are you saying, Sanjeev?"

The man half stands at his table, and shouts to be heard: "News about your plane crash was on the radio. Some terrorist groups took credit for shooting you down. They said there were no survivors, and now the British are going to hit us with more air strikes to show they won't tolerate such immoral behavior."

"Don't worry, Sanjeev, I'll let them know the truth." Smitty shakes his head and laughs a little over the absurdity of it all. "And so it goes…"

"I have to get back in the air," says Constance, with a sense of urgency. "No matter how serious the problems are, they seem petty above the clouds. It's when I feel joy."

"Only then?" Smitty studies her. He had admired her unshakable resolve during the stakeout in the trench. And he enjoyed the intimacy of touching her hand a minute ago. Her light-brown eyes are framed by long straight black lashes that add a touch of melancholy to her expression, a quality that melts his heart. He likes the shape of her mouth and the smell of her breath.

This would be the moment for a kiss. Constance knows with certainty the Englishman won't make a move. As an outsider, he could only be invited into Rawakota society through marriage, and only after having been subjected to the DNA test that showed he possessed the thirty-one genes assuring fidelity to his wife, the test which more specifically indicates who has what is regarded as the most prized heritable trait, namely loyalty.

Constance is curious. "Are you going to mastermind our getaway?"

Putting the cards back, he grins, "You won't have to lift a finger."

"The biggest threat is going to be the weather," she says. "Or do you have power over that, too?"

"Maybe. Get a good night's sleep. I'll pass a note under your door early in the morning with an agenda. I'm familiar with the road leading up to the designated mountain range."

"What about telling the RAF you're alive?"

"Not yet. If I believed it would prevent retaliation, I would. The longer I think about it, the more certain I am that some country is dead-set on bombing this place. I feel sorry for any incoming troops."

On their way out, Lt. Col. Howling Wind bemoans the fact they've been relegated to infantryman and offers the idea of "borrowing" a plane. If the army base weren't on everybody's radar because of recent events, Smitty says he'd be game. The wind has picked up and it's grown colder. Smitty salutes then prances backwards to stay warm, keeping his eye on Constance, his co-conspirator for the next few weeks.

"It'll be fun," he laughs before hightailing it to his bunker.

Constance walks quickly to her quarters, and then hurries out of her uniform to jump under the covers, all the while thinking about what a strange adventure she's agreed to. She wants to call home, to hear the voices of her family, but she can't chance it. For the dreaming hours of the night, she finds comfort in her memories of them.

CHAPTER 21

As long as I don't watch what they're doing, I'm good to go. Uncle warned that he was going to stick me with as many as two hundred needles to help with the inflammation. I'm lying face up and slightly elevated on of all things, an equine surgical table. Next I'm told to picture a favorite place and think positive thoughts. With ear buds in place, I'm floating in a magical space, lost in Jimi Hendrix's huge power chords. Dr. Nate, Uncle's friend, showed me his collection of records from the late sixties and early seventies and recommended ones to download. He was too young to have actually experienced the hippie era, but not his older brothers and sister who converted the family farm, with their parents' approval, to a commune before eventually going their separate ways, leaving the property for him to inherit. Following their lead, he changed his last name from the German Sonnenschein to the more inspired translation, Sunshine. When introduced, I didn't know about the peace and love connection; I thought he was part Indian. I knew an Olivia Sunshine on the rez.

We're in OSU's veterinary department, with permission I assume. Maybe not. The acupuncture stuff is here. I trust Uncle, which means I trust Dr. Nate. He has been doing this to horses, cows, and dogs with good results, and I *am* an animal after all. The treatment I received last spring from the acupuncturist who was Uncle William's instructor improved my bad cold. He had used only a handful of needles. That isn't the case today, but then the damage is from head to toe.

It took a lot of convincing, but I finally persuaded Dad not to come see me again. If he were here, the heartache in his eyes would be a constant reminder of what I look like. He tried so hard to be upbeat in the hospital and mask his worries. Uncle hasn't informed him that the other lead performer in *WAKAN* was responsible for my current state. Considering my size and the fact that I was found in the street, Dad believes there was more than one attacker. My fighting skills have never been underestimated. Frankly, I don't care what Uncle tells him, as long as I never have to discuss it. I just want to wipe the entire episode from memory, starting with the afternoon I first met the dancers on campus at Mirror Lake, to when I sped away from Camila's apartment the night of the party. And though that means erasing a lot of absolutely fantastic experiences, it's the only way I can heal...because they all link to Ishmael.

Hendrix is too cool! Love listening to *All Along the Watchtower*, Sam's favorite song. Poor dead Sam. My skin starts tingling. Haven't felt any needles go in. Suddenly Sam's guitar takes over. I hear him plain as day. It's as if I were inside Lazy Al's Trading Post, but I'm not. I'm soaring high over the Black Hills, above the ponderosa pines, eye to eye with the eagles... *wow.*

My insides feel weird. It's a different scene now, and a different mood. I'm lying beside Mirror Lake. A hissing lizard scurries past me. Un-hee! He's got Jim Morrison's head on him. I'm reminded of a curious Alice resting alongside a riverbank, and of the White Rabbit she followed down a hole. I do likewise and chase after the reptile as he heads through a tunnel to a labyrinth of blood-filled streams. The lizard stops and lets me catch up to it. Sweat oozes from its spiny, shining skin. He stands motionless, eyes blinking, the tantalizing eyes of the Lizard King, who, according to Morrison's lyrics, can do anything. Heady stuff. After her curious adventures, Alice at last awakens in the lap of her sister, who then exclaims, '*What a long sleep you've had*.' Yes! That's just what Iris says to me when I wake up on her lap. Wait! She's up in Wisconsin. But I go on and tell her of my bizarre and fantastic dream, of the compelling creature. She listens to every detail and then insists, just like Alice's sister, that I run in for tea because it's getting late—*because it was truly only a long sleep ... a long, long sleep.* Dreams inside dreams. My head is spinning when I'm nudged awake by Uncle William. That was wild!

Christmas is in a couple of days. Physically I'm better. All the swelling is gone. No permanent scars. Hard to believe. Still can't take a real deep breath. And I have to be careful not to twist wrong. By all appearances, I'm normal. Mentally? Hmm. Weeks have passed and still no word from Mom. Don't care anymore. Still obsessed with the Lizard King. It isn't as easy trying to forget *WAKAN* as I had hoped. Music helps. Dr. Nate's music. I stick with an album for days. Derek and the Dominos and Lynyrd

Skynyrd have been played into the ground. Moving on. Billy Preston's got a catchy tune with a funky beat. Put it on an endless loop. Love the nonsense lyrics. My head bounces, and it goes round in circles, just like the title says. How great is this, relaxing in bed, nothing on the calendar. It's impossible to forget Camila's touch, or the rush I experienced keeping up with Ishmael's powerful stride when we crossed campus, or the fun of dancing with both of them.

I must admit, Uncle William has been extremely tolerant of me and my current break with reality. "Ow!" My eyes open to him pinching my toe. Next, he's clunking around in the closet. I pull the ear buds out and prop myself up on my elbows, puzzled by his actions. He sets my duffel bag beside me, the one used for traveling.

"Pack," he says, matter-of-fact. "You're going to Kansas City to spend the holiday with your family. Your flight leaves early in the morning, an hour after mine."

"But..."

"It will do you good to spend time with your father and be surrounded by his relatives."

"But..."

"The weather is nice. There shouldn't be delays."

"I'm not ready!"

"You're finally able to sleep lying flat. The bruising and cuts have healed. This moping must cease."

"Fuck...I don't wanna go. I'm the one to know when I'm ready, and I'm not! Just leave me alone." I almost get the ear buds back in when Uncle's paw swipes the iPod from my chest. He looms over me and asks me to repeat what I just said.

"I said..." enunciating clearly, "... I fucking don't want to go." So what's he gonna do to me? He doesn't budge. Shit, not another stand-off with him. "Nothing's going to change. I'm not going."

"But you are," he says in that damned controlled voice of his.

I shake my head and laugh a little to signify it ain't happenin'. When I lean over the side of the bed to pick up the iPod from the floor, he beats me to it and doesn't hand it back. Before exiting the room, he once again orders me to pack.

I'm tempted to yell after him *fuck you* a hundred times. I should. Yeah, I should; so I do, but only around five times, and while hurling the bag at the wall. "No one can force me to go!" I flop down on the bed, absolutely craving my music. "Fuck hiiim! Fuck'm, fuck'm, fuck'm! Fuck everyone!"

And fuck it if I don't start bawling...bawling my fuckin' eyes out.

It's odd how a special understanding just kind of creeps into people's relationships when they live together. Right now I'm riding in the car of a cousin who picked me up at the airport with an aunt I hardly know. The two are talking a mile a minute and ignoring me. I size up the changes in the neighborhoods on the way to Grandpa Cyrus and Grandma Junie's house, all the while considering the way Uncle dealt with me.

After crying for what must've been over an hour last night, I drifted off to sleep. Hunger pangs woke me around two. I felt hammered. In the fridge was a wrapped meal from dinner that was ready to be microwaved. I sat watching TV, completely spaced out, scarfing down the meatloaf and mashed potatoes. Next, I dutifully packed my bag for the trip, set the alarm for seven, and then crept under the covers still in my clothes. Uncle and I didn't speak as we got ready. On our way out the door I saw my iPod on the front desk where we keep our keys. I left it, which I'm certain he noticed. We drove to the airport in silence, got breakfast and ate without speaking. His plane left first, so he shook my hand business-like and told me to tell everyone Merry Christmas from him. He held on tight until I said I would. He's never even met Dad's relatives. And then he was gone. While waiting for my departure, I wondered what the hell was going on with me. I'd have smacked a kid mouthing off the way I had, and yet I wasn't inclined to apologize for the tantrum. I was so spent that I went right to sleep on the plane.

We're pulling in the driveway. I have no idea what to expect during this visit. Will I embarrass Dad? I'm beyond embarrassing myself. Overall I feel apathetic about life in general, about school, finding love, and especially Christmas. Why the hell did I come?

"Hello...hi...good to see you, too...yes, it's been a long time... how are you?" I say all the right things while The Doors play in my head. No devices needed; it's magical. I'm under their spell and they help me to survive the unavoidable fuss everyone is making. Dad stands in the kitchen watching, waiting his turn...waiting to greet me alone. When we're toe-to-toe he takes my face in his hands, happy to see there's been no permanent scarring from the beating. Normally I'd have already swept him up in a bear hug, but I remain composed. He can tell things are *different*. He holds my hands flat open and examines my fingers.

"See, I'm good as new." I sound convincing.

Dad draws his lips together tightly and nods. I can barely hear him above the music in my head when he tells me how glad he is that I'm here. He pats my arms and sucks up a sniffle, but he doesn't hug me either. He senses my detachment and it hurts him, so I turn up the volume in my brain. I'm led around to look at the decorations, the tree, meet the new babies and note how the old babies have grown. When I at last settle in a corner with a plate of food, Grandma Junie stops by to ask if this is all too much. I answer with a shrug.

"We're so pleased you decided to come," she says. "Go upstairs and lie down whenever you want." There's no denying that it's comforting to hear her warm familiar voice. Wearing a red velvet blazer and black satin pants, she looks stylish as always. Her big diamond earrings sparkle like crazy. Dad's got her cheekbones and kind smile. "You'll be going to the candlelight service tonight, I hope."

It hadn't occurred to me, even though we've always gone. She reminds me it isn't until ten. Cupping my chin in her hand, she kisses my cheek lightly so her bold holiday lipstick won't smudge. Before returning to the others, she informs me that my favorite cousin will be arriving later. That would be Claire.

Has it been as long as three years, I wonder...no, two at the most since I last saw her. I eat, humming along to Morrison's toe-tapping *Whiskey Bar*, annoyed that another voice is interfering with *my* music. The relatives start singing along with Ole Nat and his roasting chestnuts. *Jesus!* Claire can't come soon enough!

CHAPTER 22

"Guess this'll teach me to volunteer for assignments in the future," proclaims Howling Wind angrily.

"What do you mean?" asks Smitty.

"This...Kashmir." She trails closely behind him as they steer their horses through a narrow pass in a precipitous area, trying to make it to yet another outlying hamlet before nightfall when the bitter cold makes it hard to breathe.

"Are you saying it could have been another officer who got stuck with the regiment at Pulwama?"

She laughs. "Would you believe I actually asked to come here for a well-deserved R & R. My orders changed while en route to a hotel. It's between here and Srinagar."

"So, in actual fact, the military didn't necessarily want to lose one of its ace pilots, specifically the highly regarded Lieutenant Colonel. You were simply in the area...and therefore available?"

His comment strikes a chord with her. "In truth, everyone in the military is available for sacrifice, right? I shouldn't be so arrogant to believe my life is worth more than anybody else's. How would you *not* know my situation...having been sent by the Rawakota to assist me at the base?"

"I was doing nothing other than training. If my plane hadn't crashed, I would have returned to the airfield in Kargil. I only recognized you because of stories I'd heard."

"But the cards? If the jawan in the kitchen was an operative, who was the second one? When I mentioned his sleight of hand, you said you had expected it?"

Smitty reaches over and grabs the reins to stop her horse. Neither had bothered to bring up the subject since embarking from the camp. The assumptions come as a surprise.

"As scouts we're always accounted for," he says. "The Rawakota can detect our location anywhere. I figured when I arrived in Pulwama after leaving the scene of the crash, I'd be informed about my next move. Don't you think that I scrutinized every person I encountered? I had no prior knowledge of the soldier in the kitchen. I wasn't certain you were going to play a role in whatever mission they had in mind for me. But the cards were delivered, with you sitting at the table...so here we are."

As they look at each other, it's obvious they're both mentally reviewing all the faces they've come across, wondering who it was that helped them. A guard at the gate, perhaps? It's true that an agent didn't necessarily have to be in their proximity. Smitty clicks his tongue and the horses move on. Something on the ground ahead obstructs their only way out of the hills. They dismount and step carefully over to it. A hand is visible; the head is not, having been cleanly severed from the torso and presumably taken as a trophy.

"He's been frozen a while," says Smitty as he surveys the scene. "There's no sign of him being dragged here...and yet, it's an odd spot to find someone."

"What do you mean? We're here."

Smitty laughs lightly. "Right."

"And we should be *there*." Constance removes her goggles and points to nearby lights, of which there aren't many, but at least they're electric unlike the oil lamps used at their previous two stays. Smitty tells her that years ago the place served as a barracks for the Indian army, which has since moved its operations to Srinagar. She surmises that the village was this unfortunate soul's destination.

"Or...he was making a run *from* it," says Smitty.

Faraway, a blazing sunset has turned the snow-capped peaks gold and pink. Beneath them, a soft lavender mist obscures the long, formidable mountain range. From this vantage point, their destination looks sublime and inviting. In reality, their northerly trek only leads to a bleaker and more inhospitable landscape. Wearing layers of clothes designed for frigid conditions, the two should stay reasonably warm. This would be the perfect place to load up on provisions and allow the horses to rest.

"When it's dark, I'll chance it," says Smitty. "A friend lives on the farm closest to us. We can sleep in a stall. I'll signal if I feel it's safe."

"If you *feel* it's safe?" Constance realizes he has solid connections, but his choice of words could be more assuring. Tomorrow is supposedly their last day on horseback. They should reach the National Highway leading to Baltal, which is close to the coordinates they'll be investigating, although they still have no clue why. Considering no snow has been forecast, they can flag down a driver who will be happy to transport them for a fee. They had chosen an indirect path when leaving Pulwama, well-traveled mostly by herders with their yaks and goats. There are too many checkpoints on the main roads between Pulwama and Srinagar for them to escape detection, in particular Smitty who is recognized in these parts. In the ten years that he has flown missions in northern India, he claims to have set foot in all of the five hundred plus villages, many of which lie in isolated rocky areas no vehicle can access. Sometimes a rickety improvised bridge is all that hangs across a dangerously deep gorge. His physical appearance is a type not easily forgotten, nor is his broad smile. The corridor they're following has occasionally been used by sleeper cells to operate their drug trade. After many recent arrests, Smitty was optimistic when they headed out that they would benefit from the current slackened security.

Because of her height and strong build, Constance thought about disguising herself as a man for the journey. Women always draw unusual attention. But then there was the problem of whether she should portray herself as a Muslim or Hindu. Since both are at odds with each other in the valley, Smitty suggested they go with the story of them being the pilots they are. If captured and questioned, they would state they were lost on account of a crash. The Indian Army, as well as any NATO units, would be able to verify their identities and let them go. Al Qaeda, the Taliban, and ISIS presented another complication entirely. One learns of their whereabouts by being an astute listener, in town markets, in bars, and in the rice fields. He instructs Constance to heed the whisperings of lowly workers and to observe the emotion in their eyes. "Utter fear has its own quality; it's a dead give-away." Nothing she doesn't already know, he realizes. Whereas he has the advantage of understanding a multitude of dialects, he trusts Howling Wind's ability to smell a rat—literally, an uncanny trait shared by all Rawakota. Creatures, including humans, emit different odors under different conditions, and these Natives with their heightened senses can detect it. When Smitty married into his wife's tribe, he learned that the people's origins dated back to a suborder of species that existed before its branch of the primate family split with what was to eventually become present day humans, a fact contrary to what he knew to be true regarding evolution. Rawakota DNA shows they cannot claim the same human evolutionary ties to chimpanzees as Homo sapiens, whose sense of smell diminished over time. Rawakota can still track sounds as well as scents over great distances, thanks to their long-extinct giant lemur ancestors that once inhabited Madagascar and Africa.

Cloaked in a special tarp made from advanced material, and big enough to include the horse under him, Smitty heads out into the dark open field with confidence. The normal infrared radiation given off by their bodies will elude any of the military's heat searching devices. He should arrive at the farm in about fifteen minutes, and that's without resorting to a full gallop. No need to stress the horse's lungs in this cold.

Constance watches and waits. Her horse stands patiently, indifferent to a similar thermal deflection tent hanging over him. The rock-like corpse on the ground is also draped, just to be on the safe side. Three attack helicopters pass overhead. They don't seem interested in this spot and continue on toward the Himalayas. She thinks about how commonplace the smells and sounds of war have become. Suddenly her left breast tingles twice, indicating it's a go. Without removing her implant, she's able to secure the wafer-thin gadget between her fingers and press it to acknowledge having received his message. Somewhere on his body, Smitty will feel a buzz. The location of subdermal devices is kept secret. The placement is a scout's own personal choice. The signal that was sent was a random one. Any Rawakota spy in the region would also have experienced a vibration. They won't know what it means, but having one's tribesmen nearby is heartening.

The horse delivers her safely. The stall feels wonderfully cozy. She's amused by the goats' curiosity as the animals circle around yet another intruder in their barn this evening. They begin bleating in unison. A loaf of bread and marmalade have been set atop a big bale of hay along with a small battery-operated lamp. Her eyes adjust to the dimly lit surroundings. Smitty helps unload the horse before sitting to eat dinner. The door creaks open, allowing light to enter from the main house a few yards away. The backlit figure moves toward them. His weathered but kind features are revealed when he reaches their makeshift table. He hands them a jug of cider and a bowl filled with chunks of mutton in a gravy. When Smitty pays him, the grateful gentleman bows repeatedly, offering thanks as he steps backwards to the door. The disturbance got the goats going again but they settle down quickly. It's peaceful—no jets, no bombings, not even in the distance.

"It wasn't like this last week," says Smitty. "ISIS stormed through grabbing animals and snatching up girls before continuing on toward the mountains. The body we saw was a distraught brother who begged them to leave his sister. This man's family got a goat stolen; their neighbor was robbed of his horses."

"These stories get old," says Constance. "Nothing changes." After a second she asks, "ISIS? In India? They can't be harboring them."

"I questioned it, too, but that's what the farmer said. They drove in on jeeps, around a dozen of them, aimed their rifles at the villagers and stole what they wanted. The girls they abducted were forced to ride the horses. They headed northeast. I'm guessing they've established a camp in the Himalayas, perhaps the Karakoram Range. If they gain a foothold in Kashmir..." He shakes his head over the grim possibility.

Both contemplate the enormity of this invasion, the global scope of the action. As the leftovers are placed in a satchel for tomorrow's ride, Smitty gently takes his comrade by the arm.

"Constance...I'd like time with my wife now." He looks to the corner behind them, to a stack of straw bales. There's barely enough room for him and Constance to lie beside each other tonight; however, at the moment, he would like to reserve alone time for himself and his carnal thoughts.

"Go ahead, Smitty. The horses could use a brushing."

"Do you desire to be with your husband, too?"

"No. Go on."

The matter-of-fact tone used to convey the yearning for sexual intimacy is typical of Rawakota couples. In Chohkahn, spouses think nothing of meeting up during the day and then returning to work. It's a way of life. Off the reservation among outsiders, scheduling the rendezvous often requires a degree of resourcefulness. And when apart from their partners, like Constance and Smitty are now, vivid imaginations keep the marital bond strong.

Grooming the horse is therapeutic. It evokes good memories. While Constance works the tangles out of the mane, she listens in on Smitty's passionate whisperings about devotion. They are the confidences Rawakota men are noted for, and apparently some Englishmen, too; the kind Lukas had once upon a time crooned in her ear. The words prove

Smitty a tender soul. It's improbable that a Rawakota woman could fall for an outsider if he were unable to express his inner emotions. It's tantamount to a man's overall integrity. She reflects on her own relationship with Solomon. That he would end up having feelings for her was never part of the deal. In exchange for accepting guardianship of her children, he would receive the financial backing needed to open his own auto shop. If Solomon questioned how she could possibly entrust an ex-felon, someone she barely knew, with such an important responsibility, he didn't voice it. She had developed a knack for recognizing trustworthy characters, just like the white owl told her she would, which is when Solomon caught her eye. It was evident to her that he had seen the light and turned his life around. He was, and remains, eternally grateful. But he is also a man who happened to fall in love with his wife, and that quandary will stay on the back burner until Constance decides how to address it, if ever. She's never truly come to terms with the fact that she would have married Lukas if circumstances had been different, and his addiction to alcohol hadn't derailed his life.

As soon as Smitty is still, Constance pulls off her boots and wriggles under the blanket to get comfortable against his back. If she should roll off the bales, it's a short drop to the ground. She lets out a wide yawn as her eyes close. Smitty reaches behind himself to pat her hip. They have fostered a comfortable friendship. Besides the bond they share with the Rawakota, they also belong to a fraternity of elite pilots that claims its own superlative birds-eye-view of the earth, which others on the planet will never know. She taps his hand and then nods off.

Snow showers are the norm in the middle of winter at this altitude, so it seems a good omen for the sun to be shining so brightly when Constance and Smitty set out the next morning to continue their travels up into the mountains, especially since the temperature won't budge above ten degrees for the rest of the day. To show their gratitude to the farmer who helped them, they offer him their horses in return for a ride with his neighbors on their mule-driven cart. They're headed in their direction to visit relatives. The trip from this northern region outside of Srinagar to the valley base camp in Baltal is only forty miles, but it will take almost five hours to reach it. Half an hour after getting dropped off, Smitty and Constance find themselves staring out a window at whiteout conditions from inside a tiny bungalow, one of hundreds built in several rows. The wind screams, shaking the thin walls and tin roof. Fine bits of frozen snow that sound like shards of glass pelt the structure.

"How's that for timing." Smitty looks for rags to stuff along the ledges. "I don't understand why they wouldn't construct shutters for these places. It's still cold in the summer when the people make their pilgrimage."

"Considering that most of the thousands who visit set up flimsy tents, I don't think shutters are a primary concern. These are probably the quarters for those who run tourist packages to the Hindu shrine of Amarnath."

"I feel bad for the couple that brought us," says Smitty. "They'll have to overnight at the big central building and bring their mules inside. It has heat, but it must smell bloody awful. Mostly mail runners and the wretchedly poor from the isolated communities around here travel this road during the winter. They can barely eke out a living. The people take their chances, knowing that when the snow hits they could be stranded for a while. Fortunately, merchants from Srinagar also stop by the building with sacks of flour, wheat, and rice loaded on their ponies."

"True beasts of burden."

"The provisions are meant for the Indian Army which has several outposts along the highway. Their ongoing battles with Pakistani soldiers have become a way of life."

Constance warms her hands over the portable battery heater. Within minutes the small space feels toasty. "Does anyone call you Nigel…Uncle Nigel…son Nigel?"

"Not in ages. How 'bout you? What's your call sign?"

She grumbles something unintelligible.

"C'mon. You don't get out of flight school without one…I can find out." He tries guessing: "Lakota…*Da*kota! I'll pester you till you break." His brain busies itself with possibilities. "Got it! Squaw!"

The merriment in those eyes and his toothy broad grin are disarming. Constance holds his gaze while taking a bite of bread. Chewing slowly, she nonchalantly gives him what he wants.

"Howler," he repeats to himself. "That's good; I like that."

Though they've spent three full days together, the conversations have never turned personal. They've compared aircraft and shared experiences about the Air bases in different countries.

"It's disconcerting being at target level," says Constance, who's used to being in the air.

He regards the comment. "That's how you think of Earth?"

She searches his eyes. "Flying rescue missions in a helicopter, you get close enough to see the look of terror in people's faces all the time. And yet you are able to smile."

"Terror, yes...but then there's relief, and gratitude."

"The recent landslides after the flooding must have been gruesome. Does your wife work for the RAF, too?"

"No, Mina's a nurse with the Red Cross in Kargil." Presuming Constance might be curious for more information, he adds, "We met in Canada. She grew up on the Sioux Valley Dakota reservation in Manitoba."

"The next obvious question is how a British lad met a winyan?"

Smitty is pleased by her interest and the rare, animated expression in her tone. When a smile crosses her face, she's so beautiful. Granted, it's never been that generous of one, but the suggestion of it hints to an underlying disposition that isn't so stern.

"My grandfather had been obsessed with stories about the start-up of America, which of course included tales about the Indians. He passed that interest along to me. His own Scottish and Dutch ancestors had emigrated from Europe to the New World and fought against the British. When I entered the University of Manchester to study engineering, he planted the idea of becoming an exchange student."

"When did you start flying?"

"Mm...that's more involved. Best left for another time."

She can't fathom how his romance with Mina could be less complicated than his chosen career.

Smitty has his own questions. All of Chohkahn stays abreast of the events surrounding Howling Wind's children's lives, mainly because they keep tabs on her life, which he assumes she knows. He wants to ask if she worries that her son will become resentful when he learns how much is riding on the choices he makes; after all, according to this important organization named the Council of First Nations, a group often discussed in Chohkahn, the young man is thought to be a rising star, an Indian who could one day wield enormous influence within his Native community. But he doesn't bring it up, thinking that he might ruin the agreeable vibe between them at the moment.

A cup of tea is shared before turning in. It's only 1900 hours but the plan is to depart early on foot in the dark, regardless of the weather. Half asleep, Constance asks Smitty if his wife likes him with a beard, considering that Rawakota men have dense manes but no body or facial hair. His is quite thick after only a couple days growth. "Hates it," he mumbles. "I have to be clean-shaven," adding a second later, "only my face, though… thank goodness."

Constance conjures up a naked, hairy-chested Solomon and takes pleasure in the image, always has.

Following a sound sleep, they are up for whatever challenges this new day has in store for them. Having veered off the main road almost as soon as they began their hike in the dark, Smitty and Constance continue along a winding canyon, hugging its sides in case of snipers. They're well-protected from the wind, which has lessened considerably. Every so often a big blast rolls through, slapping them hard. As they trudge over the uneven ground, they watch as a massive storm cloud continues to build. It's headed for China. The trailing edge reveals more and more constellations as the cloud moves along, and then all at once a bright half-moon appears. Hours later, the mountains obscure the sun rise, but its golden rays fan out gloriously behind their tops.

Last night's blowing snow didn't stick. As a result, the trek takes less time than expected. By noon they reach their destination. Turning slowly in a circle, they examine the crags with binoculars, waiting for anything unusual to pop out. The panorama overwhelms them.

"The coordinates needed to be more precise," says Constance.

"Maybe it wasn't possible."

She takes deep breaths in every direction, wondering whether a scent might give them a clue. Foregoing the safety of the shadows, she ventures out into the narrow valley. A small stream threads through it. Her sensitive nose does catch a whiff of something: gasoline.

Stepping toward her, Smitty asks, "Don't you think it's from the number of flyovers? This is a battle zone after all."

She shakes her head. "No. It's too strong."

"Really!" It floors him that he can't pick up on the smell.

They lock eyes when suddenly, not all that far away, they hear vehicles. In a flash they skedaddle out of sight.

Peeking between the rocks, they watch as two off-road vehicles zoom out from behind the mountain. Grabbing binoculars, they count six men.

Five are wearing helmets and green camouflage. They have moustaches but no beards and are presumed to be Pakistani. Next to one of the drivers sits a man dressed in black including a black head scarf, typical of an ISIS commander. He has a long dark beard. The vehicles bounce clumsily across the rough plateau to the opposite chain of mountains and disappear.

After waiting a bit, the pilots crawl out from the ledge and head toward the spot the soldiers drove out from, which can't be more than a half mile away. Armed with rifles, they leave behind the rest of the gear. Suddenly a third vehicle blasts around the corner. It goes in another direction. As they near the area, they see an opening. With every step the space grows bigger.

What they encounter staggers the mind. Sitting there on the ground, smack-dab in the middle of two towering canyon walls, is a military helicopter. At first it's believed to be a UH 60 Black Hawk, but Smitty counts five rotor blades instead of four. They're staring at the recently developed Chinese Z-10, which the two have only seen in photos. What an unorthodox proving ground.

There's no crew. It's eerily quiet, not even a light wind blows through the mountain pass. Surveillance drones are suspected, although nothing suspicious is sighted. Smitty and Constance go back to retrieve their supplies. They'll be keeping a close eye over the region for the next few days.

CHAPTER 23

"What an effin ass!" That's what she called me!
    Claire had laid into me but good. I'm back at my apartment and her scolding still smarts. According to her, others wished to do the same but were cutting me some slack after what I'd been through. Once she arrived at Grandma Junie's house, I thought I'd be able to cope better with things, until I walked in on the family viewing a dance number from *WAKAN* on YouTube, with the devil himself taking up the full TV screen. It was Christmas day, right before dinner. When I fled the room, phone in hand, Claire caught me as I tried to find a ride back to Columbus. I relented, having lost our staredown, and ended up spending another couple of nights with the relatives, proof that my petite and charming cousin knows how to stand her ground. And though I was adamant about leaving, Claire was equally determined to spend time with me. She had missed me terribly and feared that we were going to end up strangers. It has never mattered that she's two and a half years older, or that growing up we spent only a couple of weeks in the summer and one week in the spring and over Christmas together; we were tight, and based on this visit, our relationship will never change. I had to ask about her father. Uncle Roy is generally the loudest, most abrasive and judgmental guy in the bunch, definitely not one to leave a subject alone, but this Christmas he sat withdrawn in a corner like me. Claire seemed unbothered. She said past regrets were weighing on him. It was her mom she felt sorry for.
    I like that I'm finally by myself in my own bed, with my iPod. Uncle won't return until the middle of the month. I love campus in January; it's so peaceful. A perfect amount of snow has fallen, just enough to hide the scrawny branches and mudholes. I'm starting to feel good about school again. Getting into the academic swing of things should be easy now that I've gotten the go-ahead to do research with Dr. Sharma, who is currently in India. I plan to visit her lab in the hospital after tomorrow to get acquainted with our rats.

In the meantime, I aim to give my vocal cords a rest. It wasn't my intention to talk with the passengers beside me on the flight back, but the guy in the next seat turned out to be interesting—we never shut up. He's studying astronomy at OSU and was visiting Arizona and New Mexico during winter break to check out the observatories. Our flight was his third and last connecting one to Columbus. Now my voice is hoarse, but not just because of him. Claire and I had stayed awake the previous nights, lost in discussions, which I'm going over word for word right now. They were enlightening. We've both discovered our roots in college, with me wearing braids and feathers and her switching from a smooth shoulder-length hairstyle to a huge poofy afro that dances when she moves. I couldn't keep my hands off it—very retro, according to the family. There are pictures from the 60s of Grandpa Cyrus and Grandma Junie wearing gigantic fros.

I ended up spilling my guts to Claire about all sorts of things which produced a few surprising revelations. Uncle William's name came up first. To be fair, he *has* encouraged my independence, yet he's still right there in the apartment every day where he can observe my comings and goings. Claire understood, saying there was no way she was going to commute to college from home like her parents had wanted. She shares a studio apartment with a girlfriend from high school. Then there was my take on religion. We both agreed that the Christmas Eve candlelight service celebrating the Prince of Peace, marked by the ugliest mass shopping frenzy of the year, is hypocritical beyond belief. Speaking of hypocrisy, I then angrily denounced Mom and Dad's marriage, calling it a joke. *Whoa!* Where had that come from? How could Dad not be seeing another woman when Mom is gone most the time? Claire insisted that doesn't necessarily follow. Hmm. I wonder why I didn't think Mom might be the unfaithful one.

And I confessed that I hated that Iris got married. I was used to our family the way it was. It would never again be just the two of us riding our horses on the rez. I sounded like a whiny child. After the outburst, Claire asked sweetly if I felt better... and I did. One thing I hadn't mentioned was catching Dad alone in the family room after everyone had left. Grandma Junie asked me to go find him for the group shot around the tree in the living room. I stood in the doorway and quietly watched him. He had stopped the video and was staring intently at a close-up of Ishmael whose diabolical expression affected me like some kind of voodoo witchcraft. I immediately retreated. My heart thumped so hard I thought I was going to pass out. Half of me wanted to find a ride back to OSU as fast as possible; the other half convinced me to stay with Claire.

The heat suddenly kicks on and shakes the windows. I'm glad Claire opened up about some stuff that she was dealing with, too, like the degree of resentment her father, my Uncle Roy, has felt toward Dad for most of his life. As I grew older, Dad clued me in on the friction between him and his brother. I couldn't appreciate the depth of the emotion, though. Being kids, adults and their issues didn't concern Claire and me. She only brought it up because she feels like her father is waiting for her to screw up the same way he worried that her two older brothers would. They were constantly reminded as kids not to turn out like their Uncle Solomon.

She explained that since she was little she has had to listen to her father go on about how he'd been stuck with having to bail Dad out of every cursed situation he'd gotten himself into. When Dad joined a gang and did drugs, Grandpa Cyrus and Grandma Junie couldn't bear the disappointment and sent Uncle Roy to the court hearings because he was the oldest. He was responsible for talking to his brother's teachers when Dad was out of juvy on probation. It caused a major rift between her father and his parents, besides making their own family life miserable. When Dad finally started getting his act together, it was her brothers who started messing up, which amounted to nothing more than a few bad grades and smoking a little weed, but it was enough to cause more fights in the house. When Dad came home for a visit with a wife, a pilot no less, and these kids who adored him, it was more than Uncle Roy could take. The year Dad opened his auto repair shop, Uncle Roy had gotten demoted at work. Soon after he got laid off. Claire's oldest brother lost a college basketball scholarship because he couldn't bring his grades up, and her mom had resorted to using anti-anxiety meds to cope, gradually increasing the amount.

It didn't seem possible. I remember Dad saying that Roy had it all, and I guess he did for a while, but then everything turned south. I asked if the relatives tried to help her parents. Claire said that her father's ego prevented him from accepting it. He used to love rubbing their noses in the fact that he earned more than anyone in the family, and that was without the college education his parents had always insisted he get because they placed a high value on it. When management at the railroad companies started cutting back, those without college or trade school degrees were the first out the door. Knowing what I do now, Uncle Roy's behavior did start changing around the time Claire entered middle school. He no longer had that boisterous personality that used to scare us kids. I think of how glum he looked at the dinner table this past week.

The pizza I ordered arrives. God, it smells good. I'm starving. In my head, I'm still with Claire, sitting on the landing at the top of the stairs. We would've sprawled out under the dining room table like we used to as kids, if we could fit...well, she could; she's still tiny. Instead, we had to resort to secretly observing the grown-ups from between the railings.

I turn the TV on. The basketball game doesn't hold my interest but listening to the play-by-plays is familiar and comforting. Claire was first to mention sex. She and her boyfriend decided to have a cooling off period so they could concentrate on school. They wanted to save intercourse for marriage. When she finishes at the community college this spring, she's going to transfer to a small private Christian college. Although her plans are to become a nurse, she wishes she could go on to medical school and be a surgeon, but it's simply too expensive. There has to be a way for her to achieve her dream.

I was focused on her virgin status throughout the rest of my stay... and her boyfriend's. It made my own lack of experience seem kind of normal. They obviously came close to doing it. They'd been dating since their senior year in high school. I said next to nothing on the subject. We went on watching the relatives, wondering what *our* kids and grandkids might make of us in the distant future. Grandma Junie caught sight of us and waved. Her many diamonds flashed brightly, with sparks firing every which way as she walked around. Dad came up the steps and stopped at the top to see things from our vantage point. It amused him. He gave us a wink, kissed Claire on the forehead, and continued to the bathroom.

Claire made it perfectly clear that I have little to complain about. My tuition is taken care of, which would be a godsend to any student. She got on my case about doubting Mom's love for me just because she couldn't get to my bedside immediately following the beating. She was certain that if I had really been close to death in the hospital, Mom would have come, that a woman's maternal instinct kicks in which allows her to sense these things. She actually had me convinced, for all of two minutes. I couldn't bring myself to confiding more about the attack. I know I'm damn lucky that what *could* have happened didn't, and that my eye hadn't gotten gouged out or my back broken. I ended up leaving my grandparents' home in better spirits than when I arrived, even though I'm envious of the fact that Claire has found her special guy. Iris has hers. I desperately want to meet a girl I can be close with. My recovery interrupted the search. What I don't understand is how Claire and her fiancé could agree to a cooling off period. In what world is that possible?

My belly's full and I'm tired. I curl up on the couch and fall asleep, happy knowing the place is all mine.

The guilt is unsettling. I wish there were some kind of penance I could do to get rid of it. Not even a Lakota would understand. There I stood this morning, facing the mirror with scissors in hand, fed up with my hair that I decided to braid today. Another split second and I'd have hacked it off. Anymore it's a hassle. And it wasn't the hospital experience or my recuperation that has made dealing with it a chore. The ritual that accompanies it, the one that Uncle had asked me about, of reciting a greeting to the great-grandparents as well as a slew of their ancestors, went out the window when I started practicing for *WAKAN*. Time, precious time, got ignored. It was a brutally busy period. Most my days began hours before the sun rose and lasted until past midnight. Standing in the bathroom with my braid bunched in my hands, I actually swore out loud at Winnie and Sunkwah, at their stupid-ass old world Rawakota traditions that no one pays attention to anymore. As soon as I said it, I thought for sure lightning would strike me dead. Then I could only keep repeating how sorry I was. I'm going to see them after next month. If my hair was gone, they'd be crushed. They are so proud of their great-grandson and that he takes the time to remember them in his daily life. Ah shit, I feel lousy. To make things worse, the way I treated Dad over the holiday is also eating away at me, the way I distanced myself from him. Can't I once be mouthy and defiant and not bothered by a conscience? This stinks.

It can snow again. The stuff has melted, and the world looks ugly brown. The sky is a hazy dull white, no dot of blue in sight. It isn't very cold. I decide to walk across campus—maybe stop for coffee on High Street. I just left the research department where I met Senthil and

Goundamani, our rats, named by Dr. Sharma after a famous comedy duo in India. They're curious and friendly, and I'm glad we won't be causing them physical pain. My phone goes off. I don't recognize the number and hesitate a second before answering.

"Hey, Viktor... it's Jasper. I was wondering what you're up to?"

"Jasper?"

"Yeah, the dude at the hospital with..."

"Right, I remember now ... and?"

"Like I said...I just wanna see what you're up to. Maybe we can get together, shoot some hoops?"

"Why?" To me, this is weird.

"Why not?"

He's too quick for me. How'd he get my number? There's this foggy memory of my phone ringing when I was lying helpless on the ground by the rec center. I heard this same voice talking to someone, and heard it later at the hospital. The situation reminds me of when Ishmael appeared from out of nowhere and introduced himself. Look where that landed me.

"Sorry," I tell him, "but I'm really busy.

"What are you doing this exact minute?"

"What's it to you?"

He laughs a little. "Seriously, are you on campus?"

"Do you get how this sounds?"

"Yeah, I do. So give me a chance to explain, and then you'll understand..."

"I really have to go," and I hang up. No need for any more crazies in my life. There's the coffee shop. I buy a huge foamy cappuccino and sit along a counter that butts up to a giant window that faces the sidewalk. I'm only a foot away from the people going by. They walk close to the building, in order to steer clear of the slush being slung by tires. A poor dog stops and seems lost. I have to laugh to myself, not over his predicament, but because he's got the same dopey expression as old Tucker, Grandpa Cyrus and Grandma Junie's ancient overfed, bow-legged coonhound that Claire and I used to dress up in a platinum blonde wig we had found in an attic trunk. He never even tried pawing the darn thing off. My phone buzzes. Uncle has sent a text:

Meet with Jasper. Get my car from the airport so you can use it until I get back. Thought you'd be staying longer in Kansas City.

Next my phone rings. It's Jasper. "What the fuck," I answer, keeping my voice down. "Did you really go and tattle on me just now to my uncle!"

"It's your own fault. You left me no choice. Hang up again, and I'll do it again."

"You shittin' me! Leave me alone."

"Sorry, man...not an option. Should I come to your apartment?"

"No!" What in the world is Uncle thinking? I'm so angry at this point I can't think of anything to say. There's silence on Jasper's end. If I hang up, I'm sure Uncle will call next. I tell him he's got fifteen minutes to get here. Apparently, Uncle William thinks Jasper isn't to be distrusted like Ishmael was.

As much as I try not to think about Ishmael, it's impossible not to wonder where he disappeared to, and in the sorry condition he had to have been in. If no one knows, it means he could return.

The dog doesn't take his eyes off me. A couple held out their hand to him to offer help, but he almost backed into the traffic. He looks downright miserable. The barista says it's okay to bring him inside. She hands me a dishtowel to dry him off. He's gray and wiry, some kind of terrier mix. Smallish, around twenty pounds. So glad he trusted me. I bundle him up in my jacket and place him on the counter, which is just wide enough for him. There's no let up to his shaking. I turn him slightly so he can look out the window. Maybe he'll spot his owner and start barking.

I was too far gone at the time to remember this Jasper character, other than his voice. He's got a friendly voice. I wait for about twenty minutes, promising myself to leave in another ten if he doesn't show up. Finally, a Black guy comes in and surveys the room like he's looking for someone, and then he heads over to me. His face breaks into a big smile as he reaches to shake my hand. It's a *what's up bro* thumb-grabbing kind that I hate, at least with strangers, but I go along. It doesn't bother as me as much as I thought it would. He throws his coat over the back of the next chair and taps my arm in a friendly way before heading to the back to buy a drink.

My first impression is positive despite my not wanting it to be. The fact that Uncle is behind this forced relationship bugs me. Lately, he assumes to know what's best for me, and damn if he hasn't been right. I mean...I truly believed nothing would come of going to see Dad and the relatives. If I had managed to escape before Claire came, I could've smugly told him that no miracle took place to fix my ailing spirit. But, because I *had* stayed, and Claire's insights were helpful, the trip was worth it. And now this. Here he comes.

"The girl making coffee told me to give this to you."

He hands over some crispy bacon wrapped in a napkin. I look back and nod to acknowledge her thoughtfulness. Jasper looks puzzled.

"Is she sweet on you...and this is how she shows it?"

I roll my eyes and lean to the side to reveal the dog peeking out of my jacket.

There's a short laugh, and then he straddles the wooden chair so he's facing the inside of the place. It's awkward. With his back to the window and his elbows propped on the counter, he's well into my personal space. When he reaches across me to scratch the dog's ears, I can feel his hot coffee breath on my face. It also smells of caramel. His chest is pressed against my left arm. I can't take it.

"Do you mind..." I tried to sound nice as I wriggled my arm free. Jasper kindly stands to turn around in the chair, and then scoots it over—an entire inch. I push my chair away another foot. The dog's nose sniffs the air. He's a polite eater, patiently waiting for each little bite of bacon that I tear off the strip. When it's gone, he lowers his chin on his front paws and closes his eyes. It's a relief to see his body calm. I tell Jasper about him.

We sip our coffees and watch the cars and people go by. Anytime now, I'm thinking, as I wait to hear his story. He finally looks at me...*inspects* me is more like it...and says:

"It's great to see how well you've healed. I stayed with your uncle in the ER while they ran tests on you."

"Why on earth did you do that?"

"Because he was alone, and he felt terrible over what happened. He acted like it was somehow his fault."

"Still...he's a stranger to you."

"Horse That Walks Backwards isn't a total stranger. I'd seen him before in the locker room, helping out football players with their physical therapy."

"My uncle's on staff?" This is news to me! "Do you play football?"

"Second string...but with so many players graduating this spring, I'm hoping to see the field this fall."

I've been in my own world far too long. Uncle William never mentioned what he's been up to, but then again, I haven't bothered asking him either. I knew he'd gotten his license to practice medicine in Ohio. He got that out of the way as soon as we moved to Columbus. It took around four months for him to get the paperwork squared away, then he had to study to take a test. His plan, I thought, was to apply for a position in OSU's athletic department once I became a walk-on, which is still over a year down the road. Wow. He's actually gotten a job! And with the football team, no less.

"Is he paying you to be some kind of mentor to me?"

"What can I say," he says, "I'm a sucker for helping Indians."

I really don't know what to make of this guy.

"No, Viktor... *he isn't*. God, lighten up. He thought you could use some encouragement when it came to getting back in shape. I stand to benefit, too. If you're going to try out for quarterback next year, like he told me you were aiming to do, we'll be playing together. I'm a wide receiver. It would be an advantage to learn to read each other, right?"

"You're taking my uncle's word on blind faith that I'm Big Ten material?"

"I've seen you in action. Your uncle invited me to the apartment a couple times before you came home to watch some tapes of you in high school. You've got an unbelievable arm. The accuracy of your passing is unreal. To be that good at such a young age ... man! I was, too, I'll have you know."

"Was?"

He sighs and folds his hands under his chin. They're big hands, with long slender fingers. I can't take my eyes off of his perfectly trimmed moustache, and how it connects to a goatee on his chin. The rest of his jaw is clean-shaven. It's too cool. The hair on his head is close-cut the way Dad wears his. Their skin is the same medium shade of brown.

"Ever hear of the University of Mount Union?"

I shake my head no, to which he replies, "Anyone from around here would know you're not from Ohio." He didn't have to sound so cocky.

"The Purple Raiders are the top Division III team in the Ohio Athletic Conference. They gave me a full scholarship, and I had a great freshman year there; but I blew it."

He rests against the back of the chair, knowing full-well that he's grabbed my attention.

"Got my girlfriend from high school pregnant during her senior year

—I was already at college—married her the week after she graduated, before she showed; worked around the clock in the summer back in Chillicothe where I'm from to earn money for the baby; and from that point on just made everybody's life unhappy, because I believed that I had really fucked up my future."

"Had you gone back to Mount Union in the fall?"

"Yeah, but I was trying to make the three hour drive back and forth on the weekends to see her. Then Brenda moved up, but I wanted to party. Hell, Viktor, I was on a winning team…girls didn't care that I was married. They pushed themselves on me, and I loved it."

Seems like there's much more to the story. Gazing out the window, he says he and his wife returned to Chillicothe where he worked at the local hardware store. That had to have been humiliating for him. He then adds that an assistant coach at Mount Union moved on to OSU where he had enough pull to give him another chance with the Buckeyes. He couldn't believe it.

"You still married?" I ask.

He nods yes.

"And you're a father?"

He smiles and seems glad about it. I'm also curious how old he is. He turns twenty-two in April.

"Hmm." I think about his lucky break. "You *must* be fast."

"Damn fast," he answers, without hesitating, "and with good hands…a 4-star athlete." He sits straight and leans into me. "We could make history here…Stillman and White Owl; think Rice and Montana."

I laugh; how could I not? "Like the Buckeyes don't have enough awesome players…there's Billings and Rodriguez…"

"…and they'll be gone after next year."

He's given this a lot of thought, whereas I haven't had football on the brain in what seems like forever.

"Whaddya say?" he asks. "Can we set up a time…feel each other out?"

"I'm in no condition to throw a ball yet."

"We'll start out easy." His hopeful eyes are waiting to hear yes. I suppose if I'd been on speaking terms with Uncle William, he'd have mentioned Jasper before we parted ways over the holiday. He must've witnessed his skills during practices this past season.

Suddenly the window gets slammed hard in front of us. "Un-hee!"

"Holy shit!" We both holler, nearly jumping out of our skins. The dog yelps like his tail's been trapped. With half his body tangled in my jacket, he starts frantically scratching at the glass with his front nails. He darned near flies off the counter. In seconds, the girl outside responsible for this ruckus has charged into the coffee house. I'm trying to contain the squirrely animal that obviously belongs to her, when he leaps into her outstretched arms while she's still several feet away, an impressive trick.

Hugs follow, along with endless thanks accompanied by a kissing frenzy between girl and dog, whose name turns out to be Ozzie. She says he got spooked by the garbage trucks and took off running.

Quietly laughing, Jasper and I sit and try to compose ourselves after the mad scene that sent our hearts racing. I figure I'm comfortable around him. No harm will come from meeting at the rec center later in the week to shoot some hoops and get to know each other better.

I believe we are saying our goodbyes when Jasper tells me to hurry up before rush hour starts, so he can swing by the airport for me to pick up Uncle's car. I'm speechless. Just how chummy are those two!

It was a blast playing one-on-one with Jasper. He has mastered the pump fake. My calf muscles still hurt like hell. I relax by taking long mindless drives in the country that have helped me find my bearings. Uncle's car has been put to good use. One trip led me into Amish territory. I parked on the side of the road and googled them as I watched a long line of buggies hitched to beautiful horses go clippety-clopping through the snow-covered hills. I read that the Amish don't farm as much these days, owning businesses instead that cater to the tourist industry. That's sad. They remind me of my elders and the other Rawakota who try to preserve their identity in their corner of the Buckthorn Reservation.

I've revisited my science journals, at times so lost in ideas that when I finally got my nose out of the books, hours had passed and only then did I notice my hunger pangs. I've called Iris and Grandmother and had great conversations that take me back to the reservation, to the point that I'm really hyped about attending the upcoming powwow in March...and riding Jim. Most important, I apologized to Dad. He hasn't said another word about trying to find the thugs who beat me up.

Dawg has entered my life again. I got reacquainted with him in the gym, mostly because Jasper spars with him in the ring as part of their fitness training routine. He goes by Theo now and has done a remarkable about-face since the days we played basketball together with Jake. He takes school seriously and no longer mumbles his own incomprehensible language. Jake's death, he admits, messed up his head for a while, for the better I'd say. Here was this white dude who had it all—parents who supported him, money, grades, talent, looks—and he died a stupid death at a young age just like some gangbanger from the east side of Columbus, which is where Theo grew up. He realized he was one lucky ass nigga for making it out of his neighborhood alive and getting the chance to play college ball. I do ask him to stop using the n-word when he refers to himself and other Blacks. Why do any of our Black and Native brothers think it's okay to say? I first encountered the word as a child on a visit to Rapid City where Indians were and still are referred to as "prairie niggers" by racist wasichu. It hurt to see it in so much of the graffiti around town.

Without question it's been a transformative period for all of us. Jasper brought up something that made me think of Marnie and her dire warning about people's ulterior motives. "Suppose," he said, "the OSU recruiter who went down to Wichita Falls years ago to watch J.T. Barrett at Rider High School was the same guy who just happened to get wind of this other phenom playing for a charter school league. Problem was, the kid was too young; *but,* he was smart. How 'bout OSU giving him an academic scholarship. Later, the Buckeye football program could select him as a walk on, calling dibs before any other university got a shot at him."

When I told him I doubted anyone would be so farsighted, not to mention manipulative—I like to think I earned the prestigious Herrington Scholarship, no strings attached—he reminded me football is a business, *big* business. Didn't I know, he said, that the NFL and colleges bank on genes getting passed along from star athletes to their newborns, so they keep tabs on them from the time they're born. That was good for a laugh. Jasper told me I was naïve, and I told him he was too gullible. No matter, it's been fun with him and Theo. Uncle returns tomorrow. Today I actually miss him.

CHAPTER 24

"There are no two ways about it," says Smitty, after having weighed the options, "they must be taken out."

Constance agrees. She and Smitty just returned to what they jokingly call their cabana, a deep cave they found close to where they could observe the soldiers' activities. It was a stroke of luck that it had a continuous slow leak seeping from an overhead cranny. The water has formed a pond that conveniently serves their needs. It's only partially frozen over. They had spent four days apart, in order to watch the comings and goings around the chopper from different vantage points. Not once was the aircraft taken out for drills of any kind. The soldiers adhered to a strict schedule, arriving mornings in the dark to begin their work on the helicopter's complex electrical systems and leaving right before the sun sank behind the great mountain ridges. The one group likely goes back to a post at the nearby northern Pakistan border. The ISIS leader and his same entourage head east to their camp. It isn't determined where the third vehicle goes. The soldiers wear the army's distinctive camouflage pattern. They are unmistakably in partnership with Islamic terrorists. It's no secret the Chinese have recently sold these attack helicopters to Pakistan. The craft is specifically designed for high altitudes and low temperatures.

For Smitty, the most disappointing moment of the surveillance took place on the very first day when he witnessed a fellow member of the RAF actually instructing an enemy soldier in the use of the helicopter's instrument panel. There was no mistaking who the man was. Smitty had gotten a good view of the Brit who was in the back seat of the chopper's tandem cockpit where the gunner normally sits. The pilot was in the front seat. Roughly a year ago, a British journalist reported that Group Captain Roger Harrison, member of an Air Task Unit in the Middle East, had been killed. Constance and Smitty however were among the few who knew the facts. Intelligence received at the time by way of General Roundtree, a Rawakota undercover agent who managed to secure a well-earned post within the Pentagon's power elite, revealed Harrison had defected from Great Britain to the Islamic State. Although the British pilot had begun voicing criticisms over a botched operation that he was involved with in Syria called Plan Babel, not even England's counter-terrorism chief believed a military man of Harrison's high moral caliber would become a traitor. The British, fearing more investigations into the failings and cover-ups of Plan Babel, told the press and public that the pilot died a heroic death during an assault against ISIS. Harrison eventually fell off their radar. That will change when Smitty notifies his Commander at Kargil about seeing him, as any soldier was instructed to do by General Roundtree if the missing man deemed a defector was found.

Smitty and Constance warm themselves by the space heater. There's so much to say, but too little energy this evening. They're exhausted. Constance mulls over her own conversations that she had had yesterday, one with Rolling Thunder, and one with her brother-in-law, who relayed the terrible news about Ishmael and Viktor's confrontation. Her son may well be on his road to recovery, but it hurts her to the core that she wasn't by Viktor's side in the hospital. William had sounded so positive in his earlier communication with her when he stated that Ishmael was out of the picture. How could things have changed so abruptly! And right when the cell towers were blown up in Pulwama. She can't allow herself to dwell on the situation back home. Her absence during such a critical time in Viktor's life will undoubtedly exacerbate the lack of love he feels from her, which she is acutely aware of. And what of Solomon? First he had to deal with Viktor, then there was the horrible fire at his shop that William said had injured a worker, add to that the silence from her end. If she could just call him, but it wouldn't be safe. The U.S. Air Force needs to remain in the dark about her present location, and the Rawakota devices can't be used with outsiders. She ordered William to tell Solomon that she is alive and well. The way she sees it, William botched things up; therefore, he can come up with his own reason why he knows she is okay.

The next day, the soldiers follow their usual routine of securing the helicopter with tiedown ropes before driving off as the sun slips out of sight, except that this evening, steely-gray snow clouds obscure the sunset. Winds are kicking up. No blizzard expected, though. Surface snow twirls in columns across the valley and disappears like smoke. Group Captain Harrison stays behind. He answers to a new name: Abdul-Muiz. He's dressed in black and wears an embroidered skullcap. The Englishman's light-brown beard is grown out and reaches the middle of his chest. An Indian soldier in a military-issued white parka, likely an informant, picks him up. Smitty overhears Abdul-Muiz tell the Indian as they climb into the jeep that it's a go for tomorrow's test flight, and that the two missiles are mounted in place. The men then exit this granite hangar and travel north where they disappear from view.

Smitty readies his supplies. At 2200 hours a passing satellite will make it possible for an engineer at Pratt & Whitney Canada, a man familiar with the cutting-edge Z-10 helicopter, to relay instructions about how to manipulate the rotors so they can be controlled and disabled. A main rotor is mounted on the midsection of the fuselage. It produces low vibrations at high speeds. Tampering with it could prove problematic. Likewise, the composite material of the tail rotor blades is indestructible, literally bulletproof. Whatever Smitty does, the helicopter must still be able to ascend successfully to a certain height, if only for a few minutes. He knows it would be easier to dismantle a section on the instrument panel; however, countries have learned ways to booby trap them, incorporating secret hazards within the preflight checklist. If they're activated by anyone trying to steal or meddle with the aircraft, everything blows up in an instant. Anyway, the goal is to extinguish terrorists before the world finds out about the ever-expanding influence of ISIS in Asia, not to smuggle a helicopter. This is expected to look like nothing more than a training mishap...rather like the crash he recently escaped from.

The sound of aircraft carries across the miles. Considering the proximity of the India-Pakistan border, the skies have been unusually quiet for days. At first they're believed to be U.S. Black Hawks. Americans are reportedly in the area bringing aid to flooded villages. Smitty and Constance are at the entrance of their cabana-cave when suddenly three Russian-made MiG-21s whistle by, rattling their bones.

While they wait for the satellite connection, the predicament of the kidnapped girls from the farms they had passed through is discussed. They're surely being held at a camp the vehicles drive off to every day. Not wanting to deal with pregnancies and babies, ISIS members have been known to administer birth control to the females they enslave. Having no means for escape, the girls will endure daily rapes until the men tire of them. Next they'll get sold into the sex slave trade, and the men will grab a new batch of virginal daughters and sisters from the families in these remote parts. General Roundtree described the girls' plight as hopeless. A ghastly truth that's hard to accept. It's now time for Smitty to head out. Constance will keep close watch over her partner. There is no hug, no handshake, only a clear focus on what needs to be done.

Much like it took something so small as a rubber O-ring gasket to cause the Challenger disaster, a few hair-thin wires that Smitty extracted from his embedded implant, and then secured to the rotors, will prove as deadly. When the wires heat up, the resulting spark will touch off an explosion that no one on board the helicopter can survive. Because knowledge of Smitty's implant can't be shared with British or U.S. Intelligence, when the time comes, General Roundtree will offer a complicated explanation to his superiors regarding the ingenious way Squadron Leader Nigel Smith used parts from a generator that he discovered at the mountain site, parts that were composed of specific metals which enabled him to sabotage the Z-10. Since the plan is articulated by Roundtree, an esteemed Defense expert, it won't be questioned. The material is no mystery to U.S. scientists and engineers, they have simply lacked the imagination—so far—to put the chemistry to use in ways the Rawakota have. Smitty's implant will in fact work because it contains two known rare earths, dysprosium, and samarium. That component of the plot has not been fabricated.

It also helps that there really is a generator to later serve as proof. Smitty had observed a few soldiers moving a huge boulder that looked to weigh nothing. Upon later inspection, after everyone had left for the night, he and Constance discovered that the fake boulder hid a massive storage area where fuel barrels, anti-tank missiles, and other weapons were hidden, all things to arm military aircraft with, a development that would validate General Roundtree's statement.

Immediately following the *event,* which took place without a hitch, Squadron Leader Smith and Lt. Colonel Howling Wind are ordered to collect and submit the fingerprints from everything the soldiers have touched. This is a walk in the park compared to the situation in Pulwama. Here the enemy at least stood right in front of their noses.

When Smitty and Howling Wind returned to the India-controlled camp in Kargil where he is currently stationed, they felt invigorated by a sense of triumph. Both pilots were initially detained several hours at a remote building for routine questioning. A bit of fast talking was necessary as to why they had left Pulwama without orders. They used the British defector, Captain Harrison, as their excuse. They said they'd heard rumors among the soldiers about a military operation being carried out in the mountains by an English pilot who had joined up with terrorists. Smitty was familiar with the area and believed it was imperative to move quickly, lest Harrison move on and disappear again. He didn't think it wise to go there alone, and therefore enlisted the help of Lt. Col. Howling Wind. The two were privately commended by the U.S. and the British for interrupting a scheme designed by the enemy to gain a strategic advantage in that part of the globe. There would be no future mention of their heroic exploits. Later, Constance and Smitty asked themselves why the Rawakota sent them there. The tribe had nothing to gain from this type of mission. "Sometimes," said Gen. Roundtree to them in a private conversation, "the Rawakota find opportunities that allow their spies to advance in their respective careers because it helps their own strategists in the long run. It's a means to an end."

The pilots are granted an overdue period of R&R, in which Smitty introduces Howling Wind to his friends at the camp, which is basically everybody. They're naturally overcome with emotion upon seeing their beloved flying ace alive and healthy, having been notified he was killed in a plane crash. Fortunately, his wife, Mina, had received the more positive news covertly when she was out in the field with the Red Cross, but she couldn't divulge it. Constance only now sees Smitty's wife for the first time since he and Mina had remained holed up in a room together until this afternoon. The two are busying themselves in one of several newly erected hospital tents where the large number of injured are starting to get treated. Mina describes the unnerving experience of looking for missing bodies in the decimated villages. Besides the flooding, a series of mild earthquakes had the aid workers wondering if they'd make it out. She admits to Constance that the idea of being buried alive haunts her, to the point of wanting to go back home to Chohkahn...for good. Mina is exactly how Smitty portrayed her, with a serene face and manner. The strong Rawakota accent is a bit of a surprise. Her voice, though, is pleasingly modulated and could pacify the most unruly being. There's no trace of despair. Both women sit on a cot and talk in whispers as they watch the poor displaced souls who have lost family, all belongings, and their age-old homes. It's a gut-wrenching scene, one filled with crying babies and children. Many of the adults stare vacantly into space. The situation defies thought itself. Constance quietly excuses herself to call Viktor.

She had called Solomon within minutes of arriving here in Kargil. It was curious to hear that his take on Viktor's testy disposition over Christmas was similar to William's characterization of him. Instead of being grateful to be alive after the clobbering he took, Viktor seems to be heading down a slippery slope to ruin, displaying a discontentedness with life in general. She guesses he must be angry at himself for his lack of good judgment. She's been there. He's at an age when emotions are puzzling, which makes relationships confusing, whether platonic or romantic. Alas, emotions at any age can turn a person's world upside down. There's been Sunkwah's influence on Viktor, and her own father's, too. Thanks to her marrying Solomon and moving the kids to Texas, neither man got the chance to adequately explain the male Rawakota mindset that was passed on to them by their fathers. Viktor's current disposition can't be attributed to the usual combative teenage behavior that he exhibited during his pre-adolescent phase. At his present age of almost eighteen, a Rawakota boy is considered a man, having experienced *Otiwota* years earlier, the ceremony that would have been attended by all of his male relatives. Afterward, young people are ready for *wakuwa,* the hunt for a mate, not unlike what many societies around the world consider the normal progression of events. When that challenge is met, and man and woman come together in the act of love known as *theeich ihilah,* all is right with the world. Only occasionally does impatience grab hold of a man and impair his judgement to such a degree that it causes him to feel forlorn and doomed to a loveless future—as was the case with Lukas. By age twenty-five, he was overcome with the pain of being alone and found solace in alcohol, having rejected the counsel of his tribal brothers.

Viktor doesn't answer his phone. His mother sighs but won't read much into it. She was glad to learn from William that Viktor intends to visit South Dakota in March and stay a few days with his great-grandparents, the ones who raised him during those first formative years and who were responsible for giving him a Rawakota slant on life. She hadn't given the matter much thought at the time, considering that she lived far away in Colorado where her world revolved around her studies at the Air Force Academy. Sunkwah has to take responsibility for his earlier actions. Viktor needs to understand that he missed out on the camaraderie of his male relatives during adolescence, a period that cements the bonds among the boys that will carry them through life's highpoints and upsets. It should be revealed to him that he has cousins and uncles who are here for him now, in Chohkahn—that the underground city where generations of his forebears lived still exists to this day.

In the meantime, with five days to fill, Constance searches on the computer for a map of Tiger Hill. The tall peak stood out among the mountains when she and Smitty crossed the valley as they were being driven back to the camp by a team of Kargil's soldiers. They were the ones who actually retrieved them from the helicopter site. She superimposes a view of the November sky over a region called the Dras Valley. There they are, the seven visible stars belonging to the constellation Pleiades that she was looking for. This is the known season when those earliest of peoples, whom she is descended from, embarked on their epic journey that eventually landed them on new shores, a journey that began around fifty thousand years ago. They would continue to follow the stars, until they reached the hills in what is present day South Dakota and Wyoming. There they discovered seven openings in the ground, each with tunnels that reached the very center of Mother Earth. The place mirrored the constellation in the same way their ancestral home had, so the story goes. The tribe went by a different name back then, which no one is certain of, and lived in the Americas long before the current estimate of human migration across the Bering Strait, which new research suggests happened between 17,000 to 20,000 years ago.

Next, Constance supers a map of South Dakota over the map of the Dras Valley, lining up their two highest peaks, Black Elk Peak and Tiger Hill. She then searches for a late fall or winter image of Pleiades in the night sky over North American.

A skilled map reader wouldn't guess such similarities exist between two places halfway around the world from each other. To this Native pilot who has the coordinates of the entrances to Chohkahn in the Black Hills committed to memory, and knows the landmark mounds and spires surrounding those specific locales, the odds of finding that they match the distant elevations around Tiger Hill are staggering. Constance feels compelled to act. Forget about waiting for spring, when the present-day holy man of Chohkahn, Sleeping Buffalo, has intended to explore this remote Himalayan topography. By then she'll have been given orders to go somewhere else. No, she has to see this for herself. After all the help she has given the Rawakota over the years, they can't blame her for investigating this mystery. They can track her every move; this isn't a secret excursion. A person at the door intrudes on her thoughts. Three rapid knocks in succession means it's Smitty.

"Want to join us for dinner?"

His smile meets a countenance that is completely preoccupied.

"Are you working on something?"

Constance considers the overlaying images on the screen another few moments, then she stands to leave with him, keeping her excitement to herself. He does gather that she wants to eat.

Compared to other air force bases, Kargil is nothing more than a desolate air strip. It is however in the process of being converted to a full-fledged air base by the Airport Authority of India, which only recently gained control of it. Because of the additional numbers of deployed troops and aid workers who are here to help the victims of the floods, medical and food supplies are stretched to the limits. Everything is being rationed. Constance, Smitty, and Mina regard the small unappetizing blob of nondescript mush on their plates and, without commenting, share a mutual sentiment that they can't leave here soon enough. Rather than engaging in pointless conversation, they pick at the food, mindful every second of the hungry and tired families crowded together in the tents.

At last Constance speaks. "Mina, would it be easy to get an ID that shows I'm with the Red Cross?"

Both Mina and Smitty are taken aback by the request. "Do you want to use your own name?" she asks.

"No, well, maybe...I mean, it makes no difference; whichever way works best."

"If you want to help with the rescues," says Mina, "you would be welcomed with open arms by any of the humanitarian organizations. You don't need a special ID."

Constance smiles slightly over Mina's misunderstanding of her motive. "I simply want to go to Tiger Hill. There are Indian infantry battalions along the route. If I were confronted by a soldier, I'm sure there would be fewer questions if I weren't U.S. military."

"Why the hell would you want to go back?" asks Smitty. "Aren't you relieved we both succeeded in making it through that region undetected and in one piece?"

"I only need to stay along the bottom of the mountains," says Constance. "The highway is getting so much travel now because of supplies being flown in, which must then get transported to the villages affected by the quakes. A Red Cross worker would be an easy cover for me."

"Why!" demands Smitty, sounding angry; but then this request is being made of his wife, and he doesn't want her to get into trouble.

Constance reverts to using Rawakota.

"I trust you both with this information. There's a strong possibility that the origins of the Rawakota can be found beneath Tiger Hill...that Black Elk Peak, as it's now called, was chosen ages ago during our people's migration to the Dakotas because of its similar mirroring trait of the fall night sky. That's what I was looking at when you walked in, Smitty."

She goes on to describe the sighting of the boy with the yellow eyes, and how Sleeping Buffalo expects to visit in the spring and get a sense of the place.

At that, Mina exclaims, "They really take this seriously back home."

"Definitely." Constance is pleased to witness the excitement in her eyes.

Mina tells her that it is mostly the Canadian Red Cross accessing Kargil's air strip. It shouldn't be a problem copying someone's papers, especially since they aren't being used for crossing borders or securing a person's actual identity. No soldier would bother investigating a person's background, especially a woman's, if she isn't deemed suspicious. Smitty finally relaxes. It seems a sound plan. Next thing Constance knows, he's insisting on going along with her. He still has a few days of R&R, too.

Mina watches in amusement as the pilots, hell bent on enjoying another adventure, eye each another. "You two figure it out. I'll do my end, and then I'm returning to Chohkahn." Smitty is in favor of her decision and will go back whenever he gets time off again.

"I bet Chief Rolling Thunder is going to be upset with you," says Smitty, *"and me* when he learns I accompanied you. I ought to wait for my new implant to arrive." He then adds, "It's always useful to have a translator along, right, Colonel?"

"That it is, Squadron Leader Smith."

"It is a dilemma," sighs Constance, "like looking for a needle in a haystack."

Smitty sits beside her on a rock inside the umpteenth cave they have inspected. "I'd say more like the black cat in a coal mine." She laughs, realizing the absurdity of the situation. She turns off the high powered flashlight to see exactly how dark it is. It's black all right. The low beam is good enough for now. They've worked their way through the most twisting tunnel yet, about a quarter mile from a slit in the rock that they barely fit through. The opening of the cave is hidden by a trickle of a waterfall that normally wouldn't exist in the winter because the weather is always freezing cold. From their present position, the path appears to go on forever in a straight line. Constance firmly believed this was going to be the spot. It seemed so much like the main entrance to Chohkahn. There was the waterfall. And Pleiades' brightest star, Alcyone, appeared to be in the same position in the sky.

"This might well have been a foolish venture, Constance, but it *has* been fun. The adrenaline rush alone—from the times we thought we were surely onto a lost civilization—has made the effort worthwhile. You really had me convinced in the last cave, what with the twenty-seven steps before veering left and going six of your arm lengths against a wall." He laughs, shaking his head.

"I guess sending Sleeping Buffalo over to figure out the puzzle is logical. His energy is probably like a divining rod…he'll be walking along when suddenly, oh…here it is."

"Blimey," whispers Smitty, interrupting her. He looks past her left shoulder down a dark tunnel. She follows his eyes. He grips her by the elbow. "There! Did you see that!"

She's inclined to think he's joking, but then she notices a few tiny lights in the distance beyond the throw of the flashlight. And then a number of dots appear to the right. More pop up to the left. They don't flicker and remain steadfastly suspended in the dark. The only noise comes from their own breathing. They dare not move. Smitty forces Constance's thumb off the ring on the flashlight, fearing a sudden strong light could prove deadly for them. They are riveted by the glowing spots, which are slowly moving closer together. It's unnerving. What creature moves stealthily like that... in a cave?

From out of the darkness, upright figures emerge, stopping at the edge of the light beam around fifteen meters away, comparable to a long hallway. The pilots jump to their feet, but make no move for their guns. They stand transfixed at the sight of the brilliant gold eyes. The species has retained its tapetum lucidum, the tissue responsible for reflecting light; something the Rawakota no longer have, nor other humans.

Words fail her. Constance speculates to herself whether these *people* and her own do in fact come from the same ancient bloodline. Smitty is simply blown away by the supernatural elements of the scene. After the initial shock, they count nine sets of eyes staring back at them, staring at the strangers who have invaded their sanctum. Remarkably, there's no sense of impending danger.

CHAPTER 25

The basement isn't nearly as bad as Dr. Sharma makes it out. She keeps apologizing for the small, windowless space, afraid maybe that the claustrophobic feature of the dungeon, as she refers to it, will change my decision to stay with her team. I like it...probably from spending so much time exploring caves in the Black Hills with Daniel when we were young. We loved to sleep in them overnight.

She's relegated to the bowels of the hospital until the expansion of the research floor is completed, which should be the start of summer; and which will have a panoramic birds-eye view of campus. If only the rodents on the rez were as sweet-tempered and clean as our white lab rats, whose cage gets a friendly good-bye tap on my way out. Though she was named after a man, our mamma rat, Senthil, is expecting. I look forward to witnessing the births. It's been ages since I've felt this upbeat, motivated, and strong.

As I walk, my thoughts turn to spring break and my trip back to South Dakota. Even though it's still far off, my schedule is so full, it'll be here before I know it.

"Talking White Owl!" A hollow-sounding voice echoes through the empty hall.

With a foot already inside the elevator, I turn to see a man break into a run to catch me in time. Anxious to leave, I hold the door open, not wanting to miss the ride up.

"I went to the wrong room trying to find you," he says out of breath, and with a French accent.

He follows me into the elevator, attempting a smile while still breathing hard. I don't recognize him, but he looks damned pleased to see me. He offers his hand.

"Charles Bonnaire."

Jesus! My hand stays in his while I stare in shock. The doctor politely asks if we could go somewhere to talk. He promises not to take up much of my time, realizing how he had sprung himself on me. I can hardly say no…he's the reason I'm here at the university. I'll be so pissed if the Dean of Micro told Bonnaire that I would participate in his research project.

We seat ourselves in a quiet corner of the cafeteria. Dr. Bonnaire says he would have preferred to have treated me to a nicer meal at a restaurant.

I imagined he'd be younger. The photos attached to his research articles showed him with a full head of dark hair. There was no beard. It's gotta be traumatic going bald…and gray. His lids droop over the outer corners of his eyes. They're the clearest blue. He stands as tall as my shoulder and is average weight, except for a belly that pulls at the buttons of his corduroy jacket.

Dr. Bonnaire reassures me that he's not on a mission to recruit me. *Hallelujah!* But, he admits, he is here partly on account of me. He studies my eyes much like those old biker dudes once did at that rundown pit stop off the 44 in South Dakota, which is troubling.

"You of course know who Rosalind Franklin is."

There's a chemist's name from out of the blue.

"I'm writing a book that includes her; about what led to her interest in DNA along with thorough descriptions of her experiments."

And? I'm asking myself.

"I traveled to Cambridge to examine her notebooks, which is where her papers are held. The collection includes personal letters to family as well as correspondence with colleagues during her time at King's College in London. A television reporter took note of my visit, which prompted a viewer to contact me regarding a crate of letters she had in her possession. They were from the 1950s and contained bits of information about the esteemed female scientist. This woman's uncle was a graduate student at Cambridge when Franklin was there, and he often spoke with her. He was studying viruses while Franklin was refining x-ray diffraction techniques to be used on DNA. He wrote about Franklin to a friend who was a medical student at Newcastle. The men wrote each other religiously throughout their lives. He reclaimed the friend's saved letters when he died. Because the uncle never made any breakthroughs to attain the level of distinction as some other scientists, he told the family they could burn the pile of letters for all he cared; they would never be of value to anyone. He had gotten his use out of them in his old age, rereading them countless times until the past no longer mattered. He had never married and had no children. Upon his death, this niece asked for them. She and her mother found the contents to be way over their heads, but held on to the box, in case someone, someday, might find them of interest."

While he pauses to sip his coffee, I wait to hear how I fit in the story.

"In one letter, her uncle describes in great detail the Harvard-educated graduate student who came to work specifically with Rosalind Franklin in 1951. They developed a good professional relationship, unlike that of Franklin and another student Wilkins, who went on to fame and glory with Crick and Watson. The uncle wrote that the American is an astute listener, offering meaningful insights into his own experiments. A couple of years later, he wrote his friend that Franklin had once made an off-handed remark about the young man, that he should have been credited for driving the research forward regarding the helical structure of DNA. His ideas proved visionary. But he refused to be acknowledged for his contribution; telling her what mattered most was for him to work in a funded facility. He wanted to take the results back home so he could further his research in the Black Hills of South Dakota—this tall, handsome, yellow-eyed Indian."

"That would be Winter Crow."

"You know of him!" Bonnaire damned near chokes in disbelief.

I want to laugh; laugh at this *Wasichu* who, judging by his tone, can't reckon with his own ignorance. He'll love this: "Winter Crow lived on a ranch close to my grandparents' home. As kids we picked plums and cherries from his yard. I was too little to understand his importance. He worked out of his laboratory near Rapid City. I think he died around eight or ten years ago."

The look on Bonnaire's face is priceless.

"But there's been absolutely no mention of him in publications...ever! And how strange that neither Franklin nor Wilkins had a thing to say about him in the volumes of papers and notebooks left behind...for that matter, by anyone who was in the department during that period. It's downright mystifying."

Bonnaire sounds almost angry. I shrug my shoulders, indifferent to what he's uncovered. What does he expect from me?

"When the cheater was caught who stole my research...thanks to you, Viktor...I learned a bit about your background, in order to help me write a recommendation for the scholarship. A photograph was included. Your eye color was unusual, and I didn't make much of it at the time, thinking it was due to a strong presence of pheomelanin in the iris."

I never thought of that, since it isn't the case. I hear him out.

"During a visit to America in 1956 for a conference, this woman's uncle wrote to his friend that he had met up with Winter Crow and two of his research partners to discuss the nature of their current work. These men were also Indians, and they also had deep yellow-colored eyes, the likes of which he believed didn't exist in any other group of people. That intrigued me. I remembered the picture of you. As a scientist who searches for mutations and the reasons behind their occurrence, I must ask, are there many more of you with this feature on the reservation in South Dakota?"

"Yes, although *many* is open to interpretation." I know he means more than five or ten. It's the answer Bonnaire wants.

He leans back in his seat, laughs a little through his hands, then rubs his eyes as though he were waking from a nap. Next he folds his fingers together on the table like he's praying.

"Dear Talking White Owl…this trait is beyond fascinating. Would you permit me to study your genome?"

"Just because of my eyes?"

"No, not *only* that. You, Winter Crow, and the other scientists don't physically resemble the others on your reservation. I toured the region with a member from the Bureau of Indian Affairs before heading to Rapid City. I wanted to see the facility this man wrote about. When I inquired about the Rawakota, which is what he called the tribe that the scientists belonged to in his letters, the guide waved me off and muttered something under his breath as if it were nonsense."

The degree to which Dr. Bonnaire has put himself out, in order to investigate our people's genetics, shows a resolve that won't lessen. He's committed to his project. Considering his field of study, his curiosity is understandable. For whatever reason, the guide apparently didn't inform him about my family's neck of the woods. I'm not sure I want to join the ranks of our lab rats Goundamani and Senthil by becoming his guinea pig. He might discover something scary, like a mental illness that's going to be my undoing at a young age. Sometimes it feels like that's where things are headed for me. He continues:

"The doctors and technicians I observed at the laboratory were quite tall, the women, too. They're evidently also intelligent. And only the men had yellow eyes—so the females carry the trait, right? And they're all considered Rawakota?"

"Correct."

This could easily turn into a long string of questions. I tell him that I'm leaving town for a while, but that I'll get back to him later with an answer. Out of curiosity, I ask if it's true that he came to OSU for some other reason besides me being here.

"Yes." he says. "I'm helping Dr. Wu in neurology get to the bottom of a disorder with debilitating symptoms that has afflicted generations of families in an isolated area of China. I'll be traveling between Columbus and Paris throughout the year."

I wonder if a trip to Paris might be in the cards if I sign on. We part ways in front of the hospital. I have to catch a shuttle to get home. My brain fast forwards to racing through the snow on Jim, my best and only friend on the rez right now. I'm assuming there'll be snow on the Plains come March...always is.

CHAPTER 26

Smitty and Constance backtrack to the opening of the cave and wait until they clear the waterfall before erupting in joy. The more exuberant Smitty grabs Constance by the waist and spins her around. She can't resist the man's unbridled glee.

"Bloody mind-blowing...incredible..." He abruptly lets go and begins pacing furiously along the edge of a rocky slope, and then stops dead in front of Constance. They stare at each other with a profoundness akin to the instant a skeptic turns believer.

"They're splendidly stunning, or stunningly splendid. Do you think they're saying the same of us?"

Like Smitty, Constance is struck by the fact they're the only people on the planet who have met members of this community on their own turf. Through the ages, this singular clan has managed to remain hidden from the warring tribes above them. What must their overlapping timelines reveal! To think their progeny live on in Chohkahn. *They...them...* what to call them?

Smitty at last wears himself out. "I want to record our observations, so as not to forget a single detail about what they sound like and look like." He sits and pulls out a notepad and pen from his satchel. He checks the hour. There's still plenty of time before a medical team returning to Kargil is expected to pass on the road below. Mina arranged the rendezvous.

"Why not simply talk into your phone?"

"What if it got stolen? Anyone could check the coordinates of our location and wonder who the description is of."

"And if a boulder were to fall on your head at this moment, the notepad would be discovered along with your cell and a person could still put two and two together."

Smitty pretends not to have heard and begins the all-consuming task. "Nine beings...human-like beings...hmm ... *ninety-percent* human."

Constance glances over his shoulder at his first entry. "Make that ninety-five." He mulls over the stat and agrees, changing his number. She was joking. After every sentence he asks that she substantiate his observation, which gets old fast. Yes, she agrees, they appeared to be males...and of different races perhaps. Two had black skin as soft as suede, but their hands and freakishly long fingers felt tough as hardened leather. The faces of the others were creamy white, as best he could tell in the light from the lanterns they carried. Once the group approached and circled them, their spokesman had motioned for Constance to turn off her flashlight. They stood her height. She confirms Smitty's guess of 178cm, or five feet, ten inches.

Mujahzee is the name the leader used to refer to the group, having repeated the word several times with a sweeping arm gesture that took in the other members. For as long as Smitty has been stationed in the region, he'd never heard of such people, not even in the myths of local villages. He had drawn upon his vast knowledge of dialects to see if they, the Mujahzee, might recognize names stemming from Chinese and Indian histories, particularly those associated with Tibetan cultures. They lit up at the mention of the Khro-nasa and Kle. He then used pantomime to act out clues. When he pounded the ground and pointed below to signify the Khro people; they all nodded, seeming to understand. When he next pointed above their heads, they again nodded in affirmation. They next took an enthusiastic stab at pantomime. Back and forth their long fingers fluttered, suggesting the idea of rain coming down. It was a crazy moment, one of shared humanity. Constance was let in on the Himalayan legend. Smitty explained that the Khro-nasa of the Underworld united with the Kle of Earth. Khro-nasa brought with them vegetation and the Kle offered rain. The alliance created a harmonious balance in the world.

"I'm going to call them Khro," says Smitty, "for the sake of simplicity. Mujahzee might be comparable to a name like Sioux, in that it includes many more subtribes." He writes down the story, his face so close to the paper that his nose appears to be doing the writing. The occasional, compulsive three hard taps of the tip of the pen onto the notepad propel his thoughts. "What chatterboxes they turned out to be, huh?"

"How will you describe that?"

He at last looks up and smiles broadly, showing off what surely must be an extra dozen newly sprouted teeth. She can only wonder what the Khro thought of him. Their mouths were tiny by comparison...yet so expressive.

They had thin, straight noses with small busy nostrils that seemed to be perpetually taking in her and Smitty's scent.

"Overall, Constance, do you consider them as attractive a species as I do? What with their oval heads and narrow chins...they possess an inquisitive expression that's absolutely charming."

"Like lemurs."

And for the second time they lock eyes, silently marveling at their unprecedented find.

"Mina, Mina, Mina...my beautiful Mina." Smitty's tight embrace almost causes the pair of eager lovebirds to topple to the ground. Constance hops out of the Red Cross truck behind him and collects their gear. The women shake hands. Constance excuses herself to make some phone calls, allowing Smitty time with his wife. He definitely needs physical activity to squelch the fever pitch of his excitement.

Lt. Colonel Howling Wind's response to their discovery is no less enthusiastic, merely contained. Her brain hasn't quieted for a moment since leaving the cave. The most astounding, or rather confounding, aspect to the experience was the absence of any perceived threat. Not only was it extraordinary; it was not to be believed. Did the Khro have the ability, the technology, to detect a nearby foreign presence? And if they could, how would they know to trust them? They weren't the least curious about the guns she and Smitty had placed on the ground to convey their good intentions. When she used her high-tech smartwatch to project a holographic image of the constellation Pleiades, in order to show how she ascertained the entrance to their hideaway, there were no oohs and aahs over the *magic*. No one tried to poke their hand through the picture floating in the air. They had listened politely...had studied the strangers...and touched their skin and hair. They allowed her and Smitty to inspect them in similar fashion. It was then that the leader spoke the name Mujahzee. His voice was high-pitched, and the syllables ran together, making him hard to understand. Smitty had broken it down, saying it slowly, which made them giggle. Next the leader had pointed to her and said *pte oyate*. It wasn't possible, and a look of bewilderment crossed her face. Pte oyate, he repeated. Constance used her watch again. A life-sized 3-D buffalo suddenly stood before the men. This elicited a sound of astonishment, and they began nodding yes. How could they know the term Buffalo People? No way does an Asian bovine resemble an American bison, yet they recognized the animal, and it had sparked animated discussions among them. Smitty recorded their vocalizations and hoped to make sense of it later. He said their speech incorporates a pattern of rising and falling pitch similar to Mandarin, but it could just as well be a form of Tibetan dialect, and an ancient one at that. For some reason, Hindi was ruled out. He could hardly wait to begin the research and had enlightened her during their ride back about this inhospitable region claimed by both China and India, depending on the century. This was, after all, where early 20TH century European explorers came to search for the secret valley of Shangri-La. Although it was a fictional place dreamt up for a novel, many wished to believe in such a paradise. Perhaps spurring them on were sightings of these beguiling human-like beings in the mountains that seemingly appeared from out of thin air, and disappeared as magically. Constance had listened with interest, impatient herself to see Chief Rolling Thunder and Sleeping Buffalo in person, in order to apprise them of the encounter.

It was a stroke of luck for Constance when she learned earlier today that she'd be reporting for duty at Ellsworth Air Force Base in South Dakota within the week. She curls up on her cot and daydreams about home. Solomon can fly up and meet her on the reservation. They'll be able to spend time with Viktor during his school break. Hopefully Iris and Hashke can join them. How she would welcome having her husband's arms around her this evening, to be able to take pleasure in his confident grip and clever tongue. She closes her eyes and immerses herself in the fantasy, enjoying the strong pelvis pressed against hers, and the clean smell of his aftershave. Amply aroused, she savors the sensation of receiving him inside her.

CHAPTER 27

"What the...!"

White powder explodes from behind my head just as I'm ready to knock on the door. I do an about face...*KAPOW!* My ear gets clipped. Fast as a cornered cockroach, I slap together a snowball and fire back; but Iris is too quick.

"And you wanna be a quarterback!"

"Them's fightin' words, woman!"

"Yeah, yeah...you're all talk."

I leap off the porch and tackle her in a single bound, but not before getting pelted again smack dab on my forehead. It's a blast rolling in the fresh snow. I pack snow inside her coat collar. "Not used to little brother having the upper hand, are you!" Iris screams and laughs and manages to keep grabbing handfuls of the stuff and dumping it on my head, even though I've got her pinned.

Bam! A weight equal to mine lands full force on top of me. Next I'm trying to reach behind to grab whoever's back there, but it's impossible; impossible because it's a case of *Newfies gone wild*. Hank and Zunta pounce on my back like it's a trampoline, kicking up a flurry of snow that covers Iris and me. We hear Grandmother's big laugh. The beasts discover it's more fun to thrash around on the ground, and I can finally slide off Sister. Our eyes connect: it's understood what must be done, except Grandmother's already beaten us to the punch, hurling a snowball from each hand and *bullseye!* She gets us in the guts. Iris and I have perfected dying. We keel over then stand, reeling this way and that, grunting and screeching like bull elks in mating season, holding our bellies to keep the innards from spilling out. The dogs stand at attention with their heads cocked, wondering *what the hell...*

On our way inside, I hug Grandmother and distract her with a kiss while Iris succeeds in shoving snow down her shirt. Unfortunately, this lady commands the dogs and in a flash we're sparring with these happy big lugs, stretched to their full height and dancing around us.

The snow has stopped. Specks of clouds share the night sky with twinkling stars. A shiny three-quarter moon casts a brilliant light over everything. The dogs are curled up close and snug in front of an active fire spitting embers behind the screen, their noses and paws tucked under their chests. Grandmother got picked up by a neighbor to help deliver a baby. Iris and I lay slumped on pillows at opposite ends of the couch, our long legs crossed over each other's. I ask Sister if Claire happened to get in touch with her.

"Claire? Cousin Claire? I haven't seen or heard from her in at least a year...why?"

"Nothin'."

"C'mon...tell me." Her toes poke my thigh.

"I told her over Christmas that I missed you and me doing things together...especially riding. I figured we'd never get times alone now that you're married."

"Aw...you love your big sister."

"I do."

She scoots over and places a hand along the side of my face. "I had to come see with my own eyes that you had healed. You were a sight to behold in the hospital...absolutely frightful. Your recovery is miraculous." She smiles and kisses my cheek. "Do you want to talk about it?"

I shake my head and think to myself, *never!*

She goes back to her corner and for a while we simply look out the picture window and listen to the fire as it pops and crackles.

"Can I just say one thing, Viktor, and then that'll be the end of it."

She interprets my silence as a yes. "Dad was incredibly hurt when you didn't want his help after you were released. In a way, I understand. I don't know how much you recollect while you drifted in and out of consciousness that first week, but we tried our damndest to mask our own horror and pain. Dad was on the verge of a breakdown himself after seeing you. Later, he'd call me three and four times a day from Texas asking whether he should return to Columbus, in spite of you not wanting him there."

I picture his wet eyes at Christmas. "I was a total ass during the holiday, Iris."

"Trust me; I got an earful from him."

I sit upright on the edge of the couch, feeling a sense of shame. It's a relief to realize there's still a scrap of conscience inside this thick skull. On some level, I was aware of the hard-hearted clod I had become, but I had no idea what to do about it, and really hadn't cared.

Iris slides next to me. "Now that you're better, will you take a moment and put yourself in Dad's shoes? Think about it...Uncle William calls him to say you've landed in the hospital but doesn't offer any details. Next, he can't find a flight to take him to you fast enough. When he does arrive, he sees his son beaten beyond recognition. On top of that, he gets a call that there's a fire in his shop in Texas, so he has to go back. If it were only the building, he'd have stayed with you, but one of his employees was badly burned. When he tries to contact Mom about everything going down, she can't be reached, and her commander hadn't heard from her since an attack in a town somewhere in northern India. After all that, he learns that he can't even support his son during his recovery; the job will go to Uncle William. Really, Viktor!"

"I thought there was only *one thing* you were going to say..."

She gets up in a huff and goes to the bathroom, having succeeded in laying a major guilt trip on me. Minutes pass. A mug of hot chocolate is set on the table, sign of a truce. When next she places her arms protectively around my shoulders, all of me yields. She squeezes herself into the corner behind me on my end of the couch and pats the pillow on her lap. I stretch out on my right side to face the fireplace, and rest my head down. She strokes my hair. It's so calming. I hadn't realized to what degree I've longed for gentle feminine comfort.

The dogs bark at the arrival of Grandmother and scramble over each other in their mad dash to the door. "A boy..." she announces, "... a healthy nine pounder."

Iris and I move to the kitchen while Grandmother heats the leftover casserole in the microwave and then back we all go to the living room, back to the fire and the clear winter sky. It's late, almost the new day. Hank and Zunta are mindful of every click of the fork, which their twitching ears and eyebrows follow with precision. They might have begging eyes, but their manners are admirable. They wait patiently for their morsels, and at an acceptable distance from their kindly keeper's feet.

We talk about many things. Pahpie's name comes up, our beloved grandfather. Iris obviously knows a lot more stories than me, being much older when he died. I remember a quieter man. His heart problems began when I was around eight or nine. This would be a good time to ask a question that's been on my mind:

"Grandmother...would you prefer if I called you by another name? Someone overheard a phone conversation between us (that would've been Jasper) and found it strange that I don't call you Grandma or Nanna or our Lakota word unci. He said it sounded impersonal. He also thinks it's silly when I refer to Iris as Sister. Is that so weird?"

Grandmother grins. "After all this time, don't you think I'd have said something? As for using Sister or Brother or Cousin; that's common for here. Don't people call each other bro and sis? I hear it on TV shows ... even cuz, which I think sounds dumb."

I see her point but can't help wondering if she's partial to one of the other names.

"You called me Ganna at first. Hated that. It took you so long to pronounce your letters. But then you discovered *Red Riding Hood*. Pahpie and I had to read it over and over, and you'd repeat the lines with us: 'Oh, Grandmother, what big ears you have...Grandmother, what big eyes you have and large hands, and Grandmother, what a big mouth you have...' "

She lunges at me from her chair, scaring the shit out of me, "...all the better to eat you with!" and then goes for my neck making slurpy noises that still tickle like crazy. She wipes my neck with her sleeve, having dropped the plate to the floor on her way to the couch, then leans back giggling and takes a good look at me.

"I'm quite happy to be Grandmother. Now Mémé...that's another story."

"What!" says Iris. "What's that supposed to mean?"

She sighs: "I guess it's okay to say this, now that you're grown."

The dogs are still at it even though the plate's been licked clean a hundred times over. Grandmother leaves Iris and me hanging while she gets them some treats. I find a small log for the fire. When she returns, Sister and I are cozy in our spots, anxiously waiting for another tale from the past. Grandmother gets comfortable in her recliner, pulling the lever to elevate her feet. That signals the dogs to race in from the kitchen, biscuits in mouths, and settle beside her.

"I hated to hear French," she begins, looking at Iris. "I never knew what you and your mother talked about. You have no idea how frustrating it was. Then when Viktor came along, Constance insisted that you speak only French to him, so he'd learn it. Pahpie and I and your great-grandparents were told to speak Lakota to you kids...not *asked*, as I recall. Eventually, she figured you'd pick up English from the TV and through playing with other children." She shakes her head in a disapproving manner.

"Why'd you agree to it?" asks Iris.

"I thought I was being petty...that maybe I didn't want to go along with the idea out of jealousy. On the one hand, it seemed a good plan."

"Whoa...hold on a sec," I interrupt, confused, "please explain why Iris was speaking French in the first place...and how Mom became fluent in it?" It's been second nature to us, so I never questioned the why of it. "And Grandmother, what were you jealous of?"

"When your mom took off with Lukas and dropped out of sight, only to end up running away from him later and back home to us, she was embarrassed. She stayed in her room, terrified she had gotten pregnant. With her worst fear realized, she was inconsolable. She couldn't forgive her own stupidity in the matter. She hadn't heeded the warnings about how young she was, or the age difference...anyway; she jumped at the offer made by a couple to stay with them in their home in Canada until the baby was born. Victor and Marie Lejeune were Quakers who visited the reservation several months out of the year to educate the children. They were French, but they had learned Lakota. They told us they'd help Constance get caught up with her schooling. It hurt us that our daughter didn't want to stay with family during the pregnancy, but Pahpie and I stood by her decision. She would have felt ashamed being seen here once she started to show. We visited her up north and managed to talk her into giving birth on the reservation. We hadn't counted on her wanting to go back to live with the Lejeune couple again, and with our granddaughter no less! I don't want to speak ill of your mom, Iris, but it left a hole in our hearts when she left with you."

"I had no idea," says Iris.

Sister barely remembers the French husband and wife. Being a child, there was no thought given to which language she was speaking. It was so easy for her to switch between them. "That was inexcusable for Mom to do." I agree with Iris.

"Mémé grew on me," says Grandmother. "For some reason, that stuck instead of Unci."

Iris grins. "Since we call great-grandmother Winnie for Winona, we should call you Vicki or Tori."

"Absolutely not! Just keep saying what you've been. I'm past the point of my hairs standing on end when I hear it."

This is one of the few times that Lukas's name has come up, and it raises a question.

"What did you and Pahpie first think of Lukas?" I wonder if she'll admit I'm a dead ringer for him.

She starts rubbing a thumb hard over her folded hands, nervous-like. "*What's to say?* It was so long ago. He was a good worker...strong. He likely would have ignored Constance if she hadn't always pestered him. I was in the clinic during the week, and your grandfather was in the fields. My parents stayed at the house to supervise the construction of the porch, to keep an eye on things. Winnie totally disapproved of Constance's behavior. We couldn't lock her in her room, although looking back..." she laughs in jest. "Pahpie and I believed that a grown man like Lukas had the sense to know her teasing didn't mean anything, that her infatuation with him was simply an innocent crush. If we had gotten the porch put on in September, while she was in school all day, we could have been spared the troubles that lay ahead."

I understand what Grandmother is saying, but then Iris and I wouldn't be around. No way does she wish we hadn't been born.

"Water under the bridge..." she sighs. "If Victor Lejeune hadn't died in the car accident, and his grieving widow hadn't sent Constance back to us, he and Marie would have continued to raise Iris up in Canada while your mom went to the Air Force Academy, which was always her plan. Lukas wouldn't have entered her life again, and there'd be no baby Talking White Owl."

She removes the pin from her hair and loosens the long braid. "Time to hit the sack." On her way to the bedroom, Grandmother cups my chin in her hand and dutifully kisses the corner of my mouth, then Iris's. "I'm beat, aren't you? We'll talk more."

Yes, yes we will. I need to hear how my resemblance to Lukas as I've gotten older affects her and my great-grandparents. Iris has no clue. She was never told about the experience Dad and I had when I snapped the picture of Lukas and Mom sitting on the Harley. She definitely would have wanted to see it out of curiosity. Or so I think. Apparently she and Dad have had lots of phone discussions about me. How strange, too, after being together all day, she hasn't mentioned Uncle talking to her about the thingies in her students' heads. I'm off to bed, too. Our final dinner together will be at Winnie's and Sunkwah's, after which Iris will fly back to her husband. Grandmother will resume her schedule at the clinic, and I am to spend the remainder of the week with my great-grandparents, in order to get to know myself better, per Uncle William's request.

"Nooo...don't!" I grab Iris's hand in time before she lets go another ingredient for the pot. *"Ow!"* She steps all over my feet to hold me at bay, but I refuse to let her use up my wishes in Winnie's special "love" stew. "Put it down!" I demand. "Crossed eyes aren't important!"

"You said you don't believe in potions. It shouldn't matter then what gets mixed in. You can't honestly say you want a cross-eyed wife!"

"Winnie, please! Keep her mitts away!"

Winnie waves us both off with her wooden spoon. "Stop it! Both of you! You'll tip the pot and we'll all get burned."

One would think this was a serious situation, except we're in hysterics. Sunkwah, who's been seated at the kitchen table watching, laughs and eggs on his great-granddaughter: "Do it, Iris...do it... no crossed eyes in this family." He puts his arms up in defense as Winnie goes about giving him a pretend thrashing with the spoon she's still wielding like a weapon.

"Not for you to say," she orders, "if cross-eyed girl is okay with Viktor, we accept her."

"That's right," says Grandmother, who only now arrives after having checked in on the new mother and baby. She throws her coat over the chair and sniffs the air. "Aah...*waphi wahaŋpi*, Winnie's lucky love concoction. How many seasonings are left?"

"Viktor said the idea behind the stew was stupid," wails Iris, "and now he's getting all bent out of shape because I want to add cattail pollen to prevent his future wife, my future sister-in-law, from being cross-eyed."

Grandmother laughs and looks over the list of traits scribbled on a sheet of paper. She reads the ones checked off so far: "Sweetgrass for intelligence…definitely, milkweed so she'll be tall…hmm, stinging nettles for sense of humor…that's good, ground hickory nuts for clear skin…" She looks up at me questioningly. "Clear skin?"

Iris jumps in: "He hates tattoos, but there's nothing specific for that. Winnie picked one that came closest."

"You still have a way to go until you reach the twenty you're allowed."

"I know…and can you believe they want to waste one of my choices."

Apparently, a magic stew was never needed for Iris, since she met Hashke at such a young age. Even though we're all having a good time—at my expense—Winnie and Sunkwah trust in the power of this old world Rawakota custom, as does Grandmother, who claims she has witnessed it work. They seem sincere. I think it's dumb, but go along for the fun. It does make me stop to consider what I expect in a partner. Maybe that's the point. And the input from the family is shedding light on what they view as important, aside from the silly squabble over the eye thing. No one has yet suggested that my love interest be a Native. Perhaps they're waiting to hear it from me.

Winnie has rows of small glass bottles lined up next to the stove, all labelled. The bitter root, wild ginger, tobacco, sage, and red clover are ground into a fine powder. There are dried leaves from violets, catnip, and daylilies, even needles from pine and spruce trees. Little boxes hold hazelnuts and pecans, along with nuts I've never heard of. She assures me that she can get her hands on more spices for any trait that can't be found here, which shouldn't be necessary. In addition to the ones we started out with, I've asked to include those that will make my bride be independent; she must like horses and the outdoors, be spiritual and compassionate. I want her to be able to dance, to not be foul-mouthed or a drinker, to be ambitious, which kinda came out of nowhere. She shouldn't be shy…or a chatterbox…or a drama queen. The image of this fictitious girl is becoming surprisingly real, and I keep rattling off features, to the point of exceeding my quota; so then some have to be scrapped. By the time the persimmon is ready to be added, the final ingredient that guarantees she'll be a good cook, Winnie hesitates and looks at Sunkwah.

"Follow advice from wise Sunkwah," he says to me, his eyes narrowed real serious-like, "choose garlic, not persimmon. She can always learn to cook." Grandmother laughs to herself.

"What'll that do?"

Winnie grins: "She will love your *ché*."

Iris loses it.

Wild garlic it is, with the promise that my wife will love my penis. Seems majorly important, like it should have topped the list. Leave it to the elders.

The pot needs to simmer for several hours. The kitchen window is cracked so the aromas can drift out into the sky and beyond, as far as *wani gi yata,* the place of souls, where our deceased relatives will literally get wind of it and help with the search. I'm trying to keep a straight face as I listen to how this is supposed to go down. Because these particular ingredients are unique to me, like a fingerprint, others can safely eat it and have nothing happen to them. Once the meal is in my belly, it will be absorbed by my inner self and become part of the essence of who I am. An aura will surround me. The woman who possesses the qualities I'm looking for will be drawn to it. My job is easy; I simply wait.

Out slips a sarcastic, *"Aye-yi-yi."* Should I worry about turning into Pepé Le Pew?

Sunkwah responds with the Lakota version of *you'll be changing your tune one day.* Or maybe it's *I'll be eating my words*...whichever.

The room does smell good. Because Sister must leave now, she tastes a spoonful and smacks her lips together. "Mmm...yummy. I'll be amazed if it works, little brother. I've said it before; you're way too picky."

I walk Iris out to her rental car. We make small-talk, mostly about Dad and what a great time he missed out on tonight. I work Uncle William's name into the conversation and ask if he talked to her. I'm surprised to hear that he actually went to see her in Wisconsin, in order to discuss the research project along with the dentist's involvement. So he did take the matter more seriously than he let on. And yes, she had been completely floored. After they apologized for the oversight, the team at Winter Crow's lab gave her the specifications of the implanted devices, and then they promised to inform her on all aspects of their work in the future. That's it? That's the extent of her emotion...considering what she put me through with her phone calls and conspiracy schemes? We hug goodbye. I don't want to let go of her. She asks me to fly up some time to meet Hashke's family.

"Tell me, Iris, what do you love most about Hashke?"

Without hesitating, she answers: "What I would have put in *my* magic stew, given what I know about him, and how meaningful it is to me after being around outsiders, is his reverence for life. It's expressed in everything he does, the manner in which he treats others, the way he regards the earth when he gardens and the respect he shows animals. He upholds traditional values."

"That *is* praiseworthy." It wasn't quite what I was expecting to hear. "Not his dimples?" I ask, making light of the serious moment.

She smiles slyly, "That would be the *third* thing." If his values were the first thing? I get it, and I have no comeback.

As she pulls out of the driveway, it occurs to me that I like how our relationship is evolving as we get older. I could say the same about my Elders. What doesn't change, thankfully, is the feeling of *home*.

Laughed out and hungry, I turn on a basketball game in the living room and wait for the meal to be ready. They're still talking in the kitchen. I mute the sound, too many damn loud commercials. It's been a while since I've spent time in this house. Sunkwah and Winnie have been coming over to Grandmother's when I'm on the rez, where Dad also stays because there is usually something to fix, a dripping faucet, or a running toilet. As I look around, I think about how this room could be in a museum. Hundred-year-old buffalo hides cover the floor. The fox skin pillows propping me up, and stuffed with grasses, are the same I remember as a kid. Large harvesting bags and fur pouches used by my great-great-grandparents hang on the wall. Three-dimensional box frames display our ancestors' war bonnets and other tribal regalia. They're trimmed in beads with painstakingly detailed geometric designs. Outside the window, in the distance, I see the tepee. Descendants of the Rawakota still erect them in the yard for ceremonies, at least out here. It's a structure they liked and adopted from the Lakota Sioux. A few old-timers like Sunkwah keep them up year-round.

I twist the brackets on a frame to open the glass that protects my great-great-great-grandfather's faded "ghost shirt." Charging Bear wasn't much older than me, twenty-five, I think, when he wore this. The U.S. Government had banned the Indians from taking part in the Ghost Dance because the colonists felt threatened by it. They viewed the ritualistic circle dance as the Indians' hostile stance against their rule over them.

"Do you remember your history?" Sunkwah has walked in and rests his hand on my shoulder.

"Of course." I get a whiff of stale air from the living garment that holds the spirit of the proud brave who wore it. "Means even more nowadays."

"It is many moons when we hunted. We go before you leave us."

Sunkwah's face appears as much a relic as the old, stiffened shirt, with its deep lines and pale yellow eyes, half-covered by his lids. He still has thick braids and strong shoulders. His hair has only recently gone white along the temples. I almost ask if he feels up for hunting, then remember that questioning an elder's abilities would be insulting. Bison and elk are out of the question. He looks especially happy tonight, and that makes me happy.

"Maybe later in the week," I tell him. "We'll fish from the shore, find us a nice big rock in the river where the water pools, and catch a pheasant walking by."

He responds with a knowing nod and pats my arm. "*Ksapa*...smart."

"Why you grumble like sick bear?" asks Sunkwah, bringing Iris's horse, Ola, to a stop in front of Jim and me, his own horse being too old for day-long mountain treks.

"My *tuches* is killing me. I haven't ridden in ages."

Yiddish words never fail to tickle him; I even work them in when speaking Lakota. "Seriously, my ribs are beginning to hurt, too...all this bouncing."

"You strong young man. Sunkwah old and no complain."

"Well, you weren't beaten to a bloody pulp! I thought I was in better shape."

Before the pain grows unbearable, I slide off Jim. We passed the town of Hot Springs, which is still within view. A bed sounds really inviting. The plan was to make it to the border by nightfall and sleep in the hills under the Wyoming sky. My wobbly legs almost give way before I can lower myself onto a fallen tree trunk. How can butt muscles actually burn? Sunkwah managed to dismount without my usual help, and then comes to sit beside me.

"You in fight, Viktor?"

"You know..." If I don't shift my weight, I'm okay. "Last November," I tell him, wondering how it's possible he forgot. His mind is sharp as ever. Unless he wasn't told. *Wow!*

We eat a snack of berries and muffins in silence. Sunkwah casually pulls his cell phone out of the satchel and makes a call. It's to Winnie. It's strange to hear them speak only English to each other since I arrived. He asks her whether she knows anything about me having been hurt in a fight. He puts the phone back in the bag and goes on popping single blueberries in his mouth. The meaning of his short grunt is lost on me. Several minutes go by when he again reaches for the phone. He asks for Victoria Birdsong. Grandmother must be busy in the clinic. It takes a minute for her to answer. She gets the same question. Sunkwah rolls a berry between his thumb and fingertip as he thoughtfully listens to his daughter. He then hangs up without saying bye and remains impassive. *Now who's he calling!* There's no hello; he gives the person his name. Now he speaks Rawakota. I understand enough to know he's ticked off. There's no guessing who it might be since he uses the ancient language mostly when he's with someone around his age. Judging by his tone, he's giving the guy a piece of his mind. Meanwhile my back muscles have locked up. In his current mood, I'm afraid to ask him to head back to town. He had really looked forward to riding with me...as I had with him.

"Eat." Sunkwah hands me a capsule that was in the side pocket of his bag. "When better in morning, we leave early and ride north."

"What is it?"

"For bad pain."

"But...what's in it? Is it a narcotic...or something a medicine man gave you?"

"You not trust Great-Grandfather!"

I didn't mean to come off sounding like I was ridiculing the idea that he got it from a medicine man. His stern face softens. "Chan phezuta... from pine tree." He stands fixed in front of me, waiting.

"Come, we sit and smoke together. Is good to sleep on ground," he says, tapping it, "near healing power of Mother Earth."

There's truth in that, but I'd still rather have a soft bed tonight. His little pill, made from trees nourished by Mother Earth, does the trick in no time at all. Even though Sunkwah had wanted to keep going, we're in a beautiful spot. A stream trickles over a small dam beside us. In another month the water will flow fast as the snow melts in the mountains.

Sunkwah draws on his sacred pipe until it's ready to smoke. "It is blessing to watch you grow into man." No longer able to cross his legs, he sits with his arms resting on his knees, his body wrapped in a plain blanket spun from the long hair of Grandmother's Newfies. He watches the smoke drift upwards...up to the Great Spirit. Now he can talk to Wakan, and he begins by saying thanks for having a brave great-grandson.

Brave?

The pipe is offered to me, only the second time ever; the first being when we hunted buffalo together. I was still a boy, thirteen maybe. I'll never forget when Sunkwah asked if I had begun to roll back the foreskin from the head of my penis. It needed to be prepared for sex. He was so matter-of-fact about it. I was bummed to learn, however, that I was not to touch myself for self-pleasure; only a wife may touch her husband's ché. When I told him that my friends boasted about masturbating, he grunted and criticized them for being undisciplined. It was that summer when Sunkwah also taught me how to skin the mighty buffalo in one piece and prepare the hide that was to end up a jacket for Mr. Reuter, and how to cut up the meat. I felt incredibly accomplished afterward, connecting to our history in ways that my brothers on the rez could never understand. They had no elders to show them. When I told them that Great Granddad would be honored to instruct them, they weren't interested. There was no quick money in it. The meat could have fed their families for a month, which was a stupid thought since they didn't own freezers. By then, the realization of how poor they were—how really-really poor—was beginning to sink in, and they knew I wasn't, which is when the rift between us started, and grew with each passing summer and winter that I visited.

The combination of sweetgrass, sage, and tobacco smells good. I tell the Great Spirit how fortunate I am to be in the company of such a good man as Sunkwah. I mention Winnie's love for me, and I thank our relatives who have passed from this life into the next for watching over me.

"They help you win fight," says Sunkwah.

I understand now, and I feel somewhat embarrassed over his pride in me because...that isn't quite how I see it. I'm curious: "What makes you say I won?"

"Half Moon tell me."

Ah!...his last call was to Uncle William. Half Moon was his name when he married Mom's older sister, my Aunt Loretta. There was no reason for Sunkwah to start calling William Horse That Walks Backwards, a name Uncle adopted to endear himself to his patients on the rez, especially the kids who were calling him that anyway on account of his quirky horse. I had no idea that Uncle William was fluent in Rawakota, unless Sunkwah was merely reaming him out for not having told him about me in the language he could do it best in.

I put a heavy coat on over my sweater. The small fire doesn't give off much heat, but a bigger one wasn't necessary to cook our frozen burgers that thawed during the ride. Tomorrow we'll hunt for dinner, fish or bird …depending. Although patches of snow cover the hard ground, the day has been comfortable, around fifty degrees. The nights go below freezing, but not by much. The thick hides under us are plenty warm for sleeping outside. Stars begin to appear as the sun sets behind the walls of this small canyon where we are protected from the wind.

"So Sunkwah, you and Winnie are speaking English all of the time now?"

"Yes, to keep mind sharp. I read to Winnie…and Winnie, she read to me in afternoon. And we talk, talk about story. Make us tired end of day … but, getting easy…easier."

"That's admirable." His little grammar mistakes aren't worth pointing out. "Who chooses the book?"

He thinks about it and shrugs. "Victoria has many on shelf. Book find us. Soon finish *Hawaii*. You read book?"

"No." I have seen the monster of a book in Grandmother's house. I think it was actually Pahpie's. He loved to learn about the history of places around the world.

"Mr. Michener need one thousand pages to say: white men come…and like thief, they take and take and take. They bring disease to island people, kill spirit inside them with talk of money. " He grunts something. "Never be tempted by white man's evil greed. Listen to Indian voice inside you."

"I'll remember your advice, Sunkwah." It's not the first time I've heard it, nor will it be the last.

He seems reassured and lies down. The horses doze while standing, keeping guard in the open woods. Bears aren't a threat, but mountain lions have been spotted. I trust that an unfamiliar smell or sound would spook Jim and Ola, and I'd wake in time to react. The hunting knives stay close to our sides. The constellations stir my imagination. I fill my lungs with the fresh night air. Just when I think Sunkwah has fallen asleep, he speaks:

"Our Viktor is eighteen in spring...age of Sunkwah when Winnie and me marry. Winnie turn seventeen one day before. Sad great-grandson has no Otiwota ceremony before you find wife. Leave hole in life."

"That's kinda drastic, isn't it? I'm sure I'll be fine without it." He asks me to explain the word "drastic," and then basically repeats what he had said about the traditional ceremony. He truly believes that my future will never be as full as it should be without the experience.

Fuck that. "Is it too late?"

He motions for me to help him sit up. I poke a log to keep the fire going.

"*When you and Iris were left in our care, Winnie and I thought that the two of you were going to stay with us until you were grown.*" He has switched to Lakota, not being used to speaking so much English at one time. "*You learned the ways of our people as early as a few months old, as soon as Constance left for the Air Force school. Iris did, too, even though she was already five.*"

"You're talking about a Rawakota tradition, right, and not a Lakota one? Just making sure I'm following."

He looks at me confused and states flatly: "*Yes... Rawakota...*" then goes on to explain that Rawakota parents make time every day to hold their newborns toward the heavens, the home they just left. It's a means of comforting them. Babies need time to adjust to their Earth family. Even on the coldest nights in winter, I was bundled up and taken outdoors to view the sky. I won't bring up the fact that a baby's vision is fuzzy at best. I couldn't possibly have been aware of anything from that distance. Over time, after learning to speak, he says that I was told the history of our people, which is something I *definitely do* recall, and vividly, because incredible heroes and monsters were involved. As I grew older, the symbolism became more meaningful. Sunkwah mentions Otiwota again. I sort of remember hearing about it now, the week spent with one's father's male relatives. Being so young, any reference to it was lost on me. Sunkwah says he and Pahpie swore they would uphold the tradition when the time came. Girls have their own ceremony, which the women concern themselves with. Mom, however, put the kibosh on their plan when she came home one day with a fiancé and said she was taking us far away to Texas.

"The news made Winnie and me sick with a heavy heart. Victoria and Benjamin cried. They had already suffered great sadness when your mother left with Iris to live with the French missionary couple in Canada. It was a day filled with such joy when they came back to the reservation. And just like that, Constance suddenly disappeared on the highway on her way up to Rapid City. A scary time for everyone. The day you, our Hinhán Ska was born, brought renewed hope and happiness to our family. And for five years, having you and your sister in our home gave us peace. Think what it felt like for all of us, Viktor, knowing we were going to miss out on watching you children grow up after you moved."

"But we did end up coming back a lot."

Sunkwah has me scoot over to him. He pats my cheek and rests his hand on my knee.

"Solomon promised to carry out the instruction that Benjamin and I had begun. He is a fine man. It was not easy for your father to run his business and send you children up here during the year. He had to come, too. You were so attached to him. He is as devoted to his family as all Rawakota men are to theirs."

"Then you must have told Dad about Otiwota. If he agreed to carry on the tradition of our Rawakota narrative, why couldn't I still look forward to the ceremony?" I purposely don't mention that by the time I was in Middle School, Dad no longer pressed me about reciting the accompanying poem on a nightly basis. I did continue to always stare at the sky before going to sleep, and still do. The conditioning must have worked because my identity is definitely tied to the strong connection I feel with the universe. There's a true sense of belonging that comes from watching the heavens. I was asked not to bring up the subject with friends because it was a deeply personal matter within each family, so I never did.

Sunkwah sits in thought. "*The rituals involve too big of an idea to explain.*" He studies the stars. "*For a boy to become man, he must fully understand that he is connected to everything surrounding him. Even rocks and mountains hold spirits inside. Wakan Tanka has blessed us with a way of experiencing the greatest of mysteries while we live here on Earth.*"

I interrupt at this point because the concept isn't any different from what other Indigenous tribes around the world believe.

Sunkwah shakes his head. "*No, Viktor. You would learn what to expect during the eich ihilah. Being inside your wife for the first time, near her womb where your babies come to you, is the beginning of a long journey you both take together, a journey laid out by Wakan Tanka."*

This must've been the otherworldly business Uncle had hinted at when I was rude to him, and he told me to come here so I'd be set straight about my background. I can see why Dad was never told. This is really out-there —like the stuff I've read about in interviews with musicians from the sixties. They described altered states of consciousness from practicing transcendental meditation and taking LSD. Some people liked tripping on peyote, which has been used for centuries by various Indian tribes in spiritual cleansing ceremonies. Great Grandfather is a product of his time and can't help what he believes. That doesn't explain Uncle William's same view on the subject; he's college educated, and a man of science.

"Say that I *had* stayed on the Buckthorn Reservation, Sunkwah...who are my relatives that would show up for this ceremony? Pahpie is dead. Dad and Uncle William aren't Rawakota, so they aren't invited. That leaves only you."

"Half Moon and Solomon are not permitted because they are not blood relatives. Why do you say Half Moon is not Rawakota?"

My mind goes blank. I help Sunkwah stand so he can go pee. I might as well, too. How could I not know this about Uncle? I find a bigger piece of wood for the fire.

"Why on earth wouldn't he ever have told me that he wasn't Lakota?"

"Did you ask?"

"He has brown eyes though. I just assumed." This is an unexpected revelation. They have been brown for as far back as I can remember. Since he apparently wears colored contact lenses, wouldn't he remove them now and again, especially at home?

"Half Moon told us he wanted to fit in when he was at college studying medicine. You know how that goes. Don't outsiders often ask about your eyes?" Dr. Bonnaire's name immediately pops into my head, along with his deep interest in the genetics behind them, but I don't bother bringing it up. *"By the time he came to the reservation to work at the clinic, he was used to the way he looked. His eyes were brown when Loretta met him, and she liked it. An old timer like me had mixed feelings about him changing the color. Those of us whose grandfathers and great-grandfathers had fought beside the Lakota at the Battle of Little Big Horn appreciated that our Rawakota warriors helped them win the fight; and they called us brother,*

and the women sister, and they welcomed us into their tribe. Because of our eyes, we were recognized on sight." It sounds like the Rawakota of that period regarded this unique inherited feature as a kind of status symbol.

"So, tell me, if Uncle William and Aunt Loretta had had a son, he would have been born with yellow eyes, leading people to believe Aunt Loretta did it with the mailman."

That delights the old man and he has a good laugh. He gets back to my question. Again I'm surprised by what he says.

"*You have many relatives who would come to Otiwota. Do you forget that your Grandmother has a brother, our son High Jumping Horse? He has two sons. Your Pahpie has a living brother who has a son. My own younger sister still lives. She has only daughters, but they have sons. And the man who created you with your mother has a brother and one sister who have sons. You see, Hinhán Ska, you have many Rawakota cousins and aunts and uncles.*"

"You're telling me that if Iris and I hadn't moved to Texas, we'd know all of them...even Lukas's family, after what he did to Mom? Where does everybody live?" That just blows me away! "Does Mom know them?"

"*Of course—our families visited each other and danced together in pow-wows when Loretta and Constance were little, as did your grandmother and her brother when they were growing up, back when Winnie and I were young new parents. You played with your Rawakota cousins up at the lake house near Hot Springs before you moved to Texas. When it comes to the relatives of Lukas Born With Sun In Eyes...Constance knows where they live, but none of us has met any of them. They receive news about you and Iris.*"

Unbelievable! That's just frickin' unbelievable! Sunkwah insists it's time to let the fire die out, leaving me with all these loose ends to ponder. Where exactly in the hills does Lukas's family live? I'll never close my eyes. Lost in thought, I stare into the night. The words of the Rawakota poem, largely ignored for years, form on my lips. It occurs to me that I used to feel the presence of the ancient spirits all the time, even when I first started at Ohio State. Since then the preoccupation with schedules and deadlines has overshadowed my Lakota-Rawakota consciousness, which ignores the exact passing of time as measured by clocks.

It's 11 p.m., and I'm back inside my great-grandparents' home, having parked myself between the curtains of the living room window like a little kid as I eagerly wait for Mom and Dad to arrive. At long last, I see the glow from the headlights at the top of the hill. Following our extraordinary week together riding and camping throughout the southern part of the Black Hills, Sunkwah called it a night soon after dinner, this being our first evening back. Winnie had made tea and we sat and talked until now, when she couldn't keep her eyes open any longer. Getting a woman's perspective on Rawakota society was interesting. I discovered that the reason behind Mom's lukewarm attitude toward me these last few years has nothing to do with me resembling Lukas, which I was certain it had. All mothers, said Winnie, end up distancing themselves from their sons for a period. Even grandmothers and great-grandmothers cannot give the boys so much as a simple hug. Nor can older sisters embrace their brothers. It starts when the children turn eleven or so. It was obvious that Sunkwah's account of things was sketchy. The same holds true for fathers and daughters. At that age, kids are expected to focus solely on their interests and goals so that when they're sixteen or seventeen, they are free to start searching exclusively for a partner, without anyone's influence. There is sadness, she admitted, but it passes because everyone anticipates the day when the family is made whole by the addition of a new member. Due to this rite of passage, parents and extended family make the most of their relationships while the children are little, openly hugging and kissing them. That ticks me off. At least those sons and daughters knew what to expect when they hit that age. For me, the sudden cold shoulder treatment came without warning and explanation, as it evidently had for Winnie and Grandmother as well. Winnie said that she and her daughter never placed much stock in the outdated custom, so they were as surprised as Mom was when she learned that Sunkwah and Pahpie had been quietly grooming me for Otiwota. Am I to presume that reconciliation with Mom is in my future as soon as I meet the woman I'm going to marry? If that isn't laughable. Thank god, Dad wasn't encouraged to ignore me.

Winnie made it sound like Iris and I were anomalies in our corner of the rez. The fact that many Rawakota here maintain their traditions was news to me. They do a good job keeping it hushed up. We probably wouldn't be having this conversation, she said, if Mom had had another baby girl instead of me. Men don't interfere with the instruction of the females. In a voice filled with sadness, Winnie told me that she was sorry I never had a chance to know the fun-loving, joke-cracking side to the man I called Pahpie. By the time I was born, Benjamin One Horn had become obsessed with Native causes. He never shirked his farm duties, but he went to a lot of Indian protest rallies around the country. The more he attended, said Winnie, the more serious he became. He began to dwell on his family roots and the history of his people. Then I came along, this fatherless male child for him to pass along the ancient customs to. Winnie almost seemed angry when she recalled that with the passing years, Sunkwah, too, had become more nostalgic for the past. And there you have it, she said, two aging men in search of purpose.

I wanted to know more about everything. Winnie left me hanging in suspense like Sunkwah had done our first night out. It's unnerving! As she kissed me good night, I asked if that was allowed...given what she had just told me. She grinned and gave my chin a little shake and said, 'Who knows *what* you are?' I guess that's been the problem in a nutshell. Iris and I need to compare notes someday soon. Outside the car doors slam shut. I listen to my parents' muffled voices.

When they walk in, I'll do my best to set aside my anger. Mom has been subjected to the same mixed cultural messages her whole life like I was, and it had to have been equally confusing to her. Everyone has convinced me that she really was MIA during the period I was in the hospital and recuperating. I won't be able to hold that against her anymore. When she called recently, one of the few times, I chose not to answer.

The handshake with Dad isn't normal and makes me self-conscious. That's what I get for acting like a jerk at Christmas, even though I've since apologized. He excuses himself to go to bed after days of being on the road. He kisses Mom on the lips, a deep kiss that holds my attention because of the rare glimpses I've had into their private relationship. She stays behind in the kitchen to put some groceries away that they brought. Only the light above the sink is on, giving her features a hard edge and exaggerating the circles around her tired eyes. I continue to stand across the table from her, resting my arms on the back of a chair. I could offer to help. She's still in her uniform blouse and skirt. Dad picked her up from the Ellsworth base after driving up from Texas. Seems they could have met here, so he wouldn't have had to backtrack the hour and a half it takes to go there. If I were in the habit of making friendly chitchat with her, I'd be inclined to ask why.

She walks over and suddenly reaches for my hands, holding them in a ball against her chest. She searches my eyes then bows her head. Her warm breath passes over my skin. I can tolerate it only so long, but when I try to pull free, she tightens her grip. The agonizing memory of feeling absolutely alone makes me want to run...run from the overwhelming sense of abandonment that seized me when I looked around the hospital room and didn't find my mother at my bedside. It was unforgivable—no matter the reasons. Strange, but I get that from her.

She traces each knuckle, uncurls my fingers, and holds them flat over her heart. With her eyes half-closed eyes, she continues to follow the shape of my hands, from the fingertips to the wrists, as though committing them to memory, like one does with a newborn. Her touch is cathartic. My anxious racing heart slows to the quiet, evenly paced beats of hers. I come to be as relaxed as a cat snoozing in the sun, to the point of possibly dropping at her feet.

"Sleep tight, Viktor. I'm going to grab a bite to eat before I turn in." Her voice is soothing like a lullaby. She lets go of me, but the spell lingers.

I don't know how I found my bed, but I wake up in it with a dead arm that has lost circulation. It's late, 10:20, and bright outside. After some exercises to get the blood flowing again, I throw on my clothes then go see what the family's up to on my last day here.

"The number has grown to twenty-five percent who want the Lakota to take the money." Grandmother sounds troubled by the news. She had driven over earlier. "Just five years ago, almost everyone was against it." They're sitting around the kitchen table fired up about a recent survey. I'm invisible. I scoop the remaining sausage and eggs from the pan that was clearly saved for me. While I wait for the toast, Winnie asks if I bother keeping up with tribal issues.

Boasting a bit, I reply, "I know that last month the legislature once again rejected the Sioux' bid to take control of the million plus acres set aside for them in the Laramie Treaty. I didn't realize more Indians are willing to accept the government's money for the land that the U.S. stole from them. That goes against all principles of justice, doesn't it?"

Sunkwah grunts, which signifies that my answer merits his approval. Good thing the local paper was left in the bathroom. I squeeze into a spot between him and Grandmother.

"Would you vote to take the money, Viktor?" asks Mom. "It's now estimated to be in the billion dollar range because of accumulated interest. Think of all the lives that could be helped."

I barely get my mouth open when Sunkwah interrupts and gruffly states that corrupt tribal leaders are pushing for the sale so they can line their own pockets. The rest of the population on the reservation will be lucky if they see a dollar from the transaction. Winnie nods in agreement.

"What's the solution then?" I ask. "For things to continue as they are now?"

Dad speaks up. "There's no law…no consequences for gang violence, for dealing drugs. That's the first thing that has to be addressed. Then you can deal with the other problems. Unfortunately, they're huge problems."

"The worst thing is there's no unity among the nine tribes," says Grandmother. "They're always squabbling with each other and nothing gets resolved. They're an embarrassment to our Nation."

"So they need a leader; is that what I'm hearing?" I'm busy stuffing my mouth when I notice the silence. Was it such a naïve thing to ask?

"Name someone the young people look up to, an Indian with a message of hope." Grandmother really wants to know.

What can I say? "The brothers here admire the gangs. They follow the most charismatic leaders who best protect their turf. The goal is to move up in the organization to get closer to the power, not unlike people in general. I honestly think the situation is hopeless. You can save a few, like Iris tries to do with her mentally challenged kids, and you, Grandmother, at your clinic, but the cards are stacked against the majority of our people. It's the sad truth."

Sunkwah shakes his head, unwilling to accept my defeatist view, and then says with the authority granted the oldest in the room: "They like war so much; they can have war."

I'm not sure who *they* are, or the kind of war he's referring to, but I think I'll bow out of this conversation and give Jim a brushing before packing. Mom follows after me and suggests taking a walk. We stay on the dirt road that circles the property, seating ourselves on a stone bench that overlooks a pond. Courtship season is in full swing and the place is a running cartoon of horny bunnies scampering after each other.

"I bet you're anxious to get back to school."

"Not really. Uncle was right in telling me to come back here. Sunkwah and Winnie seem like they'll go on forever, but I realize it isn't the case, and I should visit more often...as much as I *hate flying*." The irony isn't lost on her. We smile, and it feels good.

"Why didn't I get a chance to know my cousins better? Sunkwah told me that you and Aunt Loretta vacationed with yours. And I had no idea Uncle William is Rawakota...or that Otiwota is a really big deal I'm missing out on. Why was I left in the dark?"

"Because I was."

Sitting close to Mom like this, with the sides of our bodies touching, is nice. I compare her face to the girl's on the motorcycle. I doubt Dad told her about our experience at *The Horse Rustler* a couple years back. Her shoulder length black hair is held behind her ears with a thin beaded headband. Some gray strands poke through. Her jawline seems sharper, and her eyes more deep set. She looks important...carries herself like a general, even though she claims no such ambition. I always felt proud to have such a pretty mother.

"I'm not sure how well I can explain this," she says. "Because Mom and Dad lived as Lakota, to me, when I heard the word Rawakota, I thought of Sunkwah and Winnie, a term for the older generation. It's comparable to the Jews at Hillel who aren't orthodox, but many of their grandparents were. They call themselves non-observant Jews because they no longer follow the strict rules and rituals of the Jewish religion. That's our family: non-observant Rawakota."

"If that supposedly describes Grandmother and Pahpie...it doesn't follow that they would still abide by a tradition that doesn't make sense in today's society?"

She sighs and takes a moment. "Their ancestors, the ones who chose to stay with the Lakota when they were forced onto reservations in the 1800s, were similar to today's displaced refugees, in that they had to adapt to a different people's ethnicity and customs. The Rawakota tribe falls under the banner of the Great Sioux Nation, but that's really a misnomer. After the Lakota forced the Cheyenne out of here because they regarded the territory as being vital to their own culture, they came into contact with a unique band of Indians in the forests. The tribes kept to themselves and were able to coexist in peace. Both viewed the Black Hills as a sacred place. The Lakota never revered the Rawakota, but they regarded them as special because of how they mysteriously came and went from the region, which contributed to the folklore surrounding them. Rawakota warriors aided their Lakota brothers in battle. They supplied food during droughts and floods. The two Nations felt a strong kinship with one another. The Lakota's own creation stories describe the mountains as being the center of their universe, the womb of Mother Earth—which is where they believed the Rawakota came from."

"Interesting." The history fascinates me. I learned in school that the reason there are yellow-eyed people on our reservation was because the bluecoat enemies caught Rawakota warriors as they fled the battleground during the Wounded Knee Massacre. Those who escaped supposedly died from disease or took off to Canada. I didn't think surviving offspring still existed anywhere in the Black Hills. Mom elaborates on what happened, that there were scouts who voluntarily offered to live among the Lakota on the newly established reservations, in order to spy on the white man. I had no idea.

"You're saying that Sunkwah's grandfather, my great-great-great-grandfather Charging Bear, was a spy? Was Sunkwah one? Were women spies, too?" I'm staring in disbelief.

Mom laughs a little. "Yes, no, yes."

"No shit!"

She stands and unbuttons her coat. "Let's walk."

We greet a man and boy who ride past on their horses. Mom says she went to school with the guy and the boy is his nephew. I hardly know anyone here personally, only their names from conversations. I never gave it much thought before now.

"You asked if we broke from tradition because of the strict rules. Not really. It just gradually happened." Now and then she turns toward me as we stroll, looking somewhat melancholy. Maybe she feels nostalgic. "I had heard about neighbors who remained entrenched in their old-world Rawakota ways, although I didn't grasp what it meant as a kid. Winnie once told me that too much emphasis is placed on a single aspect of a boy's journey into manhood, namely the *eich ihilah*. It was intended to give boys a deeper understanding of creation that females were thought to inherently possess, solely because they're physically equipped to bear new life. Having had daughters, Mom and Dad saw no reason to even bring it up to Loretta and me. Although we got together with our extended Rawakota family for reunions at a lakeside cabin in the hills, like you were told, we quit going when Loretta went to nursing school. I was around nine. After that, Uncle High Jumping Horse and Mom's sister, Aunt Irene Yellow Feather, would sometimes swing by with their families and stay a while. I was starting to be pretty cocky by then; could be why they stopped coming altogether." Her eyes reveal a glint of girlish satisfaction.

"By now you must've been told about my tirade when I figured out that Sunkwah and Pahpie had succeeded in brainwashing you for Otiwota, which they had every intention of you participating in when the time came."

I'm so confused. And I don't think I can take people dropping anymore bombshells on me. "A tirade?" She stops in her tracks and looks confused herself.

"They never mentioned the big blow up I had with them?"

"Believe it or not, Mom, they don't like to speak ill of you, although at times I can tell they're holding back."

We pause by a fence where horses are grazing in the field. She appreciates hearing that from me...admitting it isn't deserved. Next she asks if I recall the Rawakota word for a pregnant woman; an odd question, but I do remember. It translates as, a woman who carries it all, meaning the universe. Apparently, I used it to describe a friend's mother during one of her visits home, which gave her cause to ask me about certain other things. She learned that I had been reciting the Rawakota poem religiously to the night sky all along, the one learned for theeich ihilah. I was maybe around ten at the time, and totally clueless with regard to its significance. The confrontation must have occurred in the summer when I came up to the rez, and I missed it because I slept over at Daniel's. Everyone, including Dad, was present when she reproached them. Dad had obviously never told her about the agreement he had made with Sunkwah and her own father, which, to his mind, likely sounded good in principle. He has always wanted Iris and me to maintain ties to our Indian heritage.

"I don't know a time I was so incensed, Viktor—absolutely livid. I spit out every obscenity. I threw things. It was horrible. And finally I had to look at myself and accept it was ultimately my own doing that set you up for this. No instructions were left as to how you and Iris should be raised. You both were in safe hands, so I blindly carried on with my own life the way I saw fit."

She's never been this emotional in front of me. "What's the big deal?" I wonder. "Kids say prayers at night; it doesn't screw them up. Why would you let it get to you like that? Where's the harm?" I'm puzzled that the memory still upsets her. After a lull in the conversation, she asks what I know about theeich ihilah.

"It's basically a marriage vow, except that partners promise to be faithful to each other for eternity, not just until death do you part."

"That's how Sunkwah explained it?"

"He got into more of the spiritual nature of a relationship…I guess you could call it that. We talked about our relatives, especially the number of cousins who are around my age. Tell you the truth, Mom, Otiwota itself sounds like a wild orgy, like a bachelor party."

"Seriously! That's your interpretation of it?"

"Well…yeah. They give details about their sex lives. I don't wanna hear that from a bunch of guys. I mean…I don't know. Sunkwah actually told me he "does it" with Winnie every morning. There's a mental picture I didn't need. And he went on to say he would tell that to the others during the Otiwota ceremony."

She hikes herself onto the top rail of the wooden fence and quietly watches a couple of hawks circling around us. They've spotted something on the ground. In the meantime, I'm wondering if I should have revealed any of this.

"Don't you think it's worth noting and appreciating," she says at last, "that after seventy years of marriage, a physical expression of love is still possible? Wouldn't you want that with your own wife? Even the sixty-year olds would be inspired by his admission."

"When you put it that way…I suppose."

"And these aren't strangers or buddies who participate in Otiwota; they're your family, men you can trust your entire life to help you sort out any of your problems. They're the ones who will share your greatest joys."

"Time out, Mom—you just got through telling me how furious you were that Sunkwah and Pahpie had been preparing me for this ritual, and now you sound like you're condoning it."

"True, I'm a hypocrite. As the saying goes, Viktor, age brings new perspective. There's purpose in the old ways. I'm just beginning to comprehend the grand design."

She hops down and we slowly head back. Along the way she tells me that harboring regrets is useless. Whatever "conditioning" took hold will have to be addressed as situations arise. Sounds reasonable to me, and somewhat scary.

I feel I should ask Mom about her own life. Where to start? I'm compelled to tell her how tired she looks. She says this past winter gave her a lot to think about. It's a given that she won't discuss her job. The actor Jason Red Moon's name comes up. I agree he's a good role model for Indians, not just Apache. Based on the money that poured in for the local community college after my stint dancing in *WAKAN*, she reminds me of the good that can come from being in the public eye. The local school could finally afford upper level science classes. I picture the roomful of wealthy benefactors at Hayden's post-show party. Guess there's no point in questioning people's genuineness when it comes to the causes they support. Mom says I could be a great source of inspiration to Native youth, and to keep that in mind when I play football.

I'm curious to know more about her reaction to the news of the fight that landed me in the hospital, and at the same time I don't. I want to leave things on a good note. This has been a perfect afternoon.

Back at Sunkwah's house, it's time to apologize to Dad's face. Over the phone was too easy. While Mom goes to take a bath, I find him alone in the living room, asleep on the couch in front of the TV. I take the magazine that's about to slide off his lap and turn off the ball game. How quiet and peaceful. A snooze would be nice, and I curl up beside him. Dad rests his hand on my shoulder and gives it a gentle squeeze. We're good.

We've almost reached the Rapid City airport. Grandmother has had to tolerate my endless questions about all things Rawakota, especially after learning that females were mostly responsible for influencing the culture; and in doing so, shaped its genetic story.

Being a nurse, Grandmother is familiar with the well-known experiments carried out by the Russian geneticist, Belyaev. His goal, which she really didn't need to remind me of, was to uncover a genetic basis for behavior. He had bred only wild silver foxes that showed the least fear of people. Eventually, their descendants bore a generation with no fear of people. They were like domesticated, affectionate dogs. Surprisingly, the offspring of the tame pairs also showed physical changes. They developed spotted coats and curly tails. "Imagine instead," says Grandmother, "that it worked the same way with humans. We know that our earliest ancestors prized monogamy and permitted only those who remained faithful to their mates to reproduce. The one observable trait that corresponded to this behavior belonged to the males born with yellow eyes. And although females did not exhibit the same eye color, over time the daughters of these males were found to be monogamous, too." She believes that during the long drawn-out evolutionary process, the males and females who strayed, and who presumably were in the minority, were culled from the group. Grandmother puts forward the idea that our Rawakota common ancestor had yellow eyes, and we are therefore not linked as closely to other humans whose DNA has more in common with chimps. My brain is still reeling from all the implications.

Another custom mandated by wives and mothers was that young unmarried men should not engage in battle. Finding one's partner took precedence over anything else, because from that union life continued. If too many young braves ended up dead, the odds of a girl finding her special someone were greatly reduced. The women held that husbands and fathers have greater regard for consequences than their younger, impulsive selves. During the period when their Nation's men joined forces with the Lakota in their wars, the more mature Rawakota warriors had a reputation for being artful strategists. Few ever died.

She can't be pulling up to the departure gate—not now!

"We can talk about all this on the phone, Viktor. You have your uncle there to explain things. He'd be happy to see you taking an interest in your background."

She's right; my uncle, the Rawakota. Unbelievable. As we hug goodbye, there's something I've been meaning to tell her:

"Before I left for college, you said to watch out for girls who might fall in love with the idea of me. At the time it wasn't clear what you meant. It turned out, you should have warned me about myself. I was the one who got hung up on the idea of me."

She gives me one of those knowing looks. "An important life-lesson." Next she removes one of her countless silver rings and slides it on my little finger. "Never forget."

A baggage attendant motions to hurry it up. Off I go to Chicago to catch my connecting flight to Columbus, my mind in a fog due to information overload. Now comes the task of separating fact from what has to be mostly fiction ... has to be.

"Uncle? Leksi? Hmm."

The bedroom door is slightly open. I peek inside to find it empty, totally empty. "What the..." And to think I tried not to disturb him when I arrived early this morning in the dark. After managing a few hours of sleep, I'm anxious to speak with him. His lamp is gone. The Indian pictures and blanket and keepsakes are missing. The closet is empty. *"Unhee!"*

Some loud bumps in the hallway rattle the walls. When I go to check it out, I'm met by the backside of a guy who nearly steps on my toes. He's balancing the bottom of a huge recliner that's being driven up the stairs by someone else. I jump to the side, so he has the extra inches of my doorway to maneuver the bulky piece of furniture around the corner. I can't see them, but I recognize the voices calling out directions from below. I immediately grab a corner of the chair and march backwards into the apartment across from mine, seriously scraping my knuckles on the damn doorframe while trying to fit it through. The second it clears, we all let go. The kid beside me looks young enough to be in middle school. He flexes his sore fingers and mutters *fuck* under his breath. I agree.

"Viktor!" exclaims Jasper, happy to see me. He and Uncle scoot the chair aside to step around it and greet me. Just as Jasper is about to shake my hand, he notices blood. Uncle places an arm around me and explains the situation while walking me to the kitchen sink.

"The place literally became available overnight...make that three days ago. Because of my job at OSU, I'm able to stay in the building. It's such a convenient location. And I like the tenants. You're almost eighteen; I figured you would want to start having friends over."

He's given more thought to my future than I have. Jasper introduces me to DeShaun Rivers, a wide receiver like him, who was a redshirted freshman this year and didn't get to play either. On their way out, Jasper asks if I want to practice ball with them tomorrow. Sounds fun. Uncle grabs his wallet and pays each fifty dollars for their troubles, which seems a lot until I see the living room has a couch, a large table, and big screen TV mounted on the wall. They've been busy.

"Nate gave me these nice things, even the TV. I got a new bed, though. He let me borrow his pick-up."

"Nice," I mutter, showing no enthusiasm.

"Viktor, I realize it's sudden."

I just stand there.

"Come; help me bring the chair over so I can close the door. I'll fix us something to eat."

The obvious spot for the over-sized recliner is under the window, but he insists the area remain open as he had ordered in our place. This apartment is much smaller. I sit on a bar stool at the kitchen counter. Uncle opens the fridge, already stocked full of food, and it really hits me that I'll be living alone. Whatever I had planned to discuss with him goes out the window, along with my appetite. He sits beside me...and there we sit, in silence. At a certain point it's ridiculous. I leave to go for a walk.

"Hot Dawg! This is one effin glorious day!"

Theo laughs at the sound of his old name, or maybe it's because I won't say the word fucking in a public place. I don't know why "Dawg" slipped out; there's nothing the same about him since the summer we shot hoops together with Jake. Gone now, too, are his unruly dreadlocks, replaced by a fade haircut. He bleached the tips on top, turning them a light rust-brown color. Looks sharp.

It's half time. The stadium is packed for OSU's annual Gray versus Scarlet intrasquad spring practice game. And for once I'm not seated so high up I can touch the sky. Theo and I are in the perfect spot to observe Jasper. Most fans might not appreciate looking down center field in the B Section end zone, but the formations are easier for me to read than at the fifty yard line.

DeShaun has yet to play today, but was promised that he definitely would. I wrongly assumed he was redshirted because the team hoped he would grow a few inches. Turns out he had to concentrate on his grades. I worry for him out there, all five feet seven inches of him. Seems he'll get bulldozed over, regardless of his speed. I've witnessed how those short legs can turn on a dime and race so fast they're a blur. Jasper said it's too funny to watch him in practice, how he zips by under the radar of those behemoth linebackers.

With more than a dozen juniors and seniors leaving for the NFL after last season, the coach wanted the new Buckeyes to get a feel for playing before a huge crowd of screaming fans. He got his wish, in spades. One hundred thousand people are packed in here. I ask Theo what it's like to be on the receiving end of such loud cheering. He's had his share of raving fans during March-Madness when he filled in for an injured starter. He shakes his head and laughs. I guess the noise level of the smaller basketball crowd can't compare. The stadium holds at least four to five times more people than the basketball arena.

There's no mistaking that the girls to the left of Theo are flirting with us. We're psyched about the possibility of landing dates to a party this evening. As he passes along our huge plate of loaded nachos to share with them, he leans in and asks which one I prefer. They're both pretty brunettes with great smiles. It doesn't matter…because I have no intention of scoring with either of them, and I know he does. As usual, I'll go to the party for the fun of dancing, but leave before the drinking turns ugly. Right now, I am so unbelievably charged up to see players that I actually know on the field. Jasper and DeShaun are honest-to-god Buckeyes!

CHAPTER 28

My daily schedule keeps me busy. From 7:00 a.m. until noon, I'm on the research floor of the hospital. After lunch, it's off to the rec center for an hour of strength training. The afternoons spent with Jasper and DeShaun the past couple of weeks have been fun and productive. My flexibility has really improved. Though they'll be starters this coming year for the Buckeyes football team, they insist we still practice ball when possible along the banks of the Scioto River in an area where I used to throw passes to Hayden. They critique my form like he did. I miss seeing Hayden… miss my friendship with him. I've also begun a program in biostatistics that consumes my thoughts the remainder of my waking hours, and too often my dreams, unfortunately. Sometimes Uncle invites me for dinner. He couldn't believe that I didn't realize he was Rawakota. After showing me his yellow eyes, I agreed that brown suited him best. What a dramatic difference it makes in his appearance. His own eyes are a rather cold-looking pale yellow. The brown contacts definitely convey a warmer personality. We talk about football and the nature of the research that I'm helping Dr. Sharma with. He's as enthusiastic about the idea of altering viruses as I am! In our experiments, we'll be piggy-backing growth factor genes onto antibodies that are then injected into cancerous tumors.

Surprisingly, Mom calls on a somewhat regular basis from Arizona, which is the first time she's been assigned to a base in the desert. It's 15 miles west of Phoenix. Our conversations are short and superficial, which doesn't bother me. I'd like to believe she simply wants to hear my voice. I like hearing hers. Iris calls occasionally to discuss my love life. Or should I say, lack of one. We're silly, and it's fun. For whatever reason, she doesn't mention her work. I talk to Dad nearly every other day. He'll be coming up soon for my 18th birthday, which is the first week in May. I look forward to making it up to him for the way I behaved over winter. I cringe at the thought of how cruel it was of me to ask him to stay away while I was recovering. These days, I'm doing fairly well…just going with the flow.

I have begun to recite the Rawakota poem again on a nightly basis, with the hope of getting on the good side of my spirit ancestors. I want this "theeich ihilah" to be a positive experience for me when it happens... if it happens. At any rate, the ritual makes me feel grounded...and that's plenty enough to fulfill my needs at the moment.

Constance had just texted Viktor a picture of a coyote trotting past the kitchen window as she was pouring her morning coffee, when she heard on the TV news that Australian soldiers were killed in Kashmir, specifically in Pulwama. "And there you have it," she mutters, "the excuse the U.S. and its allies needed to redeploy their troops." *At ease,* she thinks, feeling her jaw and shoulders tighten in response to the anger and frustration growing inside her. She had arrived at the Arizona Air Force base two months ago with her guard up, worried that when she least expected it, a cabinet-level head in the Department of Defense would show up, demanding to know how she had learned about the top secret air strike set to take place at the base in Pulwama while she was there, which foiled their operation at the time. It didn't matter that Chief Rolling Thunder had assured her that none of her activities in Kashmir sent up any red flags. If anything, intercepting the Chinese helicopter like she and Squadron Leader Smith daringly did sidetracked the Americans, who gleaned critical information from both pilots about its design, along with the covert terrorist activities taking place in the mountains. The enthusiastic welcome she received in Arizona should have dispelled her concerns. She found the rugged terrain of the Sonoran Desert appealing, and the warm temperatures sure beat the freezing cold Himalayas.

Once she's at work, Constance tries to put the grim news of the soldiers' deaths behind her. It's hard to do. She keeps thinking, *that could've been me.* The ensuing relief efforts that took place following the earthquakes and floods in northern India must have delayed the Americans from acting until now. Yesterday's attack in Pulwama happened at a critical time in which to send the troops back in. North Korea's recent highly criticized underground H-bomb and nuclear warhead tests make it imperative for the Americans to maintain an ongoing military presence in Asia. It keeps a show of force in that part of the hemisphere, for what it's worth. *Such theater!* She's grateful to be out of there.

Now it's time for Howling Wind to deliver on her promise to the Rawakota Nation. Regardless whether it was plain luck that got her assigned to this base, or if the Rawakota had a hand in it, she will relay everything she learns about the extraordinarily sophisticated F-35 systems to them. This base is one of the few that trains F-35 pilots. They're an international group of aviators who account for the 1,000 flights a month out of the airfield. Constance had begun to apprise Rawakota scientists of the jet's specific capabilities over ten years ago while she was stationed in Texas, where the first stages of its development were getting underway. The F-35 combat aircraft was the first stealthy supersonic fighter of its kind to do vertical landings and short takeoffs. It could hover like a helicopter. Originally intended for both the U.S. Air Force and the Marines, other ally countries took a keen interest in what the planes could do, and they started placing orders for them. To date, the aircraft's internal computer networks and missile guidance systems incorporate the most modern electronic attack technologies. It requires an understanding of the entire range of the electromagnetic spectrum, or EMS, which includes radio waves, infrared and ultraviolet waves, microwaves, x-rays, and the like.

The upside from having been clued-in on the plane's design from its inception until now is that the Rawakotas' grasp of satellite-linked communications might presently surpasses that of the United States, the current leader when it comes to controlling the electromagnetic spectrum. If they had a mind to, the Rawakota could wage an electronic assault against any country and not worry about retaliation. China, Russia, and the U.S., the superpowers of the world, would naturally blame one another for the attack, believing their militaries solely possess this know-how. And although members of the Rawakota Nation have infiltrated the companies that design F-35 engines, along with those that produce specialized helmets and radar systems, the expertise from a pilot of Howling Wind's caliber will be helpful when it comes to finding deficiencies in the technology. Foremost to consider in this era of spectrum warfare, as it is called, is the fact that stealth systems need to be updated on an ongoing basis. The Rawakota revealed to Howling Wind that they have figured out ways in which to use weaker wavelengths. It won't be long before their jamming techniques, intended to confuse enemy radar, will be unrivaled.

"Hey, Howler!" The man within shouting distance spotted Constance the moment she stepped outside to head to the hangar for a flight test. "How's it going?"

Constance looks to the side and offers a casual wave of the hand. It's Staff Sergeant Filippo "Phil" Tardelli, nicknamed "Super Mario." He's putting Nero through his paces. The German Shepherd barks hello. The airman is one of a few handlers on the base with the additional job of training military working dogs. They're a handsome pair. Both share a slim but muscular physique. Constance had first noticed Phil's green eyes and strong Roman nose when she purposely slammed him to the ground with a blow to his side during a game of volleyball in the sand pit...because of his chauvinistic behavior. That's what he got for acting as though his skills exceeded hers. He'd been constantly interfering with her chance at the ball. The way the guy jumped to a standing position, so fast and angry, she half expected him to take a swing at her. Instead, he took the humiliation in stride and simply brushed himself off. Now they're friends.

Keeping her adrenaline in check, Howling Wind continues toward the tarmac. This afternoon she'll be testing the latest G-suit. It marks the fourth time in two weeks that she's in the air. Her opinion about the F-35 Lightning II has grown more positive this go-round. Among its previous performance issues, the ejector seat was found to be risky for pilots weighing under 75 kilos or 165 pounds. Her weight didn't come close. Flying 15 kilometers above the earth, the thought of a potential malfunction and a nine mile descent with a broken neck from the blast was hard to dismiss.

While she was stationed in Texas, she had already racked up the requisite hours needed on the simulator for training in the F-35, add to that her twenty hours in the air; but that was long before her stint in the Mideast and Asia where she flew mostly F-16s. There is an inordinate amount of new information being presented here, but it doesn't overwhelm her.

Besides the new flight suit, she must familiarize herself with the complex helmet that is custom-built for each pilot. It's spiffy...with external cameras that feed video to the face shield. A pilot can actually see through the skin of a jet. Weapons can also be aimed with the eyes, even at night. There's a missile-warning system that scans both air and ground. Yes, she is definitely enthralled by this new-fangled sensor-driven way of flying, with its 8 million lines of software code that will inevitably make a body in the cockpit obsolete. After completing the lengthy and comprehensive checklist, Howling Wind sits ready for takeoff inside the cramped cockpit, eager to tear through the blindingly blue desert sky.

Ōy·ah' ·mā·yȧn, noun • word gatherer • An ethnographic group that exists within the Rawakota Nation, credited with the creation of their people's written language. Upon reaching their destination ages ago in a region now called the Black Hills, the Oyahmayan split from the main Rawakota tribe, in order to live closer to the land and mountains. They chose not to follow their tribal brothers and sisters deeper down into the tunnels that took them to a vast cavern where they established the city of Chohkahn. Over time, the Oyahmayan people developed their own distinctive cultural identity.

During her stop-off at the Ellsworth base in South Dakota, while Howling Wind awaited new orders after returning from India, Chief Rolling Thunder and holy man, Sleeping Buffalo, invited her to join them and a team of Oyahmayan scholars at a private cabin in the Black Hills mountains, in order to discuss the Mujahzee tribe that Smitty had correctly named. Constance knew next to nothing about the Oyahmayan and looked them up. If her elders had said anything about them at all, it was only in passing. She had been impressed by their refined manner and extensive vocabulary, which made sense, considering their background in languages. Physically, they were leaner and a bit shorter than the Rawakota she had come to know in Chohkahn, who have larger and more robust frames like her family and neighbors on the Buckthorn Reservation. She is eager to enlighten Smitty about what they told her, if she could just get a word in edgewise.

"Can you believe that the shapes of the letters are not so different from the Israelites who copied them from the Egyptians over 3000 years ago!" Smitty is on the verge of yelling, he's so excited. "It boggles the mind that these age-old symbols of communication can be translated today." He is referring to the document that the Mujahzee gave him. After returning to RAF Odiham in Hampshire, England, his current base, he headed to the University of Oxford China Centre at the earliest opportunity, in order to meet with Matthew Bainbridge, Professor Emeritus of South and Inner Asia studies. Smitty's "find" had dumbfounded the retired academic, who was told it had been discovered beneath the rubble of a landslide in India.

How else could Smitty explain having the unique treasure in his possession? At first glance, the elderly gentleman could tell that the vertical system was characteristic of classical Mongolian writing. He could not give him an exact timeframe without studying it more, but suggested it was likely written around the 12th century. Smitty figured it had to have been long before that.

"It's absolutely fascinating…" begins Constance, only to have Smitty interrupt. He reels off the names of dynasties and rulers and the centuries they held power along with ways the civilizations influenced each other, until she forces him to stop.

"Breathe!" Softening her tone, she says, "It's all truly amazing, Smitty …now please let me fill you in on what I have learned, which is equally remarkable. How 'bout switching to visual mode so we can see each other."

He sinks down into a leather club chair molded to his backside. The view from his library overlooks a lovely traditional English cottage garden, thick with seasonal purple and pink blooms. Today rain hangs in the air. Constance does the same, settling instead between the corner cushions of a small sectional sofa that faces the sliding doors of the modest adobe-brick house she rents. Her panorama consists of a sunbaked hillside covered with spindly wild branching creosote shrubs. A solitary, majestic saguaro cactus stands like a sentinel holding watch. It's a venerable old-timer supporting at least a dozen arms, which Smitty can observe only a small portion of outside the glass door "Smitty, picture the planet a hundred thousand years ago. Whether the event was calamity driven—an earthquake, a flood, or disease—or a matter of simple curiosity, it's the period when the earliest humans, yours as well as my distant Rawakota-Mujahzee ancestors, left their habitats on the African continent and embarked on a journey that would lead them to Europe and Asia. One of these ancient groups had eyes that emitted light through a chemical reaction called bioluminescence, just like some other organisms found in the darkest regions of the planet. It might have been the result of an evolutionary mutation, from having lived in dark caves previously, or perhaps they ate food laced with a bacterium that contained an enzyme known to cause it. At any rate, some of those that migrated preferred the darkness and stayed underground, like the Mujahzee, while others went on to live both above the ground as well as below it. Eventually, their eyes changed, having adapted to a new environment that included sunlight."

Smitty is dying to ask questions but has been instructed to hold off until the end. Constance continues.

"There's no way of knowing how many individuals left the original population...and one must assume they communicated using only vocalizations like other species during that period." Constance jumps ahead in time, way ahead, to when this intrepid group ventured beyond the formidable Himalayas and the great desert, crossing paths with independent nomadic Mongolians who maintained an identity apart from the surrounding Chinese. "The two peoples established an unusual rapport. It was as if destiny had played a hand in their coming together; and this is known because the encounter between the cultures was documented, etched onto rolls made of copper by a band of Mujahzee tribesmen who called themselves Oyahmayan..."

"I knew it!" interjects Smitty. "They were among the first to write!"

Constance smiles. "And they could speak. They had been gathering words for a long time, from having made contact generations before with people using the Sogdian writing system. That of course means nothing to me, but I assume you can appreciate it. They met the Mongols when written languages were being devised. The biggest obstacle to this end was deciding ways to reflect the countless dialects. Oyahmayans showed the Mongols how to form numbers and create relationships between letters and sounds, which assuredly helped in the creation of trade contracts with the Chinese, as well as merchants from other countries who traveled the Silk Road. That likely served as an impetus for writing initially.

"As you've stated before, Smitty, alphabets got adopted by groups and then dismissed, sometimes on a whim—but not the Mongolian vertical script, which became part of its culture."

For the sake of convenience, Constance offers a condensed version of their later history. "The Mujahzee moved eastward, traveling on Mongol horses, true wild horses that were prized for their strength and stamina. They were led by a holy man who Sleeping Buffalo professes to be descended from. Whether by boat or land bridge, they traveled until they encountered a new land. Their trek across the open territories of what is now Canada and America, lasting tens of thousands of years, ended when they reached the landmark site of a mountain top that matched one from their ancient homeland." She doesn't have to tell him it was Black Elk Peak in South Dakota. Maps show it as Harney Peak, since the name change occurred only recently.

The two have been talking for close to an hour when Constance excuses herself to attend a party on the other side of town for the pilots on the base. Smitty still has questions, like when the Oyahmayan started using the Latin alphabet, and also why the Mujahzee changed the name of their tribe. He will get his answers soon when he takes his earned days of leave from the Royal Air Force and visits Mina, who returned to Chohkahn a while ago to be with her family.

The protest against a foreign mining company's interest in copper after it was discovered on Native land is better organized than she imagined. As a result, Lt. Colonel Howling Wind decides to stay longer in Oak Flat, a large area of 2400 acres about an hour east of Phoenix that belongs to the San Carlos Apache tribe.

She is glad to lend credibility to the cause, at least that's what she's been told by several at the rally who are pleasantly surprised to see an officer of her stature at the gathering. Wearing her military dress uniform for the dinner later in Scottsdale, Howling Wind stands out in the crowd of about two hundred. Her presence immediately grabs the attention of a TV reporter. She tells him that she has come to learn more about the controversy. In actuality, she simply wanted to observe the young actor who helped spearhead today's event, to watch the effect he has on people, both Indians and Whites. Jason Red Moon, who looks to be in his mid-twenties, speaks eloquently about the disputed issue.

"Many Apache consider the land sacred. In truth, all land is, just not to the global companies that expect to dig down 7,000 feet to extract copper out of the earth." He gives his head a shake and grins, "If only the white settlers had learned of the copper before they forced the Indians onto the reservation, onto land they thought was unfit for cultivation, and therefore worthless. Unfortunately, the company's promise of training locals for future jobs is pitting tribal members against one another. Poor rez youth want work, but you must ask yourselves if the cost in the long run is worth it to your community. Their representatives look Native leaders in the eyes while trying to convince them that they, like the Indians, are equally concerned about the environment. They promise they aren't like the historically unethical companies that, when they closed down operations, left Mother Earth totally scarred and her rivers forever ruined with poisonous chemicals. No, they want to show you they can be good stewards of the land, that the Indians will be let in on every step of the mining process. No one is fooling anybody here!"

With black eyes flashing and using a staccato style of speaking that emphasizes well his indignation, Red Moon continues to expound on his concern over back-room negotiations regarding the massive excavation project. They're the kind of shady deal-making tactics that persisted in Hawaii, where he says he raised awareness about keeping a billion dollar telescope from getting built atop a tribe's sacred mountain. Red Moon encourages the Apache on this reservation to travel to his next stop, the Grand Canyon, where the Navajo need to protect their land from developers who want it for the tourist industry. "Help the Navajo," he instructs them, "there's power in numbers." After that he's off to join the Standing Rock Sioux tribe in North Dakota to help them halt the construction of the Dakota Access Pipeline. Had he lived, her father would have surely encountered Red Moon at that rally, if not long before at another gathering for some different Native cause. Constance listens to the conversations going on behind her, and they're an eyeopener. Red Moon's words touch a raw nerve, but they're not producing the desired effect that he was certainly hoping for—which is to prevent the Apache from dealing with the mining company, period. Seems there are tribal members who don't like the actor's brash attitude. "It's like he's 'ordering' us what to do," says a man, with other voices backing him up. It turns out that the impassioned speaker is making little headway, at least with the group standing near her. Interesting, thinks Howling Wind. Red Moon concentrates so much on the big picture that he doesn't take into account the individual's point of view. He acts like he alone knows what is in the best interest of the Indians, no matter the tribe, their location, or unique circumstances. She wonders if Red Moon is the type of man who can take constructive criticism, although none will be offered this afternoon; she needs to hurry along.

Glancing at the time, she merges onto the 101 North, realizing cocktail hour is over. Her stomach is growling, and it's certain that this shindig was going to have terrific appetizers. Dinner should at least be starting when she arrives.

From one extreme to the other, notes Constance as a starched guard at the entrance to the estate checks her credentials. The automatic iron gate closes slowly and quietly behind her—securing those inside it from the riffraff element outside. An idea occurs to her: the same type of monstrosity should be erected around the Apache tribe's Oak Flat borders, in order to keep those money-grubbing conglomerates out. She weaves her leased Kia through a long, palm-lined drive, passing grand fountains and a private heliport, unimpressed by the obscene opulence. It's easy to see why the expensive ZIP code garners contempt from ordinary folk, especially during political elections. Citizens in exclusive neighborhoods like this one wield far too much influence. Tonight's party, for example, is no doubt connected with a pet project created by the super-rich couple throwing it. Ah, she shouldn't be so hard on the wealthy. Bottom line is many love the business of war, and because of it, she gets to exercise her own ambition of flying fighter jets.

The obligatory introductions and small talk tests Howling Wind's patience. She finds an opening in the crowd and escapes through the double doors to the back outdoor patio. Someone says her name. It's a familiar voice; one she welcomes.

"You've been with the Indians this whole time?"

Sergeant "Super Mario" Phil, the dog trainer, saved her a seat by the fire pit. It was also extremely thoughtful of him to have fixed her a plate stacked with goodies. She practically inhales them.

"Last year in Ethiopia, I witnessed the same problems," says Phil, in response to Howling Wind's description of the Apache's dilemma, which she managed to articulate between bites. "Except there, it's the Chinese outsourcing jobs because their own people now demand fair wages. Poor African boys and girls from small villages rush to the towns looking for work. Next, as always happens, the factories contaminate the rivers which end up polluting the groundwater that flows out to the farms. It's a sorry state of affairs for the old folks who are stuck behind with nowhere to go." Aware that she's only half-listening, he stops himself: "But then I'm not telling you anything new, right?"

With a rather unsightly full mouth, she tries mumbling that she heard him. He laughs and wipes a spot of cream cheese from her chin.

"Sorry, Phil. I'm so damn hungry."

"Did you meet our hosts?"

"No. Are they in sight?"

He scans the room. "There, the guy in the tan blazer and white pants."

"I guess I should go over…"

At that moment dinner is announced. It's a formal sit-down. Upon arrival, every guest was informed as to the color of the centerpiece he or she should look for on the table. Howling Wind is bummed that she is purple, and Phil is green.

"Did you really think they'd put our ranks together?" he asks. It's an honest comment, not intended to sound snide. "Well look at that! You get the privilege of sitting with our hostess." His green eyes sparkle with amusement. "Not that you don't deserve to, Constance; it's just that she's grabbed every male's ass who has politely indulged her in conversation tonight, including mine."

"No kidding!"

"Catch you later. Have fun."

Lt. Colonel Howling Wind greets the six officers at the round table, all men, which is usually the case. Other airmen who came with wives or girlfriends are seated elsewhere. Sandwiched between two broad-shouldered colonels is the glitzy hostess, Mrs. Falcone. Constance shakes her hand and introduces herself. She knows that Col. "Borg" Johansson is divorced, and that Col. "Raz" Edelman has a wife and children back in Israel. She walks to the last open seat. It's opposite Falcone's, a location that discourages dialogue between them, which is perfectly fine with her as she awaits the food. She wonders if the married woman is simply a tease, or a brazen adulteress who shares an *understanding* with her husband. Mr. Falcone, head of the family's lucrative scrap-metal industry, is seated several tables away. He seems indifferent to his wife's flirtations with their guests.

As dinner gets underway, Howling Wind is entertained by the pilots' stories of their exploits. They invariably follow a pattern of good-natured one-upmanship. Their boasts are aimed at impressing one another, other pilots, not Mrs. Falcone, whose interruptions go unnoticed. It's laughable. The next thing she knows, the woman is staring at her from across the table, as if she's sizing her up. Constance doesn't flinch, but holds the woman's gaze.

When the Major seated to her left excuses himself, the vacated spot is promptly taken by Mrs. Falcone. A waiter's arm pokes between them to pour coffee. Up close, Howling Wind beholds an aging, youth-obsessed vision, and pities Falcone for what she's done to herself. Besides the telltale facial cosmetic surgery, there's the unnatural brown shade of her skin, caused by either decades of golfing in the sun unprotected or tanning booths. The elaborately coiffed brassy orange-yellow hair resembles a Celtic ceremonial helmet she once saw in a museum. The style is severe and unmoving. If the image wasn't unflattering enough, her old, stretched earlobes are definitely unsightly. Falcone's chandelier-inspired earrings, decorated in god knows how many diamonds, dangle practically to her shoulders.

"Lieutenant Colonel Howling Wind, what a treat to be surrounded by so many gorgeous hunks on a daily basis. I have to ask; how can you concentrate?"

She saw that one coming: "My husband outclasses them all."

"Do tell."

The atmosphere is relaxed. The pilots, oozing with testosterone, go on delighting Mrs. Falcone. The stories grow louder as the liquor flows. Howling Wind unabashedly goes for another guest's dessert, since he put it to the side. She makes no attempt to engage Falcone, figuring the woman moved to get nearer the men on this side of the table. Content in her own world, she finds herself being addressed again.

"What do you do if you're in the air, Lt. Colonel, and something stops working?"

Howling Wind pauses in her chewing. *Odd question,* she thinks.

"Depends on what it is...you mean like, the engine?"

Mrs. Falcone looks thoughtfully at her. "I mean the power to everything. It's all run by computers nowadays, correct?"

"Well, any aircraft can glide ... one resorts to a dead-stick landing."

"Are you serious? You can land a fighter jet like a glider? Have you ever done it?"

"Yes," says Howling Wind, noting her genuine curiosity. She almost embarks on an explanation regarding the sufficient glide ratio needed, but stops short since it would be over her head.

"Have all pilots?"

"If not firsthand, on a simulator. Why the interest?"

"Seems a vital thing to know..." And with that Mrs. Falcone abruptly stands, cornering the returning Major before he gets a chance to reclaim his seat. As she whisks him onto the dance floor, she looks back over her shoulder at Howling Wind and casually adds, "… say like in two weeks, on Thursday."

CHAPTER 29

"Hot damn! That was a hundred yarder for sure, Viktor!"

DeShaun exaggerates, but is so excited about my long pass that he won't stop shaking me. You'd have thought we won a real game. Jasper comes bounding toward us from our end zone where two perfectly spaced oak trees serve as the goal posts. He's waving the ball in his outstretched arms, making ready for a chest bump celebration, which he knows darn well isn't my thing. I race away to escape him. Using his signature long dive, DeShaun lunges at my ankles. It's like my shoelaces got tied together, and I fall right over. A second later, Jasper lands splat across my back and starts helmet butting mine, laughing like a fool.

"By next year…" he says, catching his breath, "… the three of us'll be famous." He rolls to the side and smiles up at the sky. "Boys, we are headed for the bigtime!"

"Maybe you two will have bragging rights, but there's still the matter of me making the team. And what about the current quarterback?"

"Dude!" exclaims DeShaun, looking to Jasper. "Can you believe this guy? Viktor, my man, you gotta show more confidence…shit."

"I'm being realistic."

Jasper helps pull me up. "What are we gonna do with you!" He takes holds of my facemask and orders me to repeat after him: "I am going to be the greatest college quarterback in history."

"That's overstating things…how 'bout the best Buckeye…"

"Stop it already! I am going to be the greatest college quarterback in history. Say it!"

"Say it!" urges DeShaun. "I don't wanna be playin' with no one but the best, 'cuz that's what I'm gonna be, and what Jasper's gonna be."

Aye-yi-yi. They're on me till I do it.

"I, Viktor Talking White Owl, intend to be the greatest quarterback in the history of the game, *iwáhoyA*—my promise to you." They're not sold.

"Man that's lame! Show some conviction, dude!" yells DeShaun, pushing me off balance.

Jasper hangs his head and makes annoying tsk sounds. "Pitiful...just pitiful."

"You're gonna say those words every day, you hear!" barks DeShaun like a drill sergeant. "But mean them!"

"C'mon guys..."

Jasper takes me by the arm. "Every morning, every night ..."

DeShaun cuts in, "*What* did you say!" having caught the *Jesus* I muttered under my breath.

"Okay, okay."

With helmets in hand and feeling charged after the killer practice, we head up the hill to their cars, poking and tripping each other up. The positive chemistry we share when we're together reminds me of how I had clicked with Hayden. He is never far from my thoughts when the guys and I toss the ball around on this spot by the Scioto River.

I ride back to campus with Jasper. He asks why I've turned quiet.

"A year ago, I didn't know *WAKAN* was in my future, and now look at me—I am seriously preparing for football." I almost say how becoming involved with *WAKAN* proved disastrous to my life, and that I find it scary at times to think about the consequences of my decisions, but then I realize that Jasper knows nothing about Ishmael or the actual circumstances surrounding the attack that landed me in the hospital. I do tell him that I thought football wasn't in the cards anymore.

"Hell, man, don't let that beating screw with your head." I sniffle back the tears welling up in my eyes, which isn't embarrassing around him. "You've come a long way, Viktor. And that experience led you to DeShaun and me. This is a fresh start; it's the road you were meant to travel, my friend. I feel it in my bones ... don't you?"

"Having yellow eyes is the only reason this scientist wants to study you?" asks Uncle.

"He's beyond curious; I'd say he's obsessed with my eyes." I give him a quick account of how the French scientist Bonnaire, who he knows recommended me for the Herrington scholarship, learned about Winter

Crow's contribution to genetic research through letters written by the British researcher Rosalind Franklin in the 1950s.

"It's strictly up to you, Viktor." He crosses his arms and leans against the counter, ready to pull a pizza from the oven the second the buzzer goes off. "Since he is an evolutionist, your chromosomes will reveal that our closest cousins are lemurs—giant ones, all now extinct. That information might astound the science world, but it won't tell them anything about our culture."

That fact blows me away. "Lemurs...really?" It's what Grandmother was talking about on our way to the airport. When Uncle said *our* closest cousins, he was referring to the Rawakota. It's the first time he has ever alluded to his authentic background. "Why have I been kept in the dark about the Rawakota?" I ask. "Mom tried explaining Otiwota and theeich ihilah over break, because Sunkwah apparently didn't do an adequate job. Did she tell you?"

Uncle grunts, the kind that means not to hold out hope for an explanation. In the meantime he cuts the pizza. For once Lakota music isn't playing. He asks about the practice sessions with Jasper and DeShaun. It's obvious he likes both of them. He surprises me when he says, "Soon, with any luck, you will understand."

"That's vague...what determines the right time?"

"It's complicated."

"Why?"

"Because no one can guess how much the teachings of your great-grandparents affected you in your early life...the lasting impression they made. Or for that matter, things that Benjamin, your Pahpie, may have told you before he died."

"That's plain stupid! It's exactly what Mom said. Wouldn't I have already felt some kind of effect from it? Please tell me how reciting a poem every night could amount to such a big deal, big enough to cause a rift between Mom and her family when she learned about it? You must have done it, too, when you were growing up, right?"

"Eat. Don't worry yourself."

"Like that's going to happen! Did theeich ihilah cause Lukas to go off the deep end?"

His eyes give him away.

"And you say not to worry?" I further vent my frustration with a fitting

Yiddish expression that basically means *screw you,* which he wouldn't know. Judging by the way he's glowering at me, he guessed it by my tone. "Can you at least give me a hint of what to look out for?" I'm tempted to grunt right back to him in the face.

I keep pace with the fast and steady tribal drums that I haven't listened to in a while. It's a fine morning for walking, even though my ribs feel every step. I had better take a break from football and shooting hoops. After all these months, I'm still not a hundred percent. *Turn in paper.* Check. *Talk to Bonnaire.* Check. *Buy underwear.* Check. Only thing left to do is meet my teammates who are joining Dr. Sharma's research project. Then it's off to the Oval to relax. Can't wait. Plenty of students will be out with their dogs on a day like this, throwing Frisbees. Wish I had the time for a pet.

"Viktor Talking White Owl, meet Paige Kirkpatrick from Boston University, Ben Churchill from Duke, and Ernst Busch from the University of Freiburg."

They're all white people, blonde and blue-eyed ones no less. It's not a problem, just odd to me. But then I'm sure they've never met a Native American. I tower above Paige and Ben. The German might be an inch or so under six feet. His eyes are level with my collarbone, which is how I gauge heights.

We're led to a conference room where Dr. Sharma gives a short presentation about the various aspects of our investigation. Afterward, since I don't need a tour of the floor, Dr. Sharma excuses me but suggests that I poke my head in a room down the hall to have a look-see at our new state-of-the-art DNA sequencing machine. I nod okay, masking my impatience…just wanna hit the Oval, let the sun bake me…reward myself later with a dinner of all-you-can-eat pancakes for having gotten caught up in my classes.

Gonna make this quick—in, out. There it is on the counter…whoop di-doo. Guess I better glance at the manual, in case I'm quizzed over it. Don't know why people are working in here already; our official start date isn't until after next week.

"Hey, Viktor."

I turn and help Dr. Wu with a stack of boxes he's about to drop.

"Will your students be in with us, too, Dr. Wu?" I figure this is his crew.

"No, no...didn't you hear about the flood in the blood lab?"

He says a pipe burst in the ceiling. Any department with an open area is helping out until the problem is fixed. He assures me that nothing being tested is contagious. Great, because it hadn't crossed my mind. After arranging the boxes on a cart beside a girl glued to the eyepiece of her microscope, I ask what she's looking at. She holds up an index finger indicating to wait a sec while her thumb carefully rotates the focus knob. Suddenly my breathing picks up. Next, all I notice is her left ear lobe, and how I want to place my teeth on the fleshy bud and touch my tongue to the skin. *What's up with that?* The small back part of her neck that sticks out from under her lab coat makes me hot, so do the soft coppery curls that have fallen from her hairclip. As my heart starts doing some serious thumping, my dick's growing hard, fast. It's bizarre, considering I have no clue what she looks like.

"Sorry," she says, turning her chair. "Just want to make sure I don't mistake yeast cells for something else."

If only I had a witty comeback, instead I choke. She is beautiful. And her voice is beautiful. Like a fool I reach out to shake her hand for no reason. She politely responds to my awkward gesture and removes a glove. Her long fingers are beautiful, too. I can't believe I'm holding them. My height doesn't appear to faze her. Her big, smoky-blue colored eyes look directly into mine. She's got the fairest complexion I've ever seen. We tell our names. Her fingertips glide over my palm as we let go of each other. My entire being reacts to the sensation. We manage a few sentences before Dr. Wu interrupts to ask for my help in moving a cabinet back in his office. Tess says she needs to get back to work; she has a set number of slides to look at before the end of the hour.

"Will you be here tomorrow?" I ask, praying this is a daily job.

"No. I'm on call. Sometimes I'm here at night. The supervisor has my class schedule, so she knows when I'm available."

And with that she's back to the world in the viewfinder. I'm afraid to ask for her number in front of the other techs sitting around the table. Such a pretty girl probably has a boyfriend. Besides, I promised myself no distractions; it's just going to be about school and football this year. *But she's so beautiful.* On my way out, I wonder how I'm going to ignore what just happened.

CHAPTER 30

Lt. Col. Howling Wind watches from the tarmac as the last of four pilots executes a vertical take-off in his F-35, and then streaks forward into the cloudless stretch of blue sky to join his group's formation. Together they shoot north across the mountains.

There is no reason for Constance to be on the base this morning, having been given a few days leave. She wanted to lend her support to these trainees who completed their hours on the simulators this past week. She hesitates before walking away, taking a moment to rub her sore knees. Too much sparring in the ring yesterday. She's out of shape. Perhaps she should head north, too, she thinks, and play tourist among the red rocks in Sedona. Why not?

Driving with the windows and sunroof open in the car, Constance cruises toward the I-17, wishing Solomon were along for the trip. Down time is unwelcomed; her thoughts are all over the place. She isn't twenty minutes out when she notices the faraway jets growing bigger. They're returning, and far too soon. The emergency alert on her phone startles her. With no exit in sight, she veers onto the stony median of this section of empty road, in order to make a U-turn, carefully dodging bush after bush covered in long sharp spines. She then hightails it back to the base all the while checking for hidden traffic cops.

Upon her return, Constance quickly reports to the wing commander, who is waiting for word to scramble. Next, she suits up and in nothing flat is checking the cockpit displays in the F-16 as she readies for takeoff—this being a real perceived threat.

Before 9/11, who would have thought that a perfectly serene blue sky was a harbinger of bad things to come? Might it also be the case on this fine April morning, with "severe clear" conditions forecast coast to coast. Gnawing on Howling Wind's conscience since she woke up is the fact that today is the Thursday Mrs. Falcone had cautioned her about. There is no telling the scope of the crisis.

Visual identification is made by the U.S. Air Force pilots. A Boeing 737-800 en route from San Diego to Dallas, with 127 passengers and a six member crew, is definitely off course and flying directly toward the Palo Verde Nuclear Generating Station, situated not even 50 miles west of Phoenix and 40 miles west of the Air Force base.

The image of the commercial airliner sailing over a nuclear power plant and nearly shearing off the domes of its reactor containment buildings is the stuff of Hollywood action thrillers. Whoever *directed* the stunt knew the scene would instantly go viral and play to a world audience. Viewers at first wondered if the near-miss was faked, but too many on-lookers on the ground witnessed the unbelievable sight and were able to substantiate that it truly happened. And of course there were the passengers on the plane who, to their utter disbelief, lived to tell about it. Three of them, along with the co-pilot, experienced chest pains and were rushed to the hospital where they were expected to make a full recovery.

It's the second day of a Q&A session for Lt. Col. Howling Wind and Major Collins, the F-16 pilots, as well as for Col. Braverman, who flew the F-35. Today they'll be offering the same details as they had reported yesterday to Brigadier General Chafey, their Commander at the base. This afternoon the room will include chief intelligence officers from the Department of Defense, directors and commanders from the Federal Aviation Administration and North American Aerospace Defense, as well as leading physicists and engineers, all of whom will try to figure out what on earth happened. It's a matter of national security that the commercial airline pilots can't be privy to the highly secretive information that will be discussed here with the FAA and NORAD. A different investigative unit is dealing with them.

Following a night fraught with quiet trepidation, the glassed-over, red eyes of the roomful of rumpled looking souls are no indication that anyone is running short of adrenaline. To the contrary, the heightened focus is that of cornered prey—unable as yet to see the danger, but tortured by having every fiber of its being alerted to it. The high stakes whodunit is sure to stump this collection of brilliant minds. They are enlisted to pick apart the multiple safeguards put in place at each level of operations and then determine why they all failed.

Granted, no physical damage resulted, but the action exposed the vulnerabilities of the United States, the world's most dominant military superpower. It's quite embarrassing in light of the country's scandalous defense expenditure. In addition to the big security-related questions, there is also the matter of how to spin this fiasco for a public that is both outraged and terrified by what could have potentially happened.

Lt. Col. Howling Wind watches the latest arrivals with interest, many of whom are civilians. General Chafey has their full attention. He pauses before he starts, as though for a split second the light bulb went off, and he had a credible explanation for the preposterous incident. Howling Wind recognizes these moments of insight, for he excels at thinking outside the box and formulating theories others miss, a trait she witnessed firsthand when they served together in Yemen. Then, as now, his wickedly arched eyebrows come together to form a deep line that furrows halfway up his long forehead. Everyone is hanging on the next words out of his mouth. Alas, the vision is lost. The general proceeds to describe the dry facts as they unfolded on Thursday morning.

"DesertXpress Flight 3296 disappeared from radar forty-five minutes after departing the San Diego International Airport at 8:53 a.m. Up to that point, there had been no deviation in its flight path to Dallas. Suddenly all communications were lost. Its transponder was not set to the standard emergency frequency, which was highly unusual. The Phoenix Sky Harbor Airport notified the FAA, which contacted NORAD, prompting the scrambling of two F-16s and one F-35 from our Air Force base. It was dumb luck that a couple of retired gentlemen from Oregon—who happened to belong to a fraternity of ham radio enthusiasts—were the first to report something out of the ordinary to the Phoenix tower when they stopped for a break in the Harqua area, which is approximately sixty miles west of the city. They, Mr. Robert Medina and his friend Larry Wolek, had just driven through Nevada and northern Arizona, stopping at ghost towns along the way. They were headed for Yuma. During their trip, they had been meeting up with fellow ham operators, whom they had only ever spoken to on their radios. They carried in-car handsets. Reading from Robert Medina's report: 'We were parked along the road with our car doors open, getting ready to check for signals. As I turned around to grab some sandwiches in the back seat, I saw this plane heading straight for us...a regular looking passenger jet. But it was low, way too low. I jumped out of the car screaming to Larry to run for his life. While we were racing away, we couldn't believe the plane was flying steady, not nosediving...like it was going to crash.'

"It occurred to the men that the plane might be headed for Tonopah ...that terrorists could be onboard. They had driven past the nuclear plant earlier. By then our pilots had a visual of the Boeing. You have the timeline of the events in the reports given to you. Also noted are the distances of the aircraft from each other and the ground. You can study them later. What you need to know now is that the jets the Air Force sent up to intercept the airliner experienced abrupt total electrical system failure at a distance of 1600 meters from Flight 3296, roughly a mile away from it, which they were unable to communicate to the base's air traffic control tower. The multiple layers of redundancy, all the many separate components designed to act as fail-safe backups for crucial tasks, were inadequate."

That key information sets the room abuzz, but the voices quickly hush when the general straightens his posture and rests his hands on his hips. Howling Wind observes how deeply people are breathing; they'd gotten themselves so worked up. He continues.

"The city of Phoenix's air traffic control tower received a message from Mr. Medina on a radio band he used to contact it. There was no interference with his transmission, which obviously needs to be examined. By then we were able to ascertain how low the aircraft was flying and feared it was going to be intentionally flown into the power plant. As the plane neared the nuclear facility, at an altitude of perhaps 300 to 400 feet—think about that—the place lost its electricity, including its backup power. All systems were back online at the plant as soon as the plane cleared the restricted air space on the other side of the structures, which is when it began climbing ... on its own. It still didn't show up on the radar, and the Boeing pilots stated that they had yet to gain control of their instruments. By then, police were getting calls from panic-stricken witnesses saying a passenger plane had just buzzed over their heads, temporarily causing their cars to act up and their cell phones to stop working. Soon afterward, when those people received a signal again, pictures and reports began appearing on the Internet along with descriptions of a doomsday scenario that included explosions at the plant, which were untrue. You have certainly heard the hysterical accounts. At 5000 feet, the airline pilots regained control and brought the flight in for an emergency landing at

Phoenix Sky Harbor International Airport. In the meantime, the fighter pilots were forced to make dead-stick, unpowered, landings. Once on the ground, their displays and communications systems were restored. Go figure. One would think that when the Boeing airliner flew beyond a mile of the fighter jets, the distance they'd been from it when the electrical systems initially shut down, everything would have started up again, but that wasn't the case."

The General invites the Air Force's Director of Engineering to take over the meeting. He'll be responsible for assigning people to teams. They're expected to work around the clock until they can answer what kind of technology is capable of besting the most up-to-date artificial intelligence used so far around the world, even in a simulation environment, and whether the perpetrators of this alarming, illegal act were Americans or foreigners.

A break is called when food arrives. Howling Wind wanders through the crowd while she eats, listening as the military people expound upon assorted political motives. The computer science wizards, presumably well-known in hacker circles, are interested in biometrics and sensors and algorithms. She ponders the types of questions that'll be asked of her and the two other pilots who are next to take the floor.

"What are you thinking?" Howling Wind looks up from her plate at General Chafey.

"For some reason, General, everyone shrugs off the idea that it could have been North Korea. India has been developing sophisticated weapons and software in its standoff with Pakistan. The U.S. doesn't interest them. The Chinese have been successful at converting electricity into microwaves resulting in some seriously high-powered weapons...but that would have fried our control systems. You told us last night that nothing was corrupted. The Russians? Hmm...I don't know; they might be colluding with the Chinese. I still don't think they have the means to have pulled this off. I tend to side with the camp that's been critical over all the sharing that goes on between the U.S. and Israel. They possess incredibly advanced radar systems, besides always staying ahead of the latest technology. Just how many of their mini spy satellites are in orbit these days? And they're in the lead when it comes to robotics. There hasn't been much success when it comes to locating their unmanned patrol ships."

General Chafey studies the room. "Mind?" he asks, reaching for a stuffed mushroom on her plate. "Anything else?"

"Suppose a weapons manufacturing company is to blame?"

As he chews, Gen. Chafey looks at Howling Wind like she might be onto something, or more likely it's that the idea had also occurred to him. He expands on that thought. "The Air Force could finally brag about the impressive performance of the F-35A at the recent Red Flag exercises in Nevada, where it was shown to excel in electronic warfare. Now this happens. It's inevitable that for every stealth system that has been dreamed up, there is an anti-craft system on the horizon that can destroy it...the speed of innovation boggles the mind. The interference had to originate from above. It acted like a tractor beam, specifically targeting the aircrafts. The people on the ground, the way the electrical components in their cars and phones were affected...that was incidental, occurring only when the beam swept over them. The same goes for the power plant. It could be a form of laser technology."

"If some employees at a private corporation are responsible," says Howling Wind, "the purpose might have been to display their technical superiority, to show the military they no longer have the upper hand. Truth be told, a lot of people could have been annihilated. My guess is they intend to remain anonymous, using this know-how as leverage in the future."

"Agreed. No terrorist group has made demands or claimed responsibility. I believe it's safe for our airports to resume operations." Once more General Chafey scans the odd mix of characters who are presently returning to their seats. "The 1967 Outer Space Treaty never envisioned a day there'd be so many international players involved in space operations, let alone private contractors. Any one of the individuals behind this demonstration of power could be right under our noses. They may well believe they are hands down the cleverest geniuses in the world, but we're going to smoke them out." Howling Wind sees a man on a mission. "All set for questions, Lieutenant Colonel?"

"Yes, sir." Howling Wind goes to join the panel of her fellow airmen. As they sit waiting for the conversations to die down, she considers the confidential information she hadn't shared with her commander. No matter how fantastic the science behind the pretend attack turns out to be, Howling Wind knows that the complexity of the undertaking would remain outside the realm of believability if she were to reveal that...surprise!...redskins did it. *Bravo, Chief Rolling Thunder!* Her Rawakota co-conspirators must be basking in the glory of their success, exactly what she is doing.

Later at home, brimming with energy, Constance calls Solomon. "Did I wake you?"

"It's okay. I must have dozed off during the news. I got your text, but I would have preferred to hear your voice after all that's happened. I figured you had a lot on your plate. Were you personally involved with the close-call of that plane over the nuclear plant?"

"Please...you know not to ask. Can you come out here? Like right away?"

"But there aren't any flights ..."

"The ground stop has been lifted. All commercial flights have resumed."

"It's pretty late, but I guess I can message Brody to run things in the shop."

"I would greatly appreciate it, Solomon."

Silence.

"I need to hold you inside me."

That's met with a quick call to action! "I'll drive to Dallas to catch the red-eye."

CHAPTER 31

I frantically race up the steps three at a time, repeating "Dad" over and over in my head like some mantra. Uncle William picked him up at the airport an hour ago. I burst through the door and swoop him up in a big bear hug, darn near lifting him off his toes. "Dad!"

"Jesus, Viktor! Easy does it!" he laughs. "Hey...Iris promised she wouldn't let the cat out of the bag."

"What?" I ask, wondering what he meant. "Can't a guy be happy to see his dad?"

"You bet," he says, squeezing my arms, "just surprised by your enthusiasm."

I peck him on the cheek and get a whiff of his spicy after shave that I've always liked. "So what's this about Iris, and a secret?"

"Never you mind. Come sit. Look at this terrific dinner!"

Ray Charles pining away for his Georgia is playing in the background. Lucky for Dad that he got to choose the music. We dig in. As usual, Uncle has outdone himself. Dad wants to know if I ever cook for myself. It hadn't occurred to me before now, but sandwiches are about it.

"If Uncle would stop fixing such good meals and giving me the leftovers...I guess I'd be forced to cook, if I wanted something different to eat. It's not like I've been on my own for very long." That leads to a conversation about Winnie's ground-up smoked turkey "wasna" and Pahpie's grilled duck that he used to love to make, which brings on a bout of homesickness.

"Take the braided turnips to hang in your kitchen," says Uncle, "maybe it will inspire you to try your hand at a few recipes."

Dad says he feels bad for having missed my birthday. He was in Arizona with Mom for almost three weeks, his longest visit to date. By now I've deduced that she was one of the pilots called upon to intercept the DesertXpress flight, even though their names have been kept under wraps for security reasons. The story continues to be a national obsession, and rightly so. There are too many conflicting accounts of what actually happened. I ask Dad if he knows the truth because no one believes the Defense Department's official statement. Supposedly a satellite was getting overhauled at the same time the passenger plane unintentionally veered off course, which is when it entered the air space surrounding a remote desert government test site. The Air Force insisted it was always in control of the situation. There was never any fear of the airliner crashing into the nuclear plant.

"I mean...jeez! If they were so in control, why not divert the plane *around* the buildings, instead of nearly shearing off the domes of its reactors and scaring the living daylights out of the workers? There are so many holes in their report."

Dad takes a swig of Coke, forgoing his preference for beer when he's around us Indians, then stares at the bottle. "I think it's one helluva breach that has everyone tripping over each other trying to find the cause, which is scary in and of itself. I've never witnessed so many serious faces."

"Including Mom's?"

"No. Not at all," he says, grinning. "Nothing riles her ... at least not at work. She's up for promotion in two months."

It's interesting to watch my uncle and my father together. They have an easy relationship. They're always touching the other's arm and leaning into each other as they speak. It's as though they've invited me into their circle today, and it makes the occasion feel special. Uncle's eyes light up when Aunt Loretta's name is mentioned. It gets me thinking...

"Uncle, I know you met Mom's sister when you came to work on the rez, but what were the circumstances? Did Grandmother introduce the two of you? Was the attraction mutual?"

He takes his time answering.

"I was in a deep state of depression the day I arrived on the Buckthorn Reservation, suffering from *yahzahn choh lah* ... the pain of being without a partner. Finding myself alone, after almost a decade of living for the chase, I decided to leave a hospital in Sioux Falls and finish my residency at the Health Center in Kyle, where I knew other Rawakota worked. I needed to be among my own people, in a community that understood my sense of desperation."

"But why didn't you go back to your family's hometown in the Black Hills where you've said you're from?" That seems like the solution to me.

Uncle answers that none of the girls he grew up with interested him. It was a small population. He thought for sure he would find someone at a big college. That's not encouraging to hear, since it's been my plan, too.

"The job included working out of a trailer three days a week in the eastern region of the reservation alongside a well-respected nurse, Victoria Birdsong, your grandmother. Late in the afternoon on my first day, after seeing several patients in the morning, an old Chevy van pulled up carrying a boy covered in bee stings. That was our ambulance. The nurse who had taken the call and driven out to get him was Birdsong's daughter, Loretta Wildrose. We moved fast to stabilize him and then, while we were cleaning up, Loretta and I finally had a chance to introduce ourselves. One look in those eyes...*ascu!*" His hands fly in the air. "Love at first sight...like being struck by lightning!"

"Un-hee!" I'm glued to his every word. To think that's how it was for me with the girl in the lab. It's suddenly quiet. I hadn't noticed the music ended. We can hear the muffled conversations and laughter of our neighbors on the floor below us. This is when they normally come home. Their door slams shut.

"Was it like that for you and Mom, too?" I ask Dad.

"Oh God, no!"

That was quick, and negative. I know only that they had met at Sheppard Air Force Base in Texas. Mom was enrolled in its pilot training program after graduating from the Academy, and Dad had signed up for a university-sponsored rehabilitation program that partnered with the base to help low risk inmates learn a trade. He slumps back in the chair. Perhaps it's a horrible memory. To my surprise, Uncle eggs him on, never having heard the story himself.

"You're kidding!" I tell him. They've known each other how many years...and this never came up?

"No," says Uncle to me. "Not kidding." His voice is deep and serious. "Constance showed up on the rez unexpectedly with Solomon and said they were going to get married in a few weeks. The family was extremely upset. Next we learned he had been in prison, and that she met him just a couple of months before. We thought she had lost her mind."

"I didn't know that," says Dad.

It's strange to hear one of Uncle's annoying grunts directed at Dad. It sounds like a scolding, as if he were saying to him: *What the hell were they supposed to think!*

Uncle goes on to say that Mom should have had the decency to call about the news before coming, especially to prepare them for the fact that she and this acquaintance planned on taking me and Iris back to Wichita Falls, Texas. He looks directly at Dad. "Imagine how heartbroken Sunkwah and Winnie were…the children had been in their great-grandparents' care for five years."

Dad sits forward and folds his arms on the table. The men exchange a long look that speaks volumes. Being older, I can appreciate how devastating the news must have been. When I was little, though, nothing could have made me happier than getting a dad.

I hate to interrupt their "moment," but I'm not going to miss this opportunity to find out what sparked Mom and Dad's interest in each other. Dad looks at me and smiles.

"I won the lottery the day your mother asked me if I'd be willing to marry her. Don't think I wasn't surprised." He's talking in a whisper, as if to himself. "God only knows what she saw in me." He shrugs his shoulders and shakes his head. There's a short laugh, and next he asks what it is I always say when I eat Aunt Junie's sweet potato pie.

"What?" How stupid.

"What do you *say*?"

"I don't say anything…I go mmm-mmm-mmm!"

"Exactly! Which is what I said when this hot babe walked by me while I was working on a jet engine at the base. No one heard me but her. She was in a blouse and skirt, a close fitting one that showed off her fine figure. She stopped in her tracks and just stared at me. Before I could say Jack Robinson, two Air Force guys were standing at attention beside her. My boss hurried over to us. You'd have thought I groped her. Right away he told her that, whatever had happened, I would apologize for it. The nerve …he didn't even know what I'd done, which I wasn't sure of anyway. He had addressed her as Ma'am. One of the guards, or whatever they were, corrected him and gave him her rank and name. I think he said Lieutenant…I don't remember, but her name was Howling Wind. By then I realized I was up shit creek. It had been drilled into us at the prison not to have any contact with people on the base, other than our instructors. Next the boss asked if she intended to file a report. At that point, I believed I was going to get booted out of the program, and for what? Letting a girl know I thought she was pretty? Maybe it was worse coming from a Black man. I *did* tell her that I meant no disrespect."

So Mom struck him as being super attractive when he first laid eyes on her. "Did you get the sense that she liked how you looked, too?"

"I didn't know what to make of her, neither did the others who were waiting to hear what she was going to do. She gave me the once over, the way you've seen people do when they're trying to figure out a goofy piece of art. It grabs their attention, but it doesn't mean they like it."

I have to laugh. That perfectly describes the way Mom looks at things, including me sometimes. "You got your certification, so she must not have held it against you?"

"After what seemed an eternity, she finally said, 'No offense taken.' And then she asked me my name, which I wasn't keen on giving, thinking I might still have hell to pay. A few months later, after I had completed the training and earned an early release, she called the prison the day before I was set to leave and asked if I'd be interested in taking her to dinner."

"I'd have done the same thing as Mom," I tell him. "You come off as a good guy." I'd do cartwheels if Tess O'Shea called to ask me out. I can't count the number of times I have replayed the instant the girl at the microscope turned in her chair to face me, as well as the introductions that followed. Images of her ear and neck and the touch of her hand constantly turn up in my fantasies, no matter how hard I try to stay focused on classes and football.

"Did you at least experience a magical moment when you met for dinner?"

"It was all business." He turns to Uncle. "That was the deal: fatherhood, in exchange for any kind of a company I wanted to start up, a fair swap in her eyes. Were you aware of that?"

Uncle is quiet, strangely quiet.

"There you have it," says Dad. He sits up straight and stretches his arms back.

Uncle can't believe he agreed to the offer without first meeting Iris and me.

"Constance told me all about Viktor and Iris...showed me pictures. I learned about her family and Indian background, and that I'd be expected to travel with them to the reservation during school breaks, and that she wished to enroll them in Hillel in Texas, even though no one was Jewish. Every detail had been considered. Basically, it would be up to me to continue to raise them."

Now I'm the one staring in disbelief. "And you bought into that plan? Owning your own shop meant that much to you?"

"Being a father meant that much to me."

"It honestly never crossed your mind that you wouldn't like us?"

"Your mom was convinced I'd fall in love with you kids on the spot, and that you and your sister would return the love. I realize it sounds crazy. The idea of owning a business was the icing on the cake. It was a way to gain respectability. I'd be able to hold my head high in the community, not to mention within my own family, who by then had written me off. The Lord blessed me that year, as He's done ever since."

He uses a thumb to swipe a tear from the corner of his eye. Uncle wraps an arm around his shoulders, unembarrassed by the emotion. It makes me uncomfortable to watch him, not because he feels so thankful—I understand where he's coming from—it's just odd to hear who he's giving credit to. The Lord? That title, along with the names Jesus and God are generally spoken in an outburst of profanity when things go wrong.

"Solomon," says Uncle, in the kindliest voice, "you of course know the story of the white owl that spoke to Constance while she was pregnant with Viktor. She never shared those conversations with anyone, not even her sister. The owl must have told her that the right man was going to come along who would play a key role in her life."

Goosebumps time. He sounds like a mysterious Wakan. I haven't lived among outsiders for so long that I don't give credence to our Native beliefs. If an animal spirit talks to you, you listen. I wonder what else my namesake and mother discussed. Am I supposed to make something out of the tale I loved to hear growing up, about the red-tailed hawk that swooped down to grab a mouse away from the owl that had captured it?

Over coffee, Dad asks if he can come watch me practice with Jasper and DeShaun. I'm thrilled. "We were actually going to go down along the river after tomorrow where there's the perfect open field to play, but I cancelled because I wanted to spend time with you. I'd love for you to meet them."

"Great. You can show off the new set of wheels we're gonna buy you in the morning. Happy Birthday, Son."

"Wha...that's the surprise? Un-hee!"

Uncle goes to his bedroom and returns with a tall chocolate cake. Unbelievable. I had celebrated with friends back on the seventh, but felt sad that all Mom and Dad did was call. Eighteen in my book is a frickin big deal. I realized they were dealing with far more important stuff, still.

"Viktor, my man!" shouts DeShaun out the window of Jasper's truck as they pull in the spot beside me.

"Hey, DeShaun." I step out of my shiny car, beaming with pride and high fiving him back.

"Sweet," says Jasper, "but Wolverine *blue?* What were you thinking!"

"Screw you, Jasper...you're not going to ruin this for me."

"That's plain unacceptable," says DeShaun, shaking his head, trying to shame me more. Jasper's arm comes out from behind his back. He presents me with a license plate frame, a Buckeyes one. "We just saved your ass," laughs DeShaun. "You owe us." They're both standing by the trunk, checking out my Mazda hatchback, when Dad emerges from the passenger side and greets them with a big hello. They knew I was bringing him, so that isn't why they suddenly look confused. They might think they're being pranked...a Black man? Dad ignores the reaction and right away strikes up a conversation:

"He passed up a really sharp red Dodge Challenger. Can you believe it?"

I introduce him as Mr. Davis, and they shake hands. Next they tell Dad they thought for sure I was going to show up in a Nissan Murano. Now *my* face is a big ole question mark.

"Whenever I'm drivin' us somewhere," says Jasper, "or even if we're just walking around campus, Viktor stares after every black Murano that goes by."

Talk about being clueless! Can it be that Jake's death still haunts me?

The phone rings; it's Constance. "He looks healthy," says Solomon enthusiastically. "I met a couple of his pals, nice guys who are already on the football team. They're completely in sync when they practice together. The receiver, Jasper, had no idea Viktor can see so much of the sideline when he's looking straight ahead. I suggested that he hold back more instead of racing ahead to make the catch."

Constance smiles. It's good to hear Solomon talking football again. He doesn't realize that Viktor's exceptional peripheral vision is a trait inherently common to Rawakota, as is their excellent sense of smell, which has proven to be more advantageous in her line of work.

"And DeShaun, my god is he fast!" He laughs as he describes the short, stocky player who, while flying horizontal to the ground, can repeatedly connect with the ball a split-second before going down. "They'll be calling for replays with that move." Taking stock of Viktor's current situation, Solomon assures his wife that their son is in a good place.

Solomon had returned to their Texas home earlier in the afternoon. He hears himself and realizes that he's been preoccupied with football since leaving Ohio. "Sorry, Constance. How 'bout you? Did you find out where you're going next?"

"If I weren't moving up in the ranks, I'd be heading to the Middle East because of Syria, in spite of it being an unwinnable mess. As it stands, I'll continue training pilots here. In the fall, I want to take a week to see what's happening on the reservation. Mother said people are feeling a lot safer and optimistic ever since Billy Spotted Horse's testimony put many of the Mérrauders behind bars. Local gangs still create trouble, but the cash-strapped police are slowly getting a handle on the situation. More money needs to be earmarked for law enforcement."

"That was decent of Billy. He's considered a snitch, though."

"I know. The prison staff is keeping a close eye on him."

"Give me a time frame, so I can start making plans to meet up with you. Brody managed things well in the shop while I was gone."

"A new era awaits the Indians, Solomon. The future at last offers a degree of hope."

CHAPTER 32

That's them! The students are packed tightly around a table in the corner. Yesterday at the hospital, while riding the elevator, I overheard one of Dr. Avedon's researchers telling another one that his team was meeting here at the pizzeria for lunch today. And then he mentioned the name Tess. He wondered if Avedon had included her. My thought was, *how many Tesses can there be?* I had already googled her name without luck. I made Theo look her up on Facebook since I don't have an account. I found nothing, other than there were other Tess and Tessie O'Sheas, just not the right one. I couldn't give up hope of seeing her again. She hadn't been in the lab the many times I had stopped by. And then, voila! A new lead on the elevator! I swear I see red hair out of the corner of my eye. My heart just exploded in my chest. Will somebody over there please notice me. I head to the register like I'm ordering carry-out.

"Hey, White Owl."

Thank you, Jesus...or rather, Carl. I turn and act surprised to see them, then casually ask, "Celebrating a birthday?"

"Better," says Dr. Avedon, waving me over. With his bald head, fat face, and wooly moustache, he's like a friendly walrus. "We received a long-awaited NIH grant that will fund us another four years. Come join us."

"Congratulations...but it doesn't seem right."

At once they start scooting their chairs to make room, telling me the more the merrier. It's a loud group, most of whom I've gotten to know in passing. Based on the number of empty pitchers of beer on the table, they must be soused by now. My eyes land on Tess. Carl sits between us. She's wearing her hair down today. I simply wish to stare at her, but a waitress interrupts my view, not to mention Carl's arms which are all over the place as he tells a story to a colleague across the table from him. I catch only glimpses of her. I decline the glass of beer set in front of me.

"Oh, c'mon," insists Carl. "One beer for lunch is nothing to a big guy like you."

"Unless you want to be out of a job when Dr. Avedon loses his position for buying an underage person alcohol…"

"What! How old are you?"

All eyes are on me, really curious eyes. "Eighteen."

"Holy Moly! How'd I end up between the juveniles?" Carl turns to Tess. "What a shame; that means neither of you can go out drinking with us after lunch."

Dr. Avedon strokes his bushy whiskers as he figures the bill and then excuses himself, stating he has to be somewhat coherent for a meeting later this evening. A couple of his students need a ride back to campus and they leave with him. The remaining ones toss around the names of bars where they can continue partying. Brewster's Tavern, a few blocks away, wins out, but then they feel bad for bailing on Tess and me. Tess speaks up and says it's fine; she'll stay and keep me company until I'm through eating. That's good enough for them, and out the door they fly, ready for a night of serious celebrating. Left suddenly alone in the wake of that posthaste departure, Tess and I smile shyly at each other. She slides over to the chair next to mine. Wow, is this my lucky day or what?

She orders coffee…I pass, grateful that my nerves have finally calmed. We watch as the extra two tables get pulled away from ours to get cleaned and set for the dinner crowd. A few stragglers like us are quietly talking. It's relaxing.

"So…are you close to legal age?" I ask.

"I'll be eighteen in a month."

I'm guessing she's a Virgo, an earth sign like me. Iris was on an astrology kick a few years back and sucked me into it. Neither of us took it seriously, but it made for fun reading. I'm still eating my calzone when Tess's coffee arrives. Pack after pack of sugar goes into it. I'm curious about the circumstances that brought her to OSU. She must've skipped a grade or two herself in high school. "If you aren't a graduate student, how did you hook up with Avedon?"

"When the lab got flooded, and we were in the room you saw me in, Dr. Avedon approached us and asked if any tech was interested in making slides strictly for his team. It would be fewer hours, and with more pay. I jumped at the chance. I figured the experience might also give me a leg up when the time comes to land a research position."

"That's smart. What does he study?"

"He's trying to create artificial blood...as are plenty of other scientists around the world. It's extremely complicated; they've been at it for decades. I planned on majoring in chemical engineering, but bioengineering is fascinating. It's hard choosing what to specialize in...I don't know. How did you manage to get on a team already?"

"I was accepted into a combined BS/MS program. A while ago I did a lot of reading about the mitochondrial theory of ageing, which I had forgotten about until I met Dr. Sharma last year at a lecture she gave on "stress genes" and free radicals. I presumed I got the okay to work under her because I possessed a deeper understanding of the subject matter, but later I realized she had an ulterior motive. I was, after all, inexperienced when it came to carrying out research. Being Native-American, I help her satisfy a quota, so she receives more federal money."

"I qualified for a Women in Engineering scholarship. Maybe there's one for being Irish."

"You'd be surprised. At any rate, I like her a lot, and I'm convinced she likes me, too."

"Where do you want to get your doctorate? I daydream about going to France...or New Zealand."

I like her giggle. "It hasn't crossed my mind."

She checks the time and says she must leave to meet a friend. Next she asks if I drove. I tell her I'm parked in the alley.

"Would it be a hassle to drop me off near the Oval?"

"Not at all..." to which I teasingly add, "... if you'll give me your number in return."

CHAPTER 33

The summer months blurred together for newly promoted Colonel Howling Wind, who was kept busy every waking moment on the sun-baked Arizona Air Force base. The two week leave she is presently enjoying is well-earned. Apart from spending time with family on the reservation, she has made a quick trip *down under* to Chohkahn to visit Chief Rolling Thunder.

The victorious climate prevails in the sacred city, even though the show of military might meant to humble the major global powers is months old. Wherever the Chief and Howling Wind stroll, people greet them with the tribal version of a fist bump, which doesn't include physical contact. Instead, one's own clenched hands are raised in front of the chest and punched together a couple of times, knuckles to knuckles. At sporting events, the gesture is accompanied by a shrill call that mimics the noisy one made by the "flying fox," a highly evolved bat endowed with mythic stamina that inhabits these subterranean spaces. Thankfully, Chohkahn's citizens act with more decorum around their leader. To the Rawakota, the success of the operation means that their math worked, their science worked; modern technology has been mastered. They can protect themselves below the ground and their Lakota brothers and sisters above it. For the day is coming when all non-Natives in the Black Hills, with few exceptions, are going to get ousted from the towns and open lands that fall within the geographical boundaries originally promised to the Plains Indians.

The Rawakota leader and the U.S. pilot say goodbye at the central Loozh station. Howling Wind continues her trip, traveling the twenty minutes on the magnetic rail to where Smitty and Mina live. While enroute, she reflects on the day she first met Rolling Thunder. She has grown fonder of him over time. His face and ways have softened, typical of warriors approaching their sixties. He is still a shrewd leader, but gone is the brashness of his earlier years. His black hair has lost its sheen. To compensate, he has increased the number of feathers he weaves through his braids. She can't wait to open the file he gave her. Chohkahn's citizens, especially its youth, have reached a consensus on certain proposals they wish to see enacted, in order for them to mingle more freely with outside tribes on the reservations.

"Hey ho, Howler!" Smitty plants a big wet kiss on her cheek, which no Rawakota would ever dream of doing. "Mina went out with her mum." He hands her a cup of tea before they head to the living room. "Did the meeting with the security advisers go well?"

Squadron Leader Smith, known in his wife's community as Straw Hair, is trusted by the tribe, but he must be full Rawakota to take part in some of their high-level strategy meetings. In handing over the Himalayan Mujahzee document to the word-gathering Oyahmayan, he was at least privy to their discussions. He felt honored to meet with the esteemed Sleeping Buffalo, who looked to him for advice in his upcoming journey to Kashmir, half a world away.

Constance gets comfortable on the sofa, carefully balancing the cup of tea in her hand as she kicks off her shoes and slides her legs up onto the cushion.

"It was enlightening. There's far more information to read through on this." She hands over a Rawakota USB-type of flash drive for him to project.

"It isn't hush-hush top secret?"

"Just a single hush...permission granted."

He chuckles and slumps beside her, hiking up his long legs to rest them on the coffee table. "Let the show begin." The data stick is in the reader, ready for him to open.

"Egad this is wordy!" Smitty groans as he fast-forwards through part of it. "How 'bout I take a nap, and you summarize it for me later."

Constance, annoyed by his lack of enthusiasm, regards his remark, and then offers one of her own, which she mutters under her breath. He so enjoys getting her goat! "Kid-DING," he says smiling broadly, gently poking her arm with his elbow in jest.

Sunkwah and Winnie sit in their daughter Victoria's kitchen, taking in the wonderful smells as she and Constance prepare dinner. Normally

Winnie would be involved, but her legs have been hurting a lot this month. Victoria bites her tongue as she watches how slowly her daughter chops the vegetables. Constance clearly isn't suited for this job, never was. Sunkwah finds it amusing. Victoria insists he take over: "Dad, even with your twisted fingers, you can peel potatoes ten times faster than this child." These days it's good-natured ribbing, not so when Constance was a young girl and flat out refused doing any household chores. In order to draw attention away from herself, Constance brings up the report she finished reading at Smitty's home. She wants to hear her family's opinions about the ideas put forth by Chohkahn's people. Being Rawakota themselves, Sunkwah, Winnie, and Victoria, as well as their neighbors, were entitled to provide input. It sparks an impassioned conversation. They speak Lakota when it's just them.

Sunkwah offers his perspective first. "The Rawakota in Chohkahn say they have no interest in ruling anyone up here, yet they have considered every angle of how our Lakota Nation should be organized in the future. They want only to *influence* what goes on. That's the word they use. My question is: How much influence?" Winnie nods, showing she shares his concern.

"What do you think, Mom?" asks Constance, surprised by her grandparents' misgivings.

Victoria wants peace at the dinner table and will only discuss the weather and the upcoming powwow. When the dishes are cleared and coffee is served, she returns to the subject.

"Chohkahn's people have spent decades deliberating the kinds of problems that might arise, namely because generations of Lakota aren't experienced at self-governance. Not only that, too many are ignorant of their Native history. Sure they can name a few famous chiefs and battles. Then there's the matter of dealing with centuries worth of pent-up anger, and the dysfunctional families created by it. The Rawakota are merely being realistic. They're showing us ways to approach the problems." Her necklaces and bracelets jingle wildly. "Indians must embrace a new mindset if total sovereignty is to be achieved…if in fact it's truly possible. *Somebody* needs to guide our brothers and sisters on the rez."

They sit deep in thought.

Constance reflects on their comments. "There are aspects of the plan I don't think anyone will argue with." She looks at Sunkwah and Winnie.

"Like growing the buffalo population and maintaining our horse-centric culture. The Rawakota have successfully woven their age-old traditions into modern life." She rethinks the last comment. Maybe it only appears they've been successful. How would she really know, without living among them for a long time.

"They are going to come across sounding like *know-it-alls*," says Winnie.

"*They?*" Constance realizes the predicament that her grandparents find themselves in. It's one most Indians face—any group, really, that has weakened its ties with a larger cultural entity to which they owe their identity. The people that break away have to decide which customs are best to hold on to, and which ones are okay to let go of.

Winnie continues her train of thought: "What works in Chohkahn, won't on the reservation. Their culture is strong because no one tore it apart. And they don't use money. The world we know *only* understands money. White people have contaminated the Indian spirit with their greed."

Constance walks over to her grandmother and hugs her.

"I agree Winnie. One can only dream that the Rawakota's guiding principle of learning for the joy of learning can be instilled in the Lakota and other Sioux tribes. If it's modeled in early childhood, kids' natural curiosity about everything should continue into adulthood." Winnie shakes her head and says sarcastically, "Should."

Talk of Chohkahn ceases the second Solomon enters the room, as does their speaking in Lakota. Although he can understand most of what gets said by now, he simply doesn't have a knack for languages. After embracing Constance, he moves on to hugging his in-laws, which is when he announces he's hungry as a bear. Victoria has a plate ready to go in the microwave. He and Constance arrived on the rez together a couple of weeks ago. Because he isn't aware there's a thriving city underneath the Black Hills, Constance lied about having to report to the nearby Badlands for a few days. She said she'd be consulting with an Air Force unit in charge of the clean-up project for an area used as a WW II bombing range, which is half true; there truly is such a project. She suggested he see a friend in Rapid City. Based on his happy mood, he had a good time.

"Are you ready for this!" He beams like he's set to pull a puppy from under his arm. The family sits there with anticipation, glad for a change in topic. "Viktor has himself a girl he really, really likes."

He immediately gets bombarded with questions. "Who told him? Is it serious? Will Viktor be bringing her to the rez? What does she do…?"

"Hold on…" he laughs, "… give me a sec." He scarfs down a mouthful of stew. "William and I spoke on the phone yesterday, and he said he believed Viktor was truly serious about someone. Viktor made it sound like neither of them had time to date right now. He admitted, though, that she's all he can think about."

"What kind of news is that?" asks Constance, her disappointment showing.

Solomon's warm brown eyes sparkle. There's obviously more. He grabs a few more bites and chews quickly. "I decided to call Viktor on the drive back this afternoon, to see if I could get him to open up. First he went on and on about his darn classes. I couldn't take it anymore and came right out and asked if he met a girl yet who's caught his eye."

Sunkwah lets go a whoop and playfully nudges Winnie.

"And…?" Constance is ready to bop him for taking so long to get to the point.

"I had to wrangle it out of him, but for the next half hour he poured his heart out to me." Solomon is forced to talk and eat at the same time. "Her name is Tess, and she has hair the color of the rocks in the Red Valley."

Winnie sighs, "How beautiful." She and Sunkwah have never seen hair such a color red.

Solomon continues. "She'll be a junior this coming fall, which is when she turns eighteen. We figured she'd have to be super smart, right? They met at a lab in the hospital." He looks at Constance. "He said she's as tall as you and Iris, and that she has the palest skin he's ever seen, but it doesn't make her look sickly." They laugh at that. "She has beautiful big eyes that are gray or blue, depending on the light. She's from Cincinnati but spent her childhood in rural Pennsylvania close to where a famous woman named Pearl Buck lived. That's whose life he said influenced hers growing up."

"Impressive," says Constance.

"I've heard the name Pearl Buck," says Solomon, "just don't know what she did."

"She was a writer and humanitarian…she lived an extraordinary life." Constance looks pleased. If only she could squeeze in a trip to her son before returning to Arizona. She's happy that Solomon pressed Viktor about making time to see Tess during the school year, regardless of their busy schedules. She doesn't want Viktor to suffer the same fate as his biological father, were he not to find a partner during these crucial years. Constance regards this one aspect of Rawakota society truly disturbing. The practice of wakuwa, the hunt for a mate, and theeich ihilah, with all its accompanying drama, definitely needs to be re-examined.

CHAPTER 34

Before I can catch up to Tess as she charges out the door of the hospital, and right as my tongue meets the roof of mouth to shout her name, a man suddenly appears from out of nowhere, and the two leave together. Feeling every bit the stalker, I trail a distance behind as they hurry toward High Street. *Shit!* Dad's advice to me from over a month ago takes on a sense of urgency. To hell with our busy lives, I don't want to put off dating Tess. Just then Theo calls.

"Hey, man, can't talk now." I have to pick up speed to stay on their heels. "Theo...I'm following a girl I like a lot, but she's with another guy."

He asks how they're acting. "No, he hasn't put his arm around her... bodies are *not* touching." He tells me to butt in between them and go ahead and ask her out. "That's plain dumb. I don't care what you would do. Call you later." I cut him off, certain he was in the middle of saying to text her. That's actually a great idea. I'd be able to watch her reaction.

We're on High Street. They head north toward the main part of campus. The sidewalk is crowded, and now they *are* bumping against each other. Damn. I close in on them. He's nice looking. Six feet tall. At times they laugh loudly. It feels so wrong, but I text her.

Hi Tess. I'd like to see you soon. Can I take you out to dinner on Saturday? for a date?

Her phone must be in her purse and turned off. We cross the street. They go into Starbucks. I would go in, too, and play like it was a happy accident running into her... but she might look at her messages then and see mine, which could put her on the spot. She can see me out the window if she turns around. Where does a giant Indian hide? A delivery truck is parked next to the alley. I can stand behind it and still have a good view of them.

I hate myself. Jealousy is horrible...it's degrading. I leave. My car is back at the Medical Center. Fuck.

The rest of the afternoon drags on, and I don't hear from Tess. I should've met with Theo, had some fun. I almost nod off in front of the TV when my phone buzzes. The voice jumpstarts my brain.

"Hi, Tess."

"Viktor, I'm sorry it took so long to get back to you. A date, huh? Okay. I'm actually not working this Saturday, but I do have plans to go to a lecture in the physics department. I signed up for it earlier in the summer. It's about the importance of binary systems. I checked; there aren't any seats left."

"Sounds interesting. When is it over? I could pick you up there."

"It goes until four. Will you be coming from the hospital?"

I lie and say yes. I'm going to the football game, but will leave right before it's over to get her. I can't miss watching Jasper and DeShaun play, although the season didn't get off to a good start. They haven't had opportunities to shine. After hearing Tess go on about how much she hated football a few weeks ago, I better try hard to win her over quickly before I try out for the team next spring. We happened to be passing each other on the Oval, and I suggested we go to a game together. Her reaction sure took the wind out of my sails. The guy she went to Starbucks with must have been a friend.

Hell, I'm not in the mood for noisy crowds today...or the traffic; I just want it to be four o'clock. It's a Big Ten matchup with Penn State. Rain clouds hang above the stadium. Sixty-five degrees isn't bad for the end of October. Feels like a football Saturday, and for once it isn't an evening game. Uncle William confided that the quarterback is dealing with a knee injury which hasn't been made public. The backup is supposedly outstanding.

Kickoff time, and my main thought is having Tess all to myself for the entire evening. I watch as our star quarterback keeps getting sacked. He's limping badly, and it's only the first quarter. The Nittany Lions are steamrolling over us. This is too painful to watch. The Medical Center's just a five minute drive from the stadium...think I'll go do some work.

Stupid me. I pushed the down button for the basement out of habit. Dr. Sharma's department was finally moved upstairs this past week. I glance at the score on the mounted screen in the coffee bar next to the elevator. It's embarrassing. Poor Jasper and DeShaun. An employee in scrubs also watching from the doorway turns to me: "A third stringer was just called in. Penn's defense is unstoppable."

"Ohhh..." we both moan as the quarterback gets hammered and buried beneath a big pileup. That has to be the backup quarterback. The hospital worker mistakenly said third stringer.

After transferring some data for Dr. Sharma, I visit a few retired rats that are now living the good life. Their plastic home of connecting tubes rests on the shelf of a huge window that overlooks west campus, which includes the stadium. I bet many of the fans will be leaving at halftime, if they aren't already heading for the exits.

My phone goes off. *Jasper?* Can't be. "Hello?" It's super noisy.

"Viktor! Where are you, bro!"

"On the research floor..."

"On game day? Listen to me...does your uncle know the building?"

"Well, yeah...why?" I check to make sure the latch is closed tight on the cage door. "You calling me from the field?" I squint at the stadium as though it were possible to see him.

"Just do what I say! If you haven't peed, go; then race to where your uncle can find you. He's gonna be in a big van with a bunch of coaches who'll throw your ass in a uniform while burning rubber to get you here to play! Run, you hear! Are you movin'!"

"Yes, yes..."

"Where are you now?"

"Shit, Jasper...by the elevator."

"Keep movin'."

Jesus! What the hell?

When the elevator doors open, I'm swooped up on the spot. It's madness. Inside the van, I lock eyes with Uncle who's looking more excited than I've ever seen. Instantly he smiles, pats my cheek, and next he says in Lakota:

"*It's your moment, Hinhán Ská. Yours...and your teammates.*"

In the middle of the flurry of changing into pads and protective gear, all these papers, or rather forms, fly in front of me, requiring my signature. Uncle gives the okay. "Waivers," he says, "insurance." The door opens and out I jump: no name Number 7. Everyone runs alongside me, steering me through the cavernous space, through the tunnel...toward the light. I dead-end into Jasper who steadies my head with his hands. Standing helmet to helmet, his dark eyes flashing behind his facemask, he yells with spit flying: "We're hittin' them with the gay play. It's set." The head coach himself materializes and looks directly up at me. He's a good head shorter than I am. Must be trying to get a read on his new QB. Good luck, I'm thinking.

I mentally go through the steps of the high-flying grand jeté that Hayden taught me, with football in hand. Gotta concentrate on my center of gravity. There's a fleeting flashback to me in Wichita Falls, Texas, the last place I ran onto a field with a team. In this one instance, Jasper controls the huddle. He apparently had enough time on my way over to describe the formation used in the gay play, his term, only because it's a ballet move. The Center shakes my hand, bops my chest friendly-like. I read his lips: "Ska, first count." Jasper has thought of everything. It occurs to me that I've never played on this kind of turf.

The powerful smells in the air hit me like a jolt of caffeine. The rain clouds have disappeared. A colorless sky holds Wakan Tanka, who will either grant me this moment, or not.

I talk to myself. Perfect snap. Go down the middle, bolt right; at the sideline, heave-ho, lift off. Great height. Spot Jasper across field. Uh-oh, I'm dropping down, throw the pass! Boom, I'm hit...*ow*. Jasper's still running...touchdown! *"Hayé hayé, Wakan!"*

Instantly I'm airborne, raised up by god knows how many hands. There's no end to the celebrating. I'm knocked about by friendly punches the whole way to the bench where the staff now takes over congratulating me. Almost halftime. I'll need the break to get a handle on what's happening. The guys are jazzed. Penn's ball gets intercepted by Number 22. We're at the thirty. In the huddle, Jasper defers to me this time. It's DeShaun's turn. He catches for a first down, then a second down. With less than two minutes, another guy is open...touchdown! I look up at the stands for the first time while the kicker runs out to score the extra point. The cheering is indescribable. The field goal is good. We run inside with our team down by seven. Not bad.

It's a relief getting this helmet off. There's a mad scramble to find a better fitting one. I hit the john. By the time I return, the room has settled and all eyes are on Coach. It's clear he's going to introduce me. Reading from the piece of paper in his hand: "Viktor...Talking White Owl." Pause. "Welcome! Meet your teammates." They greet me with a 'Hey!' "Sorry to throw you to the wolves like this, Viktor, with no preparation. It's an unfortunate situation." I'm still clueless as to why I was called. "A big thanks goes to Stillman and Rivers for coming up with the idea of using their friend, who I understand was planning to try out next spring, right?" I nod. "It appears that we might just be able to pull off a win today." He scans the room. I look around as well. Uncle's face stands out. He mouths something at me, twice. I think it's *'unbelievable.'*

The players start psyching themselves up for the second half. Next thing I know Coach is standing beside me with his hand on my shoulder. He seems calm. "So tell me, Number 7... any thoughts about the third quarter?"

Jesus! My life has just been turned upside down. Isn't this *his* job? DeShaun has my back and suggests we go with the "corkscrew."

"Great! You explain it, DeShaun. I have to call work quick." I race to the locker, glad DeShaun invented a better name than Jasper would've come up with for a dancer's step called tour en l'air.

I grab my phone and text Tess an apology for not being able to meet her at the lecture. My hands are shaking from gripping the ball so hard. *Pick you up at your place around 5?*

Then it's back to the insanity.

The new helmet fits better. During the start of the second half, I feel I can keep my emotions in check. The Bucks are hard-hitting, and Penn fails to make a first down. In the huddle, the guys are chomping at the bit.

It's too easy. Whoever Number 2 is, there he is again, in the clear in the end zone for another touchdown. I call for a two point conversion, not the Coach. DeShaun drives it home on those fast short legs, darting effortlessly between their threatening defensive linemen. We have a one point lead. The sound is deafening. Our players are so pumped up it's scary, especially the Center, whose big square frame reminds me of my childhood buddy, Billy Spotted Horse. The mouthy left guard drops one MF-bomb after another, which, unfortunately, isn't drowned out by the fans. I can't tell what he's ranting on about...must've been who I heard in the locker room. Despite the Neanderthal behavior, he *has* saved me from getting sacked a couple of times; something he apparently wasn't able to do for the other quarterbacks.

What a high! Playing with athletes of this caliber is like being on stage with the dancers in *WAKAN,* who adhered to a work-ethic I'd never before encountered. Penn State puts up a good fight, but there's no reward. We manage two more touchdowns. The pace hasn't slowed. With a minute and a half left in the fourth, I want to end with a bang ... to make this day supremely unforgettable, not so much for the Buckeyes as for the bigger Native community.

For the first time, I'm using a third count, which should create illegal motion; and it does. No one thinks we're gonna go deep. The same call is made—but just before the snap, I connect with Jasper, slightly cocking my head to the left. I run straight back, no fancy footwork, and then switch to throw left-handed for the first time. I'm well-protected. Jasper catches the ball midfield, escapes two tackles, and sprints to the sideline where he runs it in to score—*Hot dog!* Just like Jerry Rice's catch in the '88 game against the Giants. My pass wasn't as long as Montana's seventy-plus-yarder, close enough, though. There's no doubt that Wakan Tanka let the spirit of Jim Thorpe inhabit me this afternoon, or this win couldn't have been possible.

The extra point is unimportant, an afterthought. The clock runs out and in seconds scads of people swarm the field. Microphones pop up everywhere. I stay close to our players as we try to shake hands with our opponents. Avoiding the reporters, I follow the team as they run toward the band to sing Carmen Ohio with the fans. It's there I see Uncle. His arms fold around me like powerful wings. It's as if he embodies the collective pride of Dad, Mom, Iris, Grandmother, Sunkwah, and Winnie...even dead Pahpie. It touches me to the core. The hug is short-lived. Before I go sing with the players, I speak directly into his ear so he can hear:

"After this, Uncle, I need to get out of here fast. Is that possible?" He looks at me odd. I realize it sounds strange. He insists this moment is to be shared with the team. How is it going to look? I'm honest with him: "I'm having my first date with the girl I told you about. And I'm not going to miss it for the world." He breaks out into a wide smile, and then releases me so I can join the others. I fall into place and start swaying arm in arm with players who are strangers to me. Everybody sings: *Oh come let's sing Ohio's praise...* Reality sets in. No one can tell how choked up I've become except maybe Number 2, who is holding on tight to my jersey, and whose eyes are wet with tears.

... *Dear Alma Mater...Ohio!* On the final "o" I hightail it to the locker room, looking past anyone who might be with the media. Uncle is waiting and helps remove all the pads. We laugh as he throws a sweatshirt over my head while leading me to a back door. The hood covers my face.

"I'll give Coach a good reason." He points me in the direction of his car, and says he'll pick up my Mazda at the hospital lot later this evening.

At home, I immediately turn on the shower.

"What the...!" My hair's a ratted clump. Uncle had somehow tied both braids together in back when we were in the van. All I can think to do, short of cutting it off, is to dump lots of conditioner over me. "Oh, god... slow down." My nerves are churning. My stomach's growling.

I barely make it around the car to get the door for Tess; she came out of the house so fast. I'm half an hour late, on top of having changed the time for picking her up once already. She says nothing about the fact this isn't my car.

"Thanks for not bailing on me. I'm really sorry."

"Things happen. Besides, I've never been to German Village."

Ah, shit! Another thing to add to the disappointment. "Could we go there another time? With so many people here from out of state this weekend, I'm afraid the lines will be long. It's such a popular spot." The fact is, I don't want fans recognizing me, which they would there.

"Won't all restaurants be busy?"

I haven't yet pulled away from the curb. "It's somewhat of a drive, but I know a place that shouldn't be too bad...if that's okay?" She doesn't answer. "You're starving I bet."

"I am."

"Me, too. If we pass a drive-through, I'll stop and get us someth..."

"It's not necessary," she says in a flat voice, interrupting me. "I'll live."

What a lousy way to start out. She doesn't bother to ask where we're going to end up, not even when we merge onto the freeway. We ride in silence. It's misting outside. The wiper blades swipe across the windshield at long intervals. There are no stars.

"Would you like to listen to music?"

"Huh-uh."

Argh, is this how it's going to be the rest of the evening! Her hair is twisted up and held together with a pretty sparkly barrette. I admire her profile. A scarf hides her neck, but the earlobe that got me hot the first time I saw it is affecting me the same way now; not that I can see it that well in the dark...just knowing it's exposed.

The forty minute drive felt like hours, but we're here, at Mrs. Hilty's Kitchen, a cozy, off the beaten track Amish restaurant hidden in the hills.

A pleasant older woman dressed in a traditional long-sleeved plain brown dress seats us. The booth is in a toasty corner beside their huge stone fireplace. Before opening our menus, a basket of rolls is delivered, and we dive in. Tess is in heaven, slathering butter on a square of warm corn bread and drizzling it with honey up to the point when it disappears in her mouth. With closed eyes, she savors the bite.

"Sorry you had to witness this on our first date," she says, "I'm not *me* when I'm hungry."

It takes a second to make the connection to the TV Snickers ad. "No way are you as funny as Betty White," I say, recalling the memorable Super Bowl commercial, "more like the bad-tempered Dr. House from the TV show." At last! A giggle. Things are on the upswing.

She gives a little shrug suggesting she can't help it. The place has a warm glow that makes her skin appear as soft as the white fluff of a cottonwood tree back home. I want to kiss her lips this moment, or touch her ear. When she undoes her scarf, I sink down in my seat and enjoy the view. Her low-cut top shows off an inch of cleavage, enough to distract me.

I ask about the lecture. When dinner arrives, giant portions of meatloaf, mashed potatoes, and green beans, we eat without talking much. Tess mentions that she likes my hair. Considering the fit I had straightening it out, and the amount of time it wasted, I let it hang loose. She leans back and looks around the room, now that her belly is full. She likes the simple white crocheted curtains, the "delft" blue walls, the vases filled with fresh flowers, not fake ones. There are lots of paintings of all kinds of birds that are done in a Japanese style which doesn't fit the place. I'm happy the restaurant gets her stamp of approval. She then looks at me curiously.

"You know," she begins, "when you smile just a teensy bit, the right corner of your mouth curls upward slightly more than the other side. It's charming."

"I'm glad *one* particular feature of my appearance pleases you. I could go on ad infinitum about things that are charming about you; hunger not being one of them."

She does a bit of an eye-roll and holds back a smile. I'm feeling pretty stoked about now. The plates are cleared. We decide to share a piece of coconut custard pie. Families with little kids have left the restaurant while more older couples continue to arrive.

Taking advantage of the current positive vibe, I ask if she'll go out with me next week. "On Sunday, though."

"Why not Saturday?"

Hoping to sound unfazed: "I'll be out of town."

"Oh?"

From her tone, more details are in order. I gaze into the fire, wondering what to say, wishing she didn't despise football so much.

She clears her throat on purpose to get my attention. "It was thoughtful of you to come up with a place where no one would bother us tonight." *Busted!* Her expression tells all.

I sit at attention, the emotions of the day catching up to me.

"Today's been crazy, Tess ... the craziest day of my life."

She crosses her arms on the table, ready to listen. I reach for her hand to hold it in mine.

"From the moment you agreed to go out with me, that's all I've been able to think about these past days. I woke up so happy. Four o'clock couldn't come soon enough."

She gives my hand a gentle reassuring squeeze. How to explain? "A couple of guys on the Buckeyes' squad are friends of mine. We toss the ball around once in a while, just for fun. I was in the lab this afternoon when one of them called...from the field inside the stadium, during the game! He ordered me to go outside...said I was about to get snatched up in a van." I tell her the rest, every detail, including up until the time I picked her up, adding that I still don't know what in the world happened to both the quarterbacks. There hadn't been time to watch TV or go online to find out. "I haven't even spoken with my family yet."

"Seriously!"

I can't tell if she's irritated with me or sympathetic? "If you were at the lecture, how could you know anything?"

"When the program was over, everybody started checking their phones like mad. They were getting worked up over something, which is when I looked at mine and saw you had texted about the change in plans. People were really going nuts. They talked about this incredible Indian that magically appeared on the field and saved OSU from an embarrassing defeat. Your name didn't come up. Obviously I didn't think for a second it might be you. You're a scientist. And you have an academic scholarship. And you never mentioned that you ever played football, not even after the long conversation we had last week when I told you about my brothers and my parents, and how they totally turned me off to anything related to football."

"After hearing that, do you really think I'd pursue the subject?"

"Anyway, a girl who ended up giving me a ride home was also curious about the buzz on campus, so I looked up the game on my phone and was shocked to see your name. I went back to your message to see when you sent it."

"Ah jeez."

"You can bet I was anxious to hear your explanation."

We sit quietly. To think she's been waiting the entire evening for me to bring it up. I pay the check. When we step outside the drizzle has turned to snow, the first of the season. It's a light snow that won't stick. Before opening the car door, I kiss Tess's hand and pray things are okay between us.

On our way back to Columbus, she asks to hear something bluesy.

"Bluesy? Hmm." I have no idea what Uncle has in his car these days. I recently put some jazz on my playlist that meets the criteria.

Watching the snow in the headlights is hypnotic. A saxophone transports us to a smoke-filled bar in LA's oh-so-cool underworld at night: Bosch's world. Tess isn't familiar with the series or Connelly's character, but likes the sleepy mood of the music.

Shortly into it, she says, "I don't know the players' names, but after the quarterback had to sit out because of an injury, the backup went in and did an okay job. The Bucks made it to third down, when the game was stopped, and he was escorted off the field and arrested."

"What!"

"You weren't the only one with a crazy day."

Tess continues to enlighten me. "He was charged with beating up a guy he found in bed with his girlfriend last night, after which he allegedly worked her over. The third stringer was out of town because of a family funeral, which left the team searching for a fill-in. They chose a freshman tight end who had been his high school's quarterback. According to a TV reporter, he thought this player might have been up to the task, if he hadn't gotten creamed by Penn's defense before ever letting go of the pass." *Un-hee!* That'll teach me to leave a game early.

Tess then asks if I really intend to keep playing. I know it's a loaded question. The answer could ruin any chances of a future with her. I follow my headlights, glancing at her now and again. She continues to look intently at me.

"I *am* foremost a scientist. But being a scientist won't get me the name recognition that playing football will." That isn't going to win me any points...sounds like I'm chasing fame. "If it happens that I become a successful player for the Buckeyes, I'd be able to use the media to inform the public about issues that affect Native Americans, like why there is such poverty on many of the reservations. Even though Indians rightfully own their reservation lands, most people have no clue that the federal government holds it in trust, which means Indians can't sell it or use it for equity to secure bank loans. It's what keeps them poor." Maybe playing the social crusader card wasn't the route to go. I go on staring at the road, waiting for Tess to chime in with a remark. Speak from the heart I tell myself. "The bottom line is that I really love playing the game. And it is does present an opportunity for me to represent Natives in a good light." I look at her. "It matters, you know?"

Her smile makes me think it was good answer. I'm not prepared when she asks about *WAKAN*, and why I switched from dance to football of all things. Couldn't the stage serve my interests?

I have to know: "Did you see it?"

She shakes her head no. "The poster was everywhere; it was stunning ...and then, well, your name was in the news for weeks as police searched for the people who attacked you."

Fuck Ishmael. I don't want to sound pissed off, and purposely slow my angry heart.

"I did enjoy dancing, Tess. But it's not a life for me." We stay quiet and listen to the music for a long time. I can't begin to guess what she must be thinking. "So you realized who I was when we met for the first time in the lab?"

"Regardless of the show, people are going to notice anyone who's as unique looking as you. Word gets around. Just like Dr. Boris..."

We burst out laughing. "Please tell me I'm not mentioned in the same breath as Dr. Boris." He's an oncologist in the department, a towering hulking figure who shuffles straight legged through the halls. His entire body leans side to side with every step, just like Boris Karloff's Frankenstein. "Does anyone even know his real name?"

Tess, still laughing, says, "You're gonna die…it's Dr. Freekmann."

"Is not!"

"Is! Fritz Freekmann … from Freiburg, Germany."

"Stop already!" Tears blur my view.

It's almost midnight when I reach Tess's place, a tiny brick house off campus in Grandview, not too far from my apartment. "How do you like living alone?"

"I love it. It was hard convincing my parents to agree to the arrangement, and then having to ask the landlords to fill out a bunch of forms. OSU thinks they're my relatives. They're so grateful to have me watch over the place while the lady's mom is recovering from a stroke in a nursing home. Can you believe I don't even have to pay rent? Didn't you hate the dorms?"

"I never had to live in one."

"How'd you manage that, especially since you enrolled at sixteen?"

"A story for another time. I'm curious, though; you must know this couple for them to trust you like this?"

"The husband, Roger, is a nurse I met at the hospital. His wife is a tech for a doctor in Upper Arlington. In fact, earlier in the week he told me it's doubtful his mother-in-law will return home. He wanted to assure me they have no intention of selling her property, and if, god forbid, she dies, I can stay."

"By any chance were you with him in Starbucks?" She nods and looks at me questioningly. A few steps and we're at her front door. "Can I say goodbye inside where it's warm?" I have to duck going through the doorway. A colored lampshade makes the walls glow orange. It's an itty-bitty space. Tess lays her coat across an antique-looking red sofa with huge curved arms that takes up most of the room. It's like ones in the old westerns I used to watch.

My move.

As I pull her toward me, she lays her hands on my chest, over my pounding heart. I kiss her. It's the softest kiss. The tips of our tongues brush slightly together through our teeth. My lips glide across her cheek to her ear. I lightly trace it with my tongue. At last I get to nibble her delicate earlobe. Taking hold of her wrists, I deliberately draw her arms around my waist inside my jacket. There's a slow and steady rhythm to her breathing that blows warm on my neck. I wrap her tightly in my arms, feeling her pubic bone through her skirt. I don't dare move. Her hands slide down to my tailbone. I want her so bad. My erection pushes against her belly.

It kills me to step back. Right now I need to regain my senses. "Sunday, right?"

"German Village, right?"

I stop in my tracks as I head out the door and, without overthinking it, ask, "Tess, will you be my girlfriend? May I call you that?"

She sits on the curved arm of the sofa with her hands folded primly on her lap, and then says in a kidding voice, "And to whom are you going to call me your girlfriend?"

Answering deadpan, "There's my family, of course. My friends, my research colleagues, and now that I have teammates, them, too. That about does it. Oh, and Jim, my horse."

She takes a moment. "Yes, you may. But will Jim approve?"

I'm grinning the whole way home, floating on cloud nine.

"She's *got* to be one helluva gal, Viktor, if you can't even take a second to call your old man to tell him you just won a game for the Buckeyes!"

"She is, Dad! And then some!"

I know Uncle gave him the lowdown of yesterday's mind-blowing events. I immediately fell into bed last night when I came home. As soon as I woke, five minutes ago at 11, I called.

Are we ever a couple motormouths! I don't know when I've felt so frickin' happy. It's strange…last night I didn't talk a word of football, and now it's the only thing. We end with Dad telling me he's flying up this week. He's going to see about accompanying me to the next game, which is out of state. I'm ordered to call Mom and Iris. I see that Jasper and DeShaun and Coach have also been trying to reach me. A single solid knock on the door tells me it's Uncle.

When the door closes behind him, he throws me for a loop when he greets me like he did Pahpie when he was alive, and the way he does Dad and Dr. Nate, and any adult male he regards with respect, by holding me slightly at bay with his arms, and then brushing his cheek against mine. This is a Rawakota gesture, not Lakota. Perhaps Sunkwah will also think of me as an adult the next time I visit him.

"Was your date worth it?"

It must be obvious. He smiles and says that he simply wanted to give me a rundown on what to expect this week. "Relax today," he says, "because starting tomorrow, your life will revolve around football, morning, noon, and night. The schedule begins with a complete physical. It's up to you to figure out what to do about the Research program. Any questions, ask Coach today. He is expecting you to return his call ASAP."

Halfway out the door, he turns. "Oh, and to give you a heads up, Viktor, there was too much confusion and excitement in the locker room to bother giving anyone an account of your whereabouts. You make up a story."

Great. After a quick lunch, I call Coach and address him as Mister. It seems weird to say Coach when I don't know him. Right off the bat he wonders why the hell I took off after the game.

"Well, sir...it was crucial that I get back to the research department in the Medical Center. I left during the middle of an experimental procedure that I was responsible for completing." I should have added, when you guys unexpectedly *abducted* me.

"I see."

That was easy. He follows up with heartfelt thanks for stepping in to help out the team, adding that the circumstances took everyone by complete surprise. He goes on to clarify that there are still important details which need to get ironed out before I can continue to play, like what to do with the third backup quarterback, who was out of town for a legitimate reason. I assume my performance during the practices on the field this week will be under scrutiny. He and his staff probably fear the win was a one-time fluke. Before signing off, he bluntly states how crucial it is that my blood test results turn out negative for anything illegal. If a few days are necessary after celebrating this weekend—to clear things from my system—I better tell him now.

I don't appreciate the implication. I assure him that it's not a problem. In time he'll learn I'm not a party animal. Like Cardale Jones after the Sugar Bowl victory, I must prove I have staying power. I'm ready. Bring it on!

Monday: Had physical. 6'7" – 242 lbs. Un-hee! I don't want to be a giant! Damn scary to think I might still be growing. Got introduced to several players. Liked everyone except offensive guard Damien Slaughter, a beast of a guy who goes by Demon—suits him. Has same foul mouth off the field as he had during Saturday's game. I thought it was just an act for the cameras. Don't see why that's allowed. Bought this journal. Like to tap my pen or doodle while I think. Want to keep track of what's happening to me because current life is about to get super crazy, not unlike rehearsing for *WAKAN*. Now I have a girlfriend to consider. My pinkie ring from Grandmother makes me smile—a reminder not to let football consume my life, and for me not to get too big for my britches. Mom saw game. She was eating at a Chili's with some other pilots when my name appeared on one of those screen crawls at the bottom of the TV. Said she had the best time cheering me on with them. That's wild. Iris only caught bits of coverage on the late night news after Mom and Dad each called her. Talked to Tess a few minutes last night, mostly to arrange a time to meet on Wednesday. Can't wait to hold her again and kiss her. Such a clear night—watching the stars. Bedtime—exhausted.

Tuesday: Team is waiting to hear if it violated NCAA rules by playing me on Saturday. Uncle doesn't think so. I'm learning about the training rules—only so many hours allotted for practicing with helmets and pads. There's also a set amount of time for watching videos of games and for doing physical conditioning. Jasper and DeShaun want to get together to practice on our own late Thursday afternoon. They asked the team's Center, Rhett Holgersson, to join our Scioto River League, as we like to call it. I'm fine with that—we should get to know each other better. Met more coordinators and assistant coaches—too many new faces and names. Ran around like a fool trying to track down Dr. Sharma. Relieved to get her permission to stick with the project. Switching roles with the Australian student. I'm now responsible for organizing the data collected during the next six-month period, which I'll have access to on the computer. Hate that I won't be involved in conducting the actual experiments. By spring, football season will be history, and I can devote myself to wrapping up the research results. Passed kids in costumes on way home. Damn! It's Halloween!

Wednesday: Fun, fun, fun – write tomorrow. Totally done in.

Thursday: The officially designated 3rd string QB, who in reality should now be the starting QB, returned this morning. While the two of us sat next to each other waiting for a meeting with the staff and Coach, we laughed a little in disbelief over the unexpected turn of events—this was after I offered my condolences over the loss of his sister. He said she had been ill for a long time. During the meeting, we watched films of the team and me in action, including my practice with Jasper yesterday, who had been ordered to work on one-handed catches over his shoulder. I was spot on getting the ball to him. Someone was given my films from high school that showed I could already throw deep. There was, however, none of the "acrobatics" that I displayed in Saturday's game. The coach asked what all the leaps and spins were about. I told him it's fun. He shook his head and looked at me like I had a screw loose. In my opinion (which I kept to myself) too much is made about "pocket presence." Following the snap, I can successfully get the ball off quickly if I want to, but I prefer to run back before letting go. Krull, on the other hand, the QB I met today, is great dancing inside the pocket. Tiberius Krull. That's some name. He's a junior and has no college game experience yet. The staff must be scratching their heads over what to do. Right now, I'm really thankful to Hayden for having shown me how to throw on the run. He admired Andrew Luck's mobility and we went over lots of his plays, including the awesome tackle from his Stanford quarterbacking days when he unexpectedly laid USC's cornerback out on the turf. That player had managed to pick up a bouncing ball, and it looked like he'd be running it in for USC, until Luck pounced him. And although I came to admire Elway and the Broncos, Hayden said to study Aaron Rodgers. Didn't realize the guy has probably chalked up more passing yards outside the pocket than any other QB. Later today, met with Jasper, DeShaun, and Rhett by Scioto. Damn freezing outside. Rhett was all business, which is good because the others and I tend to start goofing around after a while, and the situation calls for us to be 100% serious. We concentrated on my signaling to Rhett. At his suggestion, we worked on perfecting the under-center snap, just to throw the other team off—because he says colleges don't use the formation much anymore. I like his thinking. I'm ready for bed. Picturing Tess. We got a bite to eat at the student union last night. Kissed her hello. Love that about having a girlfriend. Enjoyed small talk about teachers we've had, and pets, although Jim is hardly a pet, neither is the fifteen-year-old dog she grew up with, a Golden Retriever named Finnegan. She had driven over in a hand-me-down Toyota Corolla. Climbed in the front seat to kiss her goodnight. Deep-kissed for a while. Staggered back to my car like a drunk. Can't stay awake for Dad tonight. Uncle picking him up at airport now.

Friday: Writing this before returning to athletic center where team will take bus to airport. Dad is still there talking to coaches and signing more papers. Grateful he came, mostly for handholding, since I'm terrified of flying. He's heading out tomorrow morning and will meet Iris and Hashke in Cedar Rapids. Nice of them to come root for me. Uncle will be in the section of the plane with the medical staff, which I might end up needing. I flew alone for the first time when Iris received her award from the governor, and I thought I was going to pass out more than once. Jasper knows I'm phobic and swore he'll stay put in the seat beside me. I've been instructed to wear big noise-canceling headphones that set Dad back $400. Going to keep eyes shut entire three hours. Hate that my stomach feels like it's in my throat. How am I my mother's child—someone so at home in the stratosphere?

CHAPTER 35

William Horse That Walks Backwards exits the Cessna bush plane carrying only a small backpack that fit on his lap. He is met by Chief Lyle Jackson from the Yakama Nation in Washington, who could be anybody under that warm, thick brown parka he's bundled in, his face hidden by a tinted face shield. Chief Jackson lifts the lid to the storage compartment of the snowmobile and hands his passenger an extra helmet in exchange for the carry-on. Waving to the pilot, they backtrack through the deep powder and zip ahead to Sherridon, a tiny dot on the map in the central Canadian province of Manitoba. The small, unincorporated community with approximately ninety citizens lies in the vicinity where the Council of First Nations held its previous conference. Remote destinations are vital, providing there is electricity and Internet. Towns like Sherridon, built up around the mining industry, are connected because of independent satellite providers. After the nearby copper mines closed decades ago, a major nickel deposit was discovered in Lynn Lake, and later gold. The residents didn't lose their jobs; Sherridon just up and moved to Lynn Lake, literally. The actual foundations of its commercial buildings, homes, and church, were dug up, loaded onto freighting sleighs, and then pulled by tractors for 120 miles to the new destination. It's worth noting that a company had the wherewithal to conduct this massive relocation, but supposedly no resources to clean up the ponds of bright red toxic acidic waste left behind when it closed, a scourge to this day.

The Council's group is small due to the last minute notice of the meeting, which is being held almost three months before the regularly scheduled one that is listed on the Bureau of Indian Affairs government website. Up for discussion—the subject that couldn't wait—the recent swell of Indigenous activism occurring not just on the northern continent, but in obscure corners of the world. Whether the issue is stopping the Dakota Access Pipeline or reclaiming tribal lands, the movements are being shared and fueled by sympathetic non-Natives who regard themselves as valuable allies to aboriginal causes. They express solidarity in their posts on the Internet, usually on Facebook. What struck the chiefs during the past year is how easy it is nowadays to organize like-minded individuals. This modern way of communicating can't be trivialized. They should use the computer network to their advantage, and quickly, in order to accelerate the momentum. It offers enormous potential for bettering their people's lives.

For the first time, a female leads them in the traditional opening chant. She is Chief Black Horse's daughter, Waneek, his confidante in tribal matters, and the one being groomed to take over the leadership of their Mohawk Nation because her father is losing his fight against cancer. Following the serious tone of the opening, Waneek breaks into a smile and adds a bit of levity by telling a joke. Based on the response, she might have done well as a comedian. She is young, in her early thirties, and attractive in an understated way, projecting a quiet strength. Her blunt, chin-length hair style might well be for convenience; as a lawyer she travels a great deal working to preserve tribal existence.

"Getting to the point," the tone shifts, but her voice remains pleasant and clear, "our tennis player and swimmer are out of the running when it comes to inspiring our Native youth on the national level. Helen Logan's promising future has hit the skids due to a cocaine addiction, and sadly, Charlene Santana doesn't want to deal with the racism she has been encountering at college and in her sport. She is still a wonderful role model who is seeking sponsors to build a recreation center on her reservation in Florida. And of course, we will help. Regarding the actor, Jason Red Moon..." Waneek pauses a moment. "... he definitely possesses the kind of charismatic leadership the Council had been hoping to find in a young person, but in talking with many of you, it appears that he no longer fits the bill. You think he is becoming too confrontational, to the point that he is alienating himself from his fellow tribesmen."

Waneek then zeros in on William Horse That Walks Backwards and addresses him personally: "Weighing in on Ohio State's football victory over the weekend, the media couldn't get enough of Viktor Talking White Owl's story. Speaking as his uncle, what do you think...is he likely to succumb to the pressures? He has seemingly pulled through one horrific experience already. Would you mind giving us your thoughts?"

Without hesitating, William answers, "True, this is a critical period.

He is mature for his age, but in reality he's still a boy. Speaking honestly …the tie to the reservation will get stronger the older he grows, just as it has for every person I know once he or she becomes a parent. The desire to preserve one's cultural identity takes on new meaning and importance. Whatever happens, Viktor's family is always there for him."

"His tribal brothers, too." says a member, offering a personal note of encouragement. A rumble of agreement follows.

"And tribal sisters as well," adds Waneek. She looks across the room. "With regard to Red Moon…his fame demands our attention, whether we like it or not. We can't ignore that he helps get stuff done which otherwise might take forever to get accomplished."

She brings up the need for protecting the actor. "Although he travels with a group of bodyguards, it isn't enough. He is a major nuisance to the wily multinational corporate giants that have billions of dollars at stake for their dubious enterprises. The protests draw attention to the big companies' shenanigans, impeding their progress. Red Moon puts himself in harm's way, more precisely, in organized-crime's kind of harm's way. Sleep on the matter, and tomorrow we will hear recommendations for a plan of action. In the meantime, and in keeping with the more informal nature of the proceedings, we will move on to the evening's entertainment. Everyone is delighted to learn they'll be watching Talking White Owl's triumphant football win.

William starts the video. He wishes he could divulge that the Rawakota are on it, that they've been keeping Jason Red Moon safe for a while now, ever since his first rallies. Howling Wind saw to that. Now, with events unfolding like they've been this past week for Viktor, security must also be stepped up to protect his privacy. A burst of enthusiastic shouting fills the room. William's eyes light up at the image of his nephew heading downfield, leaping like a powerful elk over the pile of fallen bodies.

I am standing on Tess's front stoop, hollering away while my finger wears out the doorbell: "German Village, here we come, and right on time I might add." The door cracks open, and I'm yanked inside by the sleeve, making for a funny sight gag.

"Good Lord! Do you have to broadcast it all over the neighborhood! And on Sunday when it's so quiet!"

Tess looks peeved, but I'm thinking she really isn't. I stand before her grinning like a loon, just so frickin happy to see her. She makes a little clucking noise with her tongue to show how annoyed she is, but then instantly wraps her arms around my neck and puts her lips to mine. Mmm ...*mahpiya* — heaven. It definitely won't be me who ends this kiss.

It turns humorous when we realize this can't go on indefinitely. We're laughing while still lip locked, but I refuse to give in. Before you know it, things get intense again. We finally break for air. I'm content to stare at her face; she's so beautiful.

"I'm such a lucky guy."

She holds my gaze, without blinking ... or speaking. I'm at last rewarded with the most sincere, dare I think it, *loving* smile. Tess grabs her coat and purse and out we go into the sunshine. What a fantastic day. Bright blue sky. We can see our breath. Tess heard it's going to be in the forties later. We should be able to walk around the park and neighborhood shops without freezing our butts off.

Once we get there, Tess gets excited to visit the first place she sees, a booklover's dream.

"Do you realize how long we've been holed up in here?" I ask at a certain point. Tess ignores me. I'm having as great a time as she is browsing the endless shelves of titles that are housed throughout a city-block of rooms, but there are other shops I want to take her to. I'm really glad she finds the same satisfaction in reading as I do. She has taken up residence in a corner on the floor, her coat spread out under her. The light from a window makes her red hair shimmer like its woven with shiny copper strands of tinsel. The image is committed to memory.

"This is so cool," she says, still lost in thought.

"The bookstore?"

"That, too. This chronicle on the Plains Indians."

It must be fascinating; she doesn't look up. She wants my opinion on the accuracy of the facts before buying it.

"Why is Lakota sometimes spelled with an extra "h" that's put either after the k or the final a?"

"It's a breathy language, and with not much of a written history. Linguists probably argue over which letters to use, in order for sounds to be pronounced correctly. I have no idea who has the final say."

"Is an "h" ever put in your name? And why spell Viktor with a k and not a c? Were you named after your grandmother Victoria Birdsong?"

Her nose is still in the book. I sit across from her on a footstool and reach for the massive hardback full of photographs. "Any more questions?" I ask, poking fun at her. It doesn't register. She's still in her own world. "It's a coincidence that my grandmother is Victoria. My mom lived with a Canadian Quaker couple when she was pregnant with Iris—Marie and Victor Lejeune. They didn't have kids. When he died in an accident, Mom returned home to the reservation. Later when she had me, it was her way of honoring him for everything he and Marie had done for her. As for the "k," that was Mom's way of making it native; and no, it never has an h." As I leaf through the pages, I ask if she was named after anyone.

"A saint, along with the Virgin Mary, like every Catholic girl. My parents obviously had great hopes for me."

"There's a Saint Tess?"

That cracks her up. I'm informed that her family calls her Theresa, which I find pretty. She stands and shakes out her stiff legs, happy with her find. From what I can tell the book she wants to buy is well-researched, and now I want one that will shed light on her Irish-Catholic background. Tess asks the bookseller to locate *Trinity* by Leon Uris. It's thick, and with no pictures. Right when we're paying for our treasures, Fleetwood Mac's *Gypsy* plays over the store's speakers. I can't resist. Laying our coats on the sales counter, I whisk Tess down the long, skinny aisle and twirl her around wherever there's space. She's perfectly in step with me. I dance her out to the courtyard, doing my best to keep in time with the song.

If the streets weren't so uneven, I would have gone on dancing with her the rest of the afternoon, like in a musical; instead, after collecting our coats and books, we walk hand in hand while hitting all the tourist spots. We conclude our "date" at a restaurant that Dr. Nate raved about it. There's no escaping the audible gasps of recognition rippling around the room as we're led to a table. Tess glances back over her shoulder at me, as if to say she is okay with it.

"This has got to be really pricey," she whispers when the waiter is out of ear-shot.

"I wanted the day to be memorable. Please don't give it a second thought."

"You don't think it's been memorable enough…what with the bookstore, the wonderful quirky coffee shop next to it, and the stroll through the park?"

"Glad to hear you've enjoyed yourself, but I'm greedy. I want to be with you as long as I can." I live for that subtle smile of hers. It's as fine as the daytime moon.

She opens the menu and apologizes for the sudden '*whoa*' of uncontainable surprise. "Not a second thought," I remind her, sounding more emphatic. There she goes looking at me like she does every so often, straight into my pupils, like she's probing my brain for something specific.

While we wait for our meals, a big ribeye for me and walleye for her, it's fun to watch the passers-by. Our table is directly under a window. Tess likes the cobblestone streets and says she could come here all the time. Too bad that's not practical for either of us right now.

It's only eight o'clock when we head home. Saying goodnight this early is out of the question, although yesterday's game and the plane ride ordeal are catching up to me. "Do you want to see my place?"

"You bet! But I can't stay for more than a half hour. I've allowed myself to get behind in a class. I knew Dr. Avedon and the team were going away for a convention. I planned on catching up these next few days."

She couldn't make it any clearer—I need to keep myself in check. It's not like I was expecting to have sex yet, but I was hoping for a more intimate ending to the day.

Tess comes out of the bathroom as I'm pouring the tea. "Everything's so clean. Do these apartments come with maid service?"

"My uncle lived with me until a few months ago. He drew up a cleaning schedule that has become routine. I wish you could have met him today, but he's gone at the moment. He moved in across the hall."

"My older brothers are all slobs. But then my parents overlooked it because they were always busy with sports, which took precedence over everything."

She obviously likes honey, stirring a steady stream of it into the chamomile. We take our cups to the couch. Again, she compliments me. "I think that keeping one's surroundings clean is a virtue. It shows you think enough about yourself and others to put in the work."

Good to have scored a few brownie points for being tidy. Back to the topic of her brothers, Tess mentioned the oldest one's mean streak. "My parents simply dismissed his sadistic behavior, which is the same as condoning it. I joined the swim team just to avoid facing him in the mornings. My neighbor belonged. Her mom drove us every day. Diving into cold water at 5:45 a.m. was torture. It was my only break from hearing about football. I was beyond grateful when Kevin went off to Notre Dame. That was my parents' dream, to have a son play for the Fighting Irish. My second oldest brother, Quinn, is a Bearcat at the University of Cincinnati. Next there's Thomas. He plays for Mount St. Joseph, which is also in Cincinnati. My younger brother, Ryan, is a junior in high school. He was never gung-ho about football. He likes tennis. Ryan is an interesting character, very introspective."

"That's rough. I've been around families just as obsessed about football as you're describing. Fortunately, mine isn't one of them. And I wasn't at a school where football mattered much to anyone."

"No? And you're from Texas!"

"Not at all, Tess...honest."

She drinks her tea and looks around the apartment. I don't think she believes me. The framed photos on a bookcase grab her attention. One is of me with Sunkwah and Winnie dressed in full Indian regalia at a pow-wow. Another shows Dad, Mom, Iris, and me at a Texas barbeque. There's one of Grandmother and Pahpie with their arms around each other sitting on their horses. It was taken a year before he died. The last three are of Dad's side of the family, all the many aunts, uncles, and cousins—all Black; something I never think to bring up.

Tess looks at me amused. "Now there's a cast of characters." And she leaves it at that. She comments on the piano, saying that six years of piano lessons were wasted on her. She wishes now she had learned the saxophone. I tell her it's not too late. Then she wonders why the piano isn't in the big empty spot by the window, my same question to Uncle when he was here. I tell her I've grown accustomed to the arrangement. He comes in every so often, and I want him to know I respect whatever his reason was for insisting the area stay open.

Tess walks to the sink with her empty cup. I'm right on her heels. We settle on a time we can see each other. Friday is Veteran's Day, no classes. That's too long to go. She says I can stop by her place during the week for coffee or a bite to eat. Saturday is a home game. I ask about going out on Sunday again. She offers to cook dinner instead. "We'll spend the afternoon listening to records." It sounds like the lady who owns her place has as big of a collection as Dr. Nate. Placing her arms around my neck, she glides her cheek across my jaw, across my stubble-free skin. "So smooth," she says, doing it again. The effect is…soothing, the word I read on the box of chamomile tea: a soothing antidote to life's complications.

CHAPTER 36

" 'He can throw with his right *and* with his left, jump five feet straight up, and rush like a young Michael Vick during his stint with the Falcons. A quadruple threat.' Wow, little brother! Impressive." Iris should be the one getting congratulated for memorizing that, along with all the other things the sports announcers have been saying. "I loved you being called a physical freak. How are you handling all this? Who was the clown that asked if you were really an alien?"

Laughing, I tell Sister she should have seen the way the coach looked at me when I didn't answer right away, like he was afraid I might deck the moron. I'm so glad she called.

"Hashke and I wish we could've come to this game, too. I so want to meet Tess. Any girl who has stolen my brother's heart must be one-of-a-kind."

"That she is. I worry though about her hating football. Maybe I can get Winnie to cook up another pot of waphi wahaŋpi for me. There's got to be an ingredient to make Tess accept the idea of me playing ball. The lucky soup seems to have granted me all my other wishes, except for maybe the tattoos. I haven't seen any, but I'm also afraid to ask."

"Where's the challenge! You have to put forth *some* effort to win her over. I'm just relieved she isn't cross-eyed. Tell the truth, Viktor—it *would* matter, right?"

It's great to finally get to say "my girlfriend" in a conversation. Iris hears the story about how I was smitten by the sight of Tess at the microscope before even knowing what her face looked like. "So, you see, Iris, crossed eyes would not have made a difference." I also like being able to talk about the football game with someone besides Dad. He concentrates too much on the bad calls made by the refs. Sister knows her football. She rooted for the Badgers in college and follows the Packers. She says it was thoughtful of me to have acknowledged Hayden and Skyler during the post-game interview today, my first. I truly meant it when I claimed they were instrumental to my success.

Iris figures she has taken up enough of my evening and once more says how happy she is for me, that I've found my partner to share theeich ihilah.

"*Theeich ihilah*? Where'd you come up with that?"

Silence. She hasn't hung up. "Iris?"

"You know…being together sexually with the one you want for all time."

"I know what it means." I'm not sure how else to respond. It makes sense, I guess, that she'd be familiar with the concept of theeich ihilah. Growing up, we both recited the poem to the stars, and being that she was older, she understood the reasoning behind the nightly ritual. I, on the other hand, have only recently been granted an explanation. "It's odd that you would use a Rawakota word to describe the experience when I never celebrated the ceremony of Otiwota, and you never took part in Ahtiwota, the one for girls. Seems irrelevant to me in this century, something our Elders encouraged only because it was nostalgic for them."

"Seriously? To me, if I had fallen in love with a Rawakota man and no one had told me what to expect, it would be terrifying if suddenly while we're having intercourse for the first time, he couldn't move or speak."

What on earth is she talking about? Mom never mentioned that, or maybe that's the thing being kept from me. Sounds awful. "I don't want to get into it this late, okay? I'm beat. Glad you called, Iris. Love you."

"Okay, Viktor…hope to make it to another game soon. Love you, dear Brother."

I think back over the line, "the one you want for all time." I do want Tess for all time. I can't wait to see what she's surprising me with for dinner tomorrow. Before going to sleep, I review today's game in my head from start to finish. It was fun, except for Demon Slaughter's trash-mouth. He is as vulgar off the field. The trade-off is he keeps me from getting sacked, as does Rhett, our center, a guy who's the total opposite of Slaughter.

"You mean to tell me that your brother Kevin was willing to repeat his junior year in high school simply to get noticed by Notre Dame's recruiters?"

Tess gives a little derisive snort as she searches inside her fridge. "That's nothing compared to our parents uprooting me from the wonderful life I was enjoying in Pennsylvania, just to accommodate a kid as thankless and mental as Kevin was, still is...just to play football at a Division I Catholic school in Cincinnati!"

I can see why their decision riles her. "But you, on the other hand, got placed a grade ahead. That's a plus."

Tess grabs a huge chunk of parmesan and grates it on the kitchen table, channeling her frustration in the process. "I was fine with skipping sixth grade. Physically, I looked more mature. Apparently our rural Bucks County education had been superior to the all-girls private school I was going to be attending. In Kevin's case, the high school said he didn't have enough credits, which was a bunch of malarkey...just so he could play two years and improve his stats. The fat check my father wrote the school to show his appreciation didn't hurt."

Tess sits on the chair, throws her head back and starts laughing outright, breathless from the workout. "I really thought I was beyond holding a grudge against my parents. Doesn't sound like it, does it?"

I raise my eyebrows over the mountain of parmesan, enough for a week. "Feel better?"

Dinner is ready. I knew by the aroma as soon as the door opened that Irish stew wasn't on the menu, though that's what I was half expecting. Tess pulls out a tray of sausage and spinach stuffed pasta shells from the oven.

"I was reading through the old cookbooks on the hutch, and this recipe is definitely a favorite. The page had a hard crease and it was covered in food stains...figured it must be good."

"It smells terrific."

After the insanity of yesterday's game, being alone in our own space is a welcome change of pace. I get tongue-tied singing along with *Marrakesh Express*. Tess isn't familiar with Crosby, Stills & Nash, but likes their harmonies. She grabs a wooden spoon and pokes the shells apart to cool. A burst of steam shoots up.

While she divvies up the food on our plates, I go on singing. "I can't believe the lady who owns the house has so many of the same records as Dr. Nate ... there's Dylan, Janis Joplin, Otis Retting, all the Motown artists."

"I've only begun to discover them. I find myself getting hooked on an album and then playing it over and over. Right now it's Carole King's *Tapestry*."

"Same! The Doors took over my life for the longest time." We dig in and eat. It's easy to keep conversations going with Tess. I have to make a conscious effort not to talk with food in my mouth. "Don't you think the late '60s and early '70s would have been exciting to grow up in? I'm sure I would have protested, too, though not necessarily against the Vietnam War. My grandfather, Benjamin One Horn, we called him Pahpie, occupied Wounded Knee in 1973 along with over two hundred other Indians. They wanted to impeach a corrupt tribal president and re-open treaty negotiations with the government. He spent half his life actively involved in trying to change policy on the reservation. Hard to believe how little got accomplished."

"No kidding. My maternal grandparents and their relatives were considered radicals, but back in Northern Ireland. Did you ever learn about the Troubles? The Catholic minority clashed with the British and Irish Protestants during the same years as the U.S. Vietnam protests. It was in 1972 that the Donegals came to the States to escape the violence...arriving at Boston harbor. A great uncle had been killed and another lost his legs in a bombing attack in Belfast, that's where they were from."

"What about your dad's side?"

"The O'Sheas, who'd been farmers, emigrated a century before during the Great Famine. Besides dealing with the potato blight, they left for the New World because they couldn't afford the rents they had to pay to the English and Anglo-Irish landowners. Boston had also been their port of entry. They belonged to a diocese that provided help to later generations of families, which included my mom's."

Tess and I clear the dishes from the table. I knew the English were guilty of persecuting the Catholic Irish in the largely Protestant north; however, I'd never heard they outlawed their language and history in the schools, just like they did with my people.

"Your mother's parents were nationalists, right? They wanted an independent Ireland, free from the British Crown's control, much the same as the Indians sought to be left alone." Strange how two entirely different cultures share a common bond.

"Damn monarchy," she mutters.

"Effing British bullies."

"That's what I meant. To think the colonists broke free of them only to become racist American imperialists."

We're left standing at the kitchen sink, holding hands, kind of wondering what's next. Her hair is pretty the way it curls over her shoulders. I look around. There's about as little room to dance as in the bookstore. Tess reads my mind.

"Shall we give it a whirl? See what you can find."

"How's John Coltrane, since you like the saxophone? My dad would sometimes have him on in his shop when he did his bookkeeping at the end of the day. It says on the jacket the music is seductive. That was definitely lost on me as a ten year old listening to it."

We rock gently back and forth in place, kissing now and then.

When she excuses herself to go to the bathroom, I rummage through a stack of dusty old magazines in a corner basket. The homeowner loved her art history. The ink is completely smudged along the page edges from all the times they were turned. The mailing address shows the subscriptions had been sent to a Professor Frieda Lishak at OSU more than a decade ago.

Right then Tess calls for me. I'll see what she wants before putting another record on. It's a short hallway. I've never gone beyond the bathroom. Two doors face each other. I poke my head in the room on the right. It's basically empty, just a couple of small wooden chairs. A sewing machine is on the floor in the corner with colored fabrics piled high to the side of it.

"The other one..."

"Obviously," I laugh, pushing the door open wider because I don't see her. And then I do. I squeeze the handle so hard my fingernails pierce my skin.

"Viktor?"

I might not be breathing.

"Viktor! If you don't say something this instant, I'll be so embarrassed."

Breasts, fully exposed, are within arm's reach, but my feet remain riveted to the spot.

"Am I wrong to think we have reached this stage in our relationship? Should we hold off until football season is over?"

"Tess...I don't know what favorable gods are looking down on me, but I'm forever grateful to them." Did I really say that, or just think it?

"Do you carry a condom in your wallet?"

I blink hard and stare straight at her, like a deer in headlights. "A condom? But you said once that you take birth control pills."

"That doesn't mean I'd have unprotected sex. There's always the chance of getting an infection or a disease. You realize that. Besides, the pill is mainly for treating bad cramps that I've always suffered from ... I don't sleep around."

"I didn't mean to imply that..." shut up, I warn myself. Think, think, think. "I'll buy some down the street and be back in a flash." I want to touch her breasts so bad; it kills me to leave. Fuck! I'm such an idiot!

"Viktor...hold up."

My only thought is, the faster I go the faster I'm back.

"Stop!"

She catches the back of my shirt. Next thing, her chest is puffed up against mine. She outlines my lips with her tongue. It's a dream to be holding her naked body in my arms.

"I've got to say, Tess, your breasts are beautiful."

She kisses me. I get the sense I'm not going anywhere, which makes me wonder what's next.

"If not this weekend, when were you planning on us making love?"

"I don't know. I've been so happy with the way things are going...I've never dated a girl for any length of time."

"You said you were emotionally involved with the lead in *WAKAN*."

"It was one-sided. We never had actual intercourse."

There's the fleeting image of Camila hiked up around my waist with a wet vagina that only my fingers experienced. I never brought up the fiasco in high school with Ashley. That hardly counts as having sex. Tess seems to be taking stock of the situation. It's clear this is a critical moment in our relationship. Does she trust me?

With all the sincerity I can drum up, I state with conviction that under no circumstances could she get a disease from me. I also know I won't be contracting any from her; something I never considered.

It's going to happen. I help her get my shirt over my head, then she grabs hold of me through my jeans before unzipping them. I run my hands along her curves, to her breasts. They're perfect, not droopy, and incredibly soft and squishy. When the noisy heater kicks off, it's absolutely still in the room. The double size bed causes some laughs. Lying diagonally on it doesn't help; my lower legs dangle off the end. There's barely space for me to position my elbows alongside her, but she seems okay under me.

We move together in a nice rhythm as her fingers slowly travel my spine. When they reach my shoulder blades, certain spots make me shiver. The insides of her thighs are warm and slippery, a definite "go" down there, to the point of me sliding past the target. Tess scoots around and lines me up. I enter part way. She gives a wiggle for me to keep going. I'm not about to end what's begun, but the night won't play out unless I tell her this.

"Tess," I whisper. It's hard looking in her eyes up close. "I don't expect you to say anything, but it's important to me that you know I love you." And with that I melt into her. It feels incredible…beyond belief. The scent of her permeates the air. Everywhere I see colors, amazing colors. I reach to touch them but can't raise my arms. I'm on my back. I don't know how I got this way, and I begin to feel strange and anxious. "Tess, I can't see you."

"Because your eyes are closed."

"They're not. Where are you?" Her lips brush my lids to prove it.

"I'm with you, Viktor. Right beside you."

I feel her fingertips pressing into mine, and it's electric. Next her mouth goes searching and settles on the groove in my neck between the collarbones. My pulse pounds against her tongue at the same time my ché throbs hot inside her, stoking passions designed to bring about new life. It seems we're floating in and around and through the universe, passing iridescent jets of gases and silvery spiral galaxies. Kindly spirits follow chanting, wishing us well.

I collapse on the bench beside Krull and remove my helmet.

"Get ready," he warns, "here it comes."

I look up to see Assistant Coach Mazursky marching toward us steamed as can be. Can't blame him. We brace ourselves. With hands on hips, legs spread, and feet firmly planted, he looms over me like a predator before getting down in my face and reaming me out. "How the hell do you go from playing like a pro one day to blowing it completely during practice?" I'm bound to come off sounding like a smart-ass if I inform him that his yelling tactics won't produce better results. I stare ahead as he takes a step to the side. Krull's turn. Mazursky attempts to sound sympathetic because of Krull's recent loss, the grief of which must be influencing his abilities. The fact that Krull is a third-string player with limited experience doesn't enter into the equation. Mazursky's anger quickly gets the better of him, though, and he starts screaming at both of us, "The fans are gonna have you guys for lunch if you lose to the Fighting Illini in four days! Got that, four days! Maybe you haven't heard…they're the fucking underdog!" We watch as he storms away, whacking his cap on his thigh repeatedly as he's known to do.

Krull says dryly, "Think his wife ever wonders about that bruise?"

"It's got to be a running joke in their house."

We sit motionless, having given up on the idea of going back on the field. If that was Mazursky's idea of a motivational speech, it was lost on Krull, too. While the rest of the team continues its drills, we head in silence to the locker room to shower.

We leave together, arriving first at my car. Krull holds me by the arm. His tired brown eyes come to life. "My sister's sixteenth birthday is Saturday." That was out of the blue. I understand the gravity of the statement, noting the reference to her is not in the past tense.

"What's her name?"

"Lydia."

Tears form in the corners of his eyes. The only thing I can come up with is, "That's rough." How lame. I'd probably hug him if we were closer friends.

"What's your excuse, Viktor?"

He's right to assume there must also be a reason for my lousy performance today. I'm not sure I want to go down that road with him. Tiberius Krull has a trusting manner. His distinctive military regulation haircut and clean-shaven face stand out from many guys nowadays, including ones on the team, who are covered with facial hair. Guess I'll go with my gut: "I had sex for the first time over the weekend."

"Is she someone you love and intend to marry?"

I'm relieved there's no flip remark like, *way to go, dude!* At the same time, I wasn't expecting anything as serious as that.

"I hope to."

"It's a profound experience, isn't it...when you love the person. My girlfriend and I prayed before making the decision. We refused to believe our love would be considered sinful in God's eyes, even if the Church denounced premarital sex."

I'm hardly going to discuss his religion in a parking lot, but it felt good opening up to a guy who doesn't make light of it. Krull pats my shoulder and suggests we meet early in the morning for practice while it's still dark. "Maybe a good night's sleep is all we need."

I nod. "Maybe."

I skip seeing Tess on the way home, only because I'd get an erection and my balls and groin still ache two days later. It was already noon when I woke in her bed yesterday, completely out of it. I didn't know where I was. It's a good thing the team gets Mondays off. Tess attributed it to dehydration and forced me to drink a gallon of water. I told her of the images I saw during sex. The memory reminded me of people's accounts of tripping on peyote. It was mind-expanding for sure, more powerful than immersing myself in music, which, until now, I wouldn't have believed possible. She assured me that the night had been equally meaningful to her, even if not as psychedelic. Hearing *I love you* back would have been nice.

I call Tess after dinner, happy to hear her voice. I wish I could confide to her how terrible practice went today. It hurts to a degree that she probably wouldn't be sympathetic, simply because the subject is football. I openly admit that I can only think about being inside her. She lifts my spirits when she states I'm all she can think about, too. We agree to meet Thursday instead of Wednesday. I hated having to tell her that wouldn't work for me, but it's crucial that I make up for today's sorry performance with a killer football practice tomorrow.

Lying in bed, taking in the night sky, I picture Pahpie and Sunkwah and our warrior ancestors. I feel so close to them. And it's all because of theeich ihilah. What a powerful experience. While under its spell, I had the sensation of bonding with everything, including all that is wakan, the unseeable, unknowable mysteries of our existence. I speak aloud to what I know for fact is a listening universe. I thank our creator Wakan Tanka for Tess, the woman I want to share life's adventures with, and whatever future celestial states we'll encounter in the hereafter. I look forward to the day we become *shingefora*, "life-makers." I regret how dismissive I was of Uncle William's explanation about what happens during theeich ihilah. I can see now that it's impossible to accurately convey the intensity of what a person encounters. One has a sense not only of the primordial forces that drove creation at the time of our universe's cosmic birth, but of how the event continues to play out on the tiniest of scales the instant new life is sparked in every single reproductive process. What a wild ride! I have a newfound respect for the deep-rooted Rawakota tradition. Early humans with their relatively primitive minds are to be admired; they gleaned so much about the nature of the heavens and Earth simply by star-gazing. I'm convinced there are things that should ultimately remain wakan.

CHAPTER 37

"I can't stand the suspense…so tell me already, how'd it go?"

"And hello to you, too." Iris laughs over her mother's impatience. "I *was* going to call, just as soon as I finished lunch." She realizes this is one instance when her mom won't be telling her to call back when she's done eating. "It hard to say how our conversation went. Tess seemed leery at first when I introduced myself, which was understandable. Viktor told her about me, but that didn't change the fact that this stranger was calling her unexpectedly."

"How on earth did you broach the subject?"

"I worked up to it. When I brought up German Village, and how happy Viktor sounded after his date with her, Tess said she had begun reading a book she picked up there that describes the various tribes that make up the Great Sioux Nation. She wondered why there was only a blurb about the yellow-eyed Rawakota warriors who helped the Lakota win battles."

"You couldn't have planned that any better. How fortunate."

"Wasn't it! After a brief explanation, I tied it to the main reason for the call. I said our community may identify as Lakota, but we still practice some Rawakota rituals that date far back, and which remain important to us, like one in particular called theeich ihilah. I went on and said that learning about it might play a key role in their relationship, even though Viktor thinks the idea of it is archaic. I tried to impress upon her the fact that theeich ihilah could affect him more than he realizes. I also asked her to stop me if she thought I was overstepping my bounds and getting too personal."

"She must have had questions."

"One would think, but she stayed quiet and listened, to the point that I worried she was ready to hang up on me. I guess she was mulling things over while I explained it. Afterward, I told her to please call me if she thought of anything that needed to be made clearer."

"Nothing so far I take it?"

"No, but I could tell from speaking to Viktor after his game this past Saturday that he was ready to be with her. They were going to spend Sunday together."

"Based on William's observation of Viktor's mediocre practice on Tuesday, he had to have stayed the night. He was bone-tired." The women share a knowing giggle. "You did good, Iris. Tess needed to be informed beforehand. Hopefully Viktor recognizes that he should not have downplayed the importance of his Elders' teachings; they hold a timely connection to the past."

"You've got to see our son play in person, Constance!"

"I know, I know! I'm working on it. There's a possibility of having time off over Thanksgiving. I'd be able to catch the Michigan game that weekend."

"That would be great! Iris and Hashke plan on going. I hate that none of us can make it to the one coming up. Viktor explained why his girlfriend won't go...but would it kill her to show a little support? We're not a sports-obsessed family like hers, and he's definitely not the conceited jock she makes her brother out to be!"

"Deep down, Solomon, you know Tess has a legitimate reason for not wanting any part of the game. Viktor understands. I get how proud you are of him, and that the entire world should be as enamored of his talent as we are. He has some lessons to learn yet, the biggest being how to manage the ups and downs of his emotions in such a highly charged, football-crazed environment. Tess is bound to be a grounding force."

The usual chitchat follows between them about the goings-on in their separate lives in separate places. Both have been questioning whether they can keep up being apart for these long stretches of time. Right before the goodbyes, Constance throws Solomon a curve by asking if he's up for doing the Indians a big favor. "Members from the Mérodders gang are scheduled to be released from jail soon, except for the one guy who shot young Sam Barker at Lazy Al's. Word is they intend to reorganize under a new leader in Canada then return to the Dakotas and Buckthorn Reservation to begin running drugs again...and recruiting kids to help. Billie Spotted Horse, Viktor's friend who ran with them and also landed in prison, sought to redeem himself in the eyes of his tribal family by providing law enforcement with the names of the instigators. He was promised legal immunity and protection when he gets out in a month. We both know the police on the rez don't have the resources for that. Would you take Billie in at our home in Texas...and maybe let him work at the garage?"

To Solomon it's a no-brainer.

"Looks like there's going to be another pilot in the family, Constance." William proudly passes along the news that her seven-year-old great-niece, Elena, can't wait for her favorite aunt to take her up in a plane. *"Whenever she is in the mountains, her mother says she stares endlessly at the sky and pretends she is you. She begs to leave Chohkahn all the time."*

Constance smiles over William's description of Elena. *"That's around the age I knew."*

As soon as she had hung up with Solomon, she called William to report that in January she'll be leaving Arizona for Afghanistan...again. *"The previous administration pulls us out, and a new president sends us back..."* He abruptly cuts her off with a grunt, then says:

"You signed up for the life."

"Doesn't mean I can't complain."

These days, after speaking in Rawakota to Rolling Thunder on a regular basis, she easily reverts to it when talking to William. *"With phase one out of the way, having at last gained technological superiority, phase two of Chohkahn's secret operation is well underway. The time has come to end the violence on Buckthorn Reservation. All members of Rawakota's undercover team are good to go. They've secured positions as teachers and medical workers. A couple even managed to get on Buckthorn's police force."*

"Finally," he says, having wondered himself if the day was actually going to arrive when the Rawakota Nation would act on its principles and help the Lakota Indians, covertly of course. Chohkahn's citizens have been discussing at length and for years how to rid the territory above of its criminal element. Most of the population wish to spend more time in the great outdoors, not underground in the sacred city. Personal safety should not be an issue during these extended visits. They want to mingle with their Lakota brothers and sisters like earlier generations had. *"I truly hope the matter with the gangs can be resolved once and for all."*

"Those lowlifes aren't going to hinder the process of us Indians guiding our own destiny. There is something else to share," says Constance. *"It pertains to the seventh generation and goes beyond what was prophesied by Crazy Horse and Black Elk."*

"What do you mean...beyond?"

"It's true we are living in the era which the two leaders had foretold of. The children born in the 1990s and early 2000s are still believed to be the ones who will mend the sacred hoop that was broken at the Wounded Knee massacre in 1890. According to Sleeping Buffalo, who is presently in Asia with the Mujahzee, their culture also foretells of a seventh generation."

William interrupts, *"The phrase is heard everywhere nowadays, thanks to advertisers. People talk about seventh generation this, and seventh generation that. They don't view it as a time for healing and spiritual unity like Indigenous people do... it just means that our actions impact generations to come. They use it to sell their recycled stuff. Nothing new there."*

"True, William. To the Mujahzee, though, people are accountable not only to the future generations, but to those that came before as well. A generation to them isn't the twenty-five year period the Lakota think of it as, nor is it seventy-five years, the number of years the Iroquois consider it to be. For whatever reason, the Mujahzee trace their lineage using the "powers" of seven. And the seventh generation, according to their math as it corresponds to our Gregorian calendar, will occur next year. Imagine! And it holds special meaning, too!"

"Heyah!" exclaims William gruffly. *"How long is that ... a million years!"*

"Eight hundred twenty-three thousand five hundred forty-three."

"Un-hee! Nonsense! How could an ancient civilization make such calculations? And why seven?"

"That's what I hope to learn when I go meet up with Sleeping Buffalo. He is an intuitive man who can't readily explain the technical aspects of the Mujahzee findings." She has to laugh. *"Your skepticism amuses me. What a surprising reaction from someone who grew up in Chohkahn, a hidden world that defies logic. Perhaps the Mujahzee were inspired by shamans who had visions similar to what our past leaders had. The role of number seven got lost in translation as people evolved and moved to new places."*

"It's still far-fetched. Humans emerged around...what...maybe eighty

thousand years ago. That's a far cry from eight HUNDRED thousand years!"

"Fossilized humanoid footprints have recently been discovered that date back that far. Animals resembling bison existed. Maybe stories of our creation were invented then."

"I'll wait for better proof before I get excited. In the meantime, tell me more about the reservation. The problems are so pervasive; they seem insurmountable."

"Unfortunately, it's going to take violence to rein in the violence. The Rawakota continue to surveil the plains with micro spy drones. Every vehicle, no matter how old or damaged, has been secretly fitted with a tracking device. If it runs, it has one. Scout warriors will lay in wait near the places where the drug deals, rapes, and gang attacks are planned to occur, which, as you know, are typically in isolated empty trailers. Additionally, Indians who drink will get their alcohol confiscated if they try and carry it illegally across state lines onto the rez. Next they'll be enrolled in a rehab program. It isn't a choice. Several new recovery centers have been built. Once clean, if they go back to using drugs or drinking outside the rez, they'll be banished for good, unless of course they opt for the implants to prevent relapse. It's going to be a fast, short-lived attack that will definitely make the news.

"While I think of it, William, would you look into why faculty members from Ohio State's Geodetic and Engineering Departments are at the old abandoned Black Boot gold mine on the reservation?"

I race upstairs following the game, knowing Tess is spending the night. It's late. I beat the snow. There she is, asleep in my bed, the woman I love. The thought of Thursday night comes to mind, of sitting on her couch with her bouncing on my lap. It's imperative that I eat. Some leftovers are in the fridge. There's no need to hurry. I'm just happy she's here.

Tess stirs when I climb under the warm covers. Her eyes open part way. She's got a dreamy smile. "Did you win?"

"Mm-hm." Lost in a deep kiss, we make love quietly.

In the morning, on our way out for coffee, we see Uncle in the parking lot scraping ice from his windshield. I've been anxious to introduce him to Tess, but I'd prefer it be under different circumstances. It's obvious she stayed over. Ignoring me completely, he removes a glove to shake her hand.

There's that wide smile, his special one just for the ladies. Without taking his eyes off her, he asks if we want to go riding later at Dr. Nate's farm, dinner is included. Tess is eager, saying she rode all the time during her childhood in Pennsylvania. That's great news to me, seeing as that's my favorite thing to do in the world...that is up until now. Words fail me when it comes to sex.

The invitation means she passes Uncle's test, whatever his criteria are, a test Ishmael failed from the get-go. For a fleeting second, I consider how Uncle William might have reacted to Camila, and whether he would have recognized and scorned her freewheeling promiscuity.

CHAPTER 38

Campus is dead. Not because it's cold and snowing, it's the Buckeyes and Wolverines face-off in Michigan. Fans are huddled around TVs in bars and in homes, enjoying the rivalry as they do every Thanksgiving break. Tess didn't bother going home this week. Last year she had brought a date to her family's holiday dinner in Cincinnati, an artist who knew absolutely nothing about football. The point of it was to show her parents and brothers that there were others like her who didn't give a damn about the game. Her act of defiance was lost on them.

Tess tried to ignore the buzz of excitement in the air when she shopped at a drugstore early this morning. Kickoff wasn't going to happen until later in the afternoon, and she actually contemplated watching the game, until the thought of Viktor getting hurt overwhelmed her. Having kept herself busy until now, Tess decides to treat herself to a cappuccino. The walk to the corner shop will be invigorating. She bundles up in a jacket and scarf and checks the time. The game should be about over. Just as she rounds the corner and catches a strong whiff of espresso that envelops the coffee house, she finds herself drawn to the Bar and Grill two doors down. It's standing room only, but somehow she manages to squeeze inside just as the Buckeyes victory hoopla is beginning. Hadn't she sworn to herself never to be a part of this stupid football atmosphere! The noise is hard to take, as well as the inescapable smell of beer. As she watches the cheering students, it occurs to her that this is a part of Viktor's life that he will never share with her because of her attitude. A group of arm-locked female fans squealing and hopping wildly in front of her face can't wait for the Indian to remove his helmet so they can see his eyes better.

Number 7, with cameras on him as he pushes his way through the throng of people on the field for the post-game handshakes, has so far eluded reporters. An announcer remarks about the size of the viewing audience, and that this match-up exceeded the 17 million who watched last year's game, which up until then had surpassed previous records. The man's high-pitched voice starts breaking up as he yells above the crowd noise: "No one can get enough of Viktor Talking White Owl, the composed 18-year-old Native American from Texas, who was not part of any high school powerhouse athletic program, and who rose from obscurity to secure wins in the five games he has played for the Buckeyes, a team that experienced the loss of its two top quarterbacks in one day."

Highlights of the game are shown. A second sports analyst gives Number 10, Tiberius Krull, his due. Comparisons are made regarding the quarterbacks' different playing styles. "Krull's quick feet inside the pocket keep the fans on edge. White Owl, on the other hand, is mobile. He likes to extend passing plays, giving guys more time to come open." The guy claims it's instinct, something that can't be coached. "And with receivers like Rivers and Stillman, who seem to be able to read White Owl's mind, it's magical." He concludes by saying it was White Owl's approach that wore out Michigan's defense which ultimately led to the Buckeyes' victory.

Tess has had enough. As she strolls back to her little house, cappuccino in hand, she reflects on the recent phone conversation with Viktor's sister. She couldn't believe it when Iris started talking about the most intimate aspect of a couple's relationship. According to Iris, Viktor would be all hers after they shared theeich ihilah, and she would be his—forever. There's no "till death do you part." She couldn't fathom what his sister meant, until it happened. Without question, what Viktor experienced was profound. Dare she believe what Iris told her, though? That he is all hers? She just witnessed how the girls in the bar reacted when Viktor was onscreen, yelling their brains out. He seems the type to rise above it, unlike her brother Kevin, who lived for the adulation…ate it up in fact. Viktor appears oblivious to being gawked at.

Snug in a corner on the couch, with Carole King playing in the background, Tess organizes her notes to study for finals when she gets a text from Viktor.

Dear one and only. Get ready to be loved to pieces after tomorrow.

She knows Viktor is spending Sunday with his family in Ann Arbor. There's a pang of guilt for not having gone up. Would it have killed her? She scrunches her mouth, disappointed in herself. *More than ready!* she answers back—though not ready enough to attach the word "love" to her message. She turns on the TV knowing full well that coverage of the game will continue through the rest of the evening. And sure enough, there is

Viktor twisting in mid-air in a slow motion replay. It's the moment he let go a perfect pass to Stillman, who then ran the ball downfield on the outside, skipping over a lineman, and then spinning himself free from the clutches of another player to complete an 82 yard touchdown. Seeing Viktor makes her sad; she misses him. Suddenly a picture pops on the screen of a woman dressed in a flight suit and standing beside an Air Force jet. It's Colonel Howling Wind, Viktor's mother. The reporter has done her homework. There's a photo of Hillel Academy, the school he attended in Wichita Falls, Texas. It's followed by a short video that shows a much younger and skinnier version of Viktor in action. They cut back to the reporter. She brings up the Herrington Scholarship and explains that it includes post-graduate studies. Tess hates that she feels a tinge of jealousy. The segment concludes with a scene depicting the grandeur of the Great Plains. No mention is made of the squalid living conditions usually portrayed in stories about South Dakota's Indian reservations.

After turning off the TV, Tess gets up and stops the record mid-song, and then returns to her notes. Music makes her daydream, and it's crucial that she immerse herself in her studies. She has worked hard for too long to allow herself to get side-tracked.

My relationship with Tess is heading south fast, and I don't know what to do. I'm not proud of myself, sitting in my parked car a street away from her place like a stalker, waiting for her to pull into her driveway. Fifteen minutes of this and I head home.

Racing upstairs to the apartment, I recognize the wonderful familiar aroma of food in the hallway. Uncle William is cooking. I throw my coat and gym bag inside my door on the floor, and then turn right around and knock on his door.

"It's open."

He's dumping hot water from a big pot of potatoes into the sink. The steam fills his narrow kitchen.

"You smelled the blackberry sauce and couldn't resist, eh?"

"Can I help?"

"Done. Sit." He gives it a final stir.

Two heaping plates of elk stew are set on the table along with wild cherry bark tea. We discovered a market downtown that specializes in exotic wild meats and game. Elk didn't strike me as being unusual, not like the kangaroo and alligator it sells, or rattlesnake.

Uncle asks me to give thanks to the Great Spirit.

"Let's see..." He normally does this. "In order for us to be strong and healthy, the sacrifice of the mighty heháka is recognized. Mother Earth has blessed us with plants for teas that comfort." I forget to bring up family, which is met with a grunt. But then, what's a visit without a grunt of disapproval over something or other? We dig in. I suspect he knows I've been neglecting the daily blessing, just like he suspects my love life has experienced a setback. Tess's car hasn't been in the parking lot for a couple of weeks, and I've been keeping to myself, even during practice.

We talk about the Michigan game and how great it was that everyone could fly out to it. He then asks if Tess and I want to go to Dr. Nate's again since we had so much fun on the horses. I sense he has given me an opening in which to discuss whatever is bugging me. It's too personal, though.

I do need to unload. I just don't know with whom. I almost called Hayden. I almost called Bernie at MIT…I have no clue why. Uncle snaps me out of my thoughts when he gently taps my chin, causing me to look up from my dinner, up into his kindly eyes. I can't be persuaded.

It's the end of the month and the end of the year, Bowl time for colleges. Despite my fear of flying, I actually watch as our plane lifts off the runway and takes to the air. Because of the poor showing at the start of the season, the Buckeyes didn't qualify for the Championship Game, but we were selected to go to the Fiesta Bowl in Arizona. The decision has many sports analysts baffled. According to their stats, OSU should be playing TCU in the Orange Bowl. I only know it's a complex system. The plane banks to the left. I can make out campus and Grandview, the name of the area where Uncle and I live. My imagination allows me to believe I can spot Tess's street. How can she not be thinking about me today? After almost a week, I've half given up expecting to hear from her. I continue to stare out the window, remembering how things were when I came back from Michigan. Tess was happy. She was positive she was going to do well on her finals. Dr. Avedon had given her an unexpected bonus in her pay. She smiled around the clock, especially when we decided to buy a little tree to decorate for Christmas. If only I hadn't fucked things up, not once, but twice; after which she decided to go home for the rest of the break, and I threw myself into preparing for this game.

Jasper leans in front of my face to see the clouds. "How'd you get over your phobia?"

I shrug. "Not sure I have." He annoys the hell out of me anymore. It used to be he flirted with girls who were all over him at the away games. I know for a fact he met up with them later. Jersey chasers, that's what they're called, athletic groupies. They hang out at the practice field and know the bars the players go to, dead-set on hooking up with them. I caught him once holding a girl's ass tight up to him, blatantly grinding his hips against her pelvis. He saw my disgust and laughed it off. I feel sorry for Brenda, his wife, and his sweet little daughter. I adjust my noise-cancelling headphones and open Dr. Sharma's folder on the laptop. A member of our team is experiencing interference from an unknown source. It's ruining his outcomes, so he asked for my insights. I hope I can offer my scientific expertise. I haven't really been confronted with an intellectual challenge of this nature before. To an outsider, doing research probably looks to be a calming and introspective endeavor. It is for the most part, but there are times when ideas get to spinning so fast in my head, it physically feels like my brain cells are undergoing the same kind of workout as my body's muscles during training exercises.

The past days in Arizona have been a treat, what with the constant warm sunny weather and palm trees and clear blue skies—it can't really be winter! Mom has got this gargantuan saguaro cactus in her yard with human-like welcoming arms. The football team has breakfast at the hotel, following which we complete our early morning practice drills. The remainder of the time is ours to do with as we like. For me, that means hanging out in the west valley where Mom lives and where the Air Force base is. It's a big complex that trains new pilots. I got the grand tour. Now that I'm older, it's really bizarre to think anybody chooses to make a career from war, let alone my own mother. Why put yourself in harm's way except to defend one's own borders?

And I wish Dad would stop shaking his head in disbelief just about every time he looks at me. I'm equally amazed over how far I've gotten so fast, but I can do without the constant reminder. The fact that it's a bowl game doesn't rattle me. I want the National Championship next year. The three of us doing things together has been great. Our conversations cover so much more than when we're on the phone.

I've been curious about what Afghanistan and northern India were like. Mom goes on about the beauty of the Himalayas and the countless isolated villages that are scattered across the region. Not once does she hint at what her job entailed there. How does Dad stand it?

Dad says business is better than ever. He'll be hiring more help when he returns to Texas. Suddenly he stops himself midsentence, as if he were about to reveal something he shouldn't. His face lights up big time. I wish I could read his mind. They ask if Tess went home for the holiday, wondering if perhaps they can meet her during their next visit.

Aargh. I change the subject. They can think the reason is simply because I miss her so much it hurts to talk about her.

While Dad prepares steaks inside for the grill, Mom corners me on the patio. "What an important stage in your young life. Surely the situation must overwhelm you at times?"

I nod. It's true.

Mom laughs. "You're a pygmy next to that thing."

The sun hits me square in the eyes when I look to the tip of the saguaro behind me. "No shit. What's your guess…13 meters?"

"Very good…44 feet to be exact. I used a laser to measure it."

I trail her as we go sit in the shade, impressed by how buff she is. "I don't know the last time I saw you in shorts and a tee."

"The desert uniform is liberating." Her barefoot toes wiggle in the air. Then, without holding back, she says, "First you couldn't talk enough about Tess, and now nothing." She sounds sympathetic. A swell of unwanted emotion rises from my gut, forming a hard lump in my throat. I really can't hold this in any longer.

"Tess's last words to me were…" my chin starts to quiver, '… what are you going to do next," I clench my teeth together to fight off tears, then whisper, "rape me?" The shame is unbearable. Mom strokes my cheek with the back of her hand, as if to show she doesn't think me a monster. Of all the people I thought about opening up to, I can't believe I did it with her.

"What brought it on?"

"It'll sound really stupid."

"It started when I…" she begins, encouraging me to recount the details.

Dad offers a momentary diversion when he announces the steaks are going on. "It started when I...went to Tess's house a few days before Christmas. Since I was spending most of my time on the field, and she was busy at her job and studying, we hadn't seen much of each other at the beginning of the month. And with the team flying here this week, there was this short window of opportunity for us, you know...to be alone together."

"What happened?"

"I shouldn't have brought this up with you; it's not right." I sit brooding, fidgeting with the ring on my pinkie from Grandmother.

"Spit it out."

"Fine. Like I said, I went over to her place. I was standing at the door when she yelled for me to let myself in. I found her bent over the back of a chair in the kitchen, in serious pain from menstrual cramps." I hate replaying the scene in my head. Its outcome tortures me. "I'd been thinking about her nonstop, and to finally be with her made me crazy...to the point of finding towels to put down while trying to convince her that making love would relax her muscles, and she'd feel better. I didn't let up and continued to push the idea. She looked at me like I'd lost my mind. Next she said *that,* about raping her." I cross my arms in front, hugging myself. "To think that my desire for her could be construed as anything so despicable." Dad is singing away in the corner, happily tending the meat. I sound even more the fool after hearing what I'd done out loud.

"Did you ever tell her about me or Lukas?"

"Huh-uh."

"Then her comment was nothing more than an off-handed remark, nothing to get bent out of shape about. Don't beat yourself up over it."

I glance around the yard before admitting there was something else. "It wasn't just that."

"Ah jeez...you dug yourself into a deeper hole?"

I'll be staying tight-lipped from here on out.

"Will talking to Dad help?"

"No! No way!"

"Sunkwah?"

That certainly never occurred to me.

"My son is not a rapist. Lukas was not a rapist. Technically, I suppose he was. Consent wasn't given."

Well now I'm really confused. "I thought that was the reason Iris is here…and me. The newspaper story about your kidnapping said you were found in a cabin with your ankle chained to a bed post."

Mom pauses a moment then asks, "How old were you when you looked it up?"

"I dunno," I shrug, "maybe nine. You can't blame Iris and me for being curious."

"Lukas went to jail on kidnapping charges, which he confessed to. He never would've believed he violated me. He obsessed over me becoming the mother of his children, the central tenet of theeich ihilah—nothing that I as a 13 or 14 year-old could comprehend. And by 19, when he followed me and cut me off on the road as I was driving back to the rez, there was no convincing him I didn't love him. I had after all told him once that I did, and he held me to those words, despite the amount of time that had passed. It's a conversation for a later time. For now, realize, lusting is normal. You're 18 for heaven's sake! You're not genetically predisposed to becoming a violent rapist. It was alcohol that screwed up Lukas's brain, that and the emphasis the Rawakota place on finding a partner so early in life. That's what drove him to drink. Year after year no girl came along that he was spiritually drawn to, until he met me. And even then he might never have given me the time of day if I hadn't persisted in flirting with him and ogling his body. It's why I flew into a rage when I learned Sunkwah had been preparing you—no, brainwashing you—for the day when you would embrace the idea behind theeich ihilah."

I would actually like to have that conversation now, the one she wants to put off for later. If what I experienced with Tess during our first time of lovemaking is the result of Sunkwah's influence, I'm beholden to him. Now I'm curious how Mom manages to fly a plane when she has cramps. I learn she doesn't get them, or periods. She gets an annual shot that prevents ovulation. I follow it up with the obvious, "Why wouldn't all girls do that?"

"Because you're screwing around with hormones. It's best to have had children first. Growing up, I didn't experience serious pain, nor does Iris. If Tess is willing, acupuncture might help. Talk to William."

That was enlightening. After a great dinner, and while we wait for a driver from the base to take me back to the hotel, Mom casually mentions that she's leading the flyover tomorrow at the stadium.

"What the hell! You couldn't have said anything earlier!"

"Un-hee! Why the anger?"

For a second I'm speechless, then I stammer, "Because I have mixed feelings about your job in the military…because flyovers are such a…such a…recruiting PR stunt."

She puts me in my place with an uncharacteristic scowl. It's the exact expression Winnie and Grandmother have used when they recall the years she disrespected them and went gallivanting around with Lukas. That's what Grandmother called it, gallivanting. "I'm just wondering," she says, "are you planning on taking a knee during the anthem?"

"No. I'm not sure what to think about it."

"Wow!" says Dad under his breath, having so far stayed out of this.

"What? You think I should?" I'm assuming he does, even though he doesn't elaborate. "I admire players who do. They should, if they feel strongly about it. I just don't see what it accomplishes. It seems to be pissing people off more than anything. I understand that it represents solidarity among people of color for the way they continue to be treated in this country. But politics should stay out of sports, period. And that includes the singing of the Star Spangled Banner, which I don't do. It's certainly not the land of the free to the Indians, nor is there justice for all. I'm glad the teachers at Hillel never forced us to recite the Pledge of Allegiance."

"There *is* another way of looking at this, you know." Mom is using her professional, well-modulated voice. "You and I are positive Native role models. It gives our people hope when they see us succeeding at what we love to do. Here I am a jet pilot and you are a scientist, who also, remarkably, can play football at an elite level. Don't underestimate the enormous influence you're wielding in the Indigenous community." Constance thinks twice and forgoes including his impressive foray into dance. She wonders if Viktor is aware that parts of *WAKAN* are among the most watched videos on the Internet since he began playing football. Secretly, the mother is pleased that he won't be participating in the protest. It's in the best interest of the Council of First Nations' agenda that Viktor not become the subject of controversy, for now at least. She likes that her son can't be pressured into doing something that he isn't one hundred percent behind.

My ride arrives. Dad and Mom stand as one. He's got her wrapped up in his arms. His face beams with pride over his son, which does lift my spirits considering how wounded Tess left me feeling. He pecks Mom on the cheek and squeezes her tight as they watch the car pull out of the drive. The windows are open. Mom shouts: "Don't be an ass waiting for Tess to make the first move. Call her!"

———————

"The Injun Engine! Whaddya think!" Kevin punches his brother Thomas on the arm then chugs his beer to celebrate another OSU touchdown, not that he's a Buckeyes fan. He just prefers them over the Clemson Tigers because he hates Southerners. "Think I'll post it...bet it goes viral."

"You're a first class idiot," snipes Tess, having anticipated the same old, same old during her visit home, mainly because the Tormentor would be here.

"I'd say you're the idiot, Theresa." Kevin points to his head and circles his fingers to show his sister he thinks she's the one who's cuckoo. "What student in his right mind doesn't buy game tickets they're entitled to?"

"Enough you two!" Chevonne O'Shea looks to her husband out of exasperation. "Can we never come together as a family and enjoy a peaceful day?"

Nooo, thinks Tess to herself—not as long as that jerk is permitted in the house. And jerk he is, chanting Indian war cries when the Buckeyes are up, and saying the most ridiculous things like, *scalp those hicks!* Really! If Finnegan weren't ailing, there'd be no stopping her from simply turning around and going back to Columbus with him. But the onetime handsome and athletic Golden Retriever is now old and arthritic. He noses her to scratch behind his ears. Ah, her beloved Finn. He's the reason she still makes the trip to Cincinnati. She just has to suck it up while she's here.

It's the middle of the second quarter. The Buckeyes lead 20-3. Their kicker just botched a field goal. Tess scrutinizes the roomful of family, conscious of her growing alienation from them. Kevin, her parents' shining star, is downright fat. Once an offensive tackle, his muscles have dissolved. Permanently sidelined with a hip injury after his second year on the Notre Dame team, he came back to his high school after graduating to teach Social Studies and coach his former Knights, which is laughable considering his glaring lack of empathy. Kevin's wife, whose post-baby body is back to looking perfect, sits and laughs with Thomas's perfect-looking, high energy, blonde girlfriend, who Tess will literally throw food at if she doesn't stop using "literally" in every damn sentence. Both pay little attention to the game, except when Number 7 appears on the field. Then they gush like a couple of star struck pre-teens, especially when the camera shows a close-up of Talking White Owl's unflinching deep yellow eyes. In loud enough voices for all to hear, never guessing that Tess knows him, they wonder if sex with an Indian, in particular this magnificent six-foot, seven inch specimen of an Indian, would be the high point in any girl's life. Her brothers are so into the game, they don't respond to what Tess regards as jabs to their manhood. One would presume the guys don't satisfy their ladies.

Upstairs, the baby has begun to cry. "It's your turn," says Alexis to Kevin. Tess watches her brother. He ignores his wife and doesn't budge from his seat. She repeats herself, forcefully enunciating the words. Now, it's a direct order.

"It won't kill her to cry until halftime," he mumbles with a mouth full of food, referring to his offspring like some pesky cat mewing at the door to come in.

Tess catches her dad's eye, half expecting him to suggest that she go up and check on her niece. But he doesn't. He does continue to hold her gaze. Could it be that for once he sees what she has always seen in Kevin, the reprehensible behavior conveniently overlooked all the years she was growing up in this house? Her mom keeps peace and goes to fetch her grandbaby.

Tess slides off the chair and rests on her knees beside the coffee table, eye level with Finn now, who promptly attempts to roll on his back for a belly rub. A bit of help is required. The table is crammed with food. Just looking at it is enough to pack on the pounds. Tess searches for the sturdiest chip that won't break in the spinach-artichoke dip. Her other brothers, Quinn and Ryan, who crowd their dad on the shorter side of the sectional, try to outshout the other with his own take on what coulda-shoulda happened so far in the game. If she thinks they're noisy, what must it be like for Viktor at the center of such hysteria? God, she misses him. There's no question he's phenomenal. His last pass was astounding. His body shot straight up into the air, what seemed like five feet, and then he hurled the ball 45 yards to Stillman, after switching hands no less. He and Krull have been alternating on plays, unlike the Iowa match-up when each went in for the full quarter. This strategy makes for a fast and exciting game.

The Buckeyes just intercepted the Tigers' ball, so they'll be up after halftime. Suddenly there's a flurry of her brothers' arms across the table as near empty bowls are replaced with new batches of wings and dips. Here's to another hour of them stuffing themselves.

Tess is invisible. By now she has exhausted the amount of small talk she's capable of in a day's time. She's curious as to what Viktor thought when he watched his mother's jet go thundering above the field. The sports broadcasters really played it up. Viktor had stood stoic, holding his helmet to his side as he followed the formation until the aircraft were out of sight. "Theresa!" snaps her mom. She at once looks up. A phone is held out to her. Her mom is balancing the baby on her hip while she waits for her to take the call. "He says he's your boyfriend."

Stunned, Tess glances at the TV screen as confused as can be, then takes the phone as her mother bends to hand it to her. "Hello?" Her heart pounds at the sound of Viktor's voice. "Give me a sec," she says, and hurriedly stands to go someplace far out of earshot of the others. She winds up in the cold garage. "Hello, Viktor. This is a total surprise!"

"Tess, it's been killing me that you haven't picked up my calls or messaged me back this morning. I remembered the name of your brother's high school and looked up O'Shea in the white pages using its area code. You said your parents still had a landline."

"God, sorry Viktor...I had already reached the outer belt when I realized I'd left my phone on the kitchen table. I checked my email on my parents' computer, though."

"Stupid me! I thought of emailing, then figured it was overkill. Tess, please forgive me for the way I behaved. There's no excuse."

"How can you be calling me right now? Aren't you in the locker room? Is that allowed? Don't you have pep talks or something?"

"It was short. We're far from losing. So...we're still together, right?"

"Yes. But you *were* weird. I was feeling absolutely miserable, and that's how you show sympathy?"

She can hear all the commotion in the background while she waits for him to reply. "I know another apology won't help, Tess, but I need to apologize again anyway. I truly am sorry. Just please don't give up on us. Even though it'll be late, you're two hours ahead, can I call you tonight when I get back to the hotel?"

"I'll be looking forward to it."

"Have you actually been watching the game?"

"Yes. I wouldn't miss something so important to you, although my jackass brother takes the fun out of it."

"Watch online."

"I can't see your face clearly on such a little screen."

"As long as you still want to look at me. Gotta go. Love you, Tess."

Viktor hung up so quickly, there was no chance for Tess to tell him the same. She felt ready.

I hang up quickly on my end, not wanting to put Tess on the spot. Whatever the reason is that prevents her from openly saying she loves me, I believe that she does. "Tigers, you are history! This Buckeye is pumped!"

As the team heads down the hallway, this odd sensation creeps over me, like nothing I've ever experienced. Very bizarre. Out on the field, the Offense waits to hear their assignments. "This is how the opening play's going down," I tell them. What follows are instructions that are not mine or the coach's. My lips moved, I said them. My final words to the players are, "If you're not on board, get another stringer. Please, all I ask is that you put your faith into this one. Don't think, just act." Only Slaughter puts up a fuss, but then he's the one who has to pull off this stunt; and stunt it is. I know his ego is too big to resort to a backup player. He verbally lands into me with everything he's got.

"That's not my fucking position, you cock suckin' red pussy…"

Aye-yi-yi.

Lined up and ready for the snap, I glower back at that mean cuss and yell, "You better turn up where you're fucking supposed to!"

Back in Cincinnati in the meantime, Tess had returned to the living room where she sat back down on the floor beside a snoring Finn, aware of the family's eyes on her. Leave it to Kevin to annoy her with a snide remark.

"Was that the queer artist you brought home last year?"

Alexis apologizes for her husband. She does that a lot. Tess sighs and ignores him, content with filling her plate.

"What's his name?" asks Quinn, taking a genuine interest in his sister's life.

"Viktor Talking White Owl."

"Hah!" Kevin's knees lift in the air and he rolls back on the cushion.

His body lurches forward, and he shakes his head over her lame attempt at sarcasm. "In your dreams, Theresa!"

"Enough!" demands their dad, not wanting another earful from his wife.

"All right already," whines Kevin. "But you gotta admit, that was a doozy!" He goes on laughing under his breath.

Quinn and Tess communicate a look of quiet desperation reminiscent of their childhood days. They'd felt cursed having a maniac like him for a brother.

Tess acknowledges Quinn's sincerity in asking, although it's obvious he wouldn't believe it's Talking White Owl either. "He's someone I met at work in the hospital."

"Known him long?"

"About a half year."

Quinn smiles, happy for her.

"Whoa!" yells Kevin, jumping up and punching the air like he's sparring. "A fight between a black dude and a red skin! Bring it on!"

Number 54 is right up against Number 7's face mask and provoking him with his body language. Viktor tries to sidestep him, but Slaughter won't have it. The camera zooms in tight to a shot of Demon Slaughter ranting on about something, all the while poking his quarterback in the chest and shoving his shoulder pads. Viktor simply takes the abuse and heads toward his mark, which in this instance is not under the Center, but around seven yards behind him.

The scene puzzles the commentators who are accustomed to seeing this type of spread formation when Krull is up, but not when Talking White Owl is. The Tigers' defense reconfigures itself. "I'm not sure what they're going for here," says Mel, "you, Chris? Look at the space between those guys." And before Chris can weigh in, Number 7 catches the snap and proceeds backwards then spins on a dime in an attempt to outrun and outmaneuver the Tigers' Number 27, who, unbelievably, had no one covering him, a major oversight on the part of OSU.

Thinking back to their altercation, Mel asks what's on everyone's mind, "Did Slaughter leave his quarterback open and vulnerable on purpose? White Owl could pass to Stillman who's at the 40, if 27 weren't nipping at his heels. Number 7 is masterful at dodging out of his opponent's way."

"A running lane has opened up center field and 54 shoots right through!" shouts Chris, briefly apologizing to Mel for cutting him off. In the excitement, his voice goes up several registers. "Mittelmeier, the six-eight, 300 pound Defensive End leaps onto Slaughter's back, but the six-five, 290 pound Slaughter manages to free himself and continues in the clear! But to what end? Even if White Owl manages to throw a Hail Mary, Slaughter isn't eligible to catch the ball."

"Oh, no," hollers Mel, "27 tripped over his own feet! What a serendipitous moment for the Buckeyes! White Owl, catching a break after getting chased back to the 10 yard line, kicks a leg high into the air, and then powers the ball downfield. It's got speed but not a lot of height. Gaviston, Number 46 on Clemson's team, looks ready to intercept near the Buckeyes' end zone, but wait! Stillman suddenly shoots across the field toward him. He slams into Gaviston, who manages to tip the ball, which pops it right into the lap of OSU's Demon Slaughter, alone by the goal line! A short hop, and touchdown! Incredible!"

"He was just standing there, like he was waiting for it," reports Chris, totally flabbergasted. "Once that ball touched a Tigers' hand, Slaughter became an eligible receiver. Talk about dumb luck!"

"Or divine intervention," muses Mel.

Tess grabs the phone from the nightstand on the first ring. It's almost 2 a.m. She's been lying awake fantasizing about Viktor while waiting for his call. "Hey there." She scoots her pillow up against the headboard.

"Hi Tess. I'm not sure how long my voice will hold out…it's starting to go from all the yelling. Hope I didn't wake your parents by calling this late."

"Congratulations on the win."

"Thanks. That opening play after halftime was meant to impress you."

"*Ri-i-i-ght*."

"You had a houseful, huh?"

"I thought it was going to be only me and my parents for a change. I assumed my brothers would be hanging with their friends, especially Ryan, who's in high school. Go figure."

"It's great hearing your voice. Wish you were here in my arms. Something's come up, Tess, and I'm not sure when I'll get back to Ohio. My dad told me a friend from the reservation is near death. He didn't want to say anything before the game and upset me. I didn't think Daniel mattered to me anymore. I was wrong."

"That's terrible. I'm so sorry, Viktor. I've been looking forward to us being together, too; but school's starting…it makes for busy days. As long as we can talk to each other on a regular basis, maybe Skype? Tell me what it's like out there. Would you want to live in the desert?" After listening to his descriptions of Phoenix and its surrounding areas, and with his voice growing more hoarse by the minute, Tess asks, "Before we hang up, Viktor…will you answer a question that's been bugging me? Why would you expect a girl to want to have sex during her period? The idea of it is downright yucky."

"I don't know. This is really embarrassing. I'll have you know my cheeks are burning. When we were taught the facts of life in school, the nurse said something to the effect that you shouldn't assume that pregnancy won't occur during menstruation, which to my mind meant people did it then, too. Some guys on the rez boasted about having sex with girls on their periods. I wouldn't know if it's yucky or not. Blood doesn't faze me."

"Seriously? My guess is the nurse was driving home the point that there's really no such thing as a safe time. Aren't Jewish boys taught *never* to touch their wives during their periods?"

"That's lousy. I didn't have to attend any of the Jews' religious classes at Hillel."

"I guess it's no different than me thinking that girls could only get pregnant at night." Tess laughs over something she forgot about. "We had this nun for sixth grade health who told us that when boys hit puberty, they start having what she called were these night emissions. If the "emissions" got inside a girl, she might end up having a baby. That was it; the extent of our 'sex talk.' Thank goodness I wasn't promiscuous by day. Talk about getting the surprise of your life!"

"I'll say! I'm glad we cleared the air, Tess. When it comes to the other thing, I'll try and figure it out."

"I hope so. And Viktor, you shouldn't feel you have to hold back when it comes to talking about football. That's my issue to deal with, not yours."

"I appreciate it. When are you leaving?"

"Tomorrow, early. There shouldn't be much traffic New Year's Day."

"I'll wait for a text that you got home safe. 'Night."

"Good night, Viktor." She doesn't hang up.
"Tess?" Nothing.
"I love you, Viktor. Sleep tight."

CHAPTER 39

The plains look lonely in January, a perfect backdrop for Daniel's solitary trailer, presently under quarantine. According to Grandmother, who last checked in on him two weeks ago, he might possibly be lying dead inside by now. His wish was to be left alone. Before stepping out of the toasty warm jeep into the cold, I suit up in a disposable HazMat coverall that includes goggles, sterile gloves, and an antiviral mask. This should keep me safe from HIV, pneumonia, TB, and hepatitis B, all of which Daniel has, along with any potential rodent borne diseases. I walk slowly. It's a totally different world compared to sunny Phoenix...a washed-out empty-looking world. There are times when the winter landscape is magnificent, when a bit of sunshine passes through dark blue snow clouds and the tall grasses turn copper. But not today. A couple of crows sweep over the roof. It's like entering Poe's inner sanctum.

What's left of the storm door falls off in my hand. I yell out it's me, so he's not startled by the noise. A swift kick opens the jammed front door just enough for me to squeeze through. My heart starts thumping hard. It's all so gray. Most everything has been cleared out except for two plain wooden chairs and a cot in the middle of the room. I expected to hear a lot of coughing, but it's quiet, an eerie kind of quiet, and freezing cold.

"Daniel?" I hesitate before taking a step, as if I could possibly prepare myself.

I approach, hoping to hear breathing. A mouse sniffs inside a small metal cylinder-shaped stove, the kind that belongs outdoors. It definitely hasn't been used recently. I stare at Daniel's profile. He's unrecognizable. A tiny puff of breath appears under his nose. Then it's gone. It's a while before the next one. I made it in time, for myself that is. Can't cry when the goggles need to stay in place. I should be grateful the mask keeps out bad odors. The air is surely sour from the piss-soaked blankets tucked tightly around his wasting body. I go outside in search of wood. There's the ramshackle barn where Grandmother rescued Flapjack before he almost went lame from neglect. He's now enjoying the good life beside Ola and Jim.

I get a small fire going in the stove, and for the next few hours, I tell the stories of our childhood and laugh for us both. I muster the courage to touch his bony cheek.

"Daniel? Daniel Blue Shirt…Thohca Ogle."

His eyes roll beneath his transparent lids. Taking my bottled water, I wet an edge of the sheet then dab the dry, cracked lips. I watch in disbelief as he presses them together. I'm encouraged and go on talking.

"It worked, Daniel. People thought the pass was a fluke, but I had felt wakan in the locker room. I didn't know what the hell was going on with me. There I stood, suddenly looking at Slaughter with your eyes, and the words out of my mouth weren't my own. I'm guessing it was important that he trust himself and do something remarkable outside of his comfort zone. He sure didn't want any part of it. God, I wish I knew what was going through his mind when he caught that ball!" Watching Daniel lying there motionless, I'll never get over his transformation. "Daniel…the smallest sign that you're listening would be nice. Was what you did some kind of a redemptive act?" He wouldn't know that word. "Was it your way of making peace about something before you walk on?" I can't tie it to anything. What I do know is that the universe holds mysterious connections.

The only observable trace of life fails to form under his nose. Using Grandmother's stethoscope, I slip it under his covers and listen for even the faintest pulse. I continue to sit without a thought until the last cinder in the stove turns to ash. "Find peace my friend on your journey to the Spirit World." I plan to head over to the funeral home with the news, but first I need to find some kind of memento of our time together. Anything. The floor creaks with each step as I search the place. I spot a wallet under a dirty pot next to the kitchen sink. It's cracked and stiff. There are a few singles in it along with his faded tribal ID. No, don't want that. I'll just be crying every time I hold it. I let out a long sigh and go on looking around the messy countertop. I refuse to leave empty-handed. And then I see it, Claire's school picture. I think it's from the 9th grade…one of those little ones. Daniel stuck it in the side of the kitchen window. He developed a crush on my cousin after years of listening to me go on about the things she and I used to do at Grandpa Cyrus and Grandma Junie's house in

Kansas City. Since Dad and Iris and I had always stopped off by them first before continuing our trip to South Dakota, there were lots of fresh stories to tell my friends on the reservation. Daniel really looked forward to hearing about Claire in particular. We were probably around twelve when he asked me to bring a picture back for him. To think that he kept it all these years.

It hasn't been a week since Daniel died, and I'm feeling so low I'm scaring myself. The mix of emotions is like last Christmas all over again, except I have Tess, even though she's over a thousand miles from the rez. I've stopped calling her and am only texting because I'm not fit to be around people, let alone have a conversation with anyone. There is a troubling disconnect with my present life. Tess's simple daily *I love you* grounds me. What I would give to witness the words spoken to my face, to see her eyes when she says them and feel the touch of her lips against mine.

Sunkwah says a hanbleceya is in order, and although I can't think of anyone my age who has gone on this rite-of-passage, I'm open to the idea of a vision quest. Unlike the Lakota, Rawakota tradition holds that males follow the same trails taken by generations of braves on their father's side of the family. Lukas put the kibosh on that. We also don't purify ourselves first in a sweat lodge. I've chosen to honor Pahpie by using his path. Three times in his life he made a journey of hanbleceya. He had shown me the granite peaks across the border in Wyoming where he went, in case I ever felt the need. Being so young, I couldn't fathom what he was in search of, or that going hungry and not sleeping for almost a week could solve anything. My thoughts however ran wild when he described the magical things that appeared to him during his isolation. Sunkwah, too, had fantastic stories from his hanbleceya. His route went far north almost to Canada, land of the Chippewa. There weren't so many mountains as there were lakes for him to camp beside. Iris wouldn't dare destroy his fond memories by telling him, as she had me, of the oil pumps that now ruin the peaceful landscape, and of the endless parade of irresponsible tourists and hikers who are disturbing the natural balance in caves. They trample and litter the forests. What would he and Winnie make of zip lines and the riders' screams that intrude on animals' sanctuaries? They're just more pieces of Mother Earth for outsiders to monopolize.

Having hunted with Pahpie and Sunkwah, I know the trails and caves by the old tribal names, and I've learned the secret places wasichu will never find. I'll be joining the ranks of generations of seekers who cried out to the spirits, expecting to find purpose in their lives. But first Wakan Tanka must find me worthy, or I won't be rewarded with a vision. My educated self realizes that sleep deprivation and emotionally charged situations can cause hallucinations—nothing mystical about that—but I won't dismiss the tales I grew up with that fed my imagination. It's a given that Mom spoke with an owl while pregnant with me, that Pahpie was visited by a cloud turned warrior in front of his eyes, and that Sunkwah's great-grandfather, my fourth great-grandfather Mahkohchay, ate trout and chatted with a giant black bear that walked out of the woods and sat beside him at his campfire. The bear told Mahkohchay never to return to Chohkahn, his home deep under the Black Hills; instead, he was to join the bands of Lakota, Northern Cheyenne, and Arapaho in their struggle against the U.S. military. He was 39 when he fought in the Battle of Little Big Horn. Pahpie, himself, at 32, was instructed by a later and different cloud-spirit to go to Wounded Knee in the 1970s to protest against a corrupt tribal president. The Indians had also sought to re-open treaty negotiations with the government. They were true warriors, men of conviction.

I'll leave before daybreak, in order to reach my destination before the end of the week when a powerful storm is set to slam the north central states. Grandmother shows her concern for me by repeatedly patting my cheek and holding my hands tightly together in hers. Her eyes convey the ongoing prayer for my safety. It is not her place, nor anyone's, to stop a person from going. She gave me Pahpie's full-length buffalo skin robe to wear. There's nothing warmer. I sharpen my knife. Jim's legs still need to be wrapped.

I'm dragging. I've nearly slid off Jim a few times. A branch slaps my head right when a big gust of wind forces my hood back. It feels like shards of glass striking my skin. My fingers search for an edge of the robe to grab. After some fumbling around, I find it and pull the furry hood completely over my face, leaving only the ground to focus on. We're close to a hill that can protect Jim and me this third night. Jim is getting ornery. Can't say I blame him. Although Sunkwah was the one who suggested I do this, he also warned against going in the middle of winter, especially since I was never properly groomed for the undertaking. *Am I a total idiot or what!* If I quit now and accept defeat, I'll feel like a big wuss. Wakan Tanka will never grant me a vision.

It doesn't take long to reach the shallow cave that's normally hidden by a waterfall in the later months, July being when Pahpie and I traveled here. I dismount and carefully lead Jim in. The rocks are slippery. There's a sharp turn that instantly cuts off the blast of cold air. Tucked away on a ledge behind a rock, I locate the oil lamp that Pahpie stashed here for future use. I packed a small container of clean kerosene and wicks. A flashlight or battery-operated lantern would make more sense to bring along, but there's satisfaction in doing things like the departed relatives had. How well I recall Pahpie adjusting the flame in the lamp. Next I make a peace offering to Jim with an apple. "Sorry you have no say in this." The shaggy robe gets spread out for another night of sleeping on the ground. It's thick and cushy, but not bulky enough to keep my ass from hurting after days of riding. And again I carry out the rituals which are part of this undertaking. Sage leaves are dutifully tossed in a circle around me to invoke the spirits. Next the cloth bag I brought is ceremoniously opened. It holds the cansasa mixture I made from the inner bark of the red-twig dogwood tree, a bit of tobacco, and a few other herbs I like. As I puff on the pipe to get it lit, the smell quickly fills the space. Jim has always liked the concoction and dangles his tongue out for a dab.

The two of us have covered a lot of ground. *What to do tonight?* The anticipation of my own hanbleceya energized me the first couple of days. Tedium has since taken its place. Did I actually replay the entire Fiesta Bowl game my first night, every detail from start to finish, and in real time? Afterward, taking advantage of the bright three-quarter moon, Jim and I had hit the road well before daybreak. He loves running at night, which thankfully gave me my second wind. It wasn't until that evening, after a full day of riding, that my lids wanted to close with the sinking of the sun behind the mountains. I curled up inside a large tree hollow to rest, but ended up falling asleep. In dreams, I relived that disastrous encounter with Tess at her place when she was in such pain. That was rough...don't want to go there again.

The wonderful aroma from the cansasa fills the cave. I'm tired, but can't allow myself to go to sleep like yesterday night. "Hey, Jim, nudge me once in a while, 'kay?"

His tail switches hard and fast and he flutters his lips together loudly.

"Un-hee! Did you just say what I think you did!"

I lay my pipe to the side and inch up the wall. God, my legs are stiff. After steadying myself, I automatically start dancing in place to the old Lakota standards sung at every powwow since I was little. I am more familiar with them than the couple of Rawakota ones I was taught. Turning up the flame in the oil lamp, I laugh at the spectacle. On the wall, a shadow-partner mimics my steps. My long braids look like squiggles around his head as I jump around with him. *We* do this a while before the absurdity of it sinks in.

My attention turns to Jim's feed bag and the trail mix of apples, carrots, sunflower seeds, and grains I've been filling it with. Until now, hunger hasn't been an issue for me. I poke my head outside to size up conditions. It's too early for the blizzard. The Big Dipper shines bright.

I wander back inside, lonely as can be. I'm missing Daniel. Missing Tess. Missing Pahpie. I open up to Jim. "I thought I would feel Pahpie's presence, like he's watching over me. It's sad I don't." I have flashbacks of my grandfather, of Benjamin One Horn. An impressive name for an impressive man, a serious man. I wish I could have had a glimpse of the lighthearted person he was when he met Grandmother. The deepest wrinkle connected his eyebrows, and from out of it rose a line that split three ways up the middle of his forehead, like a pitchfork. Grandmother said his dealings with Mom caused the grooves. I get excited again about the journey. It's breezy outside, but doable. I'm slow like a turtle. It takes everything I've got to pack. Off we go in the darkness at a safe trot. We're higher up and the trail is trickier. The crunch of the frozen twigs and leaves under hoof is amplified by the cold. The lemony moon has a soft edge that blends gradually into a surrounding halo of pale blue before going black. It's beautiful ... peaceful. My breath trails Jim's. I'm feeling very Indian. I like it...miss it.

Pfft! Whoosh! There's weird shit darting among the shadows in my side view. I chalk it up to a tired mind. One more wakeful night, with my sanity slipping away, I may start attacking them. The heady smell of pine conjures up nice memories from childhood, of collecting eagle feathers with Daniel from nests built high in the hills, and of fishing trips with Sunkwah and Pahpie. Dad joined us on a few. Jim suddenly rears.

"Jesus Christ! Inazin! Stop!"

A surge of adrenaline rushes through me, but my reflexes are shot. "Enough Jim!" I can't pull hard enough on the reins as he continues to buck. I sniff the air for a mountain lion or wolf. There aren't bears now. He calms down on his own. "Aye-yi-yi." My head's still spinning, but I'm definitely awake now.

The new day's light is reassuring. Jim proceeds slowly along a grueling slope. A few nimble-footed wooly mountain goats, seemingly dangling in mid-air, make sport of us by jumping with reckless abandon across the vertical stony outcroppings. After what seems an eternity, Jim and I settle in a clearing beneath a massive overhang that's just shy of the summit of three granite peaks named The Protectors. We've made it to Wyoming, the end of the line for us. I know from having been in this spot with Pahpie that there is an opening in the top. It had served as a chimney, venting the smoke from our fire that lent magic to his stories. I grab some tinder from my fire kit along with an armload of sticks collected along the way that I secured with ropes and hung off the saddle. After all this time, I'm amazed that our circle of rocks hasn't been disturbed by bears or wolves, nor the several logs rolled to a back wall. Next, I arrange the kindling in the shape of a tepee, then reach in my shirt pocket…*empty! "Where the hell did I pack the lighter!"* I'm not so old school I want to rub sticks together, and I don't have flint. "Think hard, think hard, man."

I'm so done; I can't remember.

Jim lays a wet one on me just as I'm ready to roll to the side. He's going to keep at it until he eats. I grab onto his mane to help me stand. After strapping on his feed bag, I get the saddlebag with my pipe. I hold it open and shake it upside down, hoping the lighter will magically fall out even though I'd been careful about keeping it on me. Something does drop to the ground. I pick up a book of matches with *Lazy Al's Trading Post* written in rope letters on the cover. "No way!" It looks really old. Bet they were Pahpie's. I took his saddlebag on my journey because it's bigger than mine.

Once the fire catches, just a little one for now, I take a stab at some easy mental math. "Let's try 432 divided by 18." Well, forget that! I only know how cozy warm Pahpie's robe is, after which there's nothing.

"Un-hee! Jim!" I rub my ear. "That was no nibble! Shit!" He peels back his upper lip and snorts.

I wasn't passed out very long; the fire looks the same. I guess I should be thanking Jim. He pounds the dirt floor, first with one hoof then the other. And then he begins to whinny like he does around Ola when they talk. And I swear, a horse not too far away responds to him.

It's starting—my vision. My heart thumps wildly in my ears. I never got the sage leaves spread or my pipe lit, and yet I sense an otherworldly presence. Jim grows quiet. I stupidly reach for my knife. It won't help against things that aren't truly real. *How will I know the difference!* God, I'm wired! There are noises at the end of the stone wall, beyond which is the narrow ledge that Jim and I came up on. I tiptoe toward it. The wind whistles through the cave. I'm standing close to the rim, facing the northern part of the sky. A long black horizontal band rises from the earth and cuts off the stars. The storm is finally rolling in. A cloud of steam drifts into the chilled air from behind the wall. It floats in front of the moon beside my own breaths, hypnotizing me. Whoever is standing there is around my height.

"Hinhán ska?"

"Wha...!"

"Talking White Owl?" There's a pause. "A man should not be disturbed during hanbleceya, but bad weather is coming. This is not the time to be alone in the hills."

His voice is deep, and his clipped English sounds like Sunkwah's and Winnie's thick Native accent.

"Are you Rawakota?"

"Yes, *Rrwhkhth*." He says it the true way, exhaled in a single syllable as though he was clearing his throat. "I am your cousin Suhdeer Ihá Wakinyan."

I fall back against the wall in disbelief. Jim shows no sign of there being an intruder. Do I roll with this? When this so-called cousin rounds the bend, will he be a bear or a dragon or some other nastyass demon?

In a flash, I get jumped. Instinct steers my knife-wielding hand toward a neck. There's contact, a deep-bellied grunt, and then my only weapon gets slapped away. Pinned now against the cave wall...I'm toast.

"vik*TOHR*," whispers this thing, his mouth an inch from my face, "I am no threat. We are family."

I tell myself to go with it, *just go with it*.

The outline of a horse emerges. He's tall and looks to be all black. The guy lets me go and walks him to Jim's corner. The scene is stupefying, mostly because Jim allows the stranger in his space. The man lays a blanket beside mine. Next he lowers a fur on top, and then recites something in the language of my great-grandparents. I limp over to his side. "You carry the hide of a sacred white buffalo? You're a Holy Man?"

He smiles. "No, Cousin, no Wicasa Wakan. The skin belongs to Sleeping Buffalo, the Holy Man in Chohkahn. Our Chief instructed me to take it from the Elder's home to make sure only benevolent wakans find you. Sleeping Buffalo has been in the Himalayas, hoping soon to meet with your mother when she gets time away from her duties at a military outpost."

"No, no, no! This is insane!" I crumple to the ground, face in hands. A dull pain has settled behind my eye sockets. Then—my nose picks up a scent that's wonderful and familiar. I'm ordered to sip slowly from the cup of hot soup held to my lips. I resist. One more night of fasting is required.

"Cousin, you are weak. Your body has been working hard to keep you warm."

He has me hold the cup while he sprinkles sage leaves on the ground. His hand taps mine, motioning me to drink. I savor the mouthful of potatoes and carrots before swallowing. It tastes too good for me to be making this up; but then, I really believed I was sailing through the universe with Tess our first time together.

This man is a kindly vision who gently strokes my head. He stands and finds a couple of flat stones to scoop up the manure piles. It gets flung over the ridge. Maybe he's a projection of my inner self...the Rawakota brave I secretly long to be. His braid is as long as mine. Up until now I've pretty much shrugged off that part of my ancient bloodline, having fully accepted a Lakota identity.

I jump at the sound of beating wings. A few birds shoot past the entrance, flying right over the stranger's head. He doesn't flinch. They're three red hawks, birds too big to fly in this space, and yet they can. They orbit above, screeching in that horrible high pitch, when at once one dives straight into the fire! *"Un-hee!"* It remains calmly perched on a burning branch, flames shooting around it! Overhead, the other two keep circling, undeterred by the spitting embers. The hawk in the fire holds my attention. Will it speak? I reach for it.

"vik*TOHR*! NO!"

My arm is forcefully snatched back, and I tip over. With that, the hawk's great wings unfold and away they all fly. *"Amazing,"* I whisper, finally letting my eyes close. I yawn big and give a little laugh. "You say my name the way I say un*KAHL* to Horse That Walks Backwards."

"You mean William Half Moon?"

"Half Moon? That's...right..."

"Sleep, dear Cousin," Suhdeer's low voice hums. "You were blessed tonight. Now rest."

Tess expects to see the usual darkened windows when she turns into Viktor's parking lot, her twice a week routine since the beginning of the winter semester. Her heart skips at the sight of light shining between the gaps in the blinds. Tears cloud her view as she pulls in beside his car which hasn't moved in a month. Did Viktor postpone the trip in the mountains because of the storm, and now he plans to surprise her? Already winded from emotion, she races up the stairs and knocks on the door. It opens, and immediately the disappointment registers on her face.

"Never have I had such a terrible effect on a woman." William's attempt to ease the hurt doesn't work. "Come in, Tess."

She offers a weak smile, wipes her wet cheeks, and steps inside.

"I was clearing out the refrigerator and checking for leaks after the last cold spell. Let me take your coat. I'll make us tea."

She looks around, half hoping William is in on the surprise. Viktor really is going to jump out from behind the couch or his room and swoop her up in his arms. But he doesn't. "The weather's terrible in the Black Hills. If Viktor hasn't eaten or slept for days, how will he survive the freezing cold? I saw the light and hoped he had the good sense to come back."

"Ah, Tess...it *was* unwise of him to travel into the mountains, which is why a scout was sent to find him. He is with Viktor as we speak."

"How do you know?"

"Because he called."

"Viktor called? He said he wouldn't have his phone."

"No, no—the scout did. He knows the area. It should ease your mind to hear the storm has suddenly veered south of their location."

Tess nods with relief. "Have you ever gone on a Vision Quest?"

"Hanbleceya," he says, emphasizing the use of the Native word for the spiritual tradition. The Rawakota started using the Lakota word when they began dealing with the tribe. How he hates the empty Anglicized term "vision quest." To think that even their Indian name hanbleceya gets misrepresented by white businesspeople who use it to advertise a company's culture. "Yes. Twice."

They sit across from each other. She inhales the sweet aroma of steeping cherry bark leaves that Viktor loves. Nothing pops into her head to talk about, but she's not trying very hard. At least the swell of emotion has subsided. William grazes her knees when he moves to take a seat beside her on the couch. He gives her shoulders a squeeze and brushes his lips against her temple.

"Be assured that Viktor will definitely let you know when he's coming back." He scoots a proper distance away. "Is there something you're curious about, Tess? Any questions about…oh, I don't know…the reservation, Viktor's family? Life in general?"

She smiles at his gentlemanly behavior, remembering what Viktor had said about him charming the ladies. "What can you tell me about Daniel?"

His eyes light up at the memory of two chubby-cheeked rollicking boys, always wrestling like bear cubs at play.

We've talked ourselves hoarse and it's time to part ways. I hate that an entire day was lost to sleep, time I could have used to find out more about Suhdeer and the many relatives I apparently have in Chohkahn, who he says know *everything* about me! It's unsettling that my male cousins and uncles are sad for my soul because I've been deprived of Otiwota. Suhdeer's father, Novak, would have honored his dead brother Lukas by presiding over the ceremony.

"This experience has been fuck…er, frickin unbelievable!"

"I agree!" says Suhdeer, as enthusiastically as me.

"Do you have cuss words?"

"Never one that disrespects the union resulting in new life. Grunts say it all."

"Don't I know!"

"Swearing in German is fun, though...quatsch, scheisse, arschloch. The ancestors learned it from the settlers back in the day."

"No kidding!" He cracks me up. The words are almost the same as Yiddish. I'm sure he'd understand *fercockt*. "So why don't women grunt?"

"They do," he laughs, "under their breath."

And so, as I head back to Grandmother's house, Suhdeer rides into the woods to his home in Chohkahn. Chohkahn, the city I thought was lost to history. According to my cousin, it's right underfoot! Miles underfoot, which I question, but a distance down, nevertheless.

"Yay-yoh!" exclaims Sunkwah. "Ha, ha, ha. Maybe you heard wrong, Viktor." Winnie and Grandmother laugh, too. Iris, who came for a visit, begs for the translation. Little did I know I was setting myself up for ridicule.

Winnie, wiping her eyes then blowing her nose, says she hasn't heard the word in ages, not that it's so funny, but because Suhdeer used it to describe me, an Indian.

"Would it be in a Rawakota dictionary?" Iris searches a bookshelf.

"No," says Sunkwah, "our people called Europeans and their foolish Christian religion *yay-yoh*. Always white people worry about sins."

Suhdeer compared me to wasichu! Fuck that! After the time spent getting to know each other, I trusted confessing something really personal to this newfound cousin. It wasn't easy for me, but because I believed our paths would never cross again, I opened up to him. Otiwota or not, he assured me we are as good as blood brothers, and it was therefore okay to share our concerns. I revealed that I found the act of a woman placing her lips on a man's ché demeaning to her. He thought I was kidding. Then he came back with that word, which he couldn't adequately explain.

Before I can stop her, Grandmother has Uncle William on the phone, counting on his impressive vocabulary to help us out.

"Uh-huh...uh-huh."

"Well?" asks Iris.

"Prude."

Their faces draw a blank. Iris has some notion of its meaning and looks at me with curiosity. My cheeks are scorched from embarrassment. I feel betrayed by Suhdeer. My discomfort is obvious, and the subject gets dropped. In the meantime I'm left wondering what's wrong with me. Iris thoughtfully picks up the conversation and relays the latest news regarding Hashke's family members. I'm lost in my own thoughts until I hear my name called. Great-grandfather is smiling at me.

"Have a smoke with your old Sunkwah."

I help him up from the kitchen chair and we move to the living room. Gone are the days we'd ride horseback to his tepee at the edge of the woods. I close the door behind me like he asks, cutting off the smells from the spices sitting out for the apple and sweet potato pies that are planned for the upcoming powwow, a small local one. The oven will be going all evening.

A box is taken out of a cabinet and opened. The earthy aroma of tobacco fills the air; Pahpie's favorite smoke. Sunkwah and I prefer blends without nicotine, but we're honoring my grandfather who would have been seventy-seven today. Sunkwah says Winnie sometimes joins him for a smoke, which women don't do with men, although wives smoke among themselves for certain ceremonies.

"Why not, huh?" he shrugs as he puffs to get Pahpie's pipe lit. He then hands it to me. "Benjamin walked on too soon. Many friends and relatives younger than Winnie and me have passed on to the afterlife."

There's no tinge of melancholy to his voice. He's simply stating fact.

"Your English has really improved," I tell him, impressed that he and Winnie now use contractions and different tenses. "What are you reading?"

"Mm. Not read as much. Victoria showed us how to listen to books." He draws a square with his fingers indicating a tablet. "But…" he smiles, "… we fall asleep and forget what happens. Too many stories about crazy white people. Last good one, *Kon-Tiki*." I hand back the pipe.

His sunken eyes stay fixed on me as he lightly sucks the end. Little smoke puffs trail from his lips. The white wisps of hair that he still wears in braids, skinny as a mouse tail, barely reach his collarbone. He's looking his age, and acting it, too, sitting bundled in his blanket beside the fire. Always there's a draft. I join in a chant that rides the smoke curling out a cracked window and up to an open sky, in order to reach my admired and respected Pahpie—who now dances among the stars. Our love for the man will find him. There's a profound sense of peace. Past, present, future, all time is immaterial.

"We make our own Otiwota, Hinhán ska."

I like hearing him say my name. "Doesn't that go against tradition?" A deep noise rumbles in his chest, as if that's where his thinking takes place.

"You shared theeich ihilah. We celebrate you have wife."

Oh, no! When I told him I was in a serious relationship before taking off into the hills, I didn't guess it would be interpreted like this. Sunkwah and Winnie know better. They read and watch TV. It's a modern world, one where Rawakota rules don't apply like they once did. I have a feeling it would crush him if I said Tess and I don't view ourselves as married. And when it comes to theeich ihilah, I really don't know what to tell him.

"Hua." Yes, I nod, to make him happy.

"You go away with your Tess from full moon to next full moon?"

"That's hard to do with our schedules, Sunkwah."

"Schedules! Wasichu bullshit!" He shakes his head. "Always husband and wife have month alone together."

What to say? I hate that the pleasant mood is ruined, that he's gruff. I wouldn't call him angry. That makes twice today I've felt insulted for being part of Wasichu's world.

"Hinhán ska," he says sternly, wagging his finger, "theeich ihilah is most important part of life." He shrugs the blanket off his shoulders and leans forward. "And you go on hanbleceya, and never have Otiwota *first*! Paéchiya! It is backwards!" He looks up in the air and speaks to Pahpie, telling him he needed to live longer so I could have Otiwota with his brothers and their sons.

"But Sunkwah, how is that in keeping with the tradition? They wouldn't have been part of Lukas's family. Aren't the men supposed to be from the boy's father's family?"

He jumps up, the quickness of which both startles and amazes me. It wasn't my intent to sound sarcastic or to criticize him. "Why your cousin call great-grandson yay-yoh!"

My heart starts pounding. There's no laughing this time at the mention of the word. He stands over me waiting for an answer, but I refuse to say another thing on the subject.

Then, switching to Lakota, he tells me young and old share life lessons during Otiwota. In my case, with it being the coming-of-age ceremony,

I would have heard the story of Okajah, a fertility spirit who rides the wind. He explains that long ago, during the great journey across the continent, girls and mothers were the seed savers. Besides being in charge of growing crops, the women also created beautiful designs with the colorful seeds. Other tribes envied their decorative garments and headdresses and wanted such beaded treasures for themselves. They attacked and looted the ancient Rawakota villages. Plants were ripped out of the ground and stolen along with the many stored seeds. The women sought guidance from the kindly spirit Okajah, who told them to always keep one seed hidden. In doing so, their people would never starve, and they could continue to create beauty, which greatly pleased Wakan Tanka. Only a husband knew the secret place. "Hinhán ska, do know how to find seed?" I don't have a clue where this is going, but, like it or not, his mind is set on enlightening me.

"I don't understand, Grandmother; why can't I go to the powwow again tomorrow? It meant everything to be included in the men's dances for the first time. And the food...I could've eaten two of your pies all by myself. One more day here won't make any difference."

She just came in the bedroom with a clean load of clothes for me to pack in my suitcase which is spread open on the bed. Iris followed her in, going on about her flight getting delayed a few hours.

Grandmother cocks her head and teasingly asks, "You aren't anxious to see Tess?"

"Of course...but she's busy catching up with her best friend from high school who is home for break. She goes to art school in Italy."

The explanation satisfied her. While Iris continues her rant in the background, Grandmother takes my hand and pulls me toward the bed to sit. Next she turns to Iris and cuts her off. "Sit, Iris."

"Are we in trouble?" Iris winks at me, taking note of her serious tone. Grandmother walks to the window and just stares out of it. She tightens the belt of her long robe. Her hair hangs loose and smooth to the middle of her back. She's ready for bed and had brushed it out for the night. Her jewelry is removed. I can picture the silver and gemstone bracelets and necklaces neatly arranged in her buckskin lined drawer. Sister and I used to peek inside it as kids.

"Mémé...has something bad happened?" Iris is seemingly concerned now and links arms with me. We dutifully wait for a reply.

Grandmother turns and rests against the sill. "The time has come to put an end to the criminals running things on the reservation. It could happen tomorrow, or in a week, but it is going to take place soon. We know that the gangs like to recruit older students in the spring. The majority of teens have received poor grades throughout childhood and the idea of completing high school overwhelms them. The kids feel defeated toward the end of the school year and are at their most vulnerable. Also, the Mérrauders who went to jail for destroying Lazy Al's have been getting released; not the one who killed Sam, though. I'm sorry I can't give away any more information, other than the plan has been a long time in the making. Only a few trusted Lakota tribal members have been invited to work alongside the Rawakota. Viktor, you must return to college so you won't be connected with the violence in any way. Reporters are starting to snoop around our communities and, according to Solomon, your home in Texas, too. The job of cleaning up problems on the reservation has fallen on our shoulders even though outsiders caused them. Thanks to donations, Buckthorn's police force has grown from nine to twenty. I know the new hires. They're honest. After this ugly ordeal is over, we can finally begin the process in earnest of figuring out how to run things for ourselves. That has always been what drives us, but it can't be done before people feel safe."

"If only Pahpie could have lived to see this," says Iris, who is caught up in Grandmother's optimism. I wish I could be more positive. *Warring with gangs!* I will gladly hightail it out of here, but only after Grandmother assures us she'll be safe.

It's dusk. For once it's colder in Ohio than in South Dakota. I made it to Columbus in only three days, twenty hours to be exact, all while hauling Jim behind in a trailer. I borrowed an old truck, which means I eventually have to drive it back. I pull into Dr. Nate's driveway right as he's heading out in his truck. He lowers the window to say hi, and to say that the stall is ready with a cot for me to bunk overnight.

Inside the barn, a couple of curious horses rub noses with Jim as we pass. After standing cooped up in the small trailer for so long, he exhibits his usual testiness, which is always short-lived. His top lip curls up. He's ready to bite. I shout in time to scare his new neighbors away. It's good I'm staying with him, although I had my heart set on seeing Tess, no matter how late it ended up being. She's so close. I quickly get Jim squared away, and then call her.

"How's Jim?" she asks. "I'm looking forward to meeting him."

"Mm. He did his usual showing off. I'm brushing him now, which mellows him out. Dr. Nate left a bucket of treats...apples, carrots, watermelon. It's like finding a hundred mints on a hotel pillow, or *you* in my bed."

"*Or?* Are you saying mints might possibly take precedence over me?"

"Tess, I won't ever leave like that again with a rift between us—I promise. It's killing me we're only twenty minutes from each other."

"I'm relieved you're home safe."

"I even showered at a truck stop outside Indianapolis for you."

She giggles. "You mean you were getting too rank for even yourself? Or did Jim turn his nose away from you?"

"Are you on the couch or the bed?"

No answer.

"Tess?" I check the phone signal. "You there?"

A sudden touch, and I let go the brush. Warm fingers rest on mine. Tess hugs me so tight I can barely turn around. Hearing *I love you* in person addles my brain. I could devour her. What happens next is a blur. We're kissing...and then making love in our clothes on the crude cot that's bound to break. It's nothing more than some wooden slats nailed to a frame.

After unleashing a storm of pent-up emotions, we look at each other and laugh softly. I'm still in a daze, but I realize I can't hold this position any longer. I'm propped up on my elbows above Tess, in order to keep from rolling to the ground. Although the floor is covered in fresh straw, there's sand underneath it; and it definitely won't be staying clean for long. Jim is quiet, as are the other horses. The frogs, however, are incredibly loud. There's a big pond just outside the barn. I carefully slide off Tess to turn down the lights; the switch is by the entrance. When I return, we try laying sideways nose to nose. It's definitely not comfortable, and we're feeling the cold.

"If you don't mind driving us back in your car, would you want to stay at my place? I planned on leaving the truck here."

"Are you sure Jim will be okay?"

"Oh, yeah. He's got his party bucket of goodies to keep him occupied."

Buckthorn's spring powwow celebrating life's renewal has run its course. It's late evening on the reservation, three days following Viktor's departure. In a single week, the temperatures in the Dakotas went from being far below the average for late March to well above it today, hitting the low 60s, giving rise to the number of youths wandering around the rez in search of excitement.

Jinks De Vries, a known gang ringleader, sits on his knees on the floor, holding a drugged girl's uncooperative legs over his shoulders as he feverishly pumps away inside her, spurred on by his five partners in crime, openly masturbating as they wait their turn with the unconscious victim. When the cravings return, Jinks and the boys will have another go at her.

Suddenly Jinks looks up, his wild eyes turning confused. It's grown quiet—not a peep from his homeboys. They all look stunned, bewildered, but are too drunk at the moment to realize they're dying. By all accounts they should suffer. Each of them stares at the arrow poking through his chest, piercing the heart. Flashlights stay fixed on the targets. It's a long minute before the pitiless brutes topple over.

"Khéya!" Bullseye! The braves peer inside the deserted mobile home's broken-out window, satisfied but not gloating…there's no rejoicing in having to kill a Native brother or sister, even if it is justified. An anonymous call is made to the cops so they can retrieve the girl, who can't be more than twelve. The warriors calmly turn their horses around and move on to the next location where trouble is expected. Their resolve to rid the reservation of its terrorists just got a boost following their first success.

Howling Wind arrived early and sits waiting for Sleeping Buffalo on the outdoor veranda of a coffee shop. The shops have become the rage since she was last in Srinagar. This quaint and elegant one lies on the outskirts of town where travel has been deemed safer for the droves of tourists arriving to witness the season's tulip extravaganza. Reports of mobs in the city attacking hotels and tourist buses with stones are circulating in the media. The culprits are various Kashmiri separatists that insist the Government of India stay out of their affairs. Some want to be part of Pakistan; others demand that the Himalayan region of Jammu and Kashmir be completely independent.

Word is out that the coffees tend to be weak, teas being more popular with the locals. Howling Wind orders a chai concoction of spices and herbs that the zealous young server guarantees she'll enjoy. Within minutes, a tall glass is placed in front of her filled with leaves and citrus rinds artfully arranged in a pistachio green colored tea. A dollop of orangish foam smelling of apricots tops it off. Equally wonderful is the lakeside view with its backdrop of mountains and clear blue sky. Yesterday, Colonel Howling Wind was flying a sortie above Pakistan, intervening on behalf of someone's broken alliance. She can't keep track. Viktor had called her at the end of her day, which was a pleasant surprise. When he told her he was on his way back to Columbus with Jim, she responded by saying how absolutely boring the drive must be if he thought to call his mother for once. In her heart, she recognized he had really wanted to check in on her. The conflict in Pakistan had made the evening news in the States. She loved hearing the joy in his voice when he talked about seeing Tess soon. She looks forward to describing this place in their next conversation.

From the rows of flowers to the ladies floating through the gardens in their satin chiffon sarees, the place hums with eye-popping colors. Small houseboats with solid red, blue, and yellow rectangular canopies shading their decks stand out in an otherwise unremarkable marina. It's a peaceful scene, civilized. Howling Wind's thoughts turn to the reservation where it is eleven hours earlier, still morning. She figures the bodies of those killed are only beginning to be discovered. It will be days, no weeks, before a final tally.

"Good day, Miss."

She is roused from her trance, only to do a double take of the gentleman making himself comfortable in the sumptuous barrel-back chair opposite her.

"*Seriously?*" she declares, having expected to see the man she has known professionally for fifteen years.

Trailing close behind him are four members of the Oyahmayan team. In unison, they raise their sunglasses to meet Howling Wind's eyes and say hello before taking their seats at the next table. They accompanied Sleeping Buffalo to this part of the world to meet their distant relatives and decode their exceptional language.

"Them, too?" Howling Wind shakes her head at the American Indians passing themselves off as Asian Indians, in particular Sikhs, going so far as to attach fake moustaches and long full beards to complete the charade. What with the matching tan and white striped Kurta pajamas and navy turbans, Constance says, "They look ready to break out in song…the Punjab's answer to ZZ Top with some Motown thrown in. You don't find it offensive, somehow sacrilegious?"

"Our aim was to look dapper."

Did Sleeping Buffalo really just wink? "I admit you appear respectable in your suit." She won't go so far as to say handsome. The cream linen jacket sets off his dark features. His shoulder length hair, always pulled together with a band at the nape of his neck, has been chopped to the ears. It is still long on top and thick. In his mid-forties, there's barely a trace of gray. He caught the eye of the ladies in the coffee shop when he walked in and continues to fascinate them.

"You must resemble a Bollywood star." She turns toward his entourage at the next table, still in disbelief.

"Oyahmayan think the world of Sikhs," says Sleeping Buffalo. "They honor them by walking in their shoes, so to speak. They simply have a love for the theatrical. You should see their Mujahzee costumes. It's believed that in the late 1400s, the wise and fair-minded Mujahzee crossed paths with the first Sikh Guru, Nanak, who was open to their influence…even though an encounter with God is credited for having shaped Nanak's teachings."

Sleeping Buffalo interprets her smirk to mean she is never to be regarded as gullible.

"Could we skip the formality and use our first names, Constance? Please call me Jon, short for Jahnbatahr."

That's fine with her. Constance studies the Holy Man's expression. His title is a poor translation for what his kind represents to Chohkahn society. He is greatly respected but not revered. Jahnbatahr comes from a family line endowed with unique insights into human nature. They sense the many worlds the rest of us don't see. Though highly intuitive, they are not mind-readers or fortunetellers, nor do they possess the inside track to the mystery named Wakan Tanka. People go to him to ask for help interpreting visions.

"Here we are," says Constance, "in this peaceful setting, while back home…"

"I know, I know. It's heartbreaking."

They sit in thought and listen to the exchange among the Oyahmayan at the neighboring table. They are super-fast talkers, too fast for Constance to understand. "What language is that?"

"It's Rawakota," says Jon with a distinctive left-leaning grin. "Make no mistake, they confuse us regular Rawakota folks, too. If it were anyone else, I'd call them snobs, elitists. This aptitude comes naturally to them."

"Are they actually able to speak with the Mujahzee?"

"Mujahzee vocal cords didn't evolve in such a way as to produce human speech as we know it. Our voice box sits much lower in the throat. They communicate with complex sounds that have an incredible range. It's more like chirping. But they can write, as you know. The scroll you and the British pilot Smith were given holds unbelievable history."

Sipping her tea, Constance refers back to the long overdue events playing out in South Dakota as well as parts of Canada and several other states. She wonders how Americans will interpret what's happening.

Jon shrugs. "What matters most is that the remaining gang members take notice and either change their ways or stay off the rez for good, unless they have a death wish."

"It's a shame what people must resort to, in order to save their cultures. Day in, day out, all around the globe and at the lowest level, the pecking order persists." Constance shoots Jon a hardened look. "How have the Rawakota managed to rise above the pettiness? It stands to reason that at least one of you is greedy or power hungry."

"When you say, one of you, you obviously don't include yourself, even though you are full-blooded Rawakota. And that's after all the years you have been dealing with us in Chohkahn." He is reminded of the handful of Rawakota scientists who, to this day, question whether the aviator should be trusted. Jon rightly assumes she bears no ill will toward the people of Chohkahn simply because of the sordid actions of one of their misguided men, namely Lukas Sun In Eyes. He is earnest though when he asks how she thinks her children will react to the methods used to address crime on their reservation.

Iris is 24, and Viktor almost 19, hardly "children." She knows Jon perceives them as adults, but for some reason she balked at the word. "Iris and my mother have overseen the building of dormitory-type housing for those youngsters whose families will be affected by the attacks. They'll receive medical help and counseling, not to mention schooling. In Viktor's case…I don't know. He's at a crossroads in his life."

"Talking White Owl is gaining attention on a world-wide scale. He could be as famous as Ali or Elvis…or the actor Red Moon, who is becoming increasingly embroiled in activist campaigns."

"True, Viktor strikes a romantic figure in the minds of the public, including Natives. I used to think it would be a stroke of luck if he one day joined forces with Jason Red Moon. There's a man on a mission. Unfortunately, his tactics are proving counterproductive."

Jon, like all Rawakota, is kept in the loop by Howling Wind's reports about the business of the Council of First Nations. They have been apprised of the organization's focus on finding young leaders who can motivate their peers into acting on relevant issues.

"You could play a bigger role. You used to. The people of our Nation stand in awe of you, Constance, and you're an inspiration to outsiders."

"I don't have it in me anymore." Constance appreciates the compliment but is content with the niche she occupies. In her profession, she routinely encounters intelligent and driven individuals generally deemed to possess the "it" factor. She therefore has a wide base to draw from when it comes to sizing up her son's traits. Rallying a team to win a football game is one thing; but what about firing up hundreds of thousands to get behind a common cause, one that stirs heated controversy?

Jon senses her doubt. "There's no reason not to think that Viktor would be up to the task. Now just isn't the time. Like you said, at this juncture he's figuring things out."

Central to any discussion about Viktor at the moment is the key player figuring into his decisions, his love interest, Tess. Neither Constance nor anyone else holds sway in matters of the heart.

"I better not be dreaming this." Tess snuggles closer to show me it isn't the case.

"Being in your bed with you is nice, but there's something to be said for the horse stall. I did get to meet Jim."

"Barely."

The morning light filters in from the sides of the blinds. It's probably around seven. I stretch and kick aside the sex-soaked sheets and pull the blanket back over us. Lying wide awake, there's no rethinking what I want to do. I roll on top of Tess, careful not to squish her. I kiss her eyelids. She smiles. Her cloud of hair is so soft, like everything about her. I rub my chest against her breasts. "Will you marry me?"

Her eyes open slowly. I tease her nipple and feel a rush as I grow hard between her warm thighs. She strokes my hair.

"Shouldn't we go out a while long…"

I cut her off with a kiss. We look at each other. She starts up with another excuse so I kiss her again. She motions for me to get my weight off her. I straighten my arms and remain hovering above her breasts, waiting at her opening. She is clearly thinking about the idea.

"All right, yes."

I slide in easily. Mmm. Feels like I'm melting inside her. "Next week," I whisper, remaining still, not believing my good fortune. My love for her runs so deep it could undo me. I wish it were this week, but I don't know what's involved in getting a license. Also, on a less romantic note, I need to practice for the spring game and connect with Sharma's research team.

"Okay," she agrees, "next week."

The emptiness I suffered when WAKAN and the Fiesta Bowl were over, when I felt alone, is history. I'm completely at peace.

"It has been a morning of grisly discoveries. The Native communities on several reservations feel scared and threatened. Many are afraid to leave their homes." Uncle and I watch the evening news. After Tess left, I went back to the barn to check on Jim. When I returned just now, Uncle heard me at my door and damn near dragged me over to his place to hear this. It was like he'd been lying in wait. He turns up the volume.

"It isn't clear if regular citizens are responsible for the killings, or if these are instances of gangs seeking retribution against rival gang members. A resident from Kyle, South Dakota, who was interviewed for a tribal newspaper, referred to the night of mass murders as *thigluska,* a term that refers to putting one's own house in order. Could this in fact be a case of vigilante justice? Although the motive is yet unclear, the facts are that by noon, 227 bodies had been found, and by 5:00 o'clock this evening the number of deaths had risen to 614, with more likely. All victims were shot through the heart by an arrow, and all had been engaging in one form or another of unlawful activity when they were ambushed."

"Thank god I made it back before all this."

"Shh!"

Jeez...I said it under my breath. It hits me that these mass-murders were occurring while Tess and I had been making love. Next, a Canadian reporter up in Manitoba tells of similar type killings last night. To her credit, she offers a backstory familiar to those who live on reservations, but one that outsiders have turned a blind eye to for decades, namely that the so called victims were known thugs who perpetrated horrendous crimes against their own people, First Nations people who desire nothing more than to lead simple, honest lives.

The coverage continues with video showing the slum-like conditions that exist on many tribal lands. The reporter narrates: "These drug runners, often repeat offenders, are responsible for tearing apart the fabric of Native life because of what they offer poor communities whose overall needs continually go unmet by federal agencies that are supposed to help them."

As she reels off specific places where bodies were recovered, I watch Uncle. He's glued to the TV wearing a triumphant look.

"It's the start of a new era, Viktor!" he declares, slapping my knee.

"I suppose." It seems a bit early to make such a sweeping statement.

He nods his head in affirmation and stands. "Can I fix you dinner?"

"Ah, no...no thanks. I ate a late lunch. Tomorrow I need to wake up early to go to practice."

No more is said about the news, or football for that matter. He's busy clanging around the kitchen. Guess I'm to let myself out the door. This is the longest we've gone without seeing each other since I started school. He seems lost in his own world.

"Okay, later Uncle." But then as I'm leaving something pops into my head.

"Leksi...the cousin from Lukas's side who I met in the mountains said if I ever wanted to call him, to ask you about using your phone."

"You wish to call him now?"

He glances at me while chopping the garlic.

"No, just verifying if it's true."

"It's true."

"When you visit your daughters, is it Chohkahn you travel to? Are all three of my cousins married to Rawakota men?" He scrapes the cutting board over a pan then faces me.

"Yes."

"Why didn't you come right out and say where you were going when you visit them? Why the mystery?"

Uncle wipes his hands on a towel and steps over to me. He looks thoughtfully into my eyes. "I told you I go to the Black Hills, and I do. No mystery. You have no concept of Chohkahn. Sunkwah and Winnie and your grandparents have never gone back to visit. Some people don't. Instead, their relatives come up and meet them at cabins so the families can have fun together. Surely you remember your days at the lake and all the kids you used to play with."

"Why did it stop? Because Pahpie got sick?"

"No, Viktor. Iris started going to a camp sponsored by the Council of First Nations. She liked meeting young people from different tribes. And you preferred hanging out with your friends on the rez…riding your horses…playing football. The interest wasn't there anymore."

The memories are vivid once they're retrieved from where they'd gotten stashed in my brain. There I am, splashing in a lake with lots of other bodies, laughing, swinging on rope vines. I see me at night, dancing around campfires to the beat of drums, but then that's also what Daniel and Ron and Billie and the rest of our group did. No faces stick out. It makes me sad. "You're saying those were all my cousins."

"Hua…and aunts and uncles, and great aunts and great uncles. Can you remember your grandmother's younger brother, High Jumping Horse, and her sister, Irene Yellow Feather? Both had at least four or five grown children who brought their young ones. The One Horn family was big, too. I believe your Pahpie was the fourth child out of six. I suppose you missed out on many of the get-togethers because you were in Texas."

The hot oil starts spattering in the pan and distracts him. Before he attends to it, Uncle places a hand on my shoulder. "You surprised your family with the hanbleceya. Are you thinking of returning to your roots?"

Is he being facetious? I shrug off the comment and go across the hall to collapse. What a long day. When I call Tess to say good night, she's concerned after watching the news and asks how I'm doing considering everything going down on the reservations. She wonders if my relatives were affected. "No," I say, based on Grandmother's words before I left, "not to my knowledge. They live a safe distance from the places they're talking about."

I want to hurry and sleep. Mentally, I'm ready to get back into a routine. Physically, though, if I fall apart on the field during practice tomorrow, there will be hell to pay.

CHAPTER 40

Mazursky, our deranged assistant coach, snuck up from behind and walloped the locker next to my head so hard it damn near scared the bejeebers out of me. There isn't even a second to recover when he lays into me.

"You think you're some piss-ass prima donna..." the spit flies on the '*p*'s "... who doesn't need to follow the same rules as the guys who helped put your name on the fucking map!" He is absolutely crazed. His lips are pressed so hard together his head might explode. "You self-centered son-of-a-bitch!"

I'm frozen on the spot.

"So what if you won a big game...you oughta be thrown off the team. TEAM! Get it!" Again he whacks the locker. I flinched although I saw that one coming. "Think you can just split during the celebrations and show up when it's convenient! Huh!" He punches a fist into the palm of his other hand, showing what he'd like to do to me. *Un-hee!* I'm acutely aware of being alone in here with this nut-job.

"Zursky!"

From the hallway comes a saving voice. It's the head coach. He's with a couple of suits who continue down the hall while he excuses himself and heads over to us. Mazursky still hasn't taken his eyes off me. He's a piece of work. To think that I'm stuck having to deal with him this year with no Krull around for support. Coach looks at him and simply points toward the door. Mazursky backs off and follows the order. His body language screams, *this ain't over!*

"Thanks for not decking him," says Coach. "He was out of line, but I'm partly to blame."

"You?"

"Sit, Viktor."

He sits beside me on the bench, oblivious to the players starting to stream in for practice. They're laughing and punching each other in good fun until they catch sight of him and become more serious. Coach's voice is calm, and it puts me at ease.

"I didn't figure the conversation you and I had following the Fiesta Bowl was anyone's business. I understood how important it was for you to leave to see your sick friend."

It was so long ago, I have to think back. I recall feeling overwhelmed by all the excitement after the win. There were the post-game interviews, the parties. I longed to see Tess, which I kept to myself. The bad news I received about Daniel's condition gave me the opening I needed to escape the situation. Coach was cool with it.

"Mazursky should have been let in on why you left abruptly. Even though he has been serving as a temporary replacement to help you and Krull after we lost our top quarterbacks and their Coordinators, in my mind, he is still the trainer for the tight ends. Mazursky has given the job a hundred percent ... more, actually. I see it now."

"How does that justify his rant?"

Coach looks me square in the eyes. "What is his role with his players?"

"Is this a trick question?" Coach waits. Okay, I'll bite. "To advise them how to be better blockers and receivers."

"One would think," he says, scanning the locker room and waving to a few guys to acknowledge them. With a serious face, he adds, "The reality is that off-the-field misconduct is his biggest concern, so he resorts to using a hardline approach when it comes to deterring poor behavior. It's a growing problem that we're all facing, from Oregon to Texas, as well as here. Suspensions aren't having much of an impact. Mazursky didn't know what to expect with you. After the past year's setbacks, maintaining discipline has been paramount. It's work keeping some players out of trouble. Krull thankfully followed orders; you, on the other hand ..."

"I'm disciplined! I showed up for every practice. Just because I didn't want to dance around hacky sacks tossed at my feet..."

Coach laughs. "The team, the program...it can't handle any more bad press. Mazursky had no idea of who you were, what you were like. You appeared from out of nowhere, and this once-in-a-lifetime opportunity fell in your lap. He simply doesn't want you to blow it. None of us wants to see that happen. We're getting too many kids these days with criminal histories. I for one agree it's necessary for colleges to finally address the issue."

"God, Coach—I'm set to get a Master's. I'm committed to winning this season. What more do you want?"

"Viktor...people have lost more."

True; what can I say to that? He surprises me when he mentions that he had a few conversations with Uncle William about the type of person I am. I guess there was no other way for him to have learned anything about me. DeShaun suddenly shows up and sheepishly points to his name on the locker. Coach has to stand for him to get to it. They shake hands and Coach praises DeShaun's efforts during a practice that took place an entire week ago, singling out a difficult catch he had made. DeShaun lights up. If only the Buckeyes can find a new quarterback coach half as decent and perceptive as this man. He stops and chats with a couple of players on his way out.

"Good going, DeShaun!" It's great to hug him.

"Hey, White Owl, where you been!"

Before I can answer, Coach calls me over to the door. Now what?

"See you on the field," says DeShaun.

Out of earshot of the players, Coach asks, "Who has helped you the most in achieving the level of playing you're demonstrating?"

"That's hard to answer. I mean...there's my dad; and my coach in Texas..."

"Okay, okay...who is *mostly* responsible for your technique? You launch a ball like nobody's business."

"Thanks." He's generous with compliments today. "That would have to be Hayden Adler."

"Would he be willing to join our program to keep working with you?"

I must look like I was tasered. "You mean professionally?"

Constance holds up her uniform to ensure the hotel did a good job of dry cleaning it. "How can it be Thursday already, Jon! I appreciate you joining me for dinner on my final evening. I regret not being able to meet with the Mujahzee on this trip. Tell me some things you've learned about them?"

Jon watches as she hastily folds the last few items for the suitcase. "What I find most extraordinary," he admits, "is the bond that's been established rather quickly between such a curious people as the Mujahzee and the quirky Oyahmayan. I remain a spectator, an observer who is not privy to their conversations."

"There, there…feeling left out?"

"Certainly not!" he laughs. "They yak around the clock. Our chatty brothers and sisters are quick studies. They have deciphered most of the assorted trills and chirping patterns, to the point of communicating without the associated time-lag for translation. Besides, even if they couldn't talk to each other, the Mujahzee are perfectly capable of writing down their thoughts in English as well as various Mongolian dialects."

"Yes, you mentioned that at the coffee house, which got me thinking. Bridging the language barrier through speech evidently wasn't a useful trait to the Mujahzee."

"I would agree, at least to most of them. Vocal communication was a pivotal event in human evolution, causing the early animals to split from a common ancestor. In doing so, those who left, the original Rawakota, developed into Homo sapiens. The remaining Mujahzee became a different species over time. During this period of hybridization, both groups initially looked similar to each other, but the two populations lost the ability to reproduce. Perhaps that sparked the migration of our people with others who were gaining the capacity to speak. The Mujahzee stayed here in the Himalayas and bred with clans whose DNA more closely resembled theirs. No one can say for sure. That was around a hundred thousand years ago, right?"

"I was never good at keeping the geological periods straight."

Jon grins, "I once could, for exams."

Constance quickly runs a comb through her hair. She likes wearing it loose. Tomorrow, it's back to wearing a bun. "You speak of Oyahmayan as being Rawakota, yet historically they have kept to themselves, going so far as to live in their own area under the Black Hills. Aside from having the same eye color, why aren't they big-boned and muscular like the rest of Chohkahn's citizens?"

"You're not familiar with the role that the crystals played in our past?" Jon holds the door for her.

She gives him the once-over on her way out. The Holy Man is as "dapper" as he appeared in the coffee shop, only this evening his stylish suit is taupe-colored, or maybe lavender. The material takes on a different hue when he moves. And how could any woman not be distracted by that fetchingly friendly smile of his. He has perfect lips for a man, not too full or thin.

During the meal, Constance remains attentive while Jon informs her about an aspect of Rawakota culture she knows nothing about, mainly how the scholarly Word Gatherers, the Oyahmayan, unwittingly prevented the demise of their people following the discovery of the crystals.

"Have you never wanted to see the cavern for yourself, Constance?"

"And go even farther down than Chohkahn! No thanks!"

"Curious," says Jon with a probing look, "miles *above* ground is okay... alone in a piece of metal." Impatient for him to continue, she circles her hand in the air for him to get on with it. He obliges, after first enjoying a bite of food.

"You can stop tapping the table," he says, wiping his mouth. "In the beginning, when our ancestors finally reached Black Elk Peak in what is now South Dakota, everyone lived in the forests. They survived off the land and were true hunter-gatherers, until their spiritual leaders eventually discovered the first of the seven entrances that matched the one from the old world. Their knowledge of the constellations as they once appeared over the ancient Mujahzee site had been passed down in stories. Still, without technology, it couldn't have been easy lining up star positions to ground locations. When the tribe ventured inside the tunnels, they discovered natural airshafts, tiny vertical passages that ran throughout all the strata. The temperature remained constant. Water ran in rivulets down the walls and was easily collected. Then one day during their explorations, they stepped into an astonishingly massive opening, which they took as being the center of Mother Earth, a gift from the Creator, and they named it Chohkahn. The heart of the mountain would be home."

"For the most part, I know this, Jon. Rolling Thunder offered some history when he approached me about helping Rawakota scientists with their Defense strategies."

"Of course...a bit of a review doesn't hurt. That journey, by its very nature, lasted thousands of years. Small teams of daring explorers accomplished it, none of whom were Oyahmayan. As you've no doubt noticed, Oyahmayan are insanely social creatures. The painstakingly slow process of inching through hard rock was too lonely an endeavor. They chose to stay close to the surface to study how plants and animals communicated. They were particularly drawn to the language of the buffalo since multitudes of them roamed the landscape. All sounds and gestures interested them, not just human speech."

Constance hates to interrupt, especially since Jon is about to disclose new information, but her legs are experiencing a bit of numbness from having sat too long. It's only a problem when she makes the long brutal flight over the ocean and multiple continents. The unbelievably tight cockpits leave little room for stretching. She and the other pilots never got to enjoy a proper rest before they were ordered to take part in yesterday's attack over Pakistan. Jon is impressed by her stamina. He signals the waiter. After paying, they mosey down a path leading to the hotel's courtyard. They find the perfect bench surrounded by fragrant roses. A stone sculpture of a big-breasted female deity with three heads looks down on them. It warrants the unsuppressed giggle, and then they dive back into the conversation where they left off.

Constance pictures the subterranean maze leading to Chohkahn and beyond, and wonders how often those doing the digging might have wanted to give up. "Earlier cultures envisioned the underworld a scary place. It's odd that our distant relatives didn't presume an inferno awaited them, or that devil spirits would steal their souls."

"True. But then things at Black Elk Peak matched details from their long-lost home in the snow-covered mountains of Asia. As I said, Oyahmayan, along with the holy men of the time, my ancient relatives, kept the stories alive in the oral tradition and with pictorial narratives drawn on animal skins. The scene was therefore familiar and not frightening to them."

Constance thinks about the elevator she takes from behind the waterfall down to Chohkahn. "Does it keep going? Is that how the lower regions are accessed?"

"No, not there. A larger corridor was found at the north end that could accommodate a dual elevator system where one moving platform served as a counterweight to the other." Jon can tell she's going over the physics in her mind. He quickly adds, "Our forebears were ingenious. Like all mountains, there were veins of silver and copper ore which somebody figured out how to heat and then polish to create mirrors. These were placed at specific angles throughout the passageways. Light traveled down from the outside sky."

The science is met with skepticism. "At most it might work a few hundred feet." It isn't her aim to put him on the defensive. "Okay, so finally, miraculously, some people actually succeeded in covering the distance..." she cocks her head, overlooking the thermal constraints at that depth, among the myriad of other points glossed over, "... when they hit the motherlode."

"Basically," says Jon, annoyed she isn't displaying more of an open mind. "Can you imagine...it was as bright as day in the cave." By now he realizes how ridiculous this must sound to her. "No one could know back then it was due to fluorescing microbes. It was as if the rocks had been painted. And scattered among them were giant glowing *zaptah*."

"Rawakota kryptonite, I'm guessing."

His eyes light up. "*Yes!* Too bad countless generations were negatively affected by its properties before they deduced it." Constance listens thoughtfully as he continues. "The cave with its crystals was regarded as *the* most sacred place, a healing place. Families made pilgrimages to it, usually staying for long periods. They took pieces of zaptah back home with them. Over time, they began to change physically, growing taller, bigger and stronger. It was an era when the idea of athletic prowess took hold and preoccupied the people, except for the Oyahmayan, who remained content with the abundance of things that grew and flourished above Earth. That was the beginning of a profound cultural divide."

"Amazing," says Constance, "to think we were all once as lean as they are. What brought them together again?"

"There was great concern when adults started dying at younger ages. They were lucky to see their thirtieth winter. It was especially puzzling because they looked healthy. Ancient tales told of elders who had lived well into old age, which to them meant one's sixties. However, the Oyahmayan, who spent much of the time outdoors above ground, were living as long as eighty to ninety winters. It could have been an opportune moment in history for the clever Oyahmayan to seize power and play on their fellow tribesmen's irrational fears, who by now believed they had offended Wakan Tanka and were being punished; but Oyahmayan were too virtuous for that. Instead they convinced the people to look inside the body for answers. Until then, human dissection had been taboo. Examination of cadavers revealed that the hearts of people who spent considerable time in the cave among the zaptah were the same size as the hearts of the slender Oyahmayan. Logic dictated they should be bigger, in order to correspond to the overall bigger skeletal frames they prized so much. Of course, information about the circulatory system and bone formation was nonexistent, and they certainly had no understanding about the composition of zaptah; but there was no denying a link existed between the crystals and those repeatedly exposed to it. Rapid and exaggerated bone development had to be curtailed. It was killing them. "

"Exactly what type of mineral is zaptah?" Constance reviews in her head the properties of lesser known minerals. "Perhaps a subgroup of bridgmanite? It exists in the lower regions of Earth's mantle."

Jon admits his ignorance on the subject. "You should spend a day with the researchers at Winter Crow's lab. It's too complex for me to explain, but for a person with your science background...oh, and ultraviolet B rays play an integral role."

He has certainly piqued her curiosity. Her phone suddenly goes off in her purse, the one with her civilian contacts. "It's Viktor."

Jon stands. "You have a nice chat with your son. I'll catch you in the morning before I head out." She nods while answering.

"I'm sorry to interrupt your evening, Mom. I can hear you're with someone."

"Don't ever feel you're imposing. We were wrapping up. I have to wake early in the morning for a flight out. Speaking of early..."

"Yeah...Tess and I are just finishing breakfast. Mom, sorry to spring this on you—but I'm marrying Tess in a few hours, and I want you to have us in your thoughts."

"Marrying...today?"

"This afternoon at two o'clock, at the courthouse. It's terrible of me to phone you at the last minute, but we decided just a few days ago."

"That's wonderful news, Viktor...out-of-the-blue, mind you. Does Dad know?"

"You're the first. I'm calling him next."

"And Tess is fully on board?"

"Of course," I laugh. "I didn't have to twist her arm if that's what you're thinking."

"May I speak with her?" After a brief hesitation, which caused her to wonder if Viktor had misgivings about it, Tess gets on the line.

Constance is obviously doing most the talking. Tess interjects some yesses and uh-huhs, and finally says, "That means a lot...Constance," sounding self-conscious when she uses her soon-to-be mother-in-law's first name. Smiling, Tess hands the phone back and says, "She wishes she could have met me before this important day."

"I wish so, too, Mom." I feel sad for Mom, as well as for me.

"Tell me, Viktor—I have to know—do her earlobes remind you of acorns?"

"*Acorns?* What are you talking about?" She said it in a teasing voice.

"When you were around ten or eleven, we went riding and rested by a magnificent oak tree…"

"In Texas?"

"Yes, near Wichita Falls. It was early fall; the leaves hadn't changed. Part of the trunk ran parallel to the ground. It was an old tree, historic. I told you about Comanche marker trees, about how the Indians forced saplings to grow in unnatural ways to mark things like low-water crossings and burial grounds."

"That was so cool. I totally forgot. And the clouds were massive that day. We made up things they looked like. Oh my god—the acorns! They covered every inch of the ground. But what's the connection?"

"You loved the shape of them…said they looked like a girl's ears at school."

"Gracie Rose Hoffmann! You remember that?"

"Honestly, her name escaped me, but not the strange thing you said as you rubbed a nut back and forth across your lips, which I found oddly erotic for a young boy to do. You stated that the girl you marry would have to have earlobes as smooth as an acorn."

"No way! That's hilarious!"

"Just something a mom would take note of. So *does* she?"

I'm staring intently at Tess, thinking back to the first time I saw her, her ears that is, the left earlobe to be exact. I've heard of fetishes. Is it possible I have one? Is it bad? I ignore the question and say goodbye.

I can't stop staring at Tess's beautiful face. I run my thumb obsessively across her fingertips. These next hours are going to drag. I ache for it to be two already.

"Viktor…it isn't fair to you, if I keep something to myself that happened while you were gone." Tess pulls her hand back and folds her arms across her chest. "I was expecting you to come back to Columbus after the Bowl game, but then you said you were going to visit your sick friend on the reservation, which was totally understandable. After he died, you said you were coming back, but then you chose to go into the hills for a hanbleceya. Again, I tried to be understanding about it. When that was over, you called to say you were staying to attend a powwow…plus you needed more time to figure out how to drive Jim here. I get that you had a lot to work through, but I had my own issues I was dealing with at the time, you know?"

She slept with somebody else. The artist, I bet. And I'm to blame—the way I left things between us over Christmas.

She stands and gets her purse that's on the counter next to the breadbox. My stomach feels like it's churning rocks. I can't stand the thought of another guy touching her, having sex with her. She places a box of condoms on the table and sits back down.

"I bought these on my way to Dr. Nate's on the night I knew you were going to be back. It was irresponsible of me not to use them."

I am not connecting the dots—unless Tess didn't use protection with him, and he sleeps around like Camila had. "Were you concerned I might catch a disease?"

"*You?*"

"Well I can honestly say that I didn't hook up with anyone on the rez."

"That never occurred to me." I witness her light bulb moment. "You think *I* did?" She gives me this incredulous look. "I told you I loved you."

"Then what's going on?" I make some gesture about the condoms, afraid to say another word. She's still looking at me in disbelief.

"I knew by November the pill wasn't helping my cramps anymore. When you came over before Christmas, before we had our blow-up, I told you that I needed to see my doctor. I had to find something else to try. I wanted to wait until you returned, but I was suffering too much, and you kept drawing out the time."

I cringe at the mention of that day. I still have no clue where this is going.

"I finally went off them. The doctor said to go a few months before using a different prescription. That was two weeks ago."

Her lower lip starts to tremble a little as she tries to stay composed. It's upsetting to watch, and I want to console her, but I'm not sure for what. Following a deep breath, she says: "I had friends in high school whose moms were getting pregnant in their forties. We wondered how it was possible for mature adults, with obviously more self-discipline than teens, could let such a thing happen. I swore I'd never be so stupid."

"Tess," I whisper, "are you saying what I think you are?"

She's looking at me with the most pitiful expression. "I've tried to convince myself everything's going to be okay, that the likelihood I ovulated already is slim. The past couple of nights, though, I've woken in a panic, realizing my life could be changed forever. I get angry for having met you. I'm angry at myself for allowing emotions to interfere with my studies. I've worked so hard to reach this point. There won't be the energy, let alone the money, for me to go on to grad school."

"My God, Tess!" What she's been worrying herself sick over while I've simply been trying to get back in the swing of playing ball again. I lift her out of the kitchen chair to hold her. "Whatever happens in our lives from now on, we'll deal with it together. You still love me, right?"

"I wish I didn't. That's horrible of me, isn't it?"

"If in fact your fear comes true…" I stop myself and kiss her, realizing nothing I say can help her anxiety. My body isn't the one that's going to be affected. And it would be cruel to reveal how excited I am over the prospect of becoming a dad. First I must become a husband.

"To the matter at hand." I dab the corners of her eyes. "Go get dressed and we'll hang out in German Village. It's close to the courthouse."

Jon can't hide his reaction to Constance's appearance. He waits to comment after the server leaves with their order, which amounts to nothing but tea for his breakfast companion. "Did you sleep? Are you well?"

Constance rubs her face and laughs a little. "I'm fine, really; but no, I didn't sleep." She scans her phone, which seems rude until she holds it up for him to look at. "I sat awake all night waiting for this. The reason Viktor called was to announce his wedding later in the afternoon."

She appears wounded by the news. He overlooks it. "His wife is lovely. Intelligent eyes. Hair the color of firethorn berries."

"Please, Sleeping Buffalo, can you look deeper into me. What do you *see*?" She addresses him formally, wishing his professional expertise on the matter. "My emotions confound me. Do they go beyond a normal maternal response."

"Not at all, Constance. This is unexpected news. You're right to feel this way. Sadly, the son you withheld physical affection from for almost a decade, and now are entitled to embrace again, as is our custom, is half a world away. You have a rare occupation that takes you far from home for long periods."

"It's a stupid custom, a damn cruel one! Why did I ever subject myself and Viktor to it?"

"If you at least saw your children on a regular basis, the pain wouldn't run so deep. Scouts who serve in other countries normally do it as a couple and keep their children with them." Hopefully that didn't come off sounding like he was being critical of her? "Howling Wind, I meant no offense."

"To think that now I might never make it home to hold him…" She shakes her head and sighs, too tired to launch into a tirade against Rawakota traditions. When the tea arrives, the sweet smell of lavender is calming. Jon watches as she falls asleep, her head propped up by a hand whose arm is precariously balanced on the edge of the table. While he enjoys a plate of Kashmiri breads, spreading thick layers of butter and jam across their golden crusts, it's the image of young love displayed on her phone that holds his attention.

The inevitable happens, and Constance's elbow drops, jerking her awake. Dazed, she glances around to find her bearings. Jon reassures her she was out for maybe ten minutes, not an hour like she believes.

"Constance, before you drifted off, you spoke as if you'd never have a chance to see your son again. Why? The possibility of dying is a given for those in your field, isn't it?"

"We fighter pilots are a cocky group, never doubting our skills. That conviction in and of itself is our mantle of protection. The nature of war is changing, though. There are far too many anonymous players involved at every turn." She taps her phone to activate the screen, and then smiles at the happy couple. "I'm heading to Bahrain, a country which belongs to the Saudi-led coalition of Arab states that the Americans have supported for years. The Saudis are responsible for a horrific humanitarian crisis in the region. My assignment will be to protect their aircraft as they shoot at their own Somali civilians and Yemen refugees who have been fleeing in boats to other countries…countries that refuse to accept any more migrants. Can you believe it! Americans are not the good guys. If we were, we could prevent the attacks and keep these people safe in the water until they reach their destinations. However, countries like Italy, Greece, and Britain, the ones that are in the European Union...they make deals with each other and the U.S., pacts that sabotage earlier agreements which were intended to help these very civilians who want to escape the atrocities in their homelands. Nowadays, the massive exodus of refugees is overwhelming the safe havens of the world. There is nothing remotely humanitarian about the European Union's current goal: eliminate the asylum seekers, eliminate the crisis."

Jon sucks the air between his teeth as he laments the intentional killing of so many people. "I see." He shakes his head. "Those poor, unsuspecting souls."

Constance assumes the unflappable air of the level-headed pilot she is. She gazes beyond Jon's shoulder as if fixated on a horizon and the upcoming aerial dogfight that awaits her. "I'll be over the Gulf of Aden in the Arabian Peninsula. It's a remote area; there won't be witnesses. The problem lies with the Russians, who have control of South Yemen. They have no business interfering with this Saudi operation, but they love to show off their military advantage whenever they have a chance. They have been targeting the U.S. for the past year when we've been called in there. The U.S. is equally matched, but the Russians have been using unauthorized high-grade lasers as well as concentrated microwave beams on our pilots, seriously injuring them. It's an effective way of doing battle without violating air spaces. Presently our aircraft are vulnerable to the attacks, and there you have the cause of my apprehension. I'll be in an F-15."

Concerned about her welfare, Sleeping Buffalo says he will request that Chief Rolling Thunder intervene. The tribe's computer wizards have proven that they are up to the task. "Our scientists will communicate with you through your device using the buzzing signals you're familiar with. They can identify the ground positions where the Russian lasers originate and proceed to destroy them. Our security team will have them all scratching their heads afterward," he laughs, "it will be like the nuclear plant debacle in Arizona. You'll make it home, Constance."

His resolve is appreciated. Constance rubs her heavy lids and glances at the time. "Gotta go." She straightens her back and attempts a smile.

"Did you care to know if I ascertained anything from the picture you showed me?"

After a second, "You know I would."

Jon has had plenty of time to study the faces of Viktor and Tess. "The young wife seeks solace from you."

"Solace? From me! C'mon, you can't honestly determine that from a photo. Tess looks perfectly happy." One doesn't openly challenge a spiritual member's appraisal of people or situations, which Constance realizes she just did. Sounding kinder, she asks, "Is Viktor the reason?"

"This has more to do with her own personal journey. Her eyes beseech you. She knew that you would be on the receiving end of this picture, looking at her, forming an opinion of her."

"What can I possibly do at this distance?"

"Think of her. Return home in one piece."

"*Un-hee!* You can really frustrate the hell out of a person, you know?"

Jon shrugs, not surprised anymore at getting a rise out of her. Because Constance grew up on the outside, he accepts that she can't fully grasp the nature of the function he serves. Since there's so much on her mind right now, he chooses to forego telling her what the Mujahzee disclosed to him and the Oyahmayan. Their people need to find a new home, and soon. The number of earthquakes has been increasing in the last century, with the most severe occurring in the past two decades. The serendipitous encounter in the cave between their leaders and her and Smitty couldn't have been timed any better. The Rawakota will gladly play an instrumental role in getting them resettled in the sparsely populated sovereign nation of Mongolia, specifically in the northeastern Khentii Mountains. Mujahzee expeditions zeroed in on a particular peak in the range held sacred by the Mongols, the Great Burkhan Khaldun Mountain. UNESCO recently designated it a protected World Heritage Site. And although tourists are expected to visit the burial site of Genghis Khan, the land is off limits to any company in the excavation business. The Mujahzee can continue to live isolated and safe. Sleeping Buffalo knows Howling Wind would be fascinated by the turn of events, at the moment she needs to focus on her own survival.

"Done," I declare, grinning ear to ear, happy beyond belief. "It's totally unbelievable!"

"*Totally!*"

We look at each other and chuckle. "God, Tess...we're fucking married." As soon as I whispered the words, I wished I had come up with something more poetic. Drivers honk their congratulations as they zip past, responding to the *Just Married!* decal I stuck on the back window of the car.

"That's the best you've got?" quips Tess. "*We're fucking married! Seriously?* Up till now I believed you were an eloquent, hopeless romantic."

"Got something better?"

Tess laughs. "Jesus, Mary, and Joseph! We're fucking married!"

She squeezes my free hand while my left one tries to keep us in our lane. Sparks shoot through my fingers, my body. It's incredible, stupendous! Hearing us pronounced husband and wife was music to my ears. Tess's eyes are so bright and cheery. Though fear of pregnancy looms, she's hiding it well on this special day. Lucky for us a big group is climbing aboard their tour bus when we arrive at the restaurant in the historic cobblestone district, our second trip of the day here. I suggest we move to German Village.

"Too expensive," she says, "but I do love the area."

We're okay with sitting outside on the screened-in patio while the staff clears the main room. The surrounding trellis, covered in thick vines, makes it cozy and private. It isn't too cold for the end of March either; in fact, today is supposed to hit seventy. We decide to stay put and place our orders, following which I feel I must address her comment about not being able to afford this location. "We have never discussed money, at least not in depth."

"There's a lot we haven't discussed." She uncovers the basket of rolls, pleased to see the kitchen hadn't skimped on them. "What are you hemming and hawing about?"

Guess that's exactly what I'm doing, and I stop flicking the edge of the coaster. "As long as we're coming clean about things…"

"Oh, no…what?" She drops back in the chair and regards me with suspicion. "I was at least upfront with you *before* we got hitched."

"No, no…nothing so serious." Although, maybe to her it will be. "The artist who created the poster for WAKAN asked me at the time if he could use some of his sketches for a book he wanted to illustrate about a Tarzan-like character. I was flattered."

"You should be. I take it the book is completed?"

"Well, yes…along with a calendar that includes work by his grad students. I had also agreed to pose for his life drawing classes." There's a long pause.

"Naked...for the world to see."

I never thought about the future ramifications at the time. Next she asks: "What if I told you the artist I dated had nude drawings of me?"

I search her eyes. "I'd be crushed, but that's mostly because you and he... never mind."

"Well he doesn't." As soon as the salad arrives and the waiter leaves, Tess removes the temporary ring I gave her. My heart sinks. We ordered matching turquoise and diamond rings that we saw in a magazine. They won't be arriving anytime soon. She slides it back on my pinky. "I look forward to getting my own. There was good reason your grandmother wanted you to have her ring. Besides reminding you not to become too big for your britches, let it also remind you that your body belongs to me, despite the fact it's going to be on full display for complete strangers to lust over."

"I love you."

Without so much as a smirk, she wonders: "Were you given an ample-sized pecker?"

"True to life," I reply straight-faced, "though they eliminated my foreskin."

"Wow...artists are endowed with many skills."

I'm relieved by her attitude, to the point I almost forgot why I brought it up. "The book and calendar should bring in a decent amount of money. After winning the Bowl game, my dad said there's been a huge increase in the number of *WAKAN* posters sold. He oversees the account that was set up by Efrem Zukor, the art teacher who designed it. And after a successful season on the field this fall, sales will certainly go through the roof. Just saying." I realize how egotistical that sounded. "We *could* conceivably live here."

Tess takes a moment. "I think it's practical for the time being to stay where we are."

Our thoughtful waiter turned on the outdoor speakers. The music I think is from an old movie, one Grandma Junie likes ... maybe *Casablanca*. I recognize the melody, just can't name the song. Three other middle-aged couples, all on phones, linger over coffee.

I can only keep admiring my beautiful, sexy wife during the meal. Tess has the whitest, softest skin. The pale blue dress she bought for today hugs her curves. It's got transparent ruffled sleeves that flutter like wings in the breeze. The poppies printed on the material match the color of her hair, which she's wearing long today with one side held back by a barrette. Her earring, a small, smooth pearl, sets off her perfect ear lobe, creating a distraction. I'll be finding out how long an erection can last.

As soon as we arrive back at my apartment there's a knock at the door. It's Uncle William.

"Congratulations Viktor," he says, including Tess's name when he spots her behind me in the room. He reaches out to her, and then places her hand over mine and holds them together. "Your mother sent me news of your plans to get married. Then I talked to Solomon. You should call your grandmother." He is genuinely happy for us.

"Right away, Leksi. You aren't offended because we didn't invite you to the courthouse, are you?" He pats my cheek and says the legal formality means little. We'll all be celebrating at the next powwow.

On his way out, he asks if I intend to be at practice in the morning. My excuse for today was that I needed to see my advisor. "Yes, for sure."

Tess and I sit beside each other on the couch. She dreads breaking the news to her folks.

I pull out my phone. "Guess what, Grandmother…" She's excited to hear the news from me, even though Dad had already told her. Sunkwah and Winnie are with her. I put them on speakerphone. They offer a Rawakota blessing and each welcomes Tess into our family. Iris messaged me earlier to say that she would call at eight. It's Tess's turn to call her parents. She looks desperate, like it's the last thing in the world she wants to do.

"It's going to catch them off guard. They'll think it's a prank. I'm not in the mood for a long explanation. Even people who don't follow football know your name."

"Tell them I'm the scientist you met at work and give them my Indian name, Hinhán Ska. I could write down my full authentic name, which is a paragraph long and doesn't translate well into English. It means, the white owl that shoos away sorrows from those in low spirits."

"A visit from that owl would be welcome right now."

I hug her. "Please tell me you aren't sad."

"I'm not." She plants a great juicy kiss on my lips. "It's been a grand day, a perfect day for people in love to get married."

The call is brief and to the point. She went along with the idea of using Hinhán Ska, but then mentions to her parents that she won't be taking my name, which I never assumed. Hearing my age doesn't help her case. Tess looks for strength in my eyes. Her parents probably hoped for someone older, or at least more established. "He's smart and talented, respectful... perfect in every way, Mom." She listens for a while. "Yes, I do; I love him with all my heart. I know…I know this comes as a big shock."

Tess rolls her eyes. How to wrap this up? Ordinary decency dictates I should take the phone, introduce myself; tell her mom how much I love her daughter. Maybe her father is a traditional type who expected to be asked for his daughter's hand in marriage. Tess simply says she is tired and will talk with them later to set a date for a visit. We both realize our workloads won't allow for that before the end of June, which is about three months away.

CHAPTER 41

I think nothing about following Slaughter out of the building until he abruptly shoots a wad of spit at the wall and proceeds to smear it with his finger while cursing, "That's bullshit! Fuckers don't get respect just for being fucking women!" He then storms out the door. Damien loves that f-word, always enunciates it clearly and enthusiastically, although it's generally directed at a particular person. Maybe it was.

The guys and I stop for once at the poster outside the locker room to read it. We pass it routinely, not giving its message a second thought. **DECISIONS** · HONESTY · TREAT WOMEN WITH RESPECT— **NO** DRUGS STEALING WEAPONS. I mean, *duh!* But now we get why Slaughter was so ticked off. We're all ticked off!

After pushing ourselves to the limit for this past Saturday's Scarlet versus Gray intrasquad game, which was a blast, the team was greeted this morning with a bummer of a meeting about our morals, or presumed lack of. A new face, clean-shaven with cold blue eyes, did the preaching. He looked out of place in his boring gray business suit. The staff was equally puzzled by the unscheduled speaker. All the coaches and their assistants had been pumped and high-fiving us when we first arrived, excited over prospects for the coming season. My own performance had blown them away, having connected on 29 of 32 pass attempts for 326 yards and 4 touchdowns. Then we were told a guy was waiting to talk to us in one of the conference rooms, and the mood changed in an instant.

"Who among you," he began, pausing long until the room quieted, "knows an athlete who has either exhibited violence toward a woman or who has been abused by a staff member?"

We sat in uncomfortable silence. Was he such a dumbass to actually expect a hand to go up? He made us out to sound like liars because we hadn't responded. He concluded his hostile speech with a threat, informing us that no one was above scrutiny, including the head coach! *What!?*

There wasn't a second to digest that before he started in on the anthem controversy, wondering who has entertained the idea of taking a knee or raising a fist. Did any one of us believe such disrespectful behavior was ever warranted? Talk about loaded language. His accusatory tone was entirely self-defeating.

Though some of my teammates are not academically-minded, they operate with a sophisticated level of street-smarts. This guy was nothing more than another manipulator out to gain something for the agency he represented by putting student athletes, judged as naïve, on the defensive. Players grow sick and tired of how schools hold scholarships over their heads in an attempt to keep them in line. This particular *talking to*, intended to prevent young men from expressing their opinions, and in a university setting no less, will require damage control.

Right now, I simply want to get home to Tess. I jog to my car, and with a foot already inside the door, I hear, "Hey, kid." I'm shocked to see Hayden. We fall into each other's arms laughing, offering up manly slaps to the chest and shoulders because we don't know what else to do, short of kissing. "I was worried if you saw me again, you'd tell me to go straight to hell."

"Why?"

"*Why?*" He shoots me an odd look. "Because we parted on such bad terms."

"I choose to forget." I truly have forgotten about the personal props I had lent him for *WAKAN* that he gave to Ishmael.

He nods. "Okay then."

We lean against the hood. Hayden drapes an arm over his knee, looking as relaxed as always, just like I remember. I nudge him: "You gonna do it? Are you going to coach me?"

His head drops down, and he laughs. "God, Viktor. You should've seen my face when I read the message asking me to call one of the football coordinators in the athletic department."

I tell him the circumstances under which I gave the guy his name and number. I hadn't really expected him to pursue anything.

"It's crazy," he says, "the whole situation."

"Don't I know." We stare across the parking lot at this sprawling athletic facility. I bring up the meeting the team was just in, and the sense I got that this speaker was steering the players to answer questions from the press in a certain way…a politically correct way.

"You're their golden boy, Viktor... or should I say, *copper* boy. The number of scandals is threatening the program. Everything's hanging on your success. My background check must've passed muster with the powers that be, because I'm here to review a contract. They're talking about a ridiculous amount of money, more than I've ever dreamed of making. They'll be paying me separately out of a private alumni foundation." He turns serious. "That doesn't mean I'll allow myself to be beholding to anyone."

"Me neither; not that I'm paid...but whatever gets promised me."

"What a racket. If the higher-ups don't watch it, they'll have a mutiny on their hands. When players see people in authority skirting the rules right and left, putting athletics above ethics, they wonder what's to keep them from doing the same. No one likes feeling emasculated, especially by old white dudes, right?"

I touch his graying temples. "You're turning into an old white dude, Dude."

"Better watch out!" he warns.

"I'd love to go on talking, Hayden, but..."

He pats my leg and stands. "Same. We'll be seeing each other soon enough." We shake hands. Before he walks away, I can't resist telling him:

"I just got married, Hayden. No one here knows yet."

"You *what*?" he says, his mouth gaping wide open. "I suppose it's no more shocking than Skyler becoming a mom."

"No way!" His news is definitely more unbelievable. It's no secret that he has wanted a baby. According to him, Skyler constantly avoided the subject. "Congratulations! Boy... girl?"

"Mimi," he says, looking ever so proud. He then darts across the parking lot to the building, waving back at me before disappearing inside the door.

I pull out of the lot, all smiles now over the fact that Hayden will be my personal coach. That jerk Mazursky is history. Éyahahe! I park in front of Tess's place, anxious to hold her after a weekend apart. I use my key. It's quiet inside. I find her sleeping soundly in her room. Hmm, how to fit myself on the bed without disturbing her? She was relieved when her period started on Friday. Football was the only thing on my mind this weekend, so the timing was good. The stress of waiting for it had gotten to be unbearable for her. Tess turns toward me, eyes closed, and unzips my pants. I pull them off along with my shirt and huddle close beside her. She kisses my neck, then scoots down to where she can kiss my chest. My penis finds a snug spot between her warm, soft breasts.

———————

"Viktor, if we're to get any work done, you need to put her down for a nap," snaps Hayden. "She's overdue for one." I'm in his new studio, a huge industrial warehouse he found between campus and the county fairgrounds. We're supposed to be reviewing football strategies, but I keep getting sidetracked by Mimi.

"Oh, come on…she's irresistible!" I break out laughing again when Mimi tips to her side while attempting to sit and begins rolling over and over, ending with her toes in her mouth and staring at herself in the giant dance mirror. What a fun, goofy little creature.

While I raise her high in the air, which causes endless squeals and giggles, Hayden searches on his laptop for more personal information about my new teammates. Except for their stats, neither of us knows much about the guys. Skyler, whom I have yet to see, is in New York recruiting dance teachers, leaving Hayden in charge of the baby.

"Christ! Here's a story for you," he says. "How 'bout placing her in the bassinet for now. She needs to sleep." I do as told, but not without some grumbling.

"What have you found?"

"A link to a newspaper article from twelve years ago about Paul Martin's family."

"Number 63? Could you please stick to the offensive line, the guys I actually play beside."

"Listen to this," he says, ignoring me, "the father was ordered by the court to send his children to school after his wife died, or they would all be placed with Arizona Child Protective Services, all 16 of them!" He goes on reading to himself, then says: "The Martins were considered to be anti-government zealots who belonged to a sovereign citizens movement. They lived in a rural area and were ready to shoot any trespasser who set foot on their property, including the sheriff. *Man.*"

"You sure you've got the right Paul Martin?"

"The kids were described as being blond and blue-eyed. Get this; the only suitable reading material was the Bible. There were two sets of twins.

The mother died in childbirth along with the baby, which would have made it number 17. It's definitely him. The story goes on to say how difficult it was at first for the kids to adjust to school. Three of Paul's oldest brothers, being over 18, weren't required to go. Because of his size, Paul was encouraged to play football. Turns out he had a knack for it. He went to a 3A high school and then played for an Arizona Junior college with a coach who had ties to Ohio State."

"Do you think he's a white supremacist at heart?" The thought triggers a memory. "You know, when we were in the locker room after the Bowl game, my uncle and Paul locked eyes when Paul quickly turned away, but not before noticing I saw them. He seemed embarrassed. His face turned bright red. Maybe Uncle sensed he didn't like Indians."

"Then *maybe* you should ask Horse That Walks Backwards about it. Apparently his gut instincts don't lie."

"What's that supposed to mean? And just so you know, Uncle's gone back to using his original name, Half Moon." He looks at me with a range of emotions that I can't decipher. Next he studies the ceiling and lets out a sigh.

"I'm only going to bring this up once," he says, "because you've made it clear you don't want to be reminded of that episode in your life, which is understandable. I have never seen the life drain out of a man's face like it did your uncle's on the day he burst into the dance studio hoping to find you there, only to learn you were on your way to Ishmael's. He looked so desperate it scared me. Honest to god, he was ashen. In the blink of an eye, he was gone. I ran after him, but he was too fast. I caught the tail end of his car flying around the corner. I vividly remembered you saying that he didn't like Ishmael from the get-go."

Just hearing that name turns my stomach.

"The news reports at the time suggested you were jumped on the street, that it was likely a racially motivated attack. I knew it wasn't. Based on your uncle's state of mind, I realized he feared something terrible was in store for you."

I'm listening with detached curiosity. Hayden, though, is teary-eyed.

"Skyler and I had both witnessed that dark side to Ishmael. We shouldn't have let it slide. We saw the mean way he treated the impressionable underclassmen. Girls and guys alike fawned after him. And we glimpsed that dangerous edge to him when the two of you were onstage.

At times it appeared he really had it in for you, but you managed to hold your own, so we overlooked it. As the producers of the show, Skyler and I were fixated on our deadlines…screw the personal dramas."

He stands to stretch, and then goes to peek at Mimi who's sleeping. "It's one thing to deal with professional adults, quite another, however, when it's young students navigating their way in the world, many for the first time since leaving home. When you landed in the hospital, we blamed ourselves. The remorse was life-changing, especially for Skyler. By turning a blind eye, we had in fact created an environment that permitted this brute to have his fun with inexperienced souls, which, let's face it, included you, too."

I see his point, but at the same time think he is overstating things a bit. "You have always cared about your students, Hayden." I purposely omit Skyler's name. She cared about the dancers in a strictly technical sense, paying attention only to their form.

"There's no escaping the fact we got greedy. All those rich, self-important twits Skyler insisted you suck up to at our party were eager to back any venture we proposed. We could finally, seriously, pursue our creative vision. It's tiring year after year to rely on grant money. When you waltzed into my office and bowed out of the show…"

He wraps his arms around himself and stomps the floor. It's clear how much I hurt him, how unthinking and irresponsible I was. I go to his side intent on apologizing, but instead find myself choking on the words. In light of what happened at Camila's party, I truly wanted nothing more to do with *WAKAN's* cast and crew members, and I don't know how to adequately explain my feelings to him.

"After seeing you in the hospital, Skyler and I put the brakes on everything, in order to regroup and examine our priorities." He takes my braids in his hands and looks me directly in the eyes. If it were any other guy, standing face to face like this would be awkward. He reaches toward my head and glides his thumb across my brow, above the eye that miraculously survived. "Life's lessons shouldn't come at someone else's expense."

Our *moment* is interrupted by a loud pounding at the door. Hayden says he's getting an estimate for a new floor; it shouldn't take long. The noise didn't disturb Mimi. She remains fast asleep. I wonder who else Hayden was googling. I tap the laptop and there's Damien Slaughter, Number 54, looking like his usual badass self. Although Slaughter irks me to no end, I am curious about his background. He was born in one of the worst slums in Chicago to a mother who abandoned him at the age of three. He grew up in foster care, bouncing from one home to another until a distant relative was located in Dayton, Ohio. The older man was willing to take in the troubled teen. I watch a short interview of Damien after his first season as a starting guard for the Buckeyes. The inflated ego is laughable. His final comments however strike a nerve. I replay it. He describes his involvement in gang murders, and what it was like to be shot at. He admits he'd be dead or back in jail, having already done time, if this man from Ohio, a stranger, hadn't said yes to him moving in with him. To Damien's credit, he took that opportunity and ran with it, something none of my friends on the rez were willing to do. Dad could have been their lifeline.

Hayden looks to be finishing up with the floor people. I'm forced to consider the importance of my role this year, especially since Krull transferred to Michigan. We were good at bouncing ideas off each other. It will be this Indian's job to get the players behind me, regardless of how radically different their backgrounds are. I glance at the notes Hayden jotted down about the new kicker. He is a 26-year-old Aussie freshman who never attended college before, let alone visited the U.S. How strange being here must seem to him.

CHAPTER 42

"Hurry! Go, Colonel! Take the Raptor!" yells the black African man in French. He's wearing the green camouflage uniform of the Malian army. *"It gives us more room in the helicopter for the wounded."* The insistent soldier pushes Howling Wind toward a building where flight equipment is stored. Scores of desperate local military forces and aid workers, mostly Peace Corps volunteers, scramble to leave the base with the hope of making it out alive. There's no telling when the ISIS insurgents will catch up and ambush them the way they did the unsuspecting villagers along the Niger-Mali border she had come across yesterday. Most of the inhabitants were murdered in the bloodbath, along with some foreign UN troops. Having completed her mission in Bahrain, Howling Wind was returning a fighter jet to France when she received the order to help with the rescue of two U.S. pilots who'd been shot down near a rural community along the Niger River. The men had successfully ejected. After she was given clearance to land at a French military base in Mali, she joined a squadron familiar with the area. They told her that a UN peacekeeping team was headed to the village to offer additional security. There was a real possibility of her engaging in ground combat, which had been unsettling to her.

Howling Wind now races to a different building where the nurses' quarters are. She had stored her flight suit there upon her arrival for the assignment, since she wasn't permitted to change anywhere near men. The aircraft she had flown in on, now disabled, rests on its side far from the runway. The landing gear had collapsed when she touched down. Fortunately, a live missile wasn't attached to the wing or she would have had to bail. She quickly changes into her suit.

No time for pre-flight checks. Every move is automatic. The wheel chocks get tossed to the side. She straps herself in the cockpit, taking note that this is no modern F-22. Engines rev up fine. Fuel looks good. A Chinook transport chopper filled to maximum capacity ascends from behind and heads west to safety. From the north, a French armed H225M Caracal hovers, searching for a good landing zone. A quick review of the instruments has the pilot feeling more confident. The adrenaline really kicks in at the sight of onboard weapons. Howling Wind has never been so fired up over taking anybody out. Best of all, she knows where to find the incoming enemy. They're presently at the scene of yesterday's massacre. A young woman she had tried to help in the destroyed village yesterday, a girl really, who'd been raped and disemboweled, had overheard the terrorists' phone conversations and told Howling Wind that more fighters in tanks were going to arrive by tomorrow, meaning today.

A nurse opens the blinds. The rising sun is to the back of the building. Constance asks the date. Viktor should have received his birthday card. She had mailed it early from India, in order for it to arrive on time in May…it's been a month or so since he got married. Thank goodness she's finding her bearings. It was hard to accept that she had been going in and out of consciousness for weeks. Under the watchful eye of Nurse Farah, whose name she remembered from yesterday, she manages to stand by the bed without help. She cautiously steps to the nearest wall. Solomon comes to mind. He must be out of his mind with worry. What she puts him through! He won't believe where she ended up—the Naval Air Station in Morocco. She can't believe it herself. She had successfully dropped the bombs on the rebel tanks in Mali and had begun to set a course for France when bouts of lightheadedness began plaguing her. She realized she was severely dehydrated. Having no water, it didn't take long before delirium afflicted her. A crash-landing seemed imminent, but that wasn't going to be on the conscience of the air controller at this base who doggedly talked her down.

Back in bed following a quick shower, Constance smooths over the fresh, clothesline-crisp sheets. She recalls the first time showering here, before things became a blur. It had been a sublime experience, what with scrubbing away all the dried blood stuck on her skin, none of which, as it turned out, had been hers. She never got a chance to wash herself after leaving the site of the massacre in Mali. With luck, the wounded soldiers she'd had direct contact with there should have been vaccinated against major diseases. There was the girl, though … Diarra Cissé, a stoic teen-aged girl whom Howling Wind had told was the bravest person she'd ever met, words she prayed would give the traumatized victim the will to stay alive. Diarra lay against the tree where she had been assaulted, watching with interest as the American female pilot ligated her innards that lay tangled on the ground between her thighs. Suppose, wonders Howling Wind, the African girl harbored a virus that entered a scrape on her finger as she tried to discern a uterus from intestines. She is thankful when a doctor arrives and interrupts her grim thoughts. She is not pleased, though, when she learns he is a psychiatrist. His voice is pleasant. He flew in from Stuttgart, Germany, where U.S. AFRICOM is headquartered. He asks what she remembers. And so begins the official investigation.

"You certainly rate," says Tess as she looks inside each of my birthday cards lined up on my kitchen counter. "The Liebermans?"

"A friend's parents from high school."

"That's special. It's nice they stay in touch."

"What's so funny?"

"This one from your dad...making fun of your Indian names."

"Right...the dude waking up to the Native woman in his bed named Pink Eye. Yeah, that's his thing, finding silly Native stuff. You wouldn't believe the Thanksgiving cards. Hallmark they're not!"

"*Aw*, your mom's card is beautiful. Sent from Kashmir. Sounds exotic. '...on my way to Bahrain, won't be able to call.' Where's that?"

"Near Qatar."

"Oh, like that helps!"

She looks it up on her phone while I make coffee to go with the chocolate cake she baked for me from scratch. Nineteen candles write out 19. Uncle arrives to join us.

Half-way through eating there's a knock at the door. I'm floored to see Efrem Zukor standing there. We haven't seen each other since the *WAKAN* days.

"Happy birthday, dear friend."

"How'd you know?!"

My cheek gets a gentle pat, and next a big rectangular present is slid out from behind the wall of the hallway. "For you." Efrem steps inside, leaving me standing in the doorway with it. "Go ahead, Viktor, open it," he says casually, making himself comfortable on the couch. Why do Uncle and

Tess look like partners in crime? And Efrem, for that matter? They don't know him.

"Gee, *what could it be*?" It's wrapped in burlap and tied with rope. The knots were purposely twisted in such a way as to frustrate the hell out of me.

Efrem teases, "No scissors allowed."

"This had better not be a big letdown!" I laugh, finding it impossible to hurry. At last! I can only stare in disbelief.

"It was Tess's idea," says Uncle William. "She found Efrem in the art department, and I set it up for him to go to the barn."

"Just answer me this," says Efrem, "did I capture whatever "wakan" means to you, or is that something too elusive?" He glances at Uncle, who nods his approval.

"Damn, Efrem! The Great Spirit clearly channels his magic through you! It's magnificent!"

"I'm so happy you like it. And I got to meet your lovely wife, a muse I would have preferred over a stinky horse." He gives Tess a wink.

I hug everyone and we're back to eating cake. I zone out during a conversation about campus renovations; the portrait is too compelling. Efrem chose a favorite stance that shows off Jim's strong neck. His chin is slightly elevated, and he looks like he just got in the last word, which he always does. His eyes draw me in. I see in my horse what he sees in me, a trusted brother.

Efrem and Uncle don't stay long. After clearing the table, Tess says there's another surprise. I'm thinking, what could top this? When she goes to the bathroom, I half expect her to come out wearing something sexy, not that it's a personal fantasy; I'm happy with naked. The door opens. She motions me over. My imagination has gone into overdrive. I follow her to the sink. "Look down," she says. Her eyes remain fixed on my face. I don't have to read the box to realize what's beside it. Or what color it is.

"I don't understand..."

"It was just some spotting. By the next day it was gone."

"I wish you had said something sooner. That was weeks ago."

"I had to come to terms with it first—as if that's possible."

She rests her head against my shoulder. "We should be older."

I bury my face in her hair and hold her tight. "Let's take a walk."

CHAPTER 43

Uncle William fed us a breakfast of pancakes and eggs that I pray Tess will hold down. Her appetite magically returned a few days ago along with an improved disposition, just in time for the start of our three week trip to meet all the relatives; and I mean *all*! First stop, Cincinnati.

"I'm stoked!"

"Me, too," she says, as we wave back to Uncle who's watching from his window.

"Really, Tess? I mean...*really?*"

"I'm so grateful not to be throwing up. Anything's better than that, even seeing my family." She almost has me convinced.

"My beautiful Tess is back!"

We enjoy a long, deep kiss before turning into traffic, and then it's off to the O'Sheas.

Half-way there we pull into a rest stop. Tess tells me to park at the far end designated for pet owners, which seems odd, but I drive on down. No one else is there. As soon as I turn off the engine, she jumps out of her side and hops in the back seat, slams the door shut, and starts hiking her dress over her head.

"*Yowza, woman!*"

The party at the O'Shea house celebrating the couple's twenty-fifth wedding anniversary is in full swing. There's obviously a sense of anticipation in the air over meeting Theresa's husband. Tess's parents had offered to go up to Columbus and take the couple out to dinner a number of times, being understandably anxious to meet their new son-in-law, but their daughter always came up with an excuse. She either had finals, or was changing her major, or was too sick. It would have been inexcusable if she had tried to get out of this notable event. So now, along with the neighbors and some co-workers, friends from church, and a couple of her parents' siblings who flew in from Boston, Brian and Chevonne O'Shea await the two, embarrassed they don't even have a photo of the newlyweds to show around. Most of their friends understand that's simply how Theresa *is*. But married, at eighteen! If it were any other girl, one might assume she *had to*. But Theresa is a smart cookie and too fiercely independent to get herself in such a pickle. It makes sense she met a fellow in her own field of study; and the fact that he's from India intrigues the guests. Perhaps he wears a turban like his own doctor in Boston, says Brian's brother. The O'Sheas played dumb when it came to inquiries about their son-in-law's age, not wanting to field any more questions. No matter, concern grows because their daughter should have arrived by now. Chevonne's face lights up when she reads the text that they just found an open spot to park on the next block. Kevin moves quickly to the window to check out his brother-in-law before anyone else.

I go to grab the present out of the trunk for her parents when Tess says we can get it later. It's a huge floor basket that Winnie and Grandmother made when they were teaching Sister how to weave. After the guests leave, Tess says I can bring the car around to the driveway. She does take the framed 8x10 picture of us on our wedding day; the one I sent Mom from my phone, something I don't think she did for her family. They must think we're mighty inconsiderate.

Before turning the corner, Tess pauses on the sidewalk.

"People are going to want to talk football with you. Please don't shy away from it on my account."

"I won't." Strands of her hair appear gold in the sunlight. Our thoughts are still on sex, and probably will be the rest of the day. The break we took at the rest stop was intense.

"My parents are going to be stunned when they see you. They'll wonder why I wasn't up front with them about your name."

"Mm." She's probably right. "In your defense, you did tell them over Christmas when they were watching the Bowl game that I was your boyfriend. It isn't your fault they didn't take you seriously."

"That's right!" she exclaims, suddenly squeezing my hand tight at the sight of a man disappearing behind the curtains of her parents' house. The image sours her happy mood. "Let the fun begin," she says sarcastically. And that is my introduction to Kevin.

Tess's parents look as startled as we do. We opened the door the moment they were getting ready to, and we darn near bumped into each other.

Right then we hear, "What the fuck!" Though spoken under his breath, Kevin is within earshot of us. We're still standing in the entranceway. He emerges from the living room and with a wry laugh proclaims: "No way is *he* Theresa's husband! She's messing with you guys, like when she brought home that artist to make a point." His comment draws looks of disapproval.

"I'm sorry we're running late," says Tess, introducing me quickly as Viktor Hinhán Ska. "He goes by Talking White Owl."

"We know what he goes by, Theresa," says Kevin. "What do you take us for?"

After shaking hands with the parents, Kevin holds his out for me to take. Man, he's a bruiser!

"Seriously...you're married to my sister."

"Kevin!" his mother scolds. He maintains a tight grip. Those intense blue eyes, like his dad's, only much narrower, look unconvinced. He's baiting me. I refuse to engage him.

Mr. O'Shea won't have it, and with an arm around my shoulder, leads me to the backyard. I glance back at Tess, catching her and her mom in what I gather is a rare embrace. Mrs. O'Shea is hugging the picture to her chest. We stroll onto the patio. *Wow! What a bash!* People quickly cram the area in front of us. The talking ceases. There are a lot of confused faces. Mr. O'Shea steps away. With his arm outstretched: "Everyone... please welcome Viktor Talking White Owl into our family."

There's murmuring, and then it becomes still again. At once a man blurts out: "You rascals! Making us believe he was from India! Priceless!"

Tess and I are greeted with cheers and laughter. The guests enjoy the fact they'd been had. Her parents can only be experiencing relief. The man who spoke up, their next door neighbor, is first to personally congratulate us. "It's beyond me how they managed to keep this a secret for months!"

Tess's mom sets our photo at the end of the buffet table opposite the side displaying her own wedding picture. Chevonne O'Shea was gorgeous; she still is. The groom was as solid looking back then as he is now.

His shoulders might be broader. It appears that Brian O'Shea never had much of a neck.

"I knew there had to be a picture!" The neighbor's wife admires it. "It must have killed you, Chevonne, to have kept it hidden from us." She hugs Chevonne. "Congratulations, Theresa. We wish you and Viktor nothing but happiness." Next she asks to see the ring, which draws the attention of some other ladies. Tess smiles at me as she proudly shows it off. Scores of questions follow: *Was he injured playing football? Is that how you met in the hospital?* I'm assuming they've heard my name or seen my face on the news—they can't all follow OSU football.

We're encouraged to make a plate of appetizers before mingling. Tables are set up on the lawn for a sit-down dinner later this evening. The entire time I've been completely aware of Kevin, because Tess is. At least others seem genuinely happy for us—they don't think our marriage is bogus. He stands sneering threatening-like at me from the bar, in a way that says, *I've got your number!*

It occurs to me during a conversation with three nuns, passionate about their fantasy football leagues, that it's been a while since I last spotted my "bride," which is what the guests keep calling her. We're constantly getting separated. Kevin has vacated his lookout post. I slip inside the house and follow voices that lead to a room off the hallway. The door is slightly open. Several trophy fish are mounted on the wall. I don't see anyone, but I recognize Mr. O'Shea's voice. He sounds angry. Another guy sounds angrier yet. Just when I realize it's Kevin, he flies out the room, shooting the wickedest look my way along with giving me the finger. Next he starts yelling for his wife. In hot pursuit is Mr. O'Shea, who had flung the door wide open. Tess is standing alone, her arms wrapped around herself.

"Is everything okay?" I'm unsure about approaching her.

"I can't believe what I witnessed," she says, taking my hands in hers. Instead of offering up some details, she studies my face, moving her hand to my hair to trace the beads running through the braid. It's a tender gesture. She appears composed, serene even.

"Wanna know something?" Her hand moves to my throat where she gently touches the hollow spot between the collar bones. "You spoke to me before I ever laid eyes on you, and I instantly fell in love with your deep voice."

I embrace her in my arms. "No kidding." I think back to her peering through the microscope before turning to me. "Are you trying to change the subject?" She looks at me thoughtfully. Something bumps my leg. I reach down.

"Hey, Finn...nice to finally meet you."

The ancient dog leans into me and lowers his head as his ears get scratched. He's big and shapeless. His snoot has gone completely white. When I stop showing him attention, he stands on my foot and noses my leg.

"Tess, I won't be sidetracked. Please tell me what happened."

We get down to Finn's level, taking a seat side-by-side on a big leather ottoman. I stroke the old dog's neck and upper chest. He collapses on our feet and continues groaning with contentment while Tess and I fuss over him as we talk.

"I found Finn dozing and came in to say hi when suddenly Kevin appeared from out of nowhere. He asked what kind of a stunt this was... our marriage. Then, waving his finger in my face, like he does with everyone, he claimed I was selfish for denying Dad the joy of walking his only daughter down the aisle." She shrugs. "He didn't let up, just kept rubbing it in—said he bet Mom never dreamed she'd be gypped out of planning my wedding, especially since she and Dad have gone to so many other people's."

"Aye-yi-yi."

"That's when Dad blew up. He was in the hall. I didn't let on that I saw him out there. To tell the truth, I was actually beginning to feel shitty about myself even though I know I couldn't survive a ceremony. Dad told Kevin he had no right putting words in his mouth, and next he ordered him to go home; he didn't want the day ruined."

"Un-hee." I place my arms around her. Finn doesn't mind the petting has stopped; he's snoring.

"There's more. Kevin took that to mean he was being put out to pasture, now that there's a new star football player in the family to brag about. Dad composed himself, told him again to go home, that he was drunk and needed to sleep it off. My father did admit he had thought about giving me away one day, but it was hardly a reason for getting married. He said he and Mom only wish for their children's happiness. At that, Kevin laughed and made some snide remark."

"That's too bad."

Tess's younger brother Ryan sticks his head in the room. "Dinner is served."

We carefully slide our feet free from under the dog. Out the window, clouds are streaked crimson from the setting sun. The backyard is no less magical. All the tree trunks are wrapped in tiny lights. The white tablecloths and simple orchid centerpieces look elegant. A back corner has been sectioned off for a decent-sized portable dance floor. Tess is embarrassed to find our seats are at the main table next to her parents. She feels this should be entirely their evening. I'm with them, her parents. Our marriage *is* a big to-do. I wish to celebrate my love for their daughter!

I excuse myself to run and grab my suit jacket from the car, having anticipated the need for one during our visits.

While racing back, my phone buzzes.

"Bad timing, Dad. I'm in a real hurry."

"OK, Son. I'll talk fast. I wanted you and Tess to consider flying to Texas instead of driving. It would give us more time together." Without thinking, I tell him, fine.

The anniversary toasts begin the second I take my seat. There are moving tributes as well as funny anecdotes. It's interesting for me, given I've only heard a one-sided, critical description of the O'Sheas. When they're done, Tess grips my hand, certain the speeches aren't over.

She's right. Her father stands to face us. He goes on to say that his daughter has always been her own person. He and his wife couldn't be prouder of her accomplishments. And although the news of the marriage came as a surprise to them, especially considering our ages, they respect our decision to have gotten married in a way that was meaningful to us. The guests raise their glasses. I seize the opportunity to kiss my bride. It's a long, sensual kiss that ignites enthusiastic applause and a few whistles. I lean back and regard Tess's beaming face. Mr. O'Shea, who now stands behind me, motions toward the dance floor. Just as Tess and I are about to head toward it, I reach for her Dad's hand and place it on hers. "Please. The first dance should be yours." I'm ignorant of protocol for an event like this, and I don't know if it could possibly make up for a father not giving his daughter away in church—but it seems like the right call.

They look grand. I'm unfamiliar with the song but the guests, men and women alike, are singing the words as they wipe their eyes. The pianist continues unaccompanied while the three violinists and saxophonist simply sway to the music. Again I trust my gut and proceed to escort Mrs. O'Shea onto the floor. She is as tall as Tess and follows my lead with ease. Occasionally she dabs the corners of her eyes with her fingers. "This is a blessed moment," she says.

"It is."

Mrs. O'Shea pats my cheek as the song ends and tells her daughter to request something. Tess promptly makes a beeline for the musicians. She returns to my arms, looking pleased with herself. The violin intro offers no clue. All eyes are on us, and then the saxophonist belts out a sustained note. I wait. The second and third notes follow quickly; ones everybody knows. I step forward on *wider than a mile,* the lyrics playing out in my head. It's a soulful *Moon River,* allowing for lots of hesitations which I love. Tess and I recently got hooked on Louis Armstrong's trumpet version of the song that we discovered in her landlady's record collection. After circling the floor, Tess gestures for the guests to join in. The evening progresses along nicely—thanks to Kevin's departure. I'm glad I like my in-laws. I can't help wondering what might have happened if we had opted for a traditional wedding, what with Tess's Irish side and my African-American and Native families. And where would we have held the ceremony? I love belting out gospel songs about Jesus at Trinity Church with Grandpa Cyrus and Grandma Junie, even if I don't believe he's the savior. Tess has completely severed ties with the Catholic Church. And there's no big ceremony in non-Christian Lakota and Rawakota communities. Husband and wife create their own union with the Great Spirit. Over time the families come to know each other.

By midnight a few stragglers remain, having been boxed in by the catering vans that are almost ready to leave. I've brought the car over and am waiting to park in the driveway. Tess was talked into spending the night at the house. Her parents were offended by the thought of us even considering a hotel, like I told her they would be. I look forward to sleeping with her in her old room.

I hand the O'Sheas the woven basket. They appear to appreciate the time and sentiment involved in the making of it. I place my arm around Tess who looks spent. I can't believe she lasted as long as she did. We say good night.

"Could you come in the living room?" says Mr. O'Shea, who asks that I use his and his wife's first names. "For just a few minutes. We're tired, too, and ready for bed."

We collapse on the couch. Brian and Chevonne sit across from us. She is sitting prim with ankles crossed and her hands folded neatly on her lap. Her strong jaw, which Tess didn't inherit, is set firm. I can't read her expression.

"I suppose this could've waited until tomorrow," says Brian. He scoots forward in the chair and rests his elbows on his knees. "We want to help you get off to a good start together." He reaches for an envelope on the table and hands it to me. I remove the card, a pretty one with a picture of a horseshoe for good luck and a Celtic blessing. Inside is a check written out for twenty thousand dollars. Tess gasps.

"It's too much! Please..." she begs, "... take a nice trip with it."

"Theresa, stop!" Her mom sounds stern but not mean. "It's what we would have spent on a wedding. Maybe you'd like to put it toward a down payment on a house."

Before Tess objects anymore, I kiss her quick and whisper, "It's a gift, given out of love." She's actually trembling. Tears are welling up in her eyes.

I stand to thank them. "It's extremely generous."

Tess holds her emotions in check as she comes over to hug her mom first, and then her dad. "It is generous, Mom. Thank you, Dad. I'm sorry ...but I really do need to sleep. I'm exhausted." And with that, she heads for the staircase. I follow, wanting permission to tell them about the pregnancy, which she grants without putting up a fuss.

"Should we announce the news together?"

"Viktor, I'm running on empty. I'm fine with you doing it. Really."

I'm so excited; I raise her off her feet. In the meantime, Brian has poured his wife a glass of wine and is about to settle back in his chair with his own glass of scotch, when he asks if I'd like a drink.

"Nothing, thanks." I return to the couch and sit. The house is quiet except for the clinking sound of ice cubes getting swirled in the glass. Her parents must be bummed over Tess's hasty exit. The obligatory hug they received from her was no doubt disappointing. "I realize Tess looked the picture of health today, but you need to know she's only started feeling better over the last couple of days. She's been sick for a while."

"She did discourage us from driving to Columbus, claiming she'd been under the weather." Chevonne can't mask her suspicion that it was simply an excuse to prevent them from visiting. They must realize how uninvolved they've been in their daughter's life over the years.

"It's true," I assure them. "It's because she's pregnant." And just so there's no wondering about the time frame, I tell them she conceived the week we got married. They're struck speechless, a reaction I hadn't anticipated. Now the room is dead-quiet.

I'm not saying another thing until they give me something to go on. It doesn't appear that's going to happen. I don't bother to excuse myself as I head for the hall, upset now for not waiting until morning.

"Viktor. Viktor, wait!" Brian comes at me with an extended hand and a broad smile, more like what I'd been hoping for. "Congratulations!" Chevonne slides between us and wraps her arms around me.

"Never in a million years would we have guessed this," she says, laughing and crying at the same time. "Brian…our Theresa is going to have a baby."

We're huddled together, happy. Better me here than Tess, although I wish she were.

"And you're okay with this?" asks Chevonne. "You're only nineteen. You both have your studies, and what about football?"

"Me, I'm ecstatic!" I'm not sure what to make of her comment about football. Does she think that becoming a father will somehow interfere with my playing? "Tess still gets overwhelmed when it comes to sorting out her thoughts."

"I bet," says her dad as he hugs me now. "What a day!"

CHAPTER 44

Finding long term parking at Cincinnati's airport turns out to be easy. There's no wait for the shuttle to the terminal. Getting the bags checked at the curb goes fast. We're good to go.

"Considering the storms across the Midwest, I'm glad to be flying instead of driving," says Tess. "This worked out for the best."

I wish I could agree. While scanning the departure monitor for our flight to Dallas, my breathing picks up along with my heart rate. For some reason, I'm more affected than usual by the idea of being in the air. Must be the weather. The closer it gets to boarding, the more lightheaded I feel, to the point of seeing spots.

"Viktor...your upper lip is sweating, and your hair is wet. Are you sick? How is your throat? Maybe you have a fever."

Her touch is like ice on my forehead. "I'm not sick," I insist. She presses her fingers alongside my throbbing carotid.

"My, god! Your heart's racing!"

I grab her wrist. "Stop, Tess; please don't make a scene."

"But you can't travel like this."

My head is swimming. She sounds distant. "Let's just get to our seats. If I pass out, I pass out."

I stare at the ground as we make our way through the tunnel. Thankfully our seats are up front. We aren't stuck standing in line. Tess immediately pushes my head between my knees to increase the circulation. It helps. I look for music that's calming—a Lakota song with slow drumming should do the trick. I lean back to relax. Tess looks relieved. She positions her head beside mine on the back of the seat and caresses my hand on her lap. When all passengers have boarded, she tugs on my earbud.

"You once mentioned in passing that you didn't like to fly. You neglected to admit you're absolutely petrified of it. How do you survive traveling to away games? Have you had a scary experience?"

"No. The one thing I've read that makes sense is that a person can't handle being stuck in a situation he has no control over. I feel responsible for you, more so with the baby... and there's nothing I can do up here if something were to happen."

"Nothing is going to happen," she says, kissing me softly. "Try to sleep."

"To think we could've been stuck in Dallas overnight." I stifle a yawn.

"Tell me about it!" says Dad as he places a loaded plate of stacked pancakes, fried eggs, and sausages in front of me. Tess beat me downstairs and is already well into her breakfast. "You both lucked out on not having your connecting flight to here diverted. That fog rolled in unexpectedly."

"I believe we were luckier to have survived the drive home, Dad."

"Amen to that!" he laughs, planting a kiss on Tess's head before sitting. "It was darn near impossible to see the dividing line."

"What about the hood of the truck?" says Tess. "Phew! Vaporized! It was like being inside a cloud that went on forever."

Dad informs Tess that the two hours it took to get to the house normally takes only thirty minutes. "Still, it beat driving here from Ohio."

"So when do I receive this present that I *had* to come to Texas for?"

Dad is in a playful mood. He doesn't say a word. Tess giggles.

"Are you in on this?" I ask her.

"Don't be silly! I never met your dad before last night. I love the mystery of it."

Dad's phone goes off. He's doing all the listening.

"Gotta go...lots of fender-benders to fix. After you shower, come over to the shop."

"But what about my present?"

He downs a final swig of coffee. "See you in a few."

"Geesh." I turn to Tess. "I want my present."

"Such a whiner."

"What if it's a car? God, I hope not."

"Why?"

"Every so often a muscle car would show up in the garage. One in particular was my favorite, a beefed-up 1970 Olds 442 that I swore I would own someday. Given my current life, though, I really wouldn't want one. What if it is, Tess? Maybe that's the reason he didn't want us to drive."

"You'd accept it; after all, it's a gift, given out of love, like the twenty thousand my parents gave us."

"Touché." I set myself up for that one.

The noon sun is breaking through the haze, making for a typical muggy Texas afternoon. It doesn't prevent Tess and me from walking the twenty minutes to the shop. For some reason, she had pictured a quaint car repair shop with a folksy name like "Sol's." Davis Automotive is a well-lit, spacious, modern structure that Dad has added onto over the years. After saying "Hi" to the guys and introducing them to Tess, we wait for Dad to finish his business. We wander to a picnic table out back that's shaded by a mighty oak. It isn't exactly picturesque, unless you're a mechanic, but it's no junkyard either. Things like ladders and hoses and compressors have their designated spots. It's tidy.

"Why all the cats?"

"Cats?" I see one curled in a ball between some discarded tires. Tess points out six more that are snoozing in the shadows.

"No idea."

"Hey!" yells Dad from the doorway, gesturing for us to come in.

We follow him to the back room where I used to play after school. My jaw drops. "Un-hee!" The dingy room that I loved, my own magical cave, is shockingly bright and filled with real pieces of furniture. It's amazing. And sad.

"Are you disappointed?" he asks.

"You bet!"

"I think it's lovely," says Tess.

"Don't get me wrong, it looks great…just *so-o-o* different!" I tell her that instead of a queen mattress and wall-mounted Smart TV, there was a rickety metal cot against the wall and a boxy TV balanced on a small nightstand. The badly stained industrial-sized tub used for scrubbing the dog has been replaced by a spiffy new counter with a microwave and toaster oven. Smooth laminated woodgrain planks cover a concrete floor that had made the best sound for racing Matchbox cars.

I open the door to the broom closet. "Wow." It's been expanded to include a toilet and a large shower stall that could easily accommodate someone my size. Even though it makes absolutely no sense, a strange thought occurs to me, and I have to ask, "Is this my birthday surprise?"

"In a way," he grins.

"Why so cagey?"

Dad sits at a little round kitchen table in the corner and pushes a chair out for me. I go over, squeezing past Tess who is admiring an Indian blanket she unfolded.

"Close your eyes," he says.

"Oh, c'mon."

"Do you want your surprise or not?"

"Oy, gevalt! This had better be good."

"No peeking."

"I'm not gonna peek! Can we *pu-le-e-e-ez* get on with it!" There's the shuffling of shoes. Guess it needs to be carried in. Then it's still. A hand touches my arm. "Now?" I ask.

"Mm-hmm."

With that, my heart stops.

"Hey, little brother." It's a voice I never thought I'd hear again.

"Billie," I mouth silently, conjuring up the last picture I have of him in a police car.

It was a fun-filled outing for Solomon and Tess, who spent the afternoon getting better acquainted. They waited for Billie to take a seat at the table before sneaking out of the auto shop to leave the good buddies alone. In order to plan Viktor's surprise, Solomon had spoken briefly to his daughter-in-law on the phone, but today they had a chance to really talk… and buy the baby its very first outfit, a personalized onesie they custom-designed together at a specialty store. They picked out images of feathers and musical notes and shamrocks to cover it in, along with the phrase stenciled in red, black, and green: *KISS ME, I'm Native Afro Irish*.

They arrive back at the house to the sound of wild laughter in the living room. For Solomon, it's especially heartwarming to see his son enjoying himself with a childhood friend. "Hey, boys! Have you been going at it like this the entire time?"

I jump at the sight of them and run to thank Dad. "Yeah, but only after a gut-wrenching cry that damn near did me in! And *you*, Tess! Staying tight-lipped about this for weeks!" Hugging her close, I whisper, "This was just the best...the absolute best."

Billie stands ready to be introduced. "I can't believe Viktor has a wife and a baby on the way." He turns to me, "You're a lucky man." Getting his approval still matters to me.

Dad taps Billie's arm, suggesting enough already with the long handshake. "Wait till you see what Tess and I bought."

Tess smooths out something on the bed then moves to the side for us to see.

"Damn!" laughs Billie. I can only scratch my head in wonderment. It's so teeny-tiny.

"We've covered a lot of territory these past couple of days," says Billie. It's true—from him being a snitch while he was doing time, which led to the location of gang hideouts, to his father deciding one day to just up and leave his mom and brothers and sisters. He was embarrassed to tell anyone. The timing of it explained why he started hanging with guys who didn't know him or his circumstances.

It's evening. We're eating Chinese take-out at *Billie's* table in what is now *Billie's* room behind the garage, which I learned he redid all by himself, down to the last nail. Dad has been on the phone in his office too long. He was supposed to join us. Tess is back at the house resting in preparation for the slew of relatives she'll be meeting in Kansas City tomorrow. They've warned us they're ready to party big time. Besides celebrating our marriage and the upcoming baby, in a few days it's the Fourth of July, the one holiday that brings together all the extended families for a big outdoor barbeque.

"There's something on my mind, Viktor, but I don't know how it's going to come off sounding." I didn't think there could possibly be a subject left for us to talk about.

"Shoot." I sound like Dad.

"Right." He sets his fork down. "The tutor who came to the jail to help us study for our GEDs gave me a book to read about the Apache Indian doctor, Carlos Montezuma. When I read on the cover that he had supported the colonists' policy of sending Indian kids to boarding schools, I told her I'd pass, especially when I saw it was five hundred pages long."

"Un-hee! There's that much on him?"

"Fuck, yeah. She said it was important to be open-minded, and that people aren't one-dimensional. I should walk in his shoes and try to understand his perspective."

"Smart lady. And you actually did it?"

He presses his lips together and looks with amusement. "Only because I had a crush on her and wanted to impress her."

"Ah! In your case, killing a dragon might have been easier."

He agrees. "Anyway, turns out his story hooked me. I read a few pages every day, slowly working my through it. I finally quit checking how much was left to go. I discussed it with Miss Littlesky every week."

"While you were falling in love?"

He shrugs, then smiles. I won't ask him, but I'm wondering if his weight loss has to do with his feelings for her. He's still big and square, but his belly fat is gone, which until now I assumed was from eating prison food. Tess called him handsome. Now that he is in his twenties, he obviously looks more like a man. Having no facial hair myself, I'm jealous of his five o'clock shadow. I stop eating to give him my full attention.

"Viktor...there was a moment halfway through reading the book when I had a revelation, and it involved you, our people, and our future as a Nation. And for the first time in ages I felt hope."

I realize this was a transformative event in his life—nothing to be taken lightly. I nod, not to show I understand, but to acknowledge the significance of what happened to him.

"Montezuma aimed to represent the Indian in the best way. He was a virtuous man who loved where learning took him. After becoming a doctor, do you know he tried to abolish the Office of Indian Affairs because its members were corrupt? He began to understand how nearly every aspect of reservation life was in fact controlled by federal agencies, and that it was destroying tribal cultures. Miss Littlesky called him *high-minded*, and I immediately thought of you. I said to myself, that's Viktor."

Wow! This coming from the guy I thought the world of when we were growing up.

"The best part of Carlos Montezuma's story is that later in life he returned to his reservation in Arizona where he fought for the rights of his people until his death. He didn't care to go on being an example of what an educated Native American could accomplish in the white man's world."

There is no mistaking the message. Its implications are profound. Billie isn't only referring to me, and the successes I've been having, and will continue to enjoy outside the reservation, but he's including all Natives who leave the rez to fulfill their personal dreams. Next he asks, "Why choose to live under a government that historically can't be trusted, one that did its best to eradicate all tribes?" We look at each other with new eyes, one Native man to another.

Right then Dad enters and plops down on the chair. "Sorry so late. Save me some?"

Billie scrapes the cartons clean as he tries to fill a plate. "Here Coach." I pick at my remaining noodles just to keep Dad company.

"You fellas are awfully quiet. All talked out finally?"

"Nah," says Billie, "never. Just taking a break."

Dad says I should have heard their conversations when Billie first arrived. "Everything was *dope*, and every person, *dude*. We broke that habit fast, didn't we!"

Apparently Billie was ordered to drop and give him twenty whenever he said them, which now explains how he got buff.

Dad sighs. He lets go his fork and sits hunched over his plate. "I was on the phone with a doctor in Germany. He's concerned Mom has developed PTSD. That African raid she took part in was so horrible, it could trigger flashbacks for a long time."

"She seemed fine when I talked to her last week."

"It can strike out of the blue...a sound...bright lights. At any rate, I'll meet her up at Minot after our stop in Kansas City. She'll be seen there by another doctor before we travel down to the rez."

Billie and I say our goodbyes. Dad has a lot on his mind and heads home with me. These next couple of days with his family should do him good. I'm not looking forward to another plane ride in the morning, but it'll be short, and Dad and I can play cards to pass the time.

I didn't expect to find Tess awake. She's propped against the headboard of my old bed, busy on her tablet. Her hair is pinned up and slightly messy. She looks sexy.

"Hey, husband."

"Hey, wife. Whatcha reading?"

"I was curious about the Cheyenne River Reservation. This is fascinating stuff. There used to be so many different tribes in the region. Who knew? We never covered any of this at school. Billie's girlfriend lives there."

"Girlfriend?"

She makes a tsking noise. "Alicia, *his tutor.*"

"Oh." The clothes come off and I roll close beside her.

"Alicia is descended from Spotted Elk, Chief Sitting Bull's half-brother. He tried to lead people off the reservation in the late 1800s and was killed in the Wounded Knee Massacre."

"I know, Tess. We *do* learn our own history."

"I'm sorry. It's just that it's new to me. I think Alicia's efforts to educate Indians who are locked up is commendable. Did Billie tell you he and Alicia are seeking ways to recover Native territories?"

I smile over her enthusiasm, but would argue that my friend's cause is a lost one, and then my eyes fall shut. The air conditioner sputters to a stop. Tess starts a trail of gentle kisses beginning at my forehead. Her silky-smooth fingers stroke my shaft, automatically setting my hips in motion. Her teeth graze a nipple, and a shiver runs through me. She switches to a firm grip. When I think it can't possibly feel any better, the wet touch of her tongue and lips on my tip spurs me to get inside her, to finish the *right way;* but it's too late. I'm glad afterward. I don't want to be a yay-yoh—no, not a yay-yoh, the word the Rawakota used to describe the early white settlers and their ridiculous notions about sin.

Compared to the O'Sheas' big anniversary shindig and the Davises' loud and animated July Fourth gathering, my family's home on the reservation might end up boring Tess, who wondered if she was going to see a pow-wow. There aren't any until August. For me, I can't stop wondering what Mom will be like after receiving a diagnosis of PTSD. Grandmother, Iris, and Hashke met us at the Rapid City Airport as soon as we arrived, that was a few days ago, which is when Dad boarded a short flight to continue on to the Minot International Airport in North Dakota. He went to pick up Mom at the Air Force base that's just outside the city. Normally, she would come down on her own, but due to her current mental state, she isn't permitted to travel by herself. I haven't felt her arms around me in nearly a decade; and now, simply because I found Tess, Rawakota rules permit her to embrace me again. What if it proves too emotional for her, and the underlying stressors we've been warned about surface and she goes off the deep end? Who's to say I won't?

"Viktor! Wake up from dreamland." Grandmother pinches my arm.

She and Tess and Winnie are chuckling over something, and then I realize it's me, me and my dancing leg. I'm a bundle of nerves. The car is in sight. I run to the road. There's Dad, but where's Mom? *"What the...?"* He barely gets the door open when I corner him.

"Relax, Son. I dropped her off at Sunkwah and Winnie's to freshen up and regroup."

Fast as a relay hand-off, I grab the key and jump behind the wheel of his rental. I'm squished in tight. No time to adjust the seat. It takes but a few minutes to get to their house. They can't do this to me!

She isn't in the kitchen, nor the guest room. The bathroom is empty. I don't want to yell for her. I punch the back screen door open and find her there on the porch, looking over her shoulder at me. She had to have heard the car drive up, and me walking through the house.

"What if I was a burglar!" I sound angry, which is the last thing in the world I want to sound like. "I forgot, you can take on anyone." Darn! That came off as sarcastic instead of funny.

"I recognize your scent." Mom holds out her hands, and at long last we touch. There's no describing this moment. She appears as strong as ever, something I wasn't expecting after her recent ordeal in Africa and hospitalization in Germany. The pale blue t-shirt shows off her muscled arms. The color makes her skin look darker. Her hair is loose. I better hold my tongue, to prevent anything else I might say from being misinterpreted.

"How fortunate for me that I am able to behold my son as a man. Wakan Tanka deserves all the credit for this reunion." Her voice is raspy. She smiles and kisses my cheek, next, the corner of my mouth. I, too, thank Wakan Tanka; but I do it quietly to myself. I'm so very grateful she didn't die before today. Her hands press into my arms, as if testing to ensure I'm not an illusion. We both recognize there are issues that need to be addressed before our relationship can move forward. As she looks at me, it seems she is scrolling through every confusing thought in my head that remotely relates to her.

When I agree to a cup of tea, she asks outright if adhering to the

Rawakota law of theeich ihilah has been worth it. There's a topic I could go on about, which she must gather because of how long it's taking to answer. I didn't know it was a law. I think of Tess, of the trust I place in her. "Yes."

"Good," she nods. "Then I have to make my peace with Sunkwah."

Hashke is destroying me in this online game of cut-throat pirates. Iris teases: "Aren't you worried about what Mom is telling Tess about you?"

"Nooo. I'm an open book. I just hope Tess is having a pleasant time. Even though she likes riding, they've been gone almost three hours—that's too long on a horse when you're not used to it. Plus, she's pregnant." Once Tess's parents knew, we felt we had to tell the rest of my family.

"Relax. They're likely sprawled under a tree eating berries and coming up with baby names—*Daddy*."

Iris smiles sweetly at me. Changing the subject, Sister asks what Tess and I thought about taking the mandatory drug detection test at the border. "Offended," I reply, speaking for myself and not Tess. "Seems everyone thinks it's a great idea except me."

"Then give us your solution to ridding the rez of drunks and addicts," she says, sounding miffed by my honesty. "Rehab programs haven't worked. Did you at least read about the accuracy of the latest chip technology used in the drug and alcohol detection devices?"

"Yes, it's remarkable how molecules of different drugs can be extracted from one's breath; however, my concern deals with the violation of one's civil rights. That, and there are any number of ways to cross over the border besides the eight main roads. How can every inch of forests and mountains be patrolled? And don't tell me satellites. It takes an army of top-flight engineers to build them and monitor them. Indians don't have resources like that."

"You met our cousin from Chohkahn during your hanbleceya. You said he described their modern technology. I'm beginning to think that Mom has played a crucial role in obtaining information for them. Don't forget she knew about the experiments going on with my students."

"Iris, you honestly believe that the top ranks of the most secret military intelligence in the world can be outmatched by a group of people who live underground, whose very existence requires a leap of faith? Sometimes I think I hallucinated Suhdeer."

"Well you *didn't!*"

Sunkwah has been listening to us. I ask for his thoughts.

"Go to Chohkahn, Viktor. See for yourself. You, too, Iris. Meet your family. Viktor's cousin told him that Lukas's parents still live. I am sure they follow your journeys."

"Why do you say that?" I ask, trying to picture them.

"Because *I would.*"

I ask Sister if she ever wonders about Lukas's relatives.

"Not really. I guess it makes sense his elders would be curious about their grandchildren and how they turned out. Lukas would be in his late fifties by now. His parents might be close to Sunkwah and Winnie's age." We contemplate that extraordinary fact. Great-Grandfather's idea of meeting them maybe isn't so farfetched.

Suddenly Tess bursts through the door and comes racing at me with outstretched arms from across the room. I spin her around. "Un-hee!" she yells with delight. "That was the fastest horse I've been on in my life! We tore across the rez!" She's so frickin happy! I wish we were in a bed, alone. That's a helluva lot of energy!

Mom has parked herself in the kitchen where Grandmother is busy cooking and baking for tonight's feast. The smells fill the house, and the conversation turns to food.

During dinner, I express how this trip exceeded all expectations. I'm comfortable with Tess's family, and she's at home here with us on the rez. She fit in with the relatives she met on Dad's side. While taking a breather before dessert, I pass around my phone so everyone can have a good laugh over the video I shot of my cousins in Kansas City. Tess attempted to teach them Irish clogging. If that wasn't funny enough, they mixed it up with hip hop and traditional Lakota dance steps that I've shown them over the years.

Stuffed to the gills, Grandmother shoos us youngsters into the living room to enjoy our final evening together. Tess insists on helping with the clean-up. She has been wanting to get to know Grandmother better. Sunkwah and Winnie have earned the honor of staying put at the table while the plates get cleared. It's sweet how they sit side-by-side in constant contact. These days they walk as a single unit, too. I think it's for balance, though. Mom stays to chat with them.

Hashke comes across a silly old black and white horror movie on TV. The monster is a walking, scowling tree stump with angry white cartoon eyes. It's inhabited by the soul of an innocent man who had been wrongfully executed. Naturally, the creature won't rest until the guilty have paid. Right now he's carrying a screaming woman to a patch of quicksand where he promptly lets go of her. She must have done him wrong when he was alive. She screams and screams for help as her breasts sink below the sand, then her shoulders, then chin, then... *"Hey!"* we shout, as the sound drops out. Dad's got the remote in his hand. He isn't looking at us, or the TV for that matter, but at Mom, who we then notice is standing just inside the living room, motionless. Something off to her side on the floor has caught her eye. When Iris starts to speak, Dad shushes her and raises a finger to his lips to include the rest of us.

Mom walks to a spot and looks around the floor, and then mimes picking up imaginary things from the ground. When her arms are full, she returns to the original spot and carefully sets them down. Sister grabs my hand and holds tight. Sunkwah is in the doorway, having followed his granddaughter out. Her odd behavior likely started during the screaming scene. She is presently kneeling over her invisible pile of stuff. Her focus shifts to an area ten feet away. In French, she says, *"You are strong. You will make it."*

Sunkwah points to a wooden chair and motions for me to get it so he can sit by her. Speaking Lakota, he asks what she is doing. Surprisingly, she answers. She explains that the soldier, Army Specialist Arthur Lindenhoffer—from Iowa, wanted his feet and legs back, they were out of his reach. His parents, farmers, begged him not to go in the service, called him stupid for enlisting. He wanted to show them they were wrong. He hoped to make them proud. Now he's sorry. *"He's so very sorry,"* says Mom, *"over and over he tells his momma he's sorry."*

"And who lays over there?" asks Sunkwah, continuing in Lakota. *"Another warrior?"*

"In her own way."

At least Mom's talking to someone real. Sunkwah has her attention. He strokes her hair and continues to speak softly to her:

"Like my father Kicking Horse, and his father Charging Bear, and his

father the great leader Mahkohchay, the blood of proud Rawakota warriors runs through our Howling Wind's veins. Your own father, Benjamin One Horn, came from a long line of strong warriors. During their times, there were stories about a madness that took hold of men returning from battle, and how they would wander lost. Our spiritual leaders held special ceremonies for them. They sang songs and said prayers to kill the evil spirits that had poisoned the mind. You will be whole again, Constance. Look at me."

Iris and I are rattled by the dramatic turn of events, as are Hashke and Dad, I'm sure. Sunkwah hasn't asserted his authority like this in ages. Mom maintains a faraway look. He vows no one in his family will ever succumb to anything caused by Wasichu. Next, if I didn't see it, I'd never believe it. Sunkwah taps out a code on the beads of his leather bracelet and starts a dialogue in Rawakota with another man. His wristband acts as a speaker phone. It's like one worn by cousin Suhdeer. Their conversation is short, maybe a minute.

Sunkwah tells us that the leader himself from Chohkahn will organize a gathering of warriors who can heal what ails Mom. He promises us that she will find her center again.

Seems a tall order. "Should we be there, too?" I ask, meaning the entire family.

"That won't be necessary."

'But..."

At that moment, Dad goes to raise her from the floor. Mom folds herself up in his arms. It's scary to see her so vulnerable. We leave them alone.

CHAPTER 45

We're at the doctor's office. As soon as we returned to Columbus, Tess made an appointment with an ob-gyn for the end of July, and then never brought it up again. She has been coming over to my place to sleep because the bed is bigger, but then she goes back to her house in the morning to shower and dress. An odd arrangement for newlyweds, to be sure, but we're fine with it until we locate a bigger apartment. Uncle William put forward the idea of him buying a house as an investment, and having us live there. How lucky for us if he does that.

Tess just got out of her clothes and changed into a silly-looking powder blue paper gown that tents up around her waist when she goes to sit on the exam table. We laugh. It takes the edge off our nerves. Reality is setting in. I wheel a chair over. We hold hands and wait, fortunately not too long. There's a perfunctory knock at the door. The doctor enters, hand extended. "Good afternoon. I'm Dr. Flanagan."

I reciprocate, half-standing.

"Hello," says Tess, figuring he knows her name from her chart.

He's pleasant looking. Average build. Medium brown hair and eyes, a well-groomed moustache. I'm guessing early forties. I wonder if he tires of introductions. The bulletin board behind him is thick with photos of newborns, the most recent having been carefully tacked on top of the older ones, so as not to cover their teeny faces and upset the parents. Some babies look really scrawny, but there are a few pudgy ones. Their hats and bows are cute. Dr. Flanagan takes a seat behind a cart with a laptop and skims over Tess's vitals.

"Blood pressure's great. No nausea, dizziness. Taking vitamins with folic acid." He rolls to the exam table. With elbows on knees and hands folded, he smiles at us: "Congratulations!"

"Thanks." I alone answer. Tess tightens her grip on my fingers.

"Any concerns before we get started?"

Tess and I look at each other. She so wants to be out of here. I try to gauge if she's okay with the male doctor. Two other females make up the practice. Dr. Flanagan was recommended by one of Tess's former co-workers, the only pregnant woman she had come across while at school. Tess said that gender was never a concern. She'd have felt comfortable going to Uncle William if he were still in the business.

She is told to lie down. An assistant comes in, a woman with a friendly face and short spiked fuchsia hair. She's wearing neon lime-green scrubs you could spot a mile away. Measurements are taken of the abdomen. There's a noticeable bulge, which I presume is normal at four months. While the doctor checks her thyroid and breasts, he informs us about the ultrasound, which will happen in another room down the hall. He is going to perform this one, but the next one will be done by a sonographer. Tess doesn't flinch during the internal exam. I kiss her hand. She is told she can put her clothes back on.

We walk the short distance and find the neon lady waiting. Again Tess lies on a table, belly exposed. Gel is applied to her skin. Dr. Flanagan arrives and goes to work, gently moving the transducer around as we all watch the computer screen. It's such a grainy image. Tess and I can see there's movement, but the picture is so distorted it's impossible to identify the form of our baby. We listen closely to the swishing sounds, straining to hear the heartbeat. And then it's clear. Our eyes light up.

"Is that normal," asks Tess, "for it to be galloping so fast?"

"The beats are overlapping, not fast," says Dr. Flanagan.

Tess pushes herself on her elbows. "A heart defect?"

"No, no, no, nothing like that." He gently touches her shoulder to get her to lie back down, and then glides the transducer around some more. We still can't make heads or tails of the body, and his silence isn't appreciated.

"Sorry," he says finally. "The anatomy isn't always easy to decipher. I'm curious; do twins happen to run in either of your families?"

It's spoken so casually, like...you think it's going to rain today? He freezes the image and points to the screen, to the two fetuses and their profiles. They're facing each other from opposite sides of the womb. We're dumbstruck.

"You'll be able to follow the video better now," and he clicks on the key to continue. The left baby bounces up. Dr. Flanagan turns to us and smiles. "He just hiccupped." I can't help but laugh a little. Tess strokes my cheek and forces a smile. "I'll play it again," he says, pausing halfway through the bounce.

It gives us extra time to study our blurred little treasures. The doctor asks us if we notice something. We stare at him questioningly.

"Brace yourselves," he says. "Spot the third head that was hidden behind the one that bopped up?"

I mutter the f-word under my breath—out of disbelief. Tess's hand goes limp in mine. Her eyes search the ceiling, and then they close. I catch a big tear headed for her ear. I kiss her forehead, worried over her state of mind. I continue to stroke her hair while the doctor says he suspected multiple births based on the size of Tess's abdomen. "Sometimes women are farther along than they think they are and therefore the belly is bigger, but we knew the exact date Tess conceived, which made me think there was more than one fetus."

Dr. Flanagan wipes the gel from her belly, and then leaves to give us a few minutes.

"Tess, look at me. *Please,* look at me."

She does, briefly. I kiss her softly over and over, her neck, her shoulders. We move to the chairs by the window where she pulls her hair back in a ponytail. A box of tissues is within reach. She grabs a handful and holds them over her face as she quietly sobs. Dr. Flanagan reappears. He admits it's a lot to process. We schedule the next appointment at the desk and receive an order for a routine blood test, which is handed to me because Tess has already exited the office. I run to catch up. Once in the car, she falls apart, gasping for air as she cries uncontrollably. Sitting huddled against the window, it's evident she wants no part of me, or, to be more exact, anyone.

She scares me when I pull up to the curb of her place, and she flies out of the car before the engine is off.

Inside, Tess's phone rings. It's in the side pocket of her purse. I answer.

"Viktor?" Her mother's confusion is understandable. "I thought I would have heard from Theresa by now. I marked the date of her appointment on the calendar. Nothing's wrong is there? Why did you answer her phone?" She managed all this in the same breath.

"She's resting, Chevonne. I saw it was you and know you're anxious to hear how things went." I quickly head to the front stoop, out of earshot.

"And?" she asks, probably ready to jump out of her skin with worry.

"We're having triplets!" There's a gasp and squeal. The news is passed along to Brian, who lets out a hearty Santa-like Ho-Ho-Ho in the background. I send her the ultrasound pics and video, which I also do for my family. She asks how her daughter is doing, knowing full well it can't be good.

Next she says, "Theresa once confided to me that she didn't think she would ever be able to wrap her head around the idea of having a baby, and now she's going to have three!"

I'm honest with Chevonne, to a degree. "I can't relate at all to what Tess will be stuck dealing with the next months, both psychologically and physically. Dr. Flanigan promised us that he and his staff are there for us." My own phone starts ringing. It's Dad. I excuse myself, but not before reassuring Chevonne that I'll keep her posted about Tess.

With Dad I can be totally upfront about Tess's reaction since she isn't his daughter.

"That's rough," he says. "I don't know what to tell you, Son. Just give her some space for a while." Hearing his voice makes me feel better.

"I intend to, but define a *while*." I ask to speak with Mom, but she is out for a walk with Winnie. Dad remained on the rez until her "therapy sessions" ended; that's what he referred to them as. I ask if he knows what the Rawakota warriors did for Mom exactly, the people who Sunkwah said would be helping her. From what Mom told him, she was encouraged to relive the haunting event that took place in Africa over and over again, in great detail, until the emotions stemming from the trauma no longer overwhelmed her. He feels it's likely too early to conclude anything. Her R&R has ended, however, and they need to get back to Texas tomorrow so she can start training pilots at Sheppard. He says she sounds up for it, but not the ceremony that was planned to award her a combat medal for her participation in the ground operation in Mali. He states it is quite the honor. In the meantime, I ask if he would tell everyone I'll talk to them soon. I'm due at the athletic center shortly for a meeting.

I check in on Tess before leaving and find her lying on the edge of her bed, facing away from me. I so want to hold and comfort her. The sobbing has ceased, thank God. I get that this is a nightmare for her. She had finally begun to accept the reality of being pregnant, when this happened. Carrying three babies must be way different than having a single one inside you. I can't begin to imagine what raising three kids at one time will be like for us. I stroke her hair, and then write a short note to stick on the bathroom mirror. Time to switch gears and focus on football—like that's possible.

It takes a second for Tess to realize it's night when she opens her eyes. White horizontal stripes cover the wall. As usual the neighbor's back porch light is streaming between the slats of the Venetian blinds. It's bright enough for her to find her way to the bathroom. Still groggy, she teeters on the toilet seat and nearly falls off. With that, she reaches for the pull chain on the wall sconce mounted beside the mirror. The note is at eye level. She splashes cold water on her face before reading it. Viktor let her know that he'd be going back to his apartment tonight after practice, but he'd come over in a flash, if she wanted him to. That, and he loves her.

Back in the bedroom, after turning on a lamp and closing the blinds, Tess goes to sit on the stool in front of the small mirrored dresser. She feels emotionally disconnected from the girl looking back at her, the one harboring three humans inside her. Staring at herself gets her nowhere. Without any thought to the hour, Tess decides to call her mother. Her mom clears her throat, having been woken up, and then immediately offers her daughter a rather subdued congratulations.

Tess doesn't hesitate, but right away asks her mother if she would do her a favor. "Mom, if you could speak your mind without worrying about my reaction, what would you tell me?"

"I can't do that, Theresa. You've always been flip with us when it comes to any advice your dad and I have tried to give you."

"I promise; I'll hear you out. Please. I know you've discussed my situation. If I were a fly on the wall..."

"You're not going to like it."

"Please, Mom," she begs.

Without further coaxing, Chevonne says: "You mapped out this future for yourself in high school and did an amazing job of sticking to your plan. I assumed nothing would stand in your way. After telling us you got married, I thought, okay; that shouldn't keep you from getting your degree. I figured the boy must be really special—you wouldn't take such a serious commitment lightly. It's easy to see how Viktor swept you off your feet. He's a true gentleman, and he loves you with all his heart. You have no idea how gratifying that is to a mother.

"That being said, Theresa, the pregnancy floored us. Not that we aren't thrilled about it. I wondered how you of all people could have allowed this to happen. Unfortunately, lapses in judgement are the downside to loving someone. I worry because a baby *does* interfere with goals, especially the kind of ambitious ones you've always had. It is likely a concern of Viktor's as well. The fact there will be thr..." She stops short of finishing the sentence.

Hearing her mother's voice has an undeniable calming and grounding effect.

"It's funny," says Tess, "getting through school isn't what's on my mind. Knowing there was one life growing inside me freaked me out...but three! It's the stuff of science fiction. I can't process it intellectually. If I'm not handling it well now, how will I deal when I'm huge? I'm going to be *huge*, Mom."

"You approach it like you did your swimming: one race at a time. That experience taught you great discipline. You live in the moment, and you don't overthink things. Do stuff with Viktor. Have fun right now."

"You're right."

When had Chevonne last heard that! She doesn't want to blow this moment, but there's something else she feels compelled to say, because she sincerely believes it.

"When you were old enough to understand that I'd had a couple of miscarriages, and I explained that sometimes God's plan includes trials which help us grow spiritually, you became so upset, insisting that people rationalize what they can't make sense of. Theresa...your babies are meant to be. Interpret that however you like. I'm finished now...except to add that Viktor is ecstatic about becoming a father. How terrific is that!"

Tess quietly replies, "Pretty terrific."

On that note, mother and daughter say goodnight. Tess wishes that she could hear Viktor's voice. It's late now. In his last text at ten, he said he was beat and going to bed—unhappy to be doing so alone. She looks back over her behavior. How hurt he must have been by the way she ran out of the doctor's office. She completely dismissed his emotions. He also mentioned in the text that his Uncle found a house for them to go look at. Too bad the address wasn't included. She's wide awake and would have gone to check it out even at this hour.

Balancing a cup of tea and a scone in her hands, she curls up in the corner of the couch, then rereads Viktor's hourly *I love you* messages that he had sent earlier throughout the day. He would definitely appreciate knowing that she is currently in a better frame of mind but, alas, he is sleeping right now. She contemplates researching multiple births. No, that's best left for another day. The thought of live things moving around inside her makes her shudder with fear, to the point of almost spilling the tea on herself. With months of mobility left, she should keep thoughts of the growing fetuses at bay. Once this is over, she'll never have to endure another pregnancy. How did her mother go through the experience so many times? And what about Viktor's mom, giving birth at fourteen, and again at nineteen, her own age in a couple of months? *Jesus!*

Tess reflects on the absurdly different cultures Viktor grew up in: there's the Native Indian, the African-American and Jewish, and now he'll be contending with the Irish-Catholic whites on her side. She adores her new in-laws and their families. What an adventure the trip this summer had been. The openness of the Plains was magnificent. It will be her happy, go-to place for surviving the pregnancy.

Before she knows it, she is at Viktor's door letting herself in. She just managed to beat the rain, a sprinkle so far, but they're fat drops that strike the cars below with a splat. Viktor's bedroom window is wide open. She lowers it some and finds a towel to keep the sill dry, just in case it rains harder. A speck of moon briefly appears behind the fast-traveling clouds. She takes in the heady smell of the air and the freshly mown grass. Barely any light reaches the room from the streetlamps that line the perimeter of the parking lot. Viktor's naked body, half covered by the sheet, tempts her. Is it possible they were fated to meet and have these babies, as her mother believes?

She doesn't bother removing her shorts or T-shirt before lying next to him. Her skin is as clammy as his. It still feels like ninety degrees out. He doesn't like sleeping with the air on, which she has gotten accustomed to. She rests her hand along his pubic bone. His penis comes to life. She leaves it alone and simply observes him sleeping. His breaths grow deeper, and his chest rises and falls harder. They're slow breaths, relaxed ones. His eyes are another story, darting wildly under closed lids. Is he dreaming of her?

A constant low grumble from deep inside him excites her. Her hand moves to his diaphragm where the vibrations are strongest. She slips out of her clothes and sits astride his lower chest. Within minutes she experiences an orgasm, along with the momentary stabbing headache that never fails to accompany it. She slides off his hip and rubs her forehead while Viktor's fantasies trigger a "nightly emission." Without waking, he grabs at the air and holds his breath when it happens. She wipes it up with a tissue and then slips off to sleep beside him.

The obnoxious beeping of a truck backing up interrupts an otherwise peaceful morning. *"Un-hee!"* It's too early for the damn garbage truck! I have no energy to close the window. God, what a racket! I glance at the time and roll to my stomach, with the hope of dozing off for another hour. The truck finally drives away. I start remembering the dream I had. I was in the mountains with cousin Suhdeer. He was demonstrating how to produce a deep growl that drives the wives crazy with desire, an important lesson I would have learned during Otiwota. I copied him, humming through my abdomen when, *"Whoa! What the...!"* I sit on my knees and check the sheets. Nothing. I know for certain I got off. Man, did I ever!

I'm definitely awake now, but confused. The sun should be up soon. It smells of rain. The birds are going crazy...must be lots of worms. Where did the towel come from that's in the window? And it's only cracked open now. I sniff the air and smell cinnamon. Did Uncle come over to make breakfast? I sprint to the kitchen.

"Leksi?"

There are dishes in the sink. The oven is on. "Uncle?" Maybe he went back across the hall for something.

The bathroom door opens and out strolls Tess. She must have showered; her hair is wrapped in a towel. She's in shorts and a tee shirt. As for myself, I'm standing there butt naked.

She smiles as she gives me the once-over. "Now that's the way to greet a girl!"

"Did you come over this morning?"

"Midnight."

We hug. She slaps my ass lightly.

"Did we have sex?"

"Yes."

I describe my dream. She describes what she did, confirming that the Rawakota know whereof they speak.

"And you really get a headache when you climax? That's terrible. Can it be prevented?"

"I blame my parents. They named me after the patron saint of headache sufferers."

"You're pulling my leg, Tess; there's no such thing."

"Sure there is! The Catholics have a saint for everything. St. Teresa of Avila. Go on, google it. Then there's the patron saint of dickheads."

"No there isn't."

"The Pope."

"Jesus, Tess!" I jump away.

She laughs. "Why'd you do that?"

"I don't want to be near you when the lightning strikes! Isn't that blasphemy?"

"Yeah, *right!* Like he's holy...giving reprieves to pedophile and rapist priests. She shakes her head. "Anyway, forget him. The French toast should be done in a minute."

"Mmm...yum. In the oven?"

"Thought I'd try it once after seeing your Grandma Junie do it."

For a second, as we look at each other, Tess can tell I want to bring up the subject of our babies, and I recognize she hopes I don't. The timer goes off. She is bummed when I hurry to throw on a shirt and pants, to which I tease, "I don't eat naked. Do you take me for a savage?"

"Actually, I do. How 'bout putting just the pants on?"

"Hmm...half-savage. Okay." The playful sparkle in her eyes raises my spirits. They're still puffy from yesterday's crying marathon. I yield to her request and sit at the table bare-chested. As I reach for the syrup, I tell her it's only fair if she were to do the same for me. She rests her fork on the plate and appears to be thinking about it. Next she pulls her shirt up over her head and casually lifts her breasts over the top of her bra. "You realize you're inviting trouble." Now there's a wicked smile if I ever saw one!

CHAPTER 46

Due to the locations of her Air Force assignments, Howling Wind hadn't attended a Council of First Nations' conference in years. Its leaders had convened this past winter as usual, but later called for this emergency meeting in the Canadian city of Brandon. They needed to discuss this past spring's extermination of the most violent and controlling gangs on North and South Dakota's reservations, as well as on the bordering Reserves in this Manitoba province. The late July date the Council chose happened to coincide with an airshow in Brandon. Howling Wind asked to join a group of training instructors from Sheppard Air Force Base who were heading up to fly vintage WWII aircraft in the show. It would be easy for her to slip away for a few days. She found a bush pilot named Captain Nick to take her to the Council's retreat, a no-frills community center used by the small populations in the surrounding towns. After two tours in Vietnam, Captain Nick, a member of the Canupawakpa Dakota First Nation, returned home severely depressed. He found new purpose serving the many outliers who didn't have easy access to supplies by delivering things to them in a plane. He routinely flies over the remote lake-dotted wilderness in his own Cessna and knew the building that Howling Wind wanted to go to. She was impressed with the 30,000 plus miles in the air he has logged so far.

The Council's tribal leaders gave Howling Wind a warm welcome when she walked through the door. She was pleased to see the addition of four female chiefs. Apparently the fallout from the mass execution of gang members affected tribes across the continent, even ones with no ties to the Plains Indians. The Lakota and Dakota Indians repeatedly denied any involvement in the murders, even though the majority of the attacks occurred on their lands. It begged the question: Who then were these vigilantes? Were they U.S. military or ex-military? It's true that crossbows, the assailants' weapon of choice, had become increasingly popular with the military because they're fast and quiet. Or maybe the avenging group was a throwback to the GOON squads of the early 1970s, private police forces funded by tribal governments. If that were the case, Council members would have gotten wind of who they were. One thing for sure, the killers were expert marksmen. Rumors were spreading of them striking again, which is going to be explored today. The uncertainty is creating fear on other reservations that are similarly torn apart by gang violence. Word is out that snitches contributed to the massacre. As a result, families are beginning to eye one another with suspicion. Such mistrust will be their undoing.

There are the few tribal leaders who share a surprisingly different concern. Their people have historically maintained successful joint ventures with outside companies, and they worry that if the killings continue, it could fracture their solid, long-standing relationships with them. These are Nations that have gained clear title to their lands, which means they can manage their own governments and resources. That's a pipe dream for most Indians who aren't allowed to buy the land they live on. Because it's held in trust by the government, they can't build equity. Without collateral, it's impossible for them to secure personal or business loans.

Considering the life-and-death struggles Howling Wind was faced with while overseas these past months, Native gang warfare was far from her mind. And that is her story to the Council members, who had hoped she might shed light on the identity of the perpetrators of the attacks, which had everyone calling them heroes. How she wishes she could tell them the truth about the heroes, that the Rawakota warriors who carried out the deeds belong to a Nation that's still around. She'd like to explain what a dedicated and industrious people the Rawakota are, and creative. But she can't. She can't divulge that the blitz against rez gangs was well-conceived by the citizens of Chohkahn, or that she knew when the "clean-up" was expected to take place, as did her mother and grandparents, and all their Rawakota neighbors whose recent descendants chose to remain with the Lakota after they were forced onto the Buckthorn Reservation.

Howling Wind ponders a future in which Chief Rolling Thunder might play a role in the Council of First Nations organization. Chohkahn can still remain secret. Rawakota scientists and scholars could act as confidential advisors and trustworthy intermediaries in the future when it comes to helping other Indian Nations govern themselves. Her own inner turmoil stemming from the horrific events in Mali still weighs heavily on her, or she'd be willing to step up and become more involved. She isn't even sure whether she will continue to spy for the Rawakota. As it is, she has turned down speaking engagements on behalf of the Air Force altogether, a side job that initially brought her a lot of satisfaction. Viktor's name recognition certainly continues to grow, and with it, greater national interest in all things Native. It will be interesting to see if one day, a few years down the road, he takes up a particular cause and runs with it.

On her way back from the restroom, Howling Wind spots Greg Chupko wandering the hallway. He'd been a close friend of her father's. The elderly Seminole leader from Florida, once the chairman of his clan, is delighted to see her after such a long time. They catch up on family news. He asks about Viktor, and whether she has concerns about him playing football. He only brings it up because the group had been discussing Charlene Santana, the swimmer at the University of Florida who had previously made the Council's short list of young influential Indians.

"It's a pity Miss Sanatana was the object of such hateful racism at school," says Howling Wind. "My son would have also faced it, had he gone to college in South Dakota, where stereotypes of drunken Indians are perpetuated. It's easier at Ohio State. There probably aren't more than a hundred Native Americans. It helps that Viktor fits old Hollywood's romanticized image of what an Indian should look like."

Chupko shakes his head and says coolly: "Hollywood."

She looks questioningly at him, noting the rarity of his thick moustache, gone completely white. It's quite arresting next to his dark skin.

"That actor Red Moon is worshipped like true warriors used to be," he says gruffly.

Howling Wind considers Chupko's advanced age when it comes to his disdain for the actor. She believes he's in his mid-eighties. Red Moon's profession is probably what he really has an issue with, regarding it as unmanly. It's a mindset that would disqualify many a candidate from being thought of as a warrior in this elderly leader's eyes, including Viktor, simply because the distinction wasn't earned in battle.

Howling Wind won't drop the subject. "I had the pleasure of meeting the popular young actor in Arizona," she tells him. "With all due respect, Chupko, Jason Red Moon is a man of conviction, someone who displays great moral strength. There is no proving ground like the old days. As was the case with my father, your dear friend, Benjamin One Horn, today's warriors put their lives on the line with their activism. Red Moon takes stands on issues that inflame big industry. These businesses use their clout to strongarm projects that hurt communities and the environment. They don't take kindly to interference. Protestors need to watch their backs. The actor's love for all Indigenous peoples is fierce, and his followers are equally impassioned and courageous."

He scrutinizes her. She studies him as well, and finds herself captivated by the deep-set creases spanning his forehead and the unique cleft in his chin. He springs a question on her that she wasn't expecting: "Why do you fight alongside wasichu," he asks, "against strangers in faraway lands who have never harmed us Indians?"

She answers honestly while maintaining an air of secrecy: "A war is on the horizon, Chupko, between us, the Lakota, and the United States of America. It won't require face-to-face combat, but will rely instead on technology. I, for one, am proud for having contributed to the creation of a Native American defense, which is solidly in place. I was able to help because of the work I do in the United States Air Force. Make no mistake, the time is coming when tribal justice wins the day."

The former Seminole leader is puzzled. Howling Wind elaborates a bit more.

"Of all the tribes, the Seminole story is one that spurs the Council's leaders to stay the course when it comes to recouping their stolen lands and gaining full equality for their people. Considering that your ancestors were ejected from Florida, it's truly remarkable that a few hundred remaining Seminole, who dodged getting captured by hiding in the swamps, eventually organized and won their sovereignty. That probably couldn't happen in today's world, and you probably have your doubts about other tribes in the Council reclaiming their lands in our current political climate. I think you deserve to know what the future holds."

Having returned to the central meeting room, the elderly Chupko looks around and takes note of the different tribes represented in the Council, and for the first time he feels hope. In his heart he *had* given up on them achieving their goals, mostly because tyrannical gangs maintain such a stranglehold over everything. What a game-changer, though, if they can be defeated. His own people have been able to preserve the rule of law, but their numbers are considerably fewer than those of other tribes. And what about this upcoming battle involving technology? He is no stranger to technology and its applications. The Seminole after all control Florida's online sports betting interests. But what Howling Wind is hinting at is unimaginable. Details are surely confidential, but he is curious.

"Will I live to see this day you speak of?"

Howling Wind mulls it over. "Take good care of yourself for another decade."

He chuckles. "You, too, Warrior-Sister; you, too." After a moment, he asks, "When you say Native defense, do you mean only *your* tribe?"

He's fishing. She wears her best poker face and stays tight-lipped, knowing he is familiar with their Rawakota ancestry, but unaware of any hidden tribe of them. "I'm talking about Indians in general," she says, adding, "don't you agree we should know how to carry out a land-grab by now? We've learned from the best, the United States government."

"Amen to that," he says dryly.

Next they lament the fact that around the world and throughout the ages, European invaders have swindled Indigenous societies out of untold millions of acres; no, make that billions of acres.

Excusing herself, she goes to sit outside for some alone time. There's a bench beside a stream where she can admire the rolling hills. Feathery clouds fill the entire sky. The fact she remembers they're Cirrus uncinus evokes a sigh. It's ridiculous that a Swedish man chose to categorize every damned thing on the planet using Latin words and, to add insult to injury, that other scientists, elitist self-absorbed white men, went along! Wouldn't it stand to reason that the names aborigines created to describe their surroundings should have been used, people who actually lived among creatures and plants in nature, and who slept at night under their roof of celestial objects, as many of their descendants still do. She pictures them, the wise elders from non-European civilizations, pointing to *Ursa Major,* or *Capricornus,* and telling their young about their own wonderful sky stories. And she laughs to herself over what to call the fragrant blossoms of purple prairie clover that grows wild on the reservation, if not *Petalostemon purpurea?* It's baffling, the completely useless things one has stored in a brain!

"Mind?" asks a woman who looks to the empty end of the bench. The stranger immediately apologizes, seeing as how she interrupted a train of thought.

Howling Wind isn't startled, having noticed the woman strolling toward the creek a good distance behind. She in fact wondered if she was being followed.

They sit in silence, which grows more comfortable. Perhaps she sought solitude, too, thinks Howling Wind. There is but a single bench. Dragonflies skim across the water, snagging bugs on cattails with lightning speed. Butterflies flit around, confident there's no threat, or too foolish to recognize it.

"Oh!" groan the women, surprised by the attack on a monarch. They watch the mid-air life-and-death struggle with fascination, realizing full-well the outcome. Dragonflies are vicious.

"And so it goes," says the woman. She smiles at Howling Wind, who has no problem smiling back. "My name is Patience Bone. I represent Kinonjeoshtegon First Nations. I am here as a guest. We joined five other bands of Chippewa in the area to form the Interlake Community. Collectively we have more power."

"Good plan. It's a beautiful homeland," says Howling Wind, warming to the idea of company, specifically female company. Both are around the same age. Patience Bone wears her straight black hair in a stylish chin-length cut that flatters her round face. She is in jeans and a light-weight tan jacket that doesn't incorporate any tribal designs. Nor is she wearing Native jewelry. "Are you yourself a chief?" asks Howling Wind.

"No…no more chiefs in these parts," says Patience. "Not after they were sent to prison for fraud. That was over ten years ago."

"Sounds like a mafia connection. I'm Constance Howling Wind, by the way."

"Yes, I know," says Patience. "Everyone was excited when they learned you were coming. You have accomplished a lot and seen much in the world."

Constance almost says she has seen too much of the ugliness in it, but instead simply acknowledges the kind sentiment.

"I encountered your son this past winter on Buckthorn Reservation. What a handsome young man! Sadly, he was grieving at the time. He had stopped by the funeral home to say his friend, a boy named Daniel, had died and needed to be picked up. He had some questions about cremation."

"Were you there for a service?" It seems an odd coincidence.

"No, I was looking over records with Thomas Flatwater, hoping to discover the whereabouts of children that had been abducted from our families as long ago as the sixties."

"Heavens! Did you have any luck?" She knows the healer named Flatwater. He would indeed be the person to contact. His spiritual journey began early, while yet an adolescent. He serves the entire Black Hills region, helping people make sound decisions about their choices. That includes interpreting visions. "I've heard of cases where children were removed and adopted by non-Natives, but you have facts suggesting that other Indians took them?"

"Oh, yes," says Patience. "Whenever disease swept through the land, babies being the most vulnerable, parents went in search of healthy infants and young children on other reservations to keep their lineage alive."

"And you do this work by yourself?"

"I took over the project from my mother. Plenty of people help."

Continuing on a first name basis, the talk turns to the recent drought and wildfires. Captain Nick evidently saved the day, using his plane to carry residents to safety, including six from the Bone family. Patience wasn't among them. By early summer she had moved on to Nebraska's reservations where she would still be, were it not for this meeting in Brandon.

Constance is asked if she has heard how they joke about UFO sightings in Manitoba. "One supposedly crashed in a nearby lake four years ago. It was great for business," says Patience, with an amused smile. "Believers came from around the world, glued to their phones everywhere they went. Outsiders are entertaining."

"Since we're on the subject of cover-ups and conspiracy theories," says Constance, "how is the lawsuit going against Bear Lumber Company up north?"

"They've finally been ordered to stop dumping chemicals in the ditches they dug that go to our lakes; but the damage is done, right? At least the new government won't protect loggers with legislation anymore. It's a start."

Constance sighs. "The water in the stream looks pristine. That's how insidious polluted runoff can be. Should I worry about eating the fish for dinner?"

"Eh, one meal won't kill you."

They laugh, enjoying the camaraderie. Patience reckons the time is right.

"Constance...I deliberately followed you."

After a pause that lasts too long, Constance asks, "Am I supposed to guess why?"

"Sorry...just trying to figure how to say this without it sounding absurd. It's about Viktor."

Constance is all ears, as any mother would be. "Is it dire?"

"Goodness no! I didn't mean to give that impression." She inches closer to Constance and looks her directly in the eyes. "The gift of prophecy has long been associated with the Bone family. My reason for traveling to the reservations was twofold: besides finding the children, I went to talk to shamans and medicine men in tune with forces in the universe.

"Being Lakota yourself, you of course know that Black Elk predicted in his time that the Lakota would find new hope in the seventh generation, meaning the present generation of young adults. For other tribes, a generation is a period marked by a different set of years, which they deem significant. Some of my own people believe that the upcoming fifth generation is the one that is going to produce children who will be instrumental in shaping the future. There are in fact more prophesied births expected to be occurring soon, within the year. It's an astonishing coincidence."

Constance remembers mentioning this to both William and Viktor.

"This past January," continues Patience, "I started sensing something different in the air, a feeling out of the ordinary for even me. I reported it to several tribal healers in Canada and the States, who in turn confessed feeling the same."

Constance wonders how this might relate to things she had heard.

Patience mentally edits her list of examples. "A storm tore through a Haudenosaunee reservation in New York, toppling three trees that fell in the shape of a perfect triangle at the doorstep of a young couple. Late February, fireballs streaked across the evening sky in Oklahoma and exploded in the atmosphere, dropping rocks on the ground of a Shawnee couple's yard. During a Jicarilla Apache powwow in southern Colorado, a solitary mountain lion casually walked out into the open and sat at the feet of a terrified couple before retreating back to the hills. Tribesmen armed with bows and arrows stood in awe as he quietly left."

"I see," says Constance, "and you take these for signs?"

As the sun sinks behind the hills, and the clouds turn pink and lavender, a voice yells out to them from the lodge, "Dinner, ladies." The women wave to show they're coming.

"All the wives became pregnant afterward," says Patience, "which created quite a stir. The couples are believed to be especially blessed. We're wondering—the healers and I—whether it's their offspring, not the parents, who will actually be responsible for forcing change in the unfolding era. The timing for the births will be late fall, between the new moon in November and full moon mid-December."

They take their time strolling back while Patience explains that she had felt a particularly strong disturbance at the Buckthorn Reservation funeral home, as had the healer Flatwater, to the point of them almost falling down they had become so dizzy. "Mr. McLaren, the Funeral Director, who doesn't share our unique abilities, noticed nothing unusual. The ground beneath our feet kept shifting. It was like trying to catch your balance while standing in a canoe. Flatwater called it wakan. Here we say manito. At that moment, Mr. McLaren went to the front desk to see who had rung the service bell."

"Viktor, I take it?"

"We could see him through the doorway. Flatwater told me his name and went on about his accomplishments. I wanted to meet the young man who is held in such high regard. We could overhear the conversation. I used it as an excuse to approach your son to offer my condolences. He was cried out; his gaze empty."

It hurts Constance to think of Viktor without Daniel.

"Flatwater and I were certain it was Viktor's presence we were reacting to."

The women are about to step inside when Patience unexpectedly holds Constance by the elbow. "Now that you have the backstory, I hope you understand when I ask...might Viktor become a father by year's end? Could he possibly have received a sign?"

Constance stops in her tracks. Patience worries she overstepped her bounds. This is after all a really personal matter. She holds the door open as Constance speeds past without answering. Patience feels slighted, but also guilty for asking the question in the first place. It doesn't cross her mind that the woman she had hoped to make friends with is merely absorbed in thought.

That Patience Bone read so much into her encounter with Viktor is wild. The more Constance thinks about it, though…Viktor *had* received a vision during his hanbleceya, the content of which he communicated to no one. The only thing he revealed was that his cousin Suhdeer saved his hand from going into a fire. Then, no sooner had he returned to Columbus, Tess became pregnant. *Lordy,* she thinks, quoting Solomon when he's amazed.

Constance can't stop herself from connecting-the-dots in her head when Patience motions toward the couple of open chairs. As soon as they sit, she apologizes to Patience for getting sidetracked, adding, "Your insights are fascinating." Just then the food arrives: venison and noodles with an interesting blackberry sauce. Four men are also seated at the table, four hungry men not interested in chitchat. Before digging in, Patience asks:

"And plausible?"

"It's too early to say," says Constance, and then a moment later admits, "Yes, it is plausible."

She doesn't mention Viktor's marriage and Tess's pregnancy, let alone the fact they're having triplets. After hearing what Patience had to say about these predictive signs, she intends to pursue the subject with Sleeping Buffalo. The Rawakota have surely heard these stories. Their perspective on the anticipated winter births should be interesting.

Well, there's nothing to be done about the matter tonight. The women are invited to join a game of poker after dessert, which doesn't interest them, especially since some of the men smoke. The plain dormitory-style sleeping quarters don't offer the kind of pleasant atmosphere that's conducive to friendly conversation. They're located in the adjoining building. This place has got to be the most disappointing the Council has ever chosen to stay at over the years. The women agreed that they'd like to continue talking, but where? They could return to the bench by the stream, or walk along the banks of it, but the bugs are a nuisance in the evening. The beds will have to do. Each of the women has a pillow to balance the tea they bought in the hall vending machine. They're pleased to see that the screen in the sliding door isn't torn up. The breeze is wonderful. It's almost too warm, but it carries the scents of the surrounding flowers.

Out of curiosity, Constance asks Patience Bone if, during the course of the evening, she had gotten a specific vibe from her. Patience eyes her thoughtfully.

"You slipped away," whispers Patience, "far, far away. It's a miracle you regained your bearings ... which you are keenly aware of. It has brought you an inordinate degree of peace."

It's reassuring to hear it from a person with true clairvoyant credentials. Constance knew she had been making good progress—no gruesome flashbacks of her experience in Mali in nearly three weeks, the longest period to date. Constance guesses that Patience Bone knows the answer to the question she had asked her about Viktor. The woman likely wanted to hear what his mother had to say about the upcoming "blessed" event.

CHAPTER 47

"He's unstoppable! Definitely no flash-in-the-pan!"

That pretty much depletes veteran sportscaster Grant Welbourne's bank of superlatives used for Number 7's performance against Nebraska's Cornhuskers today. The sportscaster continues, "This athlete who arrived on the scene from out of nowhere last year has proven he's got what it takes to lead a football powerhouse. Clearly the lack of experience among OSU's previously redshirted freshmen and last season's second stringers, playing for the first time this fall, has been offset by their tenacity. The Buckeyes are currently 5 - 0. Marring any injuries...or arrests," he jokes, "the team could easily have another winning season."

His voice wearing thin, Welbourne isn't able to rein in his excitement as he yells into the microphone, "With two minutes left, OSU has just gained possession of the ball after Thornton got sacked yet again. The Buckeyes have one timeout remain...*hold on, folks!* White Owl floats the ball downfield to Stillman, who's open on the sideline...and it's an easy catch! He charges past the 20, past the 10...and runs it in for touchdown number nine! These guys are spoiling their fans! Edwards, the dynamic rookie kicker from New Zealand, is set to make this final score read 63 to 6!"

Tess quietly watches the football game in her new home, which William did in fact buy as an "investment property." It's a lovely, renovated 1928 two-story brick with a big enclosed front porch and a multi-tiered deck that overlooks the quarter-acre lot. William discovered it when he took a wrong turn on his way to a different address. She and Viktor loved the style and the secluded setting immediately. It's tucked atop a hill on a cul-de-sac lined with tall mature trees. The street isn't even a five minute drive from William's apartment, which makes them still close to campus, but now they're on OSU's south end. The realtor had assured William that the other homes on the winding lane belonged to professionals like himself, that no students would be living in them, which struck him as odd. That's when he learned about the growing trend of parents buying homes for their kids to stay in during school. He hadn't let on that his nephew and his wife were the ones who were going to be occupying the place.

With the game now over, and her stomach growling, Tess contemplates heating up some leftovers. Unfortunately, it requires that she move. She's fairly content with staying in the deep corner of the sectional. She sits like a fat jolly Buddha who's ready to burst with babies, not laughter. A big pillow keeps her back straight. *Only a couple more months* she tells herself. The former owner left this massive sectional sofa along with an obscenely huge wall-mounted TV. She and Viktor accepted the items so they wouldn't have to shop for furniture right away.

Tess is in the house by herself, but definitely not alone. Three pair of feet battle for space inside her. Too often a heel catches under a rib and leaves her fighting for a breath. As they grow they're bound to run out of room. She envisions an arm stretching up through her esophagus in search of freedom. As she stares at the monster screen, there is a disconnect between the mortal man she calls husband and the larger than life character, in both the figurative and literal sense, who is causing such a frenzy in the stadium. She strokes her belly. "Hmm...*unstoppable*." She can think of a multitude of adjectives to describe Viktor, in particular his insecurities. Little do they know.

"One thing for sure," says Tess loudly, "this TV has *got* to go!"

She is about to switch channels when Welbourne states how excited everyone is to finally get to hear Talking White Owl at a post-game press conference. Viktor told her he might be taking part in it today, but he wasn't certain. So far the quarterback has avoided the limelight. Now she is as curious to see him as the rest of Buckeye Nation.

In preparation for the post-game interview, and all future ones, Uncle William and Hayden commanded me to: *THINK! THINK! THINK before answering!* They emphasized that I always be on the defensive with reporters. "Those guys are tricky," warned Hayden. He said they love coming up with hypothetical situations. It puts athletes on the spot, and that's when they say things they later regret, which of course *becomes* the story.

An assistant from the TV station comes to tell me it's time. I follow him to a meeting room around the corner from our lockers.

Jasper's session is almost over. Reporters love him. I still hold it against him that he cheats on his wife, but I have to admit he's funny. Too many players have boring, scripted responses to reporters' routine and uninspired questions, except Jasper, who has a natural ability for using language the way southern storytellers do. His delivery is priceless, no doubt picked up from the Alabama side of his family. He notices me in the wings. A reporter wonders if the long pass I threw to him in the final minute surprised him. "Didn't you assume," the reporter asks Jasper, "that Talking White Owl would just run down the clock?"

Without hesitating, Jasper says, "In our minds, it's always a tie game. I was in the clear. Viktor knows my speed. Truth be told, I didn't need to find the ball. It sailed right into my arms. All I had to do was hug it." He winks at me.

What a mischievous rascal. Jasper shakes my hand as he leaves, an honest to goodness gentlemanly handshake, no crazy fist-bumping, hand-slapping one. He goes on looking at me teasingly, and I half expect him to wink again. Damn…why is he so hard to dislike? God knows I try.

As I go to take my place at the desk, I am reminded of how I mentally prepared myself backstage for *WAKAN*, and of Skyler's spot-on painful criticism of me before opening night when she compared me to a eunuch. To boost my confidence right now, I don't dare channel Wakan Tanka like I did back then. I believe I paid the price for my hubris when I landed in the hospital. Maybe I'll take my cue from the marching band which calls itself The Best Damn Band in the Land. It's not so egotistical to claim that I'm The Best Damn QB in the Land—we're not talking the universe.

Guard is up. Fire away. All eyes are focused on me, on my every gesture and word. And the first person at the mic is Si Fogelman, a thoughtful, graying old-school journalist with hunched shoulders and a lean frame whose well-written pieces I've actually read.

"Hello, Viktor. Congratulations." He doesn't sound hoarse from chain smoking like I'd imagined. That's only because he reminds me of the men from the old black and white movies, where everybody smoked in the newsroom."

"Thank you."

Next he admits he has never met an Indian and wants to make sure that he uses the correct term when describing my background. "I thought American Indian was politically correct until I researched it and learned many Native people don't like the label American. One doesn't always know their tribe, which seems to be the preference."

"Yes, well, you're right about the tribe. And the controversy is a heated one, even among Indians. I prefer Native, and that's simply because there are so many citizens from India at Ohio State who obviously call themselves Indians. I never met an Asian Indian growing up. We in the U.S. should adopt the term First Nations from the Canadians, which perfectly describes any of the groups indigenous to this continent."

I'm cut off by a female voice that blurts out, "What about the name "Injun Engine" used for the Buckeyes that's gone viral? Isn't that a racial slur?"

"I haven't heard it before now," I reply, annoyed with myself after answering because she hadn't been formally recognized by the moderator. I also lied. Tess told me that when she was watching the game with her family last year, her brother Kevin came up with that and said he was going to post it online...hopefully it was some other idiot.

"You must be kidding!" she yells, refusing to let it go. "It's everywhere. Even if you haven't seen it, which I *really* doubt, is it okay to call you an injun?"

Do not engage her. A security guard escorts her out. The questions keep coming, and I make a point of carefully wording my responses. One reporter has a hard time believing that the subject of concussions doesn't weigh heavily on my mind, given that I have a "keen one," his words. I tell him that I simply don't dwell on it.

After replaying that answer in my head, I think I came off sounding too glib. If I misspeak, there could be ramifications. "I don't mean to downplay the seriousness of the topic. The safety of the game is a legitimate issue. What I am about to say is not in jest. My teammates excel at protecting me, and for that I'm truly grateful. If I were sacked as often as some guys, it would be a different story. I'm aware that getting hit hard just one time might be one time too many."

I realize Tess is probably watching this. She promised that she wasn't going to miss seeing the game. It was early in our relationship when we had this conversation about CTE, the horrible brain condition caused by repeated hits to the head. She feared that I would one day suffer from it.

Dad and Uncle William both confirmed that I never suffered a serious blow to the head while playing in high school, but she didn't buy it. Her older brothers had to sit out a few games because of concussions, and it angered her that their parents had allowed them to play again.

Next question: "Do you think college athletes, particularly football and basketball players, should get paid...especially at Division I schools like Ohio State where the stakes are so high?"

"Yes." I'm sure he wants me to elaborate but there's enough written about it. Hell, the school paper just published a terrific piece about how much revenue the school takes in every year, some ridiculous figure like 100 million dollars. I don't want to get my facts wrong, but I clearly remember reading that the Buckeyes football team would be worth $1 billion on the open market, if it could be bought and sold like a pro franchise. "And the band should get paid, too...anyone connected with the total college football experience." That causes a stir in the room. The guy wants to pursue it, but I turn my attention to a beat writer for the city's paper.

"Considering your mother is a highly decorated Air Force officer, how do you feel about players disrespecting our flag and taking a knee during the playing of the national anthem?"

That's filled with presumptions. In as calm a tone as I can muster, I reply, "I don't see the connection. Citizens have the right to peacefully protest social injustice."

He becomes excited. "What do you mean there's no connec..."

The moderator announces that time is almost up. "We'll take one last question. You, sir, in the last row." The previous reporter, believing he was shortchanged due to his line of questioning, throws his hands in the air and utters an audible *shit!*

"Mr. Talking White Owl," says the fellow whose entire face is taken up by his big, square, black-rimmed glasses. "Your talent has been described as transcendent. You can throw equally well with both hands. The athleticism you display on the field wows everyone, even non-sports fans. Your own head coach has asserted that you possess the patience of a seasoned pro. Could you tell us what *you* believe your strong suit is?"

Un-hee! Talk about compliments! I proceed to thank him, and then I take a second to think about it, to give him something more than a sound bite.

I look straight at his glasses and admit to having exceptional peripheral vision. "To my immediate left, outside the window, there's a truck with men loading chairs onto it. One guy standing by the driver's door is on his phone. He's waving his arms around like he's upset." People turn to see what I'm talking about. I never once glance to the side, but maintain eye contact with the guy in the giant glasses. When he realizes what I'm doing, he steps over to the center aisle to get a better view out the window. I continue. "The man is now tucking his phone in his back pocket while he heads toward the rear of the truck. A woman wearing a dark blue dress is walking over to the three men, no, make that four; one just jumped out the back. Oops. She dropped her folder." The demonstration sets the room abuzz. "I'd say that being able to detect what's happening over such a wide area gives me an advantage."

"That's amazing. Aren't you worried other teams will somehow try and exploit this secret weapon?"

"I don't see how possessing good side vision is a secret weapon. It certainly allows me to locate more openings on the field. Nevertheless, split-second timing is required for my job. Our rivals can't second-guess me, because, quite frankly, I can't second-guess me. Things just happen too fast once the ball is in play." I purposely don't mention how mentally draining having this gift is. There is a high degree of concentration needed for what amounts to a few seconds. As early as my high school playing days, I discovered that the intensity of that concentration provided an interesting benefit. When we'd be on the sidelines waiting to go in again, my brain seemed to go into overdrive, and I'd come up with ways to solve math and chemistry problems. Ideas popped into my head for my English papers. I loved how those insights came to me. They still do, and I continue the practice of jotting down notes during a game. They'd be meaningless to anyone who got hold of them. The brain definitely works in mysterious ways.

Mr. Black Glasses waves a thanks. That's it. Now to rush home to Tess!

Tess marveled at her husband's composure during the interview. She also thought he looked unbelievably handsome, downright beautiful. How often had the camera zoomed in on his golden eyes, his slow-blinking captivating eyes. They lacked the usual glint of merriment and adoration he reserves for her, but there was a different and intriguing quality to them. He had tucked his jet-black hair loosely behind his ears. A thin braid with two long white feathers hung over the front of his crisp white cotton shirt trimmed with colorful beads, the kind worn by his uncle. Viktor had curiously held his chin slightly up throughout the session, which isn't typical, and something that wouldn't have been noticed by anyone who wasn't close to him. She turns off the TV and strokes her belly, content to daydream for a while.

CHAPTER 48

"Hey, Mom. I just got off the phone with Iris. Sorry to hear about your friend dying."

Iris had filled me in with the details surrounding the unfortunate death of Phil Tardelli, a dog trainer Mom had hung out with at the base in Arizona. I met him during my visit and found him to be a super friendly guy. A wrong way driver hit his car head on...and in the middle of the day. Neither speed nor alcohol was involved, but Iris said witnesses claimed the woman behind the wheel had been texting. Apparently Mom is fixated on acquiring Tardelli's dog, Nero, who is officially retired from duty after having been wounded a couple of times. This has created a rift between her and Dad because he nixed the idea, arguing that no one is home enough to care for the dog. Iris thought it best I don't speak to him about it. I'm siding with Dad on this one, but also because when Phil and Mom were together, they just naturally clicked with each other. It's hard to describe. I could tell Dad was aware of their chemistry. I'm certain nothing came of it, but who needs a reminder of that under foot every day?

"Will you be flying to Arizona to attend the funeral on the base?"

"I appreciate you calling, Viktor, but I don't want to discuss it. Did Tess ace her finals?"

"She did, but they were for the first session of the semester. There are still ones in December she is going to ask about taking earlier. I can't picture what the size of her belly will be by then."

Mom sounds defeated, as anyone would, having just lost a friend. It won't stop me from insisting she get over her obsession with the dog. True, the company of an animal might help her cope, but I'm sticking to my guns. This isn't Dad's cause.

"We're naturally worried about you, Mom. We don't want you to suffer a setback. Only last month you were telling me how much better things were going, and that you hadn't had any flashbacks in the longest time. And now this. It's horrible. But that doesn't mean you can downplay the fact that Dad has always been there for you, not to mention Iris and me. You should respect his feelings on this. I'm sure someone can be found to give the dog a good home."

"I said I don't want to talk about it."

"You're not being fair to Dad."

"*Not being fair...*"

"Hear me out. Please, Mom." I glance at the time. I was all set to make it to an early practice this morning while Tess was till sleeping, then Iris called. I should have waited to talk to Mom later. There's no putting off this conversation, so I take a seat on the front porch. Texas is an hour behind us, but I knew she'd be up. Her body's internal alarm goes off at 4 a.m. sharp, without exception, whereas mine is regulated by the hours of daylight in a season; and right now I should be cozy under the covers. I attempt to stifle a yawn.

"Sorry. It's just too damn early for me." Returning to the subject, "Iris said Dad is worried that this tragedy could send you over the edge."

"I want Nero. End of story. Your dad likes dogs. He's being a real prick about this."

Name-calling is beneath her. "Do you hear yourself? Your friend's dog isn't your everyday run-of-the-mill dog. When Dad used to get in trouble as a teen, maybe he had a nasty encounter with a police dog...that's why he isn't gung-ho about having one under his roof." I'm hoping she'll buy this, so I don't have to go into the business about Phil's feelings for her.

"Nero is a *detector* dog; he was trained to sniff out explosives and drugs. *Patrol* dogs attack."

"When your friend Sergeant Tardelli showed me around the kennel on the base, he stated that *all* Air Force canines are first patrol trained, which means they're taught to attack, right!"

That wasn't smart of me to corner her like that. There's a long pause. "Mom?"

"Wow, Viktor. You *really* pay attention to people, don't you?" I don't care that she sounds irritated with me.

"Must I spell it out for you? Un-hee! Dad's jealous. It's one thing for him to face you being gone most of the time, and living among kick-ass male fighter pilots no less, but now you want this dog, in order to hold on to the memory of a guy who liked you *a lot*! It smacks of a lack of empathy to want to continue a relationship with Tardelli beyond the grave!"

"How can you suggest he ever had a thing for me!"

"Regardless of whether you accept it or not, that's the reality. I felt bad for Dad when I was there on the base and Phil came around. Your wants shouldn't take precedence in this case."

The words spilled out of me. Who am I to be telling my mother what to do? And it's just as odd to be defending Dad's position. My conscience gets the better of me.

"All I'm asking is that you rethink it." She hasn't hung up on me...yet. "A fellow trainer will see to it that Nero goes to a good home."

That did it, and she says bye. Right then Tess opens the door and wonders who I'm talking to in the dark that's gotten me so upset. I really need to get going at this point and offer the briefest of explanations about the car accident involving my mother's friend, which has orphaned his dog. The quick kiss turns into a long one. Now I want to stay home. I plant three little kisses on the top of Tess's active belly. As I pull out of the drive, Tess stands in the headlights holding the collar of her robe tightly around her neck in the cold, then says something that I'm sure is *I love you.* I mouth it back and wave.

Back inside, Tess surprises Constance with her second early call of the morning. "Hi, Constance. Before Viktor left for the athletic center a few minutes ago, he informed me about the dog that was left behind following the unexpected death of one of your colleagues. I'm terribly sorry for your loss." After offering her condolences, Tess tells her mother-in-law how much her own dog, Finn, meant to her growing up. "I would love for our children to experience that special bond. Would it be okay," she asks tentatively, "for us to take Nero?"

It happened fast. When Howling Wind put in the request to adopt Nero, she learned he had been flown to the military canine training center in Texas. Though no longer available for combat, the dog could still prove useful working the Mexican border. It took persistence, but she finally succeeded in procuring him. Nero was at last a civilian.

The half day return drive to Wichita Falls was easy. The seventy-five pound Shepherd sat straight and relaxed in the passenger seat. He watched the scenery and traffic with interest. When Howling Wind spoke, he gave his full attention, connecting with her like a good friend.

She admired his unusual reddish tan head, his jet black muzzle, and the way the black faded into the tan framing his eyes. The markings had grown more defined since she last saw him. He was striking, not unlike "Super Mario" Phil, whom she remembered with fondness. His beguiling green eyes would likely forever haunt her.

All in all, Howling Wind felt confident that she was taking home an animal in command of his emotions, an essential trait since he is going to end up with Viktor and Tess…and three infants. She purposely omitted this fact when filling out the paperwork because it would have put the kibosh on the deal before the adoption process ever got started.

Now, back home in time for dinner, Constance anxiously waits for Solomon, who has yet to meet the dog. He called to say he had to stay late at the shop, which she doubts was truly necessary. That's okay. He finally agreed to let Nero come, but only because the dog's final destination will be in Ohio, and soon, within two weeks. In the meantime, using a coping mechanism for post-traumatic stress disorder that was suggested by the Rawakota team treating her for it, she allows herself a good cathartic cry. She cries out of sadness. Phil is gone, really gone. She cries out of gratitude—for Tess coming to the rescue. She cries for surviving all her deployments, and for a future filled with hope. And she cries because of Solomon, a man true to his promises. She doesn't dare permit Nero to sleep in the bedroom. He appears content on the back porch.

Constance wakes to an empty bed. It's apparent though that Solomon had slept beside her at some point in the night. She hugs his pillow and takes pleasure from the scent of him. The bathroom is dark. She calls out his name. Nothing. Downstairs a lamp is on in the living room. There's freshly brewed coffee in the kitchen. Did he really leave for work already, by 5:20 a.m.? His car is gone. She turns on the spotlight in back and lets Nero out. The wind is brutal, causing tree limbs to creak as they rub against each other. Nero takes it in stride and squats in the middle of the yard to do his business, and then he jumps and plays with all the airborne branches twirling around his head. He amazingly shows no fear at a sudden loud clap of thunder. Upon hearing the command to come, the dog dashes to the door and sits at attention as he awaits his next order from Constance. Even though the door is held open for him, he won't budge without first being given the go-ahead to enter. And that's exactly what he does by his food bowl after Constance places it in front of him on the kitchen floor. She's curious how long his patience can hold out, but not so cruel as to test him. While she enjoys her coffee, and Nero inhales his kibble, she remembers Phil. Wherever he has "walked on" to, she hopes he knows that his wingman Nero will be well-taken care of.

Solomon is busy at the computer in his office when Constance arrives during the middle of the morning. He is oblivious to her standing in the open doorway. Her only thought is of the completely separate lives they lead anymore. It was wrong of her not to have shared any part of the healing process of PTSD with him. And now that she has been living at the house again, their strained relationship seems to be worsening, and through no fault of Solomon. He has had his share of adversity which he's had to shoulder alone. The attack on Viktor coinciding with the fire in his shop took a toll on him. Then to make matters worse, the Air Force wasn't able to contact her in India to let her know about the events, which only added to his worries. She knocks and takes a seat in the customer chair in front of his desk.

"Good morning." She tries to sound friendly, even though she is hurt to the core that he left the house the way he did. Perhaps he had kissed her tenderly on the cheek before heading out.

He looks up and mumbles a hello. "Glad to see you made it back before the bad weather sets in."

They're interrupted by a worker who stops by with a question. The phone rings. It has to do with the inventory. He checks something online. She waits. Showing up impromptu was a bad idea. He's back on the phone. She motions that she's leaving. He raises his chin in an *okay, bye* kind of way as he goes on speaking to the person. Rebuffed again. She stands to leave the same second he hangs up. "A hug would be nice," she says.

"Do I hug you at your workplace?"

Constance flinches. His tone is flat and stings. This is a moment unlike any other between them. As she turns to go, she quietly says, "You could."

"Solomon! We're racing against time here to get our stealth fighters up to Tinker. The evacuation has been ordered, and I can't get back home to care for Nero."

"I've got it, Constance; don't worry. But why are there big jets on a training base?"

"Eglin flew in four F-35s and a couple of F-16s as part of a base road tour for undergrad pilot training."

"Why can't the guys who brought them in fly them out?"

"God, Solomon...I don't have time. Long story short, they attended a function a day ago and everyone got food poisoning. Some are even in the hospital. It supposedly made the news. Anyway, I feel bad. You didn't want Nero, and you shouldn't have to be responsible for…"

"Go, Constance! It's fine. The Blumbergs are with me, and I'm waiting for the Feldmans to arrive. Billie is helping Mrs. Katz cross the street as we speak. The wind upended her. We'll pile in the storm cellar as soon as everybody is here. Just go. Really, it's okay."

"Thanks Solomon. Bye. I love you."

"Be safe." After a second, "I love you, too."

She briefly revels in the words, and then runs through buildings alongside staff reporting to their stations. She is responsible for an F-16 Fighting Falcon still in the hangar. At first, only severe hail was forecast. Constance is all too familiar with bumpy rides. The biggest concern that can't be planned for is flying debris. A tree limb or shard of glass can prove deadly. At high speeds they become projectiles capable of ripping apart a plane's skin.

The supercell, as it's being called, the strongest and most severe type of thunderstorms, had begun forming earlier in the week along New Mexico's southern border. The air mass quickly picked up speed, spawning thirteen EF-2 tornados over the region. The National Weather Service warned others are expected as the system moves across northern Texas, southern Arkansas, central Mississippi, and Alabama. Sheppard Air Base lies directly in its path. The dynamics of the jet streams indicate the place is sure to get pummeled later this evening by winds possibly as high as 170 mph.

The neighbors can't hear what's happening outside from the safety of Solomon's concrete storm shelter, most of which lies underground directly behind his home's garage. They're fortunate to get cell phone service. It's comforting being able to contact family members. Everyone is doing a good job of remaining calm, including Nero, who seems as intrigued by the Feldmans' two Siamese cats as they are by him. The felines continue to inch their way closer to his paws, meowing all the while as if they were egging each other on. Solomon himself is trying to convince Iris that he'll pull through this in one piece. He reassures her that flooding won't be a problem either because the house, as well as his bunker, are on high ground. He installed it about the time she had left home for college because of the number of damaging storms Texas was starting to be routinely faced with.

"Famous last words," quips Iris. She and Hashke had flown to Ohio to attend the Wisconsin game tomorrow. She says she'll pass the news on to Viktor and Tess when they join them for dinner.

CHAPTER 49

Tess's parents take their seats at our kitchen island for breakfast, having driven up from Cincinnati to Columbus last night. They are as enthusiastic as a couple of ten-year-olds who'd won a trip to Disneyland. "Thanksgiving...on a reservation, with honest-to-goodness Indians!" Brian shakes his head. "Now there's something I never dreamed I'd hear myself saying!"

I already broke the news to him that Natives regard the day differently than whites. Yes, it's true that many families do gather for a feast, but that's because they thank Mother Earth for her bounty throughout the year. It isn't modeled after a supposed meal that the Pilgrims of Plymouth, Massachusetts shared with the local Natives. There are tribal citizens who openly protest the official American holiday every year because it trivializes the actual events that took place between the Indians and English colonists. They use Internet blogs to express their anger and write impassioned essays to local newspapers. Some carry signs in front of city halls to draw attention to the fact that this was a dark period in our history. Brian understands. What confounds him and his wife is that they have lived on American soil their entire lives and have never come across a person who was native to this land, and they likely never would have if their daughter hadn't met me.

Their high spirits elicit a smile from Tess, which is quite a feat these days. My poor, Tess. I have to keep from wincing when I'm around her. Chevonne recognizes it and offers me a comforting look. If the size of her belly warrants raised eyebrows from her mom, who's been pregnant several times, then Tess must truly be as insanely huge as I think she is. Five more weeks until her due date in December, and she wants to hold out and go full term even though Dr. Flanagan doesn't recommend it. He also tried to discourage her from traveling, but she got it in her head that our babies are to be born on the reservation, which thrills Grandmother.

"All the bags are loaded," says Dad, who, through connections, got his hands on a brand new Lincoln Navigator and drove it up from Texas for the O'Sheas to travel to South Dakota in. It's mostly for Tess's comfort. While Dad gives Brian instructions, Chevonne takes me aside in the kitchen when Tess goes to the bathroom.

"Please convince Theresa to have the babies early, and with a C-section like her doctor advises. Please, Viktor. Too much can go wrong."

"I know...trust me, I know. He scared us both when he mentioned the risk of uterine rupture. My uncle agreed, which carries weight with her. Hopefully, she won't go into labor before I can get up there, which won't be until after November tenth. I can't believe Brian took his vacation and sick days to spend an entire month on Buckthorn."

Chevonne hugs me tight then wipes away her tears before Tess sees. "It's exciting. Three grandbabies all at once! And we're anxious to meet your relatives, Viktor. Do you think we're nuts for wanting to see a reservation?"

"Yes," I laugh. "I'm glad you and Brian view it as a positive thing...having your grandchildren born on our tribal lands."

Tess catches the tail-end of our conversation. "I'm glad they do, too."

I'm pleased to tell Chevonne that at least the mood has changed for the better on the rez. "It's way different than when gangs ruled."

"I can't wait to get there. Are you good to go?" she asks Tess.

Tess and I stare at each other. The emotion welling up in my chest is unbearable. Chevonne pats my cheek and goes outside.

"God, Tess. I knew this moment would hurt, but it's excruciating."

She looks at me with sad eyes and places her hands over my heart. They'll have to pry my arms off her, and my lips. This kiss needs to tide me over until next week. The plan is to hop a plane to be with her right after the Maryland game. I'd have passed on staying if Coach hadn't begged me to play. Last season the Terrapins embarrassed the Buckeyes when they gave the team a run for their money. OSU lost by a single point in overtime. That was just prior to the game in which the starting quarterback had gotten injured and the backup was arrested on the field...the day my life changed.

No one in the athletic department or on the team knows yet that I'm about to become a dad. Hell, they don't know I'm married. My hands swell from tossing the ball repeatedly, so I don't wear my wedding ring on the field. And Tess and I haven't gone anywhere on campus together recently. She quit her job at the end of the summer to focus on her two classes. We've been buying baby stuff like bottles and car seats and cribs online. That's been fun. There really is no reason to go out. The beautiful setting of our house makes it feel like we're on vacation. We moved in right when the leaves were changing colors. The deck is our favorite spot to hang out. We could sit there gazing at the sky around the clock. Hayden also insisted that I shouldn't volunteer the info with the team. According to him, the news would overshadow the games. Players and coaches alike would be on pins and needles worried I'd be called out when Tess went into labor. I see his point; but it's damn hard to keep it to myself. If Tess didn't feel the same, I would shout it directly into a camera for the world to hear. As it stands now, I'll be missing the following week's Rutgers' game. They aren't much of a threat. I simply told Coach that I was needed by my family on the rez, which is true.

Tess's brothers and neighbors back in Cincinnati aren't aware she is expecting either, which is hard on her parents, but they understand why we don't want word of it leaked to the media. The people who attended their anniversary bash have so far held to their promises of keeping the news of our marriage private. Tess and I are in some of their Facebook photos from the anniversary party, but that was to be expected. The O'Sheas' youngest son, Ryan, who is still in high school, only now learned about the babies. He wondered why his father was taking an entire month off of work to visit Columbus when he and his mother could just as easily drive back and forth from Cincinnati to drop in on his sister. His parents' explanation made sense to him. Ryan agreed that his oldest brother Kevin might post something mean and stupid if he got wind of the pregnancy, simply to get back at the world for his own personal failings. Apparently, Kevin is growing more spiteful than ever since his wife wants out of their marriage. No one blames her. Kevin had already been warned by his dad not to mention our marriage, to allow us our privacy. As it is, Kevin has provoked administrators at the high school where he works because of his cruel tweets. So far they've only involved some of his former Notre Dame teammates who'd been drafted by the NFL. Brian and Chevonne half-expect he'll get fired soon. He certainly isn't a role model for the young and impressionable students he coaches.

It's been difficult for the O'Sheas to face the truth about their athletically gifted but rotten-to-the-core son. Luckily, Ryan is the antithesis of Kevin, more so than his two other brothers, Quinn and Thomas. I like him a lot. He's a quiet, contemplative sort of a guy, but not shy. He willingly shares his opinions about any topic that comes up. To his credit, his views are based on reliable sources. He is well-read for his age. I suspect he has plans for college, but so far hasn't let his folks in on them. Football holds no interest, but he is a top scorer on his basketball team. That said, Brian and Chevonne seem to have had their fill of tailgate parties unless, they hinted, the Buckeyes go to the championship game.

Shortly after the O'Sheas pull out, I give Theo a call. "We still on?"

The plan is to shoot hoops with him this afternoon at the Rec Center. I realized if I didn't stay busy during this bye weekend with no scheduled game, I'd fall apart thinking about my unusual situation. Time was when Jasper would have been included, but he's too busy partying with his new girlfriends. I have come to terms with the fact that his wife and daughter are better off without him. Later this evening, Dad and I will be joining Uncle William for dinner at Dr. Nate's place, after which I look forward to taking Jim out for a ride in the dark and the cold, a double treat for us. The entire day tomorrow is going to be devoted to course work for my second master's. I'm grateful to have been accepted in a non-thesis program this time. It allows me to work independently at my own pace. No more Uncle William to the rescue. He was a lifesaver last spring. I had been so self-absorbed when I went on the hanbleceya that I neglected some of my academic responsibilities. Uncle was informed enough about my research project to step in and help me organize the results after I finished interpreting the data, otherwise I would have missed Dr. Sharma's deadline. Knowing Uncle, he would have preferred that I missed it and faced the music, in order to learn a valuable lesson about not shirking one's responsibilities. Fortunately for me, he still carried tremendous guilt over the Ishmael fiasco, and then he felt sorry for me when Daniel died.

This coming week, I intend to make the most of my football workout sessions, and then drop in bed exhausted at night. I can't stop wishing the Maryland game was already over. Tess's womb better hold out.

So far, things are going as planned—we beat the Maryland Terrapins, barely. They gave us a run for our money. Mom had arranged a private jet charter for Dad and me that operates out of Ohio State's airport. It will fly us to Nebraska. Dad came to the home game, having stayed in Columbus this week after driving up from Texas in that Lincoln for Tess's parents. The second the final quarter ended, I ran to the locker room to shower quickly, and then I made a dash for a waiting limo. Dad was already inside. At the airport, a shuttle drove us out on the tarmac where we just now boarded the small aircraft. It holds up to thirty passengers, but we have it to ourselves. The distant rumbling of thunder along the way made me uneasy. It has grown considerably louder.

Upon take-off, the winds are so powerful, I believe we are going to be goners before we ever reach our cruising altitude. My babies will never know me. The plane continues to lurch from side to side as we climb. Suddenly it drops into freefall, and my stomach with it, but then it fires forward and upward, until it happens again. The sense of dread makes me queasy. The pilot apologizes for the turbulence, but says we can't escape the weather and to brace ourselves for a bumpy ride.

"*Oy vey iz mir,*" I moan, between bouts of throwing up, just like Bernie had when he was struck with appendicitis in high school and lay writhing in pain on the floor during class. With me, it's nerves. Dad tries to comfort me by rubbing my back, which he does for the next two hours.

"Thank god it wasn't a longer flight," says Mom, who has come to pick us up at Nebraska's Chadron Airport. She helps Dad support me as we amble inside the building. They steer me to a restroom, which is unnecessary at this point; nothing's left in my gut. We've never been to the Chadron Airport before, even though it's conveniently close to the Buckthorn Reservation near the South Dakota border. It's relatively small, making it easy to get out of here.

We drive up Highway 385 toward Oglala. It's 3 a.m. and the border patrol waves us through when they recognize Mom. I hate for Tess to see me in this state. Did I honestly win a football game a few hours earlier? It's hard to sprawl out in the backseat.

Mom and Dad are quiet up front. She's driving. Dad turns to me once in a while. I'm sure I'm still moaning. The engine and road noise drown it out. Not a star in sight … just mile after lonely mile of darkness.

"Wake up, Son," I hear as my feet are jiggled. The car door is open, revealing the entrance to the hotel. First Mom goes past, then Dad, each hauling a suitcase. I roll onto all fours and back out slowly. The cold air feels great, although my abs ache and my throat burns.

Dad points across the road to the recently completed hospital on our rez, which he adds isn't fully staffed. Most rooms are dark. "You're *that* close!" he says. "There's Tess's room." Staring at the faint glow coming from the second floor window, my heart starts to race at the thought of holding her. "First you're going to splash cold water on your face, brush your teeth for sure, and then you can go over. The sun might even be up then."

"We agreed on the C-section, Tess." I glance at Dr. Pinto to see if things have changed. She is a good-natured doctor who heads the maternity wing. At the moment, she remains focused on the instruments, which says to me that they're still intending to do a C-section.

Tess is on the bed, sitting upright on her knees. Her ginormous belly rests on some pillows under it. She isn't sweating, only shaking something fierce. "At least let the first one be a vaginal birth," she begs. Her eyes roll around and she's breathless. "Tell her, Viktor…please," she whispers. "He's ready to pop out this minute!"

I hate that she's putting me on the spot like this.

Dr. Pinto shakes her head no, and from that moment a slew of nurses appear. They move fast, I mean fast, and with purpose. It's a job rearranging Tess's body. I'm told to step back, that I can sit beside her in a minute. Tess already received an epidural a while ago. Some other drug is administered to control hemorrhage. Dr. Pinto calmly explains that the cervix isn't fully dilated. The chance of the uterus tearing at this stage is great. I trust her. I know Tess does, too. Still, I can't help wishing Dr. Flanagan were here. Before we know it, a baby is lifted out of her, one of the boys. *"Un-hee!"* Tess and I barely get a peek at him. Waiting hands whisk him away the moment the umbilical cord is cut. There's no time for this miracle to sink in when Dr. Pinto is already holding up our second boy, and then he disappears in a flash. I eagerly await the arrival of our daughter. The doctor pushes on Tess's belly when no baby appears. There's so much blood. Where is she? Do they get stuck? I kiss Tess on the head. She holds my hand tight. This is taking too long…and then our baby girl is raised above the drape for us to see.

"They're out, Tess," I declare, and with such a tremendous feeling of relief. "They're all out." Tess smiles and closes her eyes. I'll never forget the calm that came over her.

Three distinct cries are testament to them breathing. I'm in a daze. A nurse catches me staring at all the blood and reassures me that Tess will be fine. I don't see how that's possible after losing so much. Suddenly one of the babies is gently placed in my arms. He's tightly wrapped in a blue blanket. The other two are laid on Tess's exposed breasts. Our daughter is wrapped in a yellow blanket and our second son is in a mint-colored one. Tess looks from one to the other. "They're enchanting," she beams. The emotion is indescribable. I'm quietly thanking our Creator. Each baby is healthy. I pray then for Tess to make a full recovery after her ordeal.

CHAPTER 50

Claire sees Uncle William and me from the escalator and starts waving excitedly. Uncle and I pick up our pace. No crowds to dodge in the Columbus terminal today. He's never met Dad's niece, my favorite cousin, but feels he knows her after hearing my many stories.

Boom! We collide in a hug, laughing. I grab her by the waist and spin her around. What a featherweight. Thankfully, people have license for behaving this way at airports. Following introductions, we head toward baggage claim.

"Oh my goodness, Viktor, I can't believe any of this is really happening. I'm in Columbus, and you're a dad!"

Taking a finger to his lips, Uncle quietly shushes her and looks around. "We're keeping the news under wraps for the moment."

"Yes, I get that...sure."

She looks so pretty, which I openly tell her. Her bushy afro has been tamed, which I kind of miss. After being around a super-pregnant Tess this past week, Claire seems especially tiny. I worry her ribs will crack if I squeeze her too hard. But I can't stop. We go on hugging and acting a bit silly. Based on Uncle's expression, he is somewhat miffed at our lack of decorum. I make no excuse for it and readily tell him: "Hey, I'm on cloud nine; be glad I'm not swinging *you* around by the waist!" I catch him grinning as he walks ahead of us. "This is just the best having you here, Claire!"

"It *is*." She kisses my hand and holds onto it as we walk. I need to get my own suitcase, too, having taken a regular flight back to Ohio from South Dakota, which I timed to coincide with Claire's arrival from Kansas City. I missed one game, in order to be with Tess and witness the births of our babies, but there's no way I could be a no-show for Saturday's game with Penn State. I figured Claire could stay in my apartment, which I'll continue to use as my school address for now. Uncle won't move out of the building. He likes the convenience of the location for his work, although I know he'd prefer to live among the horses on Dr. Nate's property. I almost forgot Nero is there now. Mom flew the dog up from Texas herself. Dr. Nate volunteered to watch him until things settle down in my life; I should say until Tess returns—there'll be no *settling* with three crying newborns. This animal supposedly has nerves of steel. He can serve as my model for patience.

Before I can even get my second foot in the car, Claire eagerly asks the babies' names.

"Tess and I had a bunch picked out, and didn't go with any of them. We waited a couple of days to find better names that suited them. All three will share a last name of Red Hawk, on account of Tess's red-haired family." I pull up the photos on my phone. "The biggest boy, who was six pounds, two ounces, is Holt. Then there's Raif, and our daughter is Honor Red Hawk." Claire is visibly moved and wipes away a few tears.

When we arrive at the apartment, Claire gives it the onceover after I hand her the extra key, then it's time for Uncle to drive me to my house. It won't seem right without Tess. I would have invited Claire to stay with me, but I can't afford any distractions, and I know for a fact we'd be up all night talking. She and I make plans to meet at the training center tomorrow afternoon. Uncle offers to drive her over, and then I can give her my car to use while she's here discovering what's involved in applying to OSU's medical school. I've got Tess's old car to drive in a pinch, but I don't foresee that happening. As we go to say goodbye, the enormity of what's occurring in our lives hits us. Gone is the childishness. When we embrace, it's as if we're holding on for dear life. Uncle allows us our moment, but then insists we leave so I can get to bed early in preparation for the intense workouts demanded of the players over the next few days.

"Awesome practice!" yells Jasper to me, as he's drying himself off outside the locker room shower. "We're gonna kick ass tomorrow!"

"You know it!" I'm trying to stay as positive as I can around my teammates because I feel bad for missing practice earlier in the week, and I'm going to miss three days next week, right before the Michigan game. A quick pep talk is in order.

"Hey, guys!" I shout. "Before you take off..." I make sure I have their attention. Most players are dressed and closing up their bags. "Every receiver should expect to get the ball at least ten times, if not fifty, so BE

READY!" That ignites a deafening Buckeye cheer with clenched fists circling the air. I plant myself by the door to shake every hand and check for that *give em hell* glint in the eyes. Slaughter passes behind me, but he fails to appear on my other side. I feel his chest against my back shoulder. His voice is low and menacing in my ear:

"If you ever pull another fucking stunt like you fucking did last year, see if you get any fucking protection in the fucking future."

Un-hee! That's been bottled up a long time. He's just now saying something when the season is almost over? I'm tempted to tell him, *you caught the ball; you didn't have to.* But I pledged not to rock the boat today. He's talking about the unbelievable play that I'm convinced Daniel orchestrated from his deathbed, the one where he was inadvertently cast in the role of receiver. That pass was one for the books. I think Slaughter resents me because something rattled him when he caught the ball. I could tell in the video that I've since viewed numerous times of the play. He turned to his left immediately after the catch and looked around…as if he heard something. A voice perhaps? I zoomed in tight to see his expression. It wasn't of a guy who had just scored a dazzling touchdown. Whatever it was, it clearly spooked him. Slaughter's threat falls on deaf ears, especially since I believe it was a one-time occurrence. Unless, of course, Daniel has more up his ghostly sleeve. One should never underestimate the spirit world.

After the locker room empties, I spot my backup, the junior rookie Rufus Burlee, sitting on the bench watching me. He looks bummed, and I understand why. He got a chance to shine in last Saturday's match up with Rutgers; instead, he succumbed to the pressure.

I feel for him and shrug my shoulders. "There's no right thing to say is there?"

"I appreciate you calling afterwards. Talk about hitting rock bottom."

"Hey man, we didn't lose. That's all fans care about."

"But I didn't win it. The points all came from field goals. And shit… that last snap. If the guys hadn't pulled me across the end zone for a touchdown, I'd be history here. I couldn't even carry it a yard. That's humiliating."

"You were at least on top of the mountain of players, and not under them a yard short of the line. Jumping high instead of drilling it forward was smart."

He looks at me like, who are you kidding? "C'mon, I'll walk out with you." The best thing I can do is simply listen to him. I ask what's so different about being here than back at the University of Virginia where he transferred from, and where he had led his team to two perfect seasons. He might not have had huge yardage numbers there, but he did complete over seventy percent of his passes. While he talks, I find myself fixated on his Crayola yellow hair. He's a nappy-headed white guy, with matching curly hair that carpets his arms and chest. A patch grows up his throat where it connects to a frizzy beard. Even at rest, his cheeks are flushed. At six-four, he could definitely pack on a few pounds, not that that could've helped in the Rutgers game, but future games for sure. Looking down the hall, I catch a glimpse of Slaughter before he disappears around the corner.

Lost in thought, Damien Slaughter walks angrily toward the exit. He would love nothing better than to let Number 7 get royally sacked once. However, the long-armed, intimidating athlete known for tormenting his opponents has attracted the attention of the NFL, and with the amount of money going to guards these days, he isn't about to squander a future multi-million dollar deal. All of a sudden, he's aware of this girl standing by the door. She has the face of an angel, and he can't take his eyes off of her.

"Hello," she says, smiling at him.

Bam! It's like he smacked the wall. Slaughter manages a "Hi." Her expression is one of such joy, and those eyes!

"Do you train here?" he asks, unsure where the words are coming from.

Claire laughs a little at the thought. "No…I'm meeting someone."

Damien Slaughter remains planted by the door. People step around him to get out. Beads of sweat form on his neck, his temples. This reaction is altogether new to him. At that moment she eyes the person over his shoulder she's been waiting for. He glances back. His two teammates are busy talking and haven't spotted her. Slaughter turns to her again. Her head is cocked slightly to the side. She is a vision of kindness, an image that, for the most part, is foreign to him. He escapes outside and heads to his car.

He watches from behind the wheel as the three head across the lot. White Owl and the girl wave to Rufus Burlee, who runs to his waiting ride. "Fuck you, Viktor!" It figures *he'd* be the one she knows.

Damien goes on watching with interest as the two join hands and start swinging their arms like schoolyard buddies. What's next, skipping? Envy consumes him. He follows them, making certain to stay a fixed distance behind. The girl is at the wheel. She drives slow, ridiculously slow. They weave around a couple of long roads when the car turns onto a steep drive with no outlet. Fearing he'll be spotted, he stops alongside the curb. There's no telling which of the several homes on the hill they're going to. Just when he convinces himself to stop being a total ass over a girl he knows nothing about, she drives right past him, alone. And once again his heart begins thumping hard in his chest. He impulsively gives the car gas and goes on following her. A wet snow begins falling. Does she always drive like a ninety year old, he wonders. They end up in the far back lot of an apartment complex where she hurries inside the building. He waits to see which window will light up. The lamps around the parking lot go on automatically. Snow starts sticking to the windshield. The wiper blades scrape across the glass at long intervals. And then a light appears in the left third-floor window. He jumps at the chance to catch the door when another person comes home.

Mail slots line the wall. Apartment 3E belongs to Talking White Owl. He sees that 3F belongs to Half Moon, Viktor's uncle. Damien ventures up the flight of stairs and listens. Viktor's apartment is quiet inside, as is his uncle's across the hall. He knows that Half Moon went to a nearby sports medicine center to help a few players after practice. This is crazy, he tells himself. Why is he acting like such a dumbass? It's killing him not to knock on the door. What would he say? She'd think he was stalking her. He gets an idea and races out.

Damien reaches the center in minutes flat, then sprints inside, passing Fred Gorski, a defensive lineman who regularly receives acupuncture treatment from Half Moon. That means the witch doctor hasn't already left! He considers what the Indian does as voodoo, and calls the players who resort to using acupuncture as "pincushions." Gorski can be his excuse to talk to Half Moon. He finds Viktor's uncle organizing a cart in the treatment room. Having never spoken to him, he isn't sure how to address him.

"Hey, Doc...is Gorski around?" He remains standing in the doorway.

Half Moon looks up. "You just missed him."

"Fuck." Slaughter pretends to leave, but then asks, "Mind if I ask something I've been curious about?"

This ought to be good, thinks Half Moon to himself. "Ask away," he says, washing his hands to leave.

"I happened to see Viktor with his girlfriend today, and I got to wondering if you Indians think it's wrong not to stick with your own kind."

"His girlfriend?"

"Yeah, that perky little black chick on his arm with the big fro."

Grabbing some paper towels, Half Moon saunters over to Slaughter and studies him a few seconds. It seemed an odd question. Number 54 is not wearing his usual menacing face. He actually looks vulnerable. So that's it. He's got a thing for her. Half Moon is amused that he's got the arrogant, boastful player over a barrel.

"Did you follow them?" asks Half Moon.

"What! You crazy?"

"Did you?"

Slaughter's flared nostrils grow even bigger, he's breathing so hard.

William Half Moon surmises that the fellow's feelings must run deep; after all, he is not the sort who tolerates being at the mercy of another. Besides, this "witch doctor" already got his answer. On his way out, in a kindly voice, Half Moon says, "Our people understand that the heart knows no color." Outside, it's snowing. He felt Slaughter following close at his heels and waits for him on the steps. He has decided to disclose a pertinent detail. The player breezes past, preoccupied with zipping up his jacket when the Indian startles him.

"Damien, the girl wasn't Viktor's girlfriend. Claire is his cousin, his favorite cousin I might add."

Hearing that gives Damien hope, which shows plainly on his face.

Noting the player's sudden humble demeanor, Half Moon says, "She has come to OSU from Missouri to check out the med school." Damien actually thanks him, and then apologizes for having always called him a witch doctor. Half Moon grunts and proceeds to his car, stepping carefully to avoid possible icy patches on the pavement. If Viktor knew what he had just done, he wouldn't hesitate punching his elder in the nose. The uncle realizes there is something bigger at play here. That's the beauty of wakan, those mysterious connections that abound in the universe, playing with our notions of things from time to time. Nevertheless, he will find an opportune moment in the locker room to take one of Slaughter's used towels and submit it to Winter Crow's lab for DNA testing—for Claire's sake. He is certain the results will show that the athlete possesses the combination of genes that constitute the "loyalty" trait. William Half Moon gets a completely different and positive vibe from the player with the reputation for being a hellraiser. He's been able to trust his instincts so far. Maybe there is a bit of "witch doctor" in him after all.

"That was one hell of a weird game! You sick?" asks Jasper of me. "And what's so urgent that you have to leave again?"

I don't bother answering, but I know everyone is wondering the same thing. There was no foreseeing how tired I'd be today. I gave my all at practice these past few days. I'm on the brink of telling them exactly what I've gone through in the last week, but then reconsider. Poor DeShaun was on the receiving end of my endless short passes. For the first time, it took two and three downs to go ten yards. Penn State was on him in a flash. It was all I could do to move the ball forward. We lucked out because their coach anticipated that at some point I'd be going for a long pass, and they set themselves up for it, as did Jasper. It simply wasn't in the cards today. We did win by three touchdowns, nothing to sneeze at. Our defense was great in stopping their big guys.

The players are low key as they undress to shower. Anyone would have thought we lost. Uncle comes and hands me my phone. He holds on to it during games because I don't trust placing it in the locker.

"Should I tell them, Uncle? I honestly don't know what to do."

"It would show you trust them."

I search his eyes while thinking about the ramifications. "Reporters will descend on the reservation and ruin this time for my family as well as the people in the community."

"Everyone is screened at the border. They won't be allowed in."

I can't help from laughing. Is he really that naïve? "The *border*...like that's the only place they would think to enter the rez."

"Believe it, Viktor; these days the Indians have high tech surveillance tools. Our territory is a protected fortress."

He's serious. Suddenly Rhett, our Center and my good friend, speaks up.

"Have you made a deal with the NFL?" The guys stop in their tracks. I'm in disbelief. From the looks on their faces, he's not the only one who's been thinking that. This came so far out of left field, I'm speechless.

Rhett persists, "It's as if you were saving your arm today, like a price is on it. We need you before our biggest game with Michigan next week, and you're cutting out again."

I've been so consumed by the events occurring in my own world, it never crossed my mind how my teammates might interpret my absence. *Un-hee!* I can see how my behavior would raise suspicion. Some of the players seem guilty for thinking such thoughts, and they look at one another instead of at me. Then there are those who are outright glaring at me with disgust. I spot Jasper standing by his locker.

"Is that what you think, Jasper?"

"Look…no one can fault you. It's what we all wish for, to be noticed by the NFL. How would you explain what you did today? And what about the secrecy?"

I feel like crying. I am spent. Rhett gently squeezes my neck and rests his hand on my shoulder. I find the picture on my phone of Tess and me and our little babies. We're on the bed in the hospital room. I show him the picture and ask him to pass it around for everyone to see.

"It truly hurts that any of you could believe I'd purposely let my team down. That's where I've been, with my wife Tess and our triplets. They were born the day after the Rutgers' game…on the reservation." Now the whole team is curious. The players crowd around each other to see what's on my phone. "Her due date was the first week in December. I didn't want to say anything because then everyone would be scared if she went into labor during the big game. And I didn't want the media to play it up."

A murmur of relief is audible. I mention that the doctor was concerned for Tess's health and convinced us an earlier C-section would be safer. "We wanted privacy, that's all. I'm sorry I wasn't up front with you from the start. I'd still prefer if nobody knew until after Michigan."

Jasper walks over and hugs me unexpectedly. He presses his forehead to mine. "I'm so happy for you, man. Congratulations, Viktor." He faces the room. "This stays in here, right team!"

The mood instantly changes. My teammates come at me left and right, offering congrats and nearly knocking me off my feet! The coaches promise the news won't get leaked. I solemnly swear to be ready for next

Saturday's game against Michigan's Wolverines in Ann Arbor. I plan to report back on Wednesday and go up with the guys on Friday.

DeShaun grabs my hand for a bro shake and pulls me in for a hug. "You know I love you, right?" I nod, unsure where this is going. "I am *not* going to hold it against you if you never throw the ball to me next week." He turns to Uncle. "You got a few hours to work on me?"

It's a light moment, and we laugh, but then I ask if he really is okay. He took such a beating.

"Who cares; my stats are through the roof!"

I hurry and shower in order to meet Claire before I fly out tonight with Dad, on a regular jetliner this time, and from the Columbus airport. Winds or no winds, this is one instance when I'm going to fall fast asleep on the plane. Of course, I say that with the knowledge that the skies are predicted to remain calm. I'm enjoying the positive vibe in the locker room and grateful to have finally shared the news. I love everyone calling me dad, everyone that is except Slaughter, who oddly hasn't spouted off obscenities like he usually does. Must be fighting a bug. As always, he protected his quarterback well during the game.

Claire is waiting outside the door. "God, you're a sight for sore eyes! I'm so thankful for you." I take her pretty face in my hands and kiss her forehead. "Aren't you cold?"

"The air feels good...fresh. "I've been in the apartment all day talking to mom and calling some friends."

"Homesick after only a week?"

"Nah. If anything, I'm so excited about the reality of living far from home and going to OSU, I don't know what to do with myself. The college adviser I saw was really supportive. I'm going to do it, Viktor...work on your reservation one day. I can't believe I never thought of pursuing a loan forgiveness program until you brought it up. The fact that I am already a nurse helped my case."

Slaughter appears. He ignores me but stares at Claire. He's all teeth his grin is so wide. Claire beams from the attention.

"You two-timing your wife with this ray of sunshine, White Owl?"

"Can you ever say anything that doesn't make someone want to beat the shit out of you!" I grab Claire by the elbow and steer her toward the car. Damn if Slaughter doesn't jump in front of us.

"Chill, Viktor. Where's your sense of humor. I'd like to meet your friend."

I forcibly push him to the side. Claire wriggles her way out of my grasp.

"Viktor…you can at least introduce me."

"Nope. Let's go!" I've got her by the waist now and lift her off her feet. She looks over my shoulder.

"I'm Claire," she yells.

He calls out his name to her.

Too bad I have to drive past him to get out of the lot. He's still standing by the entrance waiting for us. Claire waves enthusiastically back to him.

"Claire, cut it out!"

"Whaaat? What have you got against him?"

Where to begin? "The guy is trouble. His nickname is Demon for a reason. He's not the type you want to get involved with."

"I'm a grown woman, Viktor. I can take care of myself. I think he's gorgeous…exotic. I love his straight nose and big nostrils. He's like a magnificent bull. His skin is such a rich coal black. He reminds me of a majestic Minotaur."

"Oh, *please!* That monster Minotaur could fell you with one swoop of his hand."

"Why would he do that?"

"God, Claire." I can only shake my head. The attraction totally baffles me. We ride to the house in silence. Since I'm taking an Uber to the airport, she gets my car again. Off to the rez, one last time for a while.

Claire and I hug goodbye. Before she gets behind the wheel, I tell her there are other players I'd be only too happy to hook her up with, ones just as black and magnificent, if that's her thing. She laughs.

"It isn't my *thing*. I simply find him intriguing. Have you always had a *thing* for tall, busty redheads?"

I roll my eyes and kiss her cheek. "You're exasperating. Just stay busy with what you came here for. Get to know the campus. Busty, huh…that's funny."

CHAPTER 51

Here I am back on the Buckthorn Reservation. Sister and I are curious about what Sunkwah and Winnie want. He called from his hotel room and asked to see us before brunch. Both of our family members are staying at the hotel, the one across the street from the new hospital where Tess gave birth a week ago. She was discharged and is here in a suite. The triplets sleep together in a bassinet next to the bed. I arrived late last night. I don't know how I'm keeping it together. One minute I'm staring downfield in a stadium filled with screaming fans, and the next minute I'm in quiet rural South Dakota. Tess slept in an upright position with pillows packed by her waist to support the babies during nursing. Chevonne had been helping her, but I insisted on taking over the job. I was instructed to remove the one baby from the breast after thirty minutes, allow Tess a short break, although she looked to be sleeping through the feedings, and then place the next one at her opposite breast, following it up with the last baby. Sucking noises indicated the first one was ready to go again. Aye yi-yi, what an ongoing process. After the second set of feedings, I could really appreciate how physically draining this is going to be for Tess. As for me, I couldn't stop gazing in awe at the itty bitty creations that I am now responsible for. I will be a good dad. I have had the best one imaginable to learn from.

Sister meets me in front of our great-grandparents' door. "I expected you to have dark circles around your eyes. You actually slept?"

"I did on the plane, if you can believe that. I'm just so relieved Tess is finally getting stronger."

"I know. She had a downright ghostly face for a few days."

"You haven't worn traditional clothes in ages. That's a really pretty top. It isn't Lakota, though, is it?"

"Hashke's mother made it for me. I *do* wear a lot of Indian clothes. You just aren't around much to see me in them."

We knock and wait, realizing their gait has grown much slower. Happy eyes greet us. We haven't sat long when Sunkwah says he has a request to make on behalf of Lukas's family. That certainly piques our curiosity.

It's an easy yes, if it's something he wants. Our relatives traveled from Chohkahn to welcome the new generation into the family, if that's okay with Iris and me. They wait for word that we are open to the idea. Tess already gave her consent. Our cousin Suhdeer is included in the group. Iris knows I saw him during the hanbleceya and can't wait to meet him. Suhdeer came with his wife, their children, and his older brother and sister. More cousins for us to meet. His parents will also be there. It's going to be strange seeing Novak, Lukas's identical twin brother…like seeing myself in the future. Suhdeer's paternal grandfather has also accompanied them. That would be Lukas's father.

"It had to be a hard decision for them to make," says Winnie, "especially for the Elder, but the man needed to see his great-grandchildren. The family still suffers the humiliation caused by Lukas kidnapping your mother."

"Is there going to be a ceremony?" asks Iris.

"We don't even know these people," I tell them, wanting to celebrate the births with only those closest to us. "I was with cousin Suhdeer in the mountains for all of two days."

A look of sadness fills our great-grandparents' old eyes. It's disarming.

"We wish it," says Sunkwah, without further explanation.

Sister turns to me. I'm a big question mark. Her expression however is one of resolve, one that says, if they wish to put on some kind of a ceremony, by god we're doing it!

Lukas's family erected a few tepees on the grounds of the hotel. The designers of the medical complex understood the importance of setting aside an area for tribal members to gather and carry out healing rituals for those undergoing treatments in the hospital. As we head out, we meet up with Mom in the lobby of the hotel. She gets an earful from me after I learn she won't be attending the event.

"Darn it, Mom! You haven't been with me for so many things, but this really takes the cake! I mean it! Why am I being railroaded into doing this?"

With that, she holds me by the arms. I make no attempt to extricate myself. There's obviously something bigger I'm missing here. In my years growing up, our family and Lukas's had no contact with each other. And now Sunkwah and Winnie suddenly want to appease these strangers and include them in what should be a private affair with only our family members.

"I realize it's the principle that's got your goat," says Mom. She takes my hand and reaches for Iris's. "Listen up, you two. These people are foreign to us, but we aren't to them. They have followed your growth and progress since the day each of you was born. You're their blood relatives. It wouldn't have been right to deny them knowledge of your lives."

Suhdeer had told me in the cave during my hanbleceya that he learned about Iris and me when he was around eight. From that point on, he couldn't wait to meet his Lakota cousins who lived up top on the Buckthorn Reservation. I can't relate. Considering that Lukas was in his late thirties when he made Mom pregnant with me, Novak, his twin, must be nearing sixty.

Just then Dad, Chevonne, and Grandmother exit the elevator with cradleboards strapped to their backs holding our babies in them.

"What's the point of these?" I ask. "It takes all of two minutes to walk to the tepees from here. We can easily carry them."

"Because it's important to me," says Grandmother. "My Rawakota grandparents constructed them when they still lived down in Chohkahn. My own mother and siblings were carried in them as well as me and my brother and sister. You were, too, Viktor. Think how old these cradleboards are."

It was a thoughtless remark on my part. Of course it's an heirloom. I worry that symbolic items are becoming lost on me. I see that this gathering is having a profound effect on everyone else. Right now, my college life feels real, not this.

I ask Mom why Dad gets to meet Lukas's relatives.

"They wish to convey their gratitude to him for raising you and Iris."

"*What!* Like you had no hand in our upbringing!"

"Un-hee, Viktor! Please just go along. My presence will only make the Elder and your Uncle Novak self-conscious because of what Lukas did to me. This joyous celebration shouldn't be marred by events that occurred decades ago. Let them fully enjoy the day."

She goes and taps each baby lightly on the nose, proudly smiling at me afterward. Dad is staying on the sidelines, which is unlike him—really unlike him.

I help Tess into her coat. She says she is up for the short walk. We trail the others, admiring the itty bitty sleeping faces poking through their pretty blankets that are not old like the carved cradleboards they're strapped to, but newly knitted by Grandmother and Winnie.

Tess and I are last to enter the spacious tepee of Lukas's family. Around thirty of his family members from Chohkahn stand together on the one side. The excitement in the air is palpable. The babies are clearly the stars. A couple of women wearing surgical masks help unstrap the cradleboards and ask if they can hold the infants for the rest to see. Winnie and Grandmother lock arms with Chevonne. They're all smiles, including Brian, whose attitude toward seeing authentic Indians is positively reverential. I remain guarded. Dad's mood has oddly picked up now that Mom isn't around. Tess, for the most part, has been concentrating on her and the triplets' health and therefore hasn't had the luxury to think much about any of this. The babies are technically premature, but you'd never guess it from looking at them. Tess said this morning that she was anxious to meet the tribe, not so much because they represent my biological father's side of the family, but because they live in a place the rest of the world doesn't know exists. She never would have learned about the hidden city if she hadn't first been thoroughly vetted by the Rawakota DNA researchers at Winter Crow's lab. I played no part in that decision. Iris had asked Tess if she would voluntarily submit to the blood test if she planned on pursuing a serious relationship with me, which she evidently did. Tess was made privy to the information only after she swore never to share it with anyone, including her own parents and closest friends. Growing up, the stories that my grandparents and great-grandparents told us about their ancestors' homeland below the Black Hills were real to me. I bought into the idea that Chohkahn was hidden under my feet. However, given recent facts about its supposed distance, the location of the sacred city is the stuff of fiction. Either Mom has been duped by somebody, which is highly unlikely, or she is perpetuating false facts to protect the secrecy of its actual site. The entire Rawakota community must be in on it. During my hanbleceya, when confronted by Suhdeer, he had insisted his home in Chohkahn was down so deep inside the earth it defied logic. Speaking of which, here comes our cousin, accompanied by a petite woman I assume is his wife.

Following introductions, cousin Suhdeer motions for his father to come over. Our Uncle Novak approaches on the arm of the man we presume is his own father, Suhdeer's grandfather. Standing face to face with Lukas's twin brother is unsettling. My resemblance to my uncle is uncanny. Iris squeezes my arm, the likeness proving as strange to her. Dad comes to the rescue. I don't pay attention to what gets said. The room grows silent when the Elder is introduced to us. Daywidah is his name. It means beacon of light, as in a person who inspires others. He is without a doubt distinguished looking. Iris does the unthinkable when she embraces him, this total stranger. She forces my hand onto his.

"Viktor, think what this moment means to our grandfather."

I know she's right. My fingers fold around his hand. I rest my other hand on his forearm. An entire life's experiences are stored in those old eyes, a journey that should have included Iris and me. They aren't the big, round eyes I inherited from Lukas, which are of course like Novak's. Neither is his face square like ours. It's on the long side, and he has a distinctly different nose, one with a high bridge. He might even be an inch taller than I am.

"Daywidah, it is an honor." I can't think of anything else to say. Mom told us they all understand English even though many don't use it regularly, especially the older generation. He responds with something in Rawakota that Suhdeer is set to translate. The old man's low-pitched voice is impressive.

Suhdeer explains that his grandmother will soon pass. "My grandfather says that his wife wishes to carry a treasure with her into the next world from their son Lukas's children and grandchildren. It will bring peace to her spirit, which in turn will ease the pain of Grandfather's loss when the time comes for her to walk on. Might they be given a locket of hair from all of you?"

I turn to Sister. "Mom should be here." She agrees.

Suhdeer's family members quietly discuss our request to have our mother present. Iris and I can't fathom why they harbor this lingering shame. The situation exasperates Dad who leaves to fetch Mom without waiting for an answer. At least the triplets have hair to spare; each baby was born with a shock of dark red hair, not black, that comically shoots out in all directions.

CHAPTER 52

The issue that bugged Damien in his dorm room at night, preventing his sleep, was how to bump into Claire without it looking planned. He couldn't just show up at White Owl's apartment like a friend would. It's no secret he tops Viktor's shit list. Besides, everyone knew the Indian was going to be out of town. Why make up a story at all? He'll tell Claire he felt a connection when they laid eyes on each other, and then ask if she'd like to hang out with him. Hopefully it won't come up how he learned where she was staying, that he followed her and Viktor from the athletic center that day. He needs her last name and phone number. Viktor's witch doctor uncle must have it, but then he'd have to confront Half Moon again. He's suddenly interrupted by his roommate.

"Yo, Demon…I gotta go. Have a nice Thanksgiving."

"Same, bro. Need help with your bags? Dude, how much stuff you taking!"

"Souvenirs."

Damien laughs. "I'm sure folks in Alabama *love* wearing OSU shirts and caps."

"They do in my family!"

After the player known as T-bone leaves, Damien picks up where he left off with his thoughts. The dorm is eerily quiet. His other two roommates in the adjoining bedroom probably won't stir until noon. The gray, wet morning is perfect for sleeping in. Any other Sunday he'd be waking with a hangover in some girl's bed, having picked her up at a club during the night. Sitting alone like this is new to him. He grabs his phone and scrolls through the names of the athletic staff. The worst that can happen is the doc says no. At least it won't be to his face.

He showers and shaves quickly. Half Moon gave him Claire's number straight away when he called him, no questions asked, which is hard to believe. He takes the time to brush his tongue. The eyes staring back at him in the mirror lack their normal cocksure smugness. When he tries to imagine what a classy girl like Claire sees in him, he comes up empty. She's no jersey chasing party-girl looking to nab a popular football player's attention. One thing is certain; the caramel-skinned beauty isn't turned off by his jet-black complexion. He thinks about calling first, but then decides to surprise her.

This time Damien uses the outdoor speaker to get buzzed inside. It took a second for Claire to recognize his name. Hadn't he left a more memorable impression? He bounds up the stairs three at a time.

"I don't believe this!" says Claire, her eyes big with delight. A glorious smile greets him. "I know for a fact this isn't Viktor's doing."

Damien grins. "You got that right. His uncle told me you were here."

"Really?" She looks unconvinced.

He's taken aback when she crosses in front of him and knocks on the door opposite hers. Half Moon appears. She asks him whether Damien's claim is indeed true. William glances at him and nods yes, aware that the nervous suitor just breathed a sigh of relief.

Next she asks, "And you think Viktor would be okay with him being here?"

"No."

"But you are?"

"Yes."

"I see. Thanks, Uncle William."

She kisses his cheek, and he goes back inside. Next Claire invites her company into her new place. Damien removes his wet shoes and jacket. It was raining when he got out of his car. She brings a towel for his dreads.

"You call the doc, uncle?"

"Sure. If he's Viktor's, then he's mine, too."

That doesn't make sense in his world, especially since he can't accept that she and Viktor consider themselves really related. What truly baffles him is why the old dude is being nice to him. He's certain his bad behavior bugs the hell out of the witch doctor just as much as everyone else, which is part of his game, along with being the undisputed top-ranked blocker this season. He gets comfortable on the couch and sips the bland tea set beside him. "Got whiskey?"

"I'll put it on the list."

Her relaxed manner puts him at ease. She's so graceful. He looks around the room at the empty walls. Claire curls up on the cushion a foot or so from him. He can feel the heat radiating from her leg.

"Just so you know, I plan on decorating once I'm enrolled and living here."

"You mean, White Owl didn't leave behind a bunch of Buckeye posters and banners? Where'd he move to?"

Claire describes the house at the top of a hill on a dead-end street in a nearby neighborhood. He realizes that's where he had watched her and Viktor disappear to in the car she'd been driving when he first saw her. While they talk, he pictures cupping her firm round breasts in his hands. They'd be a perfect fit. She is wearing a body-hugging top with a low-cut neck. There's no bulging cleavage. For once he doesn't care. He asks what she's studying, and then proceeds to apologize for the "fuck" that slipped out, having promised himself on the way over not to use it.

"A heart surgeon! Don't people decide something like that when they're already *in* med school?"

"I have a four year nursing degree. This past winter I worked in a cardiology unit and loved it. I've always wanted to be a doctor but would never saddle myself with such huge debt. However, I found out that if I work with underserved Native Americans after I graduate, I'll qualify for getting most of my tuition erased. Viktor's parents, my Uncle Sol and Aunt Constance, will go on paying for this apartment, which is a huge savings."

Her goal blows him away. "That's really big of them. You've got a long road ahead of you."

"Nose to the grindstone. How 'bout you? I assume most players aspire to getting drafted by the NFL."

"Yeah...a lot dream it, but few end up making the pros." For the first time Damien opens up to someone about the never ending violence he was exposed to growing up on Chicago's south side. He explains how he showed up on the doorstep of an unknown relative in Dayton who was willing to take a chance on him, thanks to the help of a social worker.

Claire senses he's reticent about his past, and appreciates that he feels safe disclosing some details. "How lucky we are to know people who believe so strongly in our abilities."

Lucky? He reckons he is.

The sound of hail pelting the glass draws them to the window. With winds too dangerous to go out in, Claire offers to make lunch. She finds a package of macaroni and jars of spaghetti sauce in the pantry. Damien moves to a tall chair at the kitchen counter. It occurs to him that they must be around the same age. Close; he turns 23 in March, a few months before she does. Claire admires that he had the gumption to get his GED at 19, and then followed it up by going to Ohio State. He had to be really talented to make the football team. That said, he can't help but wonder if she believes he might have been given a pass by his teachers. Who isn't familiar with the stereotype of the failing athlete, allowed to move on because they win games for their schools? In Damien's case, he seldom completed all the required written assignments, but he did pay attention to the lessons because he is by nature a curious person, and most subjects, including math and science, interested him. He always scored well on exams.

While they talk, Damien is simultaneously trying to figure out ways to make this relationship work. They're from such totally different worlds. It's as though he had no choice in the matter of meeting Claire. There was an element of compulsion to it. On the tough streets of Chicago where he grew up, it was normal to regard the entire lot of females as subpar—eye candy. He didn't think it possible to be affected by a girl to this degree. Despite the strong attraction between them, it's evident that Claire's primary focus is school. Any other day, before she caught his eye, football was his. This is new territory for him.

He's totally enjoying the backside view of her while she attends to the pots on the stove. Her leggings reveal a cute, firm round ass. Now and then, Claire glances over her shoulder to find Damien staring at her butt. How brazen of him, she thinks, knowing full well he's charmed by her. And as wildly seductive as she finds him, the student in her won't permit some guy's attention to interfere with her studies. This is fun, though.

Following their meal at the coffee table, where they sat side-by-side on the floor and watched the Kansas City Chiefs, her home team, on a 19 inch TV she bought for sixty bucks at Target, they decide to call it a day. There has been a break in the weather, but the icy rains are expected to last until morning. Were it any other girl, Damien would be spending the night.

It's necessary that he hold her before he leaves. He's got to do it before she reaches the door. Her upper arms appear lost inside his big hands. Damien meets resistance when he tries to pull her closer. Claire gently presses her palms against his chest, in order to maintain a proper distance between them, the space needed for his erection not to be obvious to her. He slides an arm around the back of her neck. They study each other a moment, and then she lets him kiss her. It's a long, enjoyable kiss, with their tongues only slightly touching.

Damien can't stop replaying what happened. Last night after he drove back to his dorm from his cousin Gabe's house in Dayton, his belly full from the huge Thanksgiving spread the neighbors cooked a day early, just for his sake so he could return to OSU in time for practice before the Michigan game, he called Claire. She agreed to meet him at the Student Union today for the annual Thanksgiving dinner. Football players are among those who volunteer to serve meals to students and staff who aren't able to travel home. He wasn't about to admit that this commendable activity wasn't on his schedule. Claire appreciated the tradition since this was the first time in her entire life she wasn't going to be with her parents for the holiday, and it seemed a good way to ward off the loneliness.

They were having the best time when later in the afternoon some of his friends stopped by, and the laughs continued—for them. Once they left, Claire announced she'd been appalled by their gutter language. One word in particular so offended her that she thought it best they didn't see each other again. In all likelihood, the subject for the rift was bound to come up at some point; he only wishes it would have happened after the Michigan game.

He thinks back to how his heart skipped when he laid eyes on her walking into the Student Union. She wore a straight plaid skirt and a soft peachy-colored sweater that hugged her perfect round breasts. A headband kept her afro pulled back, showing off her pretty shaped face. When she spotted him and smiled, he felt warm all over. Now, unfortunately, the expression that haunts him is her look of disappointment. How can he salvage the relationship when he believes she got bent out of shape over nothing? And to think the entire time he'd been fighting to keep the fucks out of his vocabulary.

What really put him in the doghouse was when he claimed she was naïve for presuming her brothers never used the n-word around their friends—she couldn't even say it. And then he dug himself in a deeper hole when he added that they simply didn't say it around the house!

"Uppity bitch!"

He stuffs his clothes and shoes into an oversized leather duffel bag, punches the side hard with his fist, and then hurls it at the wall full force, startling his teammates in the next room who were finishing a video game when everything around them suddenly rattled. "Fuck," he roars, drawing out the word. They stare at each other, wondering what's next. Poor T-bone wants to go to bed, but he's scared to go over and face his roommate.

"Give him ten minutes," says one of the guys.

Slaughter pounces on Claire and pins her to the bed. In his mind, she's real. He slides his hand in his pants as he prepares to vent his anger on her, when the unforgettable image of her walking toward him in the Student Union stops him from going any further. The closer she comes, the faster his heart races. Their hello hug is magic. He clutches his pillow and relives the emotion. How could he allow a fucking female to get under his skin like this?

Hayden waits in bed for Skyler who is trying to get their daughter to sleep, a problem this week since the baby is fighting a cold. Her crying ruined the Thanksgiving meal which was a simple dinner Skyler cooked for only the three of them. Nevertheless, she put in hours to make it a memorable one. He feels bad for being away so much these past few days, but with the Michigan game looming, he has been at Viktor's side since he came back from the rez on Tuesday. He is thinking about the stories Viktor had to tell about his biological father's family, with characters too over-the-top to be real, yet he doesn't doubt they're true. His friend has never been one to exaggerate.

"What are you pondering all by your lonesome?" asks Skyler, dropping splayed across the bed, her hair damp from having washed the baby's spit-up from it.

"Does she have a fever?"

"Not bad...a hundred." She scoots up toward the headboard, grunting as she goes, then forces a weak smile to convey that the drudgery of motherhood is worth it.

They lean against each other and stare out the window at the stars. It's a crystal clear night, freezing cold but beautiful. They've not had a moment to themselves in weeks. Tomorrow Hayden leaves with the team to Michigan. Skyler has been taking little Mimi with her to the studio where the troupe continues to rehearse long hours for a December show.

"You won't believe Viktor's trip. Talk about drama!"

An exhausted Skyler welcomes hearing about anything that isn't dance. She easily pictures Viktor in a tepee with his Indian relatives. As if the backstory about his biological father weren't interesting enough, Hayden goes on to describe the brief hair-cutting ceremony.

A yawning fit overtakes her, but she enjoys her husband's breath in her ear as he talks and the touch of his skin. "Go on," she says, settling deeper into the pillow.

"Thirty or so members of his extended family rode down on horses from their homes in the Black Hills to personally congratulate him and Tess. They stayed in their own tepees and invited them to vacation together in the future. They want their children to grow up knowing each other."

"What a wonderful surprise! We should make a point of doing the same. Mimi should see Wyoming and her cousins."

"I miss you and me working together," says Hayden. "I'll quit this football gig in a second if you want me to."

"I like having different news to share. Besides, me dealing with the dancers is good for my personal growth."

He laughs. "You mean you're actually viewing them as entities with feelings, not merely as physical instruments?"

It was a lighthearted remark, but the words hurt because that's exactly what she has been doing, for she is dead serious about showing more empathy. "Sorry," he whispers.

They listen to make sure Mimi is sleeping before tucking the comforter around their shoulders. Next they admire the razor-thin crescent moon that's come into view. Hayden holds his wife close. His thoughts turn to the practice field. The dancer turned coach was initially the butt of endless jokes. He didn't take kindly to the nickname "twinkle toes." But once the squad witnessed Number 7's unbelievable balance and flexibility, a few linemen did an about-face and sheepishly approached him for pointers. These past days he's been observing the burly players, encouraging them to pivot in a way that feels more natural and not to follow blanket rules imposed on them, like never using their heels. He also has them focusing on their hip roll. His contrasting ideas have created a degree of tension among the trainers and him, but they can't ignore the results they're witnessing. Watching those enormous bodies in action reminds him of the chorus of dancing hippos in *Fantasia*. What a fun job he landed—thanks to Viktor.

"Viktor is incredible," he says, thinking back to the earlier conversation they were having about him. "We realized during *WAKAN* that he possessed an aptitude for dance, but now that I'm around him more I recognize how truly exceptional his talents are. And when you consider how young he still is."

"True," says Skyler. "He's got a rare combination of brains and brawn, besides having good sense and looks. To think that such a wonderful life force was almost extinguished." Both have avoided mentioning Ishmael's name since he mysteriously disappeared.

Their lids grow heavy, but they enjoy talking like this in bed. Before nodding off, Hayden makes a prediction about this Saturday.

"Skyler...this team is magic, as is Michigan's, and that's strictly because Krull is there now. It's going to be a game more historical than 2006's when both were top ranked. The guys play with remarkable maturity, even the freshmen. They have good instincts. OSU's captain, Rhett Holgersson, deserves a good deal of the credit. He plays the center position and is a fifth-year senior who should already be in the NFL. He stayed so his sick father can watch him play one last season for his alma mater. Then there's Krull, who dances around the pocket like nobody else. Fans at both schools have a soft spot in their hearts for the kid who dreamt of wearing a Wolverines jersey, but resigned himself to playing for the Buckeyes while his sister was undergoing cancer treatments here in Columbus."

"What sad circumstances."

"The only jerk who could put the kibosh on us winning is 54. Slaughter loves to get in everyone's face, not just the opponent's. The one time he sat out due to unsportsmanlike conduct was the one game Viktor got royally sacked."

Friday afternoon and everyone is restless as our plane nears Detroit, including me. We're eager for it to be Saturday already, game day inside

The Big House at the University of Michigan. Before our final approach, I walk the aisle and stop beside every row of seats, demanding to know: "What's our goal?"

In unison, the guys answer with a resounding: "Play smart!"

Two-thirds of the way down, I reach our most recent recruit from Tennessee, a second-stringer who is seated beside Slaughter. "Whatcha gonna do if you get a chance to start?"

"Play smart!" he barks back to me like a private to his Drill Sergeant.

Demon Slaughter, our loose cannon, laughs at us both. God, I'd love to blow him to smithereens!

CHAPTER 53

In the broadcast booth, Welbourne's familiar old-time radio announcer voice is beginning to show signs of strain. "Tiberius Krull, Michigan's fleet-footed quarterback fakes the pass and marches the ball over the goal line! With only seconds remaining in the first half, he forgoes any end zone celebration as the kicking team runs onto the field. And the ball is up...and over! Well done! The Wolverines tie the Buckeyes at 42. Folks, we are witnessing history in the making. These teams have played at an exhausting tempo and dazzled us with their extraordinary athleticism."

Word is out! Even people who don't give a damn about football sit riveted to the action in front of a screen somewhere in the country, enthralled by the high-stakes matchup of this granddaddy of college football rivalries. Tess along with her mom and Claire enjoy listening to the observations in the comfort of her and Viktor's secluded home, though they could do without the men's five-foot tall heads displayed across the wall on the unforgiving HD screen. The coverage returns to the analyst desk on the field where the marching bands in the background are doing a good job of drowning out the six men who shamelessly talk over one another. Fortunately, the decision is made to cut back to the announcers in the quieter booth. Welbourne and his young partner, color commentator Andy Salazar, a former NFL wide receiver who'd gotten passed around several teams over his twelve year career, offer their insightful views that help one appreciate the complexity of the game. The three women laugh at Salazar's plastic-looking, ridiculously white teeth. They distract from how handsome the black-haired former athlete is. His dark stubble beard accentuates the teeth even more. Both teams, they learn, are blessed with explosive safeties that can play multiple positions, which the announcers go on to better explain.

And though fans were undoubtedly pleased that no penalties got called throughout both quarters, Welbourne drives home the fact that this is unheard of. "When have rivals played such a clean game! There's been no rushing the passer, no false starts, and no grabbing the facemask. The only targeting foul was dismissed after review. It's a monumental feat considering all the new rules."

Welbourne adds that the constant adjustments each side made, when they organized blitzes and changed up blocking formations, speak volumes about the experience of the coaches and the discipline of several former redshirted freshmen who are making their debut this season.

Salazar agrees. "Their level of maturity is incredible. Some guys in the NFL could learn a thing or two," he quips.

"This is fun," says Tess, as she plows a chip through the artichoke-spinach dip.

Chevonne checks her daughter's forehead for a fever. "Since when?" she asks in jest.

Claire gets the joke, having learned about Tess's deep-rooted disdain for football from Viktor. She likes Tess's mom, whom she met yesterday for the first time when mother and daughter and triplets arrived in Columbus after the long three-day drive from South Dakota. Tess's father didn't accompany them. Brian went directly to Michigan from the Buckthorn Reservation, in order to catch the game before returning to his job in Cincinnati. During their trip, Tess had called Claire to see if she might give them a hand with the babies as soon as they returned to the house. Chevonne was the one to invite Claire to watch the Buckeyes and Wolverines go at it today. The car had to be fitted with three infant carriers for the newborns. The babies are presently huddled together and sleeping on a padded floor mat in the corner. Claire is filled with questions about the birthing experience, but refrains from asking anything simply because this day is clearly all about football for Tess's mom.

A camera slowly pans the rows of fans from one end of the stadium to the other. "Wouldn't it be a hoot," says Chevonne excitedly, "if we saw your dad or the others in the stands?" The "others" she is referring to are Tess's brother, Quinn, who flew up to Michigan from Cincinnati, Solomon and Constance, and Iris and Hashke. "Maybe we have seen them and don't realize it. Everyone's so bundled up in the cold. They should've made a big sign for us to spot them easily." Most of the banners and homemade signs show the names of the teams and the quarterbacks. Here and there are ones for other player positions. OSU's top receiver, Jasper Stillman, has his cheering section, as does DeShaun Rivers.

Claire is tempted to announce that she is a "Demon" lover. She can't stop thinking about the fine-looking athlete. The much-maligned player with the outlaw reputation has so far garnered praise for his composure during the first half, leaving the announcer to wonder if Slaughter is sick. Claire wants to believe Damien is keeping his behavior and tongue in check on account of her. He knows she'd be watching the game, if only to see Viktor play. But then again, they parted on such bad terms.

At halftime, I get an idea. Coach stares at me as though I've lost my mind, but I believe I came up with a terrific suggestion. The guys are too wired to have paid attention to it. They're chomping at the bit, anxious for another crack at taking down the Wolverines. What a harebrained idea I'm told, considering that this is our most important game of the season. 'Why?' he asks. To which I reply, "Because it is exactly that, a game." His tone was condescending with me, which I wasn't prepared for. It isn't typical of him. I chalk it up to nerves. Coach gets the gist of what I'm saying, but he isn't about to entertain the possibility of allowing second stringers on the field. Rhett moves to my side and places his arm around my shoulder. I can tell he's on board. By now Coach's patience has worn thin. Rhett nods in the affirmative and says to him, "Why not? They've proven their willingness to work hard. They know the playbook and are thoroughly prepared." When the veteran team captain speaks up, one as well-respected as Rhett, it's an entirely different matter. Rhett obviously carries more clout than this Indian, which I'm okay with since he is by far the most mature and unflappable guy around. The players are lit! We race out at full throttle!

In the meantime, in the broadcast booth, Grant Welbourne and Andy Salazar focus on the competing quarterbacks' contrasting styles, which is nothing new to these fans, but, having just learned that the Twitter audience increased in the last half hour, the announcers review the latest stats and get everyone up to speed in the few minutes before the second half kickoff. The video editor had been hustling during the break to find footage of Krull's mastery of keeping the play alive in the pocket, as well as examples of Talking White Owl's mind-boggling on-target passing accuracy.

The game resumes after the Buckeyes' explosive kick returner sensibly takes a knee in the end zone after catching the ball. At this point, Welbourne admits that all bets are off as to who will win. "We'll see if Talking White Owl goes deep…" Salazar at once nudges him and is met with a scowl for the interruption.

"Look who's starting!" he says. "It's Rufus Burlee, White Owl's backup." Salazar sounds incredulous, and rightly so. "There was no mention of an injury before halftime."

"Holy Smokes! What are they thinking?" mutters Welbourne under his breath. "The entire second string offense is on the line." After too long a pause, Welbourne continues, "Michigan's defense is as baffled as the rest of us. There are a lot of flailing arms. The frustrated players are looking to the sideline for direction. Tiberius Krull and the coaches are conferring, all the while gesturing wildly. The Defensive Coordinator just stepped away. He immediately signals the starters to return to their sideline."

"What's Krull doing!" In the excitement, Salazar's voice jumps an octave higher. "He is at the bench and physically pulling the guys to their feet and pushing them toward the field. 'Go, go, go,' he's yelling to them!"

Welbourne tries to maintain a sense of calm. "In light of the Bucks' audacious move to permit the backups to play, Michigan responds with its own substitutions, which is allowed before the snap." Welbourne watches the activity, then continues. "This will surely go down as one of the most dramatic and unorthodox decisions ever to have been made in college football. And to what purpose, we wonder, especially when the score is tied." He sighs loudly. "The teams are finally in position. Burlee, Number 11, is presently under center. The decibel level in the stadium is off the charts."

"Surprisingly, the bench-warmers don't disappoint," says Salazar during a timeout. "Flags have been tossed for the first time this afternoon, penalties for pass interference; and despite them, each side has managed to get a hard-won touchdown. It took them longer than the starting players, but these untested backups have exhibited the same grit as their counterparts. It was gratifying to witness their teammates cheering them on from the sidelines like crazed parents at a Little League tournament. We anticipate the high octane action to resume, now that the true starting lineups return to the field."

Back in Columbus, Claire is secretly pleased over the kudos Damien has earned from the announcers. Apparently he normally uses his long powerful arms to swing opposing players to the ground, even the three hundred pound tacklers. Today, however, he's been driving his shoulder into the linemen, creating openings for DeShaun Rivers to shoot through.

"Michigan is concentrating on Viktor too much," says Chevonne. "Their defense is taking their team out of the play." A second later Salazar states the exact same thing, noting that their coach will swiftly correct that losing strategy. He goes on to credit each team for its ability to make constant decisive adjustments that ultimately leads to a tied game, which puts them into overtime.

"How are they even standing?" marvels Tess. She compares them to a bunch of hard-driven horses the way they're dripping in sweat and spewing steam from their nostrils,

"They're good," says Chevonne, who is focused on the action. "Their eyes show they're just as hungry to win as when they started."

"You're intense, Mrs. O'Shea," says Claire as she picks up a crying baby, ready for a meal. It's obvious the grandmother can't be bothered by such distractions during the game.

"Nothing new," says Tess to Claire, pushing her shirt up. "I'm really thankful you're here."

The Wolverines get nowhere fast. The three-point field goal puts them ahead, temporarily. Chevonne sits on the arm of the couch and absentmindedly glides the back of her hand across the nursing baby's soft cheek. "This is it," she says quietly, her eyes glued to the screen. Tess and Claire are quite aware it is, too.

"The Bucks are going for the shotgun formation," says Welbourne, which he assumed they would. "It's a perfect snap as White Owl drops back to throw. He drills it down centerfield to Number 6, who is in the clear at the 20…but wait! Michigan's Trent Yarborough fends off Landers and races toward the ball. Oh! both players collide in the air, and the ball strikes Trent's helmet and bounces away! He whips around to catch it. The ball dances on his fingertips. By Golly, he hauls it in and scurries out of the Bucks territory! Amazing! The day's first interception. This would give the Wolverines the game! It's clear sailing as he proceeds past the line of scrimmage, but now White Owl is back on his feet, having tripped over Slaughter after he got decked by the defense. It's a desperate final charge for this quarterback who is running a lateral route to ambush Trent. What an unbelievably chaotic drive!"

"White Owl's long strides catapult him across the field," continues Salazar, "but it appears Yarborough might be just outside his grasp. No, it's not possible...White Owl lunges forward and grabs Yarborough by the foot, toppling him, but not before the ball pops into the air yet again...and it's Number 80, Jasper Stillman, who zips past and catches it. He'd been trailing the action at a distance. Jasper Stillman, the nation's top receiver, is now making a mad dash along the sideline back to the other end of the field!"

The ladies in Columbus are on their feet, jumping and screaming, "Run, Jasper, run!" The baby, intent on feeding, is apparently okay with being jostled against a vigorously shaking breast. Claire laughs, "From now on, Holt is always going to expect milkshakes." They laugh and hug.

Jasper's teammates are laughing, too, and hopping all over him, punching each other good naturedly, and dancing. The festive atmosphere in the stadium is short-lived. The crowd watches as coaches and doctors run toward the downed players. Viktor, whose front side slammed the ground with tremendous force, has since rolled to his back and isn't moving. Damien is writhing in pain on the ground. Three of Michigan's linemen are woozy and can't stand.

Chevonne instantly saves Holt when Tess goes limp. She returns him to the corner with his siblings. Of course Honor is now fussing and wants to eat. Tess stares at the screen, at her helpless husband. Claire gets her to sit. Tess gently pushes the next hungry infant away. Her mother coaxes her into feeding Honor. Little Raif will be the one who gets a bottle this go-round.

"Theresa, trust me. I've encountered this so many times with your brothers. Viktor got winded. Give him a couple minutes; he'll be on his feet. Really."

And what of Damien, wonders Claire. The players' teammates take a knee as they wait for word about the injuries. She tears up when Damien is placed on a stretcher. Mrs. O'Shea kisses her forehead, believing Claire's concern is strictly due to her cousin Viktor's unknown physical state. Naturally, the station cuts to an endless string of commercials, allowing too much time for Tess and Claire to envision worst case scenarios.

As it turns out, Tess's mom knew what she was talking about. With the game officially over, Viktor and his teammates are presently singing and slowly swaying to the melody of *Carmen Ohio* with their fans, as is tradition. It appears that Jasper has a good hold on Viktor around the waist for support. Tess squeezes Claire's hand, and then nuzzles Honor's soft hair as the baby nurses. Damien is suspected of having a bruised kidney, which Claire knows can be serious. The other hurt Michigan players aren't as lucky, with each suffering broken bones. The announcer notes, sounding somewhat unsympathetic, that at least they aren't faced with a Big Ten Championship Game next weekend like the Buckeyes are.

Tess worries about Viktor's poor family sitting in the stands. "What must have been going through their minds as they witnessed Viktor go down? I refuse to watch any more games. If the outcome had been more tragic…no, I can't go there!" Tess admires her daughter's innocent face. "Why must your daddy play football? What a terrible shortcoming."

"*Seriously?*" says Claire; she can't help herself. "Would you consider it on par with cheating or lying! I can think of a slew of worse faults."

Following a night's hospitalization in Michigan, Damien Slaughter chooses to recuperate from his injury in his dorm room at OSU instead of going to his cousin Gabe's place in Dayton. He'll get access to the best physical therapists, plus he didn't want to burden Gabe, who has had to put up with enough of his antics. Gabe, however, insisted on picking him up at the Columbus airport and driving him to campus, where he then checked himself into a nearby motel. "Who doesn't need family at a time like this?" said Gabe when Damien tried to talk him out of staying for the week. After spending only a few hours with Damien on his first full day back, Gabe could tell by his young cousin's sullen mood that something was bothering him besides his injury. Three days later, and Gabe is prepared to call him out on it.

"Damien, did you get yourself involved in a situation and now find yourself in over your head? You can be honest with me." Next he tells him, "I'll help if I can." Ever since the angry youth with the chip on his shoulder took up residence in his Dayton home, Gabe vowed to have his back, no matter the circumstances. They are blood relatives, after all. And though Damien is still mighty rough around the edges, the athlete has proven he can handle his classes while playing football at an elite level. His current mental state is troubling, though. Damien told Gabe he was relieved to hear that the blow to his back wasn't bad enough to sideline him in the upcoming game, but you wouldn't guess it by his brooding behavior. He acts preoccupied and is short when asked anything. Gabe's biggest fear all along has been that Damien might get sucked back into gang life. His social worker from Illinois warned there was a strong possibility of it happening. Once he was enrolled at OSU, Gabe urged Damien to avoid the shady clubs in a crime ridden part of Columbus where he liked to party. "Steer clear of the hangers-on," he advised him. By now they know he's set to land a big dollar contract with the NFL.

Damien stares out the window, seemingly oblivious to his cousin's concern. It's annoying to Gabe, who decides it's pointless to stay and gets up to leave. Right then he hears a short laugh coming from Damien. "In over my head," snorts Damien, shaking his head. "Yes, Gabe, you hit the nail on the head, as you like to say; I *am* in over my head." Gabe's worrisome expression prompts Damien to do some fast explaining.

He tells Gabe about Claire, including what happened on Thanksgiving at the Student Union. Gabe is sympathetic, but then reminds Damien of the ultimatum he had given him after only a month in his house. No cursing, no using the Lord's name in vain, and he never wanted to hear him utter the N-word again when referring to his friends, or he could take the next flight back to Chicago. "If you could uphold those rules in my house, why then won't you show this young woman the same respect? *You,* Damien, are the one who is naïve for believing that all Blacks have at some time used that ugly word, even if only behind closed doors. I never have; and I guarantee Claire's brothers haven't either, if that's what she claims!"

The two men from distinctly different backgrounds stand facing each other. For once, surprisingly, Damien isn't on the defensive. He shrugs and slumps on the bed.

"What would you say to Claire this moment, if you could? You don't have to tell me, but think about it…and do it by tomorrow, or it will continue to eat at you."

Gabe pats Damien on the shoulder and says goodbye.

"Thanks Gabe, for driving up and sticking by me."

"Glad to help."

Alone now, and lonely as hell, Damien writes a short message to Claire, but he can't bring himself to send it. His cousin is right; he must deal with the situation, and soon, or he'll be worthless for the game this weekend.

T-bone enters and says he'd like to go to bed, hinting for Damien to sit in their common room if he intends to stay up longer. The players need to wake early to board the bus for the Big Ten Championship game in Indianapolis. The plane that was reserved for transporting the team is being used to handle an overload of stranded passengers. The airlines had to reschedule flights this first weekend of December due to the brutal weather pounding the upper Midwest.

Damien readily agrees to hit the sack. He's eager to go inside his head, to picture Claire naked in his arms. He listens to T-bone's deep breathing and mimics the rhythm, thinking it will help him nod off...but it doesn't. He reaches for his phone in the dark, rereads the words in his message, then taps send. With that, he sleeps. In the morning, his eyes open to the blinking light showing a message. He holds his breath; it could be from anyone. But it isn't. *I miss you, too.* It is perhaps the first time in his life that he thanks Jesus outright, recognizing a blessing for what it is.

"That was too easy," declares our center and team leader, Rhett Holgersson, on the Buck's win over Wisconsin as we head back to the locker room here at Lucas Oil Stadium in Indianapolis, the site of the Big Ten Championship game. "Viktor, be honest with me. They weren't that bad, right?"

"We were smokin', brother!" exclaims one of the linebackers, shaking Rhett by the shoulder pads and then hugging him. "77 to 9! Dang!" And with that, the celebration shifts into high gear. The noise gets to me, and I steal a moment for myself in a coach's room where I listen to a reporter on TV. "OSU trounced Wisconsin's Badgers. The Buckeyes could have run up the score higher, but once again the back-ups were rewarded an opportunity to initiate a drive that eventually led to a touchdown, just like in the previous game with Michigan. The players have already entered the realm of superstardom; most notably, Viktor Talking White Owl, who by all accounts is a bona fide megastar. They're deemed a shoo-in to win the Bowl game. And a National Championship victory in January will merely solidify their reputation as the greatest team in the land."

Next he makes an astute observation that I wholeheartedly agree with, that there is a spiritual component to our games. For me personally,

Wakan is ever-present. It's also gratifying to know that the Rawakota Nation cheers me on from afar, which my relatives from Chohkahn informed me of on the rez when the triplets were born. My wish is to make the entire Indigenous community proud of this Indian, no matter where they're from.

When I call my cousin Wes, one of Claire's brothers, to confirm the name of the restaurant where we'll be celebrating tonight, I discover that Slaughter will be joining us. No way! I was so looking forward to a fun time with him and his brother and Claire. They got tickets to the game for her. Wes and Vince drove up from Kansas City to Indianapolis to see me. This news puts the kibosh on enjoying the evening. I call Tess. Besides missing her to death and wanting to hear her voice, I also need to vent.

Tess is relentless. "Viktor, you march your butt over to that restaurant this second, you hear! I bet your cousins are so excited to meet you for dinner. You can't suddenly bow out! So Claire wants to date a player you can't stand, and they invited him along. It makes sense her brothers would want to get to know him. Can't you be civil to Damien for one hour? Think what a special occasion this is for Claire. Her brothers treated her with a ticket to the Championship game, and she gets to introduce her boyfriend to them."

"What! Her *boyfriend?*"

"Claire and Damien had gotten to know each other while you were in South Dakota. They obviously want to pursue a relationship. She's crazy about him."

"No frickin' way! I knew she liked his looks…but…how did this ever happen?"

"That's another story. I've only just learned about it. Right now, you need to collect yourself and go enjoy being with your family."

I hang up and start pacing. "Fuck!" This makes no fucking sense. "Shit. Fucking lunatic…" Suddenly there's a knock. Wes stands facing me in the doorway.

"What gives, bro? You okay?"

"Yeah. Come in."

After a big hug, I haven't seen him in forever, he asks what the holdup is; everyone wants to eat. At thirty, he is quite the adult. His neatly trimmed moustache and beard are new. He's always been well-groomed and style conscious. I feel I owe him an answer, but I'm too tired to get into it.

"Sorry. Just moving in slow-motion." Seeing Wes does make me excited to see Vince, too. At some point during dinner, however, I expect to corner Slaughter. I have but one question for him, which I need to put out of my mind right now. It's comforting standing shoulder-to-shoulder with Wes as we ride down the elevator. He has always had a protective quality about him. And that wide, warm smile runs throughout the Davis families. Even his tortured father was born with it. Thank goodness for photos, because events in Uncle Roy's life have taken a toll on his.

We pass Sultan's Bar and Grille, where most of the players are partying. The floor is shaking through my legs, the music's so loud. I dread it carrying over to the restaurant that's on the other side of the lobby. Once we turn the corner, the sound is muffled, and the playlist reverts to low-key Christmas songs.

I'm so happy to see Vince that I forget about my antagonist, acknowledging him with a slight nod. I sit across from my cousins and next to Claire, who, for the most part, blocks my view of Slaughter who's sitting to her left. There's no mistaking her apologetic expression. She leans in and whispers, "He was with me when they invited him to join us."

I ignore her and spear the calamari. "Hope they serve big steaks. Looking sharp, Vince." He had bleached the top of his fade haircut.

Other than shooting hoops with them occasionally, I never did much with Wes and Vince, who are considerably older than I am. Come to think of it, that's all the two ever did at our grandparents' house. We discuss a few plays from today's game then agree that's enough about football. They laugh over their little sister's and my hideout under the dining room table when we were kids. It was constantly draped with sheets and blankets when it wasn't mealtime.

"What exactly went on inside there?" grins Vince.

"I educated, Viktor," says Claire teasingly.

That spurs a round of wisecracks. She turns and looks at me affectionately. "Viktor brought his comics for me, and I used to read him my favorite books. He loved *The Secret Garden,* and I loved to hear about the reservation and his Indian friends."

"Sounds magical," says Vince. "I should've snuck in with you guys."

Not wanting to leave Slaughter out, they ask about his childhood in

Chicago. "Another place and time." He smiles at Claire. "Don't want to ruin the mood...right?" She leans back. Now he's completely in view. Next, those two exchange a look I really didn't need to witness. Vince raises his eyebrows and mouths the word "love" to me. Realizing I'm not amused, he changes the subject and asks about the babies. He and his wife have one on the way. Wes has a three-year old boy and a one-year old girl. When Claire excuses herself to use the restroom, I have my opening to talk to Slaughter. My cousins are going on about something between themselves while the waiter clears the table. I lean across the empty chair.

"Tell me, Damien, how'd you meet up with Claire?"

He looks me straight in the eye and begins with the day he saw Claire standing inside the Athletic Center, after which he followed us out of the parking lot. I listen with interest to the rest of his story.

"Let me get this straight; you trailed behind us in your car...then followed her to my apartment after she dropped me off on a street along the way, but you didn't go up to meet her right then."

"I knew better than to knock on the door, that it might freak her out. Your uncle's name was on the mailbox next to yours, so later I called him and asked if he'd give me her number."

I'm dazed, as in Wile E. Coyote dazed, when the Acme anvil drops on his head!

Claire returns at that moment. She and Slaughter thank her brothers for dinner, but hope they understand that they'd like to enjoy some alone-time. Claire offers a slight smile and kisses my cheek. She wants things to be okay. Before now, there was never an awkward moment between us. When they're gone, Wes wonders what gives, to which I reply:

"Do you guys know *anything* about Slaughter...about his background?"

"We know he's had it rough," says Wes. "We googled his name right after Claire said she was meeting him after the game. We read that he had grown up in different foster homes and spent time in juvy."

Wes and Vince share a look that I don't pretend to make sense of. Next they say they promised Claire to give the guy a chance. "He's been pleasant," says Wes, making a case for him.

"Consider this," says Vince, resting a hand on my arm, "Damien maybe isn't so different from Uncle Sol at his age. He's likely rethinking his past.

Your dad managed to redeem himself after the mistakes he made in his youth."

Wes chimes in: "Our sister has always held your mom in the highest regard. Now she is in a position to take a leap of faith, too, like Aunt Constance did once. Uncle Sol is proof that a person can genuinely reinvent himself."

My gut reaction is to throw the table across the room, my cousins included. The nerve of them, comparing Slaughter to Dad! I shake off Vince's arm and hold myself tight to keep from exploding while Wes takes care of the bill.

We walk in silence to the elevator. They exit a floor before mine, saying how glad they were to see me. I don't say squat, but watch them leave, noting the sadness in their faces. As the door closes, I smack the button for it to open again. They turn around in surprise as I step out.

"Thanks for dinner," I grumble.

"Is it too late for a game of poker?" says Vince, his eyes lighting up.

"You'll have me at a disadvantage, I'm exhausted."

"No problem," grins Wes, wrapping an arm around me, "we'll take an IOU."

Once the cards are dealt, I find I need to get something off my chest before we begin. "I'm embarrassed by my behavior. You're both well within your rights to offer an opinion about the situation. You know better than I do what Uncle Roy had to deal with when it came to getting Dad out of all his scrapes with the law. And the way you compare Claire to my mother...it's a noble quality to find the good in someone, even if it's unclear to a yutz like me."

"No kid likes to admit a parent's flaws," says Vince. "Claire seems to think that Damien's unsportsmanlike outbursts on the field stopped around the time they met. Makes you wonder, doesn't it?" What she says is true; he hasn't been as obnoxious these last few games.

Wes, looking comically serious, pours himself a glass of scotch and taps an imaginary cigar in his mouth. "OK, men, enough with the girly chit-chat—time to ante up!"

CHAPTER 54

"You've really come into your own, Viktor," says Mom, which elicits a wry smile from me. She offers Jim carrots while I continue to wipe him down after our ride. We're in Dr. Nate's barn. She took a couple of weeks off from work to help us after Tess's mother left. Dealing with one newborn is stressful enough, but to have three of them. We were grateful that Chevonne stayed on through the holidays and New Year's to help us, but her constant presence wore on Tess's patience, which I get. As much as I wished to be home with my new family, I was out of the house for the most part, practicing for the Bowl game at the end of December, and then for the national championship game in January. I promised Tess that I would do my fair share of diapering and nightly feedings once the season was over. Today, as a thank you to Mom, I thought I'd treat her to an afternoon of riding.

"Come into my own as what?" I ask. "A son…father, or perhaps an Indian?"

She reaches for a strand of hair hanging over my face and gently twists it around my ear, a tender gesture that I appreciate. "As a man," she replies.

"Did you have doubts?"

She lays her hand across my cheek and rests her thumb on my lips. "I'm lucky you still give me the time of day," she says, mindful of the years spent away from home because of her profession.

As we stand facing each other, I'm cognizant of a different dynamic between us. "You're here now, which makes Tess and me happy."

She slides her hands in her pockets and relaxes against the side of the stall, then closes her eyes. It's chilly enough to see her breaths. "Tell me something," she says.

I await the rest of her sentence, but that's it. "Like what?"

"Anything that pops into your head?" She cracks open her eyes. I laugh a little, not sure of how to answer. I could say that I think she is coming into her own, too, as a woman. Mom has beautiful soulful eyes that give her an air of vulnerability, which I only recognize now that I'm older. The airmen she works beside must find them seductive; however, once they get to know her better, I'm sure they aren't taken in by them any more than I am. She is such a capable person. There's no question that the episodes relating to her post-traumatic stress disorder have ended. I suddenly catch a whiff of decaying apples that need to get pitched. They're in a bag hanging outside the stall. I definitely won't forget to grab it on our way out. As we prepare to leave, something does pop into my head, and I find myself describing a really personal memory.

"When I returned from the rez with Jim last spring, Dr. Nate had placed a cot in the corner there. He knew I'd want to stay until Jim got settled in. Tess surprised me when she came over later in the night. If she hadn't, there'd be no Raif, no Honor, and no Holt." Mom hugs my arm. I instantly regret saying it…that should have remained private.

In Lakota, she says, "*The trio of Red Hawks was meant to be.*"

My heart starts thumping. She can't possibly know about the three hawks that materialized and flew around the cave during my hanbleceya. I told no one, not even Suhdeer who was there with me when it happened. He even insisted that I see a holy man to help interpret whatever it was I experienced when he snatched my arm from the fire. It hasn't been until recently that I thought to associate the vision with the births of my children. It's certainly going to weigh on my mind from here on out.

"Why did you use Lakota?"

Mom shrugs, "Because it sounds like something we Indians attach meaning to. Wakan, right? C'mon, let's go. We need to round up Nero."

Wakan is right! I dutifully buss Jim on the nose and stroke his neck. "Bye, Brother." He watches as I latch the bottom half of the gate. "What do you think, Jim? Is it a coincidence, the three hawks in my vision and me having triplets?"

He snorts and shakes his head no.

"You don't know what you're talking about!"

At that, he pounds the stall forcefully with a hoof and neighs angrily. Can't fault him; I did ask his opinion.

Nero sees me sprinting to the car and races in the opposite direction, not unlike a kid who doesn't want the fun to end. It's obvious that Tess and I have allowed him too much freedom in our house. His lumbering sidekick isn't helping. Dr. Nate's hundred pound Rottweiler won't stop slamming into him, which eventually grabs the attention of a dozing corgi that wants in on the action. What a hoot! His short legs are a blur as he races to keep up. Mom laughs at Nero. "It's a joy watching him be a normal dog." We both know that a simple command will reel him in.

Nero wins more playtime until the car heats up. It's nice when Mom and I get a chance to sit like this.

"Thank goodness, football season is over," she says, "your body deserves a rest."

"That's an understatement, make that body *and mind*."

"William told me about all the fan mail you've received, and from Indians, no less."

"It's overwhelming."

"You are an esteemed young man. It's remarkable enough that you and your team won the National Championship title…but the Heisman winner, too. Un-hee!"

"It was such a relief not having to keep the triplets' births under wraps any longer, or expect the team and staff to. What resonates most with the Indians, girls and guys alike, is that I don't drink, and that I love being a dad."

"What…no mention of your scholarly attributes?"

I smile. "Wishful thinking. It impressed a few."

The car is cozy warm. There's no hurry for us to be anywhere. Tess encouraged Mom and me to go out since the babies presently nap a lot. When they're awake, they're fascinated by each other. Guess that'll change when they start teething. The barren wintry landscape has its own austere beauty. We like the tangled tree branches and colorless field. It looks like a charcoal drawing. It's February; soon spring will change the mood. Four fast-moving specks high in the sky, fighter jets, are gone from view in half a minute. I normally wouldn't give them a second thought. Mom brings up the Fiesta Bowl in Arizona.

"I'm happy you stayed in Phoenix after the game and made the effort to meet Jason Red Moon in the Santa Rita Mountains. Your presence at the demonstration mattered. It really helped draw attention to the Indians' dilemma."

"It's absurd to think I can influence policy that affects the Tohono O'odham Nation simply by showing up. Fame is ridiculous. Jason's passion is commendable." It had reminded me of Marnie's zeal for Native causes, something I wasn't able to understand when I spent that day so long ago shopping with her at the mall in Rapid City, when I was all of fifteen. That fire in their bellies resembles Pahpie's warrior spirit. It floored me when Jason said that my grandfather, Benjamin One Horn, inspired his activism.

"You know, Mom...after I left the protest, I realized there's a push in probably every state by some corporation to snatch up the resources before it's too late, before Natives and environmentalists win injunctions against them." What a tired old story to us Indians; one not worth discussing—about jobs and short term interests and broken promises.

The open door is Nero's signal. He bolts toward us and flies in the back seat. To his credit, he can still respond like the disciplined four-legged airman that he is. In reality he's probably getting hungry.

As Mom backs up, she glances at me out of the corner of her eye. "You had this odd expression when I mentioned that the babies were meant to be...as if preordained. Have you heard the rumors about the current wave of births? That it's prophesized they're going to be history-changing?"

"By whom?" After a second, I add, "I thought my generation, those of us born around 2000, was predicted to be so all-fired important."

"You are, but perhaps more as mentors to this upcoming generation. The values you uphold as parents will do more to save our cultures. This is a critical period. Too many tribes are on the brink of losing their traditions and language forever. Your age group has taken a keen interest in preventing that from happening."

"Is this only in Lakota circles? What's a person to believe?"

"No," she says, mindful of my snappish tone. "The world over. Let me give you a for-instance. Several months ago in a remote part of Norway, a giant spruce tree purported to be fifteen generations old was struck by lightning and fell beside the house of an Indigenous family, sparing the lives of the parents and their baby who had just been born. A folk tale foretold of the event. The baby is said to be the reincarnation of a raven, the people's most important symbol. A generation to them counts as fifteen years, the oldest known lifespan of the bird. I'm sure you've guessed where I'm going with this. Two hundred twenty-five growth rings were counted in the tree's trunk. Fifteen times fifteen."

"Oo-oo-oo, if that isn't convincing." I normally don't dismiss stories like this. After all, I had witnessed a dead Ron Léglise up a tree plain as day when I was younger, his football jersey blowing on the cross in the ditch where he had drowned in his overturned truck. And the hawks that mesmerized me in my vision were as real as could be, to the point that I could have burned my hand reaching for the one that stared at me from its perch atop a burning log in the middle of the fire. What Mom is describing sounds more like people affected by mass hysteria. It seems implausible, even to someone like me who's been exposed to mystical events growing up. She's not giving up on this.

"The leaders who belong to the Council of First Nations are reporting similar phenomena on their reservations. There have been births of two-headed turtles and five-legged goats on the day a mother has delivered."

"Are the human babies normal?" It seems to me they wouldn't be.

"Yes. No one regards these as bad omens. They're supposedly signs that reflect a promising future. There's nothing new about the power of collective thought. Fabricated or not, the energy is real. Enough people yearning for change can make it happen."

On that note, I'm glad to be home. As I undo my seatbelt, Mom holds me by my wrist. "I don't ask that you share the details of what you saw during your hanbleceya. Receiving a vision is an extraordinary gift, as you well know. Will you at least consider that the triplets might represent harbingers of good things to come for our people, both the Lakota and Rawakota?" Now she's spooking me. "Maybe you should think about visiting Chohkahn," she says, "see the city for yourself. It might offer new insights into what it means to be Rawakota."

I tell her plainly, "I am Lakota. That's my reality." Letting go of me, she answers back, "Mine, too." Nero nudges my neck. We say our goodbyes. She has been staying at a hotel at night, in order to get work done, unlike Chevonne, who camped next to the crib in the nursery on a cot she bought. The triplets sleep best curled up together. Tess and I are dreading the fact that we need to find someone to help us on a permanent basis. Nero barks upon entering and zooms to the kitchen. I hear Tess laughing. The house smells of beef stew. There he sits, waiting patiently at attention by his food bowl. Tess turns to me still laughing at him. God, she's beautiful.

I roll back onto the pillow after hitting the snooze button, reluctant to face the rainy morning. Something unbelievably soft touches my lids. I'm not dreaming. Mmm. A nipple parts my lips, it moves on to my chin. At long last…it's been three months since the babies were born. The wait has been torture.

CHAPTER 55

Howling Wind never imagined she'd see Mrs. Falcone again, the woman who years ago had hosted a dinner party with her husband in honor of the pilots stationed at the Arizona air base. It was Falcone who had asked Howling Wind if it was possible to land a fighter jet if its engine suddenly quit working, and then alluded to the real possibility of it happening, specifically the following Thursday. Howling Wind was among the pilots whose aircraft lost power that fateful day high over the desert when they were called upon to scramble a commercial airliner in distress, after which she demanded to know from Chief Rolling Thunder what the connection was between the Rawakota and this odd pair who evidently worked as spies for the tribe. It was explained to her that the family had earned the trust of the U.S. government as far back as World War II. Because of the nature of their metals business, Falcone Industries acquired contracts from the Army and Air Force to conduct clean-up operations at bombing test sites that were kept secret from the American public. Centuries ago, their people mined copper in what is present-day New Mexico. The maid who greeted Howling Wind at the front door leads her to the backyard. Seeing the big fire pit stirs up memories of her deceased dog trainer friend, Phil Tardelli. How they had chatted and laughed there during that long-ago evening. A voice from behind interrupts her thoughts.

"Good afternoon, Colonel," says Mrs. Falcone, adjusting the swim turban along her hairline. It's startling to see her wearing a thick, boldly striped terry cloth cover-up. Howling Wind is certain no mention was made about bringing a bathing suit. "You've been having quite an adventurous career." Howling Wind soberly assesses the enigmatic figure standing before her, more so during the lingering handshake she can't escape. It's made longer yet when the hostess rests her hand over hers, stating a fact she already knew, that absolutely no one is aware of the Rawakota Nation. Nevertheless, she nods back to the woman.

Having said that, Mrs. Falcone leads the Colonel across the patio to the pool area. It's a glorious spring day in Scottsdale, with an endless blue sky, which is where Howling Wind wishes she were up flying in at the moment instead of being here. The temperature is in the mid-eighties. She has no clue why she was personally invited by the Falcones to come to their home. There are other guests as well. She is introduced to two men, Sommers and Boorman. They are CIA agents. Next is Hiram Douglass, a senator who serves on the military's Oversight Council. She recognizes the woman from her portrait that hangs in halls on air bases, being that she is four star General Abernathy, the Chief of Staff of the U.S. Air Force. Today she is dressed like a civilian, so she must not be here in an official capacity. Howling Wind wears her best poker face as she waits to hear what the unusual and highly irregular meeting is about. She notes that the host's husband, Louis Falcone, is not present. They're invited to sit beneath a huge umbrella outfitted with a cooling mist system. After the iced tea is poured, Mrs. Falcone goes to relax on a chaise lounge. Agents Sommers and Boorman get right to the point and brief her about the reason she was called.

The news is staggering. Howling Wind is told that an Air Force lieutenant general, who so far remains unnamed, is responsible for having sabotaged the F-35 fighter jet program for years, making it one of the costliest attacks ever devised against a citizen's own country. Howling Wind can't guess what role she is going to play in this matter, but they definitely have her ear.

It's no secret that the F-35 stealth combat aircraft has been plagued with design flaws throughout its decade-long development, but to discover that a military man is to blame for its deficiencies is shocking to her. Sommers adds, "This includes defects uncovered in the latest generation fighter, the Lightning Ⅱ." Howling Wind remains composed, although her brain is in overdrive. So far, various contractors like Lockheed Martin and BAE Systems had always gotten blamed for the aircraft's poor performance.

Agent Boorman continues: "Intelligence agencies have been tracking the suspected officer for years, hoping to link his offshore bank accounts with secret payments. It follows that these problems with the F-35 will go on endangering aircrew until he is stopped."

Col. Howling Wind quickly digests the information, then says, "The lieutenant general must be receiving one helluva bribe...to sacrifice one's own. Do you know whether Russia or China is behind this scheme, in order to get foreign countries to buy their own missile systems?"

"No," says Agent Boorman. "It's Germany and France. The guy has a personal stake in the "European" fighter jet plan. Those countries have wanted to manufacture fighter planes of their own to sell to the world. The Franco-German program seemed a go when the problems with the F-35 appeared insurmountable. To their dismay, our Defense department chose to keep building them, despite the fact the aircraft kept breaking down and were taking longer to fix." A testament to U.S. stupidity, thinks Howling Wind to herself.

"What a waste," she mutters.

Agent Sommers connects the dots for her. "The lieutenant general is married to a Frenchwoman whose three brothers, all aeronautical engineers, stand to benefit bigtime if the European deal succeeds. The officer is surely looking forward to his retirement," he says, "when he'll no doubt live like a king in France with his family."

Hiram Douglass with the Oversight Council glances at General Abernathy, and then leans in on his chair. He cocks his head and regards Col. Howling Wind. She in turn holds his gaze, noting his exceptionally angular features and straight mouth. He's a lanky character, thin neck. It must be time for him to share how she fits in.

"You are well familiar with this man, Colonel." Douglass has an annoying gravelly voice. There are surgical scars alongside his vocal cords. "It's Joseph van Vliet."

If anyone else charged Lt. Gen. van Vliet with being a traitor, she'd have instantly laughed off the accusation. Howling Wind has never been one to hold any man or woman in such high regard as to believe they were above reproach, but *van Vliet*—seriously? The allegations made against the decent Catholic husband and father, not to mention likeable and admired combat-proven Airman, are disturbing and puzzling.

"If you already have proof, why am I needed?'

"We require your technical expertise," says Douglass. "Three pilots have been lost in the past eighteen months due to their aircraft exploding. One was Norwegian, the other two Italian."

"They weren't shot down as reported?'

"No."

"The pressure and speeds at high altitudes somehow caused the communications to go out," reports Douglass, "the signals weren't jammed, which is what the media was told for security reasons. Also, a fellow pilot who observed one of the incidents reported seeing a fire in an area of a power module upgrade. As a result, our allies have put their orders for the Lightning II on hold. They never believed the cover-up story, anyway."

Howling Wind studies his face. "Am I to assume the same thing happened recently at Eglin?" His silence confirms her hunch.

At last General Abernathy speaks up. "These aircraft must pass rigorous inspections before they arrive on base. Systems specialists at the point of origination are not the problem. The tampering occurs only after they're flown to their destinations. Your name repeatedly comes up when we've asked about pilots who understand the engineering behind modern strike fighters. Please don't take offense, but van Vliet might not be as guarded around you since you are a friend and...dare I say it, a woman. He might perceive you as less threatening. It's imperative to find the others responsible for crippling these advanced systems. They have to be among the mechanics who work on the planes. Our case against van Vliet will be air-tight if we can tie him to an accomplice. Besides, if you study the flaws, you could maybe offer ideas to fix them."

If she accepts the job, Howling Wind has to come to terms with the idea of staying in Arizona, where the F-35 jets are, and where van Vliet is for the time being. "I wish to remain in Ohio," she says flatly, "at Wright-Patt, near my son and his family." It goes without saying that they know about the PTSD, and why she would seek more stability in her life at this stage of her career. They promise their request won't put her in danger.

"We understand your situation," says the general, now standing. She is a rather husky woman. Her clear and higher pitched girl-like voice detracts from her authority. "I implore you to help, Colonel, so it doesn't become an order."

Howling Wind grins back at her. "Some choice." Mrs. Falcone comes to life. Her dark oiled skin looks like glossy mud. She's been quietly sunning herself just beyond the umbrella, making her privy to their shoptalk.

"Think about *all* the people who will benefit," says the lizard lady in a pleasant voice. She closes her eyes again and continues to soak up the warm rays.

What a bewildering character. Howling Wind recalls asking Rolling Thunder in jest whether the Falcones were human. He simply replied "their kind" were hard to explain. Presently the Falcones are among the richest families in the world, with a net worth of at least $100 billion dollars. Their lucrative scrap metal empire, now headquartered in Santiago, Chile, near the region that was home to their ancient ancestors, is but one of a long list of privately held international firms they run. Rolling Thunder explained that the first Rawakota spies from Chohkahn to have been sent out in the field infiltrated one of the Falcones' U.S. companies and were soon discovered by their security. He said it happened ages ago, before his parents were even born, and in New Mexico, not Chile, the Falcones' ancestors having migrated north centuries earlier on account of the active volcanoes threatening their city beneath the Andes Mountains. Both parties reached an agreement to work together, since they each belonged to fiercely guarded tribes. How interesting, too, thought Howling Wind at the time she was told about them, that both cultures saw fit to use corporate espionage as a means of advancing their own technology, which has conveniently benefitted The United States Armed Forces on occasion. One can only guess how hard America's top intelligence agencies have been trying to ascertain the backstory of this ultra-private family.

Thanks to stolen diagrams that the Falcones' secret agents handed over to the Rawakota spies, in addition to information Howling Wind had been sending to Chohkahn on a steady basis, Rawakota engineers were able to follow the progression of the F-35 fighter jet since its inception. In the early stages, the Rawakota were as concerned as the U.S. contractors when ejector seats malfunctioned, or the onboard communication systems failed. The Rawakota design team paid close attention to modifications and felt that American R&D Divisions had succeeded in making the aircraft safer over the years. However, major problems popped up again, and the Rawakota couldn't figure out why, nor could the leading aircraft manufacturers. Sabotage made perfect sense. It's encouraging to Howling Wind to learn that the U.S. Defense Department has been on top of the situation…well, somewhat. How long has van Vliet been under investigation! This will be a high-profile case, one that makes both national and international news. In the future, whenever she climbs into an F-35 cockpit, it could knowingly be her last time, as opposed to hypothetically. She can bank on help from the Rawakota, who are forever indebted to her.

Howling Wind realizes the guests are anxiously awaiting her answer. They were served a lovely lunch, giving her half an hour to mull things over.

Considering that Viktor and Tess need time to themselves to adjust to parenthood, and Iris and her husband, Hashke, are currently busy with work on his family's rez, her staying in Arizona for a while won't be so bad. Solomon is still tying up ends in Texas before making the move to Buckthorn. He's really going to do it, coach a Native youth football team on the rez fulltime. And then there is the impending pandemic to worry about, the first of its kind to threaten people everywhere. Serious infections are already running rampant across Asia and Europe, causing major lockdowns in cities. She places her napkin on the table and faces the general. "Can I live in the same house that was provided for me the last time I was here training pilots?"

The satisfied group emerges from the mansion to a waiting limo, only Howling Wind stays behind, at Marsha Falcone's request. Her husband enters the living room where Howling Wind has been viewing their folk art collection. His wife had excused herself to go to the bathroom. "Compliments of Winter Crow's lab," says Louis Falcone, setting a package on the coffee table. He then extends his hand and graciously greets his guest.

She looks on with interest as he pries it open, disclosing boxes of ampules and some type of syringes. The elderly gentleman, who has the same dark, tough reptilian skin as his wife, wears a look of smug satisfaction. "As you've heard, a new virus with the potential for causing death has begun to infect people throughout a growing number of countries. Some of us Indigenous folk might be the last people left standing. How's that for irony!"

"Vaccines?" she asks, in disbelief, stunned there's already an antidote, and that Indians have it.

"An inhalable vaccine," he says. "You breathe it in with these nebulizer syringes." He hands one to her along with the package insert describing the chemistry. "The mist delivers drugs that are activated by high-frequency sound waves when they reach their target sites in the body. It's quite revolutionary."

She skims over the information, trusting the integrity of the medical scientists at Winter Crow's research facility, and then takes a seat on the sofa as he gets her dose ready. A family photo catches her attention. She isn't close enough to see if there is something reptilian about the appearance of the others in it. Louis Falcone's gentle expression reminds her of the sweet looking faces of certain species of chameleons. His slightly globular eyes, with their thick eyelids, can't move independently like a chameleon's, thank goodness, but there is something similar in the way both creature and human blink.

"That's Marsha and me with eight generations of Falcones…impressive, huh? Bet no one you know can say that!" He places his hand behind her head, in case she jerks in response to the spray when it's injected up her nose.

"Do you have a medical background?"

"Weren't you told to trust us?" he says calmly, glancing at his wife as she walks in.

Howling Wind dutifully complies, after which she asks, "What are you, around 200 years old?" She pinches the corners of her eyes that instantly started stinging, an expected and normal side-effect of the vaccine.

"Good guess," he says, laughing a little as he hands her a tissue. "138." Louis points to his grandmother in the center of the photograph, the matriarch of the bunch, and the only person seated in a chair. "*She* is 200 years old."

"Colonel."

"General."

"Strange times."

Howling Wind and van Vliet respect the recent executive order for social distancing and keep six feet apart as they exit the meeting. Staff and crew on the Air Force base were updated about the global virus, and how it will continue to impact their daily routines.

"This certainly interferes with my plans," complains van Vliet. "My family is expecting me back in Florida, but that apparently won't be happening any time soon." With a sigh of resignation he turns to Howling Wind. "How about you? Were you expecting to stay?" Knit eyebrows express his concern; otherwise, his features are just as she remembers them, kind eyes, clear aquamarine blue ones, coarse sandy hair now mixed with some white, and there's that slight limp from a parachuting incident during the Gulf War that actually gives the spry sixty-year-old a jaunty, youthful type step.

"I was supposed to head back to Wright-Patt, but I'll gladly take the weather in Arizona right now."

"Yes, well...it would be great if there were time for golf. Can you believe something invisible like this virus could possibly wipe us all out?" Howling Wind simply stares at him. He is at once embarrassed by his thoughtlessness. He knows his history, that most Indigenous peoples were lost to disease. He forgot he was talking to an Indian. "My expertise is with the physical components of aircraft and missiles. Stuff you can see."

"You don't ponder germ warfare?"

"What's to ponder? Nothing I do in my capacity can protect us. That's for the scientists to figure out."

Quite the pragmatist, thinks Howling Wind. They go their separate ways. She need not keep tabs on him. Once the mini tracking device got placed in the general's wallet, which he had left in full view on his desk in his office, he's been under constant surveillance by the Rawakota. They had given it to her, not the CIA. He likely purchased something online and forgot to pocket it. The most important information she was able to relay to the CIA about van Vliet was that he used to keep a Cessna 210 in a hangar at a nearby airport. He never told her or anyone else about it. She recalled that Phil once mentioned in passing that he had given a gun-shy dog to van Vliet. Phil said the man couldn't wait to fly the pup down to Nogales and surprise his family. He had built a small runway on the ranch he owned near the Mexican border. His wife and kids came out from Florida every summer and also during their school breaks. Whether the general still has his plane, or his ranch, is another matter. By now his kids are grown. With his wife in Florida, and while he's stuck on the base, it just might be the getaway the general needs to conduct his covert business.

Howling Wind picks up food at a drive-through and continues on to her place in the west valley outside of Phoenix, the home she was in during her last stay—as promised by General Abernathy—the same adobe house she had shared with a steadfast friend, one that still resides there in the backyard. Every morning upon waking, while the coffee brews, Constance heads outside to say good morning to the towering venerable saguaro cactus. It's outstretched arms appear frozen in a perpetually welcoming pose.

Before turning in for the night, Constance thinks about how the planet's disparate nations are at the mercy of a microbe. In the couple of weeks since she received the vaccination at the Falcones' home, news of the pandemic has been increasingly scaring the world's populations. The Natives on the Buckthorn Reservation are fortunate to be protected from the killer virus. William was shipped a small supply of vaccines, enough for Viktor's family and their closest friends, who may not be inclined to take it because it isn't FDA approved yet. The researchers at Winter Crow's lab feel a moral obligation to share the chemistry behind their vaccine, but they admit that the complexity of the delivery system is far too involved for pharmaceutical companies to quickly manufacture the amounts required to inoculate vast numbers of people. Images of her grandchildren fill her thoughts, and the future they face.

―――――――――

How easy was that, thinks Howling Wind with regard to the phone call she had made in the night to Agent Sommers. She picks up her step to grab a quick bite for lunch at the cafeteria. Her Rawakota contact notified her at midnight that General van Vliet was departing from the Glendale, Arizona airport. They were correct in assuming he was headed for his ranch in Nogales. She imagined that she'd have to fabricate a story for the CIA agent, in order to protect the identity of her Indian informant. But Sommers had simply thanked her for the info and said they'd take it from here. Fine by her. Suddenly she hears her name called out. Two young airmen rush toward her, the one yelling, "Colonel…Rogers is in trouble! His engines are dead at 40,000 feet, and he's lost communications!" Together they race to the Control Tower.

Aware of the threat of sabotage, Howling Wind is able to mitigate a disaster by talking to the pilot's wingman, who continues to fly alongside Lieutenant Rogers. Fortunately, both men are proficient in Morse Code and can speak to each other via blinker lights worn on the fingertips. After the crew and planes return safely to the base, the Commander calls her to his office. How did she know where to tell Rogers to look for smoke, and why did she tell the Air Force controllers in the tower that the troubled F-35 Lightning II couldn't be reached on any frequencies before RAP-CON controllers determined it to be the case? She keeps her guard up. Until further word, everyone is suspect to her mind. The Commander could very well be part of Lt. Gen. van Vliet's inner circle. It becomes a stand-off while he waits for her answer. She looks at him completely deadpan.

"Sir, for more information, you should call General Abernathy."

"Say *what!*"

"The general can tell you what you need to know."

"Oh, she can, eh?"

Maybe that wasn't the best idea, but Howling Wind felt she'd been ambushed by the Defense Department at the Falcones' house, in order to do this job. At this point, she just wants to be sent back to Wright Patt in Ohio, to spend time with her grandbabies in nearby Columbus. She is dismissed without further interrogation.

CHAPTER 56

I wonder how long I've been at it when I catch myself staring at the salt-shaker on the kitchen table. Tess is seated sideways on the chair across from me with her head and back against the wall, eyes shut, as spaced out as I am. She disappears as my lids close, and that's how we sit for the next few minutes, relishing the silence. Three babies teething simultaneously has reduced us to a state of utter mindlessness. I took Raif to Dr. Nate's property this past week because of his ear-splitting screeching, clearing out a shed next to the horse stall for us to sleep in. There was no way we could stay in the main house without keeping Dr. Nate awake all night, along with his recently divorced sister who has come to live with him for a while. I wore soft foam earplugs around the clock, or I couldn't have tolerated being around him. In addition to his lower front teeth, Raif's left molar is coming in, which doesn't normally happen this early. He's been tugging on his ear nonstop; it hurts so much. Infant doses of acetaminophen and ibuprofen are useless, only warm compresses seem to dull the pain. I knew Raif would miss his brother and sister terribly, and they him, but he couldn't be near them shrieking the way he was. Their crying isn't nearly as bothersome to listen to. Early this morning, he at last managed to doze off, his teeth having finally poked through the gums. I drove home and placed him in the crib beside his siblings. What a sight! All their little legs began kicking excitedly in the air. There were squeals of joy at being back together, prompting a barking fit from Nero, who jumped up on the rail to witness the action. Once the three managed to roll themselves atop each other, they fell asleep, which is when I left to find Tess. And here we sit at the kitchen table, too exhausted for words, or so I thought.

"We deserve a break," says Tess, barely audible.

"Mm," is all I can muster, agreeing. I reach over and place my hand on hers, and then lay my head down on my other arm. Ah, the gift of silence.

I feel my hand get squeezed and look up. We laugh at having passed out for ten minutes, believing we'd slept a good hour. "I'm going to ask my mom to come," says Tess. "I can't do this...we can't go on doing this. It's too much." Wow. She *is* desperate if she's willing to resort to having her mother around again full time.

"Viktor, how 'bout you go to the rez, meet the two Lakota women your grandmother recommended to be our nannies, and bring them here ASAP. I trust your judgement."

It wasn't like Tess and I hadn't taken the offer seriously when Grandmother first suggested it, but we figured since we weren't able to establish a routine with the babies so far, how could we possibly incorporate a couple of strangers into our household. The logistics were beyond us. We liked the idea of our children learning the Lakota language. Tess wants to speak it, too. The timing is good for me to go right now. Chevonne will jump at the chance to care for the kids and get out of her house in Cincinnati. Folks everywhere are going stir crazy due to the government's "stay-at-home" orders. It's been deemed the best way to control the high rates of hospitalizations from what has indeed turned out to be a highly infectious and deadly virus. Normal life, as is constantly reported in the media, has been brought to a grinding halt around the world. The worst part is that no one can say for how long we must live quarantined like this.

Fortunately, my immediate family and inner circle of friends are vaccinated; however, as of yet, a vaccine hasn't been formulated by any of the leading pharmaceutical companies which could immunize the vast populations across the globe. Our having been inoculated isn't something we tell anyone. That would be cruel. Might not hordes of angry, panicked people, hell-bent on obtaining the vaccine, storm Winter Crow's lab in South Dakota if they learned one was available, despite the fact there is only a limited supply of it?

I tell Tess I'll go and return with two nannies, come hell or high water. Maybe Iris can meet me at the rez. After we met Lukas's family during the birth of the triplets, she and I talked about going to Black Elk Peak in the Black Hills, in order to see the entrance to their underground sacred city for ourselves. Like me, Iris isn't eager about going the full distance down an elevator shaft into Earth's interior to experience the place. We would visit a level closer to the surface, the region where Rawakota scientists secretly observe the goings-on at the Sanford Underground Research

Facility, which many of us still call the Homestake Mine. A mere mile down, it was once the deepest gold mine in North America.

The open cavern that Iris and I just walked into is bright and not the least bit claustrophobic. Nor was the well-lit, roomy elevator we rode down in. Sister and I arrived at the Rapid City airport within half an hour of each other this morning, having decided to go to the Black Hills first before traveling on to Buckthorn to stay with Grandmother. We rented a car to get to the City of Lead, where we were met by an Indian who handed over a couple of horses for us to continue our journey. Two hours later, following his directions, we arrived at a clearing deep inside the woods that included a small barn. It was quite a surprise when cousin Suhdeer stepped out. He was grinning wide. Our plans hadn't included him joining us, but Iris and I were happy to see him. He'd gotten wind of us coming from Mom. Together we went on foot to the waterfall, traversing the stony, short tunnel behind it until Suhdeer directed us toward the hidden passageway housing the elevator to Chohkahn. During the ride, although I was constantly aware of the abyss we were descending into, the movement of the elevator was barely detectable. Now, forty-five minutes later, Iris and I find ourselves in an area that is home to a distinct group of Rawakota called Oyahmayan. Suhdeer had time to fill us in on their background, which Sister and I found most intriguing.

Next we pile into the Loozh, their version of rapid transit that incorporates magnets. Suhdeer explains a bit of the science behind it. The lava tubes we're zooming through fan out from a point where a volcanic eruption took place a long, long time ago, one that supposedly created the massive chambers where the sacred city of Chohkahn was later established—I'm thinking eons later. It's also at this level under the surface of the Earth that the lava tubes become too small to support the train cars, and the track therefore doesn't continue on up to the outside world. Nevertheless, the underground Loozh was constructed to transport its passengers as far away as Wyoming, Montana, and the northern parts of Canada!

I bolt upright in bed, not recalling any dream. The light streaming in from the window likely wakened me. It takes a second to find my bearings in this strange setting. Iris is in an adjoining room, and I wonder if she is presently experiencing a similar sensation. For one thing, the sunrise in these caves is manufactured. I head to the bathroom, walking slightly off-balance. It's a small space for a man my size, for any Rawakota, really. The toilet and sink are mounted on the wall. No tub. I draw the curtain to the side of the shower stall. It's just big enough to turn around in. The ceiling is unusually high, maybe twelve feet. *Expect the water to be lukewarm*, we were told...*and the shower will run for eight minutes before slowing to a trickle the final thirty seconds*. I step inside, not wanting to waste a drop of water, and turn the knob.

While I'm still toweling myself dry, I am met by Iris when I enter the bedroom. She's sitting on the edge of my bed, dressed, and no doubt impatient for the second day of our visit among the Oyahmayan to begin.

"This is wild, isn't it?" I say, throwing on my clothes in the corner, and then braiding my hair loosely for it to air dry. Suhdeer said jeans were okay here, but I chose to bring khaki pants and some cotton shirts trimmed with Lakota beadwork. Iris is in a more tailored, modern version of a traditional Native dress. I plop down beside her. We look at each other and laugh a little nervously as we contemplate where exactly we are—deep in the bowels of the Earth, though not as far down as Chohkahn, which is even more frightening to envision. We were treated to a virtual 3D tour of the sacred city last night. Iris called the dramatically lit vaulted "rooms" grotto-chic. The city looks to have sprung from the creative minds of Disney's theme park designers, whose fantastic worlds seem perfectly real. Iris and I knew darn well that the stars lighting up Chohkahn's night sky were in fact part of the rock ceiling, as they are here. Night and day cycles match the seasonal variations in light on the outside. Today we're off to the Sanford Lab location to watch how the Rawakota secretly monitor the research that's conducted there by scientists from around the world. It was the first underground area our mother was given access to when she learned that the tribe we are descended from still existed as a nation.

There's a knock; it's Suhdeer, accompanied by a smiling, cheerful fellow who will be our guide today. They've got on plain, long tunic shirts. There's a bit of embroidery around the neck. They wear them over comfortable pajama-like pants. I have yet to see a woman in pants. They prefer embroidered knee-length dresses, no beads.

Jackets aren't necessary; the temperature is maintained around seventy degrees Fahrenheit. If it weren't for the sophisticated ventilation systems that the Rawakota learned about by means of their spying, it would be closer to one hundred thirty degrees—hot, but not the two hundred I was imagining. Starting in 2006, during the lengthy process of converting the Homestake Mine to a research facility, engineers opened up passages into shafts which ran from the surface atmosphere down to this depth, creating good air flow. Before that, in the 1800s, goldminers had already dug three hundred seventy miles worth of tunnels, which they lowered huge fans into, so as not to collapse from the heat while they worked. The photos we were shown of these excavations are beyond belief. The men also had to contend with the eighty percent humidity at this level, which I admit takes some getting used to, but then I've felt worse conditions in Ohio in August.

Our visit with the Oyahmayan was admittedly short. It was Mom's idea to have Iris and me stop in on them. She said they've long been interested in meeting her children. When Mom heard about our plans to see where the main entrance to Chohkahn lies, she quickly arranged for the layover, with the help of Suhdeer. I wasn't keen on boarding the elevator, but having Iris along helped. Both of us were curious and excited about the prospect of meeting this distinct and unusual segment of the Rawakota population; we just weren't thrilled about the mode of transport.

And now here we are back in the elevator, glad for having come, but oh-so ready to go up to a natural atmosphere and landscape. We said our goodbyes to Suhdeer over breakfast. He was heading back to Chohkahn. Iris and I were baffled by his admission that he and his relatives seldom visit this level which is home to the Oyahmayan. Apparently their ways are different enough from each other that it prevents the two groups from mingling much. We see how the people here got their name, which translated means *word gatherers*. Their extensive vocabulary is evident from the get-go. In addition to being articulate, those we spent time with were quite theatrical in their use of gestures, something Iris and I found entertaining, but not Suhdeer. He did hook us up with an Oyahmayan couple on the outside, who will be hosting us at their home this evening, saying it's a popular stopover for Native travelers. They also guard the entrance.

As the platform slows to a stop, Sister and I watch with childlike anticipation as the big door opens. A rush of cool fresh air revives us, and we're immediately greeted by the friendly middle-aged husband and wife. We step carefully through the passageway that leads to the waterfall, beyond which is the great outdoors! The rain was expected. Suhdeer wanted us to remain another day until skies cleared above, but mentally I needed a break. There was no escaping the reality of being so far underground. It was doing a number on my psyche. Iris grew accustomed to being at that depth, not me. Besides, I'm anxious to get to the rez and hire Tess and me some nannies, the prime reason for my trip.

It makes sense to spend the night with Jack and Sarah, our hosts. Riding down muddy trails on horseback is dangerous. When the storm passes, the horses we rode up on will be sent to take us safely back to our rental car.

We're handed a large tarp to share. Iris and I laugh as we trudge along behind the couple, making a game out of stepping in their footprints. The slick ground has us clutching each other. Our backpacks make the going even more awkward. If one goes down, we go together. "Ten minutes," yells Jack, half-turning for us to hear. For the most part, the thick pines shield us from the thunderous downpour, which is crazy loud. Before we know it, we're standing in a huge wood-beamed room warmed by a crackling fire. An entire glass wall offers a jaw-dropping view of the Black Hills. Tree tops and mountain spires rise above a slow-rolling fog in the valley. It's eerie yet beautiful.

The seating area surrounds a large bear skin rug, head included. Its shiny glass eyes catch the light from the nearby flames. The couple's little terrier dances around our legs while a chubby-faced gray tabby looks down with mild interest from the upper shelf of a bookcase.

"Do I smell Wohanpi…" asks Iris, closing her eyes and taking a deep breath, "…and with turnips?"

It's hard not to scarf down such a damn fine meal. Sarah used bison and seasoned the stew the same as Winnie and Grandmother. Sister keeps sneaking more of the skillet bread, which I love, too. I quietly tell her to stop so I can have seconds. Sarah heard and assures me there's another tray in the kitchen.

Following dinner, Iris excuses herself to phone Hashke. Jack invites me to smoke with him outside on a wide covered deck that wraps around their bedroom. The wind is deflected by the angle of the wall. He hands me a blanket then drapes one around his shoulders before sitting. The driving rain has ended, but it's still drizzling.

I can't wait to shiver myself warm. It must be in the upper fifties, which normally wouldn't bother me. "I feel like old Sunkwah, my great-grandfather, who's always bothered by drafts these days."

"We can go in if you're uncomfortable," says Jack, handing me a pipe.

"No way! I'm so thankful to be out in the open."

He grins and offers a knowing nod, then opens a cloth pouch of Cansasa. It smells familiar, woodsy, not like what I had smoked with Suhdeer, which had a metallic taste. Jack thinks it included something in the mix that I might have had a reaction to. As we go through the process of getting the pipes started, I'm thinking how easy this stranger is to be around. "You don't look like a Jack." I hope he isn't offended; it unconsciously slipped out.

"What name would better suit me?"

Jack is tall, lean, and dignified, as is his wife. Iris called them polite, and that Jack reminded her of our favorite spaceman, Klaatu, in the old black and white version of *The Day the Earth Stood Still*. I see it; he's got the same high cheekbones and intelligent expression.

"Does Rumjaktoowahl have a nice ring to it?" he asks.

"You pulled Jack from that?"

"J, a, and k, are in all our men's names. It means to be surrounded by, or in the middle of, for example, a flower among weeds. Translated, Rum is reason…in the middle of toowahl, or conflict. Women's names contain mir, meaning to be filled with."

"That *is* more fitting. You really don't prefer it?"

"When our men gather in groups, we all greet each other as Jack, as a joke. What can I say, it's Oyahmayan humor."

"But apparently the women don't, or Sarah would go by the name Mir."

He shrugs his shoulders as if to say *go figure*. "Sarah is Serahmiroovahn, which means creature filled with wonder."

I find myself liking these *Oyahmayan*.

"Many people pass through and stay a night or two," he says, "it's easy for them to remember Jack and Sarah. Your mother and your uncle, Half Moon, call us by our given names."

It's strange to suddenly hear him refer to Mom and Uncle William. Aspects of Mom's life continue to elude me. To some extent, Uncle's, too. Before this trip, Iris and I hadn't realized just how highly regarded Mom is in these parts—she's a bona fide Rawakota hero. During our visit to the Sanford Research Lab, we learned that the tribe's defensive capabilities are largely due to the intelligence she has obtained for them. It makes sense that she would know Jack and Sarah's place, since it's near the cave entrance. I'm curious to know if Jack has children. He says his twins, a boy and girl, are away at college, and his ten-year old son is with grandparents on the Wyoming side of the mountains.

A few bright stars pop through the holes in the clouds as they drift apart. We puff on our pipes, two dads.

"Jack, considering that you're a Rawakota father, may I discuss something personal with you about my daughter, Honor?"

Sarah walks in on our conversation, delivering hot tea. He holds off answering and sets his pipe aside. His expression suggests he has my interest at heart.

"I haven't brought up the subject with anyone, other than my wife, Tess." My cheeks and chest turn hot. "Have any girls ever been born with yellow eyes?"

He is quiet for a while, studying my face as he thinks. "There are no instances that I'm aware of."

"Are you certain? Not one, not even in the families where one parent is an outsider?" I trust he would know, especially since he and his wife cross paths with so many people. "How about a folk tale or myth about a female with yellow eyes? No heroic, golden-eyed woman in Rawakota lore who is greatly admired, like a Joan of Arc?" Apparently not. I explain that I recently did some research when the triplets developed their permanent eye color because Honor's turned out yellow. "There's a condition called Androgen insensitivity syndrome. It's extremely rare." I proceed to describe how genetics are involved, and how upsetting it had been for me to break the news to Tess, who refused to believe anything was wrong with our baby.

"Consider this, Viktor...if Honor's eyes weren't yellow, you'd never know she was genetically male. Externally, any doctor she will ever see in your world is going to presume she's female. If I understand correctly, she will likely develop breasts since her body can't use male sex hormones."

"But she has no uterus. Tess agreed to having her x-rayed, to see if she had undescended testes that should be removed. Honor will never get to experience motherhood…"

"Let me stop you there, Viktor. Not all Rawakota women are able to become pregnant. It doesn't mean they can't be mothers. And think about how many women on the outside choose not to have children. Honor is barely out of the womb, and you're planning this imaginary life for her."

He's right. "I just don't want to be treating her like a daughter, only to have her tell me when she's older that she thinks of herself as a boy. I can't wrap my brain around that."

Jack sips his tea. "I believe I'd feel the same."

"*Thank you!* That's all I've needed to hear from somebody! Once Honor's eye color became obvious, my dad merely stated that our family was apparently mistaken about girls not inheriting yellow eyes. Iris understands, but she is of the same mind as Tess, that I shouldn't make such a big deal about it. Parents should love their children no matter what. Of course I love Honor. This, however, affects me on an emotional level that I have trouble coming to terms with."

I go on to tell Jack that my great-grandparents have seen Honor on video calls and refer to her now as *he*. "It hurts."

"That's an automatic response. They simply haven't dealt with this before. Be honest with them, and ask that they correct themselves right when it's said, so it becomes habit."

Seems an easy fix. The damage is done, though, because I know they will continue to think of her as a boy. If Sunkwah and Winnie had any idea they caused me such distress, they'd be apologizing up and down. I'll be seeing them soon enough, and we can discuss it.

"The one positive aspect about knowing early on," says Jack, "is that you aren't going to be blindsided by the subject one day when it comes up. You will no doubt be on the alert for any signs that your child is identifying more with one gender over another. Time is on your side to adapt to the individual she becomes. Don't obsess."

I hear him. He looks at me with concern and says, "I heard you met your birth father's family for the first time when the babies were born. It's unfortunate that you were never given the opportunity to be around them growing up. Their blood is in you, in your children. I can only imagine the joy they felt over finally meeting you and Iris. Whatever life throws at you in the future, Viktor, your blood relatives are the people you can absolutely trust and rely on for help and advice. All Rawakota."

Jack shifts his weight and looks thoughtfully at me. "It was our warriors, after all, who saved your mother's dying spirit following the atrocities she witnessed in Africa. At the request of the great-grandfather you just spoke of, who has had no contact with Chohkahn in decades, they rallied to support her when she experienced symptoms of trauma, sharing war stories only fighters understand."

I have to ask, "When you say warriors went to see her…what Rawakota in this century goes to fight? Who are they at war with?"

"You're asking about a complicated part of our society. Oyahmayan temperament differs greatly from that of tribal members in the city of Chohkahn. We have always served a different kind of role and have rarely picked up arms to join our brothers on the battlefield. Although we still abide by our Rawakota traditions, the Oyahmayan have historically interacted with other cultures, which has greatly influenced us. For example, we hold off Otiwota for another five to seven years, which allows more time for intellectual pursuits. If young men in Chohkahn don't marry and share theeich ihilah by age twenty, their pent up sexual energy becomes debilitating. Before the arrival of the colonists, boys were always hunting and fishing outdoors in the mountains. Those physical activities are a great release. Once Indians started getting rounded up onto reservations, our ancestors retreated to their underground city to prevent capture. The only people allowed to leave were the scouts. Fast forward to the present. Adults are faced with youngsters in your generation who feel hemmed in by Chohkahn's rock-solid walls. Boys and girls alike make the trek to the level we Oyahmayan reside, in order to hang out together in the spacious media center we constructed in the late 90s. There they can access the Internet and connect with their peers. You and Iris should go see it on your next visit. It's in Wyoming. There's a similar center in Canada. Our youth follow your football games and envy how outsiders are able to move freely about. It's natural for them to want to meet and do things with other Indians, too, just like their elders did. They're curious about life on other reservations. Chohkahn will always be regarded as the sacred center of our Nation. But it's so remote. No one wants to take the time going back and forth to it constantly. We Oyahmayan go down to the city only if we have to."

My thoughts are everywhere. I could go on asking questions all night. However, the air has grown colder, and I'm picturing myself curled up next to the fireplace. "Mind going in?"

Jack's ready, too, and takes a final puff on his pipe.

Sarah and Iris are on the sofa watching the news on TV about the growing numbers of viral cases in the States. I plop down on the bear skin rug, near the sizzling, red-hot logs. As the reporter cuts away to scenes of empty airports and malls, I am reminded of how the Buckeyes' Scarlet and Gray football game got cancelled in April due to social distancing rules, as did Spring training camp. Poor Theo didn't even get to finish out the basketball season his senior year. The NFL went ahead with its Draft, but from players' homes, not Vegas. Tess and I watched with anticipation to see what team wanted Damien, only because the decision was going to impact Claire's life. She was with him at his cousin's house in Dayton when his name got called to join the Indianapolis Colts. We let go a major sigh of relief, mostly because Columbus is a doable two and a half hour drive from Indiana. Claire wasn't about to change colleges. It was no secret that the Seattle Seahawks expressed an interest in drafting him. Not even ten minutes later, Claire called to tell us she was marrying Damien the end of June. *Un-hee!* That's only a month away from now! Neither Tess nor I can figure out how they plan on carrying out a wedding during a pandemic, unless they don't intend to have guests. I haven't even heard yet what's happening with my summer practice schedule. There's talk of another wave of virus coinciding with the start of flu season in the fall, which will jeopardize not only college football programs, but all sports.

The forecast calls for periodic light showers tomorrow. Iris and I are invited to stay another day. That's an easy yes, especially when we hear smoked turkey and corn pudding are on the menu. Jack and Sarah are ready to call it a day, but insist it doesn't mean that Sister and I should turn in. Sarah stands and pulls a clip from her brown hair and down it spills past her waist. She grabs the poker to make space for another log. It instantly bursts into flames with a big sounding whoosh. The dog trots on ahead of Jack, who reminds us of leftovers in the fridge.

Iris reaches for the remote, turns off the TV, and then slides off the cushion onto the floor and scoots over to me. She hugs my arm and rests her head against my shoulder. "This is nice."

"Mm-hmm." It truly is. Instead of taking advantage of the one-on-one time to enjoy a rare, uninterrupted conversation, we remain still, hypnotized by the swirling flames.

CHAPTER 57

I sit up in bed, fully dressed, with no memory of how I got here. It takes a second to register that I'm in Jack and Sarah's home, and not underground. My eyes smart. Probably from being so near the fire. I do remember watching it with Iris beside me. My phone shows it's 9:53. Can't be. I hurry putting myself together, and then hightail it to the living room, only to discover it empty. There are voices beyond the kitchen in an area that Iris and I weren't shown during our tour of the place. I stop at the hallway.

"Hello-o-o."

Iris pokes her head out of a second doorway on the right. "In here, Viktor."

"Good morning," says Jack. He's in a long white kaftan. "Guess there's no need to ask if you slept well." Sarah leaves to get me a much-needed cup of coffee. I missed breakfast, but am told that a plate of food awaits that only needs microwaved.

"You could have woken me, Iris."

"Don't think I didn't try!"

"I have no recollection of nodding off last night. How'd I get to bed?"

"I got you standing and shoved you the entire way, which was no easy feat."

"It's good you're here now," says Jack. "Sarah and I were about to show Iris the nature of our work, since she enquired about it."

I assumed their home *was* their business, a B&B for the comings and goings of Indians.

Unlike the rest of the house, which has been thoughtfully decorated, this space is just that: space. No pictures on the walls. No pretty rugs, just two huge metal desks facing each other with computers on them and lots of neatly stacked documents of some kind. Turns out they're passports. Jack explains that he and his wife invent backgrounds for students and scouts who study or work outside Chohkahn. It involves coming up with birth certificates from any number of North American hospitals, as well as creating transcripts tied to legitimate schools. They go so far as to place individuals on class rosters in case anybody goes snooping. The details are mind-boggling.

"This is a job Oyahmayan love. We have always studied cultures and languages. Anyone who ventures out into the world is schooled by us, and therefore well-prepared."

I'm in awe of this man, of Oyahmayan in general. Jack activates the monitor on the desk with his voice. A 3D image materializes in the air above it. It's Mom, and she's standing next to a row of tall, odd looking people dressed in long robes. They have saucer-sized yellow eyes. She must be introducing them; each nods as she goes down the line.

"What the hell..." I mumble, turning to Iris, who is equally bewildered.

"I want to give you both a better understanding of the vital role your mother has played in our community. Besides the fact that she has contributed to us Rawakota becoming as tech-savvy as we are today, she *found* this Indigenous group in Asia that we believed existed, but whose location we couldn't pinpoint. Please don't mention this discovery to your spouses. Our Nation pledges to protect their way of life at all costs."

Iris and I remain transfixed by the sight of this unusual group who belong to a tribe Jack calls the Mujahzee. He says they're an ancient people whom we share a remote common ancestor with, and who, to this day, live in subterranean caves in the Himalayas. That's all he's at liberty to disclose about them.

Sarah enters with my coffee and asks if Iris is ready to go. They're heading to the chicken coop, which requires a short walk. I decline the offer to join them. I'm hardly interested in gathering eggs at the moment. My head is filled with questions for Jack. After they leave, I ask him what guarding the entrance to Chohkahn entails, and how long he's been doing it.

He gestures for me to sit in the chair at the second desk while he rolls his closer to my side. "Sarah and I weren't the first to live in this house. The need to build it arose after the death of Jonah Plain Feather, which occurred a while ago. Jonah believed he had revealed where the entrance to Chohkahn was to an outsider. You of course know about the tragedy."

"What makes you say that?" To me it's an innocent enough question, but Jack's got a puzzled look on his face that I find disconcerting.

"You have never heard Jonah's name before now? Not from your mother?"

"Should I have?"

He seems reluctant to fill me in when I ask about the circumstances, but then relents.

"Going back around fifteen years," begins Jack, "a young student from Chohkahn went to New York City to study theater arts. His name was Jonah Plain Feather. He'd been looking forward to this new adventure, much like any young man about to embark on his college life.

"I'll return to Jonah later. Now follow along when I tell you about another young man, one born in the Emirates. His name was Hammad Bishara, and he was the teen-aged son of an Arab diplomat. When the father got assigned to New York City, Hammad accompanied him."

So far I'm keeping track of things. Evidently, relatives back home in the Middle East had suspicions about Hammad having impregnated his younger sister. Gross. She died presumably by suicide, although it was declared an accident. Ambassador Bishara was obsessed with gambling, and while in New York he would take his son with him to a casino run by Indians on the other side of the state, which is where Hammad got interested in theater and staging shows. Because he was too young to get a job at the casino, he changed his looks, his name, and acquired a fake tribal-issued ID, one that showed he was a member of the Seneca Deer Clan. He became romantically involved with a female card dealer, who ended up murdered on a nearby reservation. His involvement with her made him a suspect in the crime. Jack reminds me that at the time, due to his new identity, no one realized he was the son of Ambassador Bishara. The Ambassador, who also knew the woman well from the gaming tables, feared he might be implicated in the death. Despite having diplomatic immunity, he chose to leave the U.S. His son, however, stayed and reinvented himself yet again. Using a new name, he enrolled in the theater department at a university in New York. Enter Jonah Plain Feather. I assumed their paths had to eventually cross. The school assigned them to the same dorm room. The rest of the story is heartbreaking, with Jonah getting drugged by his roommate. Afterward, he experienced tremendous guilt for having likely exposed the location of the entrance to his people's hidden city. What I'm not making a connection to is why Jack thought

Mom should have passed along this story to me. Perhaps there's a moral to it?

"Is this going somewhere, Jack? Sounds like the Arab successfully disappeared from the campus before getting nabbed by police. Did he start snooping around the waterfall, trying to find the elevator? Is that when the citizens of Chohkahn began guarding it more closely?"

"Growing numbers of outsiders did start appearing in the area, but there was no telling if he was among them. Bear with me, Viktor."

Jack continues. "It's now years later when a man called Hammad Bishara shows up in Australia, of all places. No more aliases and deceptions, he is back to using his family name." Jack describes Hammad's marriage to a wealthy heiress of a mining empire. She had been successfully running her family's company, until she met the Arab. "He used mind games on her. After their son was born, he returned to the Arab Emirates with him. His wife ended up taking her own life."

"Clearly the guy was despicable." I stand to shake out my legs, unsure about telling my kind host that the story has grown tedious.

"A few years later Hammad showed up in the States..."

"Please, Jack..." I sigh, hoping my tone hasn't offended him.

"Point taken, my friend. We've reached the end anyway, to the man's final destination, Columbus, Ohio. Only now he goes by the name Ishmael Atoga, and he enrolls at Ohio State University, in order to meet you, who he knows is Rawakota. He tells you he is a Seneca Iroquois, right?"

My mind goes blank, as if a bullet zinged past my ear. We exchange looks as I lower myself down on the chair. What a fool I'd been for allowing myself to be conned. That's what Ishmael was, or rather, Hammad, a master of manipulation. I slump forward over my knees, covering my face with my hands. Just hearing his name makes my head swim. My heart's pounding in my ears. Jack gives me a minute, then says:

"Red flags immediately went up when your uncle met Ishmael. He didn't understand why, but firmly believed an investigation was in order. The Rawakota were no help; the name meant nothing to them. There had been no leads when it came to knowing the whereabouts of Jonah Plain Feather's tormentor. His roommate, who we later discovered was Hammad, immediately disappeared from sight the day Jonah jumped to his death. Your uncle's concern worried your mother, so she took it upon herself to contact a fellow pilot named Jim Blacksnake, an Iroquois from New

York, to have him check into the background of this new acquaintance of yours. At the time, Blacksnake was stationed at a base in Australia. Right away he learned that Ishmael was no Indian. After more digging, he came across news of a casino employee's murder on a reservation, and of her ties to a diplomat named Bishara. Being stationed in Australia, Blacksnake was familiar with that name from the news and local gossip. The mystery surrounding Ishmael grew more intriguing to him. If it weren't for Blacksnake, none of the details of Hammad Bishara's past would have come to light. He made the connection between the identities.

"You can see, Viktor, why we wanted the Arab's hide. By the time all the facts surfaced linking the man you knew as Ishmael to Jonah's death, we received the news of you having been attacked. It happened just when the Rawakota were set on apprehending him themselves. Your uncle beat us to it. He had to act fast, in order to prevent Ishmael from escaping Columbus. I wrongly assumed that when your mother got the chance to explain why she didn't see you in the hospital, she would have also told you about the man who put you there. You can well imagine how worried we Rawakota were that this scoundrel may have also ruined your chance of experiencing the *eich ihilah* with your future wife like he had for Jonah Plain Feather."

My cheeks turn hot from embarrassment. It never occurred to me that anyone outside of Uncle William was aware of that possibility. I'm left with a bigger question for Jack.

"The police investigation came up empty. They didn't know about Ishmael. Maybe he did in fact get away."

"No, Viktor, he didn't."

That sends a shiver up my spine. The obvious person comes to mind. Jack suspects as much and swears it wasn't my uncle's doing. *Who then*, I wonder, but I don't ask.

"Considering everything your mother has dealt with since her last tour overseas, I can see how there hasn't been an opportune time for her to have had that discussion with you." He then adds, "You both share the same fighting spirit." Resting his hand on my knee in a friendly, sympathetic way, he suggests moving to the kitchen and warming up that breakfast for me.

Sounds good, but before going I ask to see a picture of Jonah Plain Feather. The face fills the computer screen. My first thought is that Jonah was close to my present age when he died. His eyes are bright and happy in the photo, characteristic of someone with a promising future, not those of a damaged young man plagued by guilt. Next, Jack plays a video of Jonah from a production he was in, a solo. "He enjoyed dancing, much like you, Viktor. Plays didn't interest him." It's a fun performance. When it's over, and Jonah is alone on stage taking his bow, exhausted but beaming with satisfaction, I hear myself promising him: *I'm going to do right by you one day, my brother, as well as your family.*

The afternoon is spent lounging beside the fireplace. After speaking with Tess on the phone and seeing the triplets, I'm confident that all is well at home. Tess hadn't known that her aunt from Pennsylvania was going to be accompanying her mother to help out. The bigger surprise was that her cousin also came along, a girl who'd been like a sister to her before the O'Sheas moved to Cincinnati. Even though people must still quarantine, Tess and her cousin have been able to take walks, giving her a welcome break from drooling, pooping babies.

Following another memorable dinner, Iris excuses herself to work on a report she needs to submit this evening. Jack and I help put things away in the kitchen, after which I want to start reading a book by an Oyahmayan author that Sarah picked out for me, a semifictional story. This oughta be interesting. I hang up the dish towel and am about to leave when Jack asks if I wouldn't mind sitting in the living room with him briefly.

I plant myself in a chair, hoping it will indeed be brief. He folds the skirt of his kaftan between his legs then sits on the side of the sofa nearest me, crossing his ankles before sinking back against the cushion. I continue to wait while he gazes out the window across the great expanse of mountains that make up his front yard. He better not be setting me up for another long story.

"It's imperative that you understand the effort that is required to keep you safe." His tone is serious, but still friendly like always. He turns to look at me and says that since the attack that landed me in the hospital, the group in Chohkahn that is comparable to the U.S. Department of Defense, the people Mom gets her spying orders from, has been tasked with protecting me...as well as Tess and the babies. I stare at him, trying to picture what that means exactly. Before then, he says that my uncle had but a few names in Columbus to go to for help if I ever got into a scrape, adding that I should take the subject up with him if I want more details.

"Viktor...you know the fenced-off wooded strip of land that runs along the driveway to your house in Columbus?" Of course, I tell him, with a degree of apprehension. "Well it's an easy hiding spot for paparazzi. On a weekly basis someone is caught staking out your place."

That's alarming to hear. Not only are photographers secretly observing me, but Rawakota military, too! "Am I supposed to feel comforted by that admission, Jack?" A sense of dread fills me, the kind that drives a man to take up arms so he can guard his family at all costs. "I've laughed at Mom for going through all of the rooms in our house with a scanning device when she comes to stay. Am I to understand that the paranoia is warranted?"

"Not at all. It is however the standard operating procedure for a person in her position. You should be grateful that there are people who have your back."

Just then Sarah enters and crosses in front of me as she goes and takes a seat beside her husband. I've worked myself up into such a state, my leg starts bouncing from nerves. I get up only to begin pacing by the window. It's Sarah who now addresses me.

"You can't continue to ignore how famous you are. Being a student on campus has, for the most part, allowed you to exist in a bubble because the media aren't permitted to follow athletes to classes. But you're fair game away from school. Once this pandemic is over, and people see you around the neighborhood, having a private life will be impossible...unless you accept help."

She's well-meaning. They both are. It isn't like Mom hasn't tried to drive this point home to me recently. "How do they do it?" I ask. "The Rawakota. Are there surveillance cameras aimed at my house...or a disguised undercover security guard who follows me wherever I go?"

"Ask Half Moon," says Jack. "Your uncle is still the primary person responsible for your safety at Ohio State. One can assume there are cameras in the trees on your street. A security team has no doubt been assigned to you. You really ought to be having this conversation with Howling Wind. Nothing gets implemented without your mother's approval. There is something else I want to bring to your attention. It's deeply disturbing and keeps our citizens on the defensive."

I let go a little laugh. "Thought this was going to be brief." Grinning back at me, he promises not to be long-winded.

"You're familiar with the abandoned mine on the east side of Buckthorn Reservation. A professor at The Black Hills School of Technology has taken her students there for years to witness firsthand the contamination of nearby creeks. The company that ceased its operations a decade ago has yet to accept responsibility for the clean-up. Last fall when she went with her classes, the site was suddenly up and running—quietly up and running. When confronted about the project, the men in the reopened offices told her they were environmental geologists from Ohio State University, there to solve the pollution issues. They claimed to be working in partnership with the Lakota Nation, a joint venture resulting from OSU wanting to help their star football player's people. I guess they thought that using you as an excuse wouldn't raise any red flags when it came to their presence in Indian territory. The professor wasn't convinced and notified the county Sheriff about her concerns. Unfortunately, the group at the mine site didn't hang around long enough for their criminal activity to get exposed."

"And what kind of criminal activity were they believed to be involved in?" I ask as I mosey on back to my chair, curious about what these outsiders had been up to.

"Among the fingerprints lifted from inside the offices were ones belonging to an ambassador named Bishara from the Arab Emirates."

"Un-hee! He winds up back in the States, and on our reservation of all places...and after suspicions were raised linking him to the murder of the Native woman he knew from the casino in New York!"

"What interested the Arabs was a byproduct that can be recovered from the old copper and nickel mining pit, a rare earth element called iridium, the most corrosion-resistant metal on Earth. Iridium satellite connections are vital for updating positions."

I'm familiar with it from science journals. "Sounds like a small amount goes a long way. Must be pretty pricey stuff."

"Its price has soared in trading on the global market. The sad part is, Bishara took off in the night with his band of conspirators. He must've run scared by the sudden interest in his operation. Their exit also ended the drone sightings in the Black Hills, specifically overhead here. The Rawakota shot them down. The technology behind them was highly sophisticated. They weren't the kind of drones found in hobby shops."

Jack stands and pats my knee. "That's it. If you'll excuse me now, I have some work to do. You go read your book. See you at dinner." Their cat jumps up onto Sarah's lap and buries her head between her legs, which signals she's ready to have her ears rubbed. Sarah dutifully complies, then tells me to expect dinner around five. That must be my cue to leave, and I proceed to the bedroom where I was headed in the first place.

Sitting propped against the pillows on the bed, book in hand, I can't help but get lost in the dazzling display of nature beyond my window. Gone are the mean clouds. The trees, still coated with water droplets, sparkle in the sunlight. I can't stop thinking about the Bisharas. It would appear that the man I knew as Ishmael inherited his villainous nature from his father. Perhaps the entire family is made up of depraved individuals, and Ishmael's son, born to his Australian wife, and whom he stole back to the Emirates, will turn out to be just like his dad and grandfather. How unfortunate that Jonah Plain Feather led outsiders to our sacred mountain. I flip to the opening chapter, ready to put the subject behind me. Funny or sad, I'm definitely curious about seeing things from an Oyahmayan author's perspective.

CHAPTER 58

I tell Iris to meet me in the corner of the master bedroom that Pahpie called his office when she ends her phone conversation with Mom. We're interested in seeing what's in the boxes Dad dropped off at Grandmother's house. He is storing them here until he can find a permanent new home on the Buckthorn Reservation. It's weird to think there'll be no returning to Texas. I uncover several manila envelopes filled with childhood photos of the Davises in Kansas City. They're stuffed inside boxes of company tax documents too old to be saving anymore. The pictures get dumped on the floor where I'm sitting cross-legged.

After spending a second night at Jack and Sarah's place, Iris and I got an early start this morning. First we rode the horses down the long hill to the rental car we left in a parking lot in the City of Lead. Next we drove to Sunkwah and Winnie's house, arriving in time for lunch, which included the two Lakota women who were looking forward to being my babies' nannies. Ruby Iron Cloud and Naomi Weiss are perfect for the job. Between them, the farm wives raised eleven children, and love the infant stage best, to which I shook my head in disbelief. Grandmother said they share a natural affinity for teaching children. I only wish she hadn't brought up the tragic way their husbands died in a grain bin accident, which she did right before my meeting them. It happened a decade ago, but the gruesome visuals lingered in my imagination while we talked and ate. The women, both in their middle forties, with grown adult children who've taken over the management of the farms, spoke matter-of-factly about the recent rise of grain bin deaths. I learned that the mishaps occur more during late harvests when the wheat is damp and sticks to the sides of the bins, clogging the flow. "At least there's no suffering," Ruby had said. "A person suffocates real fast." *Un-hee*, I thought. That's what you tell yourself, in order to survive traumatic loss?

Iris suddenly bursts into the room, excited over the news that Mom was largely responsible for catching a hotshot general who'd been undermining the F-35 program for years. It was a humdinger of a story that broke a few weeks ago. The media reported it as a game-changer for the Defense Department. No one, however, was privy to the details of the arrest until the investigation was over, which it apparently is now. Our allies had begun to cancel their orders for the planes because things kept going wrong with them, even after the problems had reportedly gotten resolved. This general found workers who were willing to booby-trap the U.S. jets, causing other nations to order aircraft made by a new European company that he was secretly backing.

"Will Mom get credit?"

"She doesn't want any. My guess is she'd be overwhelmed by requests for interviews." Sounding sad, "There was a time in her career when she would have jumped at the chance to talk to people. You were perhaps too young to remember the number of organizations that used to want her to speak at their meetings. She loved going to them."

"She's gotta get *something* out of it! It sounds huge."

"Oh, it is! I bet she makes general."

"You think? Have pilots died because of him?"

"Of course some died! Mom might have, too! He deserves to be kicked out of a plane without a chute! Wait'll you hear how they nabbed him… this well-respected officer and family man who has a bunch of grown kids and grandkids."

I offhandedly answer, "His mistress."

"Yes!" We giggle like kids. "Only it was a mist*er*, not a mist*ress*."

"Oh jeez."

"He had a lover for over twenty years, a Mexican artist who lives in southern Arizona near the border. He's a sculptor. Mom said that the general's ranch was in the artist's name, as well as his Cessna plane. He obviously wanted to avoid any kind of a paper trail. The government promised to make the artist's undocumented relatives legal American citizens in exchange for his help. The artist gave the agents access to a private computer that the general kept in a room below his studio."

"A sexual trap…how cliché."

"What's this about sex traps…" Grandmother enters, sounding stern but looking amused.

"I was telling Viktor about the traitor Mom helped to catch."

"Ah," she says, stepping toward us. She obviously knows all about it. "Find anything of interest in the boxes?"

"I only just got here," says Iris as she kneels down beside me and begins a search through one of them. I'm not done with the subject of our mother.

"There's something I've been meaning to ask you, Grandmother, about Mom. I only learned about her helping the people of Chohkahn from cousin Suhdeer when he surprised me during my hanbleceya. How long have you been aware of the truth behind why she's in the military?"

"Espionage isn't why she joined," says Grandmother, bending over to look at the photos strewn about the floor. "She's always wanted to fly. You know that. When your grandfather first showed symptoms of heart problems and needed a stent placed inside him, it worried Constance, and she asked that Solomon and I join her at Pahpie's bedside before the surgery because she had something important to reveal that was not to go beyond our walls." Grandmother pauses a second, smiling at the picture of her Newfies when they were pups. "She told her father that she expected his surgery to go well, but perhaps his spirit might benefit from some uplifting news. That's when we learned that tribesmen from Chohkahn came to her in secret after she graduated from the Air Force Academy, asking her if she'd be willing to work undercover for them. They planned on reclaiming our stolen lands and sought her aid. By then the cause had consumed your Pahpie's life. Your mother said she thought long and hard about their request before agreeing to help. Although Pahpie never openly voiced his disapproval about her joining the Air Force, she knew well how much he resented seeing his own flesh and blood in an American uniform. To him it represented the extinction of our people. He teared up afterward. He was so proud of her. I only wished she had told him sooner."

"That disclosure must have been hard for our Dad to hear," says Iris. "It's bad enough he had to worry about the inherent dangers his wife faced as a fighter pilot. But to find out she was also a spy!" Iris studies some papers she pulled out of a file folder, and then holds them out for me to take. "It's our official adoption record. I've never seen it, you?"

"No." Seeing Dad's signature and wondering what was going through his head that day makes me emotional.

Grandmother sweetly kisses the tops of our heads before leaving. "Little did he understand the scope of what he had signed up for when he married your mother."

"No kidding," says Iris.

"You're on your own for dinner," yells Grandmother from down the hallway.

Sister and I share stories about Dad's family while we stack and organize all the pictures. This would be an opportune time to ask whether she and Hashke have considered starting a family. Even though she married into another tribe, and is only twenty-five, women of Rawakota descent normally get pregnant right away. I'm prepared if she tells me to mind my own business.

"Bet that's been on your mind a while," she says, and with a smile... thank goodness. But then she says nothing more. We push the boxes back under the desk and agree to meet for dinner in the kitchen around seven. There are a few small jobs to keep me busy around the house. All the door hinges squeak loudly. A couple of loose boards need nailed down on the front porch before Sunkwah and Winnie trip over them and fall. Definitely want to prevent that disaster from happening, although it appears they mostly stay put at their place. Both shuffle along anymore, barely lifting their feet. While Grandmother spends more time tending to their needs, her own home is clearly showing signs of neglect. I doubt she'll have the energy to plant a garden this spring.

Seven o'clock and I'm surprised to find bags of carry-out burgers on the kitchen counter. Evidently there wasn't much in the fridge; another sign that Grandmother isn't here often. Iris and I sit slumped in our chairs as if hung over, not that either of us knows what that's like. It's been a long day, one that began on horseback. Woods after a rain are filled with such delicious earthy smells. The long ride down the mountain to the car was exhilarating. Sister's voice sounds raspy like mine. I hope it's from the amount of talking we've been doing and not that we're getting sick.

"What's with your moanin'? asks Iris when I shift in my seat.

"I've been out of the saddle too long."

We take our time eating, forgoing conversation. Then, quite unexpectedly, Iris states she won't be having any babies. Hashke's sperm count is too low. I'm surprised to hear that he survived cancer as a child, and that his infertility likely resulted from the treatments he had undergone. There is no follow-up as to the type it was, or what he had to endure. I therefore don't pursue the matter, but my heart aches for them. Should I tell her I'm sorry?

Right then my phone goes off, and I'm notified by the airline that my flight out of Rapid City tomorrow has been canceled. Shortly after, Iris gets the same news about her flight to Wisconsin. The cause is said to be pandemic related. I'm guessing that proper protocol wasn't followed for disinfecting the aircraft. What a bummer. I'm feeling waves of homesickness, although I haven't been gone a full week. I miss the babies. They're so precious and vulnerable. I miss Tess ... how she touches me. Next thing I know I'm on the phone with Mom pleading my case. She manages to locate a private pilot in Sioux Falls who can fly me to Columbus tomorrow night. I don't care that it isn't Rapid City. Sister decides to stay here a few days longer. She'll accompany me in the rental car and drive it back to the reservation.

A seizure-like shiver grips me. I had kicked the quilt off the bed during the night, as freezing air entered the room from the open window. When I go to close it, I'm momentarily captivated by the full lemon-yellow moon overhead. A few stars are still visible. Morning so soon? The sky gradually transitions from the indigo blue directly above to a lighter sapphire shade in the distance, turning a deep rosy pink along the eastern horizon. A fiery orange sliver of sun suddenly hits my retinas, too blinding to look at. I race my naked ass back to bed and pull the covers around my neck, just long enough to get warm. I'm fully awake. My thoughts turn to Tess, and I start fantasizing about being in my own bed with her tonight. That heats me up fast. There's the matter of getting through the day first, which should be fun. Because the road from the Buckthorn Reservation to the airport in Sioux Falls runs across the state, Iris and I will be able to stop at Lazy Al's Trading Post along the way. Sadly missing from the place will be Takodah and Miss Audra. I haven't traveled the route in ages. It goes through three other Indian reservations.

Breakfast was a quick cup of coffee and a muffin. Sister and I have only Grandmother left to hug, and then we'll be off. My phone rings —it's Ruby Iron Cloud. Great news. She and Naomi Weiss, the other prospective nanny, wish to spend Memorial Weekend with family, and then they'll drive to Columbus to begin caring for the triplets. That gives me time to buy three more car seats for Miss Ruby's van. Uncle put a holding deposit on a spacious apartment over a florist's shop that he thinks the women will like and also on a small two-bedroom house that's a ten minute walk to our place. It's their choice, regardless of the cost. Tess and I live in an expensive neighborhood. That was Uncle William's doing. The house is in his name. I have the artist Efrem Zukor to thank for the money in my bank account. Dad's account really—he keeps tabs on it, which, being a parent now, I should take responsibility for. The poster Efrem created for *WAKAN* along with the Tarzan stories he illustrated using me for his model continue to fly off the shelves, and not just in the States. Tess and I haven't set up a joint account yet. She's keeping the money her parents gave us in her bank for the moment.

The road is empty except for an occasional semi delivering much needed essential supplies to stores across the land. We've heard how they're presently selling out of most items. People don't feel safe traveling until a vaccine is developed for the virus. It's a shame that Winter Crow's lab doesn't have the means to produce the three hundred million needed for the country's population. At least the scientists are sharing their research with other drug companies around the world. It's the kind of grand cooperative effort that should always exist in matters of health.

"Look there," says Iris, pointing ahead to Lazy Al's. I stare unblinking as we approach the parking lot, once dirt but now covered with gravel. How familiar the building is. "I'm super excited to see it, aren't you?" I am not as quick to unbuckle my seatbelt.

We slowly climb the steps to the porch, taking it all in. Same old creaky floorboards. The rocking chairs and benches haven't been replaced. Ceremonial hand drums still fill a corner. There are the Indian dolls precariously balanced on a gnarly pine log that's been hammered into the side of the store, and which tilts down on the right. The dolls have yet to slide off. They kept the wide painted buffalo skin nailed to the wall. The photo of Al on his bucking horse hangs in the same spot next to the door, but in a new silver frame stamped with feathers. Un-hee! The memories triggered! There is no sign posted about wearing a mask inside, but we figure we should and are about to put them on when suddenly the screen door flies open. It's a Native family of four, five...no, seven, and they're not in masks. The eyes of the two young boys grow big and their mouths drop open. In their excitement, having recognized me, they start jumping all over their parents, who act embarrassed as they try to pull their kids out of our way.

"It's okay," I tell them, laughing over the boys' enthusiastic behavior. Iris takes a group picture of us on the steps. I shake hands goodbye with the parents and move on past the door.

My first whiff inside Al's reveals it's not the same store—too antiseptic. Nothing is where it should be, the magazines, the souvenirs...and where are the chips and candy? To my right, a huge space for selling produce has been added. No way.

Things used to be so crammed together. Cowboy hats were loosely stacked on the shelf beside rows of canned soups. There were always a couple of saddles for sale strapped atop sawhorses beside the cash register, which is nowhere in sight. The changes make me sad, unbelievably sad. Maybe it's for the better. How might it affect me if the scene were exactly the same as when Sam Barker got murdered, the day the gangs lit the place on fire.

"Do I detect tears, Viktor?"

There's a choking lump in my throat over what's been done to the place. Iris and I head out back to where the barn and riding ring were, still are, only now they're brand-spanking new. The thing is, kids are having fun racing their horses around barrels just like I did at their age. And they've got family and friends cheering them on from rows of bleachers that have been added, allowing for considerably more people to attend than the few here today. That's largely due to the stay-at-home orders issued by the government, in order to prevent the spread of the virus, otherwise tourists would be in the open seats. Someone yells out Iris's name. A curvy lady in a sparkly cowgirl hat and tight-fitting jeans climbs over a group in a middle section then sprints toward Sister with her arms outstretched. Iris realizes who it is and races to meet her in what turns into an energetic embrace that has them hopping in circles. When they finally let go of each other I'm introduced to Zoey Mad River, a good friend from grade school who Iris continued to see at summer camp following our move to Texas. Zoey points out her husband in the stands. They just happened to be passing through the area today on their way home to the Blackfeet Reservation in Montana. It's obvious that Iris and Zoey have some catching up to do, so I excuse myself to head to where I used to meet my football buddies, but not before asking why no one's in masks. Turns out Winter Crow's lab quietly inoculated most Indians on tribal lands in and around the Black Hills. Natives do mask up like all citizens when they go off the reservations. They don't wish to see the lab attacked by outsiders, angry there are no vaccines available for them. It's good to hear that the health of our community is safe.

I amble across the street in front of Al's, longing for the good ole days. No tourists means there's little traffic. The trees have grown unbelievably tall around the picnic spot near the roadside pull-off. I stand there looking back at Al's and relive being with Takodah and Miss Audra as we watched their property burn. It's surprising to find the same old weathered tables and benches. My fingers trace some of the initials carved into them. I find mine ... and Daniel's. "I miss you so much, Daniel." I picture him when we were little zooming around Mom with his arms spread wide and mimicking the roar of a plane. She would laugh when he'd yell to her that he was faster than any jet she ever flew. "Love you, my brother." In the distance a coach is shouting orders to his young football players. Sounds just like Dad. These pangs of nostalgia are killing me!

Enough with the past! I let go a final sniffle before strolling over to the goal post. The action is presently at the opposite end zone, with the quarterback set to throw. Oh, no, intercepted! But then the ball instantly pops into the air and lands out of bounds, which of course sparks the beginning of the blame game. I have to laugh.

"Look!" shrieks a kid, pointing straight at me. The boys are too busy yelling at each other to notice at first. The coach heard him and turns. Again the kid cries out, which now catches the attention of his teammates, who stand staring at me from downfield. I wave hello, making a sweeping arc over my head. At once they rush toward me en masse, screaming their brains out as they barrel across the field. I brace myself for the collision.

It's one thing to have fans, but this kind of hero-worship is overwhelming. Their eyes flash with joy as they go on jumping around me excitedly, bumping into each other as they grab for my arms and hands. The coach steps in and orders them to respect my space, not harshly. I tell them I'm not going anywhere at the moment, that there's plenty of time to visit. We head for the shade by the picnic tables. I feel like the Pied Piper. Next they beg me to sign their jerseys, which I agree to because I don't have the heart to tell them I don't sign autographs, not with all those pleading eyes looking at me. The coach instructs a boy to run to Al's to get a black marker, leaving nine kids crowded around me.

Each introduces himself along with the coach, Wayne Fast Dog. He says he runs a thrift store on the Rosebud Reservation. He was told about this spot by Dad, who, with Mom, recently bought the team the super-duper charter bus that's parked in the lot down the road. News to me. Wayne says it's actually for all the children that live at St. Ignatius, an orphanage run by Jesuits on Rosebud. The boys, sixth graders, chime in about how it's air-conditioned and has big comfy seats and TVs and, best of all, there's a sink with running water and a toilet. Coach and I look at each other and smile. He's a burly, middle-aged guy, not that tall, and with laugh lines growing out of the corners of his narrow dark eyes that travel across his puffy cheeks.

The boy arrives with the marker in nothing flat, completely winded, and holding an armful of OSU jerseys that he piles on the picnic table, all printed with my name and number seven on them—donated by the owner. I ask Wayne Fast Dog why the store has so many shirts on hand.

"The tourists want them. They're big sellers."

The first signed one goes to the boy who brought them. Raymond. His expression is priceless, so trusting and sweet. He hugs my arm. I almost joke that I'd like to tuck him in a pocket and steal him away with me, but then realize it might be embarrassing to him considering his size; he's the shortest player.

Wayne takes pictures using my phone. I promise to have prints made and sent to St. Ignatius. We toss the ball around a bit when I hear Iris's voice calling out that we should get a move on. Coach has the kids line up to say goodbye. I shake hands ceremoniously with each of them.

"I am so proud of my young Indian brothers," I tell them. "Keep striving to be the best you can be, and not just in football, but in your studies. I am first and foremost a scholar. Do you know what that means?" An explanation is in order, after which I tell them: "Don't be thrown off-course by setbacks. I myself promise to walk the Red Road to honor my Elders and all the departed spirits who watch over us. Will my new friends promise the same?"

"Oh chee-chee ah kay," they promise. The boys mosey along beside me in silence to the highway, at which point I join Iris on the other side.

"Mitakuye Oyasin," I yell to them.

"Mitakuye Oyasin," they shout back, waving enthusiastically with both arms. They do it until I disappear inside Al's. I want to meet the new owner and thank him for the thoughtful gesture of the free shirts. I expect to pay for them, though. He rejects the offer, but asks if I'd be in a photo with him for the wall. Now that's an honor!

As we walk to the car, Iris offers to drive. Three more hours to Sioux Falls.

Once underway, I ask, "Did you find out what became of Miss Audra and Takodah?"

"One of their sons, a teacher, moved them up to Pierre after the fire to live near his family. Which reminds me...I found some old, dusty comics in the back of the store, which I was told I could take. Made me think of you. They're on the back seat. The owner said if we had come in February, the place would have looked exactly the same. Once the virus started spreading, and the CDC described how thoroughly surfaces need to be scrubbed and sterilized, he decided it best to gut the inside and remodel. In truth, it needed to be done."

"I know. Takodah used to complain about the rotting wood beams. There was always a new leak in the roof for him to patch after a rain. At least the new owner left the front porch intact, and the name. Al's holds so many memories for everybody on the rez."

Iris and I turn quiet, taking in the miles of unchanged landscape. After a bit, I turn on the radio and find the local station. It's a call-in talk show. Can't tell what the topic is yet, but the girl on the line is responding to something the previous caller had said. It's apparent that she holds an opposing view on the subject. Ah...the discussion is about the checkpoints that were set up on the Buckthorn Reservation following the murders of the gang members. They are intended to keep the rez safe from future criminal activity. The guy on the line before her was hellbent on learning who carried out the killings. The girl, on the other hand, insists it doesn't matter. "Good riddance to them," she says. "Who cares who's responsible for killing them. They did us a huge favor. The checkpoints are working. Look how bad the violence still is on other reservations."

On that note, the DJ hosting the call-in announces it's time to move on to the next topic: "Are Indigenous influencers having a positive or negative impact on the lives of Native youth?"

"*Influencer*," I mutter sarcastically. "People and their stupid social media." Iris makes a disapproving tsk sound in response to my opinion, causing me to wonder if she pays attention to that crap. "What?" I ask, knowing full well something's on her mind.

"You do realize *you* are an influencer, whether you post stuff online or not. Think about how Jim Thorpe influenced you growing up, a dead man no less!"

She's right...up to a point. "You know darn well what I mean. It's what the word has come to represent on social media." We listen with interest to the comments. Call-in shows have always been popular on the rez, but more so now due to families isolating until the pandemic runs its course. They're a great way for everyone to stay connected. Many tribal members don't own cell phones or have access to Internet. They rely on their radios for entertainment and the latest news. As I listen to the current female caller going on about how Natives in the public eye need to hold themselves to a higher moral standard, memories of Marnie surface. I hadn't thought of her in ages—the girl who had helped me shop for clothes in Rapid City before I headed off to Ohio State. The girl who insisted I pay attention to how I dressed and acted once I was on campus because I'd be representing my people. Her well-intentioned advice made me burning mad at the time. Suddenly my name's brought up in the discussion on the radio. Why do I feel on the defensive?

The guy has only positive things to say about me, which is a relief. It's nice to hear that my efforts to act professionally on the football field are appreciated. Guess I'm the new topic. Another caller commends me for having mentioned in an interview how instrumental my high school teachers were to my success. "Must be a teacher herself," I tell Iris. "Isn't it weird listening to what total strangers have to say about your brother? Just think if it were you."

Then comes the call I was half-expecting, the one to ruffle my feathers. "If Viktor really wanted to steer his tribal brothers and sisters in a better direction, he'd return to the rez, to his people...show them that having it all in the white man's world amounts to having nothing."

"There it is," I complain, "the Indian I'm supposed to be." I reach for the knob having heard enough. "He sounds like Billie Spotted Horse. When I saw him in Texas at Dad's shop, he said I should return to Buckthorn."

"Not so fast," says Iris, brushing away my hand. "How about calling the DJ?"

I lean back, wondering what her angle is. "Why?"

"Tell him you wish to personally thank the callers who had such nice things to say about you. Mention you've been visiting your elders and are presently headed to the airport. You don't realize what a curiosity you are to the people on the neighboring reservations. They should hear how closely connected you are to your culture, despite having grown up in Texas. It makes you more relatable to them."

"And why is that important?" I ask, to which she looks at me grinning.

"Why, to *influence* more of your Indian peers. It may come in handy one day."

CHAPTER 59

Another morning slips away. For how many weeks now? It's the start of July. Neil Avenue is dead, like the rest of OSU's campus. I find a bench in the shade until I can decide where to go next. I really have no purpose at the moment. Because of the pandemic, football training was cancelled for the summer. Here and there a body briefly appears. A few research labs deemed essential are open, but with lots of restrictions. The research I was involved with is currently on hold, and not because Dr. Sharma is stuck in India for the time being. Who knows when international travel will resume. A veterinary tech on the staff of the hospital is caring for our rats, a job I wouldn't mind having. Tess shooed me out of the house to enjoy some one-on-one time with our Lakota nannies who arrived a few days ago. Miss Ruby and Miss Naomi, as they've asked to be called, have opted to live in the apartment above the florist instead of the more spacious house, primarily because it's next door to an ice cream parlor, clearly a perk.

The sky couldn't be any bluer. Mirror Lake beckons—it's right down the street. How eerie it feels to be walking along empty sidewalks. This is the first time I've truly been out and about here since returning from South Dakota over a month ago. Tess and I were busy with laundry and chores following the departure of her mother, aunt, and cousin, whom I was pleased to get a chance to meet. More redheads. Then we left for Claire and Damien's wedding in Kansas City, which they pulled off despite social distancing rules. The guest list included immediate family and closest friends, which amounted to around fifty people. Damien had no one except his older cousin, Gabe, from Dayton, who served as his best man.

A parade of ducks stops me in my tracks on the path leading down to the water, bringing me back to the present. The air smells clean. I take a few deep breaths, sucking in the heady fragrance of nearby flowers. Where's the rushing sound of the fountain? The pump's been turned off.

A single jogger and biker wearing earphones pass me, lost in their own worlds.

"Viktor?"

I turn toward the voice. "Un-hee!"

"Un-hee is right!" Hayden laughs, waving me over to where he is sprawled out on the hillside.

I collapse beside him on the long, cushy grass.

"This is frickin' spooky!" he says. "It's been months. Were you just walking around thinking you'd hang here for a while?"

"Yep, and you?"

"Same. What are the odds?" He drapes his arm around my neck. "I think it means these dudes are destined to have themselves some fun today. Whaddya say?"

"Heck, yeah!"

Instead of jumping to our feet to find some action, we fall back on the soft grass, happy for the company and the fact that neither of us needs to be anywhere.

"Aren't you going to mention my hair?" says Hayden.

"What hair?"

"Very funny. This is a month's growth."

"You can pull it off…you've got a well-shaped noggin."

He rolls his head back and forth on the ground. "Feels so good."

The noisy engine of an approaching lawn mower forces us to get our butts in gear and move.

"Let's head to High Street for coffee," he says. "I'm parked in the garage up there."

We slowly roll to a standing position and start laughing over how our grunts make us sound like old men, and then we amble across the Oval to Starbucks.

The weather is perfect for sitting outside. Half the tables have been removed on the patio to keep customers a safe distance apart. One is open by the sidewalk. As I go to shove my mask in the pocket of my cargo shorts, I remove something that's sure to slay Hayden, a diaper with a pacifier poking out of it. "Am I a good dad or what? Always prepared."

He grins and shakes his head. "God, Viktor, if I had become a father at your age. You are finally twenty, right?"

We slouch down in our seats and get comfortable. No amount of caffeine is going to perk us up. Hayden yawns. "There are going to be huge cuts in the football program. I doubt I'll be kept on as your coach."

"Yeah, it's going to be a drastically different school year. There might not be any sports if there's another spike in the number of cases of people testing positive for the virus."

"Crazy times. So tell me, how are people in general faring on Buckthorn? Good...bad?"

I take a second to think about it, and then offer a slight nod in the affirmative. "On the whole, for the first time in memory, the future looks promising. I think the Indians don't want to admit it out loud because they fear jinxing things.

"The Council's elders are moving toward working together with young people, in order to figure out policies that affect every aspect of tribal life. That's a step in the right direction, and way overdue I might add. It's like creating a new society from the ground up, much like those idealistic framers of the Constitution did for their own glorious race."

"Good for them!" says Hayden, ignoring my sarcasm. He taps my cup to toast their efforts. "Must be exciting." Next he fills me in on what Skyler's been up to and what Mimi looks like now, showing me photos of her on his phone. His daughter has been blessed with cute dimples and a gorgeous mop of light brown hair that falls in tight ringlets to her shoulders. I in turn show him recent pictures of the triplets whose hair isn't quite as wild as when they were born.

We sip our drinks and watch the traffic on High Street. Hayden brings up the topic of coaching again. "It was such a fun job at first, but I won't miss it now...not since that meeting when the coaches and staff, whom I'm considered a part of, stood together and flat out told our Black players they had better not take a knee on the field during the anthem, or else! They had no right to censure grown men for possessing a social conscience."

"Most the team let it slide. Whites are clueless."

"I resent that, Viktor! You know exactly what I'm saying. Kaepernick's career was ruined back when he took a knee, but now with the Black Lives Matter protests, it seems that everybody wants to hop on the kneeing bandwagon. It'll be interesting to see the way coaches address the issue in the future. Why is it that you don't respond to reporters when they ask for your thoughts? You realize they're going to keep pressing you for an answer in light of the media attention it draws."

"I have no interest in becoming a distraction to the game of football. Besides, I don't seek equality with whites. For me, placing myself on equal footing with whites means lowering my standards ... considerably. Indians maintain a kinship with everything in the universe. Equality is inherent. We do want freedom, freedom from outsiders who are constantly in our faces, like the governor of South Dakota who demanded that checkpoints be removed from the borders of our reservation during this pandemic, because it's important to the state's economy for the roads to stay open. In other words, Indigenous folks are dispensable—go ahead and let the virus spread on our territories, as long as goods get delivered so companies can continue to show profits. I support the Black and Native Lives Matter Movements, but I won't yield to critics who, for whatever reason, reckon I need to behave in a way that meshes with their views of the world."

I stare across the street at the sprawling campus. "Something's happening to me, Hayden. I think like a Native, but I can't find my comfort zone on the rez these days. Columbus is home. My great-grandparents sensed my impatience around them, and that makes me sad. I confronted a helluva lot on this visit, and it simply isn't relevant to my present life."

"Are you referring to the newfound clan members you said you were going to meet for the first time?"

"There's that..." I sigh, lacking the energy to explore the reasons. "It would be wrong for me to speak on behalf of *any* Indian. I don't know anymore which identity to embrace, Lakota...Rawakota. There's my Dad's Black family, and the influence of the Jewish kids I went to school with."

"It's called self-discovery, and it's perfectly normal. Your universe is expanding. I just can't believe you took the plunge and married so young. A case of different strokes." He smiles and admires my ring. I know he's thinking it was a rash and dumb thing to do, despite my having shared with him once the cultural significance behind marrying early. I didn't go into great depth, but did explain the *eich ihilah* to him, and why masturbation is disapproved of. He responded honestly saying that the idea of never touching himself required more control than he could ever muster, and that saving oneself for marriage was unrealistic.

"Tell me something, Viktor. Presuming the wait was worth it...what if you hadn't met Tess? Might you be living a monk's life until you reached thirty, or forty?"

"Yes."

"Sorry, my friend, that's plain..." he stops himself.

"Plain *stupid*, I know. I told you it was the reason my birth father drank himself to death...he couldn't wait." Hayden knows about Mom having met my birth father when she was barely a teen, and that he was already in his thirties.

He throws his head back for that last drop of coffee, then says, "You can't convince me there weren't other mitigating factors involved. When a person drinks to that degree..." He pats my cheek. "Anyway, I'm glad the theeich ihilah experience lived up to the hype. Wanna go see the studio?"

"You bet!"

As we head toward the garage, I wonder how the elders would react to hearing their valued Rawakota beliefs referred to as hype. I understand what Hayden meant by it. Children the world over are indoctrinated by the ideologies of the societies they grow up in.

When I was little, how I loved sitting outside under the stars at the feet of Pahpie and Sunkwah, listening to them go on about Great Bear and Little Bear. The bears had roamed the forests before humans existed. When they passed to the spirit world they became the constellations pointed out to me in the mysterious night sky. The story of the bears, which included elks and eagles, introduced me to the concept of loyalty, the most important trait to Rawakota people. It taught me about different kinds of friendships, especially a unique one having to do with romantic feelings, without which there could be no sacred union between a husband and his wife. When the Rawakota custom of theeich ihilah was explained more recently, I felt extremely confused. My Lakota friends on the rez had their own views about sex. As did my Health teacher in Texas, who was really vague on procedure. Considering all that I'd heard, I didn't want to take a chance on the elders being wrong, and so I refused to touch myself. As it turned out, I'm glad I listened to Sunkwah and Pahpie.

"We'll dance," says Hayden as he unlocks the car door, "like you did in *WAKAN*, when there was no mistaking you for the mighty Lakota warrior you are through and through."

Always one to bolster my confidence, I tell him, "It's going to be a sad day if you're dropped from the coaching roster. What if I choke before a play? Who's going to build me up as only you're able to do?"

"Are you kidding?" he says, followed by a shake of his head as he steers us out of the tight space. "You, my man, can successfully rely on your own instincts from here on out!"

CHAPTER 60

"What the...!" Tess scares the wits out of me when she slips off my headphones. I didn't hear her enter the study. She instantly screams, a reflex reaction to my surprise, which sets off Nero, who then starts barking wildly.

"Sorry. Jeez. You didn't answer when I called out I was home."

We laugh over the fright we gave each other, and next she leans over and kisses me full on the lips, a move that proves to Nero the situation is under control. "I am so stoked, Tess!"

"Tutoring students in chemistry online is that exciting? Have you budged at all from that chair since I left this morning?"

"Mm-hmm," I mutter, looking back at the computer screen and the virtual meeting that's been occupying me for most the afternoon. The people in the chat room have no doubt been entertained by the show Tess and I just gave them. It registers how long I've been at this and I excuse myself from the group. Tess ascertains that I was doing nothing related to chemistry.

"Oh, dear," she says, "are you turning into a social media junkie?"

"Nooo. And yes, I took breaks. You saw the pics I sent of the kids in the stroller when I walked them to Naomi and Ruby's place. They're keeping them until dinner. When I finished helping the students, I went to the website of the Native radio station that Iris and I had listened to on the rez. Remember me telling you? I thought I'd call the DJ again, just to say hi and tell him that I support this idea he'd been talking about. He wants to organize a national private online chat for us tribal members. Word spread fast that I was on the air with him, and in half an hour the station was swamped with calls. He told me that thirty-thousand people on three reservations listen to him, besides all the Indians in Rapid City, which has got to be a huge number...not a hundred thousand, but close." I'm talking a mile a minute. There's no containing my excitement.

"Tell me about it while I start dinner. Nero's ears perk up. He's got quite the vocabulary: dinner, lunch, kitchen, snack, not to mention he's completely attuned to the sound of the refrigerator door opening. I hadn't noticed when he left my feet to go greet Tess. He recognizes our cars' engines coming up the hill before the garage door rumbles open.

Tess places a knife and a bag of carrots in my hands. I dutifully head to the sink while going on about how out of the loop I am. "Kids talked about rappers I never heard of…Supaman, and DJ Shub, and they brought up these popular women filmmakers who've turned their sorry lives on the rez into comedies, as if that's possible. And there's this great folksinger, Raye Zaragoza. I tell you, Tess, it was enlightening. I suggested building a school on Buckthorn for the creative arts, with film and music … we could've gone on all night."

"Catch your breath. Do I need to remind you of your football meeting in forty minutes?"

She definitely does not. I'm the one who asked to see the QB coach. It's now late summer, and I've decided that I want the chance to play defense this year. The lateral tackle I managed to pull off last season was exhilarating, even though it winded me and scared the hell out of Tess as she watched the play unfold on TV. I haven't been able to put it out of my mind. I'm waiting to hear Coach's thoughts on it before telling Tess. "I'll leave in twenty minutes."

The Rolls-Royces are back. And the TV news trucks. I swing past the entrance of the athletic center before parking, to make sure no reporters are waiting around to highjack an unsuspecting player into giving them an easy soundbite to fill airtime. The major concern over the past couple of months is whether any college teams will play this season. The number of people infected with the virus goes up, and then down, then back up. The latest I heard is that we're set to play our first game the middle of October. Network schedules keep changing. Good luck to the head coaches, university presidents, and media bigshots, scrambling right now to keep their profits from vaporizing into thin air. I picture the anxious group in the conference room down the hall, trying to come up with ways to salvage what's left of the football season.

Coach Doyle waves me in from the doorway. He just ended a call, and based on his grim expression, there was bad news involved. No sooner do I sit and get comfortable when a new assistant coach enters his office and asks Doyle how it went. I'm assuming he's talking about the call, and

I'm right, something didn't go well. There's a revolving door of assistant coaches these days. Too many to keep track of. They're let go by teams simply for making thoughtless remarks about race or gender. Some are probably scapegoats for losing teams. And yet they manage to go on finding jobs, the white coaches that is, which he is…really white, with Highlighter-yellow hair and a freckled face. Late forties, maybe. He apologizes for the interruption, and then goes in search of something on a side table. Coach Doyle ignores him and motions for me to get on with it. He acts tense. Now I'm wishing I could reschedule.

"Coach, I've given this lots of thought…I'd like a shot at playing defense this year. It isn't a sudden whim. I was thinking a middle linebacker position behind…"

I jump in my seat when the assistant coach who's behind me slams the table hard with his fist, causing a stack of binders to slide off onto the floor. It's followed by a string of expletives. Next thing, Coach Doyle's on his feet demanding he shut up.

"Not another word, you hear me, Ron!"

But this Ron fellow doesn't listen. "That's what's wrong with this generation of players! They're nothing but a bunch of fucking prima donnas, so full of themselves. Who are they to say what's best for the team?"

"Ron! Stop! Now!"

Man, if looks could kill. Coach Doyle forcefully leads this guy out by the arm then calmly closes the door and stands staring at the floor. At first I thought he might be counting to ten to compose himself. It's more like a hundred. Hopefully not a thousand.

"Viktor, please forget what you just saw. He wasn't justified in saying any of that…but please, just forget it. Everybody's on edge, which is no excuse." With that, he walks to his chair and slumps onto it. "Finish what you were saying."

I didn't plan on having to sell the idea so much. "I'm able to recognize plays from a quarterback's perspective and shut them down." He's looking me over, probably thinking I need to pack on fifty more pounds, if he's even taking me seriously. "I'm solid; I can stand my ground. Plus I'm agile. You've seen how high I can leap. Tipping the ball will be easy."

"You're the quarterback, plain and simple. End of story."

Whoa. Now I'm ticked off. I deserve better than to be shut down like this! But then, maybe I should have made myself clearer. "I'll still play the

QB position. Not all the time. It won't be any different than when Krull was here and we alternated."

"We don't have a Tiberius Krull. We have no one! Hell, we can't even recruit a decent backup for you. Any top high school player wants to go where he can be the kind of star you are. They want the glory. And fans here pay to see you, Viktor. With college football programs hanging in limbo right now, at least students and alumni should be able to bank on watching you throw a ball again." He moans and rubs his face up and down like it's rubber. "I just got off the phone with a talented kid we believed was coming here, only to hear him tell me he is headed to Colorado. You've got teammates who have committed to staying at OSU because of you." He won't mention their names but admits that a few guys have declined contracts with the NFL because they grab so much attention playing for the Buckeyes. It's a fact that many top college players flounder once they turn pro.

His line about alumni banking on watching me raises my hackles. That's what it always comes down to in colleges sports: the alumni. And it isn't like it's a revelation to me. All football programs are funded by generous alumni. Coaches and their assistants win muti-million dollar contracts while labor gets squat. It's the players who should be compensated for taking on the risks of playing a dangerous sport. I actually feel sorry for Doyle. At what point during his career did his love for the game become compromised by money?

To think that only a few hours ago I was enjoying a discussion with my Indian brothers and sisters about returning to the sharing ways of hunter-gatherer days. The takeaway from trips to big cities is how noisy the places are and how much people care about owning stuff. Despite the poverty, reservation life still serves as a retreat from the insanity of the outside world.

"Well?" asks Coach.

I totally zoned out and have no clue what he said last. Returning to the present, I'm feeling a marked sense of empowerment. Even though I like Coach, I see him in a new and more negative light.

"Know what, Coach…I'll introduce you to Caleb Meyer, an Amish student who will make a terrific quarterback. I won't leave you in the lurch. I'm friends with his family. He would love the challenge of playing at this level."

"What the hell are you talking about? Amish don't go to college."

"Guess you haven't heard of the Bluffton University Beavers. It's a Division III school northwest of here. Don't worry about his character; he's a theology student minoring in peace and conflict studies." I leave on that note

On my way out, Doyle shouts there'll be no changing his mind.

And there's no changing mine. Seems I hold all the cards. TV ratings were up before the pandemic, not for NFL games, but for college games, primarily the ones I was in.

Outside his office, the meeting with the head honchos has wrapped up. Everyone is starting to file into the hall. I pick up my step, for once actually wanting to be seen by the reporters. I'm barraged with questions about whether the guys are prepared to play...have we had adequate practice sessions together to take on our rivals? Lucky for them I feel like shaking things up.

"Tell you what...look for me in the defensive lineup." I just had to do it, after which I run to my car. I laugh as they scurry back to corner the head coach, who's escorting the execs to their shiny waiting limos. Funny that no players were let in on their closed-door session, especially since their business is *all about us.*

On the way home, I have to figure out what to tell Tess about the stunt I pulled. The nannies wave to me as I round the corner onto our street. They returned the babies and are walking home. Fingers crossed the kids are played-out and ready for bed. I'm home in time to help Tess. We're amazed that there's not the usual kicking or squirming during diapering that they've recently been tormenting us with. "Thank you Ruby and Naomi," whispers Tess, as the trio falls asleep before our eyes. "Those ladies are a godsend."

While the soup heats on the stove, and with her backside toward me, I take Tess in my arms and gently rock her in place. "Does your brain ever feel like it's firing all over the place?" I ask, kissing her neck until she relaxes against me.

"Not in ages. I only got through breast feeding and pumping a couple of months ago. That was physically draining. Now I'm taking an online class. By late afternoon, my brain shuts down."

This isn't an ideal time for me to disclose what I did. The soup bubbles, and we sit to eat. My toes find hers under the table. I catch a smile. "Are you up for telling me how your day went with Claire in German Village?"

At once her eyes come alive. The two had planned this outing a while back, anticipating that the state-implemented shutdown of schools and businesses wouldn't last long. Fortunately restaurants have reopened, but only for take-out orders. She and Claire got to enjoy their brats and sauerkraut in the park. And they were allowed to browse our favorite bookstore, which Claire was dying to visit after she'd heard me rave about it. A limited number of customers could go inside at a time.

Raif wails. We hold our breath. It's short-lived. Whew! Tess continues to look at me as if she has something else to say. After a second…

"Claire said it was okay for me to tell you that she's pregnant. She took a home test a few days ago."

I'm dumbstruck. Damien—a dad? That clearly should not have been my first thought. "Is she happy about it?"

"Of course she's happy about it!"

"Well I don't know," I shrug. "It took us by complete surprise." Did Tess forget that I alone was thrilled by the news? The change in her expression clearly conveys she did not. Claire's response might also have been less enthusiastic if she had learned she was carrying more than one fetus. Who knows, maybe she is. It certainly complicates a pregnancy. I wonder if they planned it.

"It was fun looking for storybooks," says Tess. "Claire immediately informed her mother. She's looking forward to coming and helping out after the baby's born. I wish I hadn't minded my mom's company so much. She was as ready for a break from me as I was from her after those first months. It was my fault. Coming to terms with motherhood this early in my life is not easy, let alone the fact there are three babies to deal with. I wanted her here, and yet I didn't. The tension between us had everything to do with my own insecurities."

"And what about *my* mom?" My mother had stayed but a short time compared to Chevonne's visit, and it was long after Tess had given birth. She didn't have to face Tess's postpartum mood swings.

"*Your* mom. Hmm. Constance *gets* how to stay out of the way. She readily helped me, but only when I asked, which took me a couple of days to realize. It gave me time to study each of the babies and learn their quirks. My mother stepped in the second one cried or was wet and took over, insisting I rest."

"Please don't take this the wrong way, Tess, but, considering the circumstances, you absolutely needed the rest." She likely prefers to forget that fact.

"I'll be sure to make it up to her. It's admirable how you stick up for her. What a plus that we like our mothers-in-law. While we're on the subject of your mom, is there something going on between your parents? I don't think she brought up Solomon once while she was here."

"Iris and I thought they acted distant at Claire's wedding. Later, when I went to Texas to collect what was left of my things in the house, Dad clammed up when I mentioned her."

"Maybe they need their space right now. It happens."

"With her job, they've had far too much space. He could easily come visit her at Wright-Patt. You should have heard the way he landed into me when I called him on always having a beer in his hand, even in the morning. Said it was his house, and he could damn well drink a beer when he pleased. He argued that I didn't understand the stress he's been under, leaving a business that he built from the ground up, and a house filled with so many memories. I flat out stated it was no excuse. Not very considerate of me, was it?"

"That *doesn't* sound like him."

"I know, right?" My bowl is empty, ready for seconds. When I stand, Tess holds my hand to her cheek for a moment. I love her so much.

"The day I left, he told me he was glad I didn't let him off the hook. He at least promised to limit the beer, which I swore I would hold him to. I feel for him. It's been a lonely undertaking without Mom being involved in the move. And then there was the episode surrounding her PTSD, when the Rawakota didn't include him in her treatment. I hate that I contributed to his suffering, too. I should have let him help me when I left the hospital. That was supremely thoughtless on my part." My phone goes off on the table. I'm filling my glass and ask Tess to read the message.

"It's from Coach Doyle. When can you bring the Amish boy in? Is he talking about Caleb?"

I tell her how OSU lost out on a recruit for the backup QB position, and that I gave the coach Caleb's name for consideration. She jokes over what a marketing coup it would be for the Amish, if the straw hats the men wear catch on. The stadium might look like a hayfield on gameday from the blimp's overhead view of it. Fact is, Caleb wears a dark felt hat year round, forgoing the straw kind normally worn in summer.

"What about suspenders," I add, "to hold the players' football pants up, especially for those 350 pound Offensive Tackles." We're on a roll. Tess would hate for their style of beards to become a fad, though.

"A beard without a moustache looks stupid. Why is Caleb clean-shaven?"

"To let the ladies know he's single and available." She laughs like I made it up.

"The strange rules societies come up with. He's bound to experience culture shock at a school this size, don't you think? Would he survive a non-Amish environment?"

"Caleb's been around *the English* his entire life, that's how he became obsessed with football. As a kid, before his family opened the restaurant we go to, he'd accompany his father to a farmers market on weekends. After helping set up their stand, he got to spend the day with a regular family where he watched college games on TV. His particular community is fairly progressive as far as the Amish go. They use phones and computers to conduct business. This is his Rumspringa period. He can pretty much do as he pleases until he is baptized."

"Interesting. It's hard to imagine such a polite and quiet-spoken fellow being as competitive as one needs to be for football. He resembles a wide-eyed kitten."

"The more dangerous."

It was an off-handed comment, but for some reason I can tell it bothered her.

"Tell me honestly," she says, now serious, "what is it like to be constantly confronted by players who are dead set on hurting you?"

I don't dare sound glib or dismissive...she is after all concerned for my safety.

"History shows I'm able to outwit them...find my opening and go for it. Rest assured, Tess, no one's going to get the better of me. I harbor a killer instinct myself, you know." I have yet to reveal to her what happened between Ishmael and me, which is when I realized just how fierce and ruthless I could be when my life was on the line.

"You've heard of hubris, right? And what it leads to." Her mocking tone isn't appreciated. She continues to lock eyes with me as she stands to clear the table.

"I take it you're not convinced your husband is a legitimate threat." And with that, I scoop her up in my arms and pin her to the wall beside the pantry door. "Care to show me how to up my game?"

"With pleasure," she whispers, her lips lightly touching my ear. My tongue slips by hers as we laugh inside a kiss. Next, my hand slides under her shirt.

CHAPTER 61

"How's my favorite grandson doing?" asks Grandmother.

"Good," I answer, smiling, surprised to hear from her this early. She hasn't used that greeting in years. It hadn't dawned on me until I was around ten that I was the *only* grandson out of her five grandkids. She tells me that her parents energy level has improved, and that they sent her on back to her own home.

"The radio call-in you did has everyone excited on the rez and talking about what's important to them, young and old. It's encouraging. Keep it up, Viktor!"

"I plan to."

"And what a good idea it was to give students their own microscopes to take home. They're a big hit."

"The response amazed me. When kids called the station to say they're discovering mites and parasites on their horses and dogs, and they're learning to stain slides to look for bacteria in the water, I felt compelled to track down Mr. Reuter, my teacher from high school, to tell him about it. He retired, but I found him living in Florida. He used to say that satisfying a hunger for knowledge is as vital to a person's development as filling an empty belly."

"Can't argue that. The mood is definitely more positive here. You can sense a real change in the air," says Grandmother triumphantly. "Most families are onboard with us winning back our independence. The last meeting was packed, standing room only. There's always been a camp of tribal members who insist we go on receiving federal money, convinced that it's owed us, but this time they were shown the door when they started complaining about the rest of us wanting to officially end our ties with the government."

Grandmother has never bought into the idea that our people could sober up enough to organize anything. Their lack of purpose and discipline drove Pahpie crazy. For the first time, I, too, am believing there are workable solutions to our problems on Buckthorn. If successful, other reservations might copy our approach. Guess I shouldn't be jumping the gun.

"We're going to miss seeing you this winter," says Grandmother. "Thank goodness for computers and Zoom. We were set to watch the game together last weekend, only to hear it was cancelled at the last minute because players on the other team had gotten sick. How do you deal with that? It must be difficult emotionally."

"We hold to our workout routines. It helps."

"You enjoy your week, Hinhán Ska. Your Pahpie would have been proud of you. People look so forward to these online science sessions with you. Don't disappoint. Love you."

"Love you back, Grandmother. I think I'll give Sunkwah and Winnie a call."

With barely a foot inside the house, I belt out, "Another cancelled gayame!"

"Woohoo," shouts Tess, running at me full speed. "Aah, you're all wet! Didn't you dry off after showering?"

"They told us right as we were leaving the practice field that more of their players have tested positive for the virus. I just wanted to get home. Are the babies still napping?"

Tess slides out from my arms. "First one up the stairs calls the shots!" And, whoosh! She's gone, racing ahead to the bedroom. I could easily overtake her, if I weren't so curious as to what she has in mind for me. I find her already out of her clothes, waiting on the bed. I'm naked in no time. Next thing, her legs fly above my shoulders. And with great force, she presses me deep inside her...so fast I damn near pass out.

We listen to the triplets yammering in the playpen we put in the guest room across the hallway. It was a pain always running to the downstairs nursery when we were up here. Seems we can hold out a bit before going in.

Tess rolls over and plants little kisses on my neck. "I love you." Next she bounces off the bed, throws on her clothes and says she'll deal with the babies.

"Where'd all this energy come from?" I ask, still plainly recovering from the sex.

"Just feeling happy." She blows me a kiss and practically skips out the door. I should help. I feel guilty. I inch toward the edge of the bed and stand halfway up when a spell of lightheadedness gets the better of me, and I scoot back against the headboard. It's fun listening to my family in the other room. Tess learned a silly Lakota toe-counting rhyme similar to Mother Goose's This Little Piggy Went to Market. The kids giggle with anticipation during the countdown on their toes. When Tess reaches the pinky toe, and the last little chick goes cheep, cheep, cheep, all the way home, the three start squealing their brains out when tickled. Raif's laugh is contagious. He's seriously goofy! Tess unlatches the baby gate at the top of the stairs. There they go, backwards down the stairs on their bellies, our three little stooges. Thump…thump…more giggling. Being just a year old, there's no crawling up the steps yet, but they're fixated on shimmying down them.

This is relaxing. I glance at the clock on the nightstand. Beside it, my empty new journal beckons, a gift from Tess that she bought at the bookstore in German Village. The leather feels nice. The center of the cover has a small gold embossed outline of the Buckeyes' football stadium. The spine crackles as it's opened. The starched pages need to be pressed down hard in order to flatten them enough to write on. I find a pen in the drawer. Now, what to write about?

A story comes pouring out of me. I place the journal just so on Tess's pillow for her to discover later. Time now to get up and go play with my trio of cubs.

After bundling the kids up for a long evening wagon ride through the neighborhood streets decorated for Christmas, we sit as a family in front of the fireplace, drinking cocoa and listening to holiday songs. The little ones love watching the flames, and laugh outright when the wood pops. Nero actually does, too. I snap a picture of his wide, open-mouthed smile to show Tess, who went to change into her PJs.

When she returns in her bright green Christmas flannels, she snuggles up beside me on the floor cushions and shows little interest in Nero's funny expression. I like when she pulls her hair back in a ponytail. She kisses me tenderly, then strokes my face. I clean forgot about my journal I had left on the pillow for her to read.

"Viktor...you have no idea how curious I've been about you being adopted. If it were me, I would have asked to see the papers ages ago. How could you and your father never have discussed it?"

It would seem that she missed the point I was trying to make. "The Certificate of Adoption, in and of itself, isn't what affected me when Iris and I found all the documents; it's the fact that my legal name is really Davis, and my dad never insisted I use it. When I held that adoption record, I was instantly transported back to when I was five. I could see it plain as day ... all of us seated at the dining room table...and Mom telling Iris and me that she wanted to marry the man she had invited over. 'If you both agree to it,' I recalled her saying, 'Mr. Davis would like to be your dad.' I instantly jumped from my chair and went and climbed on his lap, and I threw my little arms around his neck—he smelled so clean, like soap —and I asked if I could call him Daddy already. 'Sure thing, Son,' he said, kissing my forehead. To me it was the luckiest day ever."

Poor Tess. Tears are streaming down her cheeks. She touches my face. I see the love in her eyes.

"So it got me thinking...after all the press I've received these past couple of years, starting with *WAKAN*, and then with playing football, it would make him incredibly proud to see Davis on my jersey." Tess nods and wipes her face with her sleeve. We sit quietly while the kids entertain each other on the carpet.

"Just think," says Tess, after some minutes, "if your name were Davis, and I had decided to change mine when we married—I'd be Tess Davis. Yuck."

"You are indisputably an O'Shea. Always will be. Although...Theresa Davis has a nice ring to it." And with that, she rolls her eyes.

"How did you manage to get a driver license without the name Davis appearing on it?"

"It was no different than when we got our marriage license and I used my tribal ID with my Lakota name. It's legal. Iris's license doesn't have Davis on it either."

Tess's phone goes off on the coffee table. She crawls over to check who's messaged her, and then looks back at me wide-eyed. "Claire's ultrasound."

"And?"

"They're having a girl!"

We're happy for them, but especially for Damien, that his wish came true. We believe that once he's experienced fatherhood, he'll change his tune about having a son, should it happen in the future. Claire told Tess that he never wanted to deal with raising a Black boy in America.

Solomon rolls down his window and engages in small talk with Lou, the affable, semi-retired security guard at the entrance gate to Wright-Patterson Air Force Base. As usual, the topic starts out about the weather, and then switches to Viktor and those Buckeyes, whose games kept getting cancelled due to the virus before it was recently contained. The men at least no longer have to wear face masks since the general public is finally vaccinated.

As Solomon drives onto the lot, he is relieved that Lou was on duty and not a stranger. Being in a rental, another guard might have called Col. Howling Wind to confirm that her guest had arrived, despite him carrying his proper credentials. That would have ruined the surprise. He had flown to Columbus yesterday, on Wednesday, expecting to meet up with Tess's dad for the big OSU-Michigan matchup this weekend, but rumors started spreading about it getting cancelled. As happens these days during the pandemic, rules can change overnight. When the men bought their tickets, a few thousand fans were going to be allowed in a stadium that seats over a hundred thousand. Then they heard that only the players' close family members could attend, which meant their trip was still a go, until today, when they learned that the teams will in fact play, but to empty stands. By Monday, more should be known regarding OSU's last game of the season. Coaches must be scrambling to figure out who else the team might play to keep the Buckeyes in contention for the conference championship title. With time on his hands now, Solomon decided to pay Constance an impromptu visit. He didn't want to overthink what he was about to do, because he feared he might talk himself out of it. Viktor's recent condemnation of his drinking was a real eye-opener. It got him thinking about where his life was headed. He was not in a good place, and he wasn't dealing with it, choosing instead to zone out like alcoholics do. It was bad enough to hear the anger in Viktor's voice, but to also witness the disappointment in his son's eyes...that was excruciating.

"Hey, Sol!"

Solomon greets the man, a colonel, whose office is next to Constance's.

He's standing just outside her door. It seems awkward not to shake hands, but people still worry about touching each other. They resort to a fist bump. The officer tells Solomon that Constance and some of the guys were heading to the food court. He could probably catch up to them.

How disappointing. He had envisioned them alone in her office. If only he hadn't taken so long at the front gate. Now he finds himself hesitating.

The group is already seated by the time he arrives. Should he still say what he had rehearsed? Considering the tension between him and Constance of late, a frosty reception could prove humiliating. He steps over to them and waits for a reaction. They are laughing about something when Constance glances at this figure who approached their table. She is visibly taken aback by the sight of her husband. Solomon smiles, indicating he is not the bearer of any bad news because, for an instant, she looked concerned. He isn't familiar with the three men she's with and apologizes for interrupting their lunch. Bracing himself against the back of an empty chair, he looks at Constance and says:

"I was in the area and thought I'd drop by to see if my wife could use a hug today."

The fact that this is a defining moment in their relationship doesn't escape either of them. Constance scoots her chair back, walks around the table, then places her arms around her husband's neck. "I definitely could," she says, loudly enough for anyone to hear.

Solomon briefly sits with the pilots. He and Constance then excuse themselves to go back to her office. She makes a few necessary calls to clear her afternoon schedule, after which he goes to his car to follow her to her house. They spend a quiet evening together, simply unloading their feelings. Neither gets angry. Considering there's no football game to get to now, he can take Constance up on her offer to stay the weekend.

Following a night of unrelenting lovemaking, brought on by the realization that they had not grown apart, despite years-worth of long absences from each other, the two enjoy a romantic late-morning coffee that includes more kissing and fondling than conversation. Solomon suggests they play tourist for the day. First stop, a Classic Cars showroom with vintage muscle cars that he's been wanting to see. Afterward, they head to a place that Constance has put off going to, Dayton's Aullwood Audubon Center, a wildlife sanctuary outside the city. The inch of snow on the ground is no deterrent to them hiking a few of the trails. Last stop, a cozy hole-in-the-wall diner she recommends that specializes in comfort food. Solomon opts for their famous meatloaf. Constance sticks to her usual fare, a heavenly tasting chicken pot pie.

Weary from the day, Solomon and Constance climb into bed and snuggle close to each other, not quite ready for sleep. There's a tenderness between them that is reflected in the way they're touching. The emotion feels different from last evening, when there existed such a desperate desire to reconnect. Tonight it's evident they've made peace.

Solomon returned to Texas on Monday, beside himself with happiness. The weekend with Constance had invigorated his soul. Here he had convinced himself that he no longer played an integral role in his wife's emotional well-being, and he wasn't sure what to do about it, or if he even cared to figure things out anymore. Ever since that episode with her disappearance in Kashmir, when he later learned that she'd been having quite the adventure in the Himalayas with a British pilot named Smitty, he believed he was losing her. Viktor lay in the hospital at the time. One of his workers who'd gotten badly burned in an accident at the auto shop was also in the hospital. He felt utterly alone as he faced these crises, and without Constance by his side, he grew more despondent with each passing day. When Constance was diagnosed with PTSD, it was the last straw when Sunkwah called upon the Rawakota to treat her, not that he could have given her the necessary help she needed, but being excluded from the process made him feel all the more estranged from her.

Solomon checks the calendar. How did it get to be Friday already? He managed to complete two weeks' worth of work in less than five days. He ponders the achievement, realizing the sudden burst of energy was due to a new sense of hope he felt, spurred on by Constance, who had called him every night. They talked like they used to, but less about the families and more about their own plans for the future. The sale of his two auto repair shops to the mechanic who had been his right-hand man from day one is almost final. Their home that he was preparing to list for sale will be rented out instead. The housing market is terrible at the moment, and not just in Wichita Falls, Texas, but across the country.

The biggest change in Constance's world is that she'll be remaining stateside from here on out. The time has come for her to weigh the pros and cons of retiring, which she swore would include Solomon's input.

Pleased to have things under control, Solomon considers his parents' invitation earlier in the week to visit them for once and watch the Buckeyes play on TV Saturday. Why not go? There's a flight tonight to Kansas City with a brief layover in Tulsa. He can sleep on the plane.

"Fingers crossed," says Solomon to his dad the next day, expecting the game wouldn't get cancelled a half hour before kick-off. It doesn't matter at this point who the Buckeyes are facing; it's been such a topsy-turvy season. His mother delivers yet another plate of food, hot wings this time, having already placed a huge batch of barbecued ribs directly in front of Solomon, as though they were his alone. An uncle and a few of Solomon's cousins who swung by to watch the game teasingly ask Junie Davis where *their* plates are.

"Coming right up, gentlemen!" she sings, heading back to the kitchen.

As the teams exit the stadium and run onto the field, minus people in the stands, but with crowd noise added by the broadcast booth, the Davis clan stands, ready to cheer on one of their family. The camera zeros in on Viktor when his name gets announced: "Buckeyes' Quarterback Number Seven, Viktor Talking White Owl Davis." As Viktor runs past the camera, DAVIS, in big letters, is the only name on his jersey. Solomon, seemingly dazed, drops back down on the couch while the rest of the family jump in the air excited, high-fiving and clapping. Cyrus sits and places his arm around his son, offering up a big hug. The others acknowledge how cool that was of Viktor to do.

"What happened?" asks Junie, looking at the screen after plunking down a heaping tray of potato skins. She turns to her husband and son, witnessing the emotion between them. Cyrus explains. Next she gives the TV her full attention, waiting to see the jersey for herself. When the announcer informs viewers that Viktor wanted to honor his dad and his family in Kansas City, she folds her hands together over her heart and looks at Solomon. "You raised a wonderful boy."

At once, everybody's phone starts ringing as relatives check in to praise Viktor's actions. Solomon makes a call of his own, to his wife. No, says Constance, she had no knowledge that Viktor planned on doing this. The loving gesture makes her tremendously proud of their son. Iris also called her father, realizing the impact it would have. And when Viktor does the unthinkable in the third quarter, switching to another number and playing a defensive position, Solomon waits to see if Davis is on that jersey. It is. Meantime, millions of confused Buckeye fans have reportedly been sounding off on social media, surprised by the sudden turn of events while also wondering who the heck this Caleb guy is standing in for Viktor during the final half.

CHAPTER 62

It's two in the afternoon, the twentieth of March. Seven pound, six ounce, Danica Celeste Slaughter, arrived punctually on Claire's due date this first day of spring at 8:02 this morning. Uncle William and Tess and I just returned home from the hospital. Damien had met us in the waiting room shortly afterward to say that the birth went fast and was relatively easy. The doctor's words, not his, he laughed. He was beside himself with joy and relief. I completely understood. It's awful to see the woman you love in pain. Claire was talkative and in good spirits when we saw her, the opposite of Tess during her scary delivery ordeal. Before we left, Uncle took Damien's hands in his and congratulated him again, saying that he knew in his heart he will be a good father. I wondered if Damien ever received such a powerful personal vote of confidence in his life. Despite having a defiant personality, he isn't diabolical in the way Ishmael was. Why Uncle supported Damien's relationship with Claire from the beginning will always baffle me.

We're starving and sit down to a late lunch of subs we bought along the way. The nannies decline our invitation to join us. They waited until we were driving home to put the triplets down for their naps, which was considerate. After a bit, Uncle says this is as good a time as any to announce he is returning to the reservation for good. I'm bowled over by the news.

"Why!"

"Come now, Viktor. I have a family. And I miss being with them, more so now because the little ones are older and can talk. I want to tell them stories about their grandmother. I've served my purpose."

"A heads-up would have been appreciated. You've grown on me, you know?"

He smiles and readily admits how important I am to him. "I am deeply grateful to your parents for letting me be your guardian. I truly had your interests at heart, which I hope you can see, especially now that you're older." He's right about that. "I'm just a phone call away," he assures me. "I still intend to visit occasionally."

No Hayden...no Uncle William. *Un-hee!* I didn't realize I had muttered my reaction out loud.

"You'll do fine, Viktor." I look at Uncle, wondering at what point this happened, him having this fervid belief in me. It's quiet at the table while we eat. Tess contributes nothing to the conversation. After his news sinks in, I have to ask:

"Please tell me, Uncle, why you're so convinced I'll be okay on my own."

Without missing a beat, he answers, "You've got clout, and what's more, you know it! No coach would risk the health of his star quarterback by playing him on a defensive line. When you mentioned that you were thinking about a different position, I didn't believe anyone would take your request seriously. I certainly didn't."

I think back to that afternoon when I first proposed the idea, ignorant of what a big deal it really was. Uncle wipes his mouth, and then leans in closer to me. "The athletic directors would love nothing more than to suspend you over what they perceive is your arrogance. The things I've overheard them say about you...when no one realized I was within earshot." He shakes his head in a woeful manner. I can well imagine. Only now do I face Tess. She's been listening with interest, but keeping her thoughts to herself, much like she had done when I finally built up the courage and informed her that I *might* be playing defense sometimes. She simply took the news in stride and went about her day. I was afraid she'd wait until bedtime to express her disappointment, refusing sex, but I was pleasantly surprised. I chalked it up to her being totally absorbed in her own life as a she tries to balance her many responsibilities. There's just no energy left in her to contemplate my particular dilemmas.

Uncle's demeanor changes. "You sure showed them what you're capable of with the jump you pulled off in the last game. The way you popped up in the middle of all those bodies and intercepted their Quarterback's pass." He sits back in his chair and laughs. "One for the books as they say. The look on their team's faces!"

Ah, yes—the jump—accurately described by a local sports reporter as a magnificent double cabriole, skillfully executed with shoulder pads, no less. Like fans in general, he likely learned the dance lingo from Hayden, who took to schooling the public in the methods he incorporated for my training. I bet people miss seeing him on TV. Hayden was comfortable around the press and enjoyed doing interviews.

There's been a slow return to normalcy over the summer. City streets are no longer empty. More businesses are beginning to reopen. Thank goodness our fall games will include fans.

This upcoming football season might feel like we're starting back at square one. Because of the past year's quarantining and cancelled games, it's been hard maintaining a fixed routine. Several sophomores who'd been redshirted are starting for the first time. Practice begins next week. It'll be interesting. We lucked out recruiting a fast freshman receiver from Alabama who runs rings around everyone. Let's hope he can catch.

It isn't until the car is fully in the garage that I feel free to howl from the pain. Tess has been waiting to help me inside. I had called to tell her that I'd gotten injured during practice. Nothing broken, I quickly assured her, simply a wrenched lower back muscle. She almost topples over from trying to support my weight as we head to the door. I never dreamed I'd hear myself say this, but I tell her that I wish Demon Slaughter were still here guarding me. What I keep to myself is, if getting sacked this often is any indication of things to come, our Amish rookie is welcome to fill in for me!

The short step up from the garage floor to the laundry room is unbearable. A shooting pain runs the length of me. "I'm sorry, Tess. Three babies, and now an invalid to take care of. Thank goodness Ruby and Naomi will be back in a couple days."

She wipes the tear trickling down my cheek, then goes to fetch Uncle William's medical bag that he left with us. She calls him to confirm the correct muscle relaxant and dosage. He swears the shot I was given before leaving the locker room should start kicking in soon, and that I have to wait to take a pill. The team doctor also gave me a prescription, but I trust Uncle's pain meds more for not making me groggy. Acupuncture is ruled out for a few days. Strict bed rest is ordered. I retreat to the main floor guest bedroom, but not before learning that our nannies won't be returning from the rez for another week. Tess had called them earlier this morning, before my call, and suggested they spend more time with their families.

The shot is working; otherwise, it would be impossible to inch my way up from the toilet seat to a semi-standing position. My insides are upset. I step over my sweatpants that lay bunched around my ankles and shuffle on back to the room. Tess brushes my hair and braids it. Next she helps ease me onto the bed. I lay motionless, grateful to be home. I had put up a good front on the field, insisting I was okay after getting knocked silly. Tess places the TV remote and phone by my hand.

"Anything else?" she asks, with a sympathetic smile.

I sheepishly nod back and thank her.

She places her hands on my naked chest, then softly kisses it. "If yelling hurts, blast the TV if you need something. Or text." We lock eyes for a moment before she walks out the room. There's the silent acknowledgement that something like this was bound to happen eventually.

I doze an hour when Theo surprises me with a call. We may not shoot hoops together anymore, but we sometimes see each other in the weight room. Theo's been a standout sharpshooter on the basketball court, but then he slipped and fell hard this past spring and seriously injured his hip. "You gonna be okay?" he asks. "I heard what happened and was trying to find you after practice."

"I'm good...sprained the ole back, just need a few days of rest. Tell me, are the 76ers still eyeing you?"

He reports they are, but that OSU wondered if he ever considered a future in coaching, which I know he hasn't. "We definitely need more coaches of color," he says, to which I agree. "I'm cool with the idea."

It sounds to me like he's made up his mind but could use some words of support.

"I'm damn good, but honestly, Viktor, I'll never play at the level of Jordan or Harden, not with this hip...or my bad elbow."

I go on to complain about our football team's weak offense, which will result in me getting sacked throughout this season, and by schools as small as Akron.

"Don't be such a whiner," he says. "The guys might be inexperienced, but you need to look at yourself, bro! What can *you* do different?"

No pity points from him. Fact is, he's absolutely right! "Wow...listen to me sounding so put out. You're already coaching, Theo. Thanks." It feels great laughing with him. He doesn't stop there. Next he advises me to start running the ball more.

"That's the key—forwards, though, not backwards," he laughs, because he knows as well as the fans that's what I do best to avoid getting trapped in the pocket. "Use it to your advantage. Find your opening fast, and bolt ...lickety-split! With your size, you can push past anyone!"

He describes any number of formations that'll get me out of a pickle and suggests I study plays from Michael Vick's career. I've heard the name, way back in grade school I think. Apparently Theo has an older brother-in-law who was a huge Vick fan...says Vick was a leader in quarterback rushing yards. I thank him again for the indispensable advice and pep talk.

As soon as we hang up, I get excited about the challenge he presented me with. Only now do I realize my confidence tanked because Uncle William is no longer around to bounce ideas off of, or Hayden, or Jasper and Rhett. Of course Damien is included in the list, jerk that he was. I could always trust his ability to protect the quarterback position—he had great instincts.

I turn on the TV, happy Theo's still in my life. We've both come a long way in a relatively short period of time. Tess appears in the doorway, kids strapped to her legs. They're begging for something in the unintelligible speech of toddlers, which their mother has learned to decipher, but not me. They want to watch Sesame Street with Daddy.

"How'd you know that's what I was getting ready to watch?" Their sweet little faces light up.

Tess gently deposits Honor and Holt on the bed and reminds them there's to be no jumping. They understand that Daddy got a big boo-boo, but they don't understand why there's no fun band aide for me to show them. Raif is relegated to the floor because he constantly bops around like he's spring-loaded. Today's letter is f, for frog, which he demonstrates by leaping from one end of the room to the other, over and over, and with an irritating, "ribbit, ribbit, ribbit." Honor sits on her knees and tucks herself under my right arm. She's holding a colorful wooden alphabet board. She points to each letter, f – r – o – g, then repeats them along with Elmo and his friends. I'm beyond impressed. She isn't yet two. Is that normal? Holt stares at the screen. Instead of saying the letters, he counts them on his fingers, proudly holding up four of them while using his other hand to hold down the thumb since it isn't included. *Un-hee!* How differently humans perceive things. Honor pushes the o and g to the side, and then slides the letters i and e in place to spell a new word. "I like fire," she says, tilting her head all the way back to look up at me. I gaze into her golden eyes with curiosity, fascinated by the learning process.

It never gets old watching my kids. Their eyes are huge, and they've got thick headfuls of black-reddish hair. Only Honor's has a touch more red in certain light. The children's skin color is hard to describe…sort of a light toasted almond.

Not a second after the show ends, Tess calls for the triplets. It's time for their afternoon nap. Honor and Holt hug me and slide off the bed. Raif kisses my hand again and again, giggling, making a game of it, until his mother threatens from afar that once the door is closed, he'll have to sleep by himself. My turn to get going. I manage to roll to a sitting position while simultaneously lowering my legs to the floor. Praise be for drugs. I slowly stand and take a step, and another, confident the pain won't return for a few hours. It'll give me the opportunity for a heart-to-heart talk with Tess about where we stand with regard to our academic programs.

Since the beginning of fall, we, like a lot of people now who've been vaccinated, have been operating at a breakneck speed in an attempt to make up for time lost due to lockdowns. I had been dragging out my doctorate as it was, simply to stay enrolled at OSU in order to play ball. Both Tess and I are researching delivery systems for drugs in the body, the difference being, my thesis concerns adding nanomagnets to proteins, particles one-billionth of a meter in size, while Tess's master's involves using gold in nanoparticles. We have seriously entertained the idea of someday working together. Several research partners at the hospital are married, and it's pretty much the norm at Winter Crow's lab up in Rapid City. And as much as I wish I didn't have to bring it up, our relationship is bound to suffer if we don't clear the air about my decision to play defense, which didn't take into account Tess's feelings. I honestly can't believe what a self-centered move that was on my part. What has been worrying me lately is that I think about football most of the day anymore. I even dream about it, which makes sense because it's football season, but it was never the case before.

I reach the kitchen where I'm pleased to find leftover coffee in the pot. Tess enters and laughs at the sight of me standing in my undershorts. I point to the sweatpants and tee shirt on the table that I had grabbed for her to help me with. After I'm dressed, she takes me up on my suggestion to talk, and we head to the living room.

The first thing I do is apologize for leaving her in the dark about my wanting to play a different position this year. I brace myself, expecting to hear that it hurt her, which in and of itself is distressing to me. But the response I get is altogether different. Before I even approached Coach Doyle with my intentions, Tess informs me that she had already discussed the subject at length with my mother, who, when she was here helping us with the babies after Chevonne left, presented Tess with just such a hypothetical situation. It was more along the lines, though, of how she would handle it if I decided I wanted to play professionally. I recall telling Mom ages ago that I fantasized about quarterbacking for the Browns. People indulge in fantasies. It wasn't a goal of mine. It occurs to me that I should be glad about Tess's reaction. It required that she confront her biases against the sport. In the final analysis, she wanted what makes me the happiest—a selfless decision on her part—while I, on the other hand, was thinking only of myself.

It's been one wild and crazy ride! Two weeks after winning the national title and I'm still floating on cloud nine, which Tess for once is excited about, too. Admittedly, it happened at the same time she received positive feedback on her research paper. We've been partying every day with family and friends, plus our neighbors on the street, who we're just now getting to know.

Fans finally got to watch their teams in person again. The noise level inside the stadiums this season was insane.

It's January and damn cold, no big snow yet in Columbus, but we hear it's on the way next week. I've reconnected with my brothers and sisters on the rez, after telling them that I wouldn't be able to continue our online chats until football season was over. The support I've received from various Native tribes across the country has been unbelievable. It's one thing to run out on a field as a Buckeye, quite another to know I'm impacting an invisible population that is significantly more real to me than the crowds in the stands on game day. My tribal brothers and sisters are wondering if I'll be attending the Council of First Nations' conference in nearby Hocking Hills, Ohio, next month. Some of them are going. I didn't think the organization's leaders included us regular citizens in their meetings, let alone teens, but they've apparently had a change of heart. Sounds like it could be a game changer. Mom and Uncle William belong to the Council…I'll check if they're going.

In the meantime, I intend to lay low, find my bearings, play with the triplets, and hopefully have lots of sex. Based on Tess's current sunny disposition, I'd say I'm in luck.

CHAPTER 63

"Good to go?" asks Mom, grabbing her receipt off the gas pump. I had gone inside the store to hit the john and buy us a few snacks, which I toss on the car seat.

"Wait...can I drive?"

I climb behind the wheel of her and Dad's new Jeep Wrangler. There's no patience for instructions, and I hit the gas. Next thing, we're winding through the scenic woods of Hocking Hills. I've never been southeast of Columbus. The area reminds me of the Black Hills in South Dakota. Mom points to a short cut. The side road is hidden beneath deep snow. The jeep easily plows through it. White powder shoots everywhere. The wipers aren't fast enough to maintain a clear view of what's ahead. Flashback to me at fifteen careening into a tree stump during the drive up to Rapid City with Dad. I doubt Mom will be as forgiving if I hit something. Forty minutes later, we arrive at our destination. I park alongside dozens of SUVs and trucks. What a spectacular setting for the conference. The lodge is impressive. It's a massive cedar A-frame with gabled dormers and a huge wrap-around porch.

A middle-aged man with two wispy short braids stands waiting at the door and offers a warm welcome. I recognize him from the Indian newsletter. He's our latest tribal president, the first leader in ages, according to our family, who is descended from spiritual leaders, and who is as highly regarded as they were. The previous president was deemed unfit to serve because he'd had sexual relations with minors. Several other Council leaders stand in a row and shake our hands as Mom introduces them to me. Only two are designated Chiefs, one being a woman, still a rarity among Native tribes. As I greet the last man in line, a familiar voice welcomes me from behind. It's Uncle William, who, after a brief but heartfelt hug, hurries us along to the big room. "There'll be time to catch up later," he says.

The place smells of food cooking. There's a big round table and a screen mounted on the opposite wall for the video conference. I'd heard that Canadian tribal leaders up in Manitoba were going to take part in the event. They presently sit facing us behind their own long desk. Rows of folding chairs circle the table here. Everyone is already seated. Mom and I almost came too late. Uncle saved us a couple of spots half way back. The room grows quiet as the chairman stands to welcome us. Following introductions, a buffet-style lunch is served by an Indigenous crew who have been busy in the kitchen. We fill our plates and return to our seats. I like how friendly and relaxed things are. There must be close to two hundred people, with at least a third surprisingly around my age. While we eat, members of Canada's First Nations' group bring us up to speed on what's been happening on their reservations. One tribal community is in the process of building a bigger police force while another is fighting to keep a uranium producer from drilling on their lands.

As kids we learned little about the formation of the alliance that was originally called the Circle of Elders, other than it predates the Council of First Nations. To his credit, our speaker who is from Oklahoma addresses the fact that much of what he and other Council leaders continue to hear about the organization is negative, the main criticism being that it's too involved with the U.S. government, and that certain tribal leaders aren't adequately representing all their people's concerns. For too long the young and old have felt left out of the decision-making process, as have the women. There's a rumble of agreement in the crowd, to which he smiles and says, "That's about to change." He scans the faces then adds how pleased he is with the turnout for the three day conference.

The agenda is laid out. It's a wide-ranging one dealing with a host of subjects that affect some reservations more than others. A slide with a list of topics is projected. The room erupts in applause as the final item is read, which has to do with returning public lands in the Black Hills to the Cheyenne and Oceti Sakowin, commonly known to outsiders as the Sioux Nation, which includes us Lakota.

Next we transition into small groups of ten, in order to brainstorm ways of handling the problems listed. Anything goes, we're told, no matter how far-fetched the idea or off-the-wall. How I love brainstorming sessions. In the afternoon we switch groups, and tomorrow we'll do the same. By the third and final day, votes will determine which plans are sound, and then we'll decide how best to actualize them.

When I asked Mom and Uncle William about the conference, after it was brought up by the Native online community, they couldn't predict whether I'd find the Council's business proceedings interesting. Allowing non-members to participate was going to be a first. They weren't sure themselves what to expect.

Already I'm impressed over how articulate this sixteen year-old girl is in our group. She's from my own reservation. Cora is her name, and she initiated a campaign last spring to rid tribal lands of the buckthorn weed. The idea came to her after she grew tired of listening to her elders complaining about the plant one too many times. The old people do go on about it, including Sunkwah and Winnie. Granted, buckthorn *is* everywhere, thanks to the colonists who brought it over from Britain in the 1800s for hedging their gardens—as if they couldn't find anything here to serve that purpose. It's true what the elders say about it being responsible for destroying our native plants. Birds spread their seeds, causing the buckthorn plants to grow out of control. They also attract undesirable pests.

"Do you see," she says, gesturing to us, "how symbolic killing off these non-native plants would be? The berries and bark and roots of the buckthorn are toxic to everything—people, animals, the environment—just like the settlers who took over our lands. Time to completely erase them from our lives."

She speaks with such conviction! It's easy to see why students at Cora's school have rallied around her idea. The Sierra Club eventually got wind of their operation. Apparently, buckthorn jungles have long been a concern of theirs. Cora says it could take up to five years to destroy the invasive species, and that's being optimistic. I am staring at one resourceful and patient individual. Listening to her, I am convinced that our people should seriously consider changing the name of our reservation. Cora hopes someone can contribute a tractor or ATV to the cause, because that's what it will take to uproot those stubborn buckthorn stems, grown so thick that chains are needed to pull them out of the ground. Such a simple request. The least I can do is buy her that. It'll be a donation from our family. Her dark eyes tears up when I tell her. The others in the group voice their support of the project, even though buckthorn doesn't exist on their lands, and they vow to spread the word in hopes of getting Cora more donations.

The two hours fly by. There's a short break, and then we move on to our next group. Mom spots me from across the room and smiles. Uncle's nearby, but his back is to me. This time I'm with an Apache, several Crow, and a few Cheyenne, no other Lakota besides me, and no woman among us. I'm congratulated for the Buckeyes' winning season, but that's where the football talk ends. One of the men is anxious to talk about starting a Farmer's Market on his rez. The problem is the land is subject to extreme weather conditions. Besides figuring out alternative growing methods, his people need to devise a way to transport the food to a central facility. Not enough roads converge anywhere, and they're all dirt. The upside to what seems like a pipe dream is that all families are willing to contribute to its success.

Because his community is one hundred percent behind it, we're determined to find a feasible solution. And for the remaining time, we take to our phones and research the latest in small wind turbines that could generate enough electricity to power a practical greenhouse system, one which individual families might easily manage. Maybe hydroponic. It can't require a huge outlay of money. We discover a number of federal grants that tribal members can apply for, only to be told by the man that his community wants nothing to do with the government. The Apache in our group suggests the grants might be worth considering, just to get their operations up and running. That's the approach some business owners have taken on his rez.

After the second session ends, everybody is free to mingle and roam around the grounds until ten o'clock. Appetizers await us in the kitchen along with some interesting blends of teas. I graciously decline an invitation to go smoke with a few Council members in an Elder's cabin. Maybe tomorrow, I tell the man. I did bring my pipe. One always does for social gatherings.

Mom surprises me from behind and hugs my arm. "Well," she asks, "think it's worthwhile so far?" She caught me with my mouth full. I can only nod yes. "Good," she says, patting my cheek. "See you back at the cabin later." Next she winds through the crowd and disappears down a hallway. Immediately someone my size takes up Mom's spot beside me, which is hard to ignore because he's close enough to be encroaching on my personal space. I don't look at him as I step away to put some needed distance between us, to which he starts laughing...a laugh I readily recognize.

"Billy Spotted Horse!" When he embraces me in those burly arms, I feel like a kid again. It was the same in Texas when he surprised me at Dad's shop. It doesn't matter that my body almost matches his. He's still a good inch taller, and his chest is broader. He's regained some of the weight he had lost since I last saw him. "What on earth are you doing here? Is your prison teacher with you?" It stuck with me what Tess had said about her being his girlfriend.

"No, Viktor...my *prison teacher*, Alicia Little Sky, didn't come because she's at home with our two-month-old son. Just so you know, she is now my wife."

We hadn't parted on good terms when I left Texas. I recall that he couldn't make sense of the fact that I was opting to stay among white people. I'm not going to bring it up, and hopefully he won't. Being proud papas, we show each other pictures of our babies. Billie says he's watched all my games, which makes me happy. I'm curious about what he's been up to job wise.

"I've been learning the construction trade. Later this spring I'll be part of the crew that's building the new college on our rez. It was originally intended to be a branch of the mining and engineering school up in Rapid City, but then a donor came along who offered to cover all the building expenses."

I'm assuming it was so the school could be run independently of any external influences. What Indian has that much money? Billie says the backers are a brother-sister team named Falcone, and although they aren't Lakota, they belong to a tribal nation in the southwest. Where have I heard that name before?

"The plans were kept under wraps until everything got finalized," he says, "which happened only a month ago. We break ground after Memorial Day."

This is a subject I will return to with Mom or Grandmother. For now, all I want is to remember our fun filled days on the rez when we used to meet up with everyone to go exploring. I want to speak our dead brothers' names...breathe life back into them, if only for a night. Daniel, Ron, and Matt. Neil and Mark and Sam.

Billie agrees, but not in the open like this. My cabin is directly behind the main lodge, closer than where Billie's is. Off we go, trying not to slip on the frozen asphalt. The parking lot had been shoveled earlier and the snow dumped along its perimeter, which is fine except that it's blocking the path to the cabin. That wasn't smart. Billie and I hike a leg over the top of the snowbank, which is chest high, and then slide down the other side, laughing as we go. The cabin is maybe fifty feet away. As we near the doorstep we feel like fools. Off to the side, only now within view, is a cleared parking spot and narrow road that no doubt runs back around through the woods to the lodge. It wouldn't have made any difference. Billy doesn't have a car. He came with another guy in his rental, and I wouldn't have left Mom in the lurch by taking our Jeep from the main lot.

Billie holds onto my arm as I'm about to open the door. He's staring up at the clear night sky. The bright stars are definitely a sight to behold. He begins reciting a Lakota prayer of gratitude. I could join in, but I like listening to him.

The morning session is winding down on this second day of the conference. I'm trying hard not to yawn. Billie and I stayed up for hours, well past when Mom arrived and went to bed. She needed to nudge us awake. We had fallen asleep on the rug in front of the stone fireplace. The place came with a bin of pre-split logs that we took advantage of.

Education was at the forefront of today's discussion, which I didn't contribute to much, mainly because other members had already given the topic considerable thought and had outlined lots of great ideas. It's a truly complex issue, which often pits tribal citizens against each other. One camp wants to improve Federal and Tribal partnerships, thereby procuring more grants for Indian students, while another faction denounces any interference whatsoever from the government, insisting Native people maintain full control of their schools.

As everyone disperses during the break for a bite to eat, I slump down in my seat and close my eyes for a moment, hoping I don't nod off to sleep.

"Hey, you!"

It's Mom. She's staring me in the face. I look around confused then sit up straight. "Man, I was out." She says it was only for ten minutes or so, but it felt like hours. Next she hands me her coffee and scoots her chair closer.

"Drink up," she orders. "Some university students are here that are big fans of yours, and they wondered if I'd wake you, in order to ask if you'd join their circle." Now I feel embarrassed that anyone was watching me. Mom directs my attention to them. I count six. Each wears his long hair in two braids. They're standing along the wall still eating, which gives me time to go splash cold water on my face.

Upon returning, I find the guys seated in the middle of the room. One of them spots me and points to an empty chair. I go over and we shake hands. They act kind of shy, until one mentions a winning pass I made in the Wisconsin game, after which each enthusiastically relates his own favorite moments from the season. It's fun, and we could probably go on talking football for hours, but that's not why we're here. As we embark on our mission of finding ways to build stronger Native communities, I'm thankful I got my second wind and am feeling alert.

I discover I'm in the company of brilliant minds. For some reason I assumed these guys were undergrads. They are in fact doctoral students in engineering and science, except for the one with a PhD in physics. All are Lakota who attended the same high school on the Rosebud Reservation, at different times, though. They credit a soft-spoken, caring teacher for their success, a Mr. Earl Spotted Tail. He'd been a Navy Submarine Officer. I'm told that after Spotted Tail retired, he returned to his reservation in South Dakota where he learned his grandson's school had no math teacher, so he stepped up and filled the vacant position. That was over fifteen years ago, and these former students of his say the man is still there sharing his love for math with a new generation of kids.

I mention my own teachers who influenced me, following which I ask if anyone has any thoughts about what we might discuss today. There's a lull in the conversation that feels a bit awkward. The one named Dennis speaks up. Thick, long-healed scars run along his cheek and neck, causing me to wonder if they are gang related. A tattoo pokes out from the bottom edge of his sleeve.

"All of us are working toward one goal," he says, "and that is to protect the Black Hills from further exploitation and intruders. The region is after all central to our identity."

His lighthearted mood has turned serious. I continue to listen with interest while he describes technologies they're each researching that are designed to secretly protect and monitor vast areas of land. Drones aren't involved, he points out, because they're such easy targets. Without delving too deeply into the science, Dennis states that, by having redirected magnetic fields, they have successfully shielded a section of tribal lands in Wyoming. He then leans forward and looks me straight in the eyes. "The military can't detect it...or any cyber-security industry out there. It's one hundred per cent possible to guard the entire region after our Great Nation wins it back."

I'm floored by the bold assertion. "Should you be saying this in the open?" I glance around. People are so immersed in their own groups, they're not paying any attention to us. Still.

Dennis continues. "We have been keeping the Lakota leadership as well as the Council informed about our work. It fell to them to investigate the backgrounds of the crews that began installing the system around two years ago."

I'm wondering what the guy who's wearing the Hocking Hills BEAR sweatshirt has to say, the one with the PhD. He sits with his legs crossed at the ankles and his hands folded on his lap. His braids were rushed, they're messy. I simply stare at him until he talks.

"I solve ways to neutralize radioactive particles in the atmosphere after a nuclear explosion."

I respond with the first thought that comes to mind. "I realize there are plenty of Indians who would love to blow up Mount Rushmore, but isn't that extreme?"

His eyes narrow, and I think he smiled. "If there's ever a face-off between tribal nations and the U.S., it won't involve nuclear war. My goal is to keep our South Dakota air clean and livable. Radioactive fallout targets all life on the planet. It isn't the realm of fantasy to imagine that a ruthless dictator somewhere in the world will resort to using weapons of mass destruction in our lifetime, which, depending on our distance from the strike zone and the wind currents, could affect our homelands."

"*Un-hee!* Glad someone's on top of it!" I take note of his left eyebrow that arches higher whenever he emphasizes an important point.

"You know," he says, using the same analytical tone, "I hadn't considered it, but based on the nature of my research, we *could* blow up that damn mountain one day. Dynamite can easily do the trick, but nuking it would really make a statement."

So true. I know a lot of people who would agree.

I remain skeptical about the things I've heard. "Say this happens, that you eventually secure the entire perimeter around the Black Hills, what then? Do the Indians divide up Rapid City and take back parts of it? And what becomes of the state parks and their gazillions of tourists, not to mention something as big as the underground research lab in Lead? The majority of the workers are non-Native. Are they simply going to be given the boot one day—adios muchachos, don't look back? You gotta admit, the scale of this plan...the logistics that are involved..." I shake my head. "Tell me what I'm missing."

"Whites can keep their racist Rapid City," says Dennis. "Winter Crow's Laboratory is our main concern. It's situated outside the city limits on the west side and could therefore continue to operate in a protected zone. In anticipation of this historic event, the scientists are slowly beginning to move their research departments to Buckthorn. One building is currently under construction near the new hospital."

There is too much conjecturing about the future. Questions pop in my head that I won't ask, because I realize the explanations will only give rise to more questions. My sense of frustration must be obvious to Dennis, who further explains that this epic takeover by the Indians isn't slated to happen for another decade. I'm beyond calculating whether that's a reasonable timeline. I need air and glance at the clock on the wall, relieved the session is ending soon. I'm anxious to call Tess and hear her voice...see what new funny pictures she has sent of the kids.

In the remaining minutes, I find out that the guys are big fans of the radio call-in show that I frequently take part in. I'm commended for being such a positive role model for rez kids, which I appreciate hearing. Dennis then suggests that I consider expanding my reach of influence.

"In what way?" I ask, impatient for this day to be over.

"None of us on tribal lands can afford to be tentative, Viktor. That's why previous attempts to win back our stolen lands have failed. It's a frustrating and challenging process, one that makes it difficult to stay the course. We presently stand at a crossroads. Our generation is passionate about saving our ancestral cultures, which includes getting our land back. Would you be willing to rally support to aid the cause, like your grandfather Benjamin One Horn did so well in his time? If we lose the momentum we've got going now, Oceti Sakowin, the Great Sioux Nation, will come to represent nothing more than lost dreams."

Dennis assumes my Pahpie's activism was wholeheartedly supported by the family. Benjamin One Horn's involvement ended up consuming him. We were of course terribly proud of Grandfather, but he became so wrapped up in problems affecting the Indigenous community at large that it began taking a toll on his health and his relationship with Grandmother. Looking back on the situation as an adult, maybe Mom's infuriating teenage behavior had something to do with it. When his daughter turned out to be more than he could handle, Pahpie found an outlet for his feelings of helplessness. Fighting for Indian rights empowered him.

People are getting up from their seats and scattering. I stand, too, and shake out my legs, aware of how intently the guys are looking at me as they step closer to say goodbye.

"How about I get back to you after I sleep on it," I tell them. I hold out my hand to shake Dennis's first.

"Please do," he insists, firmly gripping my knuckles. They likely think I'm brushing them off, which isn't the case. I'm willing to exchange phone numbers, which I reckon conveys that I'll follow through with my promise. Their spirits immediately perk up.

Next I find Billie and haul him aside a moment to see if he had ever heard anything about the installation of an invisible fence around the base of the Black Hills.

"Are you serious," he laughs. "You mean like lasers? Around the entire mountain range?" Holding a finger in the air, he gestures to someone in the crowd that he'll be a minute more. "Hey, do you want to hang out with a couple of people I met today?"

I don't. I want to find Mom—she might know—but she's nowhere in sight, so I catch a ride on a shuttle heading to the cabins.

The sun may be setting a bit later now that it's February, but it's really dark for six o'clock. There are no stars or moon. Sometimes clouds brighten the night sky, but not in this rural setting. A lamp was left on in the main room, so I don't have to flip on the harsh fluorescent ceiling light above the kitchen sink. I can see enough to microwave a bag of popcorn. Our cabin, an A-frame, is small…can't be more than 700 square feet. There's no loft. The two bedrooms and bathroom are off the living room. I think it's cozy.

The bin next to the fireplace has been restocked with logs. I wish Tess were here. Oh, to enjoy a weekend alone together in the woods. Once the fire catches, I sink into the couch, my bowl of popcorn in hand, relieved I'm not still back at the lodge. Up go my feet on the ottoman. Should have grabbed the TV remote before getting comfortable. The dancing flames will entertain me, just like they do the kids. How I miss them. At this hour, they're curled up in bed.

In no time I get lost in my thoughts. It takes a while before I realize that my bowl is empty and the dying fire needs revived. As I'm hanging the poker back on its hook, I notice something move in the bedroom out of the corner of my eye. The door is wide open and the room dark, but the fire scatters enough light to make out a figure on the bed. It registers that the body must be Mom's. I tiptoe over and stand just inside the doorway. It is her. She's lying on her side on the far side of the bed. I think her eyes are open...which is creepy. She has a full view of the corner of the couch where I'd been sitting, and also of the fireplace.

"You're awake, right?" I ask, to which she replies *mm-hm*.

"I've been here for a couple of hours, and you didn't think to come out and acknowledge me?" No response. I sit down on the edge of the bed. The fire's grown big again from the logs I added, making it easier to see her. She looks thoughtful. "Are you feeling okay?"

"I'm fine, Viktor," she whispers. "Just needed a break."

I stretch out beside her onto my back. "You could at least have had popcorn with me."

"Sorry," she says, placing her hand on my shoulder and giving it a gentle squeeze. "No Billie this evening?"

"No, we covered a lot of ground last night. Besides, he met some people he wanted to hang with. God, this quilt is the best thing ever. My tailbone feels magically healed. It's been aching all day."

"Definitely high quality goose down. To think you boys chose the floor over the bed to sleep on last night. No wonder you're in pain."

"Us *boys*. Billie is a dad now, too."

"I heard."

"So...do you ever plan on getting up?"

"In a bit. How often do I get my son all to myself?"

My eyes close as she strokes my hair. That was nice to hear.

"Since your tailbone is better, what do you say we bundle ourselves up and go for a short stroll. Maybe it's begun to snow. A front was expected to move in this evening."

"That's an excellent idea!" And although I had things I wanted to ask about the college going up on the rez, it will have to wait. I'm talked out from today, as I'm certain she is, too.

It's 4:00 p.m. The conference is officially over. Mom and I skedaddle to the outside parking lot and head for the Jeep. I automatically go for the passenger side. This time she can maneuver the car through the trees of that tricky hidden road. Too bad we'll be hitting rush hour traffic in Columbus; otherwise, I could be home sooner. I can't wait to hug my family. Mom places her hand on my thigh to steady my bouncing leg, then says it's a good thing I didn't have to take a plane home. Amen to that! I stare out the window and daydream while Mom makes some work-related calls. At one point, she gets hold of Dad, who sounds happier than I've heard him in ages. He's anxious to show Mom a plot of land on the Pine Ridge Reservation. They've been talking about building a house. That's where he coaches boys who no longer have families or relatives they can live with. After the horrible things that happened to most of my childhood friends on Buckthorn, I never thought he'd be up for coaching troubled kids again. The plan is for Mom to commute between the two places when she is working at the Ellsworth Air Base up near Rapid City.

Home, almost. As Mom winds up the driveway, I'm about ready to jump out of my skin. The triplets are waiting inside the garage, screaming and waving. As soon as the engine shuts off, Tess unleashes them on us.

Mom comes in for a cup of tea before continuing down to Wright-Patt. She is welcome to spend the night, but I get that she wants to wake up in her own bed. Dayton is only an hour away, and it's an easy stretch of road to drive.

Just like that, the house is quiet. The kids left for their first playdate at someone else's home. Ah, to have stayed in bed this morning and gone on making love to Tess. I brush out my braids and grab a quick shower. Jim's been on my mind since I left the conference yesterday. Think I'll head over to Dr. Nate's place and take him for a ride. The final thing the Council of First Nations had us do was to sit with members of our own tribe, in order to discuss aspects of our culture that we believe should be preserved at all costs. We agreed that the Lakota are foremost a Horse Nation. Although we had heard several interesting plans bandied around about improving the infrastructure on our reservations, not a one would get implemented if it didn't take that fact into account.

I feel guilty because there weren't many opportunities to see Jim during football season, and he'll certainly have a word or two to say about my neglecting him! I'm stoked to go, but not before filling a bag with sugar cubes and carrots, which should earn me his forgiveness.

After leading him out to the open field, Jim stands neighing and tossing his head vigorously while I run to take my position. He understands what I'm up to and is excited. I think I've gone far enough and turn to face him. We're about a hundred feet or so apart, plenty of distance to build the momentum needed to swing myself on his back when he's at full gallop, a trick we used to perform for the tourists at Al's back when I was a much leaner boy. I firmly believe I can defy gravity by punching the ground hard enough to catapult my body above Jim's. "Charge!" I yell, and we're off, racing headlong toward each other across the snow-dusted field. Jim looks more powerful than ever. *Focus, focus, focus* — timing is everything, and I'm up! I let go of Jim's mane and he instantly reverts to a slower gait. Nothing beats riding bareback and feeling each other's every movements. The high, fast-moving clouds capture my imagination. With arms outstretched and hair flying in the wind, I call out to Daniel, who now resides somewhere in the vast Star Nation beyond, and I implore him to join me, if only this once. There's no mistaking the sound of extra hooves suddenly pounding the ground alongside Jim and me. Lo and behold, Daniel is whooping with laughter as he and Flapjack race a few lengths ahead of us. He glances over his shoulder and playfully waves at me. "At the count of three," he yells. Next thing we're shouting at the top of our lungs, "Long live Lakota!"

"Viktor. Viktor!"

I turn toward Tess who's standing by the kitchen door, wondering why she snapped at me. Shaking her head in exasperation, she storms into the living room where Holt and I are sitting on the floor peacefully watching TV. Suddenly she's on top of us, wiping Holt with a wet towel. Only now do I realize he's covered in melted cheese. It's in his hair, on the carpet.

"I'm so sorry, Tess. I'll clean him up. Go. I'll do it!" The carpet is a sticky mess. "Tess, I'll take care of everything!" She looks at the plate on the coffee table, and then looks back at me...like how did Holt manage to grab the sandwich, pull the bread apart and smear himself from head to toe with gooey cheese without me noticing.

"What's gotten into you these past couple of weeks?" she asks tersely. "Ever since you came back from that conference you're constantly zoning out. Next she carries Holt to the bathroom for a proper cleaning, leaving me to figure out the carpet.

Tess and I barely speak the rest of the day. The tension in the air is killing me. Once dinner is over, and the triplets put to bed, I lead Tess silently by the hand to the sofa so we can talk. I expect her to sit beside me, but when she hesitates, I gently pull on her arm to draw her down on the cushion. I'm at a loss over where to begin, but not Tess, who straight away says, "I don't recognize you." And before I can respond, she adds, "You're sullen."

"*Sullen!* I'm not sullen."

"Okay, you're moody and uncommunicative."

I stare at her a long minute. She isn't wrong.

"Earlier this morning when I met with Coach Doyle to go over the spring training schedule, I told him I wasn't returning this season." My breathing picks up. Tess is sitting tall. Her arms are straight. She's got a grip on her knees that makes her look like she's bracing for bad news. "Honestly, Tess, as much as my words surprised him, they completely floored me!" She says nothing and is evidently waiting for more of an explanation.

"I can see now why my behavior concerned you. I guess I have been somewhat self-absorbed lately. Something happened to me after the conference. Meeting Indians from around the country had a profound effect on me. Everyone was incredibly enthusiastic, and we held such interesting and productive discussions. It wasn't the same as talking to people online or on the radio. The atmosphere in the room was electric."

"I'm sure it was inspiring, Viktor, but why quit football, and why so abruptly? Not that it upsets me." With that, she smiles slightly. "I'm just curious about your motive."

"Until the conference, I more or less believed I looked at life from a Lakota perspective. In truth, I need to get my priorities in order. Family means everything, and I'm blowing it, Tess. The triplets will be three years old this Christmas. There's no way I'm missing out on watching them experience the holidays. I figure we can start out at your parents' house in Cincinnati, then head over to my grandparents in Kansa City. Grandma Junie and Grandpa Cyrus go all out for Christmas. Claire will be there with her baby… and Dad and Mom. I'm sure Iris and Hashke will go. Then we'll head up to Buckthorn for the rest of winter break. They don't celebrate Christmas up there, but they make an exception for our New Year's Day. We pretend it's the start of our Lakota year, which doesn't occur until April."

I was hoping for a cheerier reaction. Tess takes a deep breath then slowly exhales.

"Wow," she whispers. "This is what you've been mulling over all this time?"

"Are you good with it?"

"Where does that leave the football team? Will Caleb start?"

"There are plenty of guys in the wings chomping at the bit to prove themselves. Caleb is headed back to his small college, where he says student-athletes are considered students first."

"Good for him, considering the only thing that truly matters to Big Ten schools these days is their TV deals." She promises not to get on her soapbox. "How about a cup of tea? Since we're taking the time to talk things out, Viktor, I could use a sounding board."

She can't leave me hanging like that. I follow her to the kitchen to find out what she meant. It turns out that she doesn't want to pursue a PhD after all, not ever. She plans to finish her master's, despite having lost interest in the subject, simply because the end is in sight. Then she wishes to take a period of time for herself and the family, just like I want to do, after which she intends to get a second master's in a different field. Apparently her research into the uses of gold nanoparticles in biology also has geological applications, namely in the treatment of toxic substances in water. A recent PBS program on the topic got her all fired up, and she immediately contacted OSU's engineering department to learn more. I admit to being as surprised by the suddenness of her decision as she was upon hearing I quit football. It's plain to see that she has found a great new strength of purpose, something I anticipate will shortly happen to me as I recommit myself to science. That we both were going through a similar reassessment of our lives struck Tess and me as odd.

    We return to the living room, mugs in hand, ready to cuddle up on the couch to watch TV, happy to be on the same page about things.

CHAPTER 64

"I don't know that I'll ever stop missing Hank and Zunta. You really don't want another dog, Grandmother?" I'm holding my phone up to her so she can view the family group shots that were taken earlier. Missing from them are her beloved Newfoundlands. Growing up, they were always front and center in pictures. Today, however, surrounded by their progeny, Sunkwah and Winnie clinched the honor.

"There's too much to deal with at the moment," she sighs. "In a few years maybe." She stares at one of the group portraits. "Five generations. Imagine." Tears well in her eyes because also absent from the photos are her husband and daughter. I hug her tightly in an attempt to console both her and me, for I miss Pahpie and my Aunt Loretta, too.

Iris, Hashke, Tess, and I moved the Adirondack chairs from the back porch of Grandmother's house to the front yard, in order to sit among the tall pines and stars. It hit sixty-seven degrees this afternoon, likely a record high for January here in South Dakota. Grandmother blows us a kiss goodnight. It was a long day for her parents, which meant it was a long day for her, since she was the one who got them ready to come over this morning. Mom and Dad gladly accompanied her back to Sunkwah and Winnie's place an hour ago to help her with their bedtime routine. They hug Grandmother, and then come over to join us. The triplets are presently asleep inside a tepee that Hashke erected for them in the dining room. He adores the children and takes his role of uncle seriously. He and Iris are aunt and uncle to seven kids on his reservation in Wisconsin. I hope he changes his mind about adopting. He'd make a terrific father.

It couldn't be a more peaceful evening. We all remark on how well Sunkwah and Winnie are doing for their age.

"They're definitely stronger than last year," says Dad, "but they've both lost considerable weight. You just can't tell when they're dressed in their native costumes."

"Speaking of which," says Iris, "you certainly cut a dashing figure today,

Viktor...all decked out in your grand ceremonial feathers and gorgeous beaded buckskin regalia."

"I could say the same about you. Thanks for letting Tess borrow one of your dresses for the picture. You were right, the deep jade green really set off the color of her hair."

Tess smiles at the compliment, but her focus is on the night sky. She's lost in the stars. The rest of us recount the fun we had over Christmas with Dad's relatives, when countless families, many with toddlers, streamed through my grandparents' door on a daily basis during the week of our visit. Fortunately, Kansas City had gotten a foot of snow, and our threesome and their cousins wanted only to play outside. Watching them teetering around on their short legs was a hoot. Mom laughs, recalling Raif when he got trapped on a small patch of ice and couldn't get up. He'd manage to stand for a split second, and then drop to his butt. The comedy would have continued if a cousin hadn't finally come to his rescue. Raif never cried for help. I observe Mom as she tells the story. She's been in such good spirits this holiday. It's hard to believe she ever suffered from PTSD. I wonder if Dad is thinking that to himself as he watches her. Their chairs are close together and he is using her armrest to hold her hand. Occasionally his thumb glides along her fingers. When she turns to him, still laughing, he kisses her hand. Their smiles are very telling. Not so long ago it seemed like they had given up on each other. Thank you, Wakan Tanka, for answering this son's prayers.

Iris asks if anyone else is hungry besides her. It's around eight-thirty. She makes a case for eating before it gets any later and recites a list of what's in the fridge. Dad holds my arm as I'm about to stand and says he'd like a word with me first.

After scooting his chair sideways to face me better, he says, "Remember yesterday when Hashke wondered about whether you missed playing football sometimes?"

"Sure. What about it?"

"I couldn't help noticing how long you hesitated before answering."

"*That* I don't remember. Maybe it's because football hasn't been on my mind during this trip, or this past season. You knew I wasn't going to be able to follow the games much, that I had to focus on my degree program. Hashke just got me thinking about it, and, to be honest, I do miss it...I miss being on the field, not the politics, though. Nowadays every decision that gets made, no matter how trivial, is scrutinized to the nth degree."

"I hear you ... still. The thrill of running out of the tunnel into a crowd of fans screaming your name must be hard to give up."

"Where is this going?" I'm curious because he never voiced an opinion about my quitting the team when I told him last spring. I can't tell if he's disappointed with me. "Perhaps having a few Indians in the stands to cheer me on would have made the experience more special."

"I had no idea, Son."

"I don't think I realized the full scope of my emotions before this year. But then, I haven't been as involved with other Indians like I am now. If I had played this season, Dad, I would have lost out on spending Christmas with Tess's family and our relatives in Kansas City. Being with everyone has given me a better perspective on what's important."

"There's no denying how much they appreciated seeing you both and the triplets." He pats my arm and smiles. "Let's go, before they eat up all the food."

As we head toward the house, he says, "I'm going to discuss our conversation with Mom."

It's unclear why he would, nothing we said seemed very important. "Fine by me," I tell him.

Once inside, I find Tess in the living room seated at a small table by a side window. It was thoughtful of her to make a sandwich for me. While we're eating, I think back on how worried we had been about taking the children on such a long trip. "Things have turned out better than expected, don't you think?" I ask.

"Hmm, let's see...the kids have behaved, for the most part, even Raif, which is truly surprising. No one has gotten sick. Haven't had to deal with blizzards. No family arguments, we're all still talking. Yep, I agree...pretty miraculous."

The rest of the evening is spent quietly talking with the others about life in general, favorite shows and actors, the current music scene. Hockey is on TV in the background. You couldn't ask for a more relaxing atmosphere. Later, when Tess and I are snuggled up in bed nose-to-nose, she whispers against my lips, "You look happiest on your own turf."

In order to stay ahead of the snow that's on the way, Tess and I need to leave the rez within the next four days. It's been a great trip, but we're feeling antsy to get home. We still need to plan our academic schedules for the spring. Mom sticks her head in the bedroom just as I'm collecting clothes to wash.

"You've got nothing going on today, right? Rumjaktoowahl is in the area and I have asked him to stop by. He's looking forward to seeing you again."

"Who?" Before she can answer, I remember. "Oh, yeah...Jack." Husband to Sarah, the couple that protects the main entrance to Chohkahn. "I'm glad Tess will get to meet him."

"He's bringing three friends, so your grandmother and I are taking the children over to Levi's to play with the rabbits and goats...let you enjoy the visit without interruptions."

"They'll get a kick out of that for sure. Thanks."

"Iris and Hashke are driving Sunkwah and Winnie to Hot Springs for the day. Dad is staying behind."

"Okay." I'm standing there holding the bundle of dirty clothes, expecting her to step aside so I can exit the doorway, but she doesn't. "Is there something else?" She definitely looks like there's more on her mind. It's so obvious, but then she walks away.

It's only a short time after the house clears out when the doorbell rings. And there stands Jack, smiling big. I introduce Tess. I bet she was hoping to see him in the kaftan I had described to her. They are all in jeans. The two people with him introduce themselves. The older man appears to be in his early sixties. He's my height and goes by Rolling Thunder. He brought along his teenage grandson, Kahlden, who admits to being a huge fan of mine. The grandfather has a heavy accent, but not the boy, who is probably around sixteen. "Wait a second..." I stop dead in my tracks right as they're about to follow Tess and me inside. "*Rolling Thunder?* Are you Chief Rolling Thunder...from Chohkahn?"

"Yes," he answers, "but for the record, I am not its so-called *chief*. No single person is in charge of all our people. Individual family lines handle various duties...always have." He looks to his grandson and adds, "Historically, our family's role has been to protect and defend our Nation's interests, much as a country's military does. There's no ranking system, unlike the rest of the world's armies. I called myself a chief when we first approached Howling Wind, so she'd think she was dealing with the person in charge. We needed to win her confidence."

Cousin Suhdeer may have explained that once, or Jack, but it went in one ear and out the other. Never in my wildest dreams did I imagine that I'd ever encounter the man who recruited my mother as a spy.

Just then Dad appears. "Come in, welcome!" He holds out his hand, "Solomon Davis." After the quick hello, Dad immediately starts helping them off with their jackets. He seems unusually animated and talkative, not that he isn't a friendly guy. He points us to the dining room where I'm taken aback when I see the fine spread of cheeses and meats and pastries on the table. Somebody's been busy. Tess cocks her head to the side in the direction of the grandson while I hold the chair out for her, indicating it should be offered to the boy, who accepts the invitation to sit beside me with childlike enthusiasm. She winds up between Kahlden and Dad. Jack is on my other side with Rolling Thunder beside him.

This in an informal visit, but at no time during the conversation, which continues to revolve around the new college under construction on the reservation, does Rolling Thunder refer to Tess and me by our first names; it's always Talking White Owl and Ms. O'Shea. The first time he addressed Dad as Mr. Davis, and Dad didn't say anything about calling him Solomon, I figured we should follow suit.

I mention that a friend of mine is helping to build the college. Next I learn there's also a stadium going up. Billie must not have realized that, or he would have told me for sure. "They break ground in late May," says Rolling Thunder, "but the stadium won't be on the reservation. It's getting built in a region between Sioux Falls and Mitchell." That's odd. I know the area well, and it's basically a no-man's-land.

Jack asks, "Did your friend happen to tell you that the university is being modeled after MIT?"

"Nooo. MIT?" I shake my head like...how is that even possible. "*The* MIT?"

"They have a football team, you know. They are solid Division 3 winners. The goal from the beginning was to establish an elite school for strictly Indigenous students. Non-native family members can attend, of course. The Lakota on the Buckthorn rez are one hundred per cent behind it, but they refuse to permit outsiders onto Indian lands for football games. We agree, it would present problems down the road. The owners of

Falcone Industries suggested the location for the stadium. The Rawakota have maintained a long-standing relationship with the family, one that predates first contact. It was the Falcones who approached the Lakota Tribal Council with the idea. It will include dormitories for the athletes to live in. Another complex is planned across from it, for other sports. These days it's possible to complete coursework online, but eventually the players will be able to attend classes at a proposed branch of the university on the nearby Yankton Reservation."

"Good heavens," says Tess, "what foresight! You must have been planning this for years."

My thoughts exactly! I turn to Dad. "Did you know about the stadium?"

"Only since yesterday, when your mother informed me about it after I told her you said you miss playing football." Tess looks at me confused. She didn't need to know that.

I fix my attention on Rolling Thunder. "I'm having trouble wrapping my head around this, particularly the location of the stadium. And why concentrate on football when you're a new university? The cost of starting a football program is staggering. Many colleges have tried recently, only to face the reality that losing teams are simply too costly to sustain, because no one starts winning fresh out of the gate."

Rolling Thunder dabs his mouth and places his napkin and plate to the side. He leans forward and crosses his arms on the table. He studies me for a minute, as I do him, observing how different his features are from the Rawakota I know. He has a fox's narrow eyes. And his face might not look so round if his hair weren't pulled back tight into a single braid. He has high cheekbones and a long and somewhat flat, straight nose. His clan's bloodline must be more closely tied to the Mongols. Kahlden's face looks similar. His golden eyes, however, are happy and shine brightly, whereas his grandfather's show a marked degree of cunning.

Jack receives a signal in the form of a clipped nod from Rolling Thunder, indicating he's to continue talking. Jack takes a sip of tea and clears his throat. "Dear friends," he begins, "the creation of a university is without a doubt an ambitious project, but that's only the half of it. The stadium will also support a newly organized NFL team, one that represents both North and South Dakota. League owners have been in talks with the Falcones for a while. The deal is basically approved. We're looking at a timeline of five years."

I'm speechless. Not Dad, though. "To think that scrap metal could make you a billionaire. The auto shops were a gold mine, and I was too naive to see it. All I can say is, it's about time we got us an NFL team in the Dakotas. That's fantastic! Don't you think, Viktor?"

I take a moment to digest the news. The room is silent. It's Tess who speaks up now.

"I get it," she mutters under her breath. "You want Viktor as the team's quarterback."

Her remark surprises me, considering that I've quit playing, which is public knowledge.

"They have it all worked out," she says, facing me.

"Tess, that's a bit farfetched…you just don't wake up one day and find yourself playing in the NFL."

"You can if it's five years from now." Her voice was flat. And her face remains blank.

Poor Kahlden glances at his grandfather, and then he stares at the table, not knowing where else to look. He gathered by Tess's tone that she isn't thrilled by the idea, and he would probably prefer not to be between us at the moment.

I proceed to ask Rolling Thunder if I should give credence to my wife's claim.

"Oh, come on…" Dad stands at this point, and with his hands on his waist he reports that Mom made no mention of the stadium being shared with the NFL. "We merely entertained the idea of you and the family moving to the rez in a couple of years, and maybe, just maybe, if you still missed playing ball, Viktor, you could enroll at the university and join its football program. It was nothing more than wishful thinking on my part." He directs his next words to Rolling Thunder. "It isn't clear to me why Constance discussed a personal matter with an outsider."

Rolling Thunder takes the remark in stride. He motions for Dad to sit. Next he offers Tess a kindly small smile and affirms that her assumption was in fact correct.

"We Rawakota have an in with just about every influential company around the globe," he explains, "just none within any top sports organizations, many of whose owners are some of the richest people in the world.

Their wealth gives them a disproportionate amount of political clout. We stand to learn a lot about the things they specifically spend their money on. It's a defensive tactic on our part ... a way of keeping tabs on individuals who may someday seek to undermine our sovereign status. We have proposed that a high end hotel with a helipad be built nearby to attract them. They are going to love the stadium's luxury suites."

"You planning on bugging the rooms?" I ask, half-joking. There's no reaction. Another thought occurs to me. "Do you expect the quarterback to penetrate their inner circles and spy for you?"

Jack grins. "Your imagination is getting the better of you, Viktor. Our plans never took you into account at all, not until Howling Wind called us and inquired about the people who'd be doing the recruiting for the university's football team. We merely want to present you with a few options to think about, should you desire to play the game again. Nothing more."

"Let us take a break and stretch our legs," says Rolling Thunder. "We have said all there is to say on the subject." He looks to Dad. "Mr. Davis, there is a matter I would like to discuss with you alone." As he scoots his chair out to stand, he asks if I'd toss a football around with Kahlden. The boy looks embarrassed by the request. True, his grandfather put me on the spot, but it actually sounds fun.

Jack and Tess look at each other, being the last two at the table. Knowing Jack, I'm confident he'll be able to mitigate Tess's concerns about my returning to football. He's an empathetic soul who's good at finding the right words. Tess didn't act like she had any qualms about me playing last year. Perhaps she simply resigned herself to it, knowing I'd be parting ways with the Buckeyes once I graduated. To me, the thought of going pro is entirely unrealistic. And why would I want to play at a Division 3 school after leading a Big Ten team?

After twenty minutes or so the others come out to watch Kahlden and me in the front yard. He is surprisingly good at both throwing and catching ... exceptionally good. Rolling Thunder thanks me and says it's time they head out. As they pull away in their car, Tess says she's going over to Levi's to see the kids, which leaves me standing there with Dad.

"I'm curious, Dad, what did Rolling Thunder want to tell you?"

He shrugs like it was nothing, but I am persistent.

Dad stares ahead and sighs. "He apologized on behalf of the Rawakota for not involving me with your mother's...what would you call it? The intervention. Her treatment. Whatever."

"That's commendable, isn't it?"

"Is it?" he says. There's anger in his eyes. "I told him, too little, too late."

"I'm sorry, Dad." It's been a while since we hugged each other like this. I know not to ask any more about it. We settle in the rocking chairs on the front porch and wait for someone to arrive. Iris and Hashke are due back soon with Sunkwah and Winnie. Now I'm wondering what Tess and Jack talked about.

Dad and I go on about the weather for a bit. Temps in the sixties are so unusual for January, one can't help but always bring it up. Far off over the mountains, snow clouds are forming.

"Too bad your Pahpie can't see the man you've become, Son. He'd be proud beyond words."

"I wish Tess could have known him."

"I wonder what he would say to having a professional football team with Indians on it."

"He'd be pleased that the owners are Indigenous."

"It's definitely going to have a positive impact on the Native community at large."

"But only if the team does well. I'm not convinced the players can hold their own when they're up against highly experienced seasoned athletes. I fear they are going to make fools of themselves." Dad must see that.

"Then there's no team until they *are* ready," he says, which seems a rather glib response. The floorboards creak in unison as we continue rocking in our chairs. The breeze has picked up. Colder air from the north is moving in.

"Consider this hypothetical situation, Viktor—and please hear me out before saying anything. You could conceivably return to playing for the Buckeyes, in a limited capacity of course, say as a third string backup QB. If they don't go for that idea, a player with your experience would be a great asset on their practice squad. What matters most is that you stay in shape, in case you want a career in the NFL. Why rule it out? You will always be a scientist. There's but a window of time, though, for a person to be a successful athlete. A new head coach has been hired at OSU for the upcoming year. His approach to the game will be different, which you can learn from. If you're not shouldering the main responsibility of winning, won't it be easier to finish your PhD...and enjoy a home life, too?"

"Those are some big ifs."

"I'm not done." He thinks for a moment. "Even with Tess going after another master's, you'll both be in a position to relocate in a couple of years. The new university on Buckthorn will have been up and running for a year. Think about how many high school players they could recruit if your name were connected to its football program."

"Are you suggesting I play for them? I can't if I'm not enrolled. By then, I will have gotten my degree. I'm done with school."

"Every college has a biology department. The administration will figure out a way for you to continue your research. According to Mom, the university is seeking a high-profile coach, a guy dead-set on creating a top rate team. The money is there, obviously. You yourself said how having a few Indians cheering you on in the stands would make playing more special. You can make that happen, Viktor, but instead of a few Indians, picture an entire stadium filled with them. What a rare opportunity this is."

I'm relieved to see the cars coming down the road. I don't want to think about this anymore. Everybody is arriving at the same time. Sister and Hashke dropped off Sunkwah and Winnie at their home and got them situated for the night, which Grandmother greatly appreciates. The kids are yelling over each other about the things they saw today as Tess and I extricate them from these infernal car seats. Next, they're all over Dad, their Pops, which is what he wanted to be called. Their excitement only increases when their mother utters the magic word *bath,* which sends them skipping inside with their Auntie Iris, who offers to supervise them. Tess follows, but not before planting a juicy kiss on my lips. I think it's to let me know there are no hard feelings left over from the meeting with our company. Dad teasingly puckers up to Mom.

"Any love for this old man?" he asks, to which Mom promptly responds with a lingering kiss of her own. It's fun to witness the mischief in his eyes.

The family squeezes together in the bathroom to watch the triplets play in the tub. They always provide entertainment. It's too crowded for me. I catch Mom alone in the kitchen. "What a day, huh!" I say, pulling a chair out from the center island. She's reading the instructions on a frozen pizza box.

"It's a testament to our stamina that we're still standing," she laughs. "Did you know Levi has pigs, baby pigs...the cutest little things. Tess and I had to talk your grandmother out of bringing a couple home. Should I put both pizzas in at the same time on different racks?"

"Separately is best." She sets the oven temperature, following which she lines up the glasses and plates in front of me. "Could you stop for a second, please. Why couldn't you have given me a heads up on the reason for Jack's visit...and that Rolling Thunder was going to be with him?"

"You might have read too much into it." I think back to her hesitating at the bedroom door yesterday after she announced that Jack was stopping by. She wanted to tell me. "They merely wished to give you some food for thought as you contemplate your future."

"Be honest with me, Mom...do you still spy for Rolling Thunder?"

"No," she answers, seemingly distracted. She spots the basil plant on the window sill. "Here," she says, handing it to me. "Make yourself useful." I begin plucking the leaves off the stem and tearing them into bits.

"I find it hard to believe that anyone would go to such great lengths and expense to buy an NFL franchise solely to snoop on people."

"Natives stand to benefit greatly from having a professional team in our region. But yes, bottom line, the entire venture is intended to serve as a smokescreen."

I shake my head and laugh to myself. "What a preposterous scheme. Why would they trust me and Dad and Tess not to divulge this to the wrong person?"

"Really, Viktor." She makes me sound foolish for suggesting it, which I get. Dad and Tess were at one point vetted by the Rawakota, making them worthy of their people's trust.

The dinger sounds, the preheat is over. Mom pops the first pizza in the oven. She then leans over and rests her elbows on the counter. Her face is about two feet from mine. She takes one of my hands in hers and holds it.

"Conspiracies abound, Viktor. Sad to say, it's the way of the world. The problem arises in determining their legitimacy. The fact is, a real plot exists that aims to expose the sacred city of Chohkahn." She has my full attention.

"I am not going to rehash the story of Jonah Plain Feather, other than to say that the boy was correct in believing he had revealed information about Chohkahn to the college roommate who had drugged him. Years after the boy's suicide, the Rawakota began noticing activity around the waterfall that hides the cave with the elevator in it. It was then that the lodge got built, in order to protect the entrance around the clock. Men with thick black hair and beards would show up sporadically throughout the years, acting like they had gotten lost hunting. Winter Crow's lab linked their DNA to the Middle East. It was easy to collect hair from their clothes. Fingerprints may have been lifted, too. The connection to the Bishara family wasn't made until you met Ishmael at Ohio State, when I asked the Iroquois colleague of mine, whom I had told you about, to investigate his background."

Mom squeezes my hand. "Sorry to bring up his name." I didn't feel anything when she mentioned Ishmael. No hair standing on end. No racing heart. That episode of my life is dead and buried. I think she senses it.

"We...me and the Rawakota, eventually learned that an older brother was living just across the mountains in Wyoming. He had managed to worm his way into a third-generation cattle ranching family... claimed he was a member of a landowning dynasty in Argentina. In the past couple of years, he has sent sophisticated miniaturized drones to the cave region, which the Rawakota have been able to take control of and neutralize. He's been tracked going into the woods alone. The manufacturer must be wondering why they continually fail. They each cost a small fortune. So you see, Viktor, one must remain vigilante. The players involved in these games of subterfuge are resourceful. They keep the Rawakota on their toes, which in turn keeps the rest of us safe."

"But why is finding Chohkahn so all-fired important to an Arab? I could see if they were archeologists. What else did Jonah Plain Feather disclose?"

"We surmised that Jonah likely described the crystals that are used to power everything in the sacred city. There's no guessing in what context he mentioned zaptah. The Bisharas might think it's a Native word for lithium or uranium. In their minds, it's valuable, and therefore worth owning. They don't strike me as people who share."

There is a sudden commotion in the hall. Three pudgy little naked bodies bounce into the kitchen, squealing with delight. A line of adults growling and howling like bears and wolves follow them in, making like they're going to gobble them up. Honor and Holt seek protection behind my legs, but Raif believes he can outwit his pursuers by hiding behind the trash can. The adults turn to each other, wondering where on earth they disappeared to. They exit the room quietly laughing, ready to catch the sneaky trio when they run back down the hall with the hope of getting chased again. What a carefree period in a child's life.

Mom doesn't have to tell me how thankful she is that Tess and I made her and Dad grandparents.

We warn Jasper not to do it; he's gonna catch hell from his football fans, but he laughs and posts the pictures online anyway of him in his Arizona Cardinal's jersey, partying with us, his old OSU buddies, who just beat the pants off his team. We go by the name of the Dakota Pronghorns. Too bad it was just a preseason match-up. What fun it is recalling our Buckeye glory days. Rhett, DeShaun, Damien, and I attempt to bribe our former teammate, who is currently the league's top receiver, into leaving the sunny Southwest and playing with us up here in the frosty north. I can only guess what DeShaun whispered in Jasper's ear when his eyes suddenly go big and he yells, *Sign me up!*

"Sign who up?" says a voice in my ear. A girl's voice.

I'm still laughing when my eyes open to a darkened room. Had to have been dreaming, although I don't remember about what. Tess is propped on her arm beside me in bed, only inches from my face. The small lamp on her nightstand silhouettes her body. The covers are bunched around our feet.

"I hate to interrupt the party," she says, "but you clunked me on the head with your arm. I believe I got in the way of a pass you were throwing."

After apologizing, and then telling her that I have no memory of the dream, she shows me my behavior on her phone.

"I woke to you laughing, thinking the kids were in bed with us. But then you just kept on talking, naming all these guys you used to play with. You just went on and on, so I figured I'd record you, in case you wouldn't believe me."

We sit against the headboard while I watch myself, my arms waving every which way while I'm shouting downfield to DeShaun. It is funny. And I do remember now, especially how absolutely real it felt being with the guys.

After getting the blankets and sheets straightened, basically remaking the bed, we climb under the covers to resume our sleep, wishing we were already back home. Tess strokes my cheek. "Apparently all that talk about football yesterday really got to you."

I cut Tess off with a kiss before she can ask if I regret my decision not to play, because that's what I sensed was coming next. She kisses me back, but with far more passion than I had summoned up when I went for her lips. It's unexpected. Exciting.

CHAPTER 65

I wake up spent, but not without a smile. It was difficult at first, balancing a research schedule with football. Last spring I did what Dad had suggested and approached OSU's new head football coach about letting me be the team's third string quarterback. He agreed to the unusual request. Taking part in the practice sessions has been a gratifying experience. Here it is the middle of fall, and the Buckeyes are undefeated. Some players have personally thanked me for my input even though I'm not in the starting lineup. Tess pokes her head in the shower, amused by my singing as I work the tangles from my hair. Normally I'm cussing when they get this bad. Can't wait to attack my busy schedule. First on the list this morning is a meeting with Dr. Bonnaire. He arrived in Columbus from France a week ago, ready to study my blood, which I once promised him he could do.

When I step off the elevator onto the hospital floor, I see him waiting for me at the reception desk. His weight loss is dramatic. The belly is gone. News reached us in the Research Department that Bonnaire had been laid up for months with pneumonia. As we walk toward his office, he complains about fatigue, but says nothing more about his ordeal. His blue eyes light up when I formally agree to be his test subject. He then hands me an order form for the lab.

"Viktor, don't be alarmed by the amount of blood that is needed." Speaking English taxes him. He continues in French to describe the particular chromosomes of interest to him, which doesn't mean a thing to me, and then he asks if I would also consent to a bone density test.

"Sure. One thing before I go, Dr. Bonnaire—you know how humans and chimpanzees share a common ancestor...well, that isn't the case with me, and yet I am human. Have fun figuring out the mystery."

He looks intently at me, and then, grinning, mutters, "L'énigme."

Unfortunately, when Bonnaire learns about my background, I will still remain an enigma to him. His curiosity about the nature of Rawakota DNA will in all likelihood consume him. The Rawakota don't care that his findings will turn evolutionary science on its head. Winter Crow's lab could have published its discovery of our people's link to the lemur ages ago. Guess they didn't want to be bothered by the attention it would garner if they had. I head downstairs to have my blood drawn; the bone test requires an appointment. Once that's over, it's off to the barn to see Jim. Riding him in the chilly fall air on a regular basis helps my brain function better. Epiphanies strike at two in the morning, causing me to bolt upright in bed and jump on the computer. Just the other night I was able to hone in on a factor that is likely disrupting the normal folding process of the protein I'm researching. Dawn sneaks up on me, and I feel primed for the new day, as does Tess, who began a swimming regimen last month. She isn't roused by ideas in the night like I am, but she is sleeping more soundly, which raises her spirits. It's a godsend that the kids, who are almost four, seldom wake us anymore throughout the night. You learn what new parents mean when they feel their sanity slipping away due to exhaustion.

After I've parked and am walking toward the barn, I notice a bright yellow flyer posted on the door. It's a note from Dr. Nate. The horses have caught a cold – nothing serious. Some have a low fever. Expect them to be out of sorts for a few days. I go in to check on Jim. He's got a runny nose and doesn't appear to be interested in food, not even the treats I brought. My phone goes off. It's an email from Dr. Nate saying the same as the note.

After hauling a couple bales of hay into Jim's stall to sit on, I run back to the car to grab my laptop. I can do some stuff while I keep him company for a while.

"Let's see who is on our Native blog." I talk out loud, hoping the sound of my voice comforts Jim. He stands close and nudges me from time to time, showing he appreciates my staying. "Un-hee, Jim! They're dealing with three feet of snow in the Dakotas, and a wind chill of minus 20 degrees. Radar shows the blizzard's gonna hit northern Ohio in a couple days." Jim drops slowly to the ground, curls himself up in a ball at my feet like a dog, and then drifts off to sleep. He really is under the weather. I continue to talk out loud, to keep myself company now. "This is interesting...an article about an environmental disaster that happened last spring in northern Russia. Twenty-one thousand tons of diesel spilled into the soil and waterways, creating a state of emergency. How does that not make headline news here in the States!" The author of the article goes on to ask readers to sign a petition that will protect the Indigenous reindeer-herding Sámi people in northern Finland from Russian extraction companies. The sheer number of drilling rigs needed for their operation will destroy the reindeers' grazing lands. The recent accident is compared to the Exxon Valdez oil spill, proving again that these conglomerates can't be trusted. "The author is right," I exclaim, adding my name to the petition, "the damage inflicted on Mother Earth is irreversible."

That done, I search the region in the Himalayas where Mom told me that a clan of our distant ancestors still live hidden from the world. Wouldn't Dr. Bonnaire be dumbfounded by that revelation! I myself don't know the exact location. Other than Mom, only a select few individuals from Chohkahn have so far made contact with them.

Jim's sudden snoring has me laughing outright. He has since changed his position and is laying on his side with his legs stretched straight out in front of him, dead to the world, poor guy. I suppose I won't be missed if I head home. Just when I'm ready to call Tess about picking up something for dinner, an emergency alert appears on my phone. It's from Ohio State —the campus is in lockdown.

I race home, worried I may have run a red light. I find Tess in front of the TV, the triplets are with the nannies in another room. Whatever happened at OSU was on the southwest side because we can hear the sirens in the distance and now helicopters circling above. I hurry to Tess's side on the couch. Not much is known at this point, she says, other than an engineering professor was fatally shot. The search is on for the shooter, who is armed with an assault rifle. Witnesses watched him run down Neil Avenue toward Mirror Lake, shooting as he ran. Some students caught a bullet, but it's too early to comment on their condition. Tess and I sit there speechless. This hits too close to home. Ruby and Naomi bring the kids out, they're hungry. I offer to walk the women down the street to their place while Tess microwaves a frozen macaroni and cheese dinner for them.

I no sooner close the door behind me after returning, when the alarms go off in our house, upstairs and downstairs. The constant low beeping sound activates Nero's guarding reflexes. With nose to the ground, the dog goes into full work mode, making a clean sweep of the kitchen before moving on to the rest of the entire house. Mom had us install a special security system, in the event that an armed person ever made it onto the lot that's on the other side of our driveway. It's the Rawakota who covertly police the wooded portion of it, not local law enforcement. Because the place contains a sprawling public self-storage facility, the company has a guard stationed inside a gatehouse that customers need to stop at first before driving onto the grounds. The Rawakota have nabbed reporters who managed to climb over the surrounding chain link fence, in order to hide in the trees and take photos of me and the family, but that alone won't set off the house alarms. Guns will.

    I turn off the alarm while Tess moves the children into the dining room at the back of the house. The kids realize something is up. Tess and I talk to them in a calm voice and ask that they quietly eat their dinner. Nero is back. He sits at attention in the middle of the living room and stares at the entrance door. We hear on the news that the residents of Grandview are being told to shelter-in-place. A passing police car on the street below announces over its loudspeaker that we are to stay indoors until further notice. I'm upset with myself for not wearing the watch the Rawakota gave me, in order to send and receive secure messages from them. I didn't bother with it once football practices started up. It's in a drawer in the bedroom. The security team has for sure been trying to reach me. I tell Tess I'll be fast, and bound up the stairs four at a time.

    I strap on the watch, glad for the positive message, and hurry back to the family. "Sit tight, they're telling us, Tess. We are safe. Have they found out more about the shooter on the news?"

    "The guy is a grad student who was suspended from the program by the professor he killed." She whispers for the kids' sake. "He highjacked a car by the hospital and got on the 315. When police spotted him, he started shooting randomly into traffic. He pulled off and drove down to Northwest Boulevard where he left the car and took off on foot. I can't believe he's in our back yard."

    Nero growls, but it's because of the flashing lights from the patrol cars swarming the neighborhood. Tess gets a puzzle for the kids to put together on the floor. They wanted dessert, but are told they must earn it tonight. Nero is noticeably twitching, as though ready to sprint into action. My watch buzzes. I show it to Tess. We brace ourselves for the sound of gunfire, which occurs seconds later, and ends just as fast. It startled the kids. We tell them the town is celebrating something with fireworks. Naturally they ask why we didn't go. They love fireworks. Nero keeps watch, the way he's been trained, only now he is next to us.

"I wish we could pack and move to the reservation tonight," says Tess. "For good."

The kids obviously heard her and are ready to go. They think she means it. Which she does, if only it weren't unrealistic…tonight that is.

Tess plays a cartoon for the children, so we can go see what's going on outside. Lots of police officers in tactical gear are packing up to leave. Tess and I were saying only last month how grateful we are that our community is safe to live in. It was after spending the day at a mall across town where a smash-and-grab robbery occurred inside at a jewelry store. We had eaten lunch at the restaurant next to it and missed it by thirty minutes. And now this happens.

"The world's gone crazy," says Tess, holding me tightly by the arm, the same thing she said after the mall event. I realize this isn't an incident we can simply put behind us.

Football season is over. The Buckeyes lost the Bowl game by one point. It's hard for the guys to accept that we didn't make it to the National Championship playoff. To think that a year ago I'd been presented with the hypothetical scenario of playing football for a university that was at the concept stage, and now I'm seriously entertaining the idea of being its quarterback. An athletic director has been hired, who in turn found himself a head coach. He's an offensive coordinator with the Miami Dolphins, a position he has held for years. I ask myself why a man with that much experience would accept a job at an unknown and unproven college. That's like a demotion. Normally coordinators become coaches within the NFL. Dad checked him out, says he is highly regarded. I'll get my chance to ask him that, along with a number of other questions, when he drops by our home to meet me in a few hours. Instead of going to a restaurant, Tess and I invited him to our house for a home cooked meal. The nannies took the triplets and Nero to their apartment for the day. I browned the meat for the beef stew this morning while Tess cut the vegetables.

He is punctual, Mr. Richard Everett. He said five o'clock, and the digital clock in the kitchen goes from 4:59 to 5:00 right as the doorbell rings, and just when we're transferring the stew to a serving bowl. Tess and I are excited. This might be the beginning of a new chapter in our lives. After a quick hug, we go to welcome our guest inside. Tess receives a gorgeous bouquet of pink roses, following which Mr. Everett shakes my hand vigorously. After I hang his coat, he stands back and checks me over from head to toe. "You, Viktor, are one formidable looking individual." He proceeds to grasp the back of my neck in a friendly way and says how much he appreciated getting the invitation to come to Columbus. A former lineman for the Patriots, he is my height, big-shouldered, and all smiles. He's got a thick crop of wavy gray hair that's impressive.

There are no lapses in the conversation during the meal, this guy's a talker. Before he sat to eat, Mr. Everett closed his eyes and inhaled deeply when he got a whiff of cabbage, stating that it really isn't a proper stew without it. The crusty rolls and Irish butter were a hit. He declined the wine that Tess would gladly have shared with him, telling us that he has given up drinking since alcohol is banned on the reservation, and therefore at the university. Apparently, it's no big sacrifice.

Mr. Everett tells us he is fifty-six and originally from Vermont. He thoroughly enjoys working with the Miami Dolphins, after having played professionally with The New England Patriots for ten years, which is why this coaching offer he received last summer baffled him. "I'm in my office in Florida when I get this call from a man who claims to be the president of a new university for Indigenous students...says it's on a South Dakota reservation, and would I consider developing its football program. Honest to God," he chuckles, "I thought I was being pranked! Next he puts me on the line with their athletic director, a guy whose name I know from my playing days. He ended up in the Canadian Football League. What can I say? They sold me on the idea of creating a team from the ground up. The timing was uncanny. My wife and I had begun thinking about doing something entirely different. We didn't figure football would play into our plans, but I love the game...and Erin is interested in learning about the different Native cultures in the Dakotas. It was an easy decision for us."

Tess and I don't go into much detail about our reasons for leaving Columbus, other than to say that we have completed our studies at OSU and now desire a change, too. We have moved to the living room for coffee. After a bit, Tess excuses herself to pick up the kids. Mr. Everett says he'd like to meet them before he takes off. He follows her to the door to grab the briefcase he had set on the floor when he arrived, which he carries back to the chair and opens on his lap, and then he pauses before going any further.

"Viktor, I hope you realize that not once was your name mentioned in connection with the football program last summer. And I certainly didn't think to ask. In interviews, you made it clear you were choosing a career in science over the NFL. Then a strange thing started happening around three weeks ago," and Mr. Everett removes a folder filled with papers that he riffles through, as if to show me how many there are. "Messages started pouring into the school. Most were emails, but some were typed letters... a few even handwritten." He hands them over and waits until I've read a couple.

"Only after I conferred with the president this past December did I learn there was a remote possibility of you, the remarkable Talking White Owl, enrolling in the college, in order to be eligible to play on the team. Imagine my surprise! Next I find out that you regularly talk with other Indians on a radio show, and on this particular occasion, you were asked if you'd consider playing for the new university...and do you remember what you said?"

"I do. I said I won't discount it." He stares thoughtfully at me.

"Many people took that to mean yes. Do you still feel that way?"

When I don't answer right away, Mr. Everett says, as though issuing an order, "You need to read all of those. They'll help you decide."

He means well. "I understand what I represent to my people and other tribal nations."

"Of course," he nods, "I didn't want to imply that..."

"It's fine. Tess and I have discussed our goals in great length, and we're both on board with moving to South Dakota, where I *will* play for you, Coach."

He sits there speechless. My acceptance will undoubtedly draw top notch talent to the school's program, which is probably reflected in the letters.

After a minute, Mr. Everett recovers from my words and shakes his head in disbelief. "You being part of the package is something I never could have anticipated. It's going to be quite the challenge, Viktor." He holds his face in his hands and rubs his temples. "I'll be pulling all-nighters like the students," he grins. "Gotta learn the latest college football rules."

"Just hire a knowledgeable staff." I'm glad Tess is back with the triplets. Nero makes a beeline to Mr. Everett's chair and sniffs the leather satchel. "Narcotics dog," I tell him, to which he laughs. He reaches inside and pulls out a Slim Jim.

"My downfall," he says, asking if Nero is allowed to have a bite. Well now the kids see it and want one, even though they don't know what a Slim Jim is. Like magic, three more appear.

As we shake hands goodbye, Mr. Everett says, "This group of players, our first team…it's going to be an interesting experiment, isn't it?"

"It is. They'll be the most self-motivated athletes you've ever encountered."

Once the kids are tucked in, I show Tess the letters, and we each grab a few to read. One especially affects her. It's from a Choctaw Indian. He's currently on the practice squad for the Chicago Bears and has never been called to the active roster. It wasn't the future he envisioned for himself during his heyday at the University of Oklahoma, where he had the best rushing record in the school's history. He admits he wasn't a good student, but vows to study hard, if the university grants him the privilege of playing with the man he most admires, Talking White Owl.

"Looks like we've got ourselves a running back." Tess smiles at me, pleased.

3 YEARS LATER

Though not ill, Sunkwah and Winnie have taken to their bed. Both agreed that a century's worth of living was enough, and they are ready to join their ancestors in the spirit life. They lay propped up with pillows, in order to watch Iris and me and our three cousins prepare for the solemn Rawakota hair-cutting ceremony. Mom requested that Sleeping Buffalo, a spiritual leader from Chohkahn, preside over the ritual and bless our gift. He respectfully sits apart from the rest of us in a corner. The triplets are seated on the floor in front of Mom and Dad. They're on Sunkwah's side of the bed. Uncle William is next to them with his grandchildren in front of him. Hashke, Tess, and my cousins' husbands sit along the wall by Sleeping Buffalo. Tess's parents really wanted to attend the event, but I had to tell Brian and Chevonne that only immediate family may take part. Grandmother sits to the side of her mother on the bed, stroking her head. The smell of burning incense fills the room. It has the soft floral scent of jasmine. Grandmother's brother and sister had a ceremony yesterday with their families. They traveled here from upstate. There was no way to jam everyone into the bedroom. Following our childhood years, Iris and I never stayed in touch with those cousins.

The five of us, standing at the foot of the bed, face our beloved Elders. Going back seven generations from the time of their births, which was in the 1920s, we take turns reciting the names of our ancestors along with a few details that defined their lives. I am responsible for acknowledging Mahkohchay, Sunkwah's great-grandfather. I name his wife and children, and also a deed for which he was known. At the age of 39, Mahkohchay fought in the 1876 Battle of the Little Bighorn, as had his father who was born in 1812. Once we finish with Sunkwah's history, we do the same with Winnie's side of the family. Then it's time for Sleeping Buffalo to step over and cut our hair. We're all wearing a single braid that's tied at the neck, to hold it together when it's cut. After the accompanying prayer, our braids are placed crosswise across both bodies. Sunkwah and Winnie lovingly caress the strands in their hands. We kiss our great-grandparents gently on the cheek and wish them well on their journey into the afterlife. So far my cousins and sister and I have managed to contain our sorrow, which we worried might not be possible. While Sleeping Buffalo leads the others in a chant, Grandmother asks us to help her lay her parents flat, so they can sleep. Next we head over to our spouses and take up chanting with them. Sleeping Buffalo prays over Sunkwah and Winnie as they drift off. I squeeze Tess's hand, fearing my emotions will suddenly get the better of me. The children remain quiet, mesmerized by the strangeness of it all, even Raif, who usually can't sit still.

Sleeping Buffalo nods for us to leave. We return to Grandmother's house and congregate in the living room, overcome with sadness at the thought of Sunkwah and Winnie being absent from our lives. Dad asks if I'd like to go for drive, just to get out and collect my thoughts. Tess agrees it might do me a world of good. I oblige them, even though I can't see it helping. Riding with the window down and the air in my face, staring at the wide-open stretches of land is therapeutic after all, that and the funny sensation of my body going airborne as Dad flies over the hills on the road, a feeling I've always loved. He wins the smile from me that he was no doubt waiting for. After a time, I realize he has a destination in mind.

We stop by the familiar picnic table where our flag football team used to gather around, so weathered now that splinters are a problem. The comings and goings at Lazy Al's on the other side of the highway entertain us, as well as the activity in the surrounding stores. It's a considerably busier corner. At least progress on the rez doesn't include high-rise buildings that obliterate the view. Dad sips an alcohol-free beer while I enjoy a milkshake. At eight-thirty, the setting sun produces a brilliant Kool Aid cherry colored stripe along the horizon that fades into a soft blue evening sky. The dust in the baking summer air is bad, but typical for mid-August, or used to be—the Plains have been dealing with drastically changing weather patterns over the past five years like the rest of the planet. An ice storm could hit us tomorrow.

"Does that even taste remotely like beer?"

Dad studies the bottle. "I think it's called a placebo effect." He takes a big swig of the fake stuff, grimacing slightly, then says, "What are the odds of Sunkwah and Winnie making it to a hundred together?"

Two semis pull in the lot behind Al's and are left idling. Stars fade into the picture ever so slowly. I love us being alone here on "our" field.

"It's mind blowing, isn't it Viktor, to think of what your great-grandparents have witnessed in their lifetime? Best of all, they got to see things turn around on the reservation." He shakes his head. "The upcoming generation has untold opportunities."

"Don't I know it. You can feel the energy everywhere. People just keep feeding off each other's ideas. We're definitely entering a new era." A hawk suddenly swoops over our heads. It circles high above the intersection near Al's. "My guess is a drone."

Dad follows it. "Probably. Folks used to get so bent out of shape over the idea of keeping the rez under constant surveillance. No one thinks twice about it anymore. Remember the guys who got caught hoarding booze underground in huge cellars? And what about the family secretly growing weed in their greenhouse. Nothing like that happens nowadays."

"It's a regular utopia." Sarcasm aside, it comes darn close to being true. I suck the bottom clean of my cup. "I shoulda gotten two." Dad goes for the last drop in his bottle and follows it up with a big aah. He reaches for my neck in what I think will be a hug, but instead he touches the blunt-cut ends of my hair and instantly I lose it, burying my face in my arms on the table. The tears end rather quickly, and with them the gut-wrenching despair I'd been repressing. My great-grandparents have been such a constant in my life. I can't picture a future without them. What must Grandmother be feeling?

"They've been ready to go for a while," says Dad, kissing my head. "They were very tired. Sunkwah had begun to stop talking mid-sentence… he just couldn't finish. And Winnie has been wandering the house, speaking Rawakota to her dead relatives."

"I know."

As we walk to the truck, I ask if he thinks the triplets, who'll soon be eight, will remember much about their ancient great-great-grandparents. "I definitely have vivid memories from that age, do you?" He does as well, which is consoling to hear.

"It was a smart move you and Tess made to allow the kids to visit them regularly these past months. They understand their beloved Sunkwah and Winnie are ready to die, and it doesn't scare them. Honor, in particular, sat with them and taught herself Rawakota from the books they have. That's one bright girl."

It's dark now, and I offer to drive back, but Dad says he's in the mood to do it. Traffic isn't bad. He is in his usual relaxed position, with the right hand hanging over the top of the steering wheel, his other arm resting on his thigh. A single finger keeps us in our lane. It has been a nostalgic period, one that causes a person to miss others who have died. Dad brings up Pahpie, and how thankful he is for the many fishing trips they enjoyed together.

"Benjamin and I had great talks. He was real curious about how the civil rights movement in the sixties affected my parents. I had no clue, so I started asking them about the times, in order to pass along the information to him. He had already been advocating for Indians for years. In the meantime, I gained a new degree of respect for my parents." Dad stares ahead at the road, smiling to himself over the happy memory. "Your Pahpie used to go on about the importance of using one's moral compass, the same thing my parents preached to us kids growing up. After everything I put them through during my teens, I'm grateful I got the chance to show them that their values weren't lost on me."

It's nice remembering the special man that Pahpie was…the special Indian. We drive in silence while my mind goes off on a tangent. After several miles, I ask:

"Do you think Raif is okay in the head? I mean…truly?" Dad erupts with laughter.

"Why on Earth would you say that?"

"Because," I shrug, "one has to wonder what's going on in that kid's brain. His head's always bopping around, and he can never simply sit or walk…he's gotta always be in motion. Holt and Honor push him out of their way constantly. He's sweet, but what a nuisance."

Dad shifts in his seat and slows as we turn onto the final stretch of road. The blue and pink digital displays on the dash play across his face. "You really don't see it, do you, Viktor? He *is* you."

"What are you talking about…he's me?"

"The only difference is you had Daniel to wrestle with when you were on the rez. You two were joined at the hip. Back in Texas, you danced around and drummed on anything you could get your hands on, like in a powwow. By ten you had mellowed."

"Huh-uh."

"Uh-huh."

I don't believe him. Dad reminds me that the kids picked out their ponies and, based on his experience with Iris and me, learning to ride and caring for their very own horses should redirect Raif's endless energy. He thinks Raif may take to trick-riding like I did. Now there's something I hadn't considered.

All is quiet as I step into the house. Only the porch and kitchen lights are on. I wave to Dad, who continues on to stay with Mom and her mother as they keep a bedside vigil tonight. Relatives have offered to take turns sitting with Sunkwah and Winnie starting tomorrow. Their families are in the hotel next to the hospital where the triplets were born. And that is how the days will proceed, until at last our Elders walk on. I plan on going to the hospital in the morning to see Claire, who is completing her cardiothoracic residency there. I admire her for following through with her commitment to serve the Indians in this region. She paid off her student loan right after marrying Damien, a move that released her from her obligations tied to OSU's medical forgiveness program. Signing with the Indianapolis Colts made Damien an instant millionaire. Claire told him at the time that she still had every intention of working a couple of years on the reservation. Carrying out a long-distance marriage with a child has not been easy for them.

I realize Claire is busy, but I was hoping for more than a quick coffee. Nevertheless, I got to hug her, that's what matters. There will be other opportunities to meet up, now that she is working here.

"Danica has her heart set on seeing her Uncle Viktor," says Claire. "The school is in the back of the hospital." She glances at her watch. "This is when all the kids are in the garden. The older children help the little ones plant stuff and do projects. She has been paired with a ten year-old boy who leads her by the hand everywhere…it's the sweetest thing." She pecks me on the cheek. "Love you."

"Love you, too."

The on-site school for the employees' children is in a separate circular building that connects to the main hospital by way of a glass enclosed walkway. The kids are presently in the quaint courtyard located in the middle of the surrounding classrooms. I spot Danica. She's with her mentor-buddy who's helping her decorate a flowerpot. He patiently shows her how to use a sponge to dab the paint on the pot. God, she's cute, with her full head of mini-pigtails and colorful barrettes. Five is a special age. Kids really start to think for themselves. Danica lets out an ear-piercing squeal when I sneak up behind her. After that, it's all giggles as I hoist her high in the air. What a smile!

She's anxious to show me her artistry. The boy stands to shake my hand. Very polite of him. His eyes light up like others his age whom I've met, thrilled to meet the football player. His name is Wyatt. He quickly answers that math is his favorite subject when I ask what he enjoys about school. His shiny black hair is worn in two braids that reach his waist. Danica insists that I draw a butterfly on her flowerpot. The boy hands me a pack of glitter and glue. I apologize for taking over his job. He seems okay with it.

As I sprinkle the glitter on my glue design, creating a mess but totally impressing Danica, the boy says, "I was named after you."

"Really! You're a Talking White Owl, too?"

Smiling shyly, he shakes his head no and says, "My name is Viktor Wyatt."

"Aah."

"My dad named me. My mom said you were his best friend when you were kids."

The revelation comes as a complete shock! Now I'm the one staring. There's no resemblance—he must take after his mom. But when I look beyond the face, I recognize the hands. "Your father was Daniel Blue Shirt?" I need to hear him confirm it. His mother named him Blue Shirt, like his dad. Danica asks me something, and I collect myself.

"It's true," I tell him, "we were like brothers. There are no words to describe how happy I am to meet his son." I'm thinking that Daniel never looked as innocent as Wyatt does. I hope his son won't end up mocking everything like his dad started doing in his teens. Right now, I wish only to find his mother. Wyatt says her name is Eileen, and she takes X-rays. I assure Danica that I will see her again soon, and no, I promise not to tell her mom about the pretty present "we" made for her. A teacher directs me toward Radiology.

There's no memory of what Eileen looked like. It was ten years ago, and I'd like to forget the shabby, dark trailer where we met. She was pregnant, but not huge yet, and it upset me to hear she was Daniel's cousin. The nurse at the desk messages Eileen, who is currently with a patient. She's told that someone is waiting for her in the break room. A few young women enter the room and head straight for the vending machines, then one walks in and our eyes connect. It's awkward at first. Where to start?

Eileen is as surprised as I was by the chance encounter with Wyatt at the school. I explain the reason for my visiting the hospital, which was to see a cousin on the cardiac floor. I am curious about how she and Daniel initially wound up together. She says they saw each other when the families got together for picnics and powwows, before her parents started getting wasted. She remembers how kind and smart Daniel was, which is why she turned to him when her home life became unbearable. Unfortunately, so did his not so long afterward.

"When Daniel started using, I begged an aunt near Sioux Falls to let me stay with her. I swore to get my GED and find a good job. Thanks to that lucky break, I'm here."

"You're to be commended, Eileen. It couldn't have been easy."

"Once I was convinced that the gangs were really gone and the place was safe, I couldn't wait to return to the rez. It's home."

"Did Daniel ever get to see his son?" She nods yes, but doesn't elaborate. It's awful recalling Daniel's sad end. Neither of us mentions it.

We sit quietly a minute. "Are you married? Does Wyatt have a dad?"

"No. I've been with my partner for three years, though."

"Would he mind if I take an interest in Wyatt's life...help him with his schooling, or whatever? Maybe take him fishing, or riding? Or to a football game," I smile. "I wouldn't want it to create a problem...make him jealous, or anything." She laughs a little.

"That's super nice of you. And *she* will be as happy as I am if you'd like a relationship with our son. Wyatt won't believe it! He's a good kid, Viktor. I'm really proud of him."

I leave in such great spirits, anxious to tell Claire about this weird twist of fate, but then I wonder if I should hold off. What purpose would it serve? Better to keep Wyatt's identity to myself until I come to terms with the surprising news. Claire knew that Daniel had a long-distance crush on her. I talked so much about her to him always. She gave me her school picture when I asked her for it, to give to him. And now...Claire and

Damien's daughter Danica is pals with his son Wyatt. That's too strange of a coincidence. It brings to mind the highly irregular pass I made to Damien that one time, the play I am convinced to this day that Daniel orchestrated from his deathbed on the rez. I doubt I'll ever get to the bottom of these unsettling connections, but Daniel is definitely at the center of them.

It's been two weeks since Sunkwah and Winnie died side-by-side in their bed. Winnie went first, Sunkwah a few hours later. The children wove flowers together and placed them on the burial shrouds. Anyone could come and pay their respects the next few days, which is when Tess's parents flew up, and also Dad's parents, which I wasn't expecting. Many of the football team's players dropped by, which was greatly appreciated. I didn't take part in our second pre-season game, but my back-up came through, and Dakota Lodestone is currently 2-0 in its very first year with the NFL.

While adults mourned, the triplets played with their cousins from Chohkahn in the back yard. Cousin Suhdeer was pleased that our children got to know his side of the family better. I made the effort to spend a little time with Lukas's brother, my Uncle Novak. Our conversations were rather superficial, with him asking mostly about the rules of football. The groups of them packed up their tepees and left within the week. I ended up feeling more in touch with my Rawakota background, which isn't a bad thing.

In accordance with Sunkwah and Winnie's final wishes, they were buried beside a centuries-old ponderosa pine tree on their daughter Victoria's property, which is where I've been sitting most days, occasionally with Grandmother, who is glad to be so near their spirits. This afternoon, however, I'm alone. My mind is finally a blank, a welcome change from the myriad of emotions I've been trying to figure out this month. On my way back to the house, I think about the meeting I'm about to have with Mom's friend, Sleeping Buffalo. There's something he wants to discuss with me, though I can't imagine what. He sees me on the path and meets me halfway, pointing to the weathered concrete bench by the pond where Mom and I once sat and enjoyed a long talk. There are no amorous rabbits to observe this time.

Jon, as he has asked me to call him, brings up the day he recently accompanied my parents to a ranch near Wind Cave, with the goal of finding Honor a horse. The place breeds Nez Perce Appaloosas, which is what she has had her heart set on. Jon speaks with a calming steady gaze. He's a seriously handsome man. I can't help from picturing him and Mom spending time together over in Kashmir, which makes me upset with myself. They share a deep friendship, nothing more.

He crosses a leg to rest his elbows on his knee, seeing as how there's no back on the bench to relax against, and continues his story about that day. "While Solomon and Constance were finalizing the sale of the filly that your daughter picked out, I followed Honor as she wandered off to a field teeming with a couple hundred bison...worried she might jump the fence rail to pet them. It's mating season. You know how dangerous the bulls can be. It turned out she was fixated on a single animal, a male calf born in the spring that, according to her, was as shiny as a new gold coin, and he glowed like the sun."

"Did he?" I inquire, not sure what Honor meant.

"No," he smiles, "but he did to her."

"You must believe there's something behind what she saw, or you'd have chalked it up to a little girl's overactive imagination."

"That's correct, particularly when she spotted a tiny white creature curled up inside its belly, which I interpreted as a fetus. I hope it doesn't bother you, Viktor, to learn that your child has prophetic abilities. Like me, she is able to tap into energies that most people are oblivious to. We recognize each other—call it a meeting-of-the-minds. We are not, however, in touch with the *same* spirits. Imagine how many exist in the universe!"

I understand what Jon is saying, but what parent wants to hear that a virtual stranger possesses a special connection with one's own child. "How about Holt and Raif?" I ask, sounding every bit as concerned as I probably look. He nods no, thank god. It does in fact weigh on me because I realized after the triplets were born that the hawks I encountered inside the cave during the hanbleceya were symbolic of them; and the possible negative aspects of that vision scare me. I have tried not to dwell on the image of the one bird gazing back at me, engulfed by fire, but, based on what Sleeping Buffalo is now telling me about Honor, it's time I shared my experience with a spiritual leader like him...just not today. "So what's your take on what she described?"

"Well…" says Jon, pausing a moment, "… he is a bull calf, and therefore won't be mothering any young. He can most assuredly father a sacred white buffalo, though."

"That's your explanation? I respect your shamanistic gift, but I'm familiar with the rancher you went to. It's near impossible for any of his bison to produce white offspring. They're considered genetically pure, and are descended from the last one hundred original American bison. The man's parents were on the forefront of saving them. Did you know there are now around 11,000 of them in the States and Canada, thanks in part to this rancher's efforts? He'll tell you that the reason you see more white buffalo in the last years is because breeds of white cattle have managed to enter fields and mate with buffalo, although some breeders cross them on purpose to produce beefalo. Their coats eventually turn brown. There's nothing sacred about them. Being from Chohkahn, perhaps you aren't aware of that. The only way for a truly white buffalo to occur is by mutation, a natural accident during DNA replication."

"When Wakan is involved, there's nothing arbitrary about it."

I can't argue that. "Is there anything you yourself have personally experienced that ties in to what Honor saw? Is that why you believe it's credible?"

"A shrewd deduction, Viktor. As a matter of fact I have, me as well as other spiritual guides and healers, and not just on our continent, but in the southern hemisphere as well. For several years now we've all had recurring dreams about a bigger than usual red moon hiding the sun."

"You're describing a lunar eclipse, right? And a super blood moon. Is it so rare? I'm almost certain there was one back when I was in high school."

"They aren't a frequent occurrence. The last time the moon was closest to the Earth in its orbit, and it coincided with a total lunar eclipse, was in 2015. Of historic interest to us now is the super blood moon that will take place on October 8, 2033. I can't expand on the significance of the event, other than to say that it will mark the beginning of a transformative period of growth for Indigenous peoples around the world. We will emerge as a force to be reckoned with."

"Sounds encouraging, and ominous, Jon. That's pretty far into the future. You're thinking the white buffalo will be born then?" Before he can answer, I am inclined to add, "Better make sure the calf isn't neutered beforehand."

"Good point," he says, smiling. "I do intend to talk to the rancher about following the course of the animal's life. It isn't just Honor who is having visions. Word is spreading about unusual sightings on other tribal lands made by children her age. They were born during that unique period when a large number of odd phenomena were observed. I'm sure it's only the start of such reports."

How well I remember Mom discussing those presumably supernatural signs to me. As we head to the house, Jon reveals that various tribal Nations have already begun preparing for the momentous occasion by updating their Constitutions and reviewing priorities. "Most territories lack an infrastructure. They're also developing health and education systems. Once that day arrives, there's to be absolutely no reliance whatsoever on governments for any kind of aid." He makes a compelling case. Jon Sleeping Buffalo is an enthralling character, for sure. After saying his goodbyes to the family, I walk him to his car where he tells me how much he looks forward to watching me play in my first pro-game next week, the preseason games being over. That was a sudden harsh jolt back to reality. I had better start concentrating on football again, and fast.

The kids, currently playing dueling Jedis with their lightsabers in the living room, are ordered outside even though it has begun to drizzle. Tess decides to relax in a hot bath, which leaves Grandmother and me sitting in front of a Star Wars episode on TV.

"You can turn it off, Viktor...if you don't mind."

I cuddle close and kiss her cheek. "Love you." There's a weak attempt at a smile from her. Although she was blessed with a steady stream of family members who came to help her care for her parents during these past few years, watching their steady decline has nevertheless chipped away at Grandmother's normally upbeat disposition, which she is painfully aware of. I have to believe she will rebound from the experience. She survived losing her husband and her daughter, my wonderful Aunt Loretta, thanks to Sunkwah and Winnie being there for her. But with both of them now gone, who can possibly fill their shoes in her hour of need?

She looks me in the eyes. "I don't want to reach a hundred, Viktor."

"Can't say I want to." We sit holding hands, listening to the clear and gentle voice of Judy Collins coming from the bathroom. There's a boom-box in there along with Grandmother's CDs. I picture Tess in the tub with her hair pinned up, her eyes closed. The smattering of raindrops against the windowpanes grows louder.

"Maybe ninety...or ninety-two," she says.

"How 'bout ninety-four. They were both still alert and themselves at that age."

She rests her head on my shoulder. "Mmm, ninety-two max."

Sunkwah and Winnie really didn't start going downhill until ninety-eight, but it's best to drop the subject. My thoughts are presently all over the place.

"Grandmother...do you think Mom is considered the most important person to the Rawakota? Look at all she's done for them to reach their current level of technical superiority."

"True, but the most valued people are the ones who keep Chohkahn's location secret, and that doesn't involve Constance."

"Oh...and who is that?"

"It's not like I know them by name. They are generations of Oyahmayan who long ago wormed their way into positions of trust with people in the military and private companies, back when they started mapping the Earth using satellites. It's a family operation. The young learned the ins and outs from their elders, which enabled them to move up through the ranks. Now there's radar and ultrasound imaging they have to deal with. We can't have the Black Hills' underground network of tunnels exposed. I don't think the technology can penetrate as far down as Chohkahn, not yet that is."

Suddenly Tess appears in comfortable sweats, her wet hair wrapped turban-style in a towel. She holds out her hands to pull Grandmother up from the couch. A warm bath awaits her. That was thoughtful. In the meantime, I volunteer to heat up one of several casseroles that was dropped off during the week.

Following dinner, the kids head to bed without a fuss, excited about getting to see their horses tomorrow. The new additions to the family can't be ridden until they're older and trained, but developing empathy begins on day one. This will be the beginning of one of the most important relationships in their lives. Tess was tired and called it a night, too. Grandmother fell asleep in her rocker on the porch while listening to the rain, and there she remains dressed in her nightgown and robe, quietly snoring. As for me, I'm wide awake.

It's call-in hour at the radio station, an opportunity for me to thank the many listeners who have offered condolences to our family. That my Elders died hours apart was big news in these parts, more so because they both made it to one hundred. Reaching sixty is remarkable for most Lakota.

I'm not on the phone ten minutes with the DJ before word spreads and the phones go crazy. I'm closed off in the kitchen. It's been difficult finding a break in my schedule to connect with my Native friends. Hearing familiar names is heartening. They share in my grief, telling of the elders they have lost. We sense it's time to move on to a different topic, and I ask my tribal brothers and sisters about their current concerns. Calls start coming in from a younger demographic, kids in middle school and high school who sound angry and frustrated…not with me, but with all the white men, long dead, who stole Indian lands and herded Native people together onto reservations. "It's the fricking 21ST century!" exclaims the fourteen-year-old girl. "So why don't we hold legal title to the land we're on?" I sounded exactly like her at that age. By the time you're a teen, it hits you that we Indians have historically been relegated to the lowest rung of society's ladder, and you ask yourself why things haven't changed much over hundreds of years. And then you demand justice. It's a tired old story, but fresh to them. The difference between when I grew up on the rez and now is—this is a proactive, educated generation, a group with a multitude of resources at their fingertips. These kids are passionate. Knowing what I do about the developments underway to protect our sacred South Dakota mountains, reclaiming the Black Hills is no longer the pipe dream I once believed it to be, and I find myself filled with fierce ambition. I'd like nothing more than to go head-to-head against those who perpetually work at holding us down.

In the remining minutes of the program, we touch upon the subject of the prophecies that have been floating around for years, as well as ponder the significance of the eclipse in 2033. A Diné caller from New Mexico says his community is mobilizing and readying itself for the event, calling what they're doing, Operation Red Moon. He suggests we all refer to it as that when we go online to discuss the nation-building projects underway on our reservations. There is a unifying aspect to that idea. The DJ interrupts; it's time for music. He thanks everyone for participating, and then wishes me well in the upcoming game.

I'm yawning as I lumber toward the bedroom, the day having finally caught up with me.

I wake to a bright room, in bed, but on top of the covers in my clothes, feeling totally disoriented. Did I sleep away the afternoon? Tess comes in and reports that it's still early in the morning. I don't believe her. "It's true," she laughs. I pull her beside me. She kisses my neck and unzips my pants. Her hair feels so soft. Times when she wears her hair down, Raif has told her he's going to marry a girl as pretty as her and his Grandma Chevonne. I welcome more redheads into the family and ignore the Freudian overtones. I lie still, waiting for what's next, because she's definitely exploring.

After breakfast, the children and I head over to Levi's place. His family has been keeping our horses while Grandmother was dealing with her parents. There used to be eight, but only Jim, Ola, and Daniel's horse, Flapjack, remain. Grandmother took him in when Daniel died. Perhaps Wyatt would like his dad's horse. He can't be ridden; his legs are weak. Even so, how very special. Levi has also offered to board the children's horses, or we never would have gotten them until later.

Honor remains with her horse when the boys take off to play with Levi's two sons. She holds the filly by the reins and proudly walks her in the small fenced enclosure next to the stable, winning her trust.

"You were once that cute," I tell Jim, who is observing them with me from a spot on the opposite side of the fence. He nudges my neck, as if he remembers. Jim is nearing his twentieth birthday and thankfully shows no signs of slowing down. Even though he liked living on Dr. Nate's property in Columbus, he's really content to be back on his old stomping ground with his childhood buddies. He and Iris's horse, Ola, still romp happily together, but both settle down around Flapjack, sensing he isn't up for their antics these days. They're extremely protective of him, too, positioning themselves between him and the rest of Levi's herd when they're in the field. Often Flapjack is seen resting his muzzle on one of their backs. The sight of them tugs at the heartstrings.

As I watch Honor, she's a sight to behold herself, marching in step beside her horse with her face turned to the sky. She's got a pretty profile, with a straight nose and nice jaw. It's too early to tell if her skin will ever be as tanned-looking as mine. Unlike the boys, whose hair has become black, Honor's glorious mane is actually a deep red chestnut brown that matches the color of the front half of her horse. The animal's rump is bright white and speckled with small brown spots. The wind blows their hair in the air, which makes me miss mine. For the briefest moment, I allow myself to picture Sleeping Buffalo placing my braid reverentially across Sunkwah and Winnie's bodies, and them holding it in their hands. Then it's back to the present. "Have you decided on a name for her?" I holler.

Honor lets go of the reins and bounces over to the fence, jumping onto the rail for me to catch her in my arms. Jim pokes his nose between us, wanting some attention. "Moonshadow," she says, planting a kiss on Jim's snout, "because Great-grandma likes the song so much."

"She sang it to your Aunt Iris and me, too, when we were little." I hum a few bars. "It makes for a beautiful name."

Honor calls out to the young horse in a sweet, coaxing manner. "Moonshadow, come here. Come meet your Uncle Jim."

"Oh wow, hear that, Jim? Being an elder means you're expected to set a good example."

Moonshadow steps cautiously toward us, only to stop a couple of feet away. Jim regards her a moment, tosses his head back, and then turns and ambles across the field, showing that he really can't be bothered with one still so new to the world. With that, Moonshadow moves in closer and begins nibbling on the fingers of Honor's outstretched arm. She giggles over how slimy it feels. It's a sight I'll always cherish.

"Spirit beings are all over the place. Can you feel them, Daddy?"

"Not at the moment," I admit, "but I do at times in other spots on the reservation."

"Sunkwah and Winnie really like Moonshadow."

A lump forms in my throat. If only I were as attuned to the unseen forces in our midst and could sense their presence. However, I trust my great-grandparents will visit me occasionally in the future. "How 'bout we find your brothers and have a quick snack with Great-grandma before we leave. Mom is anxious to hit the road and get home before midnight."

"True, being totally self-sufficient is paramount," says Mom, "but if our people aren't absolutely ready to forego outside help, all of our efforts up until now will have been in vain. If anything, Viktor, our local tribes may garner *more* support in the coming years when it comes to the Black Hills. Places where Native people's land rights are under attack are making the news more often. We're gaining allies. Governments and multi-nationals can't go on denying the damage they've inflicted on human health and the environment."

"Seriously? Folks here still believe they're going to win back those Black Hills?" Hayden overheard us as he entered the kitchen. I invited him up from Columbus to attend my first official NFL game. Mom and I exchange looks, realizing he missed the conspiratorial part of our discussion. I was merely pointing out to her that we Indians should rethink stepping up the timeline and activate that magnetic fence around the mountains sooner rather than later. Who knows what might happen in the interim—2033 is a long ways off.

Hayden pours a cup of coffee and takes a seat beside Mom at the counter. "Mornin' General," he smiles, clinking his cup against hers. "Here's to a well-deserved promotion. By the way, I like your haircut...and the wispy bangs—very sexy."

To which she responds dryly, but with the hint of a smile, "Good to hear, Hayden, considering that's what I was aiming for." He has no way of knowing that she's worn it shoulder-length for months now. "You boys have fun. I'm going to help Tess get the kids dressed. They're so excited to see their daddy play ball."

I need to make a few calls and remind Hayden that we don't leave for another half hour; he doesn't need to scarf down his muffin. Sunlight is streaming through the window. It means the stadium's retractable roof will be open. I love catching glimpses of the sky in the middle of all that madness.

I feel bad that I haven't gotten to be alone with Hayden since he arrived yesterday morning. He saw me once a couple of years ago during the first season I played for the college on the rez, which was in the same stadium we're heading to today. He was introduced to Coach Everett back then, who, remarkably, has returned to the pros to manage us Dakota Lodestones. In the meantime, Skyler recently gave birth to a baby boy, and his mom died. Their dance company in Columbus remains a profitable and creatively satisfying enterprise. He's still lean and muscular, still easy-going, and, according to Tess, grows more handsome with age. No longer sporting a buzz cut, his brown, silver-streaked, slicked-back hair looks too cool.

When it's time to go, and we're standing in the driveway, Hayden surveys the neighborhood before climbing into the car. He proceeds to sit quietly, staring pensively out the window as the house-lined streets give way to an empty stretch of road. I point out that we'll be passing the team's training facility, and in less than thirty minutes we'll arrive at the stadium's underground garage. Dad will meet us and take him to the tailgate parties that by now are well underway. Tess, Mom, and the triplets are skipping that and won't leave until it's closer to kick-off, which is 2:45 p.m.

He turns to me and then asks how many seats have been set aside for just my relatives and friends. "I don't know," I shrug. "Around fifty. They stayed after traveling here to pay their respects when Sunkwah and Winnie died." Once again there's another long gap of silence, which seems unusual. It's bugging me and I tap him on arm. "Hey...what gives?"

"It's a lot to digest, Viktor, nothing more. Take your neighborhood, for example. The fact that it's strictly an enclave for the athletes and their families is kind of odd. I realize it started out as some crypto CEO's planned community before his company went belly-up, but..." he sighs, not sure where he's going with this, but I do.

"It's convenient, Hayden. You see how close it is to the stadium. And there are advantages to us players living around each other that go beyond football. Although we're from different Indigenous Nations, we have all faced similar issues that outsiders can never fully understand. Most of us return to our so-called *real* homes off-season. I go back to Buckthorn. Our Center, who's my next-door neighbor, goes back to Hawaii, as do three other players. A couple of guys head to Canada. See, not so strange."

I was wrong to think that summed up what was bothering him. Now he wonders how well I know the Dakota Lodestone owners, the Falcone brother-sister duo. He has gone so far as to research them, which I don't consider all that strange. He was always curious about people's backgrounds. It's one of his traits. I remember him googling the players on the OSU Buckeyes squad as well as the names of the dancers in his own troupe. Apparently there's not much to find on the family's business because it's privately held. He did learn that Falcone Industries recently ventured beyond the scrap metal industry, having bought a major South American telecom provider. The owners are soon to close a deal with one of Africa's biggest communications companies.

"First off, Hayden, I've only shaken their hands, and secondly, who cares what they own?"

"I'm just looking out for your interests. I still care about you. It's been in the news that the players don't have agents and that each of you earns the same amount, a measly ten million dollars. That's unheard of. Is it true? You should have received a multi-year contract worth a hundred million bucks, minimum. It isn't like the owners can't afford it."

I laugh outright. "We're well taken care of, Hayden…maybe not in the traditional way that players in other NFL franchises are."

"You mean like with money."

I raise my hands in exasperation over his fixation on money. The stadium is within view, which prompts this comment from me, "The Falcones are the reason why over 20,000 Native families are able to attend our home games, that's one-third of the number of seats. They're completely free to them, even the transportation. There are bus locations around the state for people to travel in caravans. Those who drive can receive gas coupons to offset the cost of getting here. The logistics behind organizing all that has been no small feat."

"How charitable of them." I haven't swayed him; his tone is sarcastic. It doesn't necessarily surprise me. When I danced in *WAKAN* we sometimes discussed the ways in which the wealthy set up private foundations to support the arts, in order to evade paying taxes. I realize it's no different with sports. "Robber barons have historically bankrolled noble causes" he says, "as if their altruism could in some way make up for their unethical business practices. I'd feel better if I knew why you trust a bunch of billionaires."

"I trust them, Hayden, because my mother does. And the players trust them because I do. End of story."

"Interesting," he says, in a cryptic kind of way as if a light bulb went off in his head.

Once inside the stadium garage, I spot Dad standing by the players' door, ready to whisk Hayden off to the main parking lot where fans have already been partying for hours. I'm anxious to get to the locker room and am quick to exit the car. I tell Hayden that Tess's parents are the king and queen of tailgating. "You're gonna die when you taste Brian's Irish whiskey spare ribs and Chevonne's chile rellenos. Enjoy!"

Dad and I give each other a quick hug goodbye, and I'm expecting to do the same with Hayden, but he won't have it—the short, impersonal nature of the hug that is. He pulls me close onto his chest and wraps his arms around my shoulders, pressing his fingers into them to hold me in place. Within seconds, I feel calmer. My breathing slows. He steps back and smiles. After all these years, Hayden can still read my mood. He remains the true friend and generous mentor he always was, the guy I once said knew me better than I did myself.

"This moment can't be downplayed, Viktor. It's epic. You're clearly well-equipped for making your mark on the sports world. My guess is your teammates are, too."

As he pats my cheek, I take his hand. "Love you, Hayden."

"Love you, kid." He turns to Dad. "Can't wait to taste those ribs, Solomon."

I sprint to the locker room. The guys are just now streaming in. Our nerves appear to be in check, masking the fact that we're fired-up and ready to explode onto the field. The atmosphere is quietly electric, something Coach Everett has come to appreciate and not concern himself over. It's opposite the intense environment he endured during his time in the pros with the Dolphins, a team known for its bullying culture, and eventually investigated for it. One wouldn't expect a guy's personality to necessarily mesh with another player's, but a climate of mutual respect must prevail. Fortunately that isn't a problem with our squad. It's remarkable just how well we do get along, which is probably why we found our rhythm playing together early on. We're in sync before the first snap. I'd call us a Dream Team. An overarching shared mission clearly unites us, that of wanting to represent our Nations in the best light. Too often only the worst aspects of our communities get reported on. We aim to change that.

Following our individual pre-game rituals, it's time to suit up. Eric Lonebear, a monster-sized linebacker, gets us laughing when he starts showing off the new uniform in front of the mirror, making like he's a model posing for the cameras. The jerseys are turquoise and black and we think very classy. Eric is hands down our most threatening-looking athlete, especially when that glistening charcoal grey helmet slides down over his head. Standing seven feet tall and weighing in at over three hundred fifty pounds, he's a Transformer action-figure come to life.

The chanting begins right as we head out the locker room door. It's a ritual that's part of all of our cultures. The handful of us who played together at the college on the Buckthorn Reservation found ourselves automatically singing them under our breath before games, and then decided to keep up the practice because it does such a good job of focusing our energies.

We reach the entrance to the arena where we stand squeezed together, ready to charge, stoked by the enthusiasm of our cheering fans. The matchup is with top ranked Pittsburgh. A couple of their key players are out with injuries, an advantage for us. A booming voice announces the team over the loudspeaker and we're off to our sideline. I haven't experienced this level of noise since playing for the Buckeyes.

We win the coin toss and choose to kick off. At the snap, I don't drop back but stand my ground, faking a pass to an open receiver on my right, then instantly changing my mind. The ball drifts from my left fingertips just as my right hand snatches it, and I follow the arc as the ball sails the 50 yards downfield into the end zone, right to the outstretched arms of one of our players who suddenly shot out from behind the guy blocking him, and who then miraculously catches it. The place goes nuts! There's a thunderous response of foot-stomping in the stands. *Be bold*. I signal Coach Everett to nix sending the kicker in for the field goal, opting instead for the two-point conversion. And just like that, two more points get added to the scoreboard.

You'd have thought we already won the game the way our fans are carrying on. With arms raised high over their heads like an X, meant to represent the two crossed pickaxes of our logo, they're yelling wildly, triumphantly, "Our time, our time, our time..."

Clearly the boundaries of the game extend beyond the goal posts and sidelines. To any opponent, expect a fight-to-the-finish. You're on Indian territory after all! I don't want to consider the possibility that these battles among rivals might be a warm-up for more serious things to come. As for now, the team will go on having fun delivering the crowd's message. It absolutely *is* our people's time.

ACKNOWLEDGMENTS

Without the sustained support of several family members and friends throughout the period that it took me to write *Talking White Owl*, I could never have completed the book. I am particularly indebted to my daughter Emily's friend, Neha Locke, who looked over an early draft of the first chapters and offered wonderful advice that inspired me to approach the telling of the story in a much different way.

Finding Meg McClellan, my editor, was a godsend. If only I had met her at the outset of this undertaking rather than near the end of it when I was well on my way to hitting the thousand page mark. Meg was thorough, painfully honest, and, best of all, kind.

ABOUT THE AUTHOR

Valerie Hagenbush is the author of one other novel, *Good-bye and Good Riddance*. She spent years working in other fields before taking up writing. Valerie holds a degree in filmmaking from Ohio State University and also in veterinary technology from the University of Cincinnati. She and her husband raised their two daughters in Ohio and Illinois, then relocated to Arizona for her husband's job. Valerie taught in a local school district before retiring, writing *Talking White Owl* on the side.